J
&
HORNET FLIGHT

Ken Follett was only twenty-seven when he wrote the award-winning novel *Eye of the Needle*, which became an international bestseller. He has since written several equally successful novels including, most recently, *Whiteout*. He is also the author of the non-fiction bestseller, *On Wings of Eagles*. He lives with his family in London and Hertfordshire.

Visit the Ken Follett web site at http://www.ken-follett.com

Also by Ken Follett

KEN FOLLETT

JACKDAWS
&
HORNET
FLIGHT

PAN BOOKS

Jackdaws first published 2001 by Macmillan.
First published by Pan Books 2002
Hornet Flight first published 2002 by Macmillan.
First published by Pan Books 2003

This omnibus edition published 2005 by Pan Books
an imprint of Pan Macmillan Ltd
Pan Macmillan, 20 New Wharf Road, London N1 9RR
Basingstoke and Oxford
Associated companies throughout the world
www.panmacmillan.com

ISBN 0 330 44093 4

A CIP catalogue record for this book is available from
the British Library.

Typeset by SetSystems Ltd, Saffron Walden, Essex
Printed and bound in Great Britain by
Mackays of Chatham plc, Chatham, Kent

JACKDAWS

Exactly fifty women were sent into France as secret agents by the Special Operations Executive during the Second World War. Of those, thirty-six survived the war. The other fourteen gave their lives.

This book is dedicated to all of them.

THE FIRST DAY:
SUNDAY, 28 MAY 1944

ONE

One minute before the explosion, the square at Sainte-Cécile was at peace. The evening was warm, and a layer of still air covered the town like a blanket. The church bell tolled a lazy beat, calling worshippers to the service with little enthusiasm. To Felicity Clairet it sounded like a countdown.

The square was dominated by the seventeenth-century chateau. A small version of Versailles, it had a grand projecting front entrance, and wings on both sides that turned right angles and tailed off rearwards. There was a basement and two main floors topped by a tall roof with arched dormer windows.

Felicity, who was always called Flick, loved France. She enjoyed its graceful buildings, its mild weather, its leisurely lunches, its cultured people. She liked French paintings, French literature, and stylish French clothes. Visitors often found the French people unfriendly, but Flick had been speaking the language since she was six years old, and no one could tell she was a foreigner.

It angered her that the France she loved no longer existed. There was not enough food for leisurely lunches, the paintings had all been stolen by the Nazis, and only the whores had pretty clothes. Like most women, Flick was wearing a shapeless dress whose colours had long ago been washed to dullness. Her heart's desire was that the real France would come back. It might return soon, if she and people like her did what they were supposed to.

She might not live to see it – indeed, she might not survive the next few minutes. She was no fatalist; she wanted to live. There were a hundred things she planned to do after the war: finish her doctorate, have a baby, see New York, own a sports car, drink champagne on the beach at Cannes. But if she were about to die, she was glad to be spending her last few moments in a sunlit square, looking at a beautiful old house, with the lilting sounds of the French language soft in her ears.

The chateau had been built as a home for the local aristocracy, but the last Comte de Sainte-Cécile had lost his head on the guillotine in 1793. The ornamental gardens had long ago been turned into vineyards, for this was wine country, the heart of the Champagne district. The building now housed an important telephone exchange, sited here because the government minister responsible had been born in Sainte-Cécile.

When the Germans came they enlarged the exchange to provide connections between the French system and the new cable route to Germany. They also sited a Gestapo regional headquarters in the building, with offices on the upper floors and cells in the basement.

Four weeks ago the chateau had been bombed by

the Allies. Such precision bombing was new. The heavy four-engined Lancasters and Flying Fortresses that roared high over Europe every night were inaccurate – they sometimes missed an entire *city* – but the latest generation of fighter-bombers, the Lightnings and Thunderbolts, could sneak in by day and hit a small target, a bridge or a railway station. Much of the west wing of the chateau was now a heap of irregular seventeenth-century red bricks and square white stones.

But the air raid had failed. Repairs were made quickly, and the phone service had been disrupted only as long as it took the Germans to instal replacement switchboards. All the automatic telephone equipment and the vital amplifiers for the long-distance lines were in the basement, which had escaped serious damage.

That was why Flick was here.

The chateau was on the north side of the square, surrounded by a high wall of stone pillars and iron railings, guarded by uniformed sentries. To the east was a small medieval church, its ancient wooden doors wide open to the summer air and the arriving congregation. Opposite the church, on the west side of the square, was the town hall, run by an ultraconservative mayor who had few disagreements with the occupying Nazi rulers. The south side was a row of shops and a bar called Café des Sports. Flick sat outside the bar, waiting for the church bell to stop. On the table in front of her was a glass of the local white wine, thin and light. She had not drunk any.

She was a British officer with the rank of major. Officially, she belonged to the First Aid Nursing

Yeomanry, the all-female service that was inevitably called the FANYs. But that was a cover story. In fact she worked for a secret organization, the Special Operations Executive, responsible for sabotage behind enemy lines. At twenty-eight, she was one of the most senior agents. This was not the first time she had felt herself close to death. She had learned to live with the threat, and manage her fear, but all the same she felt the touch of a cold hand on her heart when she looked at the steel helmets and powerful rifles of the chateau guards.

Three years ago, her greatest ambition had been to become a professor of French literature in a British university, teaching students to enjoy the vigour of Hugo, the wit of Flaubert, the passion of Zola. She had been working in the War Office, translating French documents, when she had been summoned to a mysterious interview in a hotel room and asked if she were willing to do something dangerous.

She had said yes without thinking much. There was a war on, and all the boys she had been at Oxford with were risking their lives every day, so why shouldn't she do the same? Two days after Christmas 1941 she had started her SOE training.

Six months later she was a courier, carrying messages from SOE headquarters, at 64 Baker Street in London, to Resistance groups in occupied France, in the days when wireless sets were scarce and trained operators even fewer. She would parachute in, move around with her false identity papers, contact the Resistance, give them their orders, and note their replies, complaints, and requests for guns and ammunition. For the return journey she would rendezvous with a pick-up plane, usually a three-seater Westland Lysander, small enough to land on six hundred yards of grass.

From courier work she had graduated to organizing sabotage. Most SOE agents were officers, the theory being that their 'men' were the local Resistance. In practice, the Resistance were not under army discipline, and an agent had to win their co-operation by being tough, knowledgeable and authoritative.

The work was dangerous. Six men and three women had finished the training course with Flick, and she was the only one still operating two years later. Two were known to be dead: one shot by the Milice, the hated French security police, and the second killed when his parachute failed to open. The other six had been captured, interrogated and .tortured, and had then disappeared into prison camps in Germany. Flick had survived because she was ruthless, she had quick reactions, and she was careful about security to the point of paranoia.

Beside her sat her husband, Michel, leader of the Resistance circuit codenamed Bollinger, which was based in the cathedral city of Reims, ten miles away. Although about to risk his life, Michel was sitting back in his chair, his right ankle resting on his left knee, holding a tall glass of pale, watery wartime beer. His careless grin had won her heart when she was a student at the Sorbonne, writing a thesis on Molière's ethics which she had abandoned on the outbreak of war. He had been a dishevelled young philosophy lecturer with a legion of adoring students.

He was still the sexiest man she had ever met. He was tall, and he dressed with careless elegance in rumpled suits and faded blue shirts. His hair was always a little too long. He had a come-to-bed voice and an intense blue-eyed gaze that made a girl feel she was the only woman in the world.

This mission had given Flick a welcome chance to spend a few days with her husband, but it had not been a happy time. They had not quarrelled, exactly, but Michel's affection had seemed half-hearted, as if he were going through the motions; and she had felt hurt. Her instinct told her he was interested in someone else. He was only thirty-five, and his unkempt charm still worked on young women. It did not help that since their wedding they had been apart more than together, because of the war. And there were plenty of willing French girls, she thought sourly, in the Resistance and out of it.

She still loved him. Not in the same way: she no longer worshipped him as she had on their honeymoon, no longer yearned to devote her life to making him happy. The morning mists of romantic love had lifted, and in the clear daylight of married life she could see that he was vain, self-absorbed, and unreliable. But when he chose to focus his attention on her he could still make her feel unique and beautiful and cherished.

His charm worked on men, too, and he was a great leader, courageous and charismatic. He and Flick had figured out the battle plan together. They would attack the chateau in two places, dividing the defenders, then

8

regroup inside to form a single force that would penetrate the basement, find the main equipment room, and blow it up.

They had a floor plan of the building supplied by Antoinette Dupert, supervisor of the group of local women who cleaned the chateau every evening. She was also Michel's aunt. The cleaners started work at seven o'clock, the same time as vespers, and Flick could see some of them now, presenting their special passes to the guard at the wrought-iron gate. Antoinette's sketch showed the entrance to the basement, but no further details, for it was a restricted area, open to Germans only, and cleaned by soldiers.

Michel's attack plan was based on reports from MI6, the British intelligence service, which said the chateau was guarded by a Waffen SS detachment working in three shifts each of twelve men. The Gestapo personnel in the building were not fighting troops, and most would not even be armed. The Bollinger circuit had been able to muster fifteen fighters for the attack, and they were now deployed, either among the worshippers in the church, or posing as Sunday idlers around the square, concealing their weapons under their clothing or in satchels and duffel bags. If MI6 was right, the Resistance would outnumber the guards.

But a worry nagged at Flick's brain and made her heart heavy with apprehension. When she had told Antoinette of MI6's estimate, Antoinette had frowned and said: 'It seems to me there are more.' Antoinette was no fool – she had been secretary to Joseph Laperrière, the head of a champagne house, until the occupation reduced his profits and his wife became his secretary – and she could be right.

Michel had been unable to resolve the contradiction between the MI6 estimate and Antoinette's guess. He lived in Reims, and neither he nor any of his group was familiar with Sainte-Cécile. There had been no time for further reconnaissance. If the Resistance was outnumbered, Flick thought with dread, they were not likely to prevail against disciplined German troops.

She looked around the square, picking out the people she knew, apparently innocent strollers who were in fact waiting to kill or be killed. Outside the haberdashery, studying a bolt of dull green cloth in the window, stood Geneviève, a tall girl of twenty with a Sten gun under her light summer coat. The Sten was a submachine-gun much favoured by the Resistance because it could be broken into three parts and carried in a small bag. Geneviève might well be the girl Michel had his eye on, but all the same Flick felt a shudder of horror at the thought that she might be mown down by gunfire in a few seconds' time. Crossing the cobbled square, heading for the church, was Bertrand, even younger at seventeen, a blond boy with an eager face and a .45 calibre Colt automatic hidden in a folded newspaper under his arm. The Allies had dropped thousands of Colts by parachute. Flick had at first forbidden Bertrand from the team because of his age, but he had pleaded to be included, and she had needed every available man, so she had given in. She hoped his youthful bravado would survive once the shooting started. Loitering in the church porch, apparently finishing his cigarette before going in, was Albert, whose wife had given birth to their first child this morning, a girl. Albert had an extra reason to stay alive today. He carried a cloth bag that looked full of potatoes, but they were No. 36 Mark I Mills hand grenades.

The scene in the square looked normal but for one element. Beside the church was parked an enormous, powerful sports car. It was a French-built Hispano-Suiza type 68-*bis*, with a V12 aero-engine, one of the fastest cars in the world. It had a tall, arrogant-looking silver radiator topped by the flying-stork mascot, and it was painted sky blue.

It had arrived half an hour ago. The driver, a handsome man of about forty, was wearing an elegant civilian suit, but he had to be a German officer – no one else would have the nerve to flaunt such a car. His companion, a tall, striking redhead in a green silk dress and high-heeled suede shoes, was too perfectly chic to be anything but French. The man had set up a camera on a tripod and was taking photographs of the chateau. The woman wore a defiant look, as if she knew that the shabby townspeople who stared at her on their way to church were calling her *whore* in their minds.

A few minutes ago, the man had scared Flick by asking her to take a photograph of himself and his lady friend against the background of the chateau. He had spoken courteously, with an engaging smile, and only the trace of a German accent. The distraction at a crucial moment was absolutely maddening, but Flick had felt it might have caused trouble to refuse,

11

especially as she was pretending to be a local resident who had nothing better to do than lounge around at a pavement café. So she had responded as most French people would have in the circumstances: she had put on an expression of cold indifference and complied with the German's request.

It had been a farcically frightening moment: the British secret agent standing behind the camera; the German officer and his tart smiling at her, and the church bell tolling the seconds until the explosion. Then the officer had thanked her and offered to buy her a drink. She had refused very firmly: no French girl could drink with a German unless she were prepared to be called a whore. He had nodded understandingly, and she had returned to her husband.

The officer was obviously off-duty, and did not appear to be armed, so he presented no danger, but all the same he bothered Flick. She puzzled over this feeling in the last few seconds of calm, and finally realized that she did not really believe he was a tourist. There was a watchful alertness in his manner that was not appropriate for soaking up the beauty of old architecture. His woman might be exactly what she seemed, but he was something else.

Before Flick could figure out what, the bell ceased to toll.

Michel drained his glass then wiped his mouth with the back of his hand.

Flick and Michel stood up. Trying to look casual, they strolled to the café entrance and stood in the doorway, inconspicuously taking cover.

TWO

Dieter Franck had noticed the girl at the café table the moment he drove into the square. He always noticed beautiful women. This one struck him as a tiny bundle of sex appeal. She was a pale blonde with light green eyes, and she probably had German blood – it was not unusual here in the north-east of France, so close to the border. Her small, slim body was wrapped in a dress like a sack, but she had added a bright yellow scarf of cheap cotton, with a flair for style that he thought enchantingly French. When he spoke to her, he had observed the initial flash of fear usual in a French person on being approached by one of the German occupiers; but then, immediately afterwards, he had seen on her pretty face a look of ill-concealed defiance that had piqued his interest.

She was with an attractive man who was not very interested in her – probably her husband. Dieter had asked her to take a photo only because he wanted to talk to her. He had a wife and two pretty children in Cologne, and he shared his Paris apartment with Stéphanie, but that would not stop him making a play for another girl. Beautiful women were like the gorgeous French impressionist paintings he collected: having one did not stop you wanting another.

French women were the most beautiful in the world. But everything French was beautiful: their bridges, their boulevards, their furniture, even their china tableware. Dieter loved Paris nightclubs, champagne, *foie gras*, and warm baguettes. He enjoyed buying shirts and ties at Charvet, the legendary *chemisier* opposite the Ritz hotel. He could happily have lived in Paris for ever.

He did not know where he had acquired such tastes. His father was a professor of music – the one art form of which the Germans, not the French, were the undisputed masters. But to Dieter, the dry academic life his father led seemed unbearably dull, and he had horrified his parents by becoming a policeman, one of the first university graduates in Germany so to do. By 1939 he was head of the criminal intelligence department of the Cologne police. In May 1940, when General Heinz Guderian's panzer tanks crossed the river Meuse at Sedan and swept triumphantly through France to the English Channel in a week, Dieter impulsively applied for a commission in the army. Because of his police experience, he was given an intelligence posting immediately. He spoke fluent French and adequate English, so he was put to work interrogating captured prisoners. He had a talent for the work, and it gave him profound satisfaction to extract information that could help his side win battles. In north Africa his results had been noticed by Rommel himself.

He was always willing to use torture when necessary,

14

but he liked to persuade people by subtler means. That was how he had got Stéphanie. Poised, sensual and shrewd, she had been the owner of a Paris boutique selling ladies' hats that were devastatingly chic and obscenely expensive. But she had a Jewish grandmother. She had lost the boutique and spent six months in a French prison, and she had been on her way to a camp in Germany when Dieter rescued her.

He could have raped her. She had certainly expected that. No one would have raised a protest, let alone punished him. But instead he had fed her, given her new clothes, installed her in the spare bedroom in his apartment, and treated her with gentle affection until one evening, after a dinner of *foie de veau* and a bottle of La Tache, he had seduced her deliciously on the couch in front of a blazing coal fire.

Today, though, she was part of his camouflage. He was working with Rommel again. Field Marshal Erwin Rommel, the 'Desert Fox', was now Commander of Army Group B, defending northern France. German intelligence expected an Allied invasion this summer. Rommel did not have enough men to guard the hundreds of miles of vulnerable coastline, so he had adopted a daring strategy of flexible response: his battalions were miles inland, ready to be swiftly deployed wherever needed.

The British knew this – they had intelligence, too. Their counterplan was to slow Rommel's response by disrupting his communications. Night and day, British and American bombers pounded roads and railways, bridges and tunnels, stations and marshalling yards.

And the Resistance blew up power stations and factories, derailed trains, cut telephone lines, and sent teenage girls to pour grit into the oil reservoirs of trucks and tanks.

Dieter's brief was to identify key communications targets and assess the ability of the Resistance to attack them. In the last few months, from his base in Paris, he had ranged all over northern France, barking at sleepy sentries and putting the fear of God into lazy captains, tightening up security at railway signal boxes, train sheds, vehicle parks, and airfield control towers. Today he was paying a surprise visit to a telephone exchange of enormous strategic importance. Through this building passed all telephone traffic from the High Command in Berlin to German forces in northern France. That included teleprinter messages, the means by which most orders were sent nowadays. If the exchange were destroyed, German communications would be crippled.

The Allies obviously knew that, and had tried to bomb the place, with limited success. It was the perfect candidate for a Resistance attack. Yet security was infuriatingly lax, by Dieter's standards. That was probably due to the influence of the Gestapo, who had a post in the same building. The *Geheime Staatspolizei* was the state security service, and men were often promoted by reason of loyalty to Hitler and enthusiasm for Fascism rather than because of their brains or ability. Dieter had been here for half an hour, taking photographs, his anger mounting as the men responsible for guarding the place continued to ignore him.

However, as the church bell stopped ringing, a Gestapo officer in major's uniform came strutting through the tall iron gates of the chateau and headed straight for Dieter. In bad French he shouted: 'Give me that camera!'

Dieter turned away, pretending not to hear.

'It is forbidden to take photographs of the chateau, imbecile!' the man yelled. 'Can't you see this is a military installation?'

Dieter turned to him and replied quietly in German: 'You took a damn long time to notice me.'

The man was taken aback. People in civilian clothing were usually frightened of the Gestapo. 'What are you talking about?' he said less aggressively.

Dieter checked his watch. 'I've been here for thirty-two minutes. I could have taken a dozen photographs and driven away long ago. Are you in charge of security?'

'Who are you?'

'Major Dieter Franck, from Field Marshal Rommel's personal staff.'

'Franck!' said the man. 'I remember you.'

Dieter looked harder at him. 'My God,' he said as recognition dawned. 'Willi Weber.'

'*Sturmbannfuehrer* Weber, at your service.' Like most senior Gestapo men, Weber held an SS rank, which he felt was more prestigious than his ordinary police rank.

'Well, I'm damned,' Dieter said. No wonder security was slack.

Weber and Dieter had been young policemen together in Cologne in the twenties. Dieter had been a high flyer, Weber a failure. Weber resented Dieter's success and attributed it to his privileged background. (Dieter's background was not extraordinarily privileged, but it seemed so to Weber, the son of a stevedore.)

In the end, Weber had been fired. The details began to come back to Dieter: there had been a road accident, a crowd had gathered, Weber had panicked and fired his weapon, and a rubber-necking bystander had been killed.

Dieter had not seen the man for fifteen years, but he could guess the course of Weber's career: he had joined the Nazi party, become a volunteer organizer, applied for a job with the Gestapo citing his police training, and risen swiftly in that community of embittered second-raters.

Weber said: 'What are you doing here?'

'Checking your security, on behalf of the Field Marshal.'

Weber bristled. 'Our security is good.'

'Good enough for a sausage factory. Look around you.' Dieter waved a hand, indicating the town square. 'What if these people belonged to the Resistance? They could pick off your guards in a few seconds.' He pointed to a tall girl wearing a light summer coat over her dress. 'What if she had a gun under her coat? What if . . .'

He stopped.

This was not just a fantasy he was weaving to illustrate a point, he realized. His unconscious mind had seen the people in the square deploying in battle formation. The tiny blonde and her husband had taken cover in the bar. The two men in the church doorway had

18

moved behind pillars. The tall girl in the summer coat, who had been staring into a shop window until a moment ago, was now standing in the shadow of Dieter's car. As Dieter looked her coat flapped open, and to his astonishment he saw that his imagination had been prophetic: under the coat she had a submachine-gun with a skeleton-frame butt, exactly the type favoured by the Resistance. 'My God!' he said.

He reached inside his suit jacket, and remembered he was not carrying a gun.

Where was Stéphanie? He looked around, momentarily shocked into a state close to panic, but she was standing behind him, waiting patiently for him to finish his conversation with Weber. 'Get down!' he yelled.

Then there was a bang.

THREE

Flick was in the doorway of the Café des Sports, behind Michel, standing on tiptoe to look over his shoulder. She was alert, her heart pounding, her muscles tensed for action; but in her brain the blood flowed like ice water, and she watched and calculated with cool detachment.

There were eight guards in sight: two at the gate checking passes, two just inside the gate, two patrolling the grounds behind the iron railings, and two at the top of the short flight of steps leading to the chateau's grand doorway. But Michel's main force would bypass the gate.

The long north side of the church building formed part of the wall surrounding the chateau's grounds. The north transept jutted a few feet into the car park that had once been part of the ornamental garden. In the days of the *ancien régime*, the Comte had had his own personal entrance to the church, a little door in the transept wall. The doorway had been boarded up and plastered over more than a hundred years ago, and had remained that way until today.

An hour ago, a retired quarryman called Gaston had entered the empty church and carefully placed four half-pound sticks of yellow plastic explosive at the foot of the blocked doorway. He had inserted detonators, connected them together so that they would all go off at the same instant, and added a five-second fuse ignited by a thumb plunger. Then he had smeared everything with ash from his kitchen fire to make it inconspicuous, and moved an old wooden bench in front of the doorway for additional concealment. Satisfied with his handiwork, he had knelt down to pray.

When the church bell had stopped ringing a few seconds ago, Gaston had got up from his pew, walked a few paces from the nave into the transept, depressed the plunger, and ducked quickly back around the corner. The blast must have shaken centuries of dust from the gothic arches. But the transept was not occupied during services, so no one would have been injured.

After the boom of the explosion, there was a long moment of silence in the square. Everyone froze: the guards at the chateau gate, the sentries patrolling the fence, the Gestapo major, and the well-dressed German with the glamorous mistress. Flick, taut with apprehension, looked across the square and through the iron railings into the grounds. In the car park was a relic of the seventeenth-century garden, a stone fountain with three mossy cherubs sporting where jets of water had once flowed. Around the dry marble bowl were parked a truck, an armoured car, a Mercedes sedan painted the grey-green of the German army, and two black Citroëns of the 'Traction Avant' type favoured by the Gestapo in France. A soldier was filling the tank of one of the Citroëns, using a petrol pump that stood incongruously in front of a tall chateau window. For a few seconds, nothing moved. Flick waited, holding her breath.

Among the congregation in the church were ten armed men. The priest, who was not a sympathizer and therefore had had no warning, must have been pleased that so many people had shown up for the evening service, which was not normally very popular. He might have wondered why some of them wore topcoats, despite the warm weather; but after four years of austerity lots of people wore odd clothes, and a man might wear a raincoat to church because he had no jacket. By now, Flick hoped, the priest understood it all. At this moment the ten would be leaping from their seats, pulling out their guns, and rushing through the brand-new hole in the wall.

At last they came into view around the end of the church. Flick's heart leaped with pride and fear when she saw them, a motley army in old caps and worn-out shoes, running across the car park towards the grand entrance of the chateau, feet pounding the dusty soil, clutching their assorted weapons – pistols, revolvers, rifles and one submachine-gun. They had not yet begun firing them, for they were trying to get as close as possible to the building before the shooting started.

Michel saw them at the same time. He made a noise between a grunt and a sigh, and Flick knew he felt the same mixture of pride at their bravery and fear for their lives. Now was the moment to distract the guards. Michel raised his rifle, a Lee-Enfield No. 4 Mark I, the kind the Resistance called a Canadian rifle, because many of them were made in Canada. He drew a bead, took up the slack of the two-stage trigger, then fired. He worked the bolt action with a practised movement so that the weapon was immediately ready to be fired again.

The crash of the rifle ended the moment of shocked silence in the square. At the gate, one of the guards cried out and fell, and Flick felt a savage moment of satisfaction: there was one less man to shoot at her comrades. Michel's shot was the signal for everyone else to open fire. In the church porch, young Bertrand squeezed off two shots that sounded like firecrackers. He was too far from the guards for accuracy with a pistol, and he did not hit anyone. Beside him, Albert pulled the ring of a grenade and hurled it high over the railing, to land inside the grounds, where it exploded in the vineyard, uselessly scattering vegetation in the air. Flick wanted to yell angrily at them: 'Don't fire for the sake of the noise, you'll just reveal your position!' But only the best and most highly trained troops could exercise restraint once the shooting started. From behind the parked sports car, Geneviève opened up, and the deafening rattle of her Sten gun filled Flick's ears. Her shooting was more effective, and another guard fell.

At last the Germans began to act. The guards took cover behind the stone pillars, or lay flat, and brought their rifles to bear. The Gestapo major fumbled his pistol out of its holster. The redhead turned and ran, but her sexy shoes slipped on the cobblestones, and she fell. Her man lay on top of her, protecting her with his body, and Flick decided she had been right to suppose he was a soldier, for a civilian would not know that it was safer to lie down than to run.

The sentries opened fire. Almost immediately, Albert was hit. Flick saw him stagger and clutch his throat. A hand grenade he had been about to throw dropped from his grasp. Then a second round hit him, this time in the forehead. He fell like a stone, and Flick thought with sudden grief of the baby girl born this morning who now had no father. Beside Albert, Bertrand saw the turtleshell grenade roll across the age-worn stone step of the church porch. He hurled himself through the doorway as the grenade exploded. Flick waited for him to reappear, but he did not, and she thought with anguished uncertainty that he could be dead, wounded or just stunned.

In the car park, the team from the church stopped running, turned on the remaining six sentries and opened up. The four guards near the gate were caught in a crossfire, between those inside the grounds and those outside in the square, and they were wiped out in seconds, leaving only the two on the chateau steps. Michel's plan was working, Flick thought with a surge of hope.

But the enemy troops inside the building had now had time to seize their weapons and rush to the doors and windows, and they began to shoot, changing the odds again. Everything depended on how many of them there were.

For a few moments the bullets poured like rain, and

Flick stopped counting. Then she realized with dismay that there were many more guns in the chateau than she had expected. Fire seemed to be coming from at least twelve doors and windows. The men from the church, who should by now have been inside the building, retreated to take cover behind the vehicles in the car park. Antoinette had been right, and MI6 wrong, about the number of troops stationed here. Twelve was the MI6 estimate, yet the Resistance had downed six for certain and there were at least fourteen still firing.

Flick cursed passionately. In a fight like this, the Resistance could win only by sudden overwhelming violence. If they did not crush the enemy right away, they were in trouble. As the seconds ticked by, army training and discipline began to tell. In the end, regular troops would always prevail in a drawn-out conflict.

On the upper floor of the chateau, a tall seventeenth-century window was smashed open, and a machine-gun began to fire. Because of its high position, it caused horrible carnage among the Resistance in the car park. Flick was sickened as, one after another, the men there fell and lay bleeding beside the dry fountain, until there were only two or three still shooting.

It was all over, Flick realized in despair. They were outnumbered and they had failed. The sour taste of defeat rose in her throat.

Michel had been shooting at the machine-gun position. 'We can't take out that machine-gunner from the ground!' he said. He looked around the square, his gaze flying to the tops of the buildings, the bell tower of the church and the upper floor of the town hall. 'If I could get into the mayor's office I'd have a clear shot.'

'Wait.' Flick's mouth was dry. She could not stop him risking his life, much as she wanted to. But she could improve the odds. She yelled at the top of her voice: 'Geneviève!'

Geneviève turned to look at her.

'Cover Michel!'

Geneviève nodded vigorously, then dashed out from behind the sports car, spraying bullets at the chateau windows.

'Thanks,' Michel said to Flick. Then he broke cover and sprinted across the square, heading for the town hall.

Geneviève ran on, heading for the church porch. Her fire distracted the men in the chateau, giving Michel a chance of crossing the square unscathed. But then there was a flash on Flick's left. She glanced that way and saw the Gestapo major, flattened against the wall of the town hall, aiming his pistol at Michel.

It was hard to hit a moving target with a handgun at anything but close range – but the major might be lucky, Flick thought fearfully. She was under orders to observe and report back, and not to join the fighting under any circumstances, but now she thought: To hell with that. In her shoulder bag she carried her personal weapon, a Browning nine-millimetre automatic, which she preferred to the SOE standard Colt because it had thirteen rounds in the clip instead of seven, and because she could load it with the same nine-millimetre Parabellum rounds used in the Sten submachine-gun.

She snatched it out of the bag. She released the safety catch, cocked the hammer, extended her arm, and fired two hasty shots at the major.

She missed him, but her bullets chipped fragments of stone from the wall near his face, and he ducked.

Michel ran on.

The major recovered quickly and raised his weapon again.

As Michel approached his destination, he also came closer to the major, shortening the range. Michel fired his rifle in the major's direction, but the shot went wide, and the major kept his head and fired back. This time, Michel went down, and Flick let out a yell of fear.

Michel hit the ground, tried to get up, and collapsed. Flick calmed herself and thought fast. Michel was still alive. Geneviève had reached the church porch, and her submachine-gun fire continued to draw the attention of the enemy inside the chateau. Flick had a chance of rescuing Michel. It was against her orders, but no orders could make her leave her husband bleeding on the ground. Besides, if she left him there, he would be captured and interrogated. As leader of the Bollinger circuit, Michel knew every name, every address, every code word. His capture would be a catastrophe.

There was no choice.

She shot at the major again. Again she missed, but she pulled the trigger repeatedly, and the steady fire forced the man to retreat along the wall, looking for cover.

She ran out of the bar into the square. From the

corner of her eye she saw the owner of the sports car, still protecting his mistress from gunfire by lying on top of her. Flick had forgotten him, she realized with sudden fear. Was he armed? If so he could shoot her easily. But no bullets came.

She reached the supine Michel and went down on one knee. She turned towards the town hall and fired two wild shots to keep the major busy. Then she looked at her husband.

To her relief she saw that his eyes were open and he was breathing. He seemed to be bleeding from his left buttock. Her fear receded a little. 'You got a bullet in your bum,' she said in English.

He replied in French: 'It hurts like hell.'

She turned again to the town hall. The major had retreated twenty yards and crossed the narrow street to a shop doorway. This time Flick took a few seconds to aim carefully. She squeezed off four shots. The shop window exploded in a storm of glass, and the major staggered back and fell to the ground.

Flick spoke to Michel in French. 'Try to get up,' she said. He rolled over, groaning in pain, and got to one knee, but he could not move his injured leg. 'Come on,' she said harshly. 'If you stay here, you'll be killed.' She grabbed him by the front of his shirt and heaved him upright with a mighty effort. He stood on his good leg, but he could not bear his own weight, and leaned heavily against her. She realized that he was not going to be able to walk, and she groaned in despair.

She glanced over to the side of the town hall. The major was getting up. He had blood on his face, but he did not seem badly injured. She guessed that he had been cut superficially by flying glass, but might still be capable of shooting.

There was only one thing for it: she would have to pick Michel up and carry him to safety.

She bent in front of him, grasped him around the thighs, and eased him on to her shoulder in the classic fireman's lift. He was tall but thin – most French people were thin, these days. All the same, she thought she would collapse under his weight. She staggered, and felt dizzy for a second, but she stayed upright.

After a moment she took a step forward.

She lumbered across the cobblestones. She thought the major was shooting at her, but she could not be sure as there was so much gunfire from the chateau, from Geneviève, and from the Resistance fighters still alive in the car park. The fear that a bullet might hit her at any second gave her strength, and she broke into a lurching run. She made for the road leading out of the square to the south, the nearest exit. She passed the German lying on top of the redhead, and for a startled moment she met his eye and saw an expression of surprise and wry admiration. Then she crashed into a café table, sending it flying, and she almost fell, but managed to right herself and run on. A bullet hit the window of the bar, and she saw a cobweb of fracture lines maze the glass. A moment later, she was around the corner and out of the major's line of sight. Alive, she thought gratefully; both of us – for a few more minutes, at least.

Until now she had not thought where to go once she

was clear of the battlefield. Two getaway vehicles were waiting a couple of streets away, but she could not carry Michel that far. However, Antoinette Dupert lived on this street, just a few steps farther. Antoinette was not in the Resistance, but she was sympathetic enough to have provided Michel with a plan of the chateau. And Michel was her nephew, so she surely would not turn him away.

Anyway, Flick had no alternative.

Antoinette had a ground-floor apartment in a building with a courtyard. Flick came to the open gateway, a few yards along the street from the square, and staggered under the archway. She pushed open a door and lowered Michel to the tiles.

She hammered on Antoinette's door, panting with effort. She heard a frightened voice say: 'What is it?' Antoinette had been scared by the gunfire and did not want to open the door.

Breathlessly, Flick said: 'Quickly, quickly!' She tried to keep her voice low. Some of the neighbours might be Nazi sympathizers.

The door did not open, but Antoinette's voice came nearer. 'Who's there?'

Flick instinctively avoided speaking a name aloud. She replied: 'Your nephew is wounded.'

The door opened. Antoinette was a straight-backed woman of fifty wearing a cotton dress that had once been chic and was now faded but crisply pressed. She was pale with fear. 'Michel!' she said. She knelt beside him. 'Is it serious?'

'It hurts, but I'm not dying,' Michel said through clenched teeth.

'You poor thing.' She brushed his hair off his sweaty forehead with a gesture like a caress.

Flick said impatiently: 'Let's get him inside.'

She took Michel's arms and Antoinette lifted him by the knees. He grunted with pain. Together they carried him into the living room and put him down on a faded velvet sofa.

'Take care of him while I fetch the car,' Flick said. She ran back into the street.

The gunfire was dying down. She did not have long. She raced along the street and turned two corners.

Outside a closed bakery, two vehicles were parked with their engines running: one a rusty Renault, the other a van with a faded sign on the side that had once read *Blanchisserie Bisset* – Bisset's Laundry. The van was borrowed from the father of Bertrand, who was able to get fuel because he washed sheets for hotels used by the Germans. The Renault had been stolen this morning in Chalons, and Michel had changed its licence plates. Flick decided to take the car, leaving the van for any survivors who might get away from the carnage in the chateau grounds.

She spoke briefly to the driver of the van. 'Wait here for five minutes, then leave.' She ran to the car, jumped into the passenger seat, and said: 'Let's go, quickly!'

At the wheel of the Renault was Gilberte, a nineteen-year-old girl with long dark hair, pretty but stupid. Flick did not know why she was in the Resistance – she was not the usual type. Instead of pulling away, Gilberte said: 'Where to?'

'I'll direct you – for the love of Christ, move!'

Gilberte put the car in gear and drove off.

'Left, then right,' Flick said.

In the two minutes of inaction that followed, the full realization of her failure hit her. Most of the Bollinger circuit was wiped out. Albert and others had died. Geneviève, Bertrand and any others who survived would probably be tortured.

And it was all for nothing. The telephone exchange was undamaged, and German communications were intact. Flick felt worthless. She tried to think what she had done wrong. Had it been a mistake to try a frontal attack on a guarded military installation? Not necessarily – the plan might have worked but for the inaccurate intelligence supplied by MI6. However, it would have been safer, she now thought, to get inside the building by some clandestine means. That would have given the Resistance a better chance of getting to the crucial equipment.

Gilberte pulled up at the courtyard entrance. 'Turn the car around,' Flick said, and jumped out.

Michel was lying face down on Antoinette's sofa, trousers pulled down, looking undignified. Antoinette knelt beside him, holding a bloodstained towel, a pair of glasses perched on her nose, peering at his backside. 'The bleeding has slowed, but the bullet is still in there,' she said.

On the floor beside the sofa was her handbag. She had emptied the contents on to a small table, presumably while hurriedly searching for her spectacles. Flick's eye was caught by a sheet of paper, typed on and stamped, with a small photograph of Antoinette pasted to it, the whole thing in a little cardboard folder. It was the pass that permitted her to enter the chateau. In that moment, Flick had the glimmer of an idea.

'I've got a car outside,' Flick said.

Antoinette continued to study the wound. 'He shouldn't be moved.'

'If he stays here, the Boche will kill him.' Flick casually picked up Antoinette's pass. As she did so she asked Michel: 'How do you feel?'

'I might be able to walk now,' he said. 'The pain is easing.'

Flick slipped the pass into her shoulder bag. Antoinette did not notice. Flick said to her: 'Help me get him up.'

The two women raised Michel to his feet. Antoinette pulled up his blue canvas trousers and fastened his worn leather belt.

'Stay inside,' Flick said to Antoinette. 'I don't want anyone to see you with us.' She had not yet begun to work out her idea, but she already knew it would be blighted if any suspicion were to fall on Antoinette and her cleaners.

Michel put his arm around Flick's shoulders and leaned heavily on her. She took his weight and he hobbled out of the building into the street. By the time they reached the car, he was white with pain. Gilberte stared through the window at them, looking terrified.

Flick hissed at her: 'Get out and open the fucking door, dimwit!' Gilberte leaped out of the car and threw open the rear door. With her help, Flick bundled Michel on to the back seat.

The two women jumped in the front. 'Let's get out of here,' said Flick.

FOUR

Dieter was dismayed and appalled. As the shooting began to peter out, and his heartbeat returned to normal, he started to reflect on what he had seen. He had not thought the Resistance capable of such a well-planned and carefully executed attack. From everything he had learned in the last few months, he believed their raids were normally hit-and-run affairs. But this had been his first sight of them in action. They had been bristling with guns and obviously not short of ammunition – unlike the German army. Worst of all, they had been courageous. Dieter had been impressed by the rifleman who had dashed across the square, by the girl with the Sten gun who had given him covering fire, and most of all by the little blonde who had picked up the wounded rifleman and had carried him – a man six inches taller than she – out of the square to safety. Such people could not fail to be a profound threat to the occupying military force. These were not like the criminals Dieter had dealt with as a policeman in Cologne before the war. Criminals were stupid, lazy, cowardly and brutish. These French Resistance people were fighters.

But their defeat gave him a rare opportunity.

When he was sure the shooting had stopped, he got to his feet and helped Stéphanie up. Her cheeks were flushed and she was breathing hard. She held his hands and looked into his face. 'You protected me,' she said. Tears came to her eyes. 'You made yourself a shield for me.'

He brushed dirt from her hip. He was surprised by his own gallantry. The action had been instinctive. When he thought about it, he was not at all sure he would really be willing to give his life to save Stéphanie. He tried to pass over it lightly. 'No harm should come to this perfect body,' he said.

She began to cry.

He took her hand and led her across the square to the gates. 'Let's go inside,' he said. 'You can sit down for a while.' They entered the grounds. Dieter saw a hole in the wall of the church. That explained how the main force had got inside.

The Waffen SS troops had come out of the building and were disarming the attackers. Dieter looked keenly at the Resistance fighters. Most were dead, but some were only wounded, and one or two appeared to have surrendered unhurt. There should be several for him to interrogate.

Until now, his work had been defensive. The most he had been able to do was fortify key installations against the Resistance by beefing up security. The occasional prisoner had yielded little information. But having several prisoners, all from one large and evidently well-organized circuit, was a different matter.

This might be his chance of going on the attack, he thought eagerly.

He shouted at a sergeant. 'You – get a doctor for these prisoners. I want to interrogate them. Don't let any die.'

Although Dieter was not in uniform, the sergeant assumed from his manner that he was a superior officer, and said: 'Very good, sir.'

Dieter took Stéphanie up the steps and through the stately doorway into the wide hall. It was a breathtaking sight: a pink marble floor, tall windows with elaborate curtains, walls with Etruscan motifs in plaster picked out in dusty shades of pink and green, and a ceiling painted with fading cherubs. Once, Dieter assumed, the room had been filled with gorgeous furniture: pier tables under high mirrors, sideboards encrusted with ormolu, dainty chairs with gilded legs, oil paintings, huge vases, little marble statuettes. All that was gone now, of course. Instead there were rows of switchboards, each with its chair, and a snake's nest of cables on the floor.

The telephone operators seemed to have fled into the grounds at the rear but, now that the shooting had stopped, a few of them were standing at the glazed doors, still wearing their headsets and breast microphones, wondering if it was safe to come back inside. Dieter sat Stéphanie at one of the switchboards, then beckoned a middle-aged woman telephonist. 'Madame,' he said, in a polite but commanding voice. He spoke French. 'Please bring a cup of hot coffee for this lady.'

The woman came forward, shooting a look of hatred at Stéphanie. 'Very good, Monsieur.'

'And some cognac. She's had a shock.'

'We have no cognac.'

They had cognac, but she did not want to give it to the mistress of a German. Dieter did not argue the point. 'Just coffee, then, but be quick, or there will be trouble.'

He patted Stéphanie's shoulder and left her. He passed through double doors into the east wing. The chateau was laid out as a series of reception rooms, one leading into the next on the Versailles pattern, he found. The rooms were full of switchboards, but these had a more permanent look, the cables bundled into neatly made wooden trunking that disappeared through the floor into the cellar beneath. Dieter guessed the hall looked messy only because it had been brought into service as an emergency measure after the west wing had been bombed. Some of the windows were permanently blacked out, no doubt as an air-raid precaution, but others had heavy curtains drawn open, and Dieter supposed the women did not like to work in permanent night.

At the end of the east wing was a stairwell. Dieter went down. At the foot of the staircase he passed through a steel door. A small desk and a chair stood just inside, and Dieter assumed a guard normally sat there. The man on duty had presumably left his post to join in the fighting. Dieter entered unchallenged, and made a mental note of a security breach.

This was a different environment from that of the

grand principal floors. Designed as kitchens, storage, and accommodation for the dozens of staff who would have serviced this house three hundred years ago, it had low ceilings, bare walls, and floors of stone or even, in some rooms, beaten earth. Dieter walked along a broad corridor. Every door was clearly labelled in neat German signwriting, but Dieter looked inside anyway. On his left, at the front of the building, was the complex equipment of a major telephone exchange: a generator, enormous batteries, and rooms full of tangled cables. On his right, towards the back of the house, were the Gestapo's facilities: a photo lab, a large wireless listening room for eavesdropping on the Resistance, and prison cells with peepholes in the doors. The basement had been bombproofed: all windows were blocked, the walls were sandbagged, and the ceilings had been reinforced with steel girders and poured concrete. Obviously that was to prevent Allied bombers putting the phone system out of action.

At the end of the corridor was a door marked 'Interrogation Centre'. He went inside. The first room had bare white walls, bright lights and the standard furniture of a simple interview room: a cheap table, hard chairs, and an ashtray. Dieter went through to the next room. Here the lights were less bright and the walls bare brick. There was a bloodstained pillar with hooks for tying people up; an umbrella stand holding a selection of wooden clubs and steel bars; a hospital operating table with a head clamp and straps for the wrists and ankles; an electric-shock machine; and a locked cabinet that probably contained drugs and hypodermic syringes. It was a torture chamber. Dieter had been in many similar, but still they sickened him. He had to remind himself that intelligence gathered in places such as this helped save the lives of decent young German soldiers, so that they could eventually go home to their wives and children instead of dying on battlefields. All the same, the place gave him the creeps.

There was a noise behind him, startling him. He spun around. When he saw what was in the doorway he took a frightened step back. 'Christ!' he said. He was looking at a squat figure, its face thrown into shadow by the strong light from the next room. 'Who are you?' he said, and he could hear the fear in his own voice.

The figure stepped into the light and turned into a man in the uniform shirt of a Gestapo sergeant. He was short and podgy, with a fleshy face and ash-blond hair cropped so short that he looked bald. 'What are you doing here?' he said in a Frankfurt accent.

Dieter recovered his composure. The torture chamber had unnerved him, but he regained his habitual tone of authority and said: 'I am Major Franck. Your name?'

The sergeant became deferential at once. 'Becker, sir, at your service.'

'Get the prisoners down here as soon as possible, Becker,' said Dieter. 'Those who can walk should be brought immediately, the others when they have been seen by a doctor.'

'Very good, Major.'

Becker went away. Dieter returned to the interview

room and sat in the hard chair. He wondered how much information he would get out of the prisoners. Their knowledge might be limited to their own town. If his luck was bad, and their security good, each individual might know only a little about what went on in their own circuit. On the other hand, there was no such thing as perfect security. A few individuals inevitably amassed a wide knowledge of their own and other Resistance circuits. His dream was that one circuit might lead him to another in a chain, and he might be able to inflict enormous damage on the Resistance in the weeks remaining before the Allied invasion.

He heard footsteps in the corridor and looked out. The prisoners were being brought in. The first was the woman who had concealed a Sten gun beneath her coat. Dieter was pleased. It was so useful to have a woman among the prisoners. Under interrogation, women could be as tough as men; but often the way to make a man talk was to beat a woman in front of him. This one was tall and sexy, which was all the better. She seemed to be uninjured. Dieter held up a hand to the soldier escorting her, and spoke to the woman in French. 'What is your name?' he said in a friendly tone.

She looked at him with haughty eyes. 'Why should I tell you?'

He shrugged. This level of opposition was easy to overcome. He used an answer that had served him well a hundred times. 'Your relatives may enquire whether you are in custody. If we know your name, we may tell them.'

'I am Geneviève Delys.'

'A beautiful name for a beautiful woman.' He waved her on.

Next came a man in his sixties, bleeding from a head injury and limping too. Dieter said: 'You're a little old for this sort of thing, aren't you?'

The man looked proud. 'I set the charges,' he said defiantly.

'Name?'

'Gaston Lefèvre.'

'Just remember one thing, Gaston,' Dieter said in a kindly voice. 'The pain lasts as long as you choose. When you decide to end it, it will stop.'

Fear came into the man's eyes as he contemplated what faced him.

Dieter nodded, satisfied. 'Carry on.'

A youngster was next, no more than seventeen, Dieter guessed, a good-looking boy who was absolutely terrified. 'Name?'

He hesitated, seeming dazed by shock. After thinking, he said: 'Bertrand Bisset.'

'Good evening, Bertrand,' Dieter said pleasantly. 'Welcome to Hell.'

The boy looked as if he had been slapped.

Dieter pushed him on.

Willi Weber appeared, with Becker pacing behind him like a dangerous dog on a chain. 'How did you get in here?' Weber said rudely to Dieter.

'I walked in,' Dieter said. 'Your security stinks.'

'Ridiculous! You've just seen us beat off a major attack!'

'By a dozen men and some girls!'

'We defeated them, that's all that counts.'

'Think about it, Willi,' Dieter said reasonably. 'They were able to assemble close by, quite unnoticed by you, then force their way into the grounds and kill at least six good German soldiers. I suspect the only reason you defeated them was that they had underestimated the numbers against them. And I entered this basement unchallenged because the guard had left his post.'

'He's a brave German, he wanted to join the fighting.'

'God give me strength,' Dieter said in despair. 'A soldier in battle doesn't leave his post to join the fighting, he follows orders!'

'I don't need a lecture from you on military discipline.'

Dieter gave up, for now. 'And I have no desire to give one.'

'What *do* you want?'

'I'm going to interview the prisoners.'

'That's the Gestapo's job.'

'Don't be idiotic. Field Marshal Rommel has asked me, not the Gestapo, to limit the capacity of the Resistance to damage his communications in the event of an invasion. These prisoners can give me priceless information. I intend to question them.'

'Not while they're in my custody,' Weber said stubbornly. 'I shall interrogate them myself and send the results to the Field Marshal.'

'The Allies are probably going to invade this summer – isn't it time to stop fighting turf wars?'

'It is never time to abandon efficient organization.'

Dieter could have screamed. In desperation, he swallowed his pride and tried for a compromise. 'Let's interrogate them together.'

Weber smiled, sensing victory. 'Absolutely not.'

'This means I'll have to go over your head.'

'If you can.'

'Of course I can. All you will achieve is a delay.'

'So you say.'

'You damned fool,' Dieter said savagely. 'God preserve the fatherland from patriots such as you.' He turned on his heel and stalked out.

FIVE

Gilberte and Flick left the town of Sainte-Cécile behind, heading for the city of Reims on a country back road. Gilberte drove as fast as she could along the narrow lane. Flick's eyes apprehensively raked the road ahead. It rose and fell over low hills and wound through vineyards as it made its leisurely way from village to village. Their progress was slowed by many crossroads, but the number of junctions made it impossible for the Gestapo to block every route away from Sainté-Cécile. All the same, Flick gnawed her lip, worrying about the chance of being stopped at random by a patrol. She could not explain away a man in the back seat bleeding from a bullet wound.

Thinking ahead, she realized she could not take Michel to his home. After France surrendered in 1940, and Michel was demobilized, he had not returned to his lectureship at the Sorbonne, but had come back to his home town, to be deputy head of a high school, and – his real motive – to organize a Resistance circuit. He had moved into the home of his late parents, a charming town house near the cathedral. But, Flick decided, he could not go there now. It was known to too many people. Although Resistance members often did not know one another's addresses – for the sake of security, they revealed them only if necessary for a delivery or rendezvous – Michel was leader, and most people knew where he lived.

Back in Sainte-Cécile, some of the team must have been taken alive. Before long they would be under interrogation. Unlike British agents, the French Resistance did not carry suicide pills. The only reliable rule of interrogation was that everybody would talk in the long run. Sometimes the Gestapo ran out of patience, and sometimes they killed their subjects by over-enthusiasm but, if they were careful and determined, they could make the strongest personality betray his or her dearest comrades. No one could bear agony for ever.

So Flick had to treat Michel's house as known to the enemy. Where could she take him instead?

'How is he?' said Gilberte anxiously.

Flick glanced into the back seat. His eyes were closed, but he was breathing normally. He had fallen into a sleep, the best thing for him. She looked at him fondly. He needed someone to take care of him, at least for a day or two. She turned to Gilberte. Young and single, she was probably still with her parents. 'Where do you live?' Flick asked her.

'On the outskirts of town, on the Route de Cernay.'

'On your own?'

For some reason, Gilberte looked scared. 'Yes, of course on my own.'

'A house, an apartment, a bedsitting room?'

'An apartment, two rooms.'

'We'll go there.'

'No!'

'Why not? Are you scared?'

She looked injured. 'No, not scared.'

'What, then?'

'I don't trust the neighbours.'

'Is there a back entrance?'

Reluctantly, Gilberte said: 'Yes, an alley that runs along the side of a little factory.'

'It sounds ideal.'

'Okay, you're right, we should go to my place. I just . . . You surprised me, that's all.'

'I'm sorry.'

Flick was scheduled to return to London tonight. She was to rendezvous with a plane in a meadow outside the village of Chatelle, five miles north of Reims. She wondered if the plane would make it. Navigating by the stars, it was extraordinarily difficult to find a specific field near a small village. Pilots often went astray – in fact, it was a miracle they ever arrived where they were supposed to. She looked at the weather. A clear sky was darkening to the deep blue of evening. There would be moonlight, provided the weather held.

If not tonight, then tomorrow, she thought, as always.

Her mind went to the comrades she had left behind. Was young Bertrand dead or alive? What about Geneviève? They might be better off dead. Alive, they faced the agony of torture. Flick's heart seemed to convulse with grief as she thought again that she had led them to defeat. Bertrand had a crush on her, she guessed. He was young enough to feel guilty about secretly loving the wife of his commander. She wished she had ordered him to stay at home. It would have made no difference to the outcome, and he would have remained a bright, likeable youth for a little longer, instead of a corpse, or worse.

No one could succeed every time, and war meant that when leaders failed then people died. It was a hard fact, but still she cast about for consolation. She longed for a way to make sure their suffering was not in vain. Perhaps she could build on their sacrifice and get some kind of victory out of it after all.

She thought about the pass she had stolen from Antoinette, and the possibility of getting into the chateau under cover. A team could enter disguised as civilian employees. She swiftly dismissed the idea of having them pose as telephone operators: it was a skilled job that took time to learn. But anyone could use a broom.

Would the Germans notice if the cleaners were strangers? They probably paid no attention to the women who mopped the floor. What about the French telephonists – would they give the game away? It might be a risk worth taking.

SOE had a remarkable forgery department that could copy any kind of document, sometimes even making their own paper to match the original, in a couple of days. They could soon produce counterfeits of Antoinette's pass.

Flick suffered a guilty pang at having stolen it. At this moment Antoinette might be looking for it frantically, searching under the couch and in all her pockets, going out into the courtyard with a torch. When she told the Gestapo she had lost it, she would be in trouble. But in the end they would just give her a replacement. And this way she was not guilty of helping the Resistance. If interrogated, she would steadfastly maintain that she had mislaid it, for she believed that to be the truth. Besides, Flick thought grimly, if she had asked permission to borrow the thing, Antoinette might have said no.

Of course, there was one major snag with this plan. All the cleaners were women. The Resistance team that went in disguised as cleaners would have to be all-female.

But then, Flick thought, why not?

They were entering the suburbs of Reims. It was dark when Gilberte pulled up near a low industrial building surrounded by a high wire fence. She killed the engine. Flick spoke sharply to Michel. 'Wake up! We have to get you indoors.' He groaned. 'We must be quick,' she added. 'We're breaking the curfew.'

The two women got him out of the car. Gilberte pointed to the narrow alley that led along the back of the factory. Michel put his arms over their shoulders and they helped him along the alley. Gilberte opened a door in a wall that led to the back yard of a small apartment building. They crossed the yard and went in through a back door.

It was a block of cheap flats with five floors and no lift. Unfortunately, Gilberte's rooms were on the attic floor. Flick showed her how to make a carrying chair.

Crossing their arms, they linked hands under Michel's thighs and took his weight. He put an arm around the shoulders of each woman to steady himself. That way they carried him up four flights. Luckily, they met no one on the stairs.

They were breathing hard by the time they reached Gilberte's door. They stood Michel on his feet and he managed to limp inside, where he collapsed into an armchair.

Flick looked around. It was a girl's place, pretty and neat and clean. More importantly, it was not overlooked. That was the advantage of the top floor: no one could see in. Michel should be safe.

Gilberte fussed about Michel, trying to make him comfortable with cushions, wiping his face gently with a towel, offering him aspirins. She was tender but impractical, as Antoinette had been. Michel had that effect on women, though not on Flick – which was partly why he had fallen for her: he could not resist a challenge. 'You need a doctor,' Flick said brusquely. 'What about Claude Bouler? He used to help us, but last time I spoke to him, he didn't want to know me. I thought he was going to run away, he was so nervous.'

'He's become scared since he got married,' Michel replied. 'But he'll come for me.'

Flick nodded. Lots of people would make exceptions for Michel. 'Gilberte, go and fetch Dr Bouler.'

'I'd rather stay with Michel.'

Flick groaned inwardly. Someone like Gilberte was no good for anything but carrying messages, yet she could make difficulties about that. 'Please do as I ask,'

50

Flick said firmly. 'I need time alone with Michel before I return to London.'

'What about the curfew?'

'If you're stopped, say you're fetching a doctor. It's an accepted excuse. They may accompany you to Claude's house to make sure you're telling the truth. But they won't come here.'

Gilberte looked troubled, but she pulled on a cardigan and went out.

Flick sat on the arm of Michel's chair and kissed him. 'That was a catastrophe,' she said.

'I know.' He grunted with disgust. 'So much for MI6. There must have been double the number of men they told us.'

'I'll never trust those clowns again.'

'We lost Albert. I'll have to tell his wife.'

'I'm going back tonight. I'll get London to send you another radio operator.'

'Thanks.'

'You'll have to find out who else is dead, and who's alive.'

'If I can.' He sighed.

She held his hand. 'How are you feeling?'

'Foolish. It's an undignified place for a bullet wound.'

'But physically?'

'A little giddy.'

'You need something to drink. I wonder what she has.'

'Scotch would be nice.' Flick's friends in London had taught Michel to like whisky, before the war.

'That's a little strong.' The kitchen was in a corner of the living room. Flick opened a cupboard. To her surprise, she saw a bottle of Dewar's White Label. Agents from Britain often brought whisky with them, for their own use or for their comrades-in-arms, but it seemed an unlikely drink for a French girl. There was also an opened bottle of red wine, much more suitable for a wounded man. She poured half a glass and topped it up with water from the tap. Michel drank greedily: loss of blood had made him thirsty. He emptied the glass then leaned back and closed his eyes.

Flick would have liked some of the Scotch, but it seemed unkind to deny it to Michel then drink it herself. Besides, she still needed her wits about her. She would have a drink when she was back on British soil.

She looked around the room. There were a couple of sentimental pictures on the wall, a stack of old fashion magazines, no books. She poked her nose into the bedroom. Michel said sharply: 'Where are you going?'

'Just looking around.'

'Don't you think it's a little rude, when she's not here?'

Flick shrugged. 'Not really. Anyway, I need the bathroom.'

'It's outside. Down the stairs and along the corridor to the end. If I remember rightly.'

She followed his instructions. While she was in the bathroom she realized that something was bothering her, something about Gilberte's apartment. She thought hard. She never ignored her instincts: they had saved her life more than once. When she returned, she said to Michel: 'Something's wrong here. What is it?'

He shrugged, looking uncomfortable. 'I don't know.'

'You seem edgy.'

'Perhaps it's because I've just been wounded in a gunfight.'

'No, it's not that. It's the apartment.' It had something to do with Gilberte's unease, something to do with Michel's knowing where the bathroom was, something to do with the whisky. She went into the bedroom, exploring. This time Michel did not reprove her. She looked around. On the bedside table stood a photograph of a man with Gilberte's big eyes and black eyebrows, perhaps her father. There was a doll on the counterpane. In the corner was a washbasin with a mirrored cabinet over. Flick opened the cabinet door. Inside was a man's razor, bowl and shaving brush. Gilberte was not so innocent: some man stayed overnight often enough to leave his shaving tackle here.

Flick looked more closely. The razor and brush were a set, with polished bone handles. She recognized them. She had given the set to Michel for his thirty-second birthday.

So that was it.

She was so shocked that for a moment she could not move.

She had suspected him of being interested in someone else, but she had not imagined it had gone this far. Yet here was the proof, in front of her eyes.

Shock turned to hurt. How could he cuddle up to another woman when Flick was lying in bed alone in

London? She turned and looked at the bed. They had done it right here, in this room. It was unbearable.

Then she became angry. She had been loyal and faithful, she had borne the loneliness – but he had not. He had cheated. She was so furious she felt she would explode.

She strode into the other room and stood in front of him. 'You bastard,' she said in English. 'You lousy rotten bastard.'

Michel replied in the same language. 'Don't angry yourself at me.'

He knew that she found his fractured English endearing, but it was not going to work this time. She switched to French. 'How could you betray me for a nineteen-year-old nitwit?'

'It doesn't mean anything, she's just a pretty girl.'

'Do you think that makes it better?' Flick knew she had originally attracted Michel's attention, back in the days when she was a student and he a lecturer, by challenging him in class – French students were deferential by comparison with their English counterparts, and on top of that Flick was by nature disrespectful of authority. If someone similar had seduced Michel – perhaps Geneviève, a woman who would have been his equal – she could have borne it better. It was more hurtful that he had chosen Gilberte, a girl with nothing on her mind more interesting than nail varnish.

'I was lonely,' Michel said pathetically.

'Spare me the sob story. You weren't lonely – you were weak, dishonest and faithless.'

'Flick, my darling, let's not quarrel. Half our friends

have just been killed. You're going back to England. We could both die soon. Don't go away angry.'

'How can I not be angry? I'm leaving you in the arms of your floozie!'

'She's not a floozie—'

'Skip the technicalities. I'm your wife, but you're sharing her bed.'

Michel moved in his chair and winced with pain, then he fixed Flick with his intense blue eyes. 'I plead guilty,' he said. 'I'm a louse. But I'm a louse who loves you, and I'm just asking you to forgive me, this once, in case I never see you again.'

It was hard to resist. Flick weighed five years of marriage against a fling with a popsie, and gave in. She moved a step towards him. He put his arms around her legs and pressed his face into the worn cotton of her dress. She stroked his hair. 'All right,' she said. 'All right.'

'I'm so sorry,' he said. 'I feel awful. You're the most wonderful woman I ever met, or even heard of. I won't do it any more, I promise.'

The door opened, and Gilberte came in with Claude. Flick gave a guilty start, and released Michel's head from her embrace. Then she felt stupid. He was *her* husband, not Gilberte's. Why should she feel guilty about hugging him, even in Gilberte's apartment? She was angry with herself.

Gilberte looked shocked to see her lover embracing his wife here, but she swiftly recovered her composure, and her face assumed a frozen expression of indifference.

Claude, a handsome young doctor, followed her in, looking anxious.

Flick went to Claude and kissed him on both cheeks. 'Thank you for coming,' she said. 'We're truly grateful.'

Claude looked at Michel. 'How do you feel, old buddy?'

'I've got a bullet in my arse.'

'Then I'd better take it out.' He lost his worried air and became briskly professional. Turning to Flick, he said: 'Put some towels on the bed to soak up the blood, then get his trousers off and lay him face down. I'll wash my hands.'

Gilberte put old magazines on her bed and towels over the paper while Flick got Michel up and helped him hobble to the bed. As he lay down, she could not help wondering how many other times he had lain here.

Claude inserted a metal instrument into the wound and felt around for the slug. Michel cried out with pain.

'I'm sorry, old friend,' Claude said solicitously.

Flick almost took pleasure in the sight of Michel in agony on the bed where he had formerly cried out with guilty pleasure. She hoped he would always remember Gilberte's bedroom this way.

Michel said: 'Just get it over with.'

Flick's vengeful feeling passed quickly, and she felt sorry for Michel. She moved the pillow closer to his face, saying: 'Bite on this, it will help.'

Michel stuffed the pillow into his mouth.

Claude probed again, and this time got the bullet out. Blood flowed freely for a few seconds, then slowed, and Claude put a dressing on.

'Keep as still as you can for a few days,' he advised Michel. That meant Michel would have to stay at Gilberte's place. However, he would be too sore for sex, Flick thought with grim satisfaction.

'Thank you, Claude,' she said.

'Glad to be able to help.'

'I have another request.'

Claude looked scared. 'What?'

'I'm meeting a plane at a quarter to midnight. I need you to drive me to Chatelle.'

'Why can't Gilberte take you, in the car she used to come to my place?'

'Because of the curfew. But we'll be safe with you, you're a doctor.'

'Why would I have two people with me?'

'Three. We need Michel to hold a torch.' There was an unvarying procedure for pick-ups: four Resistance people held flashlights in the shape of a giant letter L, indicating the direction of the wind and where the plane should come down. The small battery-operated torches needed to be directed at the aircraft to make sure the pilot saw them. They could simply be placed in position on the ground, but that was less sure, and if the pilot did not see what he expected he might suspect a trap and decide not to land. It was better to have four people if at all possible.

Claude said: 'How would I explain you all to the police? A doctor on emergency call doesn't travel with three people in his car.'

'We'll think of some story.'

'It's too dangerous!'

'It will take only a few minutes, at this time of night.'

'Marie-Jeanne will kill me. She says I have to think of the children.'

'You don't have any.'

'She's pregnant.'

Flick nodded. That would explain why he had become so jumpy.

Michel rolled over and sat upright. He reached out and grasped Claude's arm. 'Claude, I'm begging you, this is really important. Do it for me, will you?'

It was hard to say no to Michel. Claude sighed. 'When?'

Flick looked at her watch. It was almost eleven. 'Now.'

Claude looked at Michel. 'His wound may reopen.'

'I know,' Flick said. 'Let it bleed.'

* * *

The village of Chatelle consisted of a few buildings clustered around a crossroads: three farmhouses, a strip of labourers' cottages, and a bakery that served the surrounding farms and hamlets. Flick stood in a cow pasture a mile from the crossroads, holding in her hand a torch about the size of a pack of cigarettes.

She had been on a week-long course, run by the pilots of 161 Squadron, to train her for the task of guiding an aircraft in. This location fitted the specifications they had given her. The field was almost a kilometre long – a Lysander needed six hundred metres to land and take off. The ground beneath her feet was firm, and there was no slope. A nearby pond was clearly visible from the air in the moonlight, providing a useful landmark for pilots.

Michel and Gilberte stood upwind of Flick in a straight line, also holding torches; and Claude stood a few yards to one side of Gilberte, making a flare path in the shape of an upside-down L to guide the pilot. In remote areas, bonfires could be used instead of electric lights; but here, close to a village, it was too dangerous to leave the tell-tale burn mark on the ground.

The four people formed what the agents called a reception committee. Flick's were always silent and disciplined, but less well-organized groups sometimes turned the landing into a party, with groups of men shouting jokes and smoking cigarettes, and spectators from nearby villages turning up to watch. This was dangerous. If the pilot suspected that the landing had been betrayed to the Germans, and thought the Gestapo might be lying in wait, he had to react quickly. The instructions to reception committees warned that anyone approaching the plane from the wrong angle was liable to be shot by the pilot. This had never actually happened, but on one occasion a spectator had been run over by a Hudson bomber and killed.

Waiting for the plane was always hell. If it did not arrive, Flick would face another twenty-four hours of unremitting tension and danger before the next opportunity. But an agent never knew whether a plane would show up. This was not because the RAF was unreliable. Rather, as the pilots of 161 Squadron had explained to Flick, the task of navigating a plane by moonlight across hundreds of miles of country was monumentally difficult. The pilot used dead reckoning – calculating his position by direction, speed and elapsed time – and tried to verify the result by landmarks such as rivers, towns, railway lines and forests. The problem with dead reckoning was that it was impossible to make an exact adjustment for the drift caused by wind. And the trouble with landmarks was that one river looked very much like another by moonlight. Getting to roughly the right area was difficult enough, but these pilots had to find an individual field.

If there was cloud hiding the moon it was impossible, and the plane would not even take off.

However, this was a fine night, and Flick was hopeful. Sure enough, a couple of minutes before midnight, she heard the unmistakable sound of a single-engined plane, faint at first then rapidly growing louder, like a burst of applause, and she felt a homegoing thrill. She began to flash her light in the Morse letter X. If she flashed the wrong letter, the pilot would suspect a trap, and go away without landing.

The plane circled once then came down steeply. It touched down on Flick's right, braked, turned between Michel and Claude, taxied back to Flick, and turned into the wind again, completing a long oval and finishing up ready for take-off.

The aircraft was a Westland Lysander, a small high-winged monoplane, painted matt black. It was flown by a crew of one. It had two seats for passengers, but Flick had known a 'Lizzie' to carry four, one on the floor and one on the parcel shelf.

The pilot did not stop the engine. His aim was to remain on the ground no more than a few seconds.

Flick wanted to hug Michel and wish him well, but she also wanted to slap his face and tell him to keep his hands off other women. Perhaps it was just as well that she had no time for either.

With a brief wave, Flick scrambled up the metal ladder, threw open the hatch, and climbed aboard.

The pilot glanced behind, and Flick gave him the thumbs-up. The little plane jerked forward and picked up speed, then rose into the air and climbed steeply.

Flick could see one or two lights in the village: country people were careless about the blackout. When Flick had flown in, perilously late at four in the morning, she had been able to see from the air the red glare of the baker's oven, and driving through the village she had smelt the new bread, the essence of France.

The plane banked to turn, and Flick saw the moonlit faces of Michel, Gilberte and Claude as three white smears on the black background of the pasture. As the plane levelled and headed for England, she realized with a sudden surge of grief that she might never see them again.

THE SECOND DAY:
MONDAY, 29 MAY 1944

SIX

Dieter Franck drove through the night in the big Hispano-Suiza, accompanied by his young assistant, Lieutenant Hans Hesse. The car was ten years old, but its massive eleven-litre engine was tireless. Yesterday evening, Dieter had found a neat row of bullet holes stitched in the generous curve of its offside fender, a souvenir of the skirmish in the square at Sainte-Cécile; but there was no mechanical damage, and he felt the holes added to the car's glamour, like a duelling scar on the cheek of a Prussian officer.

Lieutenant Hesse masked the headlights to drive through the blacked-out streets of Paris, then removed the covers when they got on the road to Normandy. They took turns at the wheel, two hours each, though Hesse, who adored the car and hero-worshipped its owner, would gladly have driven the whole way.

Half asleep in the passenger seat, mesmerized by the country roads unwinding in the headlights, Dieter tried to picture his future. Would the Allies reconquer France, driving the occupying forces out? The thought of Germany defeated was dismal. Perhaps there would be some kind of peace settlement, with Germany surrendering France and Poland but keeping Austria and Czechoslovakia. That seemed not much better. He found it hard to imagine everyday life back in Cologne, with his wife and family, after the excitement and sensual indulgence of Paris and Stéphanie. The only happy ending, for Dieter and for Germany, would be for Rommel's army to push the invaders back into the sea.

Before dawn on a damp morning Hesse drove into the small medieval village of La Roche-Guyon, on the Seine river between Paris and Rouen. He stopped at the roadblock at the edge of the village, but they were expected, and were quickly waved on. They went past silent, shuttered houses to another checkpoint at the gates of the ancient castle. At last they parked in the great cobbled courtyard. Dieter left Hesse with the car and went into the building.

The German commander-in-chief (West) was Field Marshal Gerd von Runstedt, a reliable senior general from the old officer class. Under him, charged with the defence of the French coast, was Field Marshal Erwin Rommel. The castle of La Roche-Guyon was Rommel's headquarters.

Dieter Franck felt an affinity with Rommel. Both were the sons of teachers – Rommel's father had been a headmaster – and consequently both had felt the icy breath of German military snobbery from such men as von Runstedt. But otherwise they were very different. Dieter was a sybarite, enjoying all the cultural and sensual pleasures France had to offer. Rommel was an obsessive worker who did not smoke or drink and often forgot to eat. He had married the only girlfriend he had ever had, and he wrote to her three times a day.

In the hall, Dieter met Rommel's aide-de-camp, Major Walter Goedel, a cold personality with a formidable brain. Dieter respected him, but could never like him. They had spoken on the phone late last night. Dieter had outlined the problem he was having with the Gestapo and said he wanted to see Rommel as soon as possible. 'Be here at four a.m.,' Goedel had said. Rommel was always at his desk by four o'clock in the morning.

Now Dieter wondered if he had done the right thing. Rommel might say: 'How dare you bother me with trivial details?' Dieter thought not. Commanders liked to feel they were on top of the details. Rommel would almost certainly give Dieter the support he was asking for. But you could never be sure, especially when the commander was under strain.

Goedel nodded a curt greeting and said: 'He wants to see you right away. Come this way.'

As they walked along the hallway, Dieter said: 'What do you hear from Italy?'

'Nothing but bad news,' Goedel said. 'We're withdrawing from Arce.'

Dieter gave a resigned nod. The Germans were fighting fiercely, but they had been depressingly unable to halt the northward advance of the enemy.

A moment later Dieter entered Rommel's office. It was a grand room on the ground floor. Dieter noticed with envy a priceless seventeenth-century Gobelin tapestry on one wall. There was little furniture but for a few chairs and a huge antique desk that looked, to Dieter, as if it might be the same age as the tapestry. On the desk stood a single lamp. Behind the desk sat a small man with receding sandy hair.

Goedel said: 'Major Franck is here, Field Marshal.'

Dieter waited nervously. Rommel continued reading for a few seconds, then made a mark on the sheet of paper. He might have been a bank manager reviewing the accounts of his more important customers – until he looked up. Dieter had seen the face before, but it never failed to make him feel threatened. It was a boxer's face, with a flat nose and a broad chin and close-set eyes, and it was suffused with the naked aggression that had made Rommel a legendary commander. Dieter recalled the story of Rommel's first military engagement, during the First World War. Leading an advance guard of three men, Rommel had come upon a group of twenty French troops. Instead of retreating and calling for reinforcements, Rommel had opened fire and dashed at the enemy. He had been lucky to survive – but Dieter recalled Napoleon's dictum: 'Send me lucky generals.' Since then, Rommel had always favoured the sudden bold assault over the cautious planned advance. In that he was the polar opposite of his desert opponent, Montgomery, whose philosophy was never to attack until you were certain of victory.

'Sit down, Franck,' said Rommel briskly. 'What's on your mind?'

Dieter had rehearsed this. 'On your instructions, I've

been visiting key installations that might be vulnerable to attack by the Resistance, and upgrading their security.'

'Good.'

'I've also been trying to assess the potential of the Resistance to inflict serious damage. Can they really hamper our response to an invasion?'

'And your conclusion?'

'The situation is worse than we imagined.'

Rommel grunted with distaste, as if an unpleasant suspicion had been confirmed. 'Reasons?'

Rommel was not going to bite his head off. Dieter relaxed a little. He recounted yesterday's attack at Sainte-Cécile: the imaginative planning, the plentiful weaponry, and most of all the bravery of the fighters. The only detail he left out was the beauty of the blonde girl.

Rommel stood up and walked across to the tapestry. He stared at it, but Dieter was sure he did not see it. 'I was afraid of this,' Rommel said. He spoke quietly, almost to himself. 'I can beat off an invasion, even with the few troops I have, if only I can remain mobile and flexible – but if my communications fail, I'm lost.'

Goedel nodded agreement.

Dieter said: 'I believe we can turn the attack on the telephone exchange into an opportunity.'

Rommel turned to him with a wry smile. 'By God, I wish all my officers were like you. Go on, how will you do this?'

Dieter began to feel the meeting was going his way. 'If I can interrogate the captured prisoners, they may lead me to other groups. With luck, we might inflict a lot of damage on the Resistance before the invasion.'

Rommel looked sceptical. 'That sounds like bragging.' Dieter's heart sank. Then Rommel went on: 'If anyone else said it, I might send him packing. But I remember your work in the desert. You got men to tell you things they hardly realized they knew.'

Dieter was pleased. Seizing his advantage, he said: 'Unfortunately, the Gestapo is refusing me access to the prisoners.'

'They are such imbeciles.'

'I need you to intervene.'

'Of course.' Rommel looked at Goedel. 'Call Avenue Foch.' The Gestapo's French headquarters was at 84 Avenue Foch in Paris. 'Tell them that Major Franck will interrogate the prisoners today, or their next phone call will come from Berchtesgaden.' He was referring to Hitler's Bavarian fortress. Rommel never hesitated to use the Field Marshal's privilege of direct access to Hitler.

'Very good,' said Goedel.

Rommel walked around his seventeenth-century desk and sat down again. 'Keep me informed, please, Franck,' he said, and returned his attention to his papers.

Dieter and Goedel left the room.

Goedel walked Dieter to the main door of the castle.

Outside, it was still dark.

SEVEN

Flick landed at RAF Tempsford, an airstrip fifty miles north of London, near the village of Sandy in Bedfordshire. She would have known, just from the cool, damp taste of the night air in her mouth, that she was back in England. She loved France, but this was home.

Walking across the airfield, she remembered coming back from holidays as a child. Her mother would always say the same thing as the house came into view: 'It's nice to go away, but it's nice to come home.' The things her mother said came back to her at the oddest moments.

A young woman in the uniform of a FANY corporal was waiting with a powerful Jaguar to drive her to London. 'This is luxurious,' Flick said as she settled into the leather seat.

'I'm to take you directly to Orchard Court,' the driver said. 'They're waiting to debrief you.'

Flick rubbed her eyes. 'Christ,' she said feelingly. 'Do they think we don't need sleep?'

The driver did not respond to that. Instead she said: 'I hope the mission went well, Major.'

'It was a snafu.'

'I beg pardon?'

'Snafu,' Flick repeated. 'It's an acronym. It stands for Situation Normal, All Fucked Up.'

The woman fell silent. Flick guessed she was embarrassed. It was nice, she thought ruefully, that there were still girls to whom the language of the barracks was shocking.

Dawn broke as the fast car sped through the Hertfordshire villages of Stevenage and Knebworth. Flick looked out at the modest houses with vegetables growing in the front gardens, the country post offices where grumpy postmistresses resentfully doled out penny stamps, and the assorted pubs with their warm beer and battered pianos, and she felt profoundly grateful that the Nazis had not got this far.

The feeling made her all the more determined to return to France. She wanted another chance to attack the chateau. She pictured the people she had left behind at Sainte-Cécile: Albert, young Bertrand, beautiful Geneviève, and the others dead or captured. She thought of their families, distraught with worry or stunned by grief. She resolved that their sacrifice should not have been fruitless.

She would have to start right away. It was a good thing she was to be debriefed immediately: she would have a chance to propose her new plan today. The men who ran SOE would be wary at first, for no one had ever sent an all-female team on such a mission. There were all sorts of snags. But there were always snags.

By the time they reached the north London suburbs it was full daylight, and the special people of the early morning were out and about: postmen and milkmen making their deliveries, train drivers and bus conductors walking to work. The signs of war were everywhere: a poster warning against waste, a notice in a butcher's window saying, 'No meat today,' a woman driving a rubbish cart, a whole row of small houses bombed into rubble. But no one here would stop Flick, and demand to see her papers, and put her in a cell, and torture her for information, then send her in a cattle truck to a camp where she would starve. She felt the high-voltage tension of living undercover drain slowly out of her, and she slumped in the car seat and closed her eyes.

She woke up when the car turned into Baker Street. It went past No. 64: agents were kept out of the headquarters building, so that they could not reveal its secrets under interrogation. Indeed, many agents did not know its address. The car turned into Portman Square and stopped outside Orchard Court, an apartment building. The driver sprang out to hold the door open.

Flick went inside and made her way to SOE's flat. Her spirits lifted when she saw Percy Thwaite. A balding man of fifty with a toothbrush moustache, he was paternally fond of Flick. He wore civilian clothing, and neither of them saluted, for SOE was impatient of military formalities.

'I can tell by your face that it went badly,' Percy said.

His sympathetic tone of voice was too much for Flick to bear. The tragedy of what had happened overwhelmed her suddenly, and she burst into tears.

Percy put his arms around her and patted her back. She buried her face in his old tweed jacket. 'All right,' he said. 'I know you did your best.'

'Oh, God, I'm sorry to be such a girl.'

'I wish all my men were such girls,' Percy said with a catch in his voice.

She detached herself from his embrace and wiped her eyes with her sleeve. 'Take no notice.'

He turned away and blew his nose into a big handkerchief. 'Tea or whisky?' he said.

'Tea, I think.' She looked around. The room was full of shabby furniture, hastily installed in 1940 and never replaced: a cheap desk, a worn rug, mismatched chairs. She sank into a sagging armchair. 'I'll fall asleep if I have booze.'

She watched Percy as he made tea. He could be tough as well as compassionate. Much-decorated in the First World War, he had become a rabble-rousing labour organizer in the twenties, and was a veteran of the 1936 Battle of Cable Street, when Cockneys attacked Fascists who were trying to march through a Jewish neighbourhood in London's East End. He would ask searching questions about her plan, but he would be open-minded.

He handed her a mug of tea with milk and sugar. 'There's a meeting later this morning,' he said. 'I have to get a briefing note to the boss by nine ack emma. Hence the hurry.'

She sipped the sweet tea and felt a pleasant jolt of energy. She told him what had happened in the square at Sainte-Cécile. He sat at the desk and made notes with a sharp pencil. 'I should have called it off,' she finished. 'Based on Antoinette's misgivings about the intelligence, I should have postponed the raid and sent you a radio message saying we were outnumbered.'

Percy shook his head sadly. 'This is no time for postponements. The invasion can't be more than a few days away. If you had consulted us, I doubt it would have made any difference. What could we do? We couldn't send you more men. I think we would have ordered you to go ahead regardless. It had to be tried. The telephone exchange is too important.'

'Well, that's some consolation.' Flick was glad she did not have to believe Albert had died because she had made a tactical error. But that would not bring him back.

'And Michel is all right?' Percy said.

'Mortified, but recovering.' When SOE had recruited Flick, she had not told them her husband was in the Resistance. If they had known, they might have steered her towards different work. But she had not really known it herself, though she had guessed. In May 1940 she had been in England, visiting her mother, and Michel had been in the army, like most able-bodied young Frenchmen, so the fall of France had left them stranded in different countries. By the time she returned as a secret agent, and learned for certain what role her husband was playing, too much training had been invested in her, and she was already too useful to SOE, for her to be fired on account of hypothetical emotional distractions.

'Everyone hates a bullet in the backside,' Percy

mused. 'People think you must have been running away.' He stood up. 'Well, you'd better go home and get some sleep.'

'Not yet,' Flick said. 'First I want to know what we're going to do next.'

'I'm going to write this report—'

'No, I mean about the telephone exchange. If it's so important, we *have* to knock it out.'

He sat down again and looked at her shrewdly. 'What have you got in mind?'

She took Antoinette's pass out of her bag and threw it on his desk. 'Here's a better way to get inside. That's used by the cleaners who go in every night at seven o'clock.'

Percy picked up the pass and scrutinized it. 'Clever girl,' he said with something like admiration in his voice. 'Go on.'

'I want to go back.'

A look of pain passed briefly over Percy's face, and Flick knew he was dreading her risking her life again. But he said nothing.

'This time I'll take a full team with me,' she went on. 'Each of them will have a pass like that. We'll substitute for the cleaners in order to get into the chateau.'

'I take it the cleaners are women?'

'Yes. I'd need an all-female team.'

He nodded. 'Not many people around here will object to that – you girls have proved yourselves. But where would you find the women? Virtually all our trained people are over there already.'

'Get approval for my plan, and I'll find the women.

I'll take SOE rejects, people who failed the training course, anybody. We must have a file of people who have dropped out for one reason or another.'

'Yes – because they were physically unfit, or couldn't keep their mouths shut, or enjoyed violence too much, or lost their nerve in parachute training and refused to jump out of the plane.'

'It doesn't matter if they're second-raters,' Flick argued earnestly. 'I can deal with that.' At the back of her mind, a voice said, *Can you, really?* But she ignored it. 'If the invasion fails, we've lost Europe. We won't try again for years. This is the turning point, we have to throw everything at the enemy.'

'You couldn't use French women who are already there, Resistance fighters?'

Flick had already considered and rejected that idea. 'If I had a few weeks, I might put together a team from women in half a dozen different Resistance circuits, but it would take too long to find them and get them to Reims.'

'It might still be possible.'

'And then we have to have a forged pass with a photo for each woman. That's hard to arrange over there. Here, we can do it in a day or two.'

'It's not that easy.' Percy held Antoinette's pass up to the light of a naked bulb hanging from the ceiling. 'But you're right, our people do work miracles in that department.' He put it down. 'All right. It has to be SOE rejects, then.'

Flick felt a surge of triumph. He was going for it.

Percy went on: 'But assuming you can find enough

French-speaking girls, will it work? What about the German guards? Don't they know the cleaners?'

'It's probably not the same women every night – they must have days off. And men never notice who cleans up after them.'

'I'm not sure. Soldiers are generally sex-hungry youngsters who pay great attention to all the women with whom they come into contact. I imagine the men in this chateau flirt with the younger ones, at least.'

'I watched these women entering the chateau last night, and I didn't see any signs of flirting.'

'Still, you can't be sure the men won't notice the appearance of a completely strange crew.'

'I can't be certain, but I'm confident enough to take the chance.'

'All right, what about the French people inside? The telephone operators are local women, aren't they?'

'Some are local, but most are brought in from Reims by bus.'

'Not every French person likes the Resistance, we both know that. There are some who approve of the Nazis' ideas. God knows, there were plenty of fools in Britain who thought Hitler offered the kind of strong modernizing government we all needed – although you don't hear much from those people nowadays.'

Flick shook her head. Percy had not been to occupied France. 'The French have had four years of Nazi rule, remember. Everyone over there is hoping desperately for the invasion. The switchboard girls will keep mum.'

'Even though the RAF bombed them?'

Flick shrugged. 'There may be a few hostile ones, but the majority will keep them under control.'

'You hope.'

'Once again, I think it's a chance worth taking.'

'You still don't know how heavily guarded that basement entrance is.'

'That didn't stop us trying yesterday.'

'Yesterday you had fifteen Resistance fighters, some of them seasoned. Next time, you'll have a handful of dropouts and rejects.'

Flick played her trump card. 'Listen, all kinds of things could go wrong, but so what? The operation is low-cost, and we're risking the lives of people who aren't contributing to the war effort anyway. What have we got to lose?'

'I was coming to that. Look, I like this plan. I'm going to put it up to the boss. But I think he will reject it, for a reason we haven't yet discussed.'

'What?'

'No one but you could lead this team. But the trip you've just returned from should be your last. You know too much. You've been going in and out for two years. You've had contact with most of the Resistance circuits in northern France. We can't send you back. If you were captured, you could give them all away.'

'I know,' Flick said grimly. 'That's why I carry a suicide pill.'

EIGHT

General Sir Bernard Montgomery, commander of the
21st Army Group that was about to invade France, had
set up improvised headquarters in west London, at a
school whose pupils had been evacuated to safer
accommodation in the countryside. By coincidence, it
was the school Monty himself had attended as a boy.
Meetings were held in the model room, and everyone
sat on the schoolboys' hard wooden benches – generals
and politicians and, on one famous occasion, the King
himself.

The Brits thought this was cute. Paul Chancellor
from Boston, Massachusetts, thought it was bullshit.
What would it have cost them to bring in a few chairs?
He liked the British, by and large, but not when they
were showing off about how eccentric they were.

Paul was on Monty's personal staff. A lot of people
thought this was because his father was a general, but
that was an unfair assumption. Paul was comfortable
with senior officers, partly because of his father, partly
because before the war the US army had been the
biggest customer for his business, which was making
educational gramophone records, language courses
mainly. He liked the military virtues of obedience,

punctuality and precision, but he could think for himself, too; and Monty had come to rely on him more and more.

His area of responsibility was intelligence. He was an organizer. He made sure the reports Monty needed were on his desk when he wanted them, chased those that came late, set up meetings with key people, and made supplementary enquiries on the boss's behalf.

He did have experience of clandestine work. He had been with the Office of Strategic Services, the American secret agency, and had served under cover in France and French-speaking north Africa. (As a child he had lived in Paris, where Pa was military attaché at the US embassy.) Paul had been wounded six months ago in a shootout with the Gestapo in Marseille. One bullet had taken off most of his left ear but harmed nothing other than his looks. The other smashed his right kneecap, which would never be the same again, and that was the real reason he had a desk job.

The work was easy, by comparison with living on the run in occupied territory, but never dull. They were planning Operation Overlord, the invasion that would end the war. Paul was one of a few hundred people in the world who knew the date, although many more could guess. In fact there were three possible dates, based on the tides, the currents, the moon, and the hours of daylight. The invasion needed a late-rising moon, so that the army's initial movements would be shrouded in darkness, but there would be moonlight later, when the first paratroopers jumped from their planes and gliders. A low tide at dawn was necessary to expose the obstacles Rommel had scattered on the beaches. And another low tide before nightfall was needed for the landing of follow-up forces. These requirements left only a narrow window: the fleet could sail next Monday, 5 June, or on the following Tuesday or Wednesday. The final decision would be made at the last minute, depending on the weather, by the Allied Supreme Commander, General Eisenhower.

Three years ago, Paul would have been desperately scheming for a place in the invasion force. He would have been itching for action and embarrassed at being a stay-at-home. Now he was older and wiser. For one thing, he had paid his dues; in high school he had captained the side that won the Massachusetts championship, but he would never again kick a ball with his right foot. More importantly, he knew that his organizational talents could do more to win the war than his ability to shoot straight.

He was thrilled to be part of the team that was planning the greatest invasion of all time. With the thrill came anxiety, of course. Battles never went according to plan (although it was a weakness of Monty's to pretend that his did). Paul knew that any error he made – a slip of the pen, a detail overlooked, a piece of intelligence not double-checked – could kill Allied troops. Despite the huge size of the invasion force, the battle could still go either way, and the smallest of mistakes could tip the balance.

Today at ten o'clock Paul had scheduled fifteen minutes on the French Resistance. It was Monty's idea.

He was nothing if not a detail man. The way to win battles, he believed, was to refrain from fighting until all preparations were in place.

At five to ten, Simon Fortescue came into the model room. He was one of the senior men at MI6, the secret intelligence department. A tall man in a pin-striped suit, he had a smoothly authoritative manner, but Paul doubted if he knew much about clandestine work in the real world. He was followed by John Graves, a nervous-looking civil servant from the Ministry of Economic Warfare, the government department that oversaw SOE. Graves wore the Whitehall uniform of black jacket and striped grey trousers. Paul frowned. He had not invited Graves. 'Mr Graves!' he said sharply. 'I didn't know you had been asked to join us.'

'I'll explain in a second,' Graves said, and he sat down on a schoolboy bench, looking flustered, and opened his briefcase.

Paul was irritated. Monty hated surprises. But Paul could not throw Graves out of the room.

A moment later, Monty walked in. He was a small man with a pointed nose and receding hair. His face was deeply lined on either side of his close-clipped moustache. He was fifty-six, but looked older. Paul liked him. Monty was so meticulous that some people became impatient with him and called him an old woman. Paul believed that Monty's fussiness saved men's lives.

With Monty was an American Paul did not know. Monty introduced him as General Pickford. 'Where's the chap from SOE?' Monty snapped, looking at Paul.

Graves answered. 'I'm afraid he was summoned by the Prime Minister, and sends his profound apologies. I hope I'll be able to help . . .'

'I doubt it,' Monty said crisply.

Paul groaned inwardly. It was a snafu, and he would be blamed. But there was something else going on here. The Brits were playing some game he did not know about. He watched them carefully, looking for clues.

Simon Fortescue said smoothly: 'I'm sure I can fill in the gaps.'

Monty looked angry. He had promised General Pickford a briefing, and the key person was absent. But he did not waste time on recriminations. 'In the coming battle,' he said, without further ado, 'the most dangerous moments will be the first.' It was unusual for him to speak of dangerous moments, Paul thought. His way was to talk as if everything would go like clockwork. 'We will be hanging by our fingertips from a cliff edge for a day.' Or two days, Paul said to himself, or a week, or more. 'This will be the enemy's best opportunity. He has only to stamp on our fingers with the heel of his jackboot.'

So easy, Paul thought. Overlord was the largest military operation in human history: thousands of boats, hundreds of thousands of men, millions of dollars, tens of millions of bullets. The future of the world depended on the outcome. Yet this vast force could be repelled so easily, if things went wrong in the first few hours.

'Anything we can do to slow the enemy's response

will be of crucial importance,' Monty finished, and he looked at Graves.

'Well, F Section of SOE has more than a hundred agents in France – in fact virtually all our people are over there,' Graves began. 'And under them, of course, are thousands of French Resistance fighters. Over the last few weeks we have dropped them many hundreds of tons of guns, ammunition and explosives.'

It was a bureaucrat's answer, Paul thought; it said everything and nothing. Graves would have gone on, but Monty interrupted with the key question: 'How effective will they be?'

The civil servant hesitated, and Fortescue jumped in. 'My expectations are modest,' he said. 'The performance of SOE is nothing if not uneven.'

There was a subtext here, Paul knew. The old-time professional spies at MI6 hated the newcomers of SOE with their swashbuckling style. When the Resistance struck at German installations they stirred up Gestapo investigations which then sometimes caught MI6's people. Paul took SOE's side: striking at the enemy was the whole point of war.

Was that the game here? A bureaucratic spat between MI6 and SOE?

'Any *particular* reason for your pessimism?' Monty asked Fortescue.

'Take last night's fiasco,' Fortescue replied promptly. 'A Resistance group under an SOE commander attacked a telephone exchange near Reims.'

General Pickford spoke for the first time. 'I thought it was our policy not to attack telephone exchanges,' he said. 'We're going to need them ourselves if the invasion is successful.'

'You're quite right,' Monty said. 'But Sainte-Cécile has been made an exception. It's an access node for the new cable route to Germany. Most of the telephone and telex traffic between the High Command in Berlin and German forces in France passes through that building. Knocking it out wouldn't do us much harm – we won't be calling Germany – but would wreak havoc with the enemy's communications.'

Pickford said: 'They'll switch to wireless communication.'

'Exactly,' said Monty. 'Then we'll be able to read their signals.'

Fortescue put in: 'Thanks to our codebreakers at Bletchley.'

Paul knew, though not many other people did, that British intelligence had cracked the codes used by the Germans, and therefore could read much of the enemy's radio traffic. MI6 was proud of this, although in truth they deserved little credit: the work had been done not by intelligence staff but by an irregular group of mathematicians and crossword-puzzle enthusiasts, many of whom would have been arrested if they had entered an MI6 office in normal times. Sir Stewart Menzies, the foxhunting head of MI6, hated intellectuals, Communists and homosexuals; but Alan Turing, the mathematical genius who led the codebreakers, was all three.

However, Pickford was right: if the Germans could not use the phone lines they would have to use radio, and then the Allies would know what they were saying. Destroying the telephone exchange at Sainte-Cécile would give the Allies a crucial advantage.

But the mission had gone wrong. 'Who was in charge?' Monty asked.

Graves said: 'I haven't seen a full report—'

'I can tell you,' Fortescue interjected. 'Major Clairet.' He paused. 'A girl.'

Paul had heard of Felicity Clairet. She was something of a legend among the small group who knew the secret of the Allies' clandestine war. She had survived under cover in France longer than anyone. Her codename was Leopardess, and people said she moved around the streets of occupied France with the silent footsteps of a dangerous cat. They also said she was a pretty girl with a heart of stone. She had killed more than once.

'And what happened?' Monty said.

'Poor planning, an inexperienced commander and a lack of discipline among the men all played their part,' Fortescue replied. 'The building was not heavily guarded, but the Germans there are trained troops, and they simply wiped out the Resistance force.'

Monty looked angry. Pickford said: 'Looks like we shouldn't rely too heavily on the French Resistance to disrupt Rommel's supply lines.'

Fortescue nodded. 'Bombing is the more reliable means to that end.'

'I'm not sure that's quite fair,' Graves protested feebly. 'Bomber Command has its successes and failures, too. And SOE is a good deal cheaper.'

'We're not here to be fair to people, for God's sake,'

Monty growled. 'We just want to win the war.' He stood up. 'I think we've heard enough,' he said to General Pickford.

Graves said: 'But what shall we do about the telephone exchange? SOE has come up with a new plan—'

'Good God,' Fortescue interrupted. 'We don't want another balls-up, do we?'

'Bomb it,' said Monty.

'We've tried that,' Graves said. 'They hit the building, but the damage was not sufficient to put the telephone exchange out of action for longer than a few hours.'

'Then bomb it again,' said Monty, and he walked out.

Graves threw a look of petulant fury at the man from MI6. 'Really, Fortescue,' he said. 'I mean to say . . . *really*.'

Fortescue did not respond.

They all left the room. In the hallway outside, two people were waiting: a man of about fifty in a tweed jacket, and a short blonde woman wearing a worn blue cardigan over a faded cotton dress. Standing in front of a display of sporting trophies, they looked almost like a head teacher chatting to a schoolgirl, except that the girl wore a bright yellow scarf tied with a touch of style that looked, to Paul, distinctly French. Fortescue hurried past them, but Graves stopped. 'They turned you down,' he said. 'They're going to bomb it again.'

Paul guessed that the woman was the Leopardess, and he looked at her with interest. She was small and slim, with curly blonde hair cut short, and – Paul noticed – rather lovely green eyes. He would not have called her pretty: her face was too grown-up for that. The initial schoolgirl impression was fleeting. There was an aggressive look to her straight nose and chisel-shaped chin. And there was something sexy about her, something that made Paul think about the slight body under the shabby dress.

She reacted with indignation to Graves's statement. 'There's no point in bombing the place from the air, the basement is reinforced. For God's sake, why did they make that decision?'

'Perhaps you should ask this gentleman,' Graves said, turning to Paul. 'Major Chancellor, meet Major Clairet and Colonel Thwaite.'

Paul was annoyed at being put in the position of defending someone else's decision. Caught off guard, he replied with undiplomatic frankness. 'I don't see that there's much to explain,' he said brusquely. 'You screwed up and you're not being given a second chance.'

The woman glared up at him – she was a foot shorter than he – and spoke angrily. 'Screwed up?' she said. 'What the hell do you mean by that?'

Paul felt himself flush. 'Maybe General Montgomery was misinformed, but wasn't this the first time you had commanded an action of this kind, Major?'

'Is *that* what you've been told? That it was my lack of experience?'

She was beautiful, he saw now. Anger made her eyes wide and her cheeks pink. But she was being very rude, so he decided to give it to her with both barrels. 'That and poor planning—'

'There was nothing wrong with the damn plan!'

' – and the fact that trained troops were defending the place against an undisciplined force.'

'You arrogant pig!'

Paul took an involuntary step back. He had never been spoken to this way by a woman. She may be five feet nothing, he thought, but I bet she scares the damn Nazis. Looking at her furious face, he realized that she was most angry with herself. 'You think it's your fault,' he said. 'No one gets this mad about other people's mistakes.'

It was her turn to be taken aback. Her mouth dropped open but she was speechless.

Colonel Thwaite spoke for the first time. 'Calm down, Flick, for God's sake,' he said. Turning to Paul, he went on: 'Let me guess – this account was given to you by Simon Fortescue of MI6, was it not?'

'That's correct,' Paul said stiffly.

'Did he mention that the attack plan was based on intelligence supplied by his organization?'

'I don't believe he did.'

'I thought not,' said Thwaite. 'Thank you, Major, I don't need to trouble you any further.'

Paul did not feel the conversation was really over, but he had been dismissed by a senior officer, and he had no choice but to walk away.

He had obviously got caught in the crossfire of a turf war between MI6 and SOE. He felt most angry with Fortescue, who had used the meeting to score points.

Had Monty made the right decision in choosing to bomb the telephone exchange rather than let SOE have another go at it? Paul was not sure.

As he turned into his own office he glanced back. Major Clairet was still arguing with Colonel Thwaite, her voice low but her face animated, expressing outrage with large gestures. She stood like a man, hand on hip, leaning forward, making her point with a belligerent forefinger; but all the same there was something enchanting about her. Paul wondered what it would be like to hold her in his arms and run his hands over her lithe body. Although she's tough, he thought, she's all woman.

But was she right? Was bombing futile?

He decided to ask some more questions.

NINE

The vast, sooty bulk of the cathedral loomed over the centre of Reims like a divine reproach. Dieter Franck's sky-blue Hispano-Suiza pulled up at midday outside the Hôtel Frankfort, taken over by the German occupiers. Dieter got out and glanced up at the stubby twin towers of the great church. The original medieval design had featured elegant pointed spires which had never been built for lack of money. So mundane obstacles frustrated the holiest of aspirations.

Dieter told Lieutenant Hesse to drive to the chateau at Sainte-Cécile and make sure the Gestapo were ready to co-operate. He did not want to risk being repulsed a second time by Major Weber. Hesse drove off, and Dieter went up to the suite where he had left Stéphanie last night.

She got up from her chair as he walked in. He drank in the welcome sight. Her red hair fell on bare shoulders, and she wore a chestnut silk *négligée* and high-heeled slippers. He kissed her hungrily and ran his hands over her slim body, grateful for the gift of her beauty.

'How nice that you're so pleased to see me,' she said with a smile. They spoke French together, as always.

Dieter inhaled the scent of her. 'Well, you smell better than Hans Hesse, especially when he's been up all night.'

She brushed his hair back with a soft hand. 'You always make fun. But you wouldn't have protected Hans with your own body.'

'True.' He sighed and let her go. 'Christ, I'm tired.'

'Come to bed.'

He shook his head. 'I have to interrogate the prisoners. Hesse's coming back for me in an hour.' He slumped on the couch.

'I'll get you something to eat.' She pressed the bell, and a minute later an elderly French waiter tapped at the door. Stéphanie knew Dieter well enough to order for him. She asked for a plate of ham with warm rolls and potato salad. 'Some wine?' she asked him.

'No – it'll send me to sleep.'

'A pot of coffee, then,' she told the waiter. When the man had gone, she sat on the couch beside Dieter and took his hand. 'Did everything go according to plan?'

'Yes. Rommel was quite complimentary to me.' He frowned anxiously. 'I just hope I can live up to the promises I made him.'

'I'm sure you will.' She did not ask for details. She knew he would tell her as much as he wanted to and no more.

He looked fondly at her, wondering whether to say what was on his mind. It might spoil the pleasant atmosphere – but it needed to be said. He sighed again. 'If the invasion is successful, and the Allies win back

France, it will be the end for you and me. You know that.'

She winced, as if at a sudden pain, and let go of his hand. 'Do I?'

He knew that her husband had been killed early in the war, and they had had no children. 'Do you have any family at all?' he asked her.

'My parents died years ago. I have a sister in Montreal.'

'Maybe we should be thinking about how to send you over there.'

She shook her head. 'No.'

'Why?'

She would not meet his eye. 'I just wish the war would be over,' she muttered.

'No, you don't.'

She showed a rare flash of irritation. 'Of course I do.'

'How uncharacteristically conventional of you,' he said with a hint of scorn.

'You can't possibly think war is a good thing!'

'You and I would not be together, were it not for the war.'

'But what about all the suffering?'

'I'm an existentialist. War enables people to be what they really are: the sadists become torturers, the psychopaths make brave front-line troops, the bullies and the victims alike have scope to play their roles to the hilt, and the whores are always busy.'

She looked angry. 'That tells me pretty clearly what part I play.'

94

He stroked her soft cheek and touched her lips with the tip of his finger. 'You're a courtesan – and very good at it.'

She moved her head away. 'You don't mean any of this. You're improvising on a tune, the way you do when you sit at the piano.'

He smiled and nodded: he could play a little jazz, much to his father's dismay. The analogy was apt. He was trying out ideas, rather than expressing a firm conviction. 'Perhaps you're right.'

Her anger evaporated, and she looked sad. 'Did you mean the part about us separating, if the Germans leave France?'

He put his arm around her shoulders and pulled her to him. She relaxed and laid her head on his chest. He kissed the top of her head and stroked her hair. 'It's not going to happen,' he said.

'Are you certain?'

'I guarantee it.'

It was the second time today he had made a promise he might not be able to keep.

The waiter returned with his lunch, and the spell was broken. Dieter was almost too tired to be hungry, but he ate a few mouthfuls and drank all of the coffee. Afterwards he washed and shaved, and then he felt better. As he was buttoning a clean uniform shirt, Lieutenant Hesse tapped at the door. Dieter kissed Stéphanie and went out.

The car was diverted around a blocked street: there had been another bombing raid overnight, and a whole row of houses near the railway station had been destroyed. They got out of town and headed for Sainte-Cécile.

Dieter had told Rommel that the interrogation of the prisoners *might* enable him to cripple the Resistance before the invasion – but Rommel, like any military commander, took a maybe for a promise, and would now expect results. Unfortunately, there was nothing guaranteed about an interrogation. Clever prisoners told lies that were impossible to check. Some found ingenious ways to kill themselves before the torture became unbearable. If security was really tight in their particular Resistance circuit, each would know only the minimum about the others, and have little information of value. Worst of all, they might have been fed false information by the perfidious Allies, so that when they finally broke under torture, what they said was part of a deception plan.

Dieter began to put himself in the mood. He needed to be completely hard-hearted and calculating. He must not allow himself to be touched by the physical and mental suffering he was about to inflict on human beings. All that mattered was whether it worked. He closed his eyes and felt a profound calm settle over him, a familiar bone-deep chill that he sometimes thought must be like the cold of death itself.

The car pulled into the grounds of the chateau. Workmen were repairing the smashed glass in the windows and filling the holes made by grenades. In the ornate hall, the telephonists murmured into their microphones in a perpetual undertone. Dieter marched through the perfectly proportioned rooms of the east wing, with Hans Hesse in tow. They went down the stairs to the fortified basement. The sentry at the door saluted and made no attempt to detain Dieter, who was in uniform. He found the door marked 'Interrogation Centre' and went in.

In the outer room, Willi Weber sat at the table. Dieter barked: 'Heil Hitler!' and saluted, forcing Weber to stand. Then Dieter pulled out a chair, sat down, and said: 'Please be seated, Major.'

Weber was furious at being invited to sit in his own headquarters, but he had no choice.

Dieter said: 'How many prisoners do we have?'

'Three.'

Dieter was disappointed. 'So few?'

'We killed eight of the enemy in the skirmish. Two more died of their wounds overnight.'

Dieter grunted with dismay. He had ordered that the wounded be kept alive. But there was no point now in questioning Weber about their treatment.

Weber went on: 'I believe two escaped—'

'Yes,' Dieter said. 'The woman in the square, and the man she carried away.'

'Exactly. So, from a total of fifteen attackers, we have three prisoners.'

'Where are they?'

Weber looked shifty. 'Two are in the cells.'

Dieter narrowed his eyes. 'And the third?'

Weber inclined his head towards the inner room. 'The third is under interrogation at this moment.'

Dieter got up, apprehensive, and opened the door. The hunched figure of Sergeant Becker stood just inside the room, holding in his hand a wooden club like a large policeman's truncheon. He was sweating and breathing hard, as if he had been taking vigorous exercise. He was staring at a prisoner who was tied to a post.

Dieter looked at the prisoner, and his fears were confirmed. Despite his self-imposed calm, he grimaced with revulsion. The prisoner was the young woman, Geneviève, who had carried a Sten gun under her coat. She was naked, tied to the pillar by a rope that passed under her arms and supported her slumped weight. Her face was so swollen that she could not have opened her eyes. Blood from her mouth covered her chin and most of her chest. Her body was discoloured with angry bruises. One arm hung at an odd angle, apparently dislocated at the shoulder. Her pubic hair was matted with blood.

Dieter said to Becker: 'What has she told you?'

Becker looked embarrassed. 'Nothing.'

Dieter nodded, suppressing his rage. It was as he had expected.

He went close to the woman. 'Geneviève, listen to me,' he said in French.

She showed no sign of having heard.

'Would you like to rest now?' he tried.

There was no response.

He turned around. Weber was standing in the doorway, looking defiant. Dieter, coldly furious, said: 'You were expressly told that I would conduct the interrogation.'

'We were ordered to give you access,' Weber replied,

with smug pedantry. 'We were not prohibited from questioning the prisoners ourselves.'

'And are you satisfied with the results you have achieved?'

Weber did not answer.

Dieter said: 'What about the other two?'

'We have not yet begun their interrogation.'

'Thank God for that.' Dieter was nonetheless dismayed. He had expected half a dozen subjects, not two. 'Take me to them.'

Weber nodded at Becker, who put down his club and led the way out of the room. In the bright lights of the corridor, Dieter could see the bloodstains on Becker's uniform. The sergeant stopped at a door with a judas peephole. Dieter slid back the panel and looked inside.

It was a bare room with a dirt floor. The only item of furniture was a bucket in the corner. Two men sat on the ground, not talking, staring into space. Dieter studied them carefully. He had seen both yesterday. The older one was Gaston, who had set the charges. He had a large piece of sticking-plaster covering a scalp wound that looked superficial. The other was very young, about seventeen, and Dieter recalled that his name was Bertrand. He had no visible injuries, but Dieter, recalling the skirmish, thought he might have been stunned by the explosion of a hand grenade.

Dieter watched them for a while, taking time to think. He had to do this right. He could not afford to waste another captive: these two were the only assets left. The kid would be scared, he foresaw, but might withstand a lot of pain. The other was too old for serious torture – he might die before he cracked – but he would be soft-hearted. Dieter began to see a strategy for interrogating them.

He closed the judas and returned to the interview room. Becker followed, reminding him again of a stupid but dangerous dog. Dieter said: 'Sergeant Becker, untie the woman and put her in the cell with the other two.'

Weber protested: 'A woman in a man's cell?'

Dieter stared at him incredulously. 'Do you think she will feel the indignity?'

Becker went into the torture chamber and re-emerged carrying the broken body of Geneviève. Dieter said: 'Make sure the old man gets a good look at her, then bring him here.'

Becker went out.

Dieter decided he would prefer to get rid of Weber. However, he knew that if he gave a direct order, Weber would resist. So he said: 'I think you should remain here to witness the interrogation. You could learn a lot from my techniques.'

As Dieter had expected, Weber did the opposite. 'I don't think so,' he said. 'Becker can keep me informed.' Dieter faked an indignant expression, and Weber went out.

Dieter caught the eye of Lieutenant Hesse, who had quietly taken a seat in the corner. Hesse understood how Dieter had manipulated Weber, and was looking admiringly at Dieter. Dieter shrugged. 'Sometimes it's too easy,' he said.

Becker returned with Gaston. The older man was

pale. No doubt he had been badly shocked by the sight of Geneviève. Dieter said in German: 'Please have a seat. Do you like to smoke?'

Gaston looked blank.

That established that he did not understand German, which was worth knowing.

Dieter motioned him to a seat and offered him cigarettes and matches. Gaston took a cigarette and lit it with shaking hands.

Some prisoners broke at this stage, before torture, just from fear of what would happen. Dieter hoped that might be the case today. He had shown Gaston the alternatives: on one hand, the dreadful sight of Geneviève; on the other, cigarettes and kindness.

Now he spoke in French, using a friendly tone. 'I'm going to ask you some questions.'

'I don't know anything,' Gaston said.

'Oh, I think you do,' Dieter said. 'You're in your sixties, and you've probably lived in or around Reims all your life.' Gaston did not deny this. Dieter went on: 'I realize that the members of a Resistance cell use codenames, and give one another the minimum of personal information, as a security precaution.' Gaston involuntarily gave a slight nod of agreement. 'But you've known most of these people for decades. A man may call himself Elephant or Priest or Aubergine when the Resistance meet, but you know his face, and you recognize him as Jean-Pierre the postman who lives in the rue du Parc and surreptitiously visits the widow Martineau on Tuesdays when his wife thinks he is playing bowls.'

Gaston looked away, unwilling to meet Dieter's eye, confirming that Dieter was right.

Dieter went on: 'I want you to understand that you are in control of everything that happens here. Pain, or the relief of pain; the sentence of death, or reprieve; all depend on your choices.' He saw with satisfaction that Gaston looked even more terrified. 'You will answer my questions,' he went on. 'Everyone does, in the end. The only imponderable is how soon.'

This was the moment when a man might break down; but Gaston did not. 'I can't tell you anything,' he said in a near-whisper. He was scared, but he still had some courage left, and he was not going to give up without a fight.

Dieter shrugged. It was to be the hard way, then. He spoke to Becker in German. 'Go back to the cell. Make the boy strip naked. Bring him here and tie him to the pillar in the next room.'

'Very good, Major,' Becker said eagerly.

Dieter turned back to Gaston. 'You're going to tell me the names and codenames of all the men and women who were with you yesterday, and any others in your Resistance circuit.' Gaston shook his head, but Dieter ignored that. 'I want to know the address of every member, and of every house used by members of the circuit.'

Gaston drew hard on his cigarette and stared at the glowing end.

In fact these were not the most important questions. Dieter's main aim was to get information that would lead him to other Resistance circuits. But he did not want Gaston to know that.

A moment later, Becker returned with Bertrand. Gaston stared open-mouthed as the naked boy was marched through the interview room into the chamber beyond.

Dieter stood up. He said to Hesse: 'Keep an eye on this old man.' Then he followed Becker into the torture chamber.

He was careful to leave the door a little ajar, so that Gaston could hear everything.

Becker tied Bertrand to the pillar. Before Dieter could intervene, Becker punched Bertrand in the stomach. It was a powerful blow from a strong man, and it made a sickening thud. The young man groaned and writhed in agony.

'No, no, no,' Dieter said. As he had expected, Becker's approach was completely unscientific. A strong young man could withstand being punched almost indefinitely. 'First, you blindfold him.' He produced a large cotton bandana from his pocket and tied it over Bertrand's eyes. 'This way, every blow comes as a dreadful shock, and every moment between blows is an agony of anticipation.'

Becker picked up his wooden club. Dieter nodded, and Becker swung the club, hitting the side of the victim's head with a loud crack of solid wood on skin and bone. Bertrand cried out in pain and fear.

'No, no,' Dieter said again. 'Never hit the head. You may dislocate the jaw, preventing the subject from speaking. Worse, you may damage the brain, then nothing he says will be of any value.' He took the wooden club from Becker and replaced it in the umbrella stand. From the selection of weapons there he chose a steel crowbar and handed it to Becker.

'Now, remember, the object is to inflict unbearable agony without endangering the subject's life or his ability to tell us what we need to know. Avoid vital organs. Concentrate on the bony parts: ankles, shins, kneecaps, fingers, elbows, shoulders, ribs.'

A crafty look came over Becker's face. He walked around the pillar then, taking careful aim, struck hard at Bertrand's elbow with the steel bar. The boy gave a scream of real agony, a sound Dieter recognized.

Becker looked pleased. God forgive me, Dieter thought, for teaching this brute how to inflict pain more efficiently.

On Dieter's orders, Becker struck at Bertrand's bony shoulder, then his hand, then his ankle. Dieter made Becker pause between blows, allowing just enough time for the pain to ease slightly and for the subject to begin to dread the next stroke.

Bertrand began to appeal for mercy. 'No more, please,' he implored, hysterical with pain and fear. Becker raised the crowbar, but Dieter stopped him. He wanted the begging to go on. 'Please don't hit me again,' Bertrand cried. 'Please, please.'

Dieter said to Becker: 'It is often a good idea to break a leg early in the interview. The pain is quite excruciating, especially when the broken bone is struck again.' He selected a sledgehammer from the umbrella stand. 'Just below the knee,' he said, handing it to Becker. 'As hard as you can.'

Becker took careful aim and swung mightily. The crack as the shin broke was loud enough to hear. Bertrand screamed and fainted. Becker picked up a bucket of water that stood in a corner and threw the water in Bertrand's face. The young man came to and screamed again.

Eventually, the screams subsided to heart-rending groans. 'What do you want?' Bertrand implored. 'Please, tell me what you want from me!' Dieter did not ask him any questions. Instead, he handed the steel crowbar to Becker and pointed to the broken leg where a jagged white edge of bone stuck through the flesh. Becker struck the leg at that point. Bertrand screamed and passed out again.

Dieter thought that might be enough.

He went into the next room. Gaston sat where Dieter had left him, but he was a different man. He was bent over in his chair, face in his hands, crying with great sobs, moaning and praying to God. Dieter knelt in front of him and prised his hands away from his wet face. Gaston looked at him through tears. Dieter said softly: 'Only you can make it stop.'

'Please, stop it, please,' Gaston moaned.

'Will you answer my questions?'

There was a pause. Bertrand screamed again. 'Yes!' Gaston yelled. 'Yes, yes, I'll tell you everything, if you just stop!'

Dieter raised his voice. 'Sergeant Becker!'

'Yes, Major?'

'No more for now.'

'Yes, Major.' Becker sounded disappointed.

Dieter reverted to French. 'Now, Gaston, let's begin with the leader of the circuit. Name and codename. Who is he?'

Gaston hesitated. Dieter looked towards the open door of the torture chamber. Gaston quickly said: 'Michel Clairet. Codename Monet.'

It was the breakthrough. The first name was the hardest. The rest would follow effortlessly. Concealing his satisfaction, Dieter gave Gaston a cigarette and held a match. 'Where does he live?'

'In Reims.' Gaston blew out smoke and his shaking began to subside. He gave an address near the cathedral.

Dieter nodded to Lieutenant Hesse, who took out a notebook and began to record Gaston's responses. Patiently, Dieter took Gaston through each member of the attack team. In a few cases Gaston knew only the codenames, and there were two men he claimed never to have seen before Sunday. Dieter believed him. There had been two getaway drivers waiting a short distance away, Gaston said: a young woman called Gilberte and a man codenamed Maréchal. There were others in the group, which was known as the Bollinger circuit.

Dieter asked about relationships between Resistance members. Were there any love affairs? Were any of them homosexual? Was anyone sleeping with someone else's wife?

Although the torture had stopped, Bertrand continued to groan and sometimes scream with the agony of his wounds, and now Gaston said: 'Is he going to be looked after?'

Dieter shrugged.

'Please, get a doctor for him.'

'Very well . . . when we have finished our talk.'

Gaston told Dieter that Michel and Gilberte were lovers, even though Michel was married to Flick, the blonde girl in the square.

So far, Gaston had been talking about a circuit that was mostly destroyed, so his information had been mainly of academic interest. Now Dieter moved on to more important questions. 'When Allied agents come to this district, how do they make contact?'

No one was supposed to know how that was handled, Gaston said. There was a cut-out. However, he knew part of the story. The agents were met by a woman codenamed Bourgeoise. Gaston did not know where she met them, but she took them to her home, then she passed them on to Michel.

No one had ever met Bourgeoise, not even Michel.

Dieter was disappointed that Gaston knew so little about the woman. But that was the idea of a cut-out.

'Do you know where she lives?'

Gaston nodded. 'One of the agents gave it away. She has a house in the rue du Bois. Number eleven.'

Dieter tried not to look jubilant. This was a key fact. The enemy would probably send more agents in an attempt to rebuild the Bollinger circuit. Dieter might be able to catch them at the safe house.

'And when they leave?'

They were picked up by plane in a field codenamed

Champ de Pierre, actually a pasture in the village of Chatelle, Gaston revealed. There was an alternative landing field, codenamed Champ d'Or, but he did not know where it was.

Dieter asked Gaston about liaison with London. Who had ordered the attack on the telephone exchange? Gaston explained that Flick – Major Clairet – was the circuit's commanding officer, and she had brought orders from London. Dieter was intrigued. A woman in command. But he had seen her courage under fire. She would make a good leader.

In the next room, Bertrand began to pray aloud for death to come. 'Please,' Gaston said. 'A doctor.'

'Just tell me about Major Clairet,' Dieter said. 'Then I'll get someone to give Bertrand an injection.'

'She is a very important person,' Gaston said, eager now to give Dieter information that would satisfy him. 'They say she has survived longer than anyone else under cover. She has been all over northern France.'

Dieter was spellbound. 'She has contact with different circuits?'

'So I believe.'

That was unusual – and it meant she could be a fountain of information about the French Resistance. Dieter said: 'She got away yesterday after the skirmish. Where do you think she went?'

'Back to London, I'm sure,' Gaston said. 'To report on the raid.'

Dieter cursed silently. He wanted her in France, where he could catch her and interrogate her. If he got his hands on her, he could destroy half the French

Resistance – as he had promised Rommel. But she was out of reach.

He stood up. 'That's all for now,' he said. 'Hans, get a doctor for the prisoners. I don't want any of them to die today – they may have more to tell us. Then type up your notes and bring them to me in the morning.'

'Very good, Major.'

'Make a copy for Major Weber – but don't give it to him until I say so.'

'Understood.'

'I'll drive myself back to the hotel.' Dieter went out. The headache began as he stepped into the open air.

Rubbing his forehead with his hand, he made his way to the car and drove out of the village, heading for Reims. The afternoon sun seemed to reflect off the road surface straight into his eyes. These migraines often struck him after an interrogation. In an hour he would be blind and helpless. He had to get back to the hotel before the attack reached its peak. Reluctant to brake, he sounded his horn constantly. Vineyard workers making their slow way home scattered out of his path. Horses reared and a cart was driven into the ditch. His eyes watered with the pain, and he felt nauseous.

He reached the town without crashing the car. He managed to steer into the centre. Outside the Hôtel Frankfort, he did not so much park the car as abandon it. Staggering inside, he made his way to the suite.

Stéphanie knew immediately what had happened. While he stripped off his uniform tunic and shirt, she

109

got the field medical kit out of her suitcase and filled a syringe with the morphine mixture. Dieter fell on the bed and she plunged the needle into his arm. Almost immediately, the pain eased. Stéphanie lay down beside him, stroking his face with gentle fingertips.

A few moments later, Dieter was unconscious.

TEN

Flick's home was a bedsitter in a big old house in Bayswater. Her room was in the attic: if a bomb came through the roof it would land on her bed. She spent little time there, not for fear of bombs, but because real life went on elsewhere – in France, at SOE headquarters, or at one of SOE's training centres around the country. There was little of her in the room: a photo of Michel playing a guitar, a shelf of Flaubert and Molière in French, a watercolour of Nice she had painted at the age of fifteen. The small chest had three drawers of clothing and one of guns and ammunition.

Feeling weary and depressed, she undressed and lay down on the bed, looking through a copy of *Parade* magazine. Berlin had been bombed by a force of one thousand five hundred planes last Wednesday, she read. It was hard to imagine. She tried to picture what it must have been like for the ordinary Germans living there, and all she could think of was a medieval painting of Hell, with naked people being burned alive in a hail of fire. She turned the page and read a silly story about second-rate 'V-cigarettes' being passed off as Woodbines.

Her mind kept returning to yesterday's failure. She

re-ran the battle in her mind, imagining a dozen decisions she might have made differently, leading to victory instead of defeat. As well as losing the battle, she feared she might be losing her husband; and she wondered if there was a link. Inadequate as a leader, inadequate as a wife, perhaps there was some flaw deep in her character.

Now that her alternative plan had been rejected, there was no prospect of redeeming herself. All those brave people had died for nothing.

Eventually she drifted into an uneasy sleep. She was awakened by someone banging on the door and calling: 'Flick! Telephone!' The voice belonged to one of the girls in the flat below.

The clock on Flick's bookshelf said six. 'Who is it?' she called.

'He just said the office.'

'I'm coming.' She pulled on a dressing-gown. Unsure whether it was six in the morning or evening, she glanced out of her little window. The sun was setting over the elegant terraces of Ladbroke Grove. She ran downstairs to the phone in the hall.

Percy Thwaite's voice said: 'Sorry to wake you.'

'That's all right.' She was always glad to hear Percy's voice on the other end of the phone. She had become very fond of him, even though he constantly sent her into danger. Running agents was a heartbreaking job, and some senior officers anaesthetized themselves by adopting a hard-hearted attitude towards the death or capture of their people; but Percy never did that. He felt every loss as a bereavement. Consequently, Flick knew he would never take an unnecessary risk with her. She trusted him.

'Can you come to Orchard Court?'

She wondered if the authorities had reconsidered her new plan for taking out the telephone exchange, and her heart leaped with hope. 'Has Monty changed his mind?'

'I'm afraid not. But I need you to brief someone.'

She bit her lip, suppressing her disappointment. 'I'll be there in a few minutes.'

She dressed quickly and took the Underground to Baker Street. Percy was waiting for her in the flat in Portman Square. 'I've found a radio operator. No experience, but he's done the training. I'm sending him to Reims tomorrow.'

Flick glanced reflexively at the window, to check the weather, as agents always did when a flight was mentioned. Percy's curtains were drawn, for security, but anyway she knew the weather was fine. 'Reims? Why?'

'We've heard nothing from Michel today. I need to know how much of the Bollinger circuit is left.'

Flick nodded. Pierre, the radio operator, had been in the attack squad. Presumably he was captured or dead. Michel might have been able to locate Pierre's radio transceiver, but he had not been trained to operate it, and he certainly did not know the codes. 'But what's the point?'

'We've sent them tons of explosives and ammunition in the last few months. I want them to light some fires. The telephone exchange is the most important target, but it's not the only one. Even if there's no one left but Michel and a couple of others, they can blow up railway lines, cut telephone wires, and shoot sentries – it all helps. But I can't direct them if I have no communication.'

Flick shrugged. To her, the chateau was the only target that mattered. Everything else was chicken feed. But what the hell? 'I'll brief him, of course.'

Percy gave her a hard look. He hesitated, then said: 'How was Michel – apart from his bullet wound?'

'Fine.' Flick was silent for a moment. Percy stared at her. She could not deceive him, he knew her too well. At last she sighed and said: 'There's a girl.'

'I was afraid of that.'

'I don't know whether there's anything left of my marriage,' she said bitterly.

'I'm sorry.'

'It would help if I could tell myself that I'd made a sacrifice for a purpose, struck a magnificent blow for our side, made the invasion more likely to succeed.'

'You've done more than most, over the last two years.'

'But there's no second prize in a war, is there?'

'No.'

She stood up. She was grateful for Percy's fond sympathy, but it was making her maudlin. 'I'd better brief the new radio man.'

'Codename Helicopter. He's waiting in the study. Not the sharpest knife in the box, I'm afraid, but a brave lad.'

This seemed sloppy to Flick. 'If he's not too bright, why send him? He might endanger others.'

'As you said earlier – this is our big chance. If the invasion fails, we've lost Europe. We've got to throw everything we have at the enemy now, because we won't get another chance.'

Flick nodded grimly. He had turned her own argument against her. But he was right. The only difference was that the lives being endangered, in this case, included Michel's. 'Okay,' she said. 'I'd better get on with it.'

'He's eager to see you.'

She frowned. 'Eager? Why?'

Percy gave a wry smile. 'Go and find out for yourself.'

Flick left the drawing room of the apartment, where Percy had his desk, and went along the corridor. His secretary was typing in the kitchen, and she directed Flick to another room.

Flick paused outside the door. This is how it is, she told herself: you pick yourself up and carry on working, hoping you will eventually forget.

She entered the study, a small room with a square table and a few mismatched chairs. Helicopter was a fair-skinned boy of about twenty-two, wearing a tweed suit in a checked pattern of mustard, orange and green. You could tell he was English from a mile away. Fortunately, before he got on the plane he would be kitted out in clothing that would look inconspicuous in a French town. SOE employed French tailors and dressmakers who sewed continental-style clothes for agents (then spent hours making the clothes look worn and shabby so that they would not attract attention by their newness). There was nothing they could do about Helicopter's pink complexion and red-blond hair, except hope that the Gestapo would think he must have some German blood.

Flick introduced herself, and he said: 'Yes, we've met before, actually.'

'I'm sorry, I don't remember.'

'You were at Oxford with my brother, Charles.'

'Charlie Standish – of course!' Flick remembered another fair boy in tweeds, taller and slimmer than Helicopter, but probably no cleverer – he had not taken a degree. Charlie spoke fluent French, she recalled – something they had had in common.

'You came to our house in Gloucestershire once, actually.'

Flick recalled a weekend in a country house in the thirties, and a family with an amiable English father and a chic French mother. Charlie had had a kid brother, Brian, an awkward adolescent in knee shorts, very excited about his new camera. She had talked to him a bit and he had developed a little crush on her. 'So how is Charlie? I haven't seen him since we graduated.'

'He's dead, actually.' Brian looked suddenly grief-stricken. 'Died in 'forty-one. Killed in the b-b-bloody desert, actually.'

Flick was afraid he would cry. She took his hand in both of hers and said: 'Brian, I'm so terribly sorry.'

'Jolly nice of you.' He swallowed hard. With an effort

he brightened. 'I've seen you since then, just once. You gave a lecture to my SOE training group. I didn't get a chance to speak to you afterwards.'

'I hope my talk was useful.'

'You spoke about traitors within the Resistance and what to do about them. "It's quite simple," you said. "You put the barrel of your pistol to the back of the bastard's head and pull the trigger twice." Scared us all to death, actually.'

He was looking at her with something like hero-worship in his eyes, and she began to see what Percy had been hinting at. It looked as if Brian still had a crush on her. She moved away from him, sat at the other side of the table, and said: 'Well, we'd better begin. You know you're going to make contact with a Resistance circuit that has been largely wiped out.'

'Yes, I'm to find out how much of it is left and what it is still capable of doing, if anything.'

'It's likely that some members were captured during the skirmish yesterday and are under Gestapo interrogation as we speak. So you'll have to be especially careful. Your contact in Reims is a woman codenamed Bourgeoise. Every day at eleven in the morning she goes to the crypt of the cathedral to pray. She's generally the only person there but, in case there are others, she'll be wearing odd shoes, one black and one brown.'

'Easy enough to remember.'

'You say to her: "Pray for me." She replies: "I pray for peace." That's the code.'

He repeated the words.

'She'll take you to her house, then put you in touch with the head of the Bollinger circuit, whose codename is Monet.' She was talking about her husband, but Brian did not need to know that. 'Don't mention the address or real name of Bourgeoise to other members of the circuit when you meet them, please: for security reasons, it's better they don't know.' Flick herself had recruited Bourgeoise and set up the cut-out. Even Michel had not met the woman.

'I understand.'

'Is there anything you want to ask me?'

'I'm sure there are a hundred things, but I can't think of any.'

She stood up and came around the table to shake his hand. 'Well, good luck.'

He kept hold of her hand. 'I never forgot that weekend you came to our house,' he said. 'I expect I was a frightful bore, but you were very kind to me.'

She smiled and said lightly: 'You were a nice kid.'

'I fell in love with you, actually.'

She wanted to jerk her hand out of his and walk away, but he might die tomorrow, and she could not bring herself to be so cruel. 'I'm flattered,' she said, trying to maintain an amiably bantering tone.

It was no good: he was in earnest. 'I was wondering . . . would you . . . just for luck, give me a kiss?'

She hesitated. Oh, hell, she thought. She stood on tiptoe and kissed him lightly on the lips. She let the kiss linger for a second, then broke away. He looked transfixed by joy. She patted his cheek softly with her hand. 'Stay alive, Brian,' she said. Then she went out.

She returned to Percy's room. He had a pile of books and a scatter of photographs on his desk. 'All done?' he said.

She nodded. 'But he's not perfect secret-agent material, Percy.'

Percy shrugged. 'He's brave, he speaks French like a Parisian, and he can shoot straight.'

'Two years ago you would have sent him back to the army.'

'True. Now I'm going to send him off to Sandy.' At a large country house in the village of Sandy, near the Tempsford airstrip, Brian would be dressed in French-style clothes and given the forged papers he needed to pass through Gestapo checkpoints and buy food. Percy got up and went to the door. 'While I'm seeing him off, have a look at that rogues' gallery, will you?' He pointed to the photos on the desk. 'Those are all the pictures MI6 has of German officers. If the man you saw in the square at Sainte-Cécile should happen to be among them, I'd be interested to know his name.' He went out.

Flick picked up one of the books. It was a graduation year book from a military academy, showing postage-stamp-size photos of a couple of hundred fresh-faced young men. There were a dozen or more similar books, and several hundred loose photos.

She did not want to spend all night looking at mug shots, but perhaps she could narrow it down. The man in the square had seemed about forty. He would have graduated at the age of twenty-two, roughly, so the year must have been about 1926. None of the books was that old.

She turned her attention to the loose photographs. As she flicked through, she recalled all she could of the man. He was quite tall and well dressed, but that would not show in a photo. He had thick dark hair, she thought, and although he was clean-shaven, he looked as if he could grow a heavy beard. She remembered dark eyes, clearly marked eyebrows, a straight nose, a square chin ... quite the matinée idol, in fact.

The loose photos had been taken in all sorts of different situations. Some were news pictures, showing officers shaking hands with Hitler, inspecting troops, or looking at tanks and aeroplanes. A few seemed to have been snapped by spies. These were the most candid shots, taken in crowds, from cars, or through windows, showing the officers shopping, talking to children, hailing a taxi, lighting a pipe.

She scanned the photos as fast as she could, tossing them to one side. She hesitated over each dark-haired man. None was as handsome as the one she recalled from the square. She passed over a photo of a man in police uniform, then went back to it. The uniform had at first put her off, but on careful study she thought this was him.

She turned the photograph over. Pasted to the back was a typewritten sheet. She read:

FRANCK, Dieter Wolfgang, sometimes 'Frankie'; born Cologne 3 June 1904; educ. Humboldt University of Berlin & Köln Police Academy; mar. 1930 Waltraud Loewe, 1 son 1 dtr; Superintendent, Criminal Investigation Department, Cologne police, to 1940; Major, Intelligence Section, Afrika Korps, to ?

A star of Rommel's intelligence staff, this officer is said to be a skilled interrogator and a ruthless torturer.

Flick shuddered to think she had been so near to such a dangerous man. An experienced police detective who had turned his skills to military intelligence was a frightening enemy. The fact that he had a family in Cologne did not prevent his having a mistress in France, it seemed.

Percy returned, and she handed him the picture. 'This is the man.'

'Dieter Franck!' said Percy. 'We know of him. How interesting. From what you overheard of his conversation in the square, Rommel seems to have given him some kind of counter-Resistance job.' He made a note on his pad. 'I'd better let MI6 know, as they loaned us their photos.'

There was a tap at the door, and Percy's secretary looked in. 'There's someone to see you, Colonel Thwaite.' The girl looked coquettish. The fatherly Percy never inspired that sort of behaviour in secretaries, so Flick guessed the visitor must be an attractive man. 'An American,' the girl added. That might explain it, Flick thought. Americans were the height of glamour, to secretaries at least.

'How did he find this place?' Percy said. Orchard Court was supposed to be a secret address.

'He went to number sixty-four Baker Street, and they sent him here.'

'They shouldn't do that. He must be very persuasive. Who is he?'

'Major Chancellor.'

Percy looked at Flick. She did not know anyone called Chancellor. Then she remembered the arrogant major who had been so rude to her this morning at Monty's headquarters. 'Oh, God, him,' she said in disgust. 'What does he want?'

'Send him in,' said Percy.

Paul Chancellor came in. He walked with a limp that Flick had not noticed this morning. It probably got worse as the day wore on. He had a pleasant American face, with a big nose and a jutting chin. Any chance he might have had of being handsome was spoiled by his left ear, or what remained of it, which was the lower one-third, mostly lobe. Flick assumed he had been wounded in action.

Chancellor saluted and said: 'Good evening, Colonel. Good evening, Major.'

Percy said: 'We don't do a lot of saluting at SOE, Chancellor. Please sit down. What brings you here?'

Chancellor took a chair and removed his uniform cap. 'I'm glad I caught you both,' he said. 'I've spent most of the day thinking about this morning's conversation.' He gave a self-effacing grin. 'Part of the time, I have to confess, I was composing wittily crushing remarks I could have made if only I had thought of them in time.'

Flick could not help smiling. She had done the same.

Chancellor went on: 'You hinted, Colonel Thwaite, that MI6 might not have told the whole truth about the attack on the telephone exchange, and that played on my mind. The fact that Major Clairet here was so rude to me did not necessarily mean she was lying about the facts.'

Flick had been half-way to forgiving him, but now she bridled. 'Rude? Me?'

Percy said: 'Shut up, Flick.'

She closed her mouth.

'So I sent for your report, Colonel. Of course the request came from Monty's office, not me personally, so it was brought to our headquarters by a FANY motorcyclist in double-quick time.'

He was a no-nonsense type who knew how to pull the levers of the military machine, Flick thought. He might be an arrogant pig, but he would make a useful ally.

'When I read it, I realized the main reason for defeat was wrong intelligence.'

'Supplied by MI6!' Flick said indignantly.

'Yes, I noticed that,' Chancellor said with mild sarcasm. 'Obviously MI6 was covering up its own incompetence. I'm not a career soldier myself, but my father is, so I'm familiar with the tricks of military bureaucrats.'

'Oh,' said Percy thoughtfully. 'Are you the son of General Chancellor?'

'Yes.'

'Go on.'

'MI6 would never have gotten away with it if your boss had been at the meeting this morning to put SOE's side of the story. It seemed too much of a coincidence that he had been called away at the last minute.'

Percy looked dubious. 'He was summoned by the Prime Minister. I don't see how MI6 could have arranged that.'

'The meeting was not attended by Churchill. A Downing Street aide took the chair. And it *had* been arranged at the instigation of MI6.'

'Well, I'm damned,' Flick said angrily. 'They're such snakes!'

Percy said: 'I wish they were as clever about gathering intelligence as they are about deceiving their colleagues.'

Chancellor said: 'I also looked in detail at your plan, Major Clairet, for taking the chateau by stealth, with a team disguised as cleaners. It's risky, of course, but it could work.'

Did that mean it would be reconsidered? Flick hardly dared to ask.

Percy gave Chancellor a level look. 'So what are you going to do about all this?'

'By chance, I had dinner with my father tonight. I told him the whole story and asked him what a general's aide should do in these circumstances. We were at the Savoy.'

'What did he say?' Flick asked impatiently. She did not care which restaurant they had gone to.

'That I should go to Monty and tell him we had made a mistake.' He grimaced. 'Not easy with any general. They never like to revisit decisions. But sometimes it has to be done.'

'And will you?' Flick said hopefully.

'I already have.'

Percy said in surprise: 'You don't waste time, do you!'

Flick held her breath. It hardly seemed possible, after a day of despair, that she might be given the second chance she longed for.

Chancellor said: 'Monty was remarkably good about it, in the end.'

Flick could not contain her agitation. 'For God's sake, what did he say about my plan?'

'He's authorized it.'

'Thank God!' She jumped up, unable to sit still. 'Another chance!'

Percy said: 'Splendid!'

Chancellor held up a warning hand. 'Two more things. The first one you may not like. He's put me in charge of the operation.'

'You!' Flick said.

'Why?' said Percy.

'You don't cross-examine the General when he gives an order. I'm sorry you seem dismayed. Monty has faith in me, even if you don't.'

Percy shrugged.

Flick said: 'What's the other stipulation?'

'There's a time constraint. I can't tell you when the invasion will be, and in fact the date has not been finally decided. But I can tell you that we have to accomplish our mission very quickly. If you haven't achieved the objective by midnight next Monday, it will probably be too late.'

'Next Monday!' said Flick.

'Yes,' said Paul Chancellor. 'We have exactly one week.'

THE THIRD DAY:
TUESDAY, 30 MAY 1944

ELEVEN

Flick left London at dawn, driving a Vincent Comet motorcycle with a powerful 500cc engine. The roads were deserted. Petrol was severely rationed, and drivers could be jailed for making 'unnecessary' journeys. She drove very fast. It was dangerous but exciting. The thrill was worth the risk.

She felt the same about the mission, scared but eager. She had stayed up late last night with Percy and Paul, drinking tea and planning. There must be six women in the team, they had decided, as it was the unvarying number of cleaners on a shift. One had to be an explosives expert; another, a telephone engineer, to decide exactly where the charges should be placed to ensure the exchange was crippled. She wanted one good marksman and two tough soldiers. With herself, that would make six.

She had one day to find them. The team would need a minimum of two days' training – they had to learn to parachute, if nothing else. That would take up Wednesday and Thursday. They would be dropped near Reims on Friday night, and enter the chateau on Saturday evening or Sunday. That left one spare day as a margin for error.

She crossed the river at London Bridge. Her motorbike roared through the bomb-ravaged wharves and tenements of Bermondsey and Rotherhithe, then she took the Old Kent Road, traditional route of pilgrims, towards Canterbury. As she left the suburbs behind, she opened the throttle and gave the bike its head. For a while she let the wind blow the worries out of her hair.

It was not yet six o'clock when she reached Somersholme, the country house of the Barons of Colefield. The baron himself, William, was in Italy, fighting his way towards Rome with the Eighth Army, Flick knew. His sister, the Honourable Diana Colefield, was the only member of the family living here now. The vast house, with its dozens of bedrooms for house-guests and their servants, was being used as a convalescent home for wounded soldiers.

Flick slowed the bike to walking speed and drove up the avenue of hundred-year-old lime trees, gazing at the great pile of pink granite ahead, with its bays, balconies, gables and roofs, acres of windows and scores of chimneys. She parked on the gravel forecourt next to an ambulance and a scatter of jeeps.

In the hall, nurses bustled about with cups of tea. The soldiers might be here to convalesce, but they still had to be woken at daybreak. Flick asked for Mrs Riley, the housekeeper, and was directed to the basement. She found her staring worriedly at the furnace in the company of two men in overalls.

'Hello, Ma,' said Flick.

Her mother hugged her hard. She was even shorter

than her daughter and just as thin, but like Flick she was stronger than she looked. The hug squeezed the breath out of Flick. Gasping and laughing, Flick extricated herself. 'Ma, you'll crush me!'

'I never know if you're alive until I see you,' her mother said. In her voice there was still a trace of the Irish accent: she had left Cork with her parents forty-five years ago.

'What's the matter with the furnace?'

'It was never designed to produce so much hot water. These nurses are mad for cleanliness, they force the poor soldiers to bathe every day. Come to my kitchen and I'll make you some breakfast.'

Flick was in a hurry, but she told herself she had time for her mother. Anyway, she had to eat. She followed her up the stairs and into the servants' quarters.

Flick had grown up in this house. She had played in the servants' hall, run wild in the woods, attended the village school a mile away, and returned here from boarding-school and university for the vacations. She had been extraordinarily privileged. Most women in her mother's position were forced to give up their jobs when they had a child. Ma had been allowed to stay, partly because the old baron had been somewhat unconventional, but mainly because she was such a good housekeeper that he had dreaded losing her. Flick's father had been butler, but he had died when she was six years old. Every February, Flick and her mother had accompanied the family to their villa in Nice, which was where Flick had learned French.

The old baron, father of William and Diana, had been fond of Flick and had encouraged her to study, even paying her school fees. He had been very proud when she had won a scholarship to Oxford University. When he died, soon after the start of the war, Flick had been as heartbroken as if he had been her real father.

The family now occupied only a small corner of the house. The old butler's pantry had become the kitchen. Flick's mother put the kettle on. 'Just a piece of toast will be fine, Ma,' said Flick.

Her mother ignored her and started frying bacon. 'Well, I can see you're all right,' she said. 'How's that handsome husband?'

'Michel's alive,' Flick said. She sat at the kitchen table. The smell of bacon made her mouth water.

'Alive, is he? But not well, evidently. Wounded?'

'He got a bullet in his bum. It won't kill him.'

'You've seen him, then.'

Flick laughed. 'Ma, stop it! I'm not supposed to say.'

'Of course not. Is he keeping his hands off other women? If *that's* not a military secret.'

Flick never ceased to be startled by the accuracy of her mother's intuition. It was quite eerie. 'I hope he is.'

'Hmm. Anyone in particular that you hope he's keeping his hands off?'

Flick did not answer the question directly. 'Have you noticed, Ma, that men sometimes don't seem to realize when a girl is really stupid?'

Her mother made a disgusted noise. 'So that's the way of it. She's pretty, I suppose.'

'Mmm.'

'Young?'

'Nineteen.'

'Have you had it out with him?'

'Yes. He promised to stop.'

'He might keep his promise – if you're not away too long.'

'I'm hopeful.'

Her mother looked crestfallen. 'So you're going back.'

'I can't say.'

'Have you not done enough?'

'We haven't won the war yet, so no, I suppose I haven't.'

She put a plate of bacon and eggs in front of Flick. It probably represented a week's rations. But Flick suppressed the protest that came to her lips. Better to accept the gift gracefully. Besides, she was suddenly ravenous. 'Thanks, Ma,' she said. 'You spoil me.'

Her mother smiled, satisfied, and Flick tucked in hungrily. As she ate, she reflected wryly that Ma had effortlessly got out of her everything she wanted to know, despite Flick's attempts to avoid answering questions. 'You should work for military intelligence,' she said through a mouthful of fried egg. 'They could use you as an interrogator. You've made me tell you everything.'

'I'm your mother, I've a right to know.'

It didn't much matter. Ma would not repeat any of it.

She sipped a cup of tea as she watched Flick eat. 'You've got to win the war all on your own, of course,' she said with fond sarcasm. 'You were that way from a child – independent to a fault.'

'I don't know why. I was always looked after. When you were busy there were half a dozen housemaids doting on me.'

'I think I encouraged you to be self-sufficient because you didn't have a father. Whenever you wanted me to do something for you, like fix a bicycle chain, or sew on a button, I used to say: 'Try it yourself, and if you can't manage I'll help you.' Nine times out of ten I heard no more about it.'

Flick finished the bacon and wiped her plate with a slice of bread. 'A lot of the time, Mark used to help me.' Mark was Flick's brother, a year older.

Her mother's face froze. 'Is that right,' she said.

Flick suppressed a sigh. Her mother had quarrelled with Mark two years ago. He worked in the theatre as a stage manager, and lived with an actor called Steve. Ma had long known that Mark was 'not the marrying kind', as she put it. But in a burst of excessive honesty Mark had been foolish enough to tell her that he loved Steve, and they were like husband and wife. She had been mortally offended and had not spoken to her son since.

Flick said: 'Mark loves you, Ma.'

'Does he, now?'

'I wish you'd see him.'

'No doubt.' She picked up Flick's empty plate and washed it in the sink.

Flick shook her head in exasperation. 'You're a bit stubborn, Ma.'

'I daresay that's where you get it from, then.'

Flick had to smile. She had often been accused of stubbornness. 'Mulish' was Percy's word. She made an effort to be conciliatory. 'Well, I suppose you can't help the way you feel. Anyway, I'm not going to argue with you, especially after such a wonderful breakfast.' All the same, it was her ambition to get the two of them to make it up.

But not today. She stood up.

Her mother smiled. 'It's lovely to see you. I worry about you.'

'I've got another reason for coming. I need to talk to Diana.'

'Whatever for?'

'Can't say.'

'I hope you're not thinking of taking her to France with you.'

'Ma, hush! Who said anything about going to France?'

'I suppose it's because she's so handy with a gun.'

'I can't say.'

'She'll get you killed! She doesn't know what discipline is, why should she? She wasn't brought up that way. Not her fault, of course. But you'd be a fool to rely on her.'

'Yes, I know,' Flick said impatiently. She had made a decision and she was not going to review it with her mother.

'She's had several war jobs, and been sacked from every one.'

'I know.' But Diana was a crack shot, and Flick did

not have time to be fussy. She had to take what she could get. Her main worry was that Diana might refuse. No one could be forced to do undercover work. It was strictly for volunteers. 'Where is Diana now, do you know?'

'I believe she's in the wood. She went out early, after rabbits.'

'Of course.' Diana loved all the blood sports: foxhunting, deerstalking, hare coursing, grouse shooting, even fishing. If there was nothing else to do, she would shoot rabbits.

'Just follow the sound of gunfire.'

Flick kissed her mother's cheek. 'Thanks for breakfast.' She went to the door.

'And don't get on the wrong side of her gun,' her mother called after her.

Flick left by the staff door, crossed the kitchen garden, and entered the woods at the rear of the house. The trees were bright with new leaves, and the nettles grew waist high. Flick tramped through the undergrowth in her heavy motorcycle boots and leather trousers. The best way to attract Diana, she thought, would be by issuing a challenge.

When she had gone a quarter of a mile into the wood, she heard the report of a shotgun. She stopped, listened, and shouted: 'Diana!' There was no reply.

She walked towards the sound, calling out every minute or so. Eventually she heard: 'Over here, you noisy idiot, whoever you are!'

'Coming, just put down the gun.'

She came upon Diana in a clearing, sitting on the ground with her back against an oak tree, smoking a cigarette. A shotgun lay across her knees, broken open for reloading, and there were half a dozen dead rabbits beside her. 'Oh, it's you!' she said. 'You scared all the game away.'

'They'll come back tomorrow.' Flick studied her childhood companion. Diana was pretty in a boyish way, with dark hair cut short and freckles across her nose. She wore a shooting jacket and corduroy trousers. 'How are you, Diana?'

'Bored. Frustrated. Depressed. Otherwise fine.'

Flick sat on the grass beside her. This might be easier than she had thought. 'What's the matter?'

'I'm rotting away in the English countryside while my brother's conquering Italy.'

'How is William?'

'He's all right, he's part of the war effort, but no one will give me a proper job.'

'I might be able to help you there.'

'You're in the FANYs.' Diana drew on her cigarette and blew out smoke. 'Darling, I can't be a *chauffeuse*.'

Flick nodded. Diana was too grand to do the menial war work that most women were offered. 'Well, I'm here to propose something more interesting.'

'What?'

'You might not like it. It's very difficult, and dangerous.'

Diana looked sceptical. 'What does it involve, driving in the blackout?'

'I can't tell you much about it, because it's secret.'

'Flick, darling, don't tell me you're involved in cloak-and-dagger stuff.'

'I didn't get promoted to Major by driving generals to meetings.'

Diana looked hard at her. 'Do you mean this?'

'Absolutely.'

'Good Lord.' Against her will, Diana was impressed.

Flick had to get her positive agreement to volunteer. 'So – are you willing to do something very dangerous? I mean it, you really are quite likely to get killed.'

Diana looked excited rather than discouraged. 'Of course I'm willing. William's risking his life, why shouldn't I?'

'You mean it?'

'I'm very serious.'

Flick concealed her relief. She had recruited her first team member.

Diana was so keen that Flick decided to press her advantage. 'There's a condition, and you may find it worse than the danger.'

'What?'

'You're two years older than I, and all our lives you've been my social superior. You're the baron's daughter, and I'm the housekeeper's brat. Nothing wrong with that, and I'm not complaining. Ma would say that's how it should be.'

'Yes, dear, so what's your point?'

'I'm in charge of the operation. You'll have to defer to me.'

Diana shrugged. 'That's fine.'

'It will be a problem,' Flick insisted. 'You'll find it strange. But I'll be hard on you until you get used to it. This is a warning.'

'Yes, sir!'

'We don't bother too much about the formalities in my department, so you won't need to call me sir, or ma'am. But we do enforce military discipline, especially once an operation has begun. If you forget that, my anger will be the least of your worries. Disobeying orders can get you killed in my line of work.'

'Darling, how dramatic! But of course I understand.'

Flick was not at all sure Diana did understand, but she had done her best. She took a scratch pad from her blouse and wrote down an address in Hampshire. 'Pack a case for three days. This is where you need to go. You get the train from Waterloo to Brockenhurst.'

Diana looked at the address. 'Why, this is Lord Montagu's estate.'

'Most of it is occupied by my department now.'

'What *is* your department?'

'The Inter Services Research Bureau,' Flick said, using the usual cover name.

'I trust it's more exciting than it sounds.'

'You can bet on that.'

'When do I start?'

'You need to get there today.' Flick got to her feet. 'Your training starts at dawn tomorrow.'

'I'll come back to the house with you and start packing.' Diana stood up. 'Tell me something?'

'If I can.'

Diana fiddled with her shotgun, seeming

embarrassed. When she looked at Flick, her face showed an expression of frankness for the first time. 'Why me?' she said. 'You must know I've been turned down by everyone.'

Flick nodded. 'I'll be blunt.' She looked at the bloodstained rabbit corpses on the ground, then lifted her gaze to Diana's pretty face. 'You're a killer,' she said. 'And that's what I need.'

TWELVE

Dieter slept until ten. He woke with a headache from the morphine, but otherwise he felt good: excited, optimistic, confident. Yesterday's bloody interrogation had given him a hot lead. The woman codenamed Bourgeoise, with her house in the rue du Bois, could be his way into the heart of the French Resistance.

Or it might go nowhere.

He drank a litre of water and took three aspirins to get rid of the morphine hangover, then he picked up the phone.

First he called Lieutenant Hesse, who was staying in a less grand room at the same hotel. 'Good morning, Hans, did you sleep well?'

'Yes, thank you, Major. Sir, I went to the town hall to check out the address in the rue du Bois.'

'Good lad,' Dieter said. 'What did you find out?'

'The house is owned and occupied by one person, a Mademoiselle Jeanne Lemas.'

'But there may be other people staying there.'

'I also drove past, just to have a look, and the place seemed quiet.'

'Be ready to leave, with my car, in an hour.'

'Very good.'

'And, Hans – well done for using your initiative.'

'Thank you, sir.'

Dieter hung up. He wondered what Mademoiselle Lemas was like. Gaston said no one in the Bollinger circuit had ever met her, and Dieter believed him: the house was a security cut-out. Incoming agents knew nothing more than where to contact the woman: if caught, they could not reveal any information about the Resistance. At least, that was the theory. There was no such thing as perfect security.

Presumably Mademoiselle Lemas was unmarried. She could be a young woman who had inherited the house from her parents, a middle-aged spinster looking for a husband, or an old maid. It might help to take a woman with him, he decided.

He returned to the bedroom. Stéphanie had brushed her abundant red hair and was sitting up in bed, with her breasts showing over the top of the sheet. She really knew how to look tempting. But he resisted the impulse to get back into bed. 'Would you do something for me?' he said.

'I would do anything for you.'

'Anything?' He sat on the bed and touched her bare shoulder. 'Would you watch me with another woman?'

'Of course,' she said. 'I would lick her nipples while you made love to her.'

'You would, I know.' He laughed with pleasure. He had had mistresses before, but none like her. 'It's not that, though. I want you to come with me while I arrest a woman in the Resistance.'

Her face showed no emotion. 'Very well,' she said calmly.

He was tempted to press her for a reaction, to ask her how she felt about this, and was she sure she was happy about it; but he decided to take her consent at face value. 'Thank you,' he said, and he returned to the living room.

Mademoiselle Lemas might be alone but, on the other hand, the house could be crawling with Allied agents, all armed to the teeth. He needed some back-up. He consulted his notebook and gave the hotel operator Rommel's number in La Roche-Guyon.

When the Germans had first occupied the country, the French telephone system had been swamped. Since then, the Germans had improved the equipment, adding thousands of kilometres of cable and installing automatic exchanges. The system was still overloaded, but it was better than it had been.

He asked for Rommel's aide, Major Goedel. A moment later he heard the familiar cold, precise voice: 'Goedel.'

'This is Dieter Franck,' he said. 'How are you, Walter?'

'Busy,' Goedel said crisply. 'What is it?'

'I'm making rapid progress here. I don't want to give details, because I'm speaking on a hotel phone, but I'm about to arrest at least one spy, perhaps several. I thought the Field Marshal might like to know that.'

'I shall tell him.'

'But I could use some assistance. I'm doing all this

with one lieutenant. I'm so desperate, I'm using my French girlfriend to help me.'

'That seems unwise.'

'Oh, she's trustworthy. But she won't be much use against trained terrorists. Can you get me half a dozen good men?'

'Use the Gestapo – that's what they're for.'

'They're unreliable. You know they're co-operating with us only reluctantly. I need people I can rely on.'

'It's out of the question,' Goedel said.

'Look, Walter, you know how important Rommel feels this is – he's given me the job of making sure the Resistance can't hamper our mobility.'

'Yes. But the Field Marshal expects you to do it without depriving him of combat troops.'

'I'm not sure I can.'

'For God's sake, man!' Goedel raised his voice. 'We're trying to defend the entire Atlantic coastline with a handful of soldiers, and you're surrounded by able-bodied men who have nothing better to do than track down scared old Jews hiding in barns. Get on with the job and don't pester me!' There was a click as the phone was hung up.

Dieter was startled. It was uncharacteristic for Goedel to blow his top. No doubt they were all tense about the threat of invasion. But the upshot was clear. Dieter had to do this on his own.

With a sigh, he jiggled the rest and placed a call to the chateau at Sainte-Cécile.

He reached Willi Weber. 'I'm going to raid a Resistance house,' he said. 'I may need some of your heavyweights. Will you send four men and a car to the Hôtel Frankfort? Or do I need to speak to Rommel again?'

The threat was unnecessary. Weber was keen to have his men along on the operation. That way, the Gestapo could claim the credit for any success. He promised a car in half an hour.

Dieter was worried about working with the Gestapo. He could not control them. But he had no choice.

While shaving he turned on the radio, which was tuned to a German station. He learned that the first-ever tank battle in the Pacific theatre had developed yesterday on the island of Biak. The occupying Japanese had driven the invading American 162nd Infantry back to their beachhead. Push them into the sea, Dieter thought.

He dressed in a dark grey worsted suit, a fine cotton shirt with pale grey stripes, and a black tie with small white dots. The dots were woven into the fabric rather than printed on it, a detail that gave him pleasure. He thought for a moment, then removed the jacket and strapped on a shoulder holster. He took his Walther P38 automatic pistol from the bureau and slid it into the holster, then put his jacket back on.

He sat down with a cup of coffee and watched Stéphanie dressing. The French made the most beautiful underwear in the world, he thought as she stepped into silk cami-knickers the colour of clotted cream. He loved to see her pull on her stockings, smoothing the silk over her thighs. 'Why did the old masters not paint this moment?' he said.

'Because Renaissance women didn't have sheer silk stockings,' said Stéphanie.

When she was ready they left.

Hans Hesse was waiting outside with Dieter's Hispano-Suiza. The young man gazed at Stéphanie with awestruck admiration. To him, she was infinitely desirable and at the same time untouchable. He made Dieter think of a poor woman staring into Cartier's shop window.

Behind Dieter's car was a black Citroën Traction Avant containing four Gestapo men in plain clothes. Major Weber had decided to come himself, Dieter saw: he sat in the front passenger seat of the Citroën, wearing a green tweed suit that made him look like a farmer on his way to church. 'Follow me,' Dieter told him. 'When we get there, please stay in your car until I call you.'

Weber said: 'Where the hell did you get a car like that?'

'It was a bribe from a Jew,' Dieter said. 'I helped him escape to America.'

Weber grunted in disbelief, but in fact the story was true.

Bravado was the best attitude to take with men such as Weber. If Dieter had tried to keep Stéphanie hidden away, Weber would immediately have suspected that she was Jewish, and might have started an investigation. But because Dieter flaunted her, the thought never crossed Weber's mind.

Hans took the wheel and they headed for the rue du Bois.

Reims was a substantial country town with a population of more than a hundred thousand, but there were few motor vehicles on the streets. Cars were used only by those on official business: the police, doctors, firemen, and of course the Germans. The citizens went about by bicycle or on foot. Petrol was available for deliveries of food and other essential supplies, but many goods were transported by horse-drawn cart. Champagne was the main industry here. Dieter loved champagne in all its forms: the nutty older vintages, the fresh, light, non-vintage *cuvées*, the refined *blanc de blancs*, the *demi-sec* dessert varieties, even the playful pink beloved of Paris courtesans.

The rue du Bois was a pleasant tree-lined street on the outskirts of town. Hans pulled up outside a tall house at the end of a row, with a little courtyard to one side. This was the home of Mademoiselle Lemas. Would Dieter be able to break her spirit? Women were more difficult than men. They cried and screamed, but held out longer. He had sometimes failed with a woman, though never with a man. If this one defeated him, his investigation was dead.

'Come if I wave to you,' he said to Stéphanie, as he got out of the car. Weber's Citroën drew up behind, but the Gestapo men stayed in the car, as instructed.

Dieter glanced into the courtyard beside the house. There was a garage. Beyond that, he saw a small garden with clipped hedges, rectangular flower beds, and a raked gravel path. The owner had a tidy mind.

Beside the front door was an old-fashioned red-and-yellow rope. He pulled it, and heard from inside the metallic ring of a mechanical bell.

The woman who opened the door was about sixty. She had white hair tied up at the back with a tortoiseshell clasp. She wore a blue dress with a pattern of small white flowers. Over it she had a crisp white apron. 'Good morning, Monsieur,' she said politely.

Dieter smiled. She was an irreproachably genteel provincial lady. Already he had thought of a way to torture her. His spirits lifted with hope.

He said: 'Good morning . . . Mademoiselle Lemas?'

She took in his suit, noticed the car at the kerb, and perhaps heard the trace of a German accent; and fear came into her eyes. There was a tremor in her voice as she said: 'How may I help you?'

'Are you alone, Mademoiselle?' He watched her face carefully.

'Yes,' she said. 'Quite alone.'

She was telling the truth. He was sure. A woman such as this could not lie without betraying herself with her eyes.

He turned and beckoned Stéphanie. 'My colleague will join us.' He was not going to need Weber's men. 'I have some questions to ask you.'

'Questions? About what?'

'May I come in?'

'Very well.'

The front parlour was furnished with dark wood, highly polished. There was a piano under a dust cover and an engraving of Reims cathedral on the wall. The mantelpiece bore a selection of ornaments: a spun-glass swan, a china flower-girl, a transparent globe containing a model of the palace at Versailles, and three wooden camels.

Dieter sat on a plush-upholstered couch. Stéphanie sat beside him, and Mademoiselle Lemas took an upright chair opposite. She was plump, Dieter observed. Not many French people were plump after four years of occupation. Food was her vice.

On a low table was a cigarette box and a heavy lighter. Dieter flipped the lid and saw that the box was full. 'Please feel free to smoke,' he said.

She looked mildly offended: women of her generation did not use tobacco. 'I don't smoke.'

'Then who are these for?'

She touched her chin, a sign of dishonesty. 'Visitors.'

'And what kind of visitors do you get?'

'Friends . . . neighbours . . .' She looked uncomfortable.

'And British spies.'

'That is absurd.'

Dieter gave her his most charming smile. 'You are obviously a respectable lady who has become mixed up in criminal activities from misguided motives,' he said, in a tone of friendly candour. 'I'm not going to toy with you, and I hope you will not be so foolish as to lie to me.'

'I shall tell you nothing,' she said.

Dieter feigned disappointment, but he was pleased to be making such rapid progress. She had already abandoned the pretence that she did not know what he was talking about. That was as good as a confession. 'I'm going to ask you some questions,' he said. 'If you don't answer them, I shall ask you again at Gestapo headquarters.'

She gave him a defiant look.

He said: 'Where do you meet the British agents?'

She said nothing.

'How do they recognize you?'

Her eyes met his in a steady gaze. She was no longer flustered, but resigned. A brave woman, he thought. She would be a challenge.

'What is the password?'

She did not answer.

'Who do you pass the agents on to? How do you contact the Resistance? Who is in charge of it?'

Silence.

Dieter stood up. 'Come with me, please.'

'Very well,' she said staunchly. 'Perhaps you will permit me to put on my hat.'

'Of course.' He nodded to Stéphanie. 'Go with Mademoiselle, please. Make sure she does not use the telephone or write anything down.' He did not want her to leave any kind of message.

He waited in the hall. When they returned, Mademoiselle Lemas had taken off her apron and wore a light coat and a cloche hat that had gone out of fashion long before the outbreak of war. She carried a sturdy tan leather handbag. As the three of them were going out of the front door, Mademoiselle Lemas said: 'Oh! I forgot my key.'

'You don't need it,' Dieter said.

'The door locks itself,' she said. 'I need a key to get back in.'

Dieter looked her in the eye. 'Don't you understand?' he said. 'You've been sheltering British terrorists in your house, you have been caught, and you are in the hands of the Gestapo.' He shook his head in an expression of sorrow that was not entirely fake. 'Whatever happens, Mademoiselle, you're never coming home again.'

She realized the full horror of what was happening to her. Her face turned white, and she staggered. She steadied herself by grabbing the edge of a kidney-shaped table. A Chinese vase containing a spray of dried grasses wobbled dangerously, but did not fall. Then Mademoiselle Lemas recovered her poise. She straightened up and let go of the table. She gave him that defiant look again, then walked out of her house with her head held high.

Dieter asked Stéphanie to take the front passenger seat, while he sat in the back of the car with the prisoner. As Hans drove them to Sainte-Cécile, Dieter made polite conversation. 'Were you born in Reims, Mademoiselle?'

'Yes. My father was a choirmaster at the cathedral.'

A religious background. This was good news for the plan that was forming in Dieter's mind. 'Is he retired?'

'He died five years ago, after a long illness.'

'And your mother?'

'Died when I was quite young.'

'So, I imagine you nursed your father through his illness?'

'For twenty years.'

'Ah.' That explained why she was single. She had spent her life caring for an invalid father. 'And he left you the house.'

She nodded.

'Small reward, some might think, for a life of dedicated service,' Dieter said sympathetically.

She gave him a haughty look. 'One does not do such things for reward.'

'Indeed not.' He did not mind the implied rebuke. It would help his plan if she could convince herself that she was somehow Dieter's superior, morally and socially. 'Do you have brothers and sisters?'

'None.'

Dieter saw the picture vividly. The agents she sheltered, all young men and women, must have been like her children. She had fed them, done their laundry, talked to them, and probably kept an eye on the relationships between the sexes, making sure there was no immorality, at least not under her roof.

And now she would die for it.

But first, he hoped, she would tell him everything.

The Gestapo Citroën followed Dieter's car to Sainte-Cécile. When they had parked in the grounds of the chateau, Dieter spoke to Weber. 'I'm going to take her upstairs and put her in an office,' he said.

'Why? There are cells in the basement.'

'You'll see.'

Dieter led the prisoner up the stairs to the Gestapo offices. Dieter looked into all the rooms and picked the busiest, a combination typing pool and post room. It was occupied by young men and women in smart shirts and ties. Leaving Mademoiselle Lemas in the corridor, he closed the door and clapped his hands for attention. In a quiet voice he said: 'I'm going to bring a French woman in here. She is a prisoner, but I want you all to be friendly and polite to her, is that understood? Treat her as a guest. It's important that she feels respected.'

He brought her in, sat her at a table and, with a murmured apology, handcuffed her ankle to the table leg. He left Stéphanie with her and took Hesse outside. 'Go to the canteen and ask them to prepare lunch on a tray. Soup, a main course, a little wine, a bottle of mineral water, and plenty of coffee. Bring cutlery, glasses, a napkin. Make it look nice.'

The lieutenant grinned admiringly. He had no idea what his boss was up to, but he felt sure it would be something clever.

A few minutes later he returned with a tray. Dieter took it from him and carried it into the office. He set it in front of Mademoiselle Lemas. 'Please,' he said. 'It's lunchtime.'

'I couldn't eat anything, thank you.'

'Perhaps just a little soup.' He poured wine into her glass.

She added water to the wine and sipped it, then tried a mouthful of soup.

'How is it?'

'Very good,' she admitted.

'French food is so refined. We Germans cannot

imitate it.' Dieter talked nonsense to her, trying to relax her, and she drank most of the soup. He poured her a glass of water.

Major Weber came in and stared incredulously at the tray in front of the prisoner. Speaking German, he said: 'Are we now rewarding people for harbouring terrorists?'

Dieter said: 'Mademoiselle is a lady. We must treat her correctly.'

'God in heaven,' Weber said, and he turned on his heel.

She refused the main course, but drank all the coffee. Dieter was pleased. Everything was going according to plan. When she had finished, he asked her all the questions again. 'Where do you meet the Allied agents? How do they recognize you? What is the password?' She looked worried, but she still refused to answer.

He looked sadly at her. 'I am very sorry that you refuse to co-operate with me, after I have treated you kindly.'

She looked somewhat bewildered. 'I appreciate your kindness, but I cannot tell you anything.'

Stéphanie, sitting beside Dieter, also looked puzzled. He guessed that she was thinking: *Did you really imagine that a nice meal would be sufficient to make this woman talk?*

'Very well,' he said. He stood up as if to go.

'And now, Monsieur,' said Mademoiselle Lemas. She looked embarrassed. 'I must ask to . . . ah . . . visit the ladies' powder room.'

In a harsh voice, Dieter said: 'You want to go to the toilet?'

She reddened. 'In a word, yes.'

'I'm sorry, Mademoiselle,' Dieter said. 'That will not be possible.'

THIRTEEN

The last thing Monty had said to Paul Chancellor, late on Monday night, had been: 'If you only do one thing in this war, make sure that telephone exchange is destroyed.'

Paul had woken this morning with those words echoing in his mind. It was a simple instruction. If he could fulfil it, he would have helped win the war. If he failed, men would die – and he might spend the rest of his life reflecting that he had helped *lose* the war.

He went to Baker Street early, but Percy Thwaite was already there, sitting in his office, puffing his pipe and staring at six boxes of files. He seemed a typical military duffer, with his check jacket and toothbrush moustache. He looked at Paul with mild hostility. 'I don't know why Monty's put you in charge of this operation,' he said. 'I don't mind that you're only a major, and I'm a colonel – that's all stuff and nonsense. But you've never run a clandestine operation, whereas I've been doing it for three years. Does it make sense to you?'

'Yes,' Paul said briskly. 'When you want to make absolutely sure that a job gets done, you give it to someone you trust. Monty trusts me.'

'But not me.'

'He doesn't know you.'

'I see,' Percy said grumpily.

Paul needed Percy's co-operation, so he decided to mollify him. Looking around the office, he saw a framed photograph of a young man in lieutenant's uniform and an older woman in a big hat. The boy could have been Percy thirty years ago. 'Your son?' Paul guessed.

Percy softened immediately. 'David's out in Cairo,' he said. 'We had some bad moments during the desert war, especially after Rommel reached Tobruk; but now, of course, he's well out of the line of fire, and I must say I'm glad.'

The woman was dark-haired and dark-eyed, with a strong face, handsome rather than pretty. 'And Mrs Thwaite?'

'Rosa Mann. She became famous as a suffragette, in the twenties, and she's always used her maiden name.'

'Suffragette?'

'Campaigner for votes for women.'

Percy liked formidable women, Paul concluded; that was why he was fond of Flick. 'You know, you're right about my shortcomings,' he said candidly. 'I have been at the sharp end of clandestine operations, but this will be my first time as an organizer. So I'll be very grateful for your help.'

Percy nodded. 'I begin to see why you have a reputation for getting things done,' he said with a hint of a smile. 'But if you'll hear a word of advice . . .'

'Please.'

'Be guided by Flick. No one else has spent as much

time under cover and survived. Her knowledge and experience are matchless. I may be in charge of her in theory, but what I do is give her the support she needs. I would never try to tell her what to do.'

Paul hesitated. He had been given command by Monty and he was not about to hand it over on anyone's advice. 'I'll bear that in mind,' he said.

Percy seemed satisfied. He gestured to the files. 'Shall we get started?'

'What are these?'

'Records of people who were considered by us as possible agents, then rejected for some reason.'

Paul took off his jacket and rolled back his cuffs.

They spent the morning going through the files together. Some of the candidates had not even been interviewed; others had been rejected after they had been seen; and many had failed some part of the SOE training course – baffled by codes, hopeless with guns, or frightened to the point of hysteria when asked to jump out of a plane with a parachute. They were mostly in their early twenties, and they had only one other thing in common: they all spoke a foreign language with native fluency.

There were a lot of files, but few suitable candidates. By the time Percy and Paul had eliminated all the men, and the women whose language was something other than French, they were left with only three names.

Paul was disheartened. They had run into a major obstacle when they had hardly begun. 'Four is the minimum number we need, even assuming that Flick recruits the woman she has gone to see this morning.'

'Diana Colefield.'

'And none of these is either an explosives expert or a telephone engineer!'

Percy was more optimistic. 'They weren't, when SOE interviewed them; but they might be now. Women have learned to do all sorts of things.'

'Well, let's find out.'

It took a while to track the three down. A further disappointment was that one was dead. The other two were in London. Ruby Romain, unfortunately, was in His Majesty's Prison for Women at Holloway, three miles north of Baker Street, awaiting trial for murder. And Maude Valentine, whose file said simply 'psychologically unsuitable', was a driver with the FANYs.

'Down to two!' Paul said despondently.

'It's not the numbers, but the quality, that bothers me,' Percy said.

'We knew from the start we'd be looking at rejects.'

Percy's tone became angry. 'But we can't risk Flick's life with people like these!'

Percy was desperate to protect Flick, Paul realised. The older man had been willing to hand over control of the operation, but was not able to give up his role as Flick's guardian angel.

Their argument was interrupted by a phone call. It was Simon Fortescue, the pinstriped spook from MI6 who had blamed SOE for the failure at Sainte-Cécile. 'What can I do for you?' Paul said guardedly. Fortescue was not a man to trust.

'I think I may be able to do something for you,'

Fortescue said. 'I know you're going ahead with Major Clairet's plan.'

'Who told you?' Paul asked suspiciously. It was supposed to be a secret.

'Let's not go into that. I naturally wish you success with your mission, even though I was against it, and I'd like to help.'

Paul was angry that the mission was being talked about, but there was no point in pursuing that. 'Do you know a female telephone engineer who speaks perfect French?' he asked.

'Not quite. But there's someone you should see. Her name is Lady Denise Bowyer. Terribly nice girl, her father was the Marquess of Inverlocky.'

Paul was not interested in her pedigree. 'How did she learn French?'

'Brought up by her French stepmother, Lord Inverlocky's second wife. She's ever so keen to do her bit.'

Paul was suspicious of Fortescue, but he was desperate for suitable recruits. 'Where do I find her?'

'She's with the RAF at Hendon.' The word 'Hendon' meant nothing to Paul, but Fortescue explained: 'It's an airfield in the north London suburbs.'

'Thank you.'

'Let me know how she gets on.' Fortescue hung up.

Paul explained the call to Percy, who said: 'Fortescue wants a spy in our camp.'

'We can't afford to turn her down for that reason.'

'Quite.'

They saw Maude Valentine first. Percy arranged for

them to meet her at the Fenchurch Hotel, around the corner from SOE headquarters. Strangers were never brought to number sixty-four, he explained. 'If we reject her, she may guess that she's been considered for secret work, but she won't know the name of the organization that interviewed her nor where its office is, so even if she blabs she can't do much harm.'

'Very good.'

'What's your mother's maiden name?'

Paul was mildly startled and had to think for a moment. 'Thomas. She was Edith Thomas.'

'So, you'll be Major Thomas and I'll be Colonel Cox. No point in giving our real names.'

Percy was not such a duffer, Paul reflected.

He met Maude in the hotel lobby. She piqued his interest right away. She was a pretty girl with a flirtatious manner. Her uniform blouse was tight across the chest and she wore her cap at a jaunty angle. Paul spoke to her in French. 'My colleague is waiting in a private room.'

She gave him an arch look and replied in the same language. 'I don't usually go to hotel rooms with strange men,' she said pertly. 'But in your case, Major, I'll make an exception.'

He blushed. 'It's a meeting room, with a table and so on, not a bedroom.'

'Oh, well, that's all right, then,' she said, mocking him.

He decided to change the subject. He had noticed that she spoke with a south of France accent, so he said: 'Where are you from?'

'I was born in Marseille.'

'And what do you do in the FANYs?'

'I drive Monty.'

'Do you?' Paul was not supposed to give any information about himself, but he could not help saying: 'I worked for Monty for a while, but I don't recall seeing you.'

'Oh, it's not always Monty. I drive all the top generals.'

'Ah. Well, come this way, please.'

He took her to the room and poured her a cup of tea. Maude was enjoying the attention, Paul realized. While Percy asked questions, he studied the girl. She was petite, though not as tiny as Flick, and she was cute: she had a rosebud mouth accentuated with red lipstick, and there was a beauty spot – which might even have been fake – on one cheek. Her dark hair was wavy.

'My family came to London when I was ten years old,' she said. 'My papa is a chef.'

'And where does he work?'

'He's the head pastry cook at Claridge's hotel.'

'Very impressive.'

Maude's file was on the table, and Percy discreetly moved it an inch closer to Paul. Paul's eye was caught by the slight movement, and his eye fell on a note made when Maude was first interviewed. *Father: Armand Valentin, 39, kitchen porter at Claridge's,* he read.

When they had finished, they asked her to wait outside. 'She lives in a fantasy world,' Percy said, as soon as she was outside the door. 'She's promoted her father to chef, and changed her name to Valentine.'

Paul nodded agreement. 'In the lobby, she told me she was Monty's driver – which I know she's not.'

'No doubt that was why she was rejected before.'

Paul thought Percy was getting ready to reject Maude. 'But now we can't afford to be so particular,' he said.

Percy looked at him in surprise. 'She'd be a menace on an undercover operation!'

Paul made a helpless gesture. 'We don't have any choice.'

'This is mad!'

Percy was half in love with Flick, Paul decided; but, being older and married, he expressed his love in a paternal, protective way. Paul liked him better for that, but realized at the same time that he would have to fight Percy's caution if he was going to get this job done. 'Listen,' he said. 'We shouldn't eliminate Maude. Flick can make up her own mind when she meets her.'

'I suppose you're right,' Percy said reluctantly. 'And the ability to invent stories can be useful under interrogation.'

'All right. Let's get her on board.' Paul called her back in. 'I'd like you to be part of a team I'm setting up,' he told her. 'How would you feel about taking on something dangerous?'

'Would we be going to Paris?' Maude said eagerly.

It was an odd response. Paul hesitated, then said: 'Why do you ask?'

'I'd love to go to Paris. I've never been. They say it's the most beautiful city in the world.'

'Wherever you go, you won't have time for sightseeing,' Percy said, letting his irritation show.

Maude did not seem to notice. 'Shame,' she said. 'I'd still like to go, though.'

'How do you feel about the danger?' Paul persisted.

'That's all right,' Maude said airily. 'I'm not scared.'

Well, you should be, Paul thought; but he kept his mouth shut.

* * *

They drove north from Baker Street and passed through a working-class neighbourhood that had suffered heavily from the bombing. In every street at least one house was a blackened shell or a pile of rubble.

Paul was to meet Flick outside the prison and they would interview Ruby Romain together. Percy would go on to Hendon to see Lady Denise Bowyer.

Percy, at the wheel, confidently wound his way through the grimy streets. Paul said: 'You know London well.'

'I was born in this neighbourhood,' Percy replied.

Paul was intrigued. He knew it was unusual for a boy from a poor family to rise as high as colonel in the British army. 'What did your father do for a living?'

'Sold coal off the back of a horse-drawn cart.'

'He had his own business?'

'No, he worked for a coal merchant.'

'Did you go to school around here?'

Percy smiled. He knew he was being probed, but he did not seem to mind. 'The local vicar helped me get a scholarship to a good school. That was where I lost my London accent.'

'Intentionally?'

'Not willingly. I'll tell you something. Before the war, when I was involved in politics, people would sometimes say to me: 'How can you be a socialist, with an accent like that?' I explained that I was flogged in school for dropping my aitches. That silenced one or two smug bastards.'

Percy stopped the car on a tree-lined street. Paul looked out and saw a fantasy castle, with battlements and turrets and a high tower. 'This is a jail?'

Percy made a gesture of helplessness. 'Victorian architecture.'

Flick was waiting at the entrance. She wore her FANY uniform: a four-pocket tunic, a divided skirt, and a little cap with a turned-up brim. The leather belt that was tightly cinched around her small waist emphasized her diminutive figure, and her fair curls spilled out from under the cap. For a moment she took Paul's breath away. 'She's such a pretty girl,' he said.

'She's married,' Percy remarked crisply.

I'm being warned off, Paul thought with amusement. 'To whom?'

Percy hesitated, then said: 'You need to know this, I think. Michel is in the French Resistance. He's the leader of the Bollinger circuit.'

'Ah. Thanks.' Paul got out of the car and Percy drove on.

He wondered if Flick would be angry that he and Percy had turned up so few prospects from the files. He had met her only twice, and on both occasions she had yelled at him. However, she seemed cheerful, and when he told her about Maude, said: 'So we have three team members, including me. That means we're half-way there, and it's only two pip emma.'

Paul nodded. That was one way of looking at it. He was worried, but there was nothing to be gained by saying so.

The entrance to Holloway was a medieval lodge with arrowslit windows. 'Why didn't they go the whole way, and build a portcullis and a drawbridge?' said Paul. They passed through the lodge into a courtyard where a few women in dark dresses were cultivating vegetables. Every patch of wasteground in London was planted with vegetables.

The prison loomed up in front of them. The entrance was guarded by stone monsters, massive winged griffins holding keys and shackles in their claws. The main gatehouse was flanked by four-storey buildings, each storey represented by a long row of narrow, pointed windows. 'What a place!' said Paul.

'This is where the suffragettes went on hunger strike,' Flick told him. 'Percy's wife was force-fed in here.'

'My God.'

They went in. The air smelt of strong bleach, as if the authorities hoped that disinfectant would kill the bacteria of crime. Paul and Flick were shown to the office of Miss Lindleigh, a barrel-shaped assistant governor with a hard, fat face. 'I don't know why you wish to see Romain,' she said. With a note of resentment she added: 'Apparently I'm not to be told.'

A scornful look came over Flick's face, and Paul could see that she was about to say something derisory, so he hastily intervened. 'I apologize for the secrecy,' he said with his most charming smile. 'We're just following orders.'

'I suppose we all have to do that,' said Miss Lindleigh, somewhat mollified. 'Anyway, I must warn you that Romain is a violent prisoner.'

'I understand she's a killer.'

'Yes. She should be hanged, but the courts are too soft nowadays.'

'They sure are,' said Paul, although he did not really think so.

'She was in here originally for drunkenness, then she killed another prisoner in a fight in the exercise yard, so now she's awaiting trial for murder.'

'A tough customer,' Flick said with interest.

'Yes, Major. She may seem reasonable at first, but don't be fooled. She's easily riled, and loses her temper faster than you can say knife.'

'And deadly when she does,' Paul said.

'You've got the picture.'

'We're short of time,' Flick said impatiently. 'I'd like to see her now.'

Paul added hastily: 'If that's convenient to you, Miss Lindleigh.'

'Very well.' The assistant governor led them out. The hard floors and bare walls made the place echo like a cathedral, and there was a constant background accompaniment of distant shouts, slamming doors, and the clang of boots on iron catwalks. They went via narrow corridors and steep stairs to an interview room.

Ruby Romain was already there. She had nut-brown skin, straight dark hair, and fierce black eyes. However, she was not the traditional gypsy beauty: her nose was hooked and her chin curved up, giving her the look of a gnome.

Miss Lindleigh left them with a warder in the next room watching through a glazed door. Flick, Paul and the prisoner sat around a cheap table with a dirty ashtray on it. Paul had brought a pack of Lucky Strikes. He put them on the table and said in French: 'Help yourself.' Ruby took two, putting one in her mouth and the other behind her ear.

Paul asked a few routine questions to break the ice. She replied clearly and politely but with a strong accent. 'My parents are travelling folk,' she said. 'When I was a girl, we went around France with a funfair. My father had a rifle range and my mother sold hot pancakes with chocolate sauce.'

'How did you come to England?'

'When I was fourteen, I fell in love with an English sailor I met in Calais. His name was Freddy. We got married – I lied about my age, of course – and came to London. He was killed two years ago, his ship was sunk by a U-boat in the Atlantic.' She shivered. 'A cold grave. Poor Freddy.'

Flick was not interested in the family history. 'Tell us why you're in here,' she said.

'I got myself a little brazier and sold pancakes in the street. But the police kept harassing me. One night, I'd had some cognac – a weakness of mine, I admit – and, anyway, I got into a dispute.' She switched to cockney-accented English. 'The copper told me to fuck off out of it, and I gave him a mouthful of abuse. He shoved me and I knocked him down.'

Paul looked at her with a touch of amusement. She was no more than average height, and wiry, but she had big hands and muscular legs. He could imagine her flattening a London policeman.

Flick asked: 'What happened next?'

'His two mates came around the corner, and I was a bit slow to leave, on account of the brandy, so they gave me a kicking and took me down the nick.' Seeing Paul's frown of incomprehension, she added: 'The police station, that is. Anyway, the first copper was ashamed to do me for assault, didn't want to admit he'd been floored by a girl, so I got fourteen days for drunk and disorderly.'

'And then you got into another fight.'

She gave Flick an appraising look. 'I don't know if I can explain to someone of your sort what it's like in here. Half the girls are mad, and they've all got weapons. You can file the edge of a spoon to make a blade, or sharpen the end of a bit of wire for a stiletto, or twist threads together for a garotte. And the warders never intervene in a fight between convicts. They like to watch us tear each other apart. That's why so many of the inmates have scars.'

Paul was shocked. He had never had contact with

people in jail. The picture painted by Ruby was horrifying. Perhaps she was exaggerating, but she seemed quietly sincere. She did not appear to care whether she was believed or not, but recited the facts in the dry, unhurried manner of someone who is not greatly interested but has nothing better to do.

Flick said: 'What happened with the woman you killed?'

'She stole something of mine.'

'What?'

'A cake of soap.'

My God, thought Paul. She killed her for a piece of soap.

Flick said: 'What did you do?'

'I took it back.'

'And then?'

'She went for me. She had a chair leg that she'd made into a club with a bit of plumber's lead fixed to the business end. She hit me over the head with it. I thought she was going to kill me. But I had a knife. I'd found a long, pointed sliver of glass, like a shard from a broken window pane, and I wrapped the broad end in a length of worn-out bicycle tyre for a handle. I stuck it in her throat. So she didn't get to hit me a second time.'

Flick suppressed a shudder and said: 'It sounds like self-defence.'

'No. You've got to prove you couldn't possibly have run away. And I'd premeditated the murder by making a knife out of a piece of glass.'

Paul stood up. 'Wait here with the guard for a moment, please,' he said to Ruby. 'We'll just step outside.'

Ruby smiled at him, and for the first time she looked, not quite pretty, but pleasant. 'You're so polite,' she said appreciatively.

In the corridor, Paul said: 'What a dreadful story!'

'Remember, everyone in here says they're innocent,' Flick said guardedly.

'All the same, I think she might be more sinned against than sinning.'

'I doubt it. I think she's a killer.'

'So we reject her.'

'On the contrary,' said Flick. 'She's exactly what I want.'

They went back into the room. Flick said to Ruby: 'If you could get out of here, would you be willing to do dangerous war work?'

She responded with another question. 'Would we be going to France?'

Flick raised her eyebrows. 'What leads you to ask that?'

'You spoke French to me at the start. I assume you were checking if I speak the language.'

'Well, I can't tell you much about the job.'

'I bet it involves sabotage behind enemy lines.'

Paul was startled: Ruby was very quick on the uptake.

Seeing his surprise, Ruby went on: 'Look, at first I thought you might want me to do a bit of translation for you, but there's nothing dangerous about that. So we must be going to France. And what would the British army do there except blow up bridges and railway lines?'

Paul said nothing, but he was impressed by her powers of deduction.

Ruby frowned. 'What I can't figure out is why it's an all-woman team.'

Flick's eyes widened. 'What makes you think that?'

'If you could use men, why would you be talking to me? You must be desperate. It can't be that easy to get a murderess out of jail, even for vital war work. So what's special about me? I'm tough, but there must be hundreds of tough men who speak perfect French and would be gung-ho for a bit of cloak-and-dagger stuff. The only reason for picking me rather than one of them is that I'm female. Perhaps women are less likely to be questioned by the Gestapo . . . is that it?'

'I can't say,' Flick said.

'Well, if you want me, I'll do it. Can I have another one of those cigarettes?'

'Sure,' said Paul.

Flick said: 'You do understand that the job is dangerous.'

'Yeah,' said Ruby, lighting a Lucky Strike. 'But not as dangerous as being in this fucking prison.'

* * *

They returned to the assistant governor's office after leaving Ruby. 'I need your help, Miss Lindleigh,' Paul said, once again flattering her. 'Tell me what you would need in order to be able to release Ruby Romain.'

172

'Release her? But she's a murderer! Why would she be released?'

'I'm afraid I can't tell you. But I can assure you that, if you knew where she was going, you wouldn't think she'd had a lucky escape – quite the contrary.'

'I see,' she said, not entirely mollified.

'I must have her out of here tonight,' Paul went on. 'But I don't want to put you in any kind of awkward position. That's why I need to know exactly what authorization you require.' What he really wanted was to make sure she would have no excuse to be obstructive.

'I can't release her under any circumstances,' said Miss Lindleigh. 'She has been remanded here by a magistrate's court, so only the court can free her.'

Paul was patient. 'And what do you think that would require?'

'She would have to be taken, in police custody, before a magistrate. The public prosecutor, or his representative, would have to tell the magistrate that all charges against Romain had been dropped. Then the magistrate would be obliged to say she was free to go.'

Paul frowned, looking ahead for snags. 'She would have to sign her army joining-up papers before seeing the magistrate, so that she would be under military discipline as soon as the court released her ... otherwise she might just walk away.'

Miss Lindleigh was still incredulous. 'Why would they drop the charges?'

'This prosecutor is a government official?'

'Yes.'

'Then it won't be a problem.' Paul stood up. 'I will be back here later this evening, with a magistrate, someone from the prosecutor's department, and an army driver to take Ruby to . . . her next port of call. Can you foresee any snags?'

Miss Lindleigh shook her head. 'I follow orders, Major, just as you do.'

'Good.'

They took their leave. When they got outside, Paul stopped and looked back. 'I've never been to a prison before,' he said. 'I don't know what I expected, but it wasn't something out of a fairy tale.'

He was making an inconsequential remark about the building, but Flick looked sour. 'Several women have been hanged here,' she said. 'Not much of a fairy tale.'

He wondered why she was grumpy. 'I guess you identify with the prisoners,' he said. Suddenly he realized why. 'It's because you might end up in a jail in France.'

She looked taken aback. 'I think you're right,' she said. 'I didn't know why I hated that place so much, but that's it.'

She might be hanged, too, he realized, but he kept that thought to himself.

They walked away, heading for the nearest Tube station. Flick was thoughtful. 'You're very perceptive,' she said. 'You understood how to keep Miss Lindleigh on our side. I would have made an enemy of her.'

'No point in that.'

'Exactly. And you turned Ruby from a tigress into a pussycat.'

'I wouldn't want a woman like that to dislike me.'

Flick laughed. 'Then you told me something that I hadn't worked out about myself.'

Paul was pleased that he had impressed her, but he was already looking ahead to the next problem. 'By midnight, we should have half a team at the training centre in Hampshire.'

'We call it the Finishing School,' Flick said. 'Yes: Diana Colefield, Maude Valentine and Ruby Romain.'

Paul nodded grimly. 'An undisciplined aristocrat, a pretty flirt who can't tell fantasy from reality, and a murdering gypsy with a short temper.' When he thought of the possibility that Flick could be hanged by the Gestapo, he felt as worried as Percy about the calibre of the recruits.

'Beggars can't be choosers,' Flick said cheerfully. Her sour mood had vanished.

'But we still don't have an explosives expert or a telephone engineer.'

Flick glanced at her wrist. 'It's still only four pip emma. And maybe the RAF has taught Denise Bowyer how to blow up a telephone exchange.'

Paul grinned. Flick's optimism was irresistible.

They reached the station and caught a train. They could not talk about the mission because there were other passengers within earshot. Paul said: 'I learned a little about Percy this morning. We drove through the neighbourhood where he was brought up.'

'He's adopted the manners and even the accent of the British upper class, but don't be fooled. Under that old tweed jacket beats the heart of a real street brawler.'

'He told me he was flogged at school for speaking with a low-class accent.'

'He was a scholarship boy. They generally have a hard time in swanky British schools. I know, I was a scholarship girl.'

'Did you have to change your accent?'

'No. I grew up in an earl's household. I always spoke like this.'

Paul guessed that was why Flick and Percy got on so well: they were both lower-class people who had climbed the social ladder. Unlike Americans, the British thought there was nothing wrong with class prejudice. Yet they were shocked at Southerners who told them Negroes were inferior. 'I think Percy's very fond of you,' Paul said.

'I love him like a father.'

The sentiment seemed genuine, Paul thought, but she was also firmly setting him straight about her relationship with Percy.

Flick had arranged to meet Percy back at Orchard Court. When they arrived, there was a car outside the building. Paul recognized the driver, one of Monty's entourage. 'Sir, there's someone in the car waiting for you,' the man said.

The back door opened and out stepped Paul's younger sister, Caroline. He grinned with delight. 'Well, I'll be damned!' he said. She stepped into his arms and he hugged her. 'What are you doing in London?'

'I can't say, but I have a couple of hours off, and I persuaded Monty's office to lend me a car to come and see you. Want to buy me a drink?'

'I don't have a minute to spare,' he said. 'Not even for you. But you can drive me to Whitehall. I have to find a man called a public prosecutor.'

'Then I'll take you there, and we'll catch up in the car.'

'Of course,' he said. 'Let's go!'

FOURTEEN

Flick turned at the building door and saw a pretty girl wearing the uniform of an American lieutenant step out of the car and throw her arms around Paul. She noted the delighted smile on his face and the force of his hug. This was obviously his wife, girlfriend or fiancée, probably making an unexpected visit to London. She must be with the US forces in Britain, preparing for the invasion. Paul jumped into her car.

Flick went into Orchard Court, feeling a little sad. Paul had a girl, they were nuts about one another, and they had been granted a surprise meeting. Flick wished Michel could show up just like that, out of the blue. But he was lying wounded on a couch in Reims with a shameless nineteen-year-old beauty nursing him.

Percy was already back from Hendon. She found him making tea. 'How was your RAF girl?' she asked.

'Lady Denise Bouverie – she's on her way to the Finishing School,' he said.

'Wonderful! Now we have four!'

'But I'm worried. She's a braggart. She boasted about the work she's doing in the air force, told me all sorts of details she should have kept quiet about. You'll have to see what you think of her in training.'

'I don't suppose she knows anything about telephone exchanges.'

'Not a thing. Nor explosives. Tea?'

'Please.'

He handed her a cup and sat behind the cheap old desk. 'Where's Paul?'

'Gone to find the public prosecutor. He's hoping to get Ruby Romain out of jail this evening.'

Percy gave her a quizzical glance. 'Do you like him?'

'More than I did initially.'

'Me, too.'

Flick smiled. 'He charmed the socks off the old battleaxe running the prison.'

'How was Ruby Romain?'

'Terrifying. She slit the throat of another inmate in a quarrel over a bar of soap.'

'Jesus.' Percy shook his head in incredulity. 'What the hell kind of a team are we putting together, Flick?'

'Dangerous. Which is what it's supposed to be. That's not the problem. Besides, the way things are going, we may have the luxury of eliminating the least satisfactory one or two during training. My worry is that we don't have the experts we need. There's no point taking a team of tough girls into France then destroying the wrong cables.'

Percy drained his teacup and began to fill his pipe. 'I know a woman explosives expert who speaks French.'

Flick was surprised. 'But this is great! Why didn't you say so before?'

'When I first thought of her, I dismissed her out of

179

hand. She's not at all suitable. But I hadn't realized how desperate we'd be.'

'How is she unsuitable?'

'She's about forty. SOE rarely uses anyone so old, especially on a parachute mission.' He struck a match.

Age was not going to be an obstacle at this stage, Flick thought. Excited, she said: 'Will she volunteer?'

'I should think there's a good chance, especially if I ask her.'

'You're friends.'

He nodded.

'How did she become an explosives expert?'

Percy looked embarrassed. Still holding the burning match, he said: 'She's a safebreaker. I met her years ago, when I was doing political work in the East End.' The match burned down, and he struck another.

'Percy, I had no idea your past was so raffish. Where is she now?'

Percy looked at his watch. 'It's six o'clock. At this time of the evening, she'll be in the private bar of the Mucky Duck.'

'A pub.'

'Yes.'

'Then get that damn pipe alight and let's go there now.'

In the car, Flick said: 'How do you know she's a safebreaker?'

Percy shrugged. 'Everyone knows.'

'Everyone? Even the police?'

'Yes. In the East End, police and villains grow up

together, go to the same schools, live in the same streets. They all know one another.'

'But if they know who the criminals are, why don't they put them in jail? I suppose they can't prove anything.'

'This is the way it works,' Percy said. 'When they need a conviction, they arrest someone who is in that line of business. If it's a burglary, they arrest a burglar. It doesn't matter whether he was responsible for that particular crime, because they can always manufacture a case: suborn witnesses, counterfeit confessions, manufacture forensic evidence. Of course, they sometimes make mistakes, and jail innocent people; and they often use the system to pay off personal grudges, and so on; but nothing in life is perfect, is it?'

'So you're saying the whole rigmarole of courts and juries is a farce?'

'A highly successful, long-running farce that provides lucrative employment for otherwise useless citizens who act the parts of detectives, solicitors, barristers and judges.'

'Has your friend the safebreaker been to jail?'

'No. You can escape prosecution if you're willing to pay hefty bribes, *and* you're careful to cultivate warm friendships with detectives. Let's say you live in the same street as Detective Inspector Callahan's dear old mum. You drop in once a week, ask her if she needs any shopping done, look at photos of her grandchildren . . . makes it hard for DI Callahan to put you in jail.'

Flick thought of the story Ruby had told a few hours

ago. For some people, life in London was almost as bad as being under the Gestapo. Could things really be so different from what she had imagined? 'I can't tell if you're serious,' she said to Percy. 'I don't know what to believe.'

'Oh, I'm serious,' he said with a smile. 'But I don't expect you to believe me.'

They were in Stepney, not far from the docks. The bomb damage here was the worst Flick had seen. Whole streets were flattened. Percy turned into a narrow cul-de-sac and parked outside a pub.

'Mucky Duck' was a humorous sobriquet: the pub was called the White Swan. The private bar was not private, but was so called to distinguish it from the public bar, where there was sawdust on the floor and the beer was a penny a pint cheaper. Flick found herself thinking about explaining these idiosyncrasies to Paul. He would be amused.

Geraldine Knight sat on a stool at the end of the bar, looking as if she might own the place. She had vivid blonde hair and heavy makeup, expertly applied. Her plump figure had the apparent firmness that could only have come from a corset. The cigarette burning in the ashtray bore a ring of bright lipstick around the end. It was hard to imagine anyone who looked less like a secret agent, Flick thought despondently.

'Percy Thwaite, as I live and breathe!' the woman said. She sounded like a Cockney who had been to elocution lessons. 'What are you doing slumming around here, you bloody old Communist?' She was obviously delighted to see him.

182

'Hello, Jelly, meet my friend Flick,' Percy said.

'Pleased to know you, I'm sure,' she said, shaking Flick's hand.

'Jelly?' Flick enquired.

'No one knows where I got that nickname.'

'Oh,' said Flick. 'Jelly Knight, gelignite.'

Jelly ignored that. 'I'll have a gin-and-It, Percy, while you're buying.'

Flick spoke to her in French. 'Do you live in this part of London?'

'Since I was ten,' she replied, speaking French with a north American accent. 'I was born in Quebec.'

That was not so good, Flick thought. Germans might not notice the accent, but the French certainly would. Jelly would have to pose as a Canadian-born French citizen. It was a perfectly plausible history, but just unusual enough to attract curiosity. Damn. 'But you consider yourself British.'

'English, not British,' said Jelly with arch indignation. She switched back to the English language. 'I'm Church of England, I vote Conservative, and I dislike foreigners, heathens and republicans.' With a glance at Percy, she added: 'Present company excepted, of course.'

Percy said: 'You ought to live in Yorkshire, on a hill farm, some place where they haven't seen a foreigner since the Vikings came. I don't know how you can bear to live in London, surrounded by Russian Bolsheviks, German Jews, Irish Catholics, and nonconformist Welshmen building little chapels all over the place like moles disfiguring the lawn.'

'London's not what it was, Perce.'

183

'Not what it was when you were a foreigner?'

This was obviously a familiar old argument. Flick interrupted it impatiently. 'I'm very glad to hear that you're so patriotic, Jelly.'

'And why would you be interested in such a thing, may I ask?'

'Because there's something you could do for your country.'

Percy put in: 'I told Flick about your . . . expertise, Jelly.'

She looked at her vermilion fingernails. 'Discretion, Percy, please. Discretion is the better part of valour, it says in the Bible.'

Flick said: 'I expect you know that there have been some fascinating recent developments in the field. Plastic explosives, I mean.'

'I try to keep up to date,' Jelly said, with airy modesty. Her expression changed, and she looked shrewdly at Flick. 'This is something to do with the war, isn't it?'

'Yes.'

'Count me in. I'll do anything for England.'

'You'll be away for a few days.'

'No problem.'

'You might not come back.'

'What the hell does that mean?'

'It will be very dangerous,' Flick said quietly.

Jelly looked dismayed. 'Oh.' She swallowed. 'Well, that makes no difference,' she said unconvincingly.

'Are you sure?'

Jelly looked thoughtful, as if she were calculating. 'You want me to blow something up.'

Flick nodded silently.

'It's not overseas, is it?'

'Could be.'

Jelly paled beneath her makeup. 'Oh, my gordon. You want me to go to France, don't you?'

Flick said nothing.

'Behind enemy lines! God's truth, I'm too bloody old for that sort of thing. I'm . . .' She hesitated. 'I'm thirty-seven.'

She was about five years older than that, Flick thought, but she said: 'Well, we're almost the same age, I'm nearly thirty. We're not too old for a bit of adventure, are we?'

'Speak for yourself, dear.'

Flick's heart sank. Jelly was not going to agree.

The whole scheme had been misconceived, she decided. It was never going to be possible to find women who could do these jobs and speak perfect French. The plan had been doomed from the start. She turned away from Jelly. She felt like crying.

Percy said: 'Jelly, we're asking you to do a job that's really crucial for the war effort.'

'Pull the other leg, Perce, it's got bells on,' she said, but her mockery was half-hearted, and she looked solemn.

He shook his head. 'No exaggeration. It could make a difference to whether we win or lose.'

She stared at him, saying nothing. Conflict twisted her face into a grimace of indecision.

Percy said: 'And you're the only person in the country who can do it.'

'Get off,' she said sceptically.

'You're a female safebreaker who speaks French – how many others do you think there are? I'll tell you: none.'

'You mean this, don't you?'

'I was never more serious in my life.'

'Bloody hell, Perce.' Jelly fell silent. She did not speak for a long moment. Flick held her breath. At last Jelly said: 'All right, you bastard, I'll do it.'

Flick was so pleased she kissed her.

Percy said: 'God bless you, Jelly.'

Jelly said: 'When do we start?'

'Now,' said Percy. 'If you'll finish up that gin, I'll take you home to pack a case, then I'll drive you to the training centre.'

'What, tonight?'

'I told you it was important.'

She swallowed the remains of her drink. 'All right, I'm ready.'

She slid her ample bottom off the bar stool, and Flick thought: I wonder how she'll manage with a parachute.

They left the pub. Percy said to Flick: 'You'll be all right going back on the Tube?'

'Of course.'

'Then we'll see you tomorrow at the Finishing School.'

'I'll be there,' said Flick, and they parted company.

She headed for the nearest station, feeling jubilant. It was a mild summer evening, and the East End was alive: a group of dirty-faced boys played cricket with a stick and a bald tennis ball; a tired man in soiled work clothes headed home for a late tea; a uniformed soldier, on leave with a packet of cigarettes and a few shillings in his pocket, strode along the pavement with a jaunty air, as if all the world's pleasures were his for the taking; three pretty girls in sleeveless dresses and straw hats giggled at the soldier. The fate of all these people would be decided in the next few days, Flick thought sombrely.

On the train to Bayswater, her spirits fell again. She still did not have the most crucial member of the team. Without a telephone engineer, Jelly might place the explosives in the wrong location. They would still do damage but, if the damage could be repaired in a day or two, the enormous effort and risk of life would have been wasted.

When she returned to her bedsitting room, she found her brother Mark waiting there. She hugged and kissed him. 'What a nice surprise!' she said.

'I've got a night off, so I thought I'd take you for a drink,' he said.

'Where's Steve?'

'Giving his Iago to the troops in Lyme Regis. We both work for ENSA most of the time, now.' ENSA was the Entertainments National Service Association, which organized shows for the armed forces. 'Where shall we go?'

Flick was tired, and her first inclination was to turn him down. Then she remembered that she was going to France on Friday, and this could be the last time she ever saw her brother. 'How about the West End?' she said.

'We'll go to a nightclub.'

'Perfect!'

They left the house and walked arm in arm along the street. Flick said: 'I saw Ma this morning.'

'How is she?'

'All right, but she hasn't softened her attitude to you and Steve, I'm sorry to say.'

'I didn't expect it. How did you happen to see her?'

'I went down to Somersholme. It would take too long to explain why.'

'Something hush-hush, I suppose.'

She smiled acknowledgement, then sighed as she remembered her problem. 'I don't suppose you happen to know a female telephone engineer who speaks French, do you?'

He stopped. 'Well,' he said, 'sort of.'

FIFTEEN

Mademoiselle Lemas was in agony. She sat rigid on the hard upright chair behind the little table, her face frozen into a mask of self-control. She did not dare to move. She still wore her cloche hat and clutched her sturdy leather handbag on her lap. Her fat little hands squeezed the handle of the bag rhythmically. Her fingers bore no rings; in fact she wore only one piece of jewellery, a small silver cross on a chain.

Around her, late-working clerks and secretaries in their well-pressed uniforms carried on typing and filing. Following Dieter's instructions, they smiled politely when they caught her eye, and every now and again one of the girls would speak a word to her, offering her water or coffee.

Dieter sat watching her, with Lieutenant Hesse on one side of him and Stéphanie on the other. Hans Hesse was the best type of sturdy, unflappable working-class German. He looked on stoically: he had seen many tortures. Stéphanie was more excitable, but she was exercising self-control. She looked unhappy, but said nothing: her aim in life was to please Dieter.

Mademoiselle Lemas' pain was not just physical, Dieter knew. Even worse than her bursting bladder was the terror of soiling herself in a room full of polite, well-dressed people going about their normal business. For a respectable elderly lady, that was the worst of nightmares. He admired her fortitude and wondered if she would break, and tell him everything, or hold out.

A young corporal clicked his heels beside Dieter and said: 'Pardon me, Major, I have been sent to ask you to step into Major Weber's office.'

Dieter considered sending a reply saying *If you want to talk to me, come and see me*, but he decided there was nothing to be gained by being combative before it was strictly necessary. Weber might even become a little more co-operative if he were allowed to score a few points. 'Very well.' He turned to Hesse. 'Hans, you know what to ask her if she breaks.'

'Yes, Major.'

'In case she doesn't . . . Stéphanie, would you go to the Café des Sports and get me a bottle of beer and a glass, please?'

'Of course.' She seemed grateful for a reason to leave the room.

Dieter followed the corporal to Willi Weber's office. It was a grand room at the front of the chateau, with three tall windows overlooking the square. Dieter gazed out at the sun setting over the town. The slanting light picked out the curved arches and buttresses of the medieval church. He saw Stéphanie crossing the square in her high heels, walking like a racehorse, dainty and powerful at the same time.

Soldiers were at work in the square, erecting three

190

stout wooden pillars in a neat row. Dieter frowned. 'A firing squad?'

'For the three terrorists who survived Sunday's skirmish,' Weber answered. 'I understand you have finished interrogating them.'

Dieter nodded. 'They have told me all they know.'

'They will be shot in public as a warning to others who may think of joining the Resistance.'

'Good idea,' Dieter said. 'However, though Gaston is fit, both Bertrand and Geneviève are seriously injured – I'll be surprised if they can walk.'

'Then they will be carried to their fate. But I did not summon you to discuss them. My superiors in Paris have been asking me what further progress has been made.'

'And what did you tell them, Willi?'

'That after forty-eight hours of investigation you have arrested one old woman who may or may not have sheltered Allied agents in her house, and who has so far told us nothing.'

'And what would you *wish* to tell them?'

Weber banged his desk theatrically. 'That we have broken the back of the French Resistance!'

'That may take longer than forty-eight hours.'

'Why don't you torture this old cow?'

'I am torturing her.'

'By refusing to let her go to the toilet! What kind of torture is that?'

'In this case, the most effective one, I believe.'

'You think you know best. You always were arrogant.

But this is the new Germany, Major. You are no longer assumed to have superior judgement just because you are the son of a professor.'

'Don't be ridiculous.'

'Do you really think you would have become the youngest-ever head of the Cologne criminal intelligence department if your father had not been an important man in the university?'

'I had to pass the same exams as everyone else.'

'How strange that other people, just as capable as you, never seemed to do quite so well.'

Was that the fantasy Weber told himself? 'For God's sake, Willi, you can't believe the entire Cologne police force conspired to give me better marks than you because my father was professor of music – it's risible!'

'Such things were commonplace in the old days.'

Dieter sighed. Weber was half right. Patronage and nepotism had existed in Germany. But that was not why Willi had failed to win promotion. The truth was that he was stupid. He would never get on anywhere except in an organization where fanaticism was more important than ability.

Dieter had had enough of this stupid talk. 'Don't worry about Mademoiselle Lemas,' he said. 'She'll talk soon.' He went to the door. 'And we will break the back of the French Resistance, too. Just wait a little longer.'

He returned to the main office. Mademoiselle Lemas was now making low moaning noises. Weber had made Dieter impatient, and he decided to speed up the process. When Stéphanie returned, he put the glass on the table, opened the bottle, and poured the beer slowly in front of the prisoner. Tears of pain squeezed from her eyes and rolled down her plump cheeks. Dieter took a long drink of beer and put the glass down. 'Your agony is almost over, Mademoiselle,' he said. 'Relief is at hand. In a few moments you will answer my questions, then you will find ease.'

She closed her eyes.

'Where do you meet the British agents?' He paused. 'How do you recognize one another?' She said nothing. 'What is the password?'

He waited a moment, then said: 'Have the answers ready, in the forefront of your mind, and make sure they are clear, so that when the time comes, you can tell me quickly, without hesitation or explanations; then you can seek rapid release from your pain.'

He took the key to the handcuffs from his pocket. 'Hans, hold her wrist firmly.' He bent down and unlocked the cuffs that fastened her ankle to the table leg. He took her by the arm. 'Come with us, Stéphanie,' he said. 'We're going to the ladies' toilet.'

They left the room, Stéphanie leading the way, Dieter and Hans holding the prisoner, who hobbled along with difficulty, bent at the waist, biting her lip. They went to the end of the corridor and stopped at a door marked *Damen*. Mademoiselle Lemas groaned loudly when she saw it.

Dieter said to Stéphanie: 'Open the door.'

She did so. It was a clean, white-tiled room, with a wash basin, a towel on a rail, and a row of cubicles. 'Now,' said Dieter. 'The pain is about to end.'

'Please,' she whispered. 'Let me go.'

'Where do you meet the British agents?'

Mademoiselle Lemas began to cry.

Dieter said gently: 'Where do you meet these people?'

'In the cathedral,' she sobbed. 'In the crypt. Please let me go!'

Dieter breathed a long sigh of satisfaction. She had broken. 'When do you meet them?'

'Three o'clock any afternoon, I go every day.'

'And how do you recognize one another?'

'I wear odd shoes, black and brown, now can I go?'

'One more question: what is the password?'

' "Pray for me." '

She tried to move forward, but Dieter held her tightly, and Hans did the same. 'Pray for me,' Dieter repeated. 'Is that what you say, or what the agent says?'

'The agent, oh, I beg you!'

'And your reply?'

' "I pray for peace", that's my reply.'

'Thank you,' Dieter said, and released her.

She rushed inside.

Dieter nodded at Stéphanie, who followed her in and closed the door.

He could not conceal his satisfaction. 'There, Hans, we make progress.'

Hans, too, was pleased. 'The cathedral crypt, three p.m. any day, black and brown shoes, "Pray for me," and the response "I pray for peace." Very good!'

'When they come out, put the prisoner in a cell and turn her over to the Gestapo. They'll arrange for her to disappear into a camp somewhere.'

Hans nodded. 'It seems harsh, sir. Her being an elderly lady, I mean.'

'It does – until you think of the German soldiers and French civilians killed by the terrorists she sheltered. Then it seems hardly punishment enough.'

'That does throw a different light on it, yes, sir.'

'You see how one thing leads to another,' Dieter said reflectively. 'Gaston gives us a house, the house gives us Mademoiselle Lemas, she gives us the crypt, and the crypt will give us . . . who knows?' He began to think about the best way to exploit the new information.

The challenge was to capture agents without letting London know. If the thing was handled right, the Allies would send more people along the same route, wasting vast resources. It had been done in Holland: more than fifty expensively trained saboteurs had parachuted straight into the arms of the Germans.

Ideally, the next agent sent by London would go to the crypt of the cathedral and find Mademoiselle Lemas waiting there. She would take the agent home, and he would send a wireless message to London saying all was well. Then, when he was out of the house, Dieter could get hold of his code books. After that, Dieter could arrest the agent but continue to send messages to London in his name – and read the replies. In effect, he would be running a Resistance circuit that was entirely fictional. It was a thrilling prospect.

Willi Weber walked by. 'Well, Major, has the prisoner talked?'

'She has.'

'Not a moment too soon. Did she say anything useful?'

'You may tell your superiors that she has revealed the location of her rendezvous, and the passwords used. We can pick up any further agents as they arrive.'

Weber looked interested despite his hostility. 'And where is the rendezvous?'

Dieter hesitated. He would have preferred not to tell Weber anything. But it was difficult to refuse without giving offence, and he needed the man's help. He had to tell him. 'The cathedral crypt, afternoons at three.'

'I shall inform Paris.' Weber walked on.

Dieter resumed thinking about his next step. The house in the rue du Bois was a cut-out. No one in the Bollinger circuit had met Mademoiselle Lemas. Agents coming in from London did not know what she looked like – hence the need for recognition signals and passwords. If he could get someone to impersonate her . . . but who?

Stéphanie came out of the ladies' toilet with Mademoiselle Lemas.

She could do it.

She was much younger than Mademoiselle Lemas, and looked completely different, but the agents would not know that. She was obviously French. All she had to do was take care of the agent for a day or so.

He took Stéphanie's arm. 'Hans will deal with the prisoner now. Come, let me buy you a glass of champagne.'

He walked her out of the chateau. In the square, the soldiers had done their work, and the three stakes threw long shadows in the evening light. A handful of local people stood silent and watchful outside the church door.

Dieter and Stéphanie went into the café. Dieter ordered a bottle of champagne. 'Thank you for helping me today,' he said. 'I appreciate it.'

'I love you,' she said. 'And you love me, I know, even though you never say it.'

'But how do you feel about what we did today? You're French, and you have that grandmother whose race we mustn't speak of, and as far as I know you're not a Fascist.'

She shook her head violently. 'I no longer believe in nationality, or race, or politics,' she said passionately. 'When I was arrested by the Gestapo, no French people helped me. No Jews helped me. No socialists or liberals or Communists either. And I was so cold in that prison.' Her face changed. Her lips lost the sexy half-smile she wore most of the time, and the glint of teasing invitation went from her eyes. She was looking at another scene in another time. She crossed her arms and shivered, although it was a warm summer evening. 'Not just cold on the outside, not just the skin. I felt cold in my heart and my bowels and my bones. I felt I would never be warm again, I would just go cold to my grave.' She was silent for a long moment, her face drawn and pale, and Dieter felt at that instant that war was a terrible thing. Then she said: 'I'll never forget the fire in your apartment. A coal fire. I had forgotten what it was like to feel that blazing warmth. It made me human again.' She came out of her trance. 'You saved me. You gave

197

me food and wine. You bought me clothes.' She smiled her old smile, the one that said *You can, if you dare.* 'And you loved me, in front of that coal fire.'

He held her hand. 'It wasn't difficult.'

'You keep me safe, in a world where almost no one is safe. So now I believe only in you.'

'If you really mean that . . .'

'Of course.'

'There's something else you could do for me.'

'Anything.'

'I want you to impersonate Mademoiselle Lemas.'

She raised one perfectly plucked eyebrow.

'Pretend to be her. Go to the cathedral crypt every afternoon at three o'clock, wearing one black shoe and one brown. When someone approaches you and says: "Pray for me," reply: "I pray for peace." Take the person to the house in the rue du Bois. Then call me.'

'It sounds simple.'

The champagne arrived, and he poured two glasses. He decided to level with her. 'It should be simple. But there is a slight risk. If the agent has met Mademoiselle Lemas before, he will know you're an impostor. Then you could be in danger. Will you take that chance?'

'Is it important to you?'

'It's important for the war.'

'I don't care about the war.'

'It's important to me, too.'

'Then I'll do it.'

He raised his glass. 'Thank you,' he said.

They clinked glasses and drank.

Outside, in the square, there was a volley of gunfire.

Dieter looked through the window. He saw three bodies tied to the wooden pillars, slumped in death; a row of soldiers lowering their rifles; and a crowd of citizens looking on, silent and still.

SIXTEEN

Wartime austerity had made little real difference to Soho, the red-light district in the heart of London's West End. The same groups of young men staggered through the streets, drunk on beer; though most of them were in uniform. The same painted girls in tight dresses strolled along the pavements, eyeing potential customers. The illuminated signs outside clubs and bars were switched off, because of the blackout, but all the establishments were open.

Mark and Flick arrived at the Criss-Cross Club at ten o'clock in the evening. The manager, a young man wearing a dinner jacket with a red bow-tie, greeted Mark like a friend. Flick's spirits were high. Mark knew a female telephone engineer. Flick was about to meet her, and she felt optimistic. Mark had not said much about her, except that her name was Greta, like the film star. When Flick tried to question him, he just said: 'You have to see her for yourself.'

As Mark paid the entrance fee and exchanged commonplaces with the manager, Flick saw an alteration come over him. He grew more extrovert, his voice took on a lilt, and his gestures became theatrical.

Flick wondered if her brother had another persona that he put on after dark.

They went down a flight of stairs to a basement. The place was dimly lit and smoky. Flick could see a five-piece band on a low stage, a small dance floor, a scatter of tables, and a number of booths around the dark perimeter of the room. She had wondered if it would be a men-only club, the kind of place that catered to chaps like Mark who were 'not the marrying kind'. Although the patrons were mostly male, there was a good sprinkling of girls, some of them very glamorously dressed.

A waiter said: 'Hello, Markie,' and put a hand on Mark's shoulder, but gave Flick a hostile glare.

'Robbie, meet my sister,' Mark said. 'Her name's Felicity, but we've always called her Flick.'

The waiter's attitude changed and he gave Flick a friendly smile. 'Very nice to meet you.' He showed them to a table.

Flick guessed that Robbie had suspected she might be a girlfriend, and had resented her for persuading Mark to change sides, as it were. Then he had warmed to her when he learned she was Mark's sister.

Mark smiled up at Robbie and said: 'How's Kit?'

'Oh, all right, I suppose,' Robbie said, with the hint of a flounce.

'You've had a row, haven't you?'

Mark was being charming and was almost flirting. This was a side of him Flick had never seen. In fact, she thought, it might be the real Mark. The other persona, his discreet daytime self, was probably the pretence.

'When have we not had a row?' Robbie said.

'He doesn't appreciate you,' Mark said, with exaggerated melancholy, touching Robbie's hand.

'You're right, bless you. Something to drink?'

Flick ordered Scotch and Mark asked for a martini.

Flick did not know much about men such as these. She had been introduced to Mark's lover, Steve, and had visited the flat they shared, but had never met any of their friends. Although she was madly curious about their world, it seemed prurient to ask questions.

She didn't even know what they called themselves. All the words she knew were more or less unpleasant: queer, homo, fairy, nancy-boy. 'Mark,' she said, 'what do *you* call men who, you know, prefer men?'

He grinned. 'Musical, darling,' he said, waving his hand in a feminine gesture.

I must remember that, Flick thought. Now I can say to Mark: 'Is he musical?' She had learned the first word of their secret code.

A tall blonde in a red cocktail dress came swishing on to the stage to a burst of applause. 'This is Greta,' said Mark. 'She's a telephone engineer by day.'

Greta began to sing 'Nobody Knows You When You're Down And Out.' She had a powerful, bluesy voice, but Flick noticed immediately that she had a German accent. Shouting into Mark's ear over the sound of the band, she said: 'I thought you said she was French.'

'She *speaks* French,' he corrected. 'But she's German.'

Flick was bitterly disappointed. This was no good.

Greta would have just as much of a German accent when she spoke French.

The audience loved Greta, clapping each number enthusiastically, cheering and whistling when she accompanied the music with bump-and-grind movements. But Flick could not relax and enjoy the show. She was too worried. She still did not have her telephone engineer, and she had wasted the latter half of the evening coming here on a wild goose chase.

But what was she going to do? She wondered how long it would take her to pick up the rudiments of telephone engineering herself. She had no difficulty with technical things. She had built a radio at school. Anyway, she needed to know only enough to destroy the equipment effectively. Could she do a two-day course, maybe with some people from the General Post Office?

The trouble was, nobody could be quite sure what kind of equipment the saboteurs would find when they entered the chateau. It could be French or German or a mixture, possibly even including imported American machinery – the USA was far ahead of France in phone technology. There were many kinds of equipment, and the chateau served several different functions. It had a manual exchange, an automatic exchange, a tandem exchange for connecting other exchanges to one another, and an amplification station for the all-important new trunk route to Germany. But only an experienced engineer could be confident of recognizing whatever he saw when he walked in.

There were engineers in France, of course, and she

might find a woman – if she had time. It was not a promising idea, but she thought it through. SOE could send a message to every Resistance circuit. If there was a woman who could fit the bill, it would take her a day or two to get to Reims, which was all right. But the plan was so uncertain. Was there a woman telephone engineer in the French Resistance? If not, Flick would waste two days to learn that the mission was doomed.

No, she needed something more sure. She thought again about Greta. She could not pass for French. The Gestapo might not notice her accent, since they spoke French the same way, but the French police would. Did she have to pretend to be French? There were plenty of German women in France: officers' wives, young women in the armed services, drivers and typists and wireless operators. Flick began to feel excited again. Why not? Greta could pose as an army secretary. No, that could cause problems – an officer might start giving her orders. It would be safer for her to pose as a civilian. She could be the young wife of an officer, living with her husband in Paris – no, Vichy, it was farther away. There would have to be a story about why Greta was travelling with a group of French women. Perhaps one of the team could pose as her French maid.

What about when they entered the chateau? Flick was pretty sure there were no German women working as cleaners in France. How could Greta evade suspicion? Once again, Germans probably would not notice her accent, but French people would. Could she avoid speaking to any French people? Pretend she had laryngitis?

She might be able to get away with it for a few minutes, Flick thought.

It was not exactly watertight, but it was better than any other option.

Greta finished her act with a hilariously suggestive blues called 'Kitchen Man', full of *double-entendres*. The audience loved the line: 'When I eat his doughnuts, all I leave is the hole.' She left the stage to gales of applause. Mark got up, saying: 'We can talk to her in her dressing room.'

Flick followed him through a door beside the stage, down a smelly concrete corridor, into a dingy area crammed with cardboard boxes of beer and gin. It was like the cellar of a run-down pub. They came to a door that had a pink paper cut-out star fixed to it with thumbtacks. Mark knocked and opened it without waiting for a reply.

The tiny room had a dressing-table, a mirror surrounded by bright makeup lights, a stool, and a movie poster showing Greta Garbo in *Two-Faced Woman*. An elaborate blonde wig rested on a stand shaped like a head. The red dress Greta had worn on stage hung from a hook on the wall. Sitting on the stool in front of the mirror, Flick saw to her utter astonishment, was a young man with a hairy chest.

She gasped.

It was Greta, no question. The face was heavily made-up, with vivid lipstick and false eyelashes, plucked eyebrows and a layer of powder hiding the shadow of a dark beard. The hair was cut brutally short, no doubt to accommodate the wig. The false bosom was presumably fixed inside the dress, but Greta still wore a half-slip, stockings, and red high-heeled shoes.

Flick rounded on Mark. 'You didn't tell me!' she accused.

He laughed delightedly. 'Flick, meet Gerhard,' he said. 'He loves it when people don't realize.'

Flick saw that Gerhard was looking pleased. Of course he would be happy that she had taken him for a real woman. It was a tribute to his art. She did not need to worry that she had insulted him.

But he was a man. And she needed a woman telephone engineer.

Flick was painfully disappointed. Greta would have been the last piece in the jigsaw, the woman who made the team complete. Now the mission was in doubt again.

She was angry with Mark. 'This was so mean of you!' she said. 'I thought you'd solved my problem, but you were just playing a joke.'

'It's not a joke,' Mark said indignantly. 'If you need a woman, take Greta.'

'I couldn't,' Flick said. It was a ridiculous idea.

Or was it? Greta had convinced *her*. She could probably do the same to the Gestapo. If they arrested her and stripped her they would learn the truth, but if they got to that stage it was generally all over anyway.

She thought of the hierarchy at SOE, and Simon Fortescue at MI6. 'The top brass would never agree to it.'

'Don't tell them,' Mark suggested.

'Not tell them!' Flick was at first shocked then

intrigued by that idea. If Greta was to fool the Gestapo, she ought also to be able to deceive everyone at SOE.

'Why not?' said Mark.

'Why not?' Flick repeated.

Gerhard said: 'Mark, sweetie, what is all this about?' His German accent was stronger in speech than in song.

'I don't really know,' Mark told him. 'My sister is involved in something hush-hush.'

'I'll explain,' Flick said. 'But, first, tell me about yourself. How did you come to London?'

'Well, sweetheart, where shall I begin?' Gerhard lit a cigarette. 'I'm from Hamburg. Twelve years ago, when I was a boy of sixteen, and an apprentice telephone engineer, it was a wonderful town, bars and nightclubs full of sailors making the most of their shore leave. I had the best time. And when I was eighteen I met the love of my life. His name was Manfred.'

Tears came to Gerhard's eyes, and Mark held his hand.

Gerhard sniffed, in a very unladylike fashion, and carried on. 'I've always adored women's clothes, lacy underwear and high heels, hats and handbags. I love the swish of a full skirt. But I did it so crudely in those days. I really didn't even know how to put on eyeliner. Manfred taught me everything. He wasn't a cross-dresser himself, you know.' A fond look came over Gerhard's face. 'He was *extremely* masculine, in fact. He worked in the docks, as a stevedore. But he loved me in drag, and he taught me how to do it right.'

'Why did you leave?'

'They took Manfred away. The bloody fucking Nazis, sweetheart. We had five years together, but one night they came for him, and I never saw him again. He's probably dead, I think prison would kill him, but I don't know anything for sure.' Tears dissolved his mascara and ran down his powdered cheeks in black streaks. 'He could still be alive in one of their bloody fucking camps, you know.'

His grief was infectious, and Flick found herself fighting back tears. What got into people that made them persecute one another? she asked herself. What made the Nazis torment harmless eccentrics such as Gerhard?

'So I came to London,' Gerhard said. 'My father was English. He was a sailor from Liverpool who got off his ship in Hamburg and fell in love with a pretty German girl and married her. He died when I was two, so I never really knew him, but he gave me my surname, which is O'Reilly, and I always had dual nationality. It still cost me all my savings to get a passport, in 1939. As things turned out, I was just in time. Happily, there's always work for a telephone engineer in any city. So here I am, the toast of London, the deviant diva.'

'It's a sad story,' Flick said. 'I'm very sorry.'

'Thank you, sweetheart. But the world is full of sad stories these days, isn't it? Why are you interested in mine?'

'I need a female telephone engineer.'

'What on earth for?'

'I can't tell you much. As Mark said, it's hush-hush.

One thing I can say is that the job is very dangerous. You might get killed.'

'How absolutely chilling! But you can imagine that I'm not very good at rough stuff. They said I was psychologically unsuited to service in the army, and quite bloody rightly. Half the squaddies would have wanted to beat me up and the other half would have been sneaking into bed with me at night.'

'I've got all the tough soldiers I need. What I want from you is your expertise.'

'Would it mean a chance to hurt those bloody fucking Nazis?'

'Absolutely. If we succeed, it will do a very great deal of damage indeed to the Hitler regime.'

'Then, sweetheart, I'm your girl.'

Flick smiled. My God, she thought; I've done it.

THE FOURTH DAY:
WEDNESDAY, 31 MAY 1944

SEVENTEEN

In the middle of the night, the roads of southern England were thronged with traffic. Great convoys of army trucks rumbled along every highway, roaring through the darkened towns, heading for the coast. Bemused villagers stood at their bedroom windows, staring in incredulity at the endless stream of traffic that was stealing their sleep.

'My God,' said Greta. 'There really is going to be an invasion.'

She and Flick had left London shortly after midnight in a borrowed car, a big white Lincoln Continental that Flick loved to drive. Greta wore one of her less eye-popping outfits, a simple black dress with a brunette wig. She would not be Gerhard again until the mission was over.

Flick hoped Greta was as expert as Mark had claimed. She worked for the General Post Office as an engineer, so presumably she knew what she was talking about. But Flick had not been able to test her. Now, as they crawled along behind a tank transporter, Flick explained the mission, anxiously hoping the conversation would not reveal gaps in Greta's knowledge. 'The chateau contains a new automatic exchange put in by the Germans to handle all the extra telephone and teleprinter traffic between Berlin and the occupying forces.'

At first Greta was sceptical about the plan. 'But, sweetheart, even if we succeed, what's to stop the Germans just rerouting calls around the network?'

'Volume of traffic. The system is overloaded. The army command centre called Zeppelin outside Berlin handles a hundred and twenty thousand long-distance calls and twenty thousand telex messages a day. There will be more when we invade France. But much of the French system still consists of manual exchanges. Now imagine that the main automatic exchange is out of service and all those calls have to be made the old-fashioned way, by hello-girls, taking ten times as long. Ninety per cent of them will never get through.'

'The military could prohibit civilian calls.'

'That won't make much difference. Civilian traffic is only a tiny fraction anyway.'

'All right.' Greta was thoughtful. 'Well, we could destroy the common equipment racks.'

'What do they do?'

'Provide the tones and ringing voltages and so on for automatic calls. And the register translators, they transform the dialled area code into a routing instruction.'

'Would that make the whole exchange unworkable?'

'No. And the damage could be repaired. You need to knock out the manual exchange, the automatic exchange, the long-distance amplifiers, the telex exchange and the telex amplifiers – which are probably all in different rooms.'

'Remember, we can't carry a great quantity of explosives with us – only what six women could hide in their everyday bags.'

'That's a problem.'

Michel had been through all this with Arnaud, a member of the Bollinger circuit who worked for the French PTT – *Postes, Télégraphes, Téléphones* – but Flick had not queried the details, and Arnaud was dead, killed in the raid. 'There must be some equipment common to all the systems.'

'Yes, there is – the MDF.'

'What's that?'

'The Main Distribution Frame. Two sets of terminals on large racks. All the cables from outside come to one side of the frame; all the cables from the exchange come to the other; and they're connected by jumper links.'

'Where would that be?'

'In a room next to the cable chamber. Ideally, you'd want a fire hot enough to melt the copper in the cables.'

'How long would it take to reconnect the cables?'

'A couple of days.'

'Are you sure? When the cables in my street were severed by a bomb, one old Post Office engineer had us reconnected in a few hours.'

'Street repairs are simple, just a matter of connecting broken ends together, red to red and blue to blue. But an MDF has hundreds of cross-connections. Two days is conservative, and that assumes the repairmen have the record cards.'

'Record cards?'

'They show how the cables are connected. They're normally kept in a cabinet in the MDF room. If we burn them, too, it will take weeks of trial and error to figure out the connections.'

Flick now recalled Michel saying the Resistance had someone in the PTT who was ready to destroy the duplicate records kept at headquarters. 'This is sounding good. Now, listen. In the morning, when I explain our mission to the others, I'm going to tell them something completely different, a cover story.'

'Why?'

'So that our mission won't be jeopardized if one of us is captured and interrogated.'

'Oh.' Greta found this a sobering thought. 'How dreadful.'

'You're the only one who knows the true story, so keep it to yourself for now.'

'Don't worry. Us queers are used to keeping secrets.'

Flick was startled by her choice of words, but made no comment.

The Finishing School was located in the grounds of one of England's grandest stately homes. Beaulieu, pronounced Bewly, was a sprawling estate in the New Forest near the south coast. The main residence, Palace House, was the home of Lord Montagu. Hidden away in the surrounding woods were numerous large country houses in extensive grounds of their own. Most of these had been vacated early in the war: younger owners had gone on active service, and older ones generally had the means to flee to safer locations. Twelve of the houses had been requisitioned by SOE and were used for training agents in security, wireless operation, map reading, and dirtier skills such as burglary, sabotage, forgery, and silent killing.

They reached the place at three o'clock in the morning. Flick drove down a rough track and crossed a cattle grid before pulling up in front of a large house. Coming here always felt like entering a fantasy world, one where deception and violence were talked of as commonplace. The house had an appropriate air of unreality. Although it had about twenty bedrooms, it was built in the style of a cottage – an architectural affectation that had been popular in the years before the First World War. It looked quaint in the moonlight, with its chimneys and dormer windows, hipped roofs and tile-hung bays. It was like an illustration in a children's novel, a big rambling house where you could play hide-and-seek all day.

The place was silent. The rest of the team were here, Flick knew, but they would be asleep. She was familiar with the house, and found two vacant rooms on the attic floor. She and Greta went gratefully to bed. Flick lay awake for a while, wondering how she would ever weld this bunch of misfits into a fighting unit; but she soon fell asleep.

She got up again at six. From her window she could see the estuary of the Solent. The water looked like mercury in the grey morning light. She boiled a kettle

217

for shaving and took it to Greta's room. Then she roused the others.

Percy and Paul were first to arrive in the big kitchen at the back of the house, Percy demanding tea and Paul coffee. Flick told them to make it themselves. She had not joined SOE to wait on men.

'I make tea for you sometimes,' Percy said indignantly.

'You do it with an air of *noblesse oblige*,' she replied. 'Like a duke holding a door for a housemaid.'

Paul laughed. 'You guys,' he said. 'You crack me up.'

An army cook arrived at half past six, and before long they were sitting around the big table eating fried eggs and thick rashers of bacon. Food was not rationed for secret agents: they needed to build up their reserves. Once they went into action, they might have to go for days without proper nourishment.

The girls came down one by one. Flick was startled by her first sight of Maude Valentine: neither Percy nor Paul had said how pretty she was. She appeared immaculately dressed and scented, her rosebud mouth accentuated by bright lipstick, looking as if she were off to lunch at the Savoy. She sat next to Paul, and said with a suggestive air: 'Sleep well, Major?'

Flick was relieved to see the dark pirate face of Ruby Romain. She would not have been surprised to learn that Ruby had run off in the night, never to be seen again. Of course, Ruby could then be rearrested for the murder. She had not been pardoned: rather, the charges had been dropped. They could always be picked up again. That ought to keep Ruby from disappearing, but she was as tough as a boot, and she might have decided to take the chance.

Jelly Knight looked her age, this early in the morning. She sat beside Percy and gave him a fond smile. 'I suppose you slept like a top,' she said.

'Clear conscience,' he replied.

She laughed. 'You haven't got a bloody conscience.'

The cook offered her a plate of bacon and eggs, but she made a face. 'No, thank you, dear,' she said. 'I've got to watch my figure.' Her breakfast was a cup of tea and several cigarettes.

When Greta came through the door, Flick held her breath.

She wore a pretty cotton dress with a small false bosom. A pink cardigan softened her shoulder line and a chiffon scarf concealed her masculine throat. She wore the short dark wig. Her face was heavily powdered, but she had used only a little lipstick and eye makeup. By contrast with her sassy on-stage personality, today she was playing the part of a rather plain young woman who was perhaps a little embarrassed about being so tall. Flick introduced her and watched the reactions of the other women. This was the first test of Greta's impersonation.

They all smiled pleasantly, showing no sign that they saw anything wrong, and Flick breathed easier.

Along with Maude, the other woman Flick had not met before was Lady Denise Bowyer. Percy had interviewed her at Hendon, and had recruited her despite signs that she was indiscreet. She turned out to be a plain girl with a lot of dark hair and a defiant air.

Although she was the daughter of a marquess, she lacked the easy self-confidence typical of upper-class girls. Flick felt a little sorry for her, but Denise was too charmless to be likeable.

This is my team, Flick thought: one flirt, one murderess, one safebreaker, one female impersonator, and one awkward aristocrat. There was someone missing, she realized: the other aristocrat. Diana had not appeared. And it was now half past seven.

Flick said to Percy: 'You did tell Diana that reveille was at six?'

'I told everyone.'

'And I banged on her door at a quarter past.' Flick stood up. 'I'd better check on her. Bedroom ten, right?'

She went upstairs and knocked at Diana's door. There was no response, so she went in. The room looked as if a bomb had hit it – a suitcase open on the rumpled bed, pillows on the floor, knickers on the dressing table – but Flick knew this was normal. Diana had always been surrounded by people whose job it was to tidy up after her. Flick's mother had been one of those people. No, Diana had simply gone off somewhere. She was going to have to realize that her time was no longer her own, Flick thought with irritation.

'She's disappeared,' she told the others. 'We'll start without her.' She stood at the head of the table. 'We have two days' training in front of us. Then, on Friday night, we parachute into France. We're an all-female team because it is much easier for women to move around occupied France – the Gestapo are less suspicious. Our mission is to blow up a railway tunnel near the village of Marles, not far from Reims, on the main railway line between Frankfurt and Paris.'

Flick glanced at Greta, who knew the story was false. She sat quietly buttering toast, and did not meet Flick's eye.

'The agent's course is normally three months,' Flick went on, 'but this tunnel has to be destroyed by Monday night. In two days, we hope to give you some basic security rules, teach you how to parachute, do some weapons training, and show you how to kill people without making a noise.'

Maude looked pale despite her makeup. 'Kill people?' she said. 'Surely you don't expect girls to do that?'

Jelly gave a grunt of disgust. 'There is a bloody war on, you know.'

Diana came in from the garden with bits of vegetation clinging to her corduroy trousers. 'I've been for a tramp in the woods,' she said enthusiastically. 'Marvellous. And look what the greenhouseman gave me.' She took a handful of ripe tomatoes from her pocket and rolled them on to the kitchen table.

Flick said: 'Sit down, Diana, you're late for the briefing.'

'I'm sorry, darling, have I missed your lovely talk?'

'You're in the military now,' Flick said with exasperation. 'When you're told to be in the kitchen by seven, it's not a suggestion.'

'You're not going to get all headmistressy with me, are you?'

'Sit down and shut up.'

'Frightfully sorry, darling.'

Flick raised her voice. 'Diana, when I say shut up, you don't say, 'Frightfully sorry,' to me, and you don't call me darling, ever. Just shut up.'

Diana sat down in silence, but she looked mutinous. Oh, hell, Flick thought, I didn't handle that very well.

The kitchen door opened with a bang and a small, muscular man of about forty came in. He had sergeant's chevrons on his uniform shirt. 'Good morning, girls!' he said heartily.

Flick said: 'This is Sergeant Bill Griffiths, one of the instructors.' She did not like Bill. An army PT instructor, he showed an unpleasant relish in physical combat, and never seemed sorry enough when he hurt someone. She had noticed that he was worse with women. 'We're just about ready for you, Sergeant, so why don't you begin?' She moved aside and leaned against the wall.

'Your wish is my command,' he said unnecessarily. He took her place at the head of the table. 'Landing with a parachute,' he began, 'is like jumping off a wall fourteen feet high. The ceiling of this kitchen is a bit less than that, so it's like leaping into the garden from upstairs.'

Flick heard Jelly say quietly: 'Oh, my gordon.'

'You cannot come down on your feet and stay upright,' Bill continued. 'If you try to land in a standing position, you will break your legs. The only safe way is to fall. So the first thing we're going to teach you is how to fall. If anyone wishes to keep their clothing clean, please go into the boot room just there and put on overalls. If you will assemble outside in three minutes, we will begin.'

While the women were changing, Paul took his leave. 'We need a parachute training flight tomorrow, and they're going to tell me there are no planes available,' he said to Flick. 'I'm going to London to kick some butt. I'll be back tonight.' Flick wondered if he was going to see his girl as well.

In the garden were an old pine table, an ugly mahogany wardrobe from the Victorian era, and a stepladder fourteen feet high. Jelly was dismayed. 'You're not going to make us jump off the top of that bloody wardrobe, are you?' she said to Flick.

'Not before we show you how,' she said. 'You'll be surprised how easy it is.'

Jelly looked at Percy. 'You bugger,' she said. 'What have you let me in for?'

When they were all ready, Bill said: 'First we're going to learn to fall from zero height. There are three ways: forwards, backwards and sideways.'

He demonstrated each method, dropping to the ground effortlessly and springing up again with a gymnast's agility. 'You must keep your legs together.' He looked arch and added: 'As all young ladies should.' No one laughed. 'Do not throw out your arms to break your fall, but keep them at your sides. Do not worry about hurting yourself. If you break an arm it will hurt a hell of a lot worse.'

As Flick expected, the younger girls had no difficulty: Diana, Maude, Ruby and Denise were all able to fall like athletes as soon as they were shown how. Ruby, having done it once from the standing position, lost patience with the exercise. She climbed to the top of the stepladder. 'Not yet!' Bill shouted at her, but he was too late. She jumped off the top and landed perfectly. Then she walked off, sat under a tree, and lit a cigarette. I think she's going to give me trouble, Flick thought.

Flick was more worried about Jelly. She was a key member of the team, the only one who knew about explosives. But she had lost her girlish suppleness some years ago. Parachuting was going to be difficult for her. However, she was game. Falling from the standing position, she hit the ground with a grunt, and cursed as she got up, but she was ready to try again.

To Flick's surprise, the worst student was Greta. 'I can't do this,' she said to Flick. 'I told you I'm no good at rough stuff.'

It was the first time Greta had spoken more than a couple of words, and Jelly frowned and muttered: 'Funny accent.'

'Let me help you,' Bill said to Greta. 'Stand still. Just relax.' He took her by the shoulders. Then, with a sudden strong motion, he threw her to the ground. She landed heavily and gave a gasp of pain. She struggled to her feet and, to Flick's dismay, she began to cry. 'For God's sake,' Bill said disgustedly. 'What kind of people are they sending us?'

Flick glared at him. She did not want to lose her telephone engineer through Bill's brutishness. 'Just go easy,' she snapped at him.

He was unrepentant. 'The Gestapo are a lot worse than me!'

Flick would have to mend the damage herself. She took Greta by the hand. 'We'll do a little special training on our own.' They went around the house to another part of the garden.

'I'm sorry,' Greta said. 'I just hate that little man.'

'I know. Now, let's do this together. Kneel down.' They knelt facing one another and held hands. 'Just do what I do.' Flick leaned slowly sideways. Greta mirrored her action. Together, they fell to the ground, still holding hands. 'There,' Flick said. 'That was all right, wasn't it?'

Greta smiled. 'Why can't he be like you?'

Flick shrugged. 'Men,' she said with a grin. 'Now, are you ready to try falling from a standing position? We'll do it the same way, holding hands.'

She took Greta through all the exercises Bill was doing with the others. Greta quickly gained confidence. They returned to the group. The others were jumping off the table. Greta joined in and landed perfectly, and they gave her a round of applause.

They progressed to jumping from the top of the wardrobe, then finally the stepladder. When Jelly jumped off the ladder, rolled perfectly, and stood upright, Flick hugged her. 'I'm proud of you,' she said. 'Well done.'

Bill looked disgusted. He turned to Percy. 'What kind of army is it when you get a hug for doing what you're bloody well told?'

'Get used to it, Bill,' said Percy.

EIGHTEEN

At the tall house in the rue du Bois, Dieter carried
Stéphanie's suitcase up the stairs and into
Mademoiselle Lemas's bedroom. He looked at the
tightly made single bed, the old-fashioned walnut chest
of drawers, and the prayer stool with the rosary on its
lectern. 'It's not going to be easy to pretend this is
your house,' he said anxiously, putting the case on the
bed.

'I'll say I've inherited it from a maiden aunt, and I've
been too lazy to fix it up to my taste,' she said.

'Clever. All the same, you'll need to mess it up a
little.'

She opened the case, took out a black *négligée*, and
draped it carelessly over the prayer stool.

'Better already,' Dieter said. 'What will you do if the
phone rings?'

Stéphanie thought for a minute. When she spoke,
her voice was lower, and her high-class Paris accent had
been replaced by the tones of provincial gentility.
'Hello, yes, this is Mademoiselle Lemas, who is calling,
please?'

'Very good,' said Dieter. The impersonation might
not fool a close friend or relative, but a casual caller

226

would notice nothing wrong, especially with the distortion of a telephone line.

They explored the house. There were four more bedrooms, each ready to receive a guest, the beds made up, a clean towel on each washstand. In the kitchen, where there should have been a selection of small saucepans and a one-cup coffee pot, they found large casserole dishes and a sack of rice that would have fed Mademoiselle Lemas for a year. The wine in the cellar was cheap *vin ordinaire*, but there was half a case of good Scotch whisky. The garage at the side of the house contained a little pre-war Simca-Cinq, the French version of the Fiat the Italians called the Topolino. It was in good condition with a tank full of petrol. He cranked the starting handle, and the engine turned over immediately. There was no way the authorities would have allowed Mademoiselle Lemas to buy scarce petrol and spare parts for a car to take her shopping. The vehicle must have been fuelled and maintained by the Resistance. He wondered what cover story she had used to explain her ability to drive around. Perhaps she pretended to be a midwife. 'The old cow was well organized,' Dieter remarked.

Stéphanie made lunch. They had shopped on the way. There was no meat or fish in the shops, but they had bought some mushrooms and a lettuce, and a loaf of *pain noir*, the bread the French bakers made with the poor flour and bran which was all they could get. Stéphanie prepared a salad, and used the mushrooms to make a risotto, and they found some cheese in the larder to finish off. With crumbs on the dining room table and dirty pans in the kitchen sink, the house began to look more lived-in.

'The war must have been the best thing that ever happened to her,' Dieter said, as they drank coffee.

'How can you say that? She's on her way to a prison camp.'

'Think of the life she led before. A woman alone, no husband, no family, her parents dead. Then into her life come all these young people, brave boys and girls on daredevil missions. They probably tell her all about their loves and their fears. She hides them in her house, gives them whisky and cigarettes, and sends them on their way, wishing them luck. It was probably the most exciting time of her life. I bet she's never been so happy.'

'Perhaps she would have preferred a peaceful life, shopping for hats with a woman friend, arranging the flowers for the cathedral, going to Paris once a year for a concert.'

'Nobody really prefers a peaceful life.' Dieter glanced out of the dining-room window. 'Damn!' A young woman was coming up the path, pushing a bicycle with a large basket over its front wheel. 'Who the hell is this?'

Stéphanie stared at the approaching visitor. 'What shall I do?'

Dieter did not answer for a moment. The intruder was a plain, fit-looking girl in muddy trousers and a work shirt with big sweat patches under the armpits. She did not ring the doorbell, but pushed her bicycle into the courtyard. He was dismayed. Was his charade to be exposed so soon? 'She's coming to the back door. She must be a friend or relation. You'll just have to improvise. Go and meet her, I'll stay here and listen.'

They heard the kitchen door open and close, and the girl called out in French: 'Good morning, it's me.'

Stéphanie went into the kitchen. Dieter stood by the dining room door. He could hear everything clearly. The girl's startled voice said: 'Who are you?'

'I'm Stéphanie, the niece of Mademoiselle Lemas.'

The visitor did not bother to conceal her suspicion. 'I didn't know she had a niece.'

'She didn't tell me about you, either.' Dieter heard the note of amiable amusement in Stéphanie's voice, and realized she was being charming. 'Would you like to sit down? What's in that basket?'

'Some provisions. I'm Marie. I live in the country. I'm able to get extra food and I bring some for . . . for Mademoiselle.'

'Ah,' said Stéphanie. 'For her . . . guests.' There was a rustling sound, and Dieter guessed she was looking through the paper-wrapped food in the basket. 'This is wonderful! Eggs . . . pork . . . strawberries . . .'

This explained how Mademoiselle Lemas managed to remain plump, Dieter thought.

'You know, then,' said Marie.

'I know about Auntie's secret life, yes.' Hearing her say 'Auntie', Dieter realized that neither he nor Stéphanie had ever asked Mademoiselle Lemas's first name. The pretence would be over if Marie found out that Stéphanie did not even know the name of her 'aunt'.

'Where is she?'

'She went to Aix. Do you remember Charles Menton, who used to be dean at the cathedral?'

'No, I don't.'

'Perhaps you're too young. He was the best friend of Auntie's father, until he retired and went to live in Provence.' Stéphanie was improvising brilliantly, Dieter thought with admiration. She had cool nerves and she was imaginative. 'He has suffered a heart-attack, and she has gone to nurse him. She asked me to take care of any guests while she's away.'

'When will she come back?'

'Charles is not expected to live long. On the other hand, the war may be over soon.'

'She didn't tell anyone about this Charles.'

'She told me.'

It looked as if Stéphanie might get away with it, Dieter thought. If she could keep this up a little longer, Marie would go away convinced. She would report what had happened, to someone or other, but Stéphanie's story was plausible, and exactly the kind of thing that happened in Resistance movements. It was not like the army: someone like Mademoiselle Lemas could easily make a unilateral decision to leave her post and put someone else in charge. It drove Resistance leaders mad, but there was nothing they could do: all their troops were volunteers.

He began to feel hopeful.

'Where are you from?' said Marie.

'I live in Paris.'

'Does your aunt Valérie have any other nieces hidden away?'

So, Dieter thought, Mademoiselle Lemas's name is Valérie.

'I don't think so – none that I know.'

'You're a liar.'

Marie's tone had changed. Something had gone wrong. Dieter sighed and drew the automatic pistol from beneath his jacket.

Stéphanie said: 'What on earth are you talking about?'

'You're lying. You don't even know her name. It's not Valérie, it's Jeanne.'

Dieter thumbed the safety lever on the left of the slide up to the fire position.

Stéphanie carried on gamely. 'I always call her Auntie. You're being very rude.'

Marie said scornfully: 'I knew from the start. Jeanne would never trust someone like you, with your high heels and perfume.'

Dieter stepped into the kitchen. 'What a shame, Marie,' he said. 'If you had been more trusting, or less clever, you might have got away. As it is, you're under arrest.'

Marie looked at Stéphanie and said: 'You're a Gestapo whore.'

It was a wounding jibe, and Stéphanie blushed.

Dieter was so infuriated that he almost pistol-whipped Marie. 'You'll regret that remark when you're in the hands of the Gestapo,' he said coldly. 'There's a man called Sergeant Becker who is going to question you. When you're screaming and bleeding and begging for mercy, remember that careless insult.'

Marie looked poised to flee. Dieter almost hoped she would. Then he could shoot her and the problem would be solved. But she did not run. After a long moment, her shoulders slumped and she began to cry.

Her tears did not move him. 'Lie face down on the floor with your hands behind your back.'

She obeyed.

He put away the gun. 'I think I saw a rope in the cellar,' he said to Stéphanie.

'I'll get it.'

She returned with a length of washing line. Dieter tied Marie's hands and feet. 'I'll have to take her to Sainte-Cécile,' he said. 'We can't have her here in case a British agent comes in today.' He looked at his watch. It was two o'clock. He had time to take her to the chateau and be back by three. 'You'll have to go to the crypt on your own,' he told Stéphanie. 'Use the little car in the garage. I'll be in the cathedral, though you may not see me.' He kissed her. Almost like a husband going to the office, he thought with grim amusement. He picked Marie up and slung her over his shoulder. 'I'll have to hurry,' he said, and went to the back door.

He stepped outside then turned back. 'Hide the bicycle.'

'Don't worry,' Stéphanie replied.

He carried the bound girl through the courtyard and into the street. He opened the boot of his car and put her inside. Had it not been for the 'whore' comment he would have put her on the back seat.

He slammed the lid and looked around. He saw no one, but there were always watchers in a street such as this, peering through their shutters. They would have seen Mademoiselle Lemas being taken away yesterday, and would have remarked the big sky-blue car. As soon as he drove away, they would be talking about the man who had put a girl into the boot of his car. In normal times, they would have called the police; but no one in occupied territory would talk to the police unless they had to, especially where the Gestapo might be involved.

The key question for Dieter was: would the Resistance hear of the arrest of Mademoiselle Lemas? Reims was a city, not a village. People were arrested every day: thieves, murderers, smugglers, black marketeers, Communists, Jews. There was a good chance that no report of the events in the rue du Bois would reach the ears of Michel Clairet.

But there was no guarantee.

Dieter got into the car and headed for Sainte-Cécile.

NINETEEN

The team had got through the morning's instruction reasonably well, to Flick's relief. Everyone had learned the falling technique that was the hardest part of parachuting. The map reading session had been less successful. Ruby had never been to school and could barely read: a map was like a page of Chinese to her. Maude was baffled by directions such as north-north-east, and fluttered her eyelids prettily at the instructor. Denise, despite her expensive education, proved completely incapable of understanding co-ordinates. If the group got split up in France, Flick thought worriedly, she would not be able to rely on them finding their own way.

In the afternoon they moved on to the rough stuff. The weapons instructor was Captain Jim Cardwell, a character quite different from Bill Griffiths. Jim was an easy-going man with a craggy face and a thick black moustache. He grinned amiably when the girls discovered how difficult it was to hit a tree at six paces with a .45 calibre Colt automatic pistol.

Ruby was comfortable with an automatic in her hand and could shoot accurately: Flick suspected she had used handguns before. Ruby was even more comfortable when Jim put his arms around her to show her how to hold the Lee Enfield 'Canadian' rifle. He murmured something in her ear, and she smiled up at him with a wicked gleam in her black eyes. She had been in a women's prison for three months, Flick reflected: no doubt she was enjoying being touched by a man.

Jelly, too, handled the firearms with relaxed familiarity. But Diana was the star of the session. Using the rifle she hit the centre of the target with every shot, emptying the magazine of both its five-round clips in a steady burst of deadly fire. 'Very good!' Jim said in surprise. 'You can have my job.'

Diana looked triumphantly at Flick. 'There are *some* things you're not best at,' she said.

What the heck did I do to deserve that? Flick asked herself. Was Diana thinking of their schooldays, when Flick had always done so much better? Did that childhood rivalry still rankle?

Greta was the only failure. Once again, she was more feminine than the real women. She put her hands over her ears, jumped nervously at every bang, and closed her eyes in terror as she pulled the trigger. Jim worked with her patiently, giving her earplugs to muffle the noise, holding her hand to teach her how to squeeze the trigger gently, but it was no good: she was too skittish ever to be a good shot. 'I'm just not cut out for this kind of thing!' she said in despair.

Jelly said: 'Then what the hell are you doing here?'

Flick interposed quickly. 'Greta's an engineer. She's going to tell you where to place the charges.'

'Why do we need a German engineer?'

'I'm English,' Greta said. 'My father was born in Liverpool.'

Jelly snorted sceptically. 'If that's a Liverpool accent, I'm the Duchess of Devonshire.'

'Save your aggression for the next session,' Flick said. 'We're about to do hand-to-hand combat.' This bickering bothered her. She needed them to trust one another.

They returned to the garden of the house, where Bill Griffiths was waiting. He had changed into shorts and tennis shoes, and was doing press-ups on the grass with his shirt off. When he stood up, Flick got the feeling he wanted them to admire his physique.

Bill liked to teach self-defence by giving the student a weapon and saying: 'Attack me.' Then he would demonstrate how an unarmed man could repel an attacker. It was a dramatic and memorable lesson. Bill was sometimes unnecessarily violent but, Flick always thought, the agents might as well get used to that.

Today he had a selection of weapons laid out on the old pine table: a wicked-looking knife that he claimed was SS equipment, a Walther P38 automatic pistol of the kind Flick had seen German officers carrying, a French policeman's truncheon, a length of black-and-yellow electrical cord that he called a garotte, and a beer bottle with the neck snapped to leave a rough circle of sharp glass.

He put his shirt back on for the training session. 'How to escape from a man who is pointing a gun at you,' he began. He picked up the Walther, thumbed the safety catch up to the firing position, and handed the gun to Maude. She pointed it at him. 'Sooner or later, your captor is going to want you to go somewhere.' He turned and put his hands in the air. 'Chances are, he'll follow close behind you, poking the gun in your back.' He walked around in a wide circle, with Maude behind. 'Now, Maude, I want you to pull the trigger the moment you think I'm trying to escape.' He quickened his pace slightly, forcing Maude to step out a little faster to keep up with him; and as she did so he moved sideways and back. He caught her right wrist under his arm and hit her hand with a sharp downward chopping motion. She cried out and dropped the gun.

'This is where you can make a bad mistake,' he said, as Maude rubbed her wrist. 'Do *not* run away at this point. Otherwise your Kraut copper will just pick up his gun and shoot you in the back. What you have to do is . . .' He picked up the Walther, pointed it at Maude, and pulled the trigger. There was a bang. Maude screamed, and so did Greta. 'This gun is loaded with blanks, of course,' Bill said.

Sometimes Flick wished Bill would not be quite so dramatic in his demonstrations.

'We'll practise all these techniques on one another in a few minutes,' he went on. He picked up the electrical cord and turned to Greta. 'Put that around my neck. When I give the word, pull it as tight as you can.' He handed her the cord. 'Your Gestapo man, or your traitorous collaborationist French *gendarme*, could kill you with the cord, but he can't hold your weight with it. All right, Greta, strangle me.' Greta hesitated, then pulled the cord tight. It dug into Bill's muscular neck. He kicked out forwards with both feet, and fell to the ground, landing on his back. Greta lost her grip on the cord.

'Unfortunately,' Bill said, 'this leaves you lying on the ground with your enemy standing over you, which is an unfavourable situation.' He got up. 'We'll do it again. But this time, before I drop to the ground I'm going to take hold of my captor by one wrist.' They resumed the position and Greta pulled the cord tight. Bill grabbed her wrist, fell to the ground, pulling her forward and down. As she fell on top of him, he bent one leg and kneed her viciously in the stomach.

She rolled off him and curled up, gasping for breath and retching. Flick said: 'For Christ's sake, Bill, that's a bit rough!'

He looked pleased. 'The Gestapo are a lot worse than me,' he said.

She went to Greta and helped her up. 'I'm sorry,' she said.

'He's a bloody fucking Nazi,' Greta gasped.

Flick helped Greta into the house and sat her down in the kitchen. The cook, who was peeling potatoes for lunch, offered her a cup of tea, and Greta accepted gratefully.

When Flick returned to the garden, Bill had picked his next victim, Ruby, and handed her the policeman's truncheon. There was a cunning look on Ruby's face, and Flick thought: If I were Bill I'd be careful with her.

Flick had seen Bill demonstrate this technique before. When Ruby raised her right hand to hit him

238

with the truncheon, Bill was going to grab her arm, turn, and throw her over his shoulder. She would land flat on her back with a painful thump.

'Right, gypsy girl,' Bill said. 'Hit me with the truncheon, as hard as you like.'

Ruby lifted her arm, and Bill moved towards her, but the action did not follow the usual pattern. When Bill reached for Ruby's arm it was not there. The truncheon fell to the ground. Ruby moved close to Bill and brought her knee up hard into his groin. He gave a sharp cry of pain. She grabbed his shirt front, pulled him towards her sharply, and butted his nose. Then, with her sturdy black-laced shoe, she kicked his shin, and he fell to the ground, blood pouring from his nose.

'You bitch, you weren't supposed to do that!' he yelled.

'The Gestapo are a lot worse than me,' said Ruby.

TWENTY

It was a minute before three when Dieter parked outside the Hôtel Frankfort. He hurried across the cobbled square to the cathedral under the stony gaze of the carved angels in the buttresses. It was almost too much to hope that an Allied agent would show up at the rendezvous on the first day. On the other hand, if the invasion really were imminent, the Allies would be throwing in every last asset.

He saw Mademoiselle Lemas's Simca-Cinq parked to one side of the square, which meant that Stéphanie was already here. He was relieved to have arrived in time. If anything should go wrong, he would not want her to have to deal with it alone.

He passed through the great west door into the cool gloom of the interior. He looked for Hans Hesse, and saw him sitting in the back row of pews. They nodded briefly to one another but did not speak.

Right away Dieter felt like a violator. The business he was engaged upon should not take place in this atmosphere. He was not very devout – less so than the average German, he thought – but he was certainly no unbeliever. He felt uncomfortable catching spies in a place that had been a holy sanctuary for hundreds of years.

He shook off the feeling as superstitious.

He crossed to the north side of the building and walked up the long north aisle, his footsteps ringing on the stone floor. When he reached the transept he saw the gate, railing and steps leading down to the crypt, which was below the high altar. Stéphanie was down there, he assumed, wearing one black shoe and one brown. From here he could see in both directions: back the way he had come the length of the north aisle, and forward around the curved ambulatory at the other end of the building. He knelt down and folded his hands in prayer.

He said: 'O Lord, forgive me for the suffering I inflict on my prisoners. You know I'm trying my best to do my duty. And forgive me for my sin with Stéphanie. I know it's wrong, but You made her so lovely that I can't resist the temptation. Watch over my dear Waltraud, and help her to care for Rudi and little Mausi, and protect them from the bombs of the RAF. And be with Field Marshal Rommel when the invasion comes, and give him the power to push the Allied invaders back into the sea. It's a short prayer to have so much in it, but You know that I have a lot to do right now. Amen.'

He looked around. There was no service going on, but a handful of people were scattered around the pews in the side chapels, praying or just sitting quietly in the sacred stillness. A few tourists walked around the aisles, talking in hushed voices about the medieval architecture, bending their necks to peer up into the vastness of the vaulting.

If an Allied agent showed up today, Dieter planned simply to watch and make sure nothing went wrong. Ideally he would not have to do anything. Stéphanie would talk to the agent, exchange passwords, and take him home to the rue du Bois.

After that, his plans were vaguer. Somehow, the agent would lead him to others. At some point, there would be a breakthrough: an unwise person would be found to have a written list of names and addresses; a wireless set and a code book would fall into Dieter's hands; or he would capture someone like Flick Clairet, who would, under torture, betray half the French Resistance.

He checked his watch. It was five past three. Probably no one would come today. He looked up. To his horror, he saw Willi Weber.

What the hell was he doing here?

Weber was in plain clothes, wearing his green tweed suit. With him was a younger Gestapo man in a check jacket. They were coming from the east end of the church, walking around the ambulatory towards Dieter, though they had not seen him. They drew level with the crypt door and stopped.

Dieter cursed under his breath. This could ruin everything. He almost hoped that no British agent would come today.

Looking along the north aisle, he saw a young man carrying a small suitcase. Dieter narrowed his eyes: most of the people in the church were older. The man was wearing a shabby blue suit of French cut, but he looked like a Viking, with red hair, blue eyes, and pale-pink skin. It was a very English combination, but could also be German. At first glance, the young man might be an officer in mufti, seeing the sights or even intending to pray.

However, his behaviour gave him away. He walked purposefully along the aisle, neither looking at the pillars like a tourist nor taking a seat like a worshipper. Dieter's heart beat faster. An agent on the first day! And the bag he carried was almost certainly a suitcase radio. That meant he had a code book, too. This was more than Dieter had dared to hope for.

But Weber was here to mess everything up.

The agent passed Dieter and slowed his walk, obviously looking for the crypt.

Weber saw the man, gave him a hard look, then turned and pretended to study the fluting on a column.

Maybe it was going to be all right, Dieter thought. Weber had done a stupid thing in coming here, but perhaps he was just planning to observe. Surely he was not such an imbecile as to interfere? He could ruin a unique opportunity.

The agent found the crypt gate and disappeared down the stone steps.

Weber looked across the north transept and gave a nod. Following his gaze, Dieter saw two more Gestapo men lurking beneath the organ-loft. That was a bad sign. Weber did not need four men just to observe.

Dieter wondered if he had time to speak to Weber, get him to call his men off. But Weber would argue, and there would be a row, and then –

As it turned out, there was no time. Almost immediately, Stéphanie came up from the crypt with the agent right behind her.

When she reached the top of the steps she saw Weber. A look of shock came over her face. She was disoriented by his unexpected presence, as if she had walked on stage and found herself in the wrong play. She stumbled, and the young agent caught her elbow and steadied her. She recovered her composure with characteristic speed, and gave him a grateful smile. Well done, my girl, Dieter thought.

Then Weber stepped forward.

'No!' Dieter said involuntarily. No one heard him.

Weber took the agent by the arm and said something. Dieter's heart sank as he realized Weber was making an arrest. Stéphanie backed away from the little tableau, looking bewildered.

Dieter got up and walked quickly towards the group. He could only think that Weber had decided to grab the glory by capturing an agent. It was insane but possible.

Before Dieter got close, the agent shook off Weber's hand and bolted.

Weber's young companion in the check jacket reacted fast. He took two big strides after the agent, flung himself forward in a flying tackle, and threw his arms around the agent's knees. The agent stumbled, but he was moving strongly, and the Gestapo man could not hold him. The agent recovered his balance, straightened up, and ran on, still clutching his suitcase.

The sudden running steps, and the grunts made by both men, sounded loud in the hushed cathedral, and everyone looked. The agent ran towards Dieter. Dieter saw what was going to happen, and groaned. The second pair of Gestapo men stepped out of the south transept. The agent saw them and seemed to guess what they were, for he swerved left; but he was too late. One of the men stuck out a foot and tripped him. He fell headlong, his chunky body hitting the stone floor with a thwack. The suitcase went flying. Both Gestapo men jumped on him. Weber came running up, looking pleased.

'Shit,' Dieter said aloud, forgetting where he was. The mad fools were ruining everything.

Maybe he could still save the situation.

He reached into his jacket, drew his Walther P38, thumbed the safety catch, and pointed it at the Gestapo men who were holding the agent down. Speaking French, he yelled at the top of his voice: 'Get off him now, or I shoot!'

Weber said: 'Major, I—'

Dieter fired into the air. The report of the pistol crashed around the cathedral vaults, drowning Weber's giveaway words. 'Silence!' Dieter shouted in German. Weber looked scared and shut up.

Dieter poked the nose of the pistol hard into the face of one of the Gestapo men. Reverting to French, he screamed: 'Off! Off! Get off him!'

With terrified faces the two men stood up and backed away.

Dieter looked at Stéphanie. Calling her by Mademoiselle Lemas's name, he shouted: 'Jeanne! Go! Get away!' Stéphanie began to run. She circled widely around the Gestapo men and dashed for the west door.

The agent was scrambling to his feet. 'Go with her! Go with her!' Dieter shouted at him, pointing. The man grabbed his suitcase and ran, vaulting over the backs of the wooden choir stalls and haring down the middle of the nave.

Weber and his three associates looked bemused. 'Lie face down!' Dieter ordered them. As they obeyed he backed away, still threatening them with the gun. Then he turned and ran after Stéphanie and the agent.

As the other two fled through the doorway, Dieter stopped and spoke to Hans, who stood near the back of the church, looking stolid. 'Talk to those damn fools,' Dieter said breathlessly. 'Explain what we're doing and make sure they don't follow us.' He holstered the pistol and ran outside.

The engine of the Simca was turning over. Dieter pushed the agent into the cramped back seat and got into the front passenger seat. Stéphanie stamped on the pedal and the little car shot out of the square like a champagne cork.

As they raced along the street, Dieter turned and looked through the back window. 'No one following,' he said. 'Slow down. We don't want to get stopped by a *gendarme.*'

The agent said in French: 'I'm Helicopter. What the hell happened in there?'

Dieter realized that 'Helicopter' must be a codename. He recalled that Gaston had told him Mademoiselle Lemas's codename. 'This is Bourgeoise,' he said, indicating Stéphanie. 'And I'm Charenton,' he improvised, thinking for some reason of the prison where the Marquis de Sade had been incarcerated. 'Bourgeoise has become suspicious, in the last few days, that the cathedral rendezvous might be watched, so she asked me to come with her. I'm not part of the Bollinger circuit – Bourgeoise is a cut-out.'

'Yes, I understand that.'

'Anyway, we now know the Gestapo had set a trap; and it's just fortunate that she had asked me to be there as back-up for her.'

'You were brilliant!' Helicopter said enthusiastically. 'God, I was so scared, I thought I'd blown it on my first day.'

You have, Dieter thought silently.

It seemed to Dieter that he might have saved the situation. Helicopter now firmly believed that Dieter was a member of the Resistance. Helicopter's French sounded perfect, but obviously he was not quite good enough to identify Dieter's slight accent. Was there anything else that might cause him to be suspicious, perhaps later when he thought things over? Dieter had stood up and said: 'No!' right at the start of the rumpus, but a plain 'No' did not mean much, and anyway he did not think anyone had heard him. Willi Weber had shouted, 'Major', in German at Dieter, and Dieter had fired his weapon to drown out any further indiscretion. Had Helicopter heard that one word, did he know what it meant, and would he remember it later and puzzle over it? No, Dieter decided. If Helicopter had understood the word he would have assumed Weber was addressing one of the other Gestapo men: they were all in plain clothes so could be any rank.

Helicopter would now trust Dieter in all things, being convinced Dieter had snatched him from the clutches of the Gestapo.

Others might not be quite so easy to fool. The existence of a new Resistance member codenamed Charenton and recruited by Mademoiselle Lemas would have to be plausibly explained, both to London and to the leader of the Bollinger circuit, Michel Clairet. Both might ask questions and run checks. Dieter would just have to deal with them in due course. It was not possible to anticipate everything.

He allowed himself a moment of triumph. He was one step closer to his goal of crippling the Resistance in northern France. He had pulled it off despite the stupidity of the Gestapo. And it had been exhilarating.

The challenge now was to make maximum use of Helicopter's trust. The agent must continue to operate, believing himself unsuspected. That way he could lead Dieter to more agents, perhaps dozens more. But it was a subtle trick to pull off.

They arrived at the rue du Bois and Stéphanie drove into Mademoiselle Lemas's garage. They entered the house by the back door and sat in the kitchen. Stéphanie got a bottle of Scotch from the cellar and poured them all a drink.

Dieter was desperately anxious to confirm that Helicopter had a radio. He said: 'You'd better send a message to London right away.'

'I'm supposed to broadcast at eight p.m. and receive at eleven.'

Dieter made a mental note. 'But you need to tell them as soon as possible that the cathedral rendezvous is compromised. We don't want them to send any more men there. And there could be someone else on his way tonight.'

'Oh, my God, yes,' the young man said. 'I'll use the emergency frequency.'

'You can set up your wireless right here in the kitchen.'

Helicopter lifted the heavy case on to the table and opened it.

Dieter hid a sigh of profound satisfaction. There it was.

The interior of the case was divided into four: two side compartments and, in the middle, one front and one back. Dieter could see immediately that the rear middle compartment contained the transmitter, with the Morse key in the lower right-hand corner, and the front middle was the receiver, with a socket for headphone connections. The right side compartment was the power supply. The function of the left side compartment became clear when the agent lifted the lid to reveal a selection of accessories and spare parts: a power lead, adaptors, aerial wire, connection cables, a headset, spare tubes, fuses and a screwdriver.

It was a neat, compact set, Dieter thought admiringly; the kind of thing the Germans would have made, not at all what he would expect from the untidy British.

He already knew Helicopter's times for transmission and reception. Now he had to learn the frequencies used and – most important – the code.

Helicopter plugged a lead into the power socket. Dieter said: 'I thought it was battery-operated.'

'Battery or mains power. I believe the Gestapo's favourite trick, when they're trying to locate the source of an illicit radio transmission, is to switch off the town's electricity block by block until the broadcast is cut off.'

Dieter nodded.

'Well, with this set, if you lose the house current, you just have to reverse this plug, and it switches to battery operation.'

'Very good.' Dieter would pass that on to the Gestapo, in case they did not already know.

Helicopter plugged the power lead into an electrical outlet, then took the aerial wire and asked Stéphanie to drape it over a tall cupboard. Dieter looked in the kitchen drawers and found a pencil and a scratch pad that Mademoiselle Lemas had probably used to make shopping lists. 'You can use this to encode your message,' he said helpfully.

'First I'd better work out what to say.' Helicopter scratched his head then began to write in English:

ARRIVED OK STOP CRYPT RENDEZVOUS
UNSAFE STOP NABBED BY GESTAPO BUT
GOT AWAY OVER

'I suppose that's it for now,' he said.

Dieter said: 'We should give them a new rendezvous for future incomers. Say the Café de la Gare next to the railway station.'

Helicopter wrote it down.

He took from the case a silk handkerchief printed with a complex table showing letters in pairs. He also took out a pad of a dozen or so sheets of paper printed with five-letter nonsense words. Dieter recognized the makings of a one-time pad encryption system. It was unbreakable – unless you had the pad.

Over the words of his message, Helicopter wrote the five-letter groups from the pad; then he used the letters he had written to select transpositions from the silk handkerchief. Over the first five letters of ARRIVED he had written the first group from his one-time pad, which was BGKRU. The first letter, B, told him which column to use from the grid on the silk handkerchief. At the top of column B were the letters Ae. That told him to replace the A of ARRIVED with the letter e.

The code could not be broken in the usual way, because the next A would be represented, not by e, but by some other letter. In fact, any letter could stand for any other letter, and the only way to decrypt the message was by using the pad with the five-letter groups. Even if the codebreakers could get hold of a coded message and its plain-language original, they could not

251

use them to read another message, because the next message would be encoded with a different sheet from the pad – which was why it was called a 'one-time' pad. Each sheet was used once then burned.

When he had encrypted his message, Helicopter flicked the ON/OFF switch and turned a knob marked in English 'Crystal Selector'. Looking carefully, Dieter saw that the dial bore three faint markings in yellow wax crayon. Helicopter had mistrusted his memory and had marked his broadcast positions. The crystal he was using would be reserved for emergencies. Of the other two, one would be for transmission and the other for reception.

Finally he tuned in, and Dieter saw that the frequency dial was also marked with yellow crayon.

Before sending his message, he checked in with the receiving station by sending:

HLCP DXDX QTC1 QRK? K

Dieter frowned, figuring. The first group had to be the call sign 'Helicopter'. The next one, 'DXDX', was a mystery. The number one at the end of 'QTC1' suggested that this group meant something like: 'I have one message to send you.' The question mark at the end of 'QRK?' made him think this asked if he was being received loud and clear. 'K' meant 'Over', he knew. That left the mysterious 'DXDX'.

He tried a guess. 'Don't forget your security tag,' he said.

'I haven't,' Helicopter said.

That must be 'DXDX', Dieter concluded.

Helicopter turned to 'Receive' and they all heard the Morse reply:

HLCP QRK QRV K

Once again, the first group was Helicopter's call sign. The second group, 'QRK', had appeared in the original message. Without the question mark, it presumably meant 'I am receiving you loud and clear.' He was not sure about 'QRV', but he guessed it must mean 'Go ahead.'

As Helicopter tapped out his message in Morse, Dieter watched, feeling elated. This was the spycatcher's dream: he had an agent in his hands and the agent did not know he had been captured.

When the message was sent, Helicopter shut down the radio quickly. Because the Gestapo used radio direction-finding equipment to track down spies, it was dangerous to operate a set for more than a few minutes.

In England, the message had to be transcribed, decoded, and passed to Helicopter's controller, who might have to consult with others before replying; all of which could take several hours, so Helicopter would wait until the appointed hour for a response.

Now Dieter had to separate him from the wireless set and, more importantly, from his coding materials. 'I presume you want to contact the Bollinger circuit now,' he said.

'Yes. London needs to know how much of it is left.'

'We'll put you in touch with Monet, that's the

codename of the leader.' He looked at his wristwatch, and suffered a moment of sheer panic: it was a standard-issue German army officer's watch, and if Helicopter recognized it the game would be up. Trying to keep the tremor out of his voice, Dieter said: 'We've got time, I'll drive you to his house.'

'Is it far?' Helicopter said eagerly.

'Centre of town.'

Monet, Michel Clairet, would not be at home. He was no longer using the house; Dieter had checked. The neighbours claimed to have no idea where he was. Dieter was not surprised. Monet had guessed that his name and address would be given away by one of his comrades under interrogation, and he had gone into hiding.

Helicopter began to close up the radio. Dieter said: 'Does that battery need recharging from time to time?'

'Yes – in fact they tell us to plug it in at every opportunity, so that it's always fully charged.'

'So why don't you leave it where it is for now? We can come back for it later, by which time it will be charged. If anyone should come in the meantime, Bourgeoise can hide it away in a few seconds.'

'Good idea.'

'Then let's go.' Dieter led the way to the garage and backed the Simca-Cinq out. Then he said: 'Wait here a minute, I have to tell Bourgeoise something.'

He went back into the house. Stéphanie was in the kitchen, staring at the suitcase radio on the kitchen table. Dieter took the one-time pad and the silk handkerchief from the accessories compartment. 'How long will it take you to copy these?' he said.

She made a face. 'All those gibberish letters? At least an hour.'

'Do it as fast as you can, but don't make any mistakes. I'll keep him out for an hour and a half.'

He returned to the car and drove Helicopter into the city centre.

Michel Clairet's home was a small, elegant town house near the cathedral. Dieter waited in the car while Helicopter went to the door. After a few minutes, the agent came back and said: 'No answer.'

'You can try again in the morning,' Dieter said. 'Meanwhile, I know a bar used by the Resistance.' He knew no such thing. 'Let's go there and see if I recognize anyone.'

He parked near the station and picked a bar at random. The two of them sat drinking watery beer for an hour, then returned to the rue du Bois.

When they entered the kitchen, Stéphanie gave Dieter a slight nod. He took it to mean she had succeeded in copying everything. 'Now,' Dieter said to Helicopter, 'you'd probably like a bath, having spent a night in the open. And you certainly should shave. I'll show you your room, and Bourgeoise will run your bath.'

'How kind you are.'

Dieter put him in an attic room, the one farthest from the bathroom. As soon as he heard the man splashing in the bath, he went into the room and searched his clothes. Helicopter had a change of underwear and socks, all bearing the labels of French shops. In his jacket pockets were French cigarettes and matches, a handkerchief with a French label, and a wallet. In the wallet was a lot of cash – half a million francs, enough to buy a luxury car, if there had been any new cars for sale. The identity papers seemed impeccable, though they had to be forgeries.

There was also a photograph.

Dieter stared at it in surprise. It showed Flick Clairet. There was no mistake. It was the woman he had seen in the square at Sainte-Cécile. Finding it was a wonderful piece of luck for Dieter – and a disaster for her.

She was wearing a swimsuit that revealed muscular legs and suntanned arms. Beneath the costume she had neat breasts, a small waist, and delightfully rounded hips. There was a glimmer of moisture, either water or perspiration, at her throat, and she was looking into the camera with a faint smile. Behind her and slightly out of focus, two young men in bathing trunks seemed about to dive into a river. The picture had obviously been taken at an innocent swimming party. But her semi-nakedness, the wetness at her throat, and the slight smile combined to make a picture that seemed sexually charged. Had it not been for the boys in the background, she might have been about to take the swimsuit off and reveal her body to the person behind the camera. That was how a woman smiled at her man when she wanted him to make love to her, Dieter thought. He could see why a young fellow would treasure the photo.

Agents were not supposed to carry photos with them into enemy territory – for very good reasons. Helicopter's passion for Flick Clairet might destroy her, and much of the French Resistance too.

Dieter slipped the photo into his pocket and left the room. All in all, he thought, he had done a very good day's work.

TWENTY-ONE

Paul Chancellor spent the day fighting the military bureaucracy – persuading, threatening, pleading, cajoling, and as a last resort using the name of Monty – and, in the end, he got a plane for the team's parachute training the following day.

When he caught the train back to Hampshire, he found he was eager to see Flick again. He liked her a lot. She was smart, tough, and a pleasure to look at. He wished to hell she was single.

On the train he read the war news in the paper. The long lull on the eastern front had been broken, yesterday, by a surprisingly powerful German attack in Romania. The continuing resilience of the Germans was formidable. They were in retreat everywhere, but they kept fighting back.

The train was delayed, and he missed six o'clock dinner at the Finishing School. After dinner there was always another lecture, then at nine the students were free to relax for an hour or so before bed. Paul found most of the team gathered in the drawing room of the house, which had a bookcase, a cupboard full of games, a wireless set, and a half-size billiards table. He sat on the sofa beside Flick and said quietly: 'How did it go today?'

'Better than we had a right to expect,' she said. 'But everything is so compressed. I don't know how much they're going to remember when they're in the field.'

'I guess anything is better than nothing.'

Percy Thwaite and Jelly were playing poker for pennies. Jelly was a real character, Paul thought. How could a professional safebreaker consider herself a respectable English lady? 'How was Jelly?' he asked Flick.

'Not bad. She has more difficulty than the others with the physical training but, my goodness, she just gritted her teeth and got on with it, and in the end she did everything the youngsters did.' Flick paused and frowned.

Paul said: 'What?'

'Her hostility to Greta is a problem.'

'It's not surprising that an Englishwoman should hate Germans.'

'It's illogical, though – Greta has suffered more from the Nazis than Jelly has.'

'Jelly doesn't know that.'

'She knows that Greta's prepared to fight against the Nazis.'

'People aren't logical about these things.'

'Too bloody right.'

Greta herself was talking to Denise. Or rather, Paul thought, Denise was talking and Greta was listening. 'My stepbrother, Lord Foules, pilots fighter-bombers,' he heard her say in her half-swallowed aristocratic accent. 'He's been training to fly support missions for the invasion troops.'

Paul frowned. 'Did you hear that?' he asked Flick.

'Yes. Either she's making it up, or she's being dangerously indiscreet.'

He studied Denise. She was a rawboned girl who always looked as if she had just been insulted. He did not think she was fantasizing. 'She doesn't seem the imaginative type,' he said.

'I agree. I think she's giving away real secrets.'

'I'd better arrange a little test tomorrow.'

'Okay.'

Paul wanted to get Flick to himself so that they could talk more freely.'Let's take a stroll around the garden,' he said.

They stepped outside. The air was warm and there was an hour of daylight left. The house had a large garden with several acres of lawn dotted with trees. Maude and Diana were sitting on a bench under a copper beech. Maude had flirted with Paul at first, but he had given her no encouragement, and she seemed to have given up. Now she was listening avidly to something Diana was saying, looking into Diana's face with an attitude almost of adoration. 'I wonder what Diana's saying?' Paul said. 'She's got Maude fascinated.'

'Maude likes to hear about the places she's been,' Flick said. 'The fashion shows, the balls, the ocean liners.'

Paul recalled that Maude had surprised him by asking whether the mission would take them to Paris. 'Maybe she wanted to go to America with me,' he said.

'I noticed her making a play for you,' Flick said. 'She's pretty.'

'Not my type, though.'

'Why not?'

'Candidly? She's not smart enough.'

'Good,' Flick said. 'I'm glad.'

He raised an eyebrow at her. 'Why?'

'I would have thought less of you otherwise.'

He thought this was a little condescending. 'I'm glad to have your approval,' he said.

'Don't be ironic,' she reprimanded him. 'I was paying you a compliment.'

He grinned. He could not help liking her, even when she was being high-handed. 'Then I'll quit while I'm ahead,' he said.

They passed close to the two women, and heard Diana say: 'So the contessa said: "Keep your painted claws off my husband," then poured a glass of champagne over Jennifer's head, whereupon Jennifer pulled the contessa's hair – and it came off in her hand, because it was a wig!'

Maude laughed. 'I wish I'd been there!'

Paul said to Flick: 'They all seem to be making friends.'

'I'm pleased. I need them to work as a team.'

The garden merged gradually with the forest, and they found themselves walking through woodland. It was only half light under the canopy of leaves. 'Why is it called the New Forest?' Paul said. 'It looks old.'

'Do you still expect English names to be logical?'

He laughed. 'I guess I don't.'

They walked in silence for a while. Paul felt quite romantic. He wanted to kiss her, but she was wearing a wedding ring.

'When I was four years old, I met the King,' Flick said.

'The present king?'

'No, his father, George V. He came to Somersholme. I was kept out of his way, of course, but he wandered into the kitchen garden on Sunday morning and saw me. He said: "Good morning, little girl, are you ready for church?" He was a small man, but he had a booming voice.'

'What did you say?'

'I said: "Who are you?" He replied: "I'm the King." And then, according to family legend, I said: "You can't be, you're not big enough." Fortunately, he laughed.'

'Even as a child, you had no respect for authority.'

'So it seems.'

Paul heard a low moan. Frowning, he looked toward the sound and saw Ruby Romain with Jim Cardwell, the firearms instructor. Ruby had her back to a tree and Jim was embracing her. They were kissing passionately. Ruby moaned again.

They were not just embracing, Paul realized, and he felt both embarrassed and aroused. Jim's hands were busy inside Ruby's blouse. Her skirt was up around her waist. Paul could see all of one brown leg and a thick patch of dark hair at her groin. The other leg was raised and bent at the knee, and Ruby's foot rested high on Jim's hip. The movement they were making together was unmistakable.

Paul looked at Flick. She had seen the same thing. She stared for a moment, her expression showing shock and something else. Then she turned quickly away. Paul followed suit, and they went back the way they had come, walking as quietly as they could.

When they were out of earshot, he said: 'I'm terribly sorry about that.'

'Not your fault,' she said.

'Still, I'm sorry I led you that way.'

'I really don't mind. I've never seen anyone ... doing that. It was rather sweet.'

'Sweet?' It was not the word he would have chosen. 'You know, you're kind of unpredictable.'

'Have you only just noticed?'

'Don't be ironic, I was paying you a compliment,' he said, repeating her own words.

She laughed. 'Then I'll quit while I'm ahead.'

They emerged from the woods. Daylight was fading fast, and the blackout curtains were drawn in the house. Maude and Diana had gone from their seat under the copper beech. 'Let's sit here for a minute,' Paul said. He was in no hurry to go inside.

Flick complied without speaking.

He sat sideways, looking at her. She bore his scrutiny without comment, but she was thoughtful. He took her hand and stroked her fingers. She looked at him, her face unreadable, but she did not pull away her hand. He said: 'I know I shouldn't, but I really want to kiss you.' She made no reply, but continued to look at him with that enigmatic expression, half amused and half sad. He took silence for assent, and kissed her.

Her mouth was soft and moist. He closed his eyes, concentrating on the sensation. To his surprise, her lips parted, and he felt the tip of her tongue. It ran along his upper lip then his lower. He opened his mouth.

He put his arms around her and pulled her to him, but she slipped out of his embrace and stood up. 'Enough,' she said. She turned away and walked toward the house.

He watched her go in the fading light. Her small, neat body suddenly seemed the most desirable thing in the world. She broke into a run, and he smiled at her athletic stride. 'Felicity,' he murmured, 'you're absolutely adorable.'

When she had disappeared inside, he followed. In the drawing room Diana sat alone, smoking a cigarette, looking thoughtful. On impulse, Paul sat close to her and said: 'You've known Flick since you were kids.'

Diana smiled with surprising warmth. 'She's delightful, isn't she?'

Paul did not want to give away too much of what was in his heart. 'I like her a lot, and I wish I knew more about her.'

'She always yearned for adventure,' Diana said. 'She loved those long trips we made to France every February. We would spend a night in Paris then take the Blue Train all the way to Nice. One winter, my father decided to go to Morocco. I think it was the best time of Flick's life. She learned a few words of Arabic and talked to the merchants in the souks. We used to read the memoirs of those doughty Victorian lady explorers who travelled the Middle East dressed as men.'

'She got on well with your father.'

'Better than I did.'

'What's her husband like?'

'All Flick's men are slightly exotic. At Oxford her best friend was a Nepalese boy, Rajendra, which caused great consternation in the senior common room at St Hilda's, I can tell you, although I'm not sure she ever, you know, misbehaved with him. A boy called Charlie Standish was desperately in love with her, but he was just too boring for her. She fell for Michel because he's charming and foreign and clever, which is what she likes.'

'Exotic,' Paul repeated.

Diana laughed. 'Don't worry, you'll do. You're American, you've only got one and a half ears, and you're as smart as a whip. You're in with a chance, at least.'

Paul stood up. The conversation was taking an uncomfortably intimate turn. 'I'll take that as a compliment,' he said, with a smile. 'Goodnight.'

On his way upstairs, he passed Flick's room. There was a light under the door.

He put on his pyjamas and got into bed, but he lay awake. He was too excited and happy to sleep. He re-lived the kiss again and again. He wished he and Flick could be like Ruby and Jim, and give in to their desires shamelessly. Why not? he thought. Why the hell not?

The house fell quiet.

A few minutes after midnight, Paul got up. He went along the corridor to Flick's room. He tapped gently on the door and stepped inside.

'Hello,' she said quietly.

'It's me.'

'I know.'

She lay on her back in the single bed, her head propped up on two pillows. The curtains were drawn back, and moonlight came in at the small window. He could see, quite clearly, the straight line of her nose and the chisel chin that he had once thought not to be pretty. Now they seemed angelic.

He knelt by the bed.

'The answer is no,' she said.

He took her hand and kissed her palm. 'Please,' he said.

'No.'

He leaned over her to kiss her, but she turned her head away.

'Just a kiss?' he said.

'If I kiss you, I'll be lost.'

That pleased him. It told him she was feeling the same way he did. He kissed her hair, then her forehead and her cheek, but she kept her face averted. He kissed her shoulder through the cotton of her nightdress, then brushed his lips over her breast. Her nipple was erect. 'You want to,' he said.

'Out,' she commanded.

'Don't say that.'

She turned to him. He bent his face to kiss her, but

she put a finger on his lips as if to hush him. 'Go,' she said. 'I mean it.'

He looked at her lovely face in the moonlight. Her expression was set with determination. Although he hardly knew her, he understood that her will could not be overridden. Reluctantly, he stood up.

He gave it one more try. 'Look, let's—'

'No more talk. Go.'

He turned away and left the room.

THE FIFTH DAY:
THURSDAY, 1 JUNE 1944

TWENTY-TWO

Dieter slept a few hours at the Hôtel Frankfort and got up at two a.m. He was alone: Stéphanie was at the house in the rue du Bois with the British agent, Helicopter. Some time this morning, Helicopter would go in search of the head of the Bollinger circuit, and Dieter had to follow him. He knew Helicopter would start at Michel Clairet's house, so he had decided to put a surveillance team there by first light.

He drove to Sainte-Cécile in the early hours, winding through the moonlit vineyards in his big car, and parked in front of the chateau. He went first to the photo lab in the basement. There was no one in the darkroom, but his prints were there, pegged on a line to dry like laundry. He had asked for two copies of Helicopter's picture of Flick Clairet. He took them off the line and studied one, remembering the way she had run through gunfire to rescue her husband. He tried to see some of that steely nerve in the carefree expression of the pretty girl in the swimsuit, but there was no sign of it. No doubt it had come with war.

He pocketed the negative and picked up the original photo, which would have to be returned surreptitiously

271

to Helicopter. He found an envelope and a sheet of plain paper, thought for a moment, and wrote:

> *My darling,*
>   *While Helicopter is shaving, please put this in his inside jacket pocket, so that it will look as if it slipped out of his wallet. Thank you.*
>   *D.*

He put the note and the picture in the envelope, sealed it, and wrote: 'Mlle Lemas' on the front. He would drop it off later.

He passed the cells and looked through a judas at Marie, the girl who had surprised him yesterday by showing up at the house in the rue du Bois with food for Mademoiselle Lemas's 'guests'. She lay on a bloodstained sheet, staring at the wall with a wide-eyed gaze of horror, emitting a constant low moan like a piece of machinery that was broken but not switched off.

Dieter had interrogated Marie last night. She had had no useful information. She had claimed she knew no one in the Resistance, only Mademoiselle Lemas. Dieter had been inclined to believe her, but he had let Sergeant Becker torture her just in case. However, she had not changed her story, and he now felt confident that her disappearance would not alert the Resistance to the impostor in the rue du Bois.

He suffered a moment of depression as he stared at the wrecked body. He remembered her coming up the path yesterday with her bicycle, a picture of vigorous health. She had been a happy girl, albeit foolish. She had made a simple mistake, and now her life was coming to a ghastly end. She deserved her fate, of course; she had helped terrorists. All the same, it was horrible to contemplate.

He put her out of his mind and went up the stairs. On the ground floor, the night shift telephonists were at their switchboards. Above that, on what had once been a floor of impossibly grand bedrooms, were the Gestapo offices.

Dieter had not seen Weber since the fiasco in the cathedral, and assumed the man was licking his wounds somewhere. However, he had spoken to Weber's deputy and asked for four Gestapo men to be here in plain clothes at three o'clock ready for a day's surveillance. Dieter had also ordered Lieutenant Hesse to be here. Now he pulled aside a blackout blind and looked out. Moonlight illuminated the car park, and he could see Hans walking across the yard, but there was no sign of anyone else.

He went to Weber's office and was surprised to find him there alone, behind his desk, pretending to work on some papers by the light of a green-shaded lamp. 'Where are the men I asked for?' Dieter said.

Weber stood up. 'You pulled a gun on me yesterday,' he said. 'What the devil do you mean by threatening an officer?'

Dieter had not expected this. Weber was being aggressive about an incident in which he had made a fool of himself. Was it possible that he did not understand what a dreadful mistake he had made? 'It was your own damn fault, you idiot,' Dieter said in exasperation. 'I didn't want that man arrested.'

'You could be court-martialled for what you did.'

Dieter was about to ridicule the idea, then he stopped himself. It was true, he realized. He had simply done what was necessary to rescue the situation; but it was not impossible, in the bureaucratic Third Reich, for an officer to be arraigned for using his initiative. His heart sank, and he had to feign confidence. 'Go ahead, report me, I think I can justify myself in front of a tribunal.'

'You actually fired your gun!'

Dieter could not resist saying: 'I suppose that's something you haven't often witnessed, in your military career.'

Weber flushed. He had never seen action. 'Guns should be used against the enemy, not fellow officers.'

'I fired into the air. I'm sorry if I frightened you. You were in the process of ruining a first-class counter-intelligence coup. Don't you think a military court would take that into account? What orders were *you* following? You were the one who showed lack of discipline.'

'I arrested a British terrorist spy.'

'And what's the point of that? He's just one. They have plenty more. But, left to go free, he will lead us to others – perhaps many others. Your insubordination would have destroyed that chance. Fortunately for you, I saved you from a ghastly error.'

Weber looked sly. 'Certain people in authority would find it highly suspicious that you're so keen to free an Allied agent.'

Dieter sighed. 'Don't be stupid. I'm not some wretched Jewish shopkeeper, to be frightened by the threat of malicious gossip. You can't pretend I'm a traitor, no one will believe you. Now, where are my men?'

'The spy must be arrested immediately.'

'No, he mustn't, and if you try I'll shoot you. Where are the men?'

'I refuse to assign much-needed men to such an irresponsible task.'

'You *refuse*?'

'Yes.'

Dieter stared at him. He had not thought Weber brave enough or foolish enough to do this. 'What do you imagine will happen to you when the Field Marshal hears about this?'

Weber looked scared but defiant. 'I am not in the army,' he said. 'This is the Gestapo.'

Unfortunately, he was right, Dieter thought despondently. It was all very well for Walter Goedel to order Dieter to use Gestapo personnel instead of taking much-needed fighting troops from the coast, but the Gestapo were not obliged to take orders from Dieter. The name of Rommel had frightened Weber for a while, but the effect had worn off.

And now Dieter was left with no staff but Lieutenant Hesse. Could he and Hans manage the shadowing of Helicopter without assistance? It would be difficult, but there was no alternative.

He tried one more threat. 'Are you sure you're willing to bear the consequences of this refusal,

Willi? You're going to get into the most dreadful trouble.'

'On the contrary, I think it is you who are in trouble.'

Dieter shook his head in despair. There was no more to be said. He had already spent too much time arguing with this idiot. He went out.

He met Hans in the hall and explained the situation. They went to the back of the chateau, where the engineering section was housed in the former servants' quarters. Last night Hans had arranged to borrow a PTT van and a moped, the kind of motorized bicycle whose small engine was started by pedalling.

Dieter wondered whether Weber might have found out about the vehicles and ordered the engineers not to lend them. He hoped not: dawn was due in half an hour, and he did not have time for more arguments. But there was no trouble. Dieter and Hans put on overalls and drove away, with the moped in the back of the van.

They went to Reims and drove along the rue du Bois. They parked around the corner and Hans walked back, in the faint light of dawn, and put the envelope containing the photo of Flick into the letterbox. Helicopter's bedroom was at the back, so there was no serious risk that he might see Hans, and recognize him later.

The sun was rising when they arrived outside Michel Clairet's house in the centre of town. Hans parked a hundred metres down the road and opened a PTT manhole. He pretended to be working while watching the house. It was a busy street with numerous parked vehicles, so the van was not conspicuous.

Dieter stayed in the van, keeping out of sight, brooding over the row with Weber. The man was stupid, but he had a point. Dieter was taking a dangerous risk. Helicopter could give him the slip and disappear. Then Dieter would have lost the thread. The safe and easy course would be to torture Helicopter. Though letting him go was risky, it promised rich rewards. If things went right, Helicopter could be solid gold. When Dieter thought of the triumph that hung just beyond his grasp, he lusted for it with a passion that made his pulse race.

On the other hand, if things went wrong, Weber would make the most of it. He would tell everyone how he had opposed Dieter's risky plan. But Dieter would not allow himself to worry about such bureaucratic point-scoring. Men such as Weber, who played those games, were the most contemptible people on earth.

The town came slowly to life. First to appear were the women walking to the bakery opposite Michel's house. The shop was closed, but they stood patiently outside, waiting and talking. Bread was rationed, but Dieter guessed it sometimes ran out anyway, so dutiful housewives shopped early to make sure they got their share. When eventually the doors opened, they all tried to get in at once – unlike German housewives, who would have formed an orderly queue, Dieter thought with a feeling of superiority. When he saw them come out with their loaves, he wished he had eaten some breakfast.

After that, the working men appeared in their boots and berets, each carrying a bag or cheap fibre case containing his lunch. The children were just beginning to set out for school when Helicopter appeared, pedalling the bicycle that had belonged to Marie. Dieter sat upright. In the bicycle's basket was a rectangular object covered with a rag: the suitcase radio, Dieter guessed.

Hans put his head up out of the manhole and watched.

Helicopter went to Michel's door and knocked. There was no reply, of course. He stood on the step for a while, then looked in at the windows, then walked up and down the street looking for a back entrance. There was none, Dieter knew.

Dieter had suggested to Helicopter what to do next. 'Go to Chez Régis, the bar along the street. Order coffee and rolls, and wait.' Dieter's hope was that the Resistance might be watching Michel's house, alert for an emissary from London. He did not expect full-time surveillance, but perhaps a sympathetic neighbour might have agreed to keep an eye on the place. Helicopter's evident guilelessness would reassure such a watcher. Anyone could tell, just by the way he walked around, that he was not a Gestapo man or agent of the Milice, the French security police. Dieter felt sure that somehow the Resistance would be alerted, and before too long someone would show up and speak to Helicopter – and *that* person might lead Dieter to the heart of the Resistance.

A minute later Helicopter did as Dieter had

suggested. He wheeled his bicycle along the street to the bar and sat at a pavement table, apparently enjoying the sunshine. He got a cup of coffee. It had to be ersatz, made with roasted grain, but he drank it with apparent relish.

After twenty minutes or so he got another coffee and a newspaper from inside. He began to read the paper thoroughly. He had a patient air, as if he were prepared to wait all day. That was good.

The morning wore on. Dieter began to wonder whether this was going to work. Maybe the Bollinger circuit had been so decimated by the slaughter at Sainte-Cécile that it was no longer operational, and there was no one left to perform even the most essential tasks. It would be a profound disappointment if Helicopter did not lead him to other terrorists. And it would please Weber no end.

The time approached when Helicopter would have to order lunch to justify continuing to use the table. A waiter came out and spoke to him, then brought him a pastis. That, too, would be ersatz, made with a synthetic substitute for aniseed, but all the same Dieter licked his lips: he would have liked a drink.

Another customer sat at the table next to Helicopter's. There were five tables, and it would have been natural to take one farther away. Dieter's hopes rose. The newcomer was a long-limbed man in his thirties. He wore a blue chambray shirt and navy canvas trousers, but to Dieter's intuition he did not have the air of a working man. He was something else, perhaps an artist who affected a proletarian look. He sat back in his chair and crossed his legs, resting his right ankle on his left knee, and the pose struck Dieter as familiar. Had he seen this man before?

The waiter came out and the customer ordered something. For a minute or so nothing happened. Was the man covertly studying Helicopter? Or just waiting for his drink? The waiter brought a glass of pale beer on a tray. The man took a long pull and wiped his mouth with a satisfied air. Dieter began to think gloomily that he was just a man with a thirst. But at the same time he felt he had seen that mouth-wiping gesture before.

Then the newcomer spoke to Helicopter.

Dieter tensed. Could this be what he had been waiting for?

They exchanged a few casual words. Even at this distance, Dieter sensed that the newcomer had an engaging personality: Helicopter was smiling and talking with enthusiasm. After a few moments Helicopter pointed to Michel's house, and Dieter guessed he was asking where the owner might be found. The other man gave a typical French shrug, and Dieter could imagine him saying: 'Me, I don't know.' But Helicopter seemed to persist.

The newcomer drained his beer glass, and Dieter had a flash of recollection. He suddenly knew exactly who this man was, and the realization so startled him that he jumped in his seat. He had seen the man in the square at Sainte-Cécile, at another café table, sitting with Flick Clairet, just before the skirmish – for this was her husband, Michel himself.

'Yes!' Dieter said, and he thumped the dashboard

with his fist in satisfaction. His strategy had been proved right – Helicopter had led him to the heart of the local Resistance.

But he had not been expecting this degree of success. He had thought a messenger might come, and the messenger might take Helicopter – and Dieter – to Michel. Now Dieter had a dilemma. Michel was a very big prize. Should Dieter arrest him right away? Or follow him, in the hope of catching even bigger fish?

Hans replaced the manhole cover and got into the van. 'Contact, sir?'

'Yes.'

'What next?'

Dieter did not know what to do next – arrest Michel, or follow him?

Michel stood up, and Helicopter did the same.

Dieter decided to follow them.

'What shall I do?' Hans said anxiously.

'Get out the bike, quick.'

Hans opened the back doors of the van and took out the moped.

The two men put money on the café tables and moved away. Dieter saw that Michel walked with a limp, and recalled that he had taken a bullet during the skirmish.

He said to Hans: 'You follow them, I'll follow you.' He started the engine of the van.

Hans climbed on the moped and starting pedalling, which fired the engine. He drove slowly along the street, keeping a hundred metres behind his quarry. Dieter followed Hans.

Michel and Helicopter turned a corner. Following a minute later, Dieter saw that they had stopped to look in a shop window. It was a pharmacy. They were not shopping for medicines, of course: this was a precaution against surveillance. As Dieter drove by, they turned and headed back the way they had come. They would be watching for a vehicle that made a U-turn, so Dieter could not pursue them. However, he saw Hans pull behind a truck and turn back, remaining on the far side of the street but keeping the two men in sight.

Dieter went around the block and caught up with them again. Michel and Helicopter were approaching the railway station, with Hans still following.

Dieter asked himself whether they knew they were being followed. The trick at the pharmacy might indicate that they were suspicious. He did not think they had noticed the PTT van, for he had been out of their sight most of the time, but they could have spotted the moped. Most likely, Dieter thought, the reversal of direction was a precaution taken routinely by Michel, who was presumably an experienced undercover operator.

The two men crossed the gardens in front of the station. There were no flowers in the beds, but a few trees were blossoming in defiance of the war. The station was a solidly classical building with pilasters and pediments, heavyweight and over-decorated, no doubt like the nineteenth-century businessmen who had built it.

What would Dieter do if Michel and Helicopter caught a train? It was too risky for Dieter to get on the same train. Helicopter would certainly recognize him, and it was even possible that Michel might remember him from the square at Sainte-Cécile. No, Hans would have to board the train, and Dieter would follow by road.

They entered the station through one of three classical arches. Hans left his moped and followed them inside. Dieter pulled up and did the same. If the two men went to the booking office, he would tell Hans to stand behind them in the queue and buy a ticket to the same destination.

They were not at the ticket window. Dieter entered the station just in time to see Hans go down a flight of steps to the tunnel beneath the lines that connected the platforms. Perhaps Michel had bought tickets in advance, Dieter thought. That was not a problem. Hans would just get on the train without a ticket.

On either side of the tunnel, steps led up to the platforms. Dieter followed Hans past all the platform entrances. Sensing danger, he quickened his pace as he mounted the stairs to the station's rear entrance. He caught up with Hans and they emerged together into the rue de Courcelles.

Several of the buildings had been bombed recently, but cars were parked on those stretches of the road that were clear of rubble. Dieter scanned the street, fear leaping in his chest. A hundred metres away, Michel and Helicopter were jumping into a black car. Dieter and Hans would never catch them. Dieter put his hand on his gun, but the range was too great for a pistol. The car pulled away. It was a black Renault Monaquatre, one of the commonest cars in France. Dieter could not read its licence plate. It tore off along the street and turned a corner.

Dieter cursed. It was a simple ploy, but infallible. By entering the tunnel, they had forced their pursuers to abandon their vehicles; then they had a car waiting at the other side, enabling them to escape. They might not even have detected their shadows: like the change of direction outside the pharmacy, the tunnel trick had probably been a routine precaution.

Dieter sunk into gloom. He had gambled and lost. Weber would be overjoyed.

'What do we do now?' said Hans.

'Go back to Sainte-Cécile.'

They returned to the van, put the moped into the back, and drove to headquarters.

Dieter had just one ray of hope. He knew Helicopter's times for radio contact, and the frequencies assigned to him. That information might yet be used to recapture him. The Gestapo had a sophisticated system, developed and refined throughout the war, for detecting illicit broadcasts and following them to their source. Many Allied agents had been captured that way. As British training improved, so the wireless operators had adopted better security precautions, always broadcasting from a different location, never staying on air longer than fifteen minutes; but careless ones could still be caught.

Would the British suspect that Helicopter had been found out? Helicopter would by now be giving Michel a full account of his adventures. Michel would question him closely about the arrest in the cathedral and subsequent escape. He would be particularly interested in the newcomer codenamed Charenton. However, he would have no reason to suspect that Mademoiselle Lemas was not who she claimed to be. Michel had never met her, so he would not be alerted even if Helicopter happened to mention that she was an attractive young redhead rather than a middle-aged spinster. And Helicopter had no idea that his one-time pad and his silk handkerchief had been meticulously copied out by Stéphanie, or that his frequencies had been noted – from the yellow wax crayon marks on the dials – by Dieter.

Perhaps, Dieter began to think, all was not yet lost.

When they got back to the chateau, Dieter ran into Weber in the hallway. Weber looked hard at him and said: 'Have you lost him?'

Jackals can smell blood, Dieter thought. 'Yes,' he admitted. It was beneath his dignity to lie to Weber.

'Hah!' Weber was triumphant. 'You should leave such work to the experts.'

'Very well, then, I shall,' Dieter said. Weber looked surprised. Dieter went on: 'He's due to broadcast to England at eight o'clock tonight. Here's your chance to prove your expertise. Show how good you are. Track him down.'

TWENTY-THREE

The Fisherman's Rest was a big pub that stood on the estuary shore like a fort, with chimneys for gun turrets and smoked-glass windows instead of observation slits. A fading sign in its front garden warned customers to stay off the beach, which had been mined back in 1940 in anticipation of a German invasion.

Since SOE had moved into the neighbourhood, the pub had been busy every night; its lights blazing behind the blackout curtains, its piano loud, its bars crowded and spilling over into the garden on warm summer evenings. The singing was raucous, the drinking was heavy, and the canoodling was kept only just within the bounds of decency. An atmosphere of abandon prevailed, for everyone knew that some of the youngsters who were laughing uproariously at the bar tonight would embark tomorrow on missions from which they would never return.

Flick and Paul took their team to the pub at the end of their two-day training course. The girls dressed up for the outing. Maude was prettier than ever in a pink summer frock. Ruby would never be pretty, but she looked sultry in a black cocktail dress she had borrowed from somewhere. Lady Denise had an oyster-coloured silk dress that looked as if it had cost a fortune, though it did nothing for her bony figure. Greta wore one of her stage outfits, an evening gown and red shoes. Even Diana was wearing a smart skirt instead of her usual country corduroys and, to Flick's astonishment, had put on a smear of lipstick.

The team had been given the codename Jackdaws. They were going to parachute in near Reims, and Flick remembered the legend of the Jackdaw of Reims, the bird that stole the bishop's ring. 'The monks couldn't figure out who had taken it, so the bishop cursed the unknown thief,' she explained to Paul, as they both sipped Scotch, hers with water and his on the rocks. 'Next thing they knew, the jackdaw appeared all bedraggled, and they realized he was suffering from the effects of the curse, and must be the culprit. I learned the whole thing at school:

'The day was gone
The night came on
The monks and the friars, they searched till dawn
When the sacristan saw
On crumpled claw
Come limping a poor little lame jackdaw
No longer gay
As on yesterday
His feathers all seemed to be turned the wrong way
His pinions drooped, he could hardly stand
His head was as bald as the palm of your hand
His eye so dim

So wasted each limb
That, heedless of grammar, they all cried: 'That's him!'

'Sure enough, they found the ring in his nest.'

Paul nodded, smiling. Flick knew he would have nodded and smiled in exactly the same way if she had been speaking Icelandic. He did not care what she said, he just wanted to watch her. She did not have vast experience of men, but she could tell when a man was in love, and Paul was in love with her.

She had got through the day on autopilot. Last night's kisses had shocked and thrilled her. She told herself that she did not want to have an illicit affair, she wanted to win back the love of her faithless husband. But Paul's passion had up-ended her priorities. She asked herself angrily why she should stand in line for Michel's affections when a man such as Paul was ready to throw himself at her feet. She had very nearly let him into her bed – in fact, she wished he had been less of a gentleman, for if he had ignored her refusal, and climbed between the sheets, she might have given in.

At other moments she was ashamed that she had even kissed him. It was frightfully common: all over England, girls were forgetting about husbands and boyfriends on the front line and falling in love with visiting American servicemen. Was she as bad as those empty-headed shop assistants who went to bed with their Yanks just because they talked like movie stars?

Worst of all, her feelings for Paul threatened to distract her from the job. She held in her hands the lives of six people, plus a crucial element in the invasion plan, and she really did not need to be thinking about whether his eyes were hazel or green. He was no matinée idol anyway, with his big chin and his shot-off ear, although there was a certain charm to his face—

'What are you thinking?' he said.

She realized she must have been staring at him. 'Wondering whether we can pull this off,' she lied.

'We can, with a little luck.'

'I've been lucky so far.'

Maude sat herself next to Paul. 'Speaking of luck,' she said, batting her eyelashes, 'can I have one of your cigarettes?'

'Help yourself.' He pushed the Lucky Strike pack along the table.

She put a cigarette between her pink lips and he lit it. Flick glanced across to the bar and caught an irritated look from Diana. Maude and Diana had become great friends, and Diana had never been good at sharing. So why was Maude flirting with Paul? To annoy Diana, perhaps. It was a good thing Paul was not coming to France, Flick thought: he could not help being a disruptive influence in a group of young women.

She looked around the room. Jelly and Percy were playing a gambling game called Spoof, which involved guessing how many coins the other player held in a closed fist. Percy was buying round after round of drinks. This was deliberate. Flick needed to know what the Jackdaws were like under the influence of booze. If any of them became rowdy, indiscreet, or aggressive, she would have to take precautions once they were in the field. She was most worried about Denise, the boastful aristocrat, who even now was sitting in a corner talking animatedly to a man in captain's uniform.

Ruby was drinking steadily, too, but Flick trusted her. She was a curious mixture: she could barely read or write, and had been hopeless in classes on map reading and encryption, but nevertheless she was the brightest and most intuitive of the group. Ruby gave Greta a hard look now and again, and she might have guessed that Greta was a man, but to her credit she had said nothing.

Ruby was sitting at the bar with Jim Cardwell, the firearms instructor, talking to the barmaid but at the same time discreetly stroking the inside of Jim's thigh with a small brown hand. They were having a whirlwind romance. They kept disappearing. During the morning coffee break, the half-hour rest period after lunch, the afternoon tea time, or at any opportunity, they would sneak off for a few minutes. Jim looked as if he had jumped out of a plane and had not yet opened his parachute. His face wore a permanent expression of bemused delight. Ruby was no beauty, with her hooked nose and turned-up chin, but she was obviously a sex bomb, and Jim was reeling from the explosion. Flick almost felt jealous. Not that Jim was her type – all the men she had ever fallen for were intellectuals, or at least very bright – but she envied Ruby's lustful happiness.

Greta was leaning on the piano with some pink cocktail in her hand, talking to three men who looked to be local residents rather than Finishing School types. It seemed they had got over the shock of her German accent – no doubt she had told the story of her Liverpudlian father – and now she held them enthralled with tales about Hamburg nightclubs. Flick could see they had no suspicions about Greta's gender: they were treating her like an exotic but attractive woman, buying her drinks and lighting her cigarettes and laughing in a pleased way when she touched them.

As Flick watched, one of the men sat at the piano, played some chords, and looked up at Greta expectantly. The bar went quiet, and Greta launched into 'Kitchen Man':

> 'How that boy can open clams
> No one else can touch my hams'

The audience quickly realized that every line was a sexual innuendo, and the laughter was uproarious. When Greta finished, she kissed the pianist on the lips, and he looked thrilled.

Maude left Paul and returned to Diana at the bar. The captain who had been talking to Denise now came over and said to Paul: 'She told me everything, sir.'

Flick nodded, disappointed but not surprised.

Paul asked him: 'What did she say?'

'That she's going in tomorrow night to blow up a railway tunnel at Marles, near Reims.'

It was the cover story, but Denise thought it was the truth, and she had revealed it to a stranger. Flick was furious.

'Thank you,' Paul said.

'I'm sorry.' The captain shrugged.

Flick said: 'Better to find out now than later.'

'Do you want to tell her, sir, or shall I deal with it?'

'I'll talk to her first,' Paul replied. 'Just wait outside for her, if you wouldn't mind.'

'Yes, sir.'

The captain left the pub, and Paul beckoned Denise.

'He left suddenly,' Denise said. 'Rather bad behaviour, I thought.' She obviously felt slighted. 'He's an explosives instructor.'

'No, he's not,' Paul said. 'He's a policeman.'

'What do you mean?' Denise was mystified. 'He's wearing a captain's uniform and he told me—'

'He told you lies,' Paul said. 'His job is to catch people who blab to strangers. And he caught you.'

Denise's jaw dropped, then she recovered her composure and became indignant. 'So it was a trick? You tried to trap me?'

'I succeeded, unfortunately,' Paul said. 'You told him everything.'

Realizing she was found out, Denise tried to make light of it. 'What's my punishment? A hundred lines and no playtime?'

Flick wanted to slap her face. Denise's boasting could have endangered the lives of the whole team.

Paul said coldly: 'There's no punishment, as such.'

'Oh. Thank you so much.'

'But you're off the team. You won't be coming with us. You'll be leaving tonight, with the captain.'

'I shall feel rather foolish going back to my old job at Hendon.'

Paul shook his head. 'He's not taking you to Hendon.'

'Why not?'

'You know too much. You can't be allowed to walk around free.'

Denise began to look worried. 'What are you going to do to me?'

'You'll be posted to some place where you can't do any damage. I believe it's usually an isolated base in Scotland where their main function is to file regimental accounts.'

'That's as bad as prison!'

Paul reflected for a moment, then nodded. 'Almost.'

'For how long?' Denise said in dismay.

'Who knows? Until the war is over, probably.'

'You absolute rotter,' Denise said furiously. 'I wish I'd never met you.'

'You may leave now,' said Paul. 'And be grateful I caught you. Otherwise it might have been the Gestapo.'

Denise stalked out.

Paul said: 'I hope that wasn't unnecessarily cruel.'

Flick did not think so. The silly cow deserved a lot worse. However, she wanted to make a good impression on Paul, so she said: 'No point in crushing her. Some people just aren't suited to this work. It's not her fault.'

Paul smiled. 'You're a rotten liar,' he said. 'You think I was too easy on her, don't you?'

'I think crucifixion would be too easy on her,' Flick said angrily; but Paul laughed, and his humour softened her wrath until she had to smile. 'I can't pull the wool over your eyes, can I?'

'I hope not.' He became serious again. 'It's fortunate that we had one team member more than we really needed. We could afford to lose Denise.'

'But now we're down to the bare minimum.' Flick stood up wearily. 'We'd better get the rest to bed. This will be their last decent night's sleep for a while.'

Paul looked around the room. 'I don't see Diana and Maude.'

'They must have stepped out for a breath of air. I'll find them if you'll round up the rest.' Paul nodded agreement, and Flick went outside.

There was no sign of the two girls. She paused for a moment to look at the evening light glowing on the calm water of the estuary. Then she walked around the side of the pub to the car park. A tan-coloured army Austin was pulling away, and Flick glimpsed Denise in the back, crying.

There was no sign of Diana or Maude. Frowning, puzzled, Flick crossed the tarmac and went to the back of the pub. She came to a yard with old barrels and stacked crates. Across the yard was a small outbuilding with a wooden door that stood open. She went in.

At first she could see nothing in the gloom, but she knew she was not alone, for she could hear breathing. Instinct told her to remain silent and still. Her eyes adjusted to the dim light. She was in a tool shed, with neat rows of spanners and shovels on hooks, and a big lawn-mower in the middle of the floor. Diana and Maude were in a far corner.

Maude was leaning against the wall and Diana was kissing her. Flick's jaw dropped. Diana's blouse was undone, revealing a large, severely practical brassière. Maude's pink gingham skirt was rucked up around her waist, and Flick could see that she was wearing matching pink panties. As the picture became clear, she saw that Diana's hand was thrust down the front of the panties.

Flick stood there for a moment, frozen with shock. Maude saw her and met her eye. 'Have you had a good look?' she said saucily. 'Or do you want to take a photo?'

Diana jumped, snatching her hand away and stepping back from Maude. She turned around, and a look of horror came over her face. 'Oh, my *God*,' she said. She pulled the front of her blouse together with one hand and covered her mouth with the other in a gesture of shame.

Flick stammered: 'I – I – I just came to say we're leaving.' Then she turned around and stumbled out.

TWENTY-FOUR

Wireless operators were not quite invisible. They lived in a spirit world where their ghostly shapes could be dimly seen. Peering into the gloom, searching for them, were the men of the Gestapo's radio detection team, housed in a cavernous, darkened hall in Paris. Dieter had visited the place. Three hundred round oscilloscope screens flickered with a greenish light. Radio broadcasts appeared as vertical lines on the monitors, the position of the line showing the frequency of the transmission, the height indicating the strength of the signal. The screens were tended, day and night, by silent, watchful operators, who made him think of angels observing the sins of humankind.

The operators knew the regular stations, either German-controlled or foreign-based, and were able to spot a rogue instantly. As soon as this happened, the operator would pick up a telephone at his desk and call three tracking stations: two in southern Germany, at Augsburg and Nuremberg, and one in Brittany, at Brest. He would give them the frequency of the rogue broadcast. The tracking stations were equipped with goniometers, apparatus for measuring angles, and each could say within seconds which direction the broadcast was coming from. They would send this information back to Paris, where the operator would draw three lines on a huge wall map. The lines intersected where the suspect radio was located. The operator then telephoned the Gestapo office nearest to the location. The local Gestapo had cars waiting in readiness, equipped with their own detection apparatus.

Dieter was now sitting in such a car, a long black Citroën parked on the outskirts of Reims. With him were three Gestapo men experienced in wireless detection. Tonight the help of the Paris centre was not required: Dieter already knew the frequency Helicopter would use, and he assumed Helicopter would broadcast from somewhere in the city (because it was too difficult for a wireless operator to lose himself in the countryside). The car's receiver was tuned to Helicopter's frequency. It measured the strength, as well as the direction, of the broadcast, and Dieter would know he was getting nearer to the transmitter when the needle rose on the dial.

In addition, the Gestapo man sitting next to Dieter wore a receiver and an aerial concealed beneath his raincoat. On his wrist was a meter like a watch that showed the strength of the signal. When the search narrowed down to a particular street, city block, or building, the walker would take over.

The Gestapo man in the front seat held on his lap a sledgehammer, for breaking doors down.

Dieter had been hunting once. He did not much like country pursuits, preferring the more refined pleasures of city life, but he was a good shot. Now he was reminded of that, as he waited for Helicopter to begin sending his coded report home to England. This was like lying in the hide in the early dawn, tense with anticipation, impatient for the deer to start moving, savouring the thrill of anticipation.

The Resistance were not deer but foxes, Dieter thought, skulking in their holes, coming out to cause carnage in the chicken house, then going to earth again. He was mortified to have lost Helicopter. He was so keen to recapture the man that he hardly minded having to rely on the help of Willi Weber. He just wanted to kill the fox.

It was a fine summer evening. The car was parked at the northern end of the city. Reims was a small town, and Dieter reckoned a car could drive from one side to the other in less than ten minutes.

He checked his watch: one minute past eight. Helicopter was late coming on air. Perhaps he would not broadcast tonight . . . but that was unlikely. Today Helicopter had met up with Michel. As soon as possible, he would want to report his success to his superiors, and tell them just how much was left of the Bollinger circuit.

Michel had phoned the house in the rue du Bois two hours ago. Dieter had been there. It was a tense moment. Stéphanie had answered, in her imitation of Mademoiselle Lemas's voice. Michel had given his codename, and asked whether 'Bourgeoise' remembered him – a question that reassured Stéphanie, because it indicated that Michel did not know Mademoiselle Lemas very well and therefore would not realize this was an impersonator.

He had asked her about her new recruit, codenamed Charenton. 'He's my cousin,' Stéphanie had said gruffly. 'I've known him since we were children, I would trust him with my life.' Michel had told her she had no right to recruit people without at least discussing it with him, but he had appeared to believe her story, and Dieter had kissed Stéphanie and told her she was a good enough actor to join the Comédie Française.

All the same, Helicopter would know that the Gestapo would be listening and trying to find him. That was a risk he had to run: if he sent no messages home he was of no use. He would stay on air only for the minimum length of time. If he had a lot of information to send, he would break it into two or more messages, and send them from different locations. Dieter's only hope was that he would be tempted to stay on the air just a little too long.

The minutes ticked by. There was silence in the car. The men smoked nervously. Then, at five past eight, the receiver beeped.

By prearrangement, the driver set off immediately, driving south.

The signal grew stronger, but slowly, making Dieter worry that they were not heading directly for the source.

Sure enough, as they passed the cathedral in the centre of town, the needle fell back.

In the passenger seat, a Gestapo man talked into a

short-wave radio. He was consulting with someone in a radio-detection truck a mile away. After a moment he said: 'North-west quarter.'

The driver immediately turned west, and the signal began to strengthen.

'Got you,' Dieter breathed.

But five minutes had elapsed.

The car raced west, and the signal strengthened, as Helicopter continued to tap on the Morse key of his suitcase radio in his hiding-place – a bathroom, an attic, a warehouse – somewhere in the north-west of the city. Back at the chateau of Sainte-Cécile, a German radio operator had tuned to the same frequency and was taking down the coded message. It was also being registered on a wire recorder. Later, Dieter would decrypt it, using the one-time pad copied by Stéphanie. But the message was not as important as the messenger.

They entered a neighbourhood of large old houses, mostly decrepit and subdivided into small apartments and bedsitting rooms for students and nurses. The signal grew louder then suddenly began to fade. 'Overshoot, overshoot!' said the Gestapo man in the front passenger seat. The driver reversed the car, then braked.

Ten minutes had passed.

Dieter and the three Gestapo men sprang out. The one with the portable detection unit under his raincoat walked rapidly along the pavement, consulting his wrist dial constantly, and the others followed. He went a hundred metres then suddenly turned back. He stopped and pointed to a house. 'That one,' he said. 'But the transmission has ended.'

Dieter noticed that there were no curtains in the windows. The Resistance liked to use derelict houses for their transmissions.

The Gestapo man carrying the sledgehammer broke the door down with two blows. They all rushed in.

The floors were bare and the place had a musty smell. Dieter threw open a door and looked into an empty room.

Dieter opened the door of the back room. He crossed the vacant room in three strides and looked into an abandoned kitchen.

He ran up the stairs. On the next floor was a window overlooking a long back garden. Dieter glanced out – and saw Helicopter and Michel running across the grass. Michel was limping, Helicopter was carrying his little suitcase. Dieter swore. They must have escaped through a back door as the Gestapo were breaking down the front. Dieter turned and yelled: 'Back garden!' The Gestapo men ran and he followed.

As he reached the garden, he saw Michel and Helicopter scrambling over the back fence into the grounds of another house. He joined in the chase, but the fugitives had a long lead. With the three Gestapo men, he climbed the fence and ran through the second garden.

They reached the next street just in time to see a black Renault Monaquatre disappearing around the corner.

'Hell,' Dieter said. For the second time in a day, Helicopter had slipped through his grasp.

TWENTY-FIVE

When they got back to the house, Flick made cocoa for the team. It was not regular military practice for officers to make cocoa for their troops, but in Flick's opinion that only showed how little the army knew about leadership.

Paul stood in the kitchen watching her as she waited for the kettle to boil. She felt his eyes on her like a caress. She knew what he was going to say, and she had prepared her reply. It would have been easy to fall in love with Paul, but she was not going to betray the husband who was risking his life fighting the Nazis in occupied France.

However, his question surprised her. 'What will you do after the war?'

'I'm looking forward to being bored,' she said.

He laughed. 'You've had enough excitement.'

'Too much.' She thought for a moment. 'I still want to be a teacher. I'd like to share my love of French culture with young people. Educate them about French literature and painting, and also about less highbrow things like cooking and fashion.'

'So you'll become a don?'

'Finish my doctorate, get a job at a university, be

condescended to by narrow-minded old male professors. Maybe write a guidebook to France, or even a cookbook.'

'Sounds tame, after this.'

'It's important, though. The more young people know about foreigners, the less likely they are to be as stupid as we were, and go to war with their neighbours.'

'I wonder if that's right.'

'What about you? What's your plan for after the war?'

'Oh, mine is real simple. I want to marry you and take you to Paris for a honeymoon. Then we'll settle down and have children.'

She stared at him. 'Were you thinking of asking my consent?' she said indignantly.

He was quite solemn. 'I haven't thought of anything else for days.'

'I already have a husband.'

'But you don't love him.'

'You have no right to say that!'

'I know, but I can't help it.'

'Why did I used to think you were a smooth talker?'

'Usually I am. That kettle's boiling.'

She took the kettle off the hob and poured boiling water over the cocoa mixture in a big stoneware jug. 'Put some mugs on a tray,' she told Paul. 'A little housework might cure you of dreams of domesticity.'

He complied. 'You can't put me off by being bossy,' he said. 'I kind of like it.'

She added milk and sugar to the cocoa and poured

it into the mugs he had laid out. 'In that case, carry that tray into the living room.'

'Right away, boss.'

When they entered the living room they found Jelly and Greta having a row, standing face to face in the middle of the room while the others looked on, half amused and half horrified.

Jelly was saying: 'You weren't using it!'

'I was resting my feet on it,' Greta replied.

'There aren't enough chairs.' Jelly was holding a small stuffed pouffe, and Flick guessed she had snatched it away from Greta rudely.

Flick said: 'Ladies, please!'

They ignored her. Greta said: 'You only had to ask, sweetheart.'

'I don't have to ask permission from foreigners in my own country.'

'I'm not a foreigner, you fat bitch.'

'Oh!' Jelly was so stung by the insult that she reached out and pulled Greta's hair. Greta's brunette wig came off in her hand.

With her head of close-cropped dark hair exposed, Greta suddenly looked unmistakably like a man. Percy and Paul were in on the secret, and Ruby had guessed, but Maude and Diana were shocked rigid. Diana said: 'Good God!' and Maude gave a little scream of fright.

Jelly was the first to recover her wits. 'A pervert!' she said triumphantly. 'Oh, my gordon, it's a foreign pervert!'

Greta was in tears. 'You bloody fucking Nazi,' she sobbed.

'I bet she's a spy!' Jelly said.

Flick said: 'Shut up, Jelly. She's not a spy. I knew she was a man.'

'You knew!'

'So did Paul. So did Percy.'

Jelly looked at Percy, who nodded solemnly.

Greta turned to leave, but Flick caught her arm. 'Don't go,' she said. 'Please. Sit down.'

Greta sat down.

'Jelly, give me the damn wig.'

Jelly handed it to Flick.

Flick stood in front of Greta and put the wig back on. Ruby, quickly understanding what Flick was trying to do, lifted the mirror from over the mantelpiece and held it in front of Greta, who studied her reflection while she adjusted the wig and blotted her tears with a handkerchief.

'Now listen to me, all of you,' said Flick. 'Greta is an engineer, and we can't accomplish our mission without an engineer. We have a much better chance of survival in occupied territory as an all-woman team. The upshot is, we need Greta and we need her to be a woman. So get used to it.'

Jelly gave a contemptuous grunt.

'There's something else I ought to explain,' Flick said. She looked hard at Jelly. 'You may have noticed that Denise is no longer with us. A little test was set for her tonight, and she failed it. She's off the team. Unfortunately, she's learned some secrets in the last two days, and she can't be allowed to return to her old posting. So she's gone to a remote base in Scotland, where she'll stay, probably for the rest of the war, with no leave.'

Jelly said: 'You can't do that!'

'Of course I can, you idiot,' Flick said impatiently. 'There's a war on, remember? And what I've done to Denise, I'll do to anyone who has to be sacked from this team.'

'I never even joined the army!' Jelly protested.

'Yes, you did. You were commissioned as an officer, yesterday, after tea. You all were. And you're getting officer's pay, although you haven't seen any yet. That means you're under military discipline. And you all know too much.'

'So we're prisoners?' Diana said.

'You're in the army,' Flick said. 'It's much the same thing. So drink your cocoa and go to bed.'

They drifted off one by one until only Diana was left. Flick had been expecting this. Seeing the two women in a sexual clinch had been a real shock. She recalled that at school some of the girls had developed crushes on one another, sending loving notes, holding hands, and sometimes even kissing; but as far as she knew it had not gone any farther. At some point she and Diana had practised French kissing on one another, so that they would know what to do when they got boyfriends, and now Flick guessed those kisses had meant more to Diana than they had to her. But she had never known a grown woman who desired other women. Theoretically, she was aware that they existed, the female equivalents of her brother Mark and of Greta, but she had never really imagined them . . . well, feeling each other up in a garden shed.

Did it matter? Not in everyday life. Mark and his kind were happy, or at least they were when people left them alone. But would Diana's relationship with Maude affect the mission? Not necessarily. Flick herself worked with her husband in the Resistance, after all. This was not quite the same, admittedly. A passionate new romance might prove a distraction.

Flick could try to keep the two lovers separate – but that might make Diana even more insubordinate. And the affair could just as easily be an inspiration. Flick had been trying desperately to get the women to work together as a team, and this might help. She had decided to leave well enough alone. But Diana wanted to talk.

'It's not what it seems, really it isn't,' Diana said, without preamble. 'Christ, you've got to believe me. It was just a stupid thing, a joke—'

'Would you like more cocoa?' Flick said. 'I think there's some left in the jug.'

Diana stared at her, nonplussed. After a moment she said: 'How can you talk about cocoa?'

'I just want you to calm down and realize that the world is not going to come to an end simply because you kissed Maude. You kissed me, once – remember?'

'I knew you'd bring that up. But that was just kids' stuff. With Maude, it wasn't just a kiss.' Diana sat down. Her proud face crumpled and she began to cry. 'You know it was more than that, you could see, oh, God, the things I did. What on earth did you think?'

Flick chose her words carefully. 'I thought the two of you looked very sweet.'

'Sweet?' Diana was incredulous. 'You weren't disgusted?'

'Certainly not. Maude is a pretty girl, and you appear to have fallen in love with her.'

'That's exactly what happened.'

'So stop being ashamed.'

'How can I not be ashamed? I'm queer!'

'I wouldn't look at it that way, if I were you. You ought to be discreet, to avoid offending narrow-minded people such as Jelly, but there's no need for shame.'

'Will I always be like this?'

Flick considered. The answer was probably yes, but she did not want to be brutal. 'Look,' she said, 'I think some people, like Maude, just love to be loved, and they can be made happy by a man or a woman.' In truth, Maude was shallow, selfish and tarty, but Flick suppressed that thought firmly. 'Others are more inflexible,' she went on. 'You should keep an open mind.'

'I suppose that's the end of the mission for me and Maude.'

'It most certainly is not.'

'You'll still take us?'

'I still need you. And I don't see why this should make any difference.'

Diana took out a handkerchief and blew her nose. Flick got up and went to the window, giving her time to recover her composure. After a minute Diana spoke in a calmer voice. 'You're frightfully kind,' she said with a touch of her old hauteur.

'Go to bed,' Flick said.

Diana got up obediently.

'And if I were you . . .'

'What?'

'I'd go to bed with Maude.'

Diana looked shocked.

Flick shrugged. 'It may be your last chance,' she said.

'Thank you,' Diana whispered. She stepped towards Flick and spread her arms, as if to hug her; then she stopped. 'You may not want me to kiss you,' she said.

'Don't be silly,' Flick said, and embraced her.

'Goodnight,' said Diana. She left the room.

Flick turned and looked out at the garden. The moon was three-quarters full. In a few days' time it would be full, and the Allies would invade France. A wind was disturbing the new leaves in the forest: the weather was going to change. She hoped there would not be a storm in the English Channel. The entire invasion plan could be ruined by the capricious British climate. She guessed a lot of people were praying for good weather.

She ought to get some sleep. She left the room and climbed the stairs. She thought of what she had said to Diana: *I'd go to bed with Maude. It may be your last chance.* She hesitated outside Paul's door. It was different for Diana – she was single. Flick was married.

But it might be her last chance.

She knocked at the door and stepped inside.

TWENTY-SIX

Sunk in gloom, Dieter returned to the chateau at
Sainte-Cécile in the Citroën with the radio detection
team. He went to the wireless listening room in the
bombproofed basement. Willi Weber was there, looking
angry. The one consolation from tonight's fiasco, Dieter
thought, was that Weber was not able to crow that he
had succeeded where Dieter had failed. But Dieter
could have put up with all the triumphalism Weber
could muster in return for having Helicopter in the
torture chamber.

'You have the message he sent?' Dieter asked.

Weber handed him a carbon copy of the typed
message. 'It has already been sent to the cryptanalysis
office in Berlin.'

Dieter looked at the meaningless strings of letters.
'They won't be able to decode it. He's using a one-time
pad.' He folded the sheet and slipped it into his pocket.

'What can you do with it?' Weber said.

'I have a copy of his code book,' Dieter said. It was a
petty victory, but he felt better.

Weber swallowed. 'The message may tell us where he
is.'

'Yes. He's scheduled to receive a reply at eleven

p.m.' He looked at his watch. It was a few minutes before eleven. 'Let's record that, and I will decrypt the two together.'

Weber left. Dieter waited in the windowless room. On the dot of eleven, a receiver tuned to Helicopter's listening frequency began to chatter with the long-and-short beeps of Morse. An operator wrote the letters down while at the same time a wire recorder ran. When the chattering stopped, the operator pulled a typewriter towards him and typed out what he had on his notepad. He gave Dieter a carbon copy.

The two messages could be everything or nothing, Dieter thought as he got behind the wheel of his own car. The moon was bright as he followed the twisting road through the vineyards to Reims and parked in the rue du Bois. It was good weather for an invasion.

Stéphanie was waiting for him in the kitchen of Mademoiselle Lemas's house. He put the coded messages on the table and took out the copies Stéphanie had made of the pad and the silk handkerchief. He rubbed his eyes and began to decode the first message, the one Helicopter had sent, writing the decrypt on the scratch pad Mademoiselle Lemas had used to make her shopping lists.

Stéphanie brewed a pot of coffee. She looked over his shoulder for a while, asked a couple of questions, then took the second message and began to decode it herself.

Dieter's decrypt gave a concise account of the incident at the cathedral, naming Dieter as Charenton and saying he had been recruited by Bourgeoise

311

(Mademoiselle Lemas) because she was worried about the security of the rendezvous. It said Monet (Michel) had taken the unusual step of phoning Bourgeoise to confirm that Charenton was trustworthy, and he was satisfied.

It listed the codenames of those members of the Bollinger circuit who had not fallen in the battle last Sunday and were still active. There were only four.

It was useful, but it did not tell him where to find the spies.

He drank a cup of coffee while he waited for Stéphanie to finish. She handed him a sheet of paper covered with her flamboyant handwriting.

When he read it, he could hardly believe his luck. It said:

PREPARE RECEIVE GROUP OF SIX NUMBER
PARACHUTISTS CODENAMED JACKDAWS LEADER
LEOPARDESS ARRIVING ELEVEN PIP EMMA
FRIDAY FIRST JUNE CHAMP DE PIERRE.

'My God,' he whispered.

Champ de Pierre was a codename, but Dieter knew what it meant, for Gaston had told him during the very first interrogation. It was a drop zone in a pasture outside Chatelle, a small village five miles from Reims. Dieter now knew exactly where Helicopter and Michel would be tomorrow night, and could pick them up.

He could also capture six more Allied agents as they parachuted to earth.

And one of them was 'Leopardess': Flick Clairet, the

312

woman who knew more than anyone else about the French Resistance, the woman who, under torture, would give him the information he needed to break the back of the Resistance – just in time to stop them aiding the invasion force.

'Jesus Christ Almighty,' Dieter said. 'What a break.'

THE SIXTH DAY:
FRIDAY, 2 JUNE 1944

TWENTY-SEVEN

Paul and Flick were talking.

They lay side by side on his bed. The lights were off, but the moon shone through the window. He was naked, as he had been when she entered the room. He always slept naked. He wore pyjamas only to walk along the corridor to the bathroom.

He had been asleep when she came in, but he had woken fast and leaped out of bed, his unconscious mind assuming that a clandestine visit in the night must mean the Gestapo. He had had his hands around her throat before he realized who it was.

He was astonished, thrilled, and grateful. He had closed the door then kissed her, standing there, for a long time. He was unprepared, and it felt like a dream. He was afraid he might wake up.

She had caressed him, feeling his shoulders and his back and his chest. Her hands were soft but her touch was firm, exploring. 'You have a lot of hair,' she had whispered.

'Like an ape.'

'But not as handsome,' she teased.

He looked at her lips, delighting in the way they moved when she spoke, thinking that in a moment he would touch them with his own, and it would be lovely. He smiled. 'Let's lie down.'

They lay on the bed, facing one another, but she did not take off any clothes, not even her shoes. He found it strangely exciting to be naked with a woman who was fully dressed. He enjoyed it so much that he was in no hurry to move to the next base. He wanted this moment to last for ever.

'Tell me something,' she said, in a lazy, sensual voice.

'What?'

'Anything. I feel I don't know you.'

What was this? He had never had a girl behave like this. She came to his room in the night, she lay on his bed but kept her clothes on, then she questioned him. 'Is that why you came?' he said lightly, watching her face. 'To interrogate me?'

She laughed softly. 'Don't worry, I want to make love to you, but not in a hurry. Tell me about your first lover.'

He stroked her cheek with light fingertips, tracing the curve of her jaw. He did not know what she wanted, where she was going. She had thrown him off balance. 'Can we touch while we talk?'

'Yes.'

He kissed her lips. 'And kiss, too?'

'Yes.'

'Then I think we should talk for just a little while, maybe a year or two.'

'What was her name?'

Flick was not as confident as she pretended to be, he decided. In fact she was nervous, and that was the reason for the questions. If it made her comfortable, he would answer. 'Her name was Linda. We were terribly young – I'm embarrassed at how young we were. The first time I kissed her, she was twelve, and I was fourteen, can you imagine?'

'Of course I can.' She giggled, and for an instant she was a girl again. 'I used to kiss boys when I was twelve.'

'We always had to pretend we were going out with a bunch of friends, and usually we started the evening that way, but pretty soon we would peel off from the crowd and go to a movie or something. We did that for a couple of years before we had real sex.'

'Where was this, in America?'

'Paris. My father was military attaché at the embassy. Linda's parents owned a hotel that catered specially for American visitors. We used to run with a whole crowd of expatriate kids.'

'Where did you make love?'

'In the hotel. We had it easy. There were always empty rooms.'

'What was it like the first time? Did you use any, you know, precautions?'

'She stole one of her father's rubbers.'

Flick's fingertips traced a course down his belly. He closed his eyes. She said: 'Who put it on?'

'She did. It was very exciting. I nearly came right then. And if you're not careful . . .'

She moved her hand to his hip. 'I'd like to have known you when you were sixteen.'

He opened his eyes. He no longer wanted to make this moment last for ever. In fact, he found he was in a great hurry to move on. 'Would you . . .' His mouth was dry, and he swallowed. 'Would you like to take off some clothes?'

'Yes. But speaking of precautions . . .'

'In my billfold. On the bedside table.'

'Good.' She sat upright and unlaced her shoes, throwing them on the floor. She stood up and unbuttoned her blouse. She was tense, he could see, so he said: 'Take your time, we have all night.'

It was a couple of years since Paul had watched a real woman undress. He had been living on a diet of pin-ups, and they always wore elaborate confections of silk and lace, corsets and garter belts and transparent *négligées*. Flick was wearing a loose cotton chemise, not a brassière, and he guessed that the small, neat breasts he could see tantalizingly outlined beneath it did not need support. She dropped her skirt. Her panties were plain white cotton with frills around the legs. Her body was tiny but muscular. She looked like a schoolgirl getting changed for hockey practice, but he found that more exciting than a pin-up.

She lay down again. 'Is that better?' she said.

He stroked her hip, feeling the warm skin, then the soft cotton, then skin again. She was not yet ready, he could tell. He forced himself to be patient and let her set the pace. 'You haven't told me about your first time,' he said.

To his surprise, she blushed. 'It wasn't as nice as yours.'

'In what way?'

'It was a horrible place, a dusty storeroom.'

He felt indignant. What kind of idiot could take a girl as special as Flick and submit her to a furtive quickie in a cupboard? 'How old were you?'

'Twenty-two.'

He had expected her to say seventeen. 'Jeepers. At that age you deserve a comfortable bed.'

'That wasn't it, though.'

She was relaxing again, Paul could tell. He encouraged her to talk some more. 'So what was wrong?'

'Probably that I didn't really want to do it. I was talked into it.'

'Didn't you love the guy?'

'Yes, I did. But I wasn't ready.'

'What was his name?'

'I don't want to tell you.'

Paul guessed it was her husband, Michel, and decided not to question her any more. He kissed her and said: 'May I touch your breasts?'

'You can touch anything you like.'

No one had ever said that to him. He found her openness startling and exciting. He began to explore her body. In his experience, most women closed their eyes at this point, but she kept hers open, studying his face with a mixture of desire and curiosity that inflamed him more. It was as if by watching him she was exploring him, instead of the other way around. His hands discovered the pert shape of her breasts, and his fingertips got to know her shy nipples, learning what they liked. He took off her panties. She had curly hair the colour of honey, lots of it, and under the hair, on the left side, a birthmark like a splash of tea. He bent his head and kissed her there, his lips feeling the crisp brush of her hair, his tongue tasting her moisture.

He sensed her yielding to pleasure. Her nervousness vanished. Her arms and legs spread out in a star shape, slack, abandoned, but her hips strained towards him eagerly. He explored the folds of her sex with slow delight. Her movements became more urgent.

She pushed his head away. Her face was flushed and she was breathing hard. She reached across to the bedside table, opened his billfold, and found the rubbers, three of them in a small paper packet. She ripped the pack with fumbling fingers, took one out and put it on him. Then she straddled him as he lay on his back. She bent to kiss him, and said into his ear: 'Oh, you feel so good inside me.' Then she sat upright and began to move.

'Take off your chemise,' he said.

She pulled it over her head.

He watched her above him, her lovely face drawn into an expression of fierce concentration, her pretty breasts moving delightfully. He felt like the luckiest man in the world. He wanted this to go on for ever: no dawn, no tomorrow, no plane, no parachute, no war.

In all of life, he thought, there was nothing better than love.

* * *

When it was over, Flick's first thought was: What will I say to Michel?

She did not feel unhappy. She was full of love and

desire for Paul. In a short time she had come to feel more intimate with him than she ever had with Michel. She wanted to make love to him every day for the rest of her life. That was the trouble. Her marriage was over. And she would have to tell Michel as soon as she saw him. She could not pretend, even for a few minutes, to feel the same about him.

Michel was the only man she had been intimate with before Paul. She would have told Paul that, but she felt disloyal talking about Michel. It seemed more of a betrayal than simple adultery. One day she would tell Paul he was only her second lover, and she might say he was her best, but she would never talk to him about how sex was with Michel.

However, it was not just sex that was different with Paul, it was herself. She had never asked Michel, the way she had questioned Paul, about his early sexual experiences. She had never said to him, *You can touch anything you like.* She had never put a rubber on him, or climbed on top of him to make love, or told him he felt good inside her.

When she had lain down on the bed beside Paul, another personality had seemed to come out of her, just as a transformation had come over Mark when he walked into the Criss-Cross Club. She suddenly felt she could say anything she liked, do anything that took her fancy, be herself without worrying what would be thought of her.

It had never been like that with Michel. Beginning as his student, wanting to impress him, she had never really got on an even footing with him. She had

323

continued to seek his approval, something he had never done with her. In bed, she tried to please him, not herself.

After a while, Paul said: 'What are you thinking?'

'About my marriage,' she said.

'What about it?'

She wondered how much to confess. He had said, earlier in the evening, that he wanted to marry her; but that was before she came to his bedroom. Men never married girls who slept with them first, according to female folklore. It was not always true, Flick knew from her own experience with Michel. But all the same she decided to tell Paul half the truth. 'That it's over.'

'A drastic decision.'

She raised herself on her elbow and looked at him. 'Does that bother you?'

'On the contrary. I hope it means we might see each other again.'

'Do you mean that?'

He put his arms around her. 'I'm scared to tell you how much I mean it.'

'Scared?'

'Of frightening you off. I said a foolish thing earlier.'

'About marrying me and having children?'

'I meant it, but I said it in an arrogant way.'

'That's okay,' she said. 'When people are perfectly polite, it usually means they don't really care. A little awkwardness is more sincere.'

'I guess you're right. I never thought of that.'

She stroked his face. She could see the bristles of his

beard, and she realized the dawn light was strengthening. She forced herself not to look at her watch: she did not want to keep checking how much time they had left.

She ran her hand over his face, mapping his features with her fingertips: the bushy eyebrows, the deep eye sockets, the big nose, the shot-off ear, the sensual lips, the lantern jaw. 'Do you have hot water?' she said suddenly.

'Yes, it's a swanky room. There's a basin in the corner.'

She got up.

He said: 'What are you doing?'

'Stay there.' She padded across the floor in her bare feet, feeling his eyes on her naked body, wishing she were not quite so broad across the hips. On a shelf over the sink was a mug containing toothpaste and a wooden toothbrush that she recognized as French. Next to the glass were a safety razor, a brush and a bowl of shaving soap. She ran the hot tap, dipped the shaving brush in it, and worked up a lather in his soap bowl. She glanced across at him. He was staring at her. 'My bum is too big,' she said.

He grinned. 'Oh, no, it's not.'

She returned to the bed.

'Come on,' he said. 'What is this?'

'I'm going to shave you.'

'Why?'

'You'll see.'

She covered his face with lather, then got his safety

razor and filled the tooth mug with hot water. She straddled him the way she had when they made love, and shaved his face with careful, tender strokes.

'How did you learn to do this?' he asked.

'Don't speak,' she said. 'I watched my mother do it for my father, many times. Dad was a drunk, and towards the end he couldn't hold the razor steady, so Ma had to shave him every day. Lift your chin.'

He did so obediently, and she shaved the sensitive skin of his throat. When she had finished she soaked a flannel in hot water and wiped his face with it, then patted him dry with a clean towel. 'I should put on some face cream, but I bet you're too masculine to use it.'

'It never occurred to me that I should.'

'Never mind.'

'What next?'

'Do you remember what you were doing to me just before I reached for your wallet?'

'Yes.'

'Did you wonder why I didn't let you go on longer?'

'I thought you were impatient for . . . intercourse.'

'No, your bristles were scratching my thighs, right where the skin is most tender.'

'Oh, I'm sorry.'

'Well, you can make it up to me.'

He frowned. 'How?'

She groaned with mock frustration. 'Come on, Einstein. Now that your bristles have gone . . .'

'Oh – I see! Is that why you shaved me? Yes, of course it is. You want me to . . .'

She lay on her back, smiling, and parted her legs. 'Is this enough of a hint?'

He laughed. 'I guess it is,' he said, and he bent over her.

She closed her eyes.

TWENTY-EIGHT

The old ballroom was in the bombed west wing of the chateau at Sainte-Cécile. The room was only partly damaged: one end was a pile of debris, square stones and carved pediments and chunks of painted wall in a dusty heap, but the other remained intact. The effect was picturesque, Dieter thought, with the morning sun shining through a great hole in the ceiling on to a row of broken pillars, like a Victorian painting of classical ruins.

Dieter had decided to hold his briefing in the ballroom. The alternative was to meet in Weber's office, and Dieter did not want to give the men the impression that Weber was in charge. There was a small dais, presumably intended for the orchestra, on which he had placed a blackboard. The men had brought chairs from other parts of the building, and had placed them in front of the dais in four neat rows of six – very German, Dieter thought with a secret smile; French men would have scattered the chairs anyhow. Weber, who had assembled the team, sat on the dais facing the men, to emphasize that he was one of the commanders, not subordinate to Dieter.

The presence of two commanders, equal in rank and

hostile to one another, was the greatest threat to the operation, Dieter thought.

On the blackboard he had chalked a neat map of the village of Chatelle. It consisted of three large houses – presumably farms or wineries – plus six cottages and a bakery. The buildings were clustered around a crossroads, with vineyards to the north, west and south, and to the east a large cow pasture, a kilometre long, bordered by a broad pond. Dieter guessed that the field was used for grazing because the ground was too wet for grapes.

'The parachutists will aim to land in the pasture,' Dieter said. 'It must be a regular landing and take-off field: it's level, plenty big enough for a Lysander, and long enough even for a Hudson. The pond next to it would be a useful landmark, visible from the air. There is a cowshed at the southern end of the field where the reception committee probably take shelter while they are waiting for the plane.'

He paused. 'The most important thing for everyone here to remember is that *we want these parachutists to land*. We must avoid any action that might betray our presence to the reception committee or the pilot. We have to be silent and invisible. If the plane turns around and returns home with the agents on board, we will have lost a golden opportunity. One of the parachutists is a woman who can give us information on most of the Resistance circuits in northern France – if only we can get our hands on her.'

Weber spoke, mainly to remind them that he was here. 'Allow me to underline what Major Franck has said. Take no risks! Do nothing ostentatious! Stick to the plan!'

'Thank you, Major,' Dieter said. 'Lieutenant Hesse has divided you into two-man teams, designated A through L. Each building on the map is marked with a team letter. We will arrive at the village at twenty hundred hours. Very swiftly, we will enter every building. All the residents will be brought to the largest of the three big houses, known as La Maison Grandin, and held there until it is all over.'

One of the men raised a hand. Weber barked: 'Schuller! You may speak.'

'Sir, what if the Resistance people call at a house? They will find it empty and they may become suspicious.'

Dieter nodded. 'Good question. But I don't think they will. My guess is the reception committee are strangers here. They don't usually have agents parachute in near where sympathizers live – it's an unnecessary security risk. I'm betting they arrive after dark and go straight to the cowshed without bothering the villagers.'

Weber spoke again. 'This would be normal Resistance procedure,' he said, with the air of a doctor giving a diagnosis.

'The Maison Grandin will be our headquarters,' Dieter continued. 'Major Weber will be in command there.' This was his scheme for keeping Weber away from the real action. 'The prisoners will be locked away in some convenient place, ideally a cellar. They must be kept quiet, so that we can hear the vehicle in which the reception committee arrive, and later the plane.'

Weber said: 'Any prisoner who persistently makes noise may be shot.'

Dieter continued: 'As soon as the villagers have been incarcerated, teams A, B, C and D will take up concealed positions on the roads leading into the village. If any vehicles or personnel enter the village, you will report by short-wave radio, but you will do nothing more. At this point, you will not prevent people entering the village and you will not do anything that might betray your presence.' Looking around the room, Dieter wondered pessimistically whether the Gestapo men had brains enough to follow these orders.

'The enemy needs transport for six parachutists plus the reception committee, so they will arrive in a truck or bus, or possibly several cars. I believe they will enter the pasture by this gate – the ground is quite dry at this time of year, so there is no danger of cars becoming bogged down – and park between the gate and the cowshed, just here.' He pointed to the spot on the map.

'Teams E, F, G and H will be in this cluster of trees beside the pond, each equipped with a large battery searchlight. Teams I and J will remain at Maison Grandin to guard the prisoners and maintain the command post with Major Weber.' Dieter did not want Weber at the scene of the arrest. 'Teams K and L will be with me, behind this hedge near the cowshed.' Hans had found out which of the men were the best shots, and assigned them to work with Dieter.

'I will be in radio contact with all teams and will be in command in the pasture. When we hear the plane – we do nothing! When we see the parachutists – we do nothing! We will watch the parachutists land and wait for the reception committee to round them up and assemble them near where the vehicles are parked.' Dieter raised his voice, mainly for the benefit of Weber. '*Not until this process has been completed will we arrest anyone!*' The men would not jump the gun unless a skittish officer told them to.

'When we are ready, I will give the signal. From this moment on, until the order to stand down is given, teams A, B, C and D will arrest anyone attempting to enter or leave the village. Teams E, F, G and H will switch on their searchlights and turn them on the enemy. Teams K and L will approach them with me and arrest them. No one is to fire on the enemy – is that clear?'

Schuller, obviously the thinker among the group, raised his hand again. 'What if they fire on us?'

'Do not return their fire. These people are useless to us dead! Lie flat and keep the lights trained on them. Only teams E and F are permitted to use their weapons, and they have orders to shoot to wound. We want to interrogate these parachutists, not kill them.'

The phone in the room rang, and Hans Hesse picked it up. 'It's for you,' he said to Dieter. 'Rommel's headquarters.'

The timing was lucky, Dieter thought as he took the phone. He had called Walter Goedel at La Roche-Guyon earlier, and had left a message asking Goedel to call back. Now he said: 'Walter, my friend, how is the Field Marshal?'

'Fine, what do you want?' said Goedel, abrupt as ever.

'I thought the Field Marshal might like to know that we expect to carry off a small coup tonight – the arrest of a group of saboteurs as they arrive.' Dieter hesitated to give details over the phone, but this was a German military line, and the risk that the Resistance might be listening was very small. And it was crucial to get Goedel's support for the operation. 'My information is that one of them could tell us a great deal about several Resistance circuits.'

'Excellent,' said Goedel. 'As it happens, I am calling you from Paris. How long would it take me to drive to Reims – two hours?'

'Three.'

'Then I will join you on the raid.'

Dieter was delighted. 'By all means,' he said, 'if that is what the Field Marshal would like. Meet us at the chateau of Sainte-Cécile not later than nineteen hundred.' He looked at Weber, who had gone slightly pale.

'Very good.' Goedel hung up.

Dieter handed the phone back to Hans. 'Field Marshal Rommel's personal aide, Major Goedel, will be joining us tonight,' he said triumphantly. 'Yet another reason for us to make sure that everything is done with impeccable efficiency.' He smiled around the room, bringing his gaze to rest finally on Weber. 'Aren't we fortunate?'

TWENTY-NINE

All morning the Jackdaws drove north in a small bus. It was a slow journey through leafy woods and fields of green wheat, zigzagging from one sleepy market town to the next, circling London to the west. The countryside seemed oblivious of the war or indeed of the twentieth century, and Flick hoped it would long remain so. As they wound their way through medieval Winchester, she thought of Reims, another cathedral city, with uniformed Nazis strutting on the streets and the Gestapo everywhere in their black cars, and she gave a short prayer of thanks that they had stopped at the English Channel. She sat next to Paul and watched the countryside for a while, then – having been awake all night making love – she fell into a blissful sleep with her head on his shoulder.

At two in the afternoon they reached the village of Sandy in Bedfordshire. The bus went down a winding country road, turned on to an unpaved lane through a wood, and arrived at a large mansion called Tempsford House. Flick had been here before: it was the assembly point for the nearby Tempsford airfield. The mood of tranquillity left her. Despite the eighteenth-century elegance of the place, to her it symbolized the unbearable tension of the hours immediately before a flight into enemy territory.

They were too late for lunch, but they got tea and sandwiches in the dining room. Flick drank her tea but felt too anxious to eat. However, the others tucked in heartily. Afterwards they were shown to their rooms.

A little later the women met in the library. The room looked more like the wardrobe of a film studio. There were racks of coats and dresses, boxes of hats and shoes, cardboard cartons labelled *Culottes, Chaussettes,* and *Mouchoirs,* and a trestle table in the middle of the room with several sewing-machines.

In charge of the operation was Madame Guillemin, a slim woman of about fifty in a shirtwaist dress with a chic little matching jacket. She had spectacles on the end of her nose and a measuring tape around her neck, and she spoke to them in perfect French with a Parisian accent. 'As you know, French clothes are distinctively different from British clothes. I won't say they are more stylish, but, you know, they are . . . more stylish.' She gave a French shrug, and the girls laughed.

It was not just a question of style, Flick thought sombrely: French jackets were normally about ten inches longer than British, and there were numerous differences of detail, any of which could be the fatal clue that betrayed an agent. So all the clothes here had been bought in France, exchanged with refugees for new British clothes, or faithfully copied from French originals then worn for a while so that they would not look new.

'Now it is summer so we have cotton dresses, light

wool suits and showerproof coats.' She waved a hand at two young women sitting at sewing-machines. 'My assistants will make alterations if the clothes don't fit quite perfectly.'

Flick said: 'We need clothes that are fairly expensive, but well worn. I want us to look like respectable women in case we're questioned by the Gestapo.' When they needed to pose as cleaners, they could quickly downgrade their appearance by taking off their hats, gloves and belts.

Madame Guillemin began with Ruby. She looked hard at her for a minute, then picked from the rack a navy dress and a tan raincoat. 'Try those. It's a man's coat, but in France today no one can afford to be particular.' She pointed across the room. 'You can change behind that screen if you wish, and for the very shy there is a little anteroom behind the desk. We think the owner of the house used to lock himself in there to read dirty books.' They laughed again, all but Flick, who had heard Madame Guillemin's jokes before.

The seamstress looked hard at Greta, then moved on, saying: 'I'll come back to you.' She picked outfits for Jelly, Diana and Maude, and they all went behind the screen. Then she turned to Flick and said in a low voice: 'Is this a joke?'

'Why do you say that?'

She turned to Greta. 'You're a man.'

Flick gave a grunt of frustration and turned away. The seamstress had seen through Greta's disguise in seconds. It was a bad omen.

Madame added: 'You might fool a lot of people, but not me. I can tell.'

Greta said: 'How?'

Madame Guillemin shrugged. 'The proportions are all wrong – your shoulders are too broad, your hips too narrow, your legs too muscular, your hands too big – it's obvious to an expert.'

Flick said irritably: 'She has to be a woman, for this mission, so please dress her as best you can.'

'Of course – but for God's sake try not to let her be seen by a dressmaker.'

'No problem. The Gestapo don't employ many of those.' Flick's confidence was faked. She did not want Madame Guillemin to know how worried she was.

The seamstress looked again at Greta. 'I'll give you a contrasting skirt and blouse, to reduce your height, and a three-quarter-length coat.' She selected clothes and handed them to Greta.

Greta looked at them with disapproval. Her taste ran to more glamorous outfits. However, she did not complain. 'I'm going to be shy and lock myself in the anteroom,' she said.

Finally Madame gave Flick an apple-green dress with a matching coat. 'The colour shows off your eyes,' she said. 'As long as you're not ostentatious, why shouldn't you look pretty? It may help you charm your way out of trouble.'

The dress was loose, and looked like a tent on Flick, but she put on a leather belt to give it a waist. 'You are so chic, just like a French girl,' said Madame Guillemin.

337

Flick did not tell her that the main purpose of the belt was to hold a gun.

They all put on their new clothes and paraded around the room, preening and giggling. Madame Guillemin had chosen well, and they liked what they had been given, but some of the garments needed adjusting. 'While we are making alterations you can choose some accessories,' Madame said.

They rapidly lost their inhibitions, and clowned around in their underwear, trying on hats and shoes, scarves and bags. They had momentarily forgotten the dangers ahead, Flick thought, and were taking simple pleasure in their new outfits.

Greta came out of the anteroom looking surprisingly glamorous. Flick studied her with interest. She had turned up the collar of the plain white blouse so that it looked stylish, and wore the shapeless coat draped over her shoulders cloak-style. Madame Guillemin raised an eyebrow but made no comment.

Flick's dress had to be shortened. While that was being done she studied the coat. Working undercover had given her a sharp eye for detail, and she anxiously checked the stitching, the lining, the buttons and the pockets to make sure they were in the normal French style. She found no fault. The label in the collar said: 'Galeries Lafayette.'

Flick showed Madame Guillemin her lapel knife. It was only three inches long, with a thin blade, but it was wickedly sharp. It had a small handle and no hilt. It came in a slim leather sheath pierced with holes for thread. 'I want you to sew this to the coat under the lapel,' Flick said.

Madame Guillemin nodded. 'I can do this.'

She gave them each a little pile of underwear, two of everything, all with the labels of French shops. With unerring accuracy she had picked not just the right size but the preferred style of each woman: corsets for Jelly, pretty lacy slips for Maude, navy knickers and boned brassières for Diana, simple chemises and panties for Ruby and Flick. 'The handkerchiefs bear the laundry marks of different *blanchisseries* in Reims,' said Madame Guillemin with a touch of pride.

Finally she produced an assortment of bags: a canvas duffel, a Gladstone bag, a rucksack, and a selection of cheap fibre suitcases in different colours and sizes. Each woman got one. Inside she found a toothbrush, toothpaste, face powder, shoe polish, cigarettes and matches – all French brands. Even though they were going in only for a short time, Flick had insisted on the full kit for each of them.

'Remember,' Flick said, 'you may not take with you *anything* that you have not been given this afternoon. Your life depends on that.'

The giggling stopped as they remembered the danger they would face in a few hours.

Flick said: 'All right, everybody, please go back to your rooms and change into your French outfits, including underwear. Then we'll meet downstairs for dinner.'

In the main drawing room of the house a bar had

been set up. When Flick walked in it was occupied by a dozen or so men, some in RAF uniform, all of them – Flick knew from previous visits – destined to make clandestine flights over France. A blackboard bore the names or codenames of those who would leave tonight, together with the times they needed to depart from the house. Flick read:

Aristotle – 19.50
Capt. Jenkins & Lieut. Ramsey – 20.05
All Jackdaws – 20.30
Colgate & Bunter – 21.00
Mr Blister, Paradox, Saxophone – 22.05

She looked at her watch. It was six thirty. Two hours to go.

She sat at the bar and looked around, wondering which of them would come back and which would die in the field. Some were terribly young, smoking and telling jokes, looking as if they had no cares. The older ones looked hardened, and savoured their whisky and gin in the grim knowledge that it might be their last. She thought about their parents, their wives or girlfriends, their babies and children. Tonight's work would leave some of them with a grief that would never entirely go away.

Her sombre reflections were interrupted by a sight that astonished her. Simon Fortescue, the slippery bureaucrat from MI6, walked into the bar in a pinstriped suit – accompanied by Denise Bowyer.

Flick's jaw dropped.

'Felicity, I'm so glad I caught you,' said Simon. Without waiting for an invitation he pulled up a stool for Denise. 'Gin and tonic, please, barman. What would you like, Lady Denise?'

'A martini, very dry.'

'And for you, Felicity?'

Flick did not answer the question. 'She's supposed to be in Scotland!' she said.

'Look, there seems to have been some misunderstanding. Denise has told me all about this policeman fellow—'

'No misunderstanding,' Flick said abruptly. 'Denise failed the course. That's all there is to it.'

Denise made a disgusted sound.

Fortescue said: 'I really don't see how a perfectly intelligent girl from a good family could fail—'

'She's a blabbermouth.'

'What?'

'She can't keep her damn mouth shut. She's not trustworthy. She shouldn't be walking around free!'

Denise said: 'You insolent cat.'

Fortescue controlled his temper with an effort and lowered his voice. 'Look, her brother is the Marquess of Inverlocky, who's *very* close to the Prime Minister. Inverlocky himself asked me to make sure Denise got a chance to do her bit. So, you see, it would be dreadfully tactless to turn her down.'

Flick raised her voice. 'Let me get this straight.' One or two of the men nearby looked up. 'As a favour to your upper-class friend, you're asking me to take someone untrustworthy on a dangerous operation behind enemy lines. Is that it?'

As she was speaking, Percy and Paul walked in. Percy glared at Fortescue with undisguised malevolence. Paul said: 'Did I hear right?'

Fortescue said: 'I've brought Denise with me because it would be, frankly, an embarrassment to the government if she were left behind—'

'And a danger to me if she were to come!' Flick interrupted. 'You're wasting your breath. She's off the team.'

'Look, I don't want to have to pull rank—'

'What rank?' said Flick.

'I resigned from the Guards as a colonel—'

'Retired!'

' – and I'm the civil service equivalent of a Brigadier.'

'Don't be ridiculous,' Flick said. 'You're not even in the army.'

'I'm *ordering* you to take Denise with you.'

'Then I'll have to consider my response,' said Flick.

'That's better. I'm sure you won't regret it.'

'All right, here is my response. Fuck off.'

Fortescue went red. He had probably never been told to fuck off by a girl. He was uncharacteristically speechless.

'Well!' said Denise. 'We've certainly found out what type of person we're dealing with.'

Paul said: 'You're dealing with me.' He turned to Fortescue. 'I'm in command of this operation, and I won't have Denise on the team at any price. If you want to argue, call Monty.'

'Well said, my boy,' Percy added.

Fortescue found his voice at last. He wagged a finger at Flick. 'The time will come, Mrs Clairet, when you will regret saying that to me.' He got off his stool. 'I'm sorry about this, Lady Denise, but I think we've done all we can here.'

They left.

'Stupid prat,' Percy muttered.

'Let's have dinner,' said Flick.

The others were already in the dining room, waiting. As the Jackdaws began their last meal in England, Percy gave each of them an expensive gift: silver cigarette cases for the smokers, gold powder compacts for the others. 'They have French hallmarks, so you can take them with you,' he said. The women were pleased, but he brought their mood back down with his next remark. 'They have a purpose, too. They are items that can easily be pawned for emergency funds if you get into real trouble.'

The food was plentiful, a banquet by wartime standards, and the Jackdaws tucked in with relish. Flick did not feel very hungry, but she forced herself to eat a big steak, knowing it was more meat than she would get in a week in France.

When they finished supper, it was time to go to the airfield. They returned to their rooms to pick up their French bags, then boarded the bus. It took them along another country lane and across a railway line, then approached what looked like a cluster of farm buildings at the edge of a large, flat field. A sign said, 'Gibraltar Farm,' but Flick knew that this was RAF Tempsford, and the barns were heavily disguised Nissen huts.

They went into what looked like a cowshed and found a uniformed RAF officer standing guard over steel racks of equipment. Before they were given their gear, each of them was searched. A box of British matches was found in Maude's suitcase; Diana had in her pocket a half-completed crossword torn from the *Daily Mirror*, which she swore she had intended to leave on the plane; and Jelly, the inveterate gambler, had a pack of playing-cards with *Made in Birmingham* printed on every one.

Paul distributed their identity cards, ration cards, and clothing coupons. Each woman was given a hundred thousand French francs, mostly in grubby thousand-franc notes. It was the equivalent of five hundred pounds, enough to buy two Ford cars.

They also got weapons, .45 calibre Colt automatic pistols and sharp double-bladed Commando knives. Flick declined both. She took her personal gun, a Browning nine-millimetre automatic. Around her waist she wore the leather belt, into which she could push the pistol or, at a pinch, the submachine-gun. She also took her lapel knife instead of the Commando knife. The Commando knife was longer and deadlier, but more cumbersome. The great advantage of the lapel knife was that when the agent was asked to produce papers, she could innocently reach towards an inside pocket then at the last moment pull the knife.

In addition there was a Lee-Enfield rifle for Diana and a Sten Mark II submachine-gun with silencer for Flick.

The plastic explosive Jelly would need was distributed evenly around the six women, so that even if one or two bags were lost there would still be enough to do the job.

Maude said: 'It might blow me up!'

Jelly explained that it was extraordinarily safe. 'I knew a bloke who thought it was chocolate and ate some,' she said. 'Mind you,' she added, 'it didn't half give him the runs.'

They were offered the usual round Mills grenades with the conventional turtleshell finish, but Flick insisted on general-purpose grenades in square cans, because they could also be used as explosive charges.

Each woman got a fountain pen with a hollow cap containing a suicide pill.

There was a compulsory visit to the bathroom before putting on the flying suit. It had a pistol pocket, so that the agent could defend herself immediately on landing, if necessary. With the suit they donned helmet and goggles, and finally shrugged into the parachute harness.

Paul asked Flick to step outside for a moment. He had held back the all-important special passes that would enable the women to enter the chateau as cleaners. If a Jackdaw were to be captured by the Gestapo, this pass would betray the true purpose of the mission. For safety, he gave all the passes to Flick, to be distributed at the last minute.

Then he kissed her. She kissed him back with desperate passion, clutching his body to hers, shamelessly thrusting her tongue into his mouth until she had to gasp for breath.

'Don't get killed,' he said into her ear.

They were interrupted by a discreet cough. Flick smelt Percy's pipe. She broke the clinch.

Percy said to Paul: 'The pilot is waiting for a word with you.'

Paul nodded and moved away.

'Make sure he understands that Flick is the officer in command,' Percy called after him.

'Sure,' Paul replied.

Percy looked grim, and Flick had a bad feeling. 'What's wrong?' she said.

He took a sheet of paper from his jacket pocket and handed it to her. 'A motorcycle courier from London brought this from SOE headquarters just before we left the house. It came in from Brian Standish last night.' He sucked anxiously on his pipe and blew out clouds of smoke.

Flick looked at the sheet of paper in the evening sunlight. It was a decrypt. Its contents hit her like a punch in the stomach. She looked up, dismayed. 'Brian has been in the hands of the Gestapo!'

'Only for a few seconds.'

'So this claims.'

'Any reason to think otherwise?'

'Ah, *fuck* it,' she said loudly. A passing airman looked up sharply, surprised to hear a woman's voice utter such words. Flick crumpled the paper and threw it on the ground.

Percy bent down, picked it up, and smoothed out the creases. 'Let's try to stay calm and think clearly.'

Flick took a deep breath. 'We have a rule,' she said insistently. 'Any agent who is captured by the enemy, *whatever the circumstances*, must immediately be returned to London for debriefing.'

'Then you'll have no wireless operator.'

'I can manage without one. And what about this Charenton?'

'I suppose it's natural that Mademoiselle Lemas might have recruited someone to help her.'

'All recruits are supposed to be vetted by London.'

'You know that rule has never been followed.'

'At a minimum they should be approved by the local commander.'

'Well, he has been now – Michel is satisfied that Charenton is trustworthy. And Charenton saved Brian from the Gestapo. That whole scene in the cathedral can't have been deliberately staged, can it?'

'Perhaps it never took place at all, and this message comes straight from Gestapo headquarters.'

'But it has all the right security codes. Anyway, they wouldn't invent a story about his being captured and then released. They'd know that would arouse our suspicions. They would just say he had arrived safely.'

'You're right, but still I don't like it.'

'No, nor do I,' he said, surprising her. 'But I don't know what to do.'

She sighed. 'We have to take the risk. There's no time for precautions. If we don't disable the telephone exchange in the next three days it will be too late. We have to go anyway.'

Percy nodded. Flick saw that there were tears in his eyes. He put his pipe in his mouth and took it out again. 'Good girl,' he said, his voice reduced to a whisper. 'Good girl.'

THE SEVENTH DAY:
SATURDAY, 3 JUNE 1944

THIRTY

SOE had no planes of its own. It had to borrow them from the RAF, which was like pulling teeth. In 1941 the air force had reluctantly handed over two Lysanders, too slow and heavy for their intended role in battlefield support, but ideal for clandestine landings in enemy territory. Later, under pressure from Churchill, two squadrons of obsolete bombers were assigned to SOE, although the head of Bomber Command, Arthur Harris, never stopped scheming to get them back. By the spring of 1944, when dozens of agents were flown into France in preparation for the invasion, SOE had the use of thirty-six aircraft.

The plane the Jackdaws boarded was an American-made twin-engined Hudson light bomber, manufactured in 1939 and since made obsolete by the four-engined Lancaster heavy bomber. A Hudson came with two machine-guns in the nose, and the RAF added a rear turret with two more. At the back of the passenger cabin was a slide like a water chute, down which the parachutists would glide into space. There were no seats inside, and the six women and their despatcher lay down on the metal floor. They were cold and uncomfortable and scared, but Jelly got a fit of the giggles, which cheered them all up.

They shared the cabin with a dozen metal containers, each as tall as a man and equipped with a parachute harness, all containing – Flick presumed – guns and ammunition to enable some other Resistance circuit to run interference behind German lines during the invasion. After dropping the Jackdaws at Chatelle, the Hudson would fly on to another destination before turning around and heading back to Tempsford.

Take-off had been delayed by a faulty altimeter, which had had to be replaced, so it was one o'clock in the morning when they left the English coastline behind. Over the Channel the pilot dropped the plane to a few hundred feet above the sea, trying to hide below the level of enemy radar, and Flick silently hoped they would not be shot at by ships of the Royal Navy; but he soon climbed again to eight thousand feet to cross the fortified French coastline. He stayed high to traverse the 'Atlantic Wall', the heavily defended coastal strip, then descended again to three hundred feet, to make navigation less difficult.

The navigator was constantly busy with his maps, calculating the plane's position by dead reckoning and trying to confirm it by landmarks. The moon was waxing, and only three days from full, so large towns were easily visible, despite the blackout. However, they generally had anti-aircraft batteries, so had to be avoided, as did army camps and military sites, for the same reason. Rivers and lakes were the most useful terrain features, especially when the moon was reflected off the water. Forests showed as dark patches, and the unexpected absence of one was a sure sign that the flight had gone astray. The gleam of railway lines, the glow of a steam engine's fire, and the headlights of the occasional blackout-breaking car were all helpful.

All the way, Flick brooded over the news about Brian Standish and the newcomer Charenton. The story was probably true. The Gestapo had learned about the cathedral crypt rendezvous from one of the prisoners they had taken last Sunday at the chateau, and they had set a trap which Brian had walked into; but he had escaped, with help from Mademoiselle Lemas's new recruit. It was all perfectly possible. However, Flick hated plausible explanations. She felt safe only when events followed standard procedure and no explanations were required.

As they approached the Champagne region, another navigation aid came into play. It was a recent invention known as Eureka-Rebecca. A radio beacon broadcast a call-sign from a secret location somewhere in Reims. The crew of the Hudson did not know exactly where it was, but Flick did, for Michel had placed it in the tower of the cathedral. This was the Eureka half. On the plane was Rebecca, a radio receiver, shoehorned into the cabin next to the navigator. They were about fifty miles north of Reims when the navigator picked up the signal from the Eureka in the cathedral.

The intention of the inventors was that the Eureka should be in the landing field with the reception committee, but this was impracticable. The equipment weighed more than a hundred pounds, it was too bulky to be transported discreetly, and it could not be explained away to even the most gullible Gestapo officer at a checkpoint. Michel and other Resistance leaders were willing to place a Eureka in a permanent position, but refused to carry them around.

So the navigator had to revert to traditional methods to find Chatelle. However, he was lucky in having Flick beside him, someone who had landed there on several occasions and could recognize the place from the air. In the event, they passed about a mile to the east of the village, but Flick spotted the pond and redirected the pilot.

They circled around and flew over the cow pasture at three hundred feet. Flick could see the flare path, four weak, flickering lights in an L shape, with the torch at the toe of the L flashing the prearranged code. The pilot climbed towards six hundred feet, the ideal altitude for a parachute drop: any higher, and the wind could blow the parachutists away from the dropping zone; much lower, and the chute might not have time to open fully before the agent hit the ground.

'Ready when you are,' said the pilot.

'I'm not ready,' Flick said.

'What's the matter?'

'Something's wrong.' Flick's instincts were sounding alarm bells. It was not just her worries about Brian Standish and Charenton. There was something else. She pointed west, to the village. 'Look, no lights.'

'That surprises you? There's a blackout. And it's after three o'clock in the morning.'

Flick shook her head. 'This is the countryside, they're careless about the blackout. And there's always someone up: a mother with a new baby, an insomniac, a student cramming for finals. I've never seen it completely dark.'

'If you really feel there's something wrong, we should get out of here fast,' the pilot said nervously.

Something else was bothering her. She tried to scratch her head and found her helmet in the way. The thought evaded her.

What should she do? She could hardly abort the mission just because the villagers of Chatelle were obeying the blackout rules for once.

The plane overflew the field and banked to turn. The pilot said anxiously: 'Remember, each time we overfly increases the risk. Everyone in that village can hear our engines, and one of them might call the police.'

'Exactly!' she said. 'We must have awakened the entire place. Yet no one has switched on a light!'

'I don't know, country folk can be very incurious. They like to keep themselves to themselves, as they always say.'

'Nonsense. They're as nosy as anyone. This is peculiar.'

The pilot looked more and more worried, but he continued circling.

Suddenly it came to her. 'The baker should have lit his oven. You can normally see the glow from the air.'

'Could he be closed today?'

'What day is it? Saturday. A baker might close on a Monday or a Tuesday, but never on a Saturday. What's happened? This is like a ghost town!'

'Then let's get out of here.'

It was as if someone had rounded up the villagers, including the baker, and locked them in a barn – which was probably what the Gestapo would have done if they were lying in wait for her.

She could not abort the mission. It was too important. But every instinct told her not to parachute into Chatelle. 'A risk is a risk,' she said.

The pilot was losing patience. 'So what do you want to do?'

Suddenly she remembered the containers of supplies in the passenger cabin. 'What's your next destination?'

'I'm not supposed to tell you.'

'Not usually, no. But now I really need to know.'

'It's a field north of Chartres.'

That meant the Vestryman circuit. 'I know them,' Flick said with mounting excitement. This could be the solution. 'You could drop us with the containers. There will be a reception committee waiting, they can take care of us. We could be in Paris this afternoon, Reims by tomorrow morning.'

He reached for the joystick. 'Is that what you want to do?'

'Is it possible?'

'I can drop you there, no problem. The tactical decision is yours. You're in command of the mission – that was made very clear to me.'

Flick considered, worrying. Her suspicions might be

unfounded, in which case she would need to get a message to Michel via Brian's radio, saying that although her landing had been aborted, she was still on her way. But in case Brian's radio was in Gestapo hands, she would have to give the minimum of information. However, that was feasible. She could write a brief radio signal for the pilot to take back to Percy: Brian would have it in a couple of hours.

She would also have to change the arrangements for picking up the Jackdaws after the mission. At present, a Hudson was scheduled to land at Chatelle at two a.m. on Sunday, and if the Jackdaws were not there, to return the following night at the same time. If Chatelle had been betrayed to the Gestapo and could no longer be used, she would have to divert the Hudson to another landing field at Laroque, to the west of Reims, codenamed Champ d'Or. The mission would take an extra day, because they would have to travel from Chartres to Reims, so the pickup flight would have to come down at two on Monday morning, with a fall-back on Tuesday at the same hour.

She weighed consequences. Diverting to Chartres meant the loss of a day. But landing at Chatelle could mean the entire mission failed and all the Jackdaws ended up in Gestapo torture chambers. It was no contest. 'Go to Chartres,' she said to the pilot.

'Roger, wilco.'

As the aircraft banked and turned, Flick went back to the cabin. The Jackdaws all looked expectantly at her. 'There's been a change of plan,' she said.

THIRTY-ONE

Dieter lay beneath a hedge and watched, bewildered, while the British plane circled over the cow pasture.

Why the delay? The pilot had made two passes over the landing site. The flare path, such as it was, was in place. Had the reception leader flashed the wrong code? Had the Gestapo men done something to arouse suspicion? It was maddening. Felicity Clairet was a few yards away from him. If he fired his pistol at the plane, a lucky shot might hit her.

Then the plane banked, turned, and roared away to the south.

Dieter was mortified. Flick Clairet had evaded him – in front of Walter Goedel, Willi Weber and twenty-four Gestapo men.

For a moment, he buried his face in his hands.

What had gone wrong? There could be a dozen reasons. As the drone of the plane's engines receded, Dieter could hear shouts of indignation in French. The Resistance seemed as perplexed as he was. His best guess was that Flick, an experienced team leader, had smelt a rat and aborted the jump.

Walter Goedel, lying in the dirt beside him, said: 'What are you going to do now?'

Dieter considered briefly. There were four Resistance people here: Michel the leader, still limping from his bullet wound; Helicopter, the British radio operator; a Frenchman Dieter did not recognize, and a young woman. What should he do with them? His strategy of letting Helicopter run free had been a good one in theory, but it had now led to two humiliating reverses, and he did not have the nerve to continue it. He had to get something out of tonight's fiasco. He was going to have to revert to traditional methods of interrogation, and hope to salvage the operation – and his reputation.

He brought the mouthpiece of the short-wave radio to his lips. 'All units, this is Major Franck,' he said softly. 'Action, I repeat, action.' Then he got to his feet and drew his automatic pistol.

The searchlights concealed in the trees blazed into life. The four terrorists in the middle of the field were mercilessly lit up, looking suddenly bewildered and vulnerable. Dieter called out in French: 'You are surrounded! Raise your hands!'

Beside him, Goedel drew his Luger. The four Gestapo men with Dieter aimed their rifles at the legs of the Resistance people. There was a moment of uncertainty: would the Resistance open fire? If they did, they would be mown down. With luck, they might be only wounded. But Dieter had not had much luck tonight. And if these four were killed, he would be left empty-handed.

They hesitated.

Dieter stepped forward, moving into the light, and

the four riflemen moved with him. 'Over twenty guns are aimed at you,' he shouted. 'Do not draw your weapons.'

One of them started to run.

Dieter swore. He saw a flash of red hair in the lights: it was Helicopter, stupid boy, heading across the field like a charging bull. 'Shoot him,' Dieter said quietly. All four riflemen took careful aim and fired. The shots crashed out in the silent meadow. Helicopter ran another two paces then fell to the ground.

Dieter looked at the other three, waiting. Slowly, they raised their hands in the air.

Dieter spoke into the short-wave radio. 'All teams in the pasture, move in and secure the prisoners.' He put away his pistol.

He walked over to where Helicopter lay. The body was still. The Gestapo riflemen had shot at his legs, but it was hard to hit a moving target in the dark, and one of them had aimed too high, putting a bullet through his neck, severing his spinal cord, or his jugular vein, or both. Dieter knelt beside him and felt for a pulse, but there was none. 'You weren't the cleverest agent I've ever met, but you were a brave boy,' he said quietly. 'God rest your soul.' He closed the eyes.

He looked over at the other three as they were disarmed and fettered. Michel would resist interrogation well: Dieter had seen him in action, and he had courage. His weakness was probably vanity. He was handsome, and a womanizer. The way to torture him would be in front of a mirror: break his nose, knock out his teeth, scar his cheeks, make him understand that with every minute that he continued to resist, he was getting irreversibly uglier.

The other man had the air of a professional, perhaps a lawyer. A Gestapo man searched him and showed Dieter a pass which permitted Dr Claude Bouler to be out after curfew. Dieter assumed it was a forgery, but when they searched the Resistance cars they found a genuine doctor's bag, full of instruments and drugs. Under arrest he looked pale but composed: he, too, would be a difficult subject.

The girl was the most promising. She was about nineteen, and pretty, with long dark hair and big eyes, but she had a vacant look. Her papers showed that she was Gilberte Duval. Dieter knew from his interrogation of Gaston that Gilberte was the lover of Michel and the rival of Flick. Handled correctly, she might prove easy to turn.

The German vehicles were brought from the barn at La Maison Grandin. The prisoners went in a truck with the Gestapo men. Dieter gave orders that they should be kept in separate cells and prevented from communicating with one another.

He and Goedel were driven back to Sainte-Cécile in Weber's Mercedes. 'What a damned farce,' Weber said scornfully. 'A complete waste of time and manpower.'

'Not quite,' said Dieter. 'We have taken four subversive agents out of circulation – which is, after all, what the Gestapo is supposed to do – and, even better, three of them are still alive for interrogation.'

Goedel said: 'What do you hope to get from them?'

'The dead man, Helicopter, was a wireless operator,' Dieter explained. 'I have a copy of his code book. Unfortunately, he did not have his set with him. If we can find the set, we can impersonate Helicopter.'

'Surely you can use any radio transmitter, so long as you know the frequency assigned to him?'

Dieter shook his head. 'Every transmitter sounds different to the experienced ear. And these little suitcase radios are particularly distinctive. All non-essential circuits are omitted, to minimize the size; and the result is poor tone quality. If we had one exactly like his, captured from another agent, it might be similar enough to take the risk.'

'We may have one somewhere.'

'If we do it will be in Berlin. It's easier to find Helicopter's.'

'How will you do that?'

'The girl will tell me where it is.'

For the rest of the journey, Dieter brooded over his interrogation strategy. He could torture the girl in front of the men, but they might resist that. More promising would be to torture the men in front of the girl. But there might be an easier way.

A plan was forming in his mind when they passed the public library in the centre of Reims. He had noticed the building before. It was a little jewel, an art deco design in tan stone, standing in a small garden. 'Would you mind stopping the car for a moment, please, Major Weber?' he said.

Weber muttered an order to his driver.

'Do you have any tools in the boot?'

'I have no idea,' said Weber. 'What is this about?'

The driver said: 'Of course, Major, we have the regulation tool kit.'

'Is there a good-sized hammer?'

'Yes.' The driver jumped out.

'This won't take a moment,' Dieter said. He got out of the car.

The driver handed him a long-handled hammer with a chunky steel head. Dieter walked past a bust of Andrew Carnegie up to the library. The place was closed and dark, of course. The glass doors were protected by an elaborate wrought-iron grille. He walked around to the side of the building and found a basement entrance with a plain wood door marked 'Archives Municipales'.

Dieter swung at the door with the hammer, hitting the lock. It broke after four blows. He went inside, turning on the lights. He ran up a narrow staircase to the main floor and crossed the lobby to the fiction section. There he located the letter F for Flaubert, and picked out a copy of the book he was looking for, *Madame Bovary*. It was not particularly lucky: that was the one book that must be available in every library in the country.

He turned to Chapter Nine and located the passage he was thinking about. He had remembered it accurately. It would serve his purpose very well.

He returned to the car. Goedel was looking amused. Weber said incredulously: 'You needed something to read?'

'Sometimes I find it difficult to get to sleep,' Dieter replied.

Goedel laughed. He took the book from Dieter and read its title. 'A classic of world literature,' he said. 'All the same, I imagine that's the first time someone broke down the library door to borrow it.'

They drove on to Sainte-Cécile. By the time they reached the chateau, Dieter's plan was fully formed.

He ordered Lieutenant Hesse to prepare Michel by stripping him naked and tying him to a chair in the torture chamber. 'Show him the instrument used for pulling out fingernails,' he said. 'Leave it on the table in front of him.' While that was being done, he got a pen, a bottle of ink, and a pad of letter paper from the offices on the upper floor. Walter Goedel ensconced himself in a corner of the torture chamber to watch.

Dieter studied Michel for a few moments. The Resistance leader was a tall man, with attractive wrinkles around his eyes. He had a kind of bad-boy look that women liked. Now he was scared but determined. He was thinking grimly about how to hold out as long as possible against torture, Dieter guessed.

Dieter put the pen, ink and paper on the table next to the fingernail pliers, to show that they were alternatives. 'Untie his hands,' he said.

Hesse complied. Michel's face showed enormous relief combined with a fear that this might not be real.

Dieter explained to Walter Goedel: 'Before questioning the prisoners, I will take samples of their handwriting.'

'Their handwriting?'

Dieter nodded, watching Michel, who seemed to

have understood the brief exchange in German. He looked hopeful.

Dieter took *Madame Bovary* from his pocket, opened it, and put it down on the table. 'Copy out Chapter Nine,' he said to Michel in French.

Michel hesitated. It seemed a harmless request. He suspected a trick, Dieter could tell, but he could not see what it was. Dieter waited. The Resistance were told to do everything they could to put off the moment when torture began. Michel was bound to see this as a means of postponement. It was unlikely to be harmless, but it had to be better than having his fingernails pulled out. 'Very well,' he said after a long pause. He began writing.

Dieter watched him. His handwriting was large and flamboyant. Two pages of the printed book took up six sheets of the letter paper. When Michel turned the page, Dieter stopped him. He told Hans to return Michel to his cell and bring Gilberte.

Goedel looked over what Michel had written, and shook his head bemusedly. 'I can't figure out what you're up to,' he said. He handed the sheets back and returned to his chair.

Dieter tore one of the pages very carefully to leave only certain words.

Gilberte came in looking terrified but defiant. She said: 'I won't tell you anything. I will never betray my friends. Besides, I don't know anything. All I do is drive cars.'

Dieter told her to sit down and offered her coffee.

'The real thing,' he said, as he handed her a cup. French people could get only ersatz coffee.

She sipped it and thanked him.

Dieter studied her. She was quite beautiful, with long dark hair and dark eyes, although there was something bovine about her expression. 'You're a lovely woman, Gilberte,' he said. 'I don't believe you are a murderer at heart.'

'No, I'm not!' she said gratefully.

'A woman does things for love, doesn't she?'

She looked at him with surprise. 'You understand.'

'I know all about you. You are in love with Michel.'

She bowed her head without replying.

'A married man, of course. This is regrettable. But you love him. And that's why you help the Resistance. Out of love, not hate.'

She nodded.

'Am I right?' he said. 'You must answer.'

She whispered: 'Yes.'

'But you have been misguided, my dear.'

'I know I've done wrong—'

'You misunderstand me. You've been misguided, not just in breaking the law, but in loving Michel.'

She looked at him in puzzlement. 'I know he's married, but—

'I'm afraid he doesn't really love you.'

'But he does!'

'No. He loves his wife. Felicity Clairet, known as Flick. An Englishwoman – not chic, not very beautiful, some years older than you – but he loves her.'

Tears came to her eyes, and she said: 'I don't believe you.'

'He writes to her, you know. I imagine he gets the couriers to take his messages back to England. He sends her love letters, saying how much he misses her. They're rather poetic, in an old-fashioned way. I've read some.'

'It's not possible.'

'He was carrying one when we arrested all of you. He tried to destroy it, just now, but we managed to save a few scraps.' Dieter took from his pocket the sheet he had torn and handed it to her. 'Isn't that his handwriting?'

'Yes.'

'And is it a love letter . . . or what?'

Gilberte read it slowly, moving her lips:

I think of you constantly. The memory of you drives me to despair. Ah! Forgive me! I will leave you! Farewell! I will go far away, so far that you will never hear of me again; and yet – today – I know not what force impelled me towards you. For one doesn't struggle against heaven; one cannot resist the smile of angels; one is carried away by that which is beautiful, charming, adorable.

She threw down the paper with a sob.

'I'm sorry to be the one to tell you,' Dieter said gently. He took the white linen handkerchief from the breast pocket of his suit and handed it to her. She buried her face in it.

It was time to turn the conversation imperceptibly towards interrogation. 'I suppose Michel has been living with you since Flick left.'

'Longer than that,' she said indignantly. 'For six months, every night except when *she* was in town.'

'In your house?'

'I have an apartment. Very small. But it was enough for two . . . two people who loved each other.' She continued to cry.

Dieter strove to maintain a light conversational tone as he obliquely approached the topic he was really interested in. 'Wasn't it difficult to have Helicopter living with you as well, in a small place?'

'He's not living there. He only came today.'

'But you must have wondered where he was going to stay.'

'No. Michel found him a place, an empty room over the old bookshop in the rue Molière.'

Walter Goedel suddenly shifted in his chair: he had realized where this was heading. Dieter carefully ignored him, and casually asked Gilberte: 'Didn't he leave his stuff at your place when you went to Chatelle to meet the plane?'

'No, he took it to the room.'

Dieter asked the key question. 'Including his little suitcase?'

'Yes.'

'Ah.' Dieter had what he wanted. Helicopter's radio set was in a room over the bookshop in the rue Molière. 'I've finished with this stupid cow,' he said to Hans in German. 'Turn her over to Becker.'

Dieter's own car, the blue Hispano-Suiza, was parked in front of the chateau. With Walter Goedel beside him and Hans Hesse in the back seat, he drove fast through the villages to Reims and quickly found the bookshop in the rue Molière.

They broke down the door and climbed a bare wooden staircase to the room over the shop. It was unfurnished but for a palliasse covered with a rough blanket. On the floor beside the rough bed stood a bottle of whisky, a bag containing toiletries, and the small suitcase.

Dieter opened it to show Goedel the radio. 'With this,' Dieter said triumphantly, 'I can become Helicopter.'

On the way back to Sainte-Cécile, they discussed what message to send. 'First, Helicopter would want to know why the parachutists did not drop,' Dieter said. 'So he will ask: 'What happened?' Do you agree?'

'And he would be angry,' Goedel said.

'So he will say, "What the blazes happened?" perhaps.'

Goedel shook his head. 'I studied in England before the war. That phrase, "what the blazes", is too polite. It's a coy euphemism for "what the hell". A young man in the military would never use it.'

'Maybe he should say "what the fuck" instead.'

'Too coarse,' Goedel objected. 'He knows the message may be decoded by a female.'

'Your English is better than mine, you choose.'

'I think he would say: "What the devil happened?" It expresses his anger, and it's a masculine curse that would not offend most women.'

'Okay. Then he wants to know what he should do next, so he will ask for further orders. What would he say?'

'Probably: "Send instructions." English people dislike the word "order", they think it's not refined.'

'All right. And we'll ask for a quick response, because Helicopter would be impatient, and so are we.'

They reached the chateau and went to the wireless listening room in the basement. A middle-aged operator called Joachim plugged the set in and tuned it to Helicopter's emergency frequency while Dieter scribbled the agreed message:

WHAT THE DEVIL HAPPENED? SEND INSTRUCTIONS. REPLY IMMEDIATELY.

Dieter forced himself to control his impatience and carefully show Joachim how to encode the message, including the security tags.

Goedel said: 'Won't they know it's not Helicopter at the machine? Can't they recognize the individual 'fist' of the sender, like handwriting?'

'Yes,' Joachim said. 'But I've listened to this chap sending a couple of times, and I can imitate him. It's a bit like mimicking someone's accent, talking like a Frankfurt man, say.'

Goedel was sceptical. 'You can do a perfect impersonation after hearing him twice?'

'Not perfect, no. But agents are often under pressure when they broadcast, in some hiding-place and worried about us catching up with them, so small variations will be put down to strain.' He began to tap out the letters.

Dieter reckoned they had a wait of at least an hour. At the British listening station, the message had to be decrypted then passed to Helicopter's controller, who was surely in bed. The controller might get the message by phone and compose a reply on the spot, but even then the reply had to be encrypted and transmitted, then decrypted by Joachim.

Dieter and Goedel went to the kitchen on the ground floor, where they found a mess corporal starting work on breakfast, and got him to give them sausages and coffee. Goedel was impatient to get back to Rommel's headquarters, but he wanted to stay and see how this turned out.

It was daylight when a young woman in SS uniform came to tell them that the reply had come in and Joachim had almost finished typing it.

They hurried downstairs. Weber was already there, with his usual knack of showing up where the action was. Joachim handed the typed message to him and carbon copies to Dieter and Goedel.

Dieter read:

JACKDAWS ABORTED DROP BUT HAVE LANDED
ELSEWHERE AWAIT CONTACT FROM
LEOPARDESS.

Weber said grumpily: 'This does not tell us much.'
Goedel agreed. 'What a disappointment.'

'You're both wrong!' Dieter said jubilantly. 'Leopardess is in France – and I have a picture of her!' He pulled the photos of Flick Clairet from his pocket with a flourish and handed one to Weber. 'Get a printer out of bed and have a thousand copies made. I want to see that picture all over Reims within the next twelve hours. Hans, get my car filled up with petrol.'

'Where are you going?' said Goedel.

'To Paris, with the other photograph, to do the same thing there. I've got her now!'

THIRTY-TWO

The parachute drop went smoothly. The containers were pushed out first, so that there was no possibility of one landing on the head of a parachutist; then the Jackdaws took turns to sit on the top of the slide and, when tapped on the shoulder by the despatcher, slither down the chute and out into space.

Flick went last. As she fell, the Hudson turned north and disappeared into the night. She wished the crew luck. It was almost dawn: because of the night's delays, they would have to fly the last part of their journey in dangerous daylight.

Flick landed perfectly, with her knees bent and her arms tucked into her sides, as she fell to the ground. She lay still for a moment. French soil, she thought with a shiver of fear; enemy territory. Now she was a criminal, a terrorist, a spy. If she were caught, she would be executed.

She put the thought out of her mind and stood up. A few yards away, a donkey stared at her in the moonlight then bent its head to graze. She could see three containers nearby. Farther away, scattered across the field, were half a dozen Resistance people, working in pairs, picking up the bulky containers and carrying them away.

She struggled out of her parachute harness, helmet and flying suit. While she was doing so, a young man ran up to her and said in breathless French: 'We weren't expecting any personnel, just supplies!'

'A change of plan,' she said. 'Don't worry about it. Is Anton with you?' Anton was the codename of the leader of the Vestryman circuit.

'Yes.'

'Tell him Leopardess is here.'

'Ah – you are Leopardess?' He was impressed.

'Yes.'

'I'm Chevalier. I'm so pleased to meet you.'

She glanced up at the sky. It was turning from black to grey. 'Find Anton as quickly as you can, please, Chevalier. Tell him we have six people who need transport. There's no time to spare.'

'Very good.' He hurried away.

She folded her parachute into a neat bundle, then set out to find the other Jackdaws. Greta had landed in a tree, and had bruised herself crashing through the upper branches, but had come to rest without serious injury, and had been able to slip out of her harness and climb down to the ground. The others had all come down safely on the grass. 'I'm very proud of myself,' said Jelly, 'but I wouldn't do it again for a million pounds.'

Flick noted that the Resistance people were carrying the containers to the southern end of the field, and she took the Jackdaws in that direction. There she found a builder's van, a horse and cart, and an old Lincoln limousine with the bonnet removed and some kind of steam motor powering it. She was not surprised: petrol was available only for essential business, and French people tried all kinds of ingenious ways to run their cars.

The Resistance men had loaded the cart with containers and were now hiding them under empty vegetable boxes. More containers were going into the back of the builder's van. Directing the operation was Anton, a thin man of forty in a greasy cap and a short blue workman's jacket, with a yellow French cigarette stuck to his lip. He stared in astonishment. 'Six women?' he said. 'Is this a sewing circle?'

Jokes about women were best ignored, Flick had found. She spoke solemnly to him. 'This is the most important operation I've ever run, and I need your help.'

'Of course.'

'We have to catch a train to Paris.'

'I can get you to Chartres.' He glanced at the sky, calculating the time until daylight, then pointed across the field to a farmhouse, dimly visible. 'You can hide in a barn for now. When we have disposed of these containers, we'll come back for you.'

'Not good enough,' Flick said firmly. 'We have to get going.'

'The first train to Paris leaves at ten. I can get you there by then.'

'Nonsense. No one knows when the trains will run.' It was true. The combination of Allied bombing,

Resistance sabotage, and deliberate mistakes by anti-Nazi railway workers had wrecked all schedules, and the only thing to do was go to the station and wait until a train came. But it was best to get there early. 'Put the containers in the barn and take us now.'

'Impossible,' he said. 'I have to stash the supplies before daylight.'

The men stopped work to listen to the argument.

Flick sighed. The guns and ammunition in the containers were the most important thing in the world to Anton. They were the source of his power and prestige. She said: 'This is more important, believe me.'

'I'm sorry . . .'

'Anton, listen to me. If you don't do this for me, I promise you, you will never again receive a single container from England. You know I can do this, don't you?'

There was a pause. Anton did not want to back down in front of his men. However, if the supply of arms dried up, the men would go elsewhere. This was the only leverage British officers had over the French Resistance.

But it worked. He glared at her. Slowly, he removed the stub of the cigarette from his mouth, pinched out the end, and threw it away. 'Very well,' he said. 'Get into the van.'

The women helped unload the containers then clambered in. The floor was filthy with cement dust, mud and oil, but they found some scraps of sacking and used them to keep the worst of the dirt off their clothes as they sat on the floor. Anton closed the door on them.

Chevalier got into the driving seat. 'So, ladies,' he said in English. 'Off we go!'

Flick replied coldly in French. 'No jokes, please, and no English.'

He drove off.

Having flown five hundred miles on the metal floor of a bomber, the Jackdaws now drove twenty miles in the back of a builder's van. Surprisingly it was Jelly – the oldest, the fattest, and the least fit of the six – who was most stoical, joking about the discomfort and laughing at herself when the van took a sharp bend and she rolled over helplessly.

But when the sun came up, and the van entered the small city of Chartres, their mood became sombre again. Maude said: 'I can't believe I'm doing this,' and Diana squeezed her hand.

Flick was planning ahead. 'From now on, we split up into pairs,' she said. The teams had been decided back at the Finishing School. Flick had put Diana with Maude, for otherwise Diana would make a fuss. Flick paired herself with Ruby, because she wanted to be able to discuss problems with someone, and Ruby was the cleverest Jackdaw. Unfortunately, that left Greta with Jelly. 'I still don't see why I have to go with the foreigner,' Jelly said.

'This isn't a tea-party,' Flick said, irritated. 'You don't get to sit by your best friend. It's a military operation and you do what you're told.'

Jelly shut up.

'We'll have to modify our cover stories, to explain the train trip,' Flick went on. 'Any ideas?'

Greta said: 'I'm the wife of Major Remmer, a German officer working in Paris, travelling with my French maid. I was to be visiting the cathedral at Reims. Now, I suppose, I could be returning from a visit to the cathedral at Chartres.'

'Good enough. Diana?'

'Maude and I are secretaries working for the electric company in Reims. We've been to Chartres because . . . Maude has lost contact with her fiancé and we thought he might be here. But he isn't.'

Flick nodded, satisfied. There were thousands of French women searching for missing relatives, especially young men, who might have been injured by bombing, arrested by the Gestapo, sent to labour camps in Germany, or recruited by the Resistance.

She said: 'And I'm the widow of a stockbroker who was killed in 1940. I went to Chartres to fetch my orphaned cousin and bring her to live with me in Reims.'

One of the great advantages women had as secret agents was that they could move around the country without attracting suspicion. By contrast, a man found outside the area where he worked would automatically be assumed to be in the Resistance, especially if he was young.

Flick spoke to the driver, Chevalier. 'Look for a quiet spot to let us out.' The sight of six respectably dressed women getting out of the back of a builder's van would be somewhat remarkable, even in occupied France where people used any means of transport they could get. 'We can find the station on our own.'

A couple of minutes later he stopped the van and reversed into a turn, then jumped out and opened the back door. The Jackdaws got out and found themselves in a narrow cobbled alley with high houses on either side. Through a gap between roofs she glimpsed part of the cathedral.

Flick reminded them of the plan. 'Go to the station, buy one-way tickets to Paris, and get the first train. Each pair will pretend not to know the others, but we'll try to sit close together on the train. We regroup in Paris: you have the address.' They were going to a flophouse called Hôtel de la Chapelle, where the proprietress, though not actually in the Resistance, could be relied upon not to ask questions. If they arrived in time, they would go on to Reims immediately; if not, they could stay overnight at the flophouse. Flick was not pleased to be going to Paris – it was crawling with Gestapo men and their collaborators, the 'Kollabos' – but there was no way around it by train.

Only Flick and Greta knew the real mission of the Jackdaws. The others still thought they were going to blow up a railway tunnel.

'Diana and Maude first, off you go, quick! Jelly and Greta next, more slowly.' They went off, looking scared. Chevalier shook their hands, wished them luck, and drove away, heading back to the field to fetch the rest of the containers. Flick and Ruby walked out of the alley.

The first few steps in a French town were always the worst. Flick felt that everyone she saw must know who she was, as if she had a sign on her back saying: 'British agent! Shoot her down!' But people walked by as if she were nobody special; and after she had safely passed a *gendarme* and a couple of German officers her pulse began to return to normal.

She still felt very strange. All her life she had been respectable, and she had been taught to regard policemen as her friends. 'I hate being on the wrong side of the law,' she murmured to Ruby in French. 'As if I've done something wicked.'

Ruby gave a low laugh. 'I'm used to it,' she said. 'The police have always been my enemies.'

Flick remembered with a start that Ruby had been in jail for murder last Tuesday. It seemed a long four days.

They reached the cathedral, at the top of the hill, and Flick felt a thrill at the sight of it, the summit of French medieval culture, a church like none other. She suffered a sharp pang of regret for the peaceful times when she might have spent a couple of hours looking around the cathedral.

They walked down the hill to the station, a modern stone building the same colour as the cathedral. They entered a square lobby in tan marble. There was a queue at the ticket window. That was good: it meant local people were optimistic that there would be a train soon. Greta and Jelly were in the queue, but there was no sign of Diana and Maude, who must already be on the platform.

They stood in line in front of an anti-Resistance

poster showing a thug with a gun and Stalin behind him. It read:

> ### THEY MURDER!
> *wrapped in the folds of*
> ### OUR FLAG

That's supposed to be me, Flick thought.

They bought their tickets without incident. On the way to the platform they had to pass a Gestapo checkpoint, and Flick's pulse beat faster. Greta and Jelly were ahead of them in line. This would be their first encounter with the enemy. Flick prayed they would be able to keep their nerve. Diana and Maude must have already passed through.

Greta spoke to the Gestapo men in German. Flick could clearly hear her giving her cover story. 'I know a Major Remmer,' said one of the men, a sergeant. 'Is he an engineer?'

'No, he's in Intelligence,' Greta replied. She seemed remarkably calm, and Flick reflected that pretending to be something she was not must be second nature to her.

'You must like cathedrals,' he said conversationally. 'There's nothing else to see in this dump.'

'Yes.'

He turned to Jelly's papers and began to speak French. 'You travel everywhere with Frau Remmer?'

'Yes, she's very kind to me,' Jelly replied. Flick heard the tremor in her voice and knew that she was terrified.

The sergeant said: 'Did you see the bishop's palace? That's quite a sight.'

381

Greta replied in French. 'We did – very impressive.'

The sergeant was looking at Jelly, waiting for her response. She looked dumbstruck for a moment, then she said: 'The bishop's wife was very gracious.'

Flick's heart sank into her boots. Jelly could speak perfect French but she knew nothing about any foreign country. She did not realize that it was only in the Church of England that bishops could have wives. France was Catholic, and priests were celibate. Jelly had given herself away at the first check.

What would happen now? Flick's Sten gun, with the skeleton butt and the silencer, was in her suitcase, disassembled into three parts; but she had her personal Browning automatic in the worn leather shoulder bag she carried. Now she discreetly unzipped the bag for quick access to her gun, and she saw Ruby put her right hand in her raincoat pocket, where her pistol was.

'Wife?' the sergeant said to Jelly. 'What wife?'

Jelly just looked nonplussed.

'You are French?' he said.

'Of course.'

Greta stepped in quickly. 'Not his wife, his housekeeper,' she said in French. It was a plausible explanation: in that language, a wife was *une femme* and a housekeeper was *une femme de ménage*.

Jelly realized she had made a mistake, and said: 'Yes, of course, his housekeeper, I meant to say.'

Flick held her breath.

The sergeant hesitated for a moment longer, then shrugged and handed back their papers. 'I hope you won't have to wait too long for a train,' he said, reverting to German.

Greta and Jelly walked on, and Flick allowed herself to breathe again.

When she and Ruby got to the head of the line, they were about to hand over their papers when two uniformed French gendarmes jumped the queue. They paused at the checkpoint and gave the Germans a sketchy salute, but did not offer their papers. The sergeant nodded and said: 'Go ahead.'

If I were running security here, Flick thought, I'd tighten up on that point. Anyone could pretend to be a cop. But the Germans were overly deferential to people in uniform: that was part of the reason they had let their country be taken over by psychopaths.

Then it was her turn to tell her story to the Gestapo. 'You're cousins?' the sergeant said, looking from her to Ruby and back again.

'Not much resemblance, is there?' Flick said, with a cheerful air she did not feel. There was none at all: Flick had blonde hair, green eyes and fair skin, whereas Ruby had dark hair and black eyes.

'She looks like a gypsy,' he said rudely.

Flick pretended to be indignant. 'Well, she's not.' By way of explanation for Ruby's colouring, she added: 'Her mother, my uncle's wife, came from Naples.'

He shrugged and addressed Ruby. 'How did your parents die?'

'In a train derailed by saboteurs,' she said.

'The Resistance?'

383

'Yes.'

'My sympathies, young lady. Those people are animals.' He handed the papers back.

'Thank you, sir,' said Ruby. Flick just nodded. They walked on.

It had not been an easy checkpoint. I hope they're not all like that, Flick thought; my heart won't stand it.

Diana and Maude had gone to the bar. Flick looked through the window and saw they were drinking champagne. She felt cross. SOE's thousand-franc notes were not for that purpose. Besides, Diana should realize she needed her wits about her at every second. But there was nothing Flick could do about it now.

Greta and Jelly were sitting on a bench. Jelly looked chastened, no doubt because her life had just been saved by someone she thought of as a foreign pervert. Flick wondered whether her attitude would improve now.

She and Ruby found another bench some distance away, and sat down to wait.

Over the next few hours more and more people crowded on to the platform. There were men in suits who looked as if they might be lawyers or local government officials with business in Paris, some relatively well-dressed French women, and a scattering of Germans in uniform. The Jackdaws, having money and forged ration books, were able to get *pain noir* and ersatz coffee from the bar.

It was eleven o'clock when a train pulled in. The coaches were full, and not many people got off, so Flick and Ruby had to stand. Greta and Jelly did, too, but

Diana and Maude managed to get seats in a six-person compartment with two middle-aged women and the two gendarmes.

The gendarmes worried Flick. She managed to squeeze into a place right outside the compartment, from where she could look through the glass and keep an eye on them. Fortunately, the combination of a restless night and the champagne they had drunk at the station put Diana and Maude to sleep as soon as the train pulled out of the station.

They chugged slowly through woods and rolling fields. An hour later the two French women got off the train, and Flick and Ruby quickly slid into the vacated seats. However, Flick regretted the decision almost immediately. The gendarmes, both in their twenties, immediately struck up a conversation, delighted to have some girls to talk to during the long journey.

Their names were Christian and Jean-Marie. Both appeared to be in their twenties. Christian was romantically handsome, with curly black hair and brown eyes; Jean-Marie had a shrewd, foxy face with a fair moustache. Christian, the talkative one, was in the middle seat, and Ruby sat next to him. Flick was on the opposite banquette, with Maude beside her, slumped the other way with her head on Diana's bosom.

The gendarmes were travelling to Paris to pick up a prisoner, they said. It was nothing to do with the war: he was a local man who had murdered his wife and stepson then fled to Paris, where he had been caught by the *flics*, the city police, and had confessed. It was their job to bring him back to Chartres to stand trial.

Christian reached into his tunic pocket and pulled out the handcuffs they would put on him, as if to prove to Flick that he was not boasting.

In the next hour Flick learned everything there was to know about Christian. She was expected to reciprocate, so she had to elaborate her cover story far beyond the basic facts she had figured out beforehand. It strained her imagination, but she told herself this was good practice for a more hostile interrogation.

They passed Versailles and crawled through bomb-ravaged train yards at St Quentin. Maude woke up. She remembered to speak French, but she forgot that she was not supposed to know Flick, so she said: 'Hello, where are we, do you know?'

The gendarmes looked puzzled. Flick had told them she and Ruby had no connection with the two sleeping girls, yet Maude had addressed Flick like a friend.

Flick kept her nerve. Smiling, she said: 'You don't know me. I think you have mistaken me for your friend on the other side. You're still half asleep.'

Maude gave her a don't-be-so-stupid frown, then caught the eye of Christian. In a pantomime of comprehension she registered surprise, put her hand over her mouth in horror, then said unconvincingly: 'Of course, you're quite right, excuse me.'

Christian was not a suspicious man, however, and he smiled at Maude and said: 'You've been asleep for two hours. We're on the outskirts of Paris. But, as you can see, the train is not moving.'

Maude gave him the benefit of her most dazzling smile. 'When do you think we will arrive?'

'There, Mademoiselle, you ask too much of me. I am merely human. Only God can tell the future.'

Maude laughed as if he had said something deliciously witty, and Flick relaxed.

Then Diana woke up and said loudly, in English: 'Good God, my head hurts, what bloody time is it?'

A moment later she saw the gendarmes and realized instantly what she had done – but it was too late.

'She spoke English!' said Christian.

Flick saw Ruby reach for her gun.

'You're British!' he said to Diana. He looked at Maude. 'You, too!' As his gaze went around the compartment he realized the truth. 'All of you!'

Flick reached across and grabbed Ruby's wrist as her gun was half way out of her raincoat pocket.

Christian saw the gesture, looked down at what Ruby had in her hand, and said: 'And armed!' His astonishment would have been comical if they had not been in danger of their lives.

Diana said: 'Oh, Christ, that's torn it.'

The train jerked and moved forward.

Christian lowered his voice. 'You're all agents of the Allies!'

Flick waited on tenterhooks to see what he would do. If he drew his gun, Ruby would shoot him. Then they would all have to jump from the train. With luck they might disappear into the slums beside the railway tracks before the Gestapo were alerted. The train picked up speed. She wondered whether they should jump now, before they were moving too fast.

Several frozen seconds passed. Then Christian

smiled. 'Good luck!' he said, lowering his voice to a whisper. 'Your secret is safe with us!'

They were sympathizers – thank God. Flick slumped with relief. 'Thank you,' she said.

Christian said: 'When will the invasion come?'

He was naïve to think that someone who really knew such a secret would reveal it so casually; but to keep him motivated she said: 'Any day now. Maybe Tuesday.'

'Truly? This is wonderful. Long live France!'

Flick said: 'I'm so glad you are on our side.'

'I have always been against the Germans.' Christian puffed himself up a little. 'In my job, I have been able to render some useful services to the Resistance, in a discreet way.' He tapped the side of his nose.

Flick did not believe him for a second. No doubt he was against the Germans: most French people were, after four years of scarce food, old clothes and curfews. But if he really had worked with the Resistance he would not have told anyone – on the contrary, he would have been terrified of people finding out.

However, that did not matter. The important thing was that he could see which way the wind was blowing, and he was not going to turn Allied agents over to the Gestapo a few days before the invasion. There was too strong a chance he would end up being punished for it.

The train slowed down, and Flick saw that they were coming into the Gare d'Orsay station. She stood up. Christian kissed her hand and said with a tremor in his voice: 'You are a brave woman. Good luck!'

She left the carriage first. As she stepped on to the

platform, she saw a workman pasting up a poster. Something struck her as familiar. She looked more closely at the poster, and her heart stopped.

It was a picture of her.

She had never seen it before, and she had no recollection of ever having had her photograph taken in a swimsuit. The background was cloudy, as if it had been painted over, so there were no clues there. The poster gave her name, plus one of her old aliases, Françoise Boule, and said she was a murderess.

The workman was just finishing his task. He picked up his bucket of paste and a stack of posters and moved on.

Flick realized her picture must be all over Paris.

This was a terrible blow. She stood frozen on the platform. She was so frightened she wanted to throw up. Then she got hold of herself.

Her first problem was how to get out of the Gare d'Orsay. She looked along the platform and saw a checkpoint at the ticket barrier. She had to assume the Gestapo officers manning it had seen the picture.

How could she get past them? She could not talk her way through. If they recognized her, they would arrest her, and no tall tale would convince German officers to do otherwise. Could the Jackdaws shoot their way out of this? They might kill the men at the checkpoint, but there would be others all over the station, plus French police who would probably shoot first and ask questions later. It was too risky.

There was a way out, she realized. She could hand over command of the operation to one of the others –

Ruby, probably – then let them pass through the checkpoint ahead of her, and finally give herself up. That way, the mission would not be doomed.

She turned around. Ruby, Diana and Maude had got off the train. Christian and Jean-Marie were about to follow. Then Flick remembered the handcuffs Christian had in his pocket, and a wild scheme occurred to her.

She pushed Christian back into the carriage and climbed in after him.

He was not sure if this was some kind of joke, and he smiled anxiously. 'What's the matter?'

'Look,' she said. 'There's a poster of me on the wall.'

Both the gendarmes looked out. Christian turned pale. Jean-Marie said: 'My God, you really are spies!'

'You have to save me,' she said.

Christian said: 'How can we? The Gestapo—'

'I must get through the checkpoint.'

'But they will arrest you.'

'Not if I've already been arrested.'

'What do you mean?'

'Put the handcuffs on me. Pretend you have captured me. March me through the checkpoint. If they stop you, say you're taking me to eighty-four Avenue Foch.' It was the address of Gestapo headquarters.

'What then?'

'Commandeer a taxi. Get in with me. Then, once we are clear of the station, take the cuffs off and let me out in a quiet street. And continue on to your real destination.'

Christian looked terrified. Flick could tell that he

wanted with all his heart to back out. But he hardly could, after his big talk about the Resistance.

Jean-Marie was calmer. 'It will work,' he said. 'They won't be suspicious of police officers in uniform.'

Ruby climbed back into the carriage. 'Flick!' she said. 'That poster—'

'I know. The gendarmes are going to march me through the checkpoint in handcuffs and release me later. If things go wrong, you're in charge of the mission.' She switched to English. 'Forget the railway tunnel, that's a cover story. The real target is the telephone exchange at Sainte-Cécile. But don't tell the others until the last minute. Now get them back in here, quickly.'

A few moments later they were all crowded into the carriage. Flick told them the plan. Then she said: 'If this doesn't work, and I get arrested, *whatever you do don't shoot.* There will be too many police at the station. If you start a gun battle you'll lose. The mission comes first. Abandon me, get out of the station, regroup at the hotel, and carry on. Ruby will be in command. No discussion, there isn't time.' She turned to Christian. 'The handcuffs.'

He hesitated.

Flick wanted to scream, *Get on with it, you big-mouthed coward,* but instead she lowered her voice to an intimate murmur and said: 'Thank you for saving my life – I'll never forget you, Christian.'

He took out the cuffs.

'The rest of you, get going,' Flick said.

Christian handcuffed Flick's right hand to Jean-

Marie's left, then they stepped down from the train and marched along the platform three abreast, Christian carrying Flick's suitcase and her shoulder bag with the automatic pistol in it. There was a queue at the checkpoint. Jean-Marie said loudly: 'Stand aside, there. Stand aside, please, ladies and gentlemen. Coming through.' They went straight to the head of the line, as they had at Chartres. Both gendarmes saluted the Gestapo officers, but they did not stop.

However, the captain in charge of the checkpoint looked up from the identity card he was examining and said quietly: 'Wait.'

All three stood still. Flick knew she was very near death.

The captain looked hard at Flick. 'She's the one on the poster.'

Christian seemed too scared to speak. After a moment, Jean-Marie answered the question. 'Yes, Captain, we arrested her in Chartres.'

Flick thanked heaven that one of them had a cool head.

'Well done,' said the captain. 'But where are you taking her?'

Jean-Marie continued to answer. 'Our orders are to deliver her to Avenue Foch.'

'Do you need transport?'

'There is a police vehicle waiting for us outside the station.'

The captain nodded, but still did not dismiss them. He continued to stare at Flick. She began to think there was something about her appearance that had given away her subterfuge, something in her face that told him she was only pretending to be a prisoner. Finally he said: 'These British. They send little girls to do their fighting for them.' He shook his head in disbelief.

Jean-Marie sensibly kept his mouth shut.

At last the captain said: 'Carry on.'

Flick and the gendarmes marched through the checkpoint and out into the sunshine.

THIRTY-THREE

Paul Chancellor had been angry with Percy Thwaite, violently angry, when he found out about the message from Brian Standish. 'You deceived me!' Paul had shouted at Percy. 'You deliberately made sure I was out of the way before you showed it to Flick!'

'It's true, but it seemed best—'

'I'm in command – you have no right to withhold information from me!'

'I thought you would have aborted the flight.'

'Perhaps I would have – maybe I *should* have.'

'But you would have done it for love of Flick, not because it was right operationally.'

There Percy had touched Paul's weak spot, for Paul had compromised his position as leader by sleeping with one of his team. That had made him more angry, but he had been forced to suppress his rage.

They could not contact Flick's plane, for flights over enemy territory had to observe radio silence, so the two men had stayed at the airfield all night, smoking and pacing and worrying about the woman they both, in different ways, loved. Paul had, in his shirt pocket, the wooden French toothbrush he and Flick had shared on Friday morning, after their night together. He was not normally superstitious, but he kept touching it, as if he were touching her, making sure she was okay.

When the plane returned, and the pilot told them how Flick had become suspicious of the reception committee at Chatelle, and had eventually dropped near Chartres, Paul had been so relieved he almost wept. Minutes later, Percy had taken a call from SOE headquarters in London and had learned of Brian Standish's message demanding to know what had gone wrong. Paul had decided to respond by sending the reply drafted by Flick and brought home by her pilot. In case Brian was still at liberty, it told him that the Jackdaws had landed and would contact him; but it gave no further information, because of the possibility that he was in the hands of the Gestapo.

Still no one was sure what had happened out there. The uncertainty was unbearable for Paul. Flick had to go to Reims, one way or another. He had to know whether she was walking into a Gestapo trap. Surely there must be a way to check whether Brian's transmissions were genuine?

His signals bore the correct security tags: Percy double-checked. But the Gestapo knew about security tags, and they could easily have tortured Brian to learn his. There were subtler methods of checking, Percy said, but they depended on the girls at the listening station. So Paul had decided to go there.

At first Percy had resisted. It was dangerous for operational people to descend on signals units, he said; they disrupted the smooth running of the service for hundreds of agents. Paul ignored that. Then the head of the station said he would be delighted for Paul to make an appointment to visit in, say, two or three weeks? No, Paul had said, two or three hours is what I had in mind. He had insisted, gently but firmly, using the threat of Monty's wrath as a last resort. And so he had gone to Grendon Underwood.

As a small boy in Sunday school, Paul had been vexed by a theological problem. He had noticed that in Arlington, Virginia, where he was living with his parents, most of the children of his age went to bed at the same time, seven thirty. That meant they were saying their prayers simultaneously. With all those voices rising to heaven, how could God hear what he, Paul, was saying? He was not satisfied with the answer of the pastor, who just said that God could do anything. Little Paul knew that was an evasion. The question troubled him for years.

If he could have seen Grendon Underwood, he would have understood.

Like God, the Special Operations Executive had to listen to innumerable messages, and it often happened that scores of them came in at the same time. Secret agents in their hideaways were all tapping their Morse keys simultaneously, like the nine-year-olds of Arlington kneeling at their bedsides at half past seven. SOE heard them all.

Grendon Underwood was another grand country house vacated by the owners and taken over by the military. Officially called Station 53a, it was a listening post. In its extensive grounds were radio aerials grouped in great arcs like the ears of God, listening to

396

messages that came from anywhere between the Arctic north of Norway to the dusty south of Spain. Four hundred wireless operators and coders, most of them young women in the FANYs, worked in the big house and lived in Nissen huts hastily erected in the grounds.

Paul was shown around by a supervisor, Jean Bevins, a heavy woman with spectacles. At first she was terrified of the visiting bigshot who represented Montgomery himself, but Paul smiled and talked softly and made her feel at ease. She took him to the transmitting room, where a hundred or so girls sat in rows, each with headphones, notebook and pencils. A big board showed agents' codenames and scheduled times for transmission – known as 'skeds' and always pronounced the American way – and the frequencies they would use. There was an atmosphere of intense concentration, the only sound being the tap of Morse code as an operator told an agent she was receiving him loud and clear.

Jean introduced Paul to Lucy Briggs, a pretty blonde girl with a Yorkshire accent so strong that he had to concentrate hard to understand her. 'Helicopter?' she said. 'Aye, I know Helicopter – he's new. He calls in at twenty hundred hours and receives at twenty-three hundred. No problems, so far.'

She never pronounced the letter aitch. Once Paul realized that, he began to find it easier to interpret the accent.

'What do you mean?' he asked her. 'What sort of problems do you get?'

'Well, some of them don't tune the transmitter right

so you have to search for the frequency. Then the signal may be weak, so that you can't hear the letters very well and you worry that you might be mistaking dashes for dots – the letter B is very like D, for instance. And the tone is always bad from those little suitcase radios, because they're so small.'

'Would you recognize his "fist"?'

She looked dubious. 'He's only broadcast three times. On Wednesday he was a bit nervous, probably because it was his first, but his pace was steady, as if he knew he had plenty of time. I was pleased – I thought he must feel reasonably safe. We worry about them, you know. We're sitting here nice and warm and they're somewhere behind enemy lines dodging the bloody Gestapo.'

'What about his second broadcast?'

'That was Thursday, and he was rushed. When they're in a hurry, it can be difficult to be sure what they mean – you know, was that two dots run together, or a short dash? Wherever he was sending from, he wanted to get out of there fast.'

'And then?'

'Friday he didn't broadcast. But I didn't worry. They don't call unless they have to, it's too dangerous. Then he came on the air on Saturday morning, just before dawn. It was an emergency message, but he didn't sound panicky, in fact I remember thinking to myself, "He's getting the hang of this." You know, it was a strong signal, the rhythm was steady, all the letters clear.'

'Could it have been someone else using his transmitter that time?'

She looked thoughtful. 'It sounded like him . . . but yes, it could have been someone else, I suppose. And if it was a German, pretending to be him, they would sound nice and steady, wouldn't they, because they'd have nothing to fear?'

Paul felt as if he were wading through gumbo. Every question he asked had two answers. He yearned for something definite. He had to fight down panic every time he recalled to mind the dreadful prospect that he might lose Flick, less than a week after she had come into his life like a gift from the gods.

Jean had disappeared, and returned now with a sheaf of papers in a plump hand. 'I've brought the decrypts of the three signals received from Helicopter,' she said. Her quiet efficiency pleased him.

He looked at the first sheet.

CALLSIGN HLCP (HELICOPTER)
SECURITY TAG PRESENT
30 MAY 1944
MESSAGE READS:
ARRIVED OK STOP CRYT RENDEVOUS UNSAFE
STOP NABBED BY GGESTAPO BUT GOT AWAY
STOP IN FUTURE RENDEZVOUS AT CAFE DE LA
GARE OVER

'He can't spell for nuts,' Paul commented.

'It's not his spelling,' Jean said. 'They always make errors in the Morse. We order the decoders to leave them in the decrypt, rather than tidy them up, in case there's some significance.'

Brian's second transmission, giving the strength of the Bollinger circuit, was longer.

CALLSIGN HLCP (HELICOPTER)
SECURITY TAG PRESENT
31 MAY 1944
MESSAGE READS:
ACTIV AGENTS NOMBER FIVE AS FOLOWS STOP
MONET WHO IS WOUNED STOP COMTESSE OK
STOP CHEVAL HELPS OCASIONLY STOP
BOURGEOISE STILL IM PLACE STOP PLUS MY
RESCUER CODNAME CHARENTON STOP

Paul looked up. 'This is much worse.'

Lucy said: 'I told you he was in a rush the second time.'

There was more of the second message, mainly a detailed account of the incident at the cathedral. Paul went on to the third:

CALLSIGN HLCP (HELICOPTER)
SECURITY TAG PRESENT
2 JUN 1944
MESSAGE READS:
WHAT THE DEVIL HAPPENED QUERY SEND
INSTRUCTIONS STOP REPLY IMEDIATELY OVER

'He's improving,' Paul said. 'Only one mistake.'

'I thought he was more relaxed on Saturday,' Lucy said.

'Either that, or someone else sent the signal.' Suddenly, Paul thought he saw a way to test whether 'Brian' was himself or a Gestapo impersonator. If it worked, it would at least give him certainty. 'Lucy, do you ever make mistakes in transmission?'

'Hardly ever.' She threw an anxious glance at her supervisor. 'If a new girl is a bit careless, the agent will kick up a hell of a stink. Quite rightly, too. There should never be any mistakes – the agents have enough problems to cope with.'

Paul turned to Jean. 'If I draft a message would you encode it exactly as it is? It would be a kind of test.'

'Of course.'

He looked at his watch. It was seven thirty p.m. 'He should broadcast at eight. Can you send it then?'

The supervisor said: 'Yes. When he calls in, we'll just tell him to stand by to receive an emergency message immediately after transmission.'

Paul sat down, thought for a moment, then wrote on a pad:

GIVE YOUR ARMS HOW MAN AUTOMATS HOW
MY STENS ALSO AMMO HOW MNY ROUNDS ECH
PLUS GREDANES REPLY IMMMEDIATLY

He considered it for a moment. It was an unreasonable request, phrased in a high-handed tone, and it appeared to be carelessly encoded and transmitted. He showed it to Jean. She frowned. 'That's a terrible message. I'd be ashamed of it.'

'What do you think an agent's reaction would be?'

She gave a humourless laugh. 'He would send an angry reply with a few swear words in it.'

'Please encode it exactly as it is and send it to Helicopter.'

She looked troubled. 'If that's what you wish.'

'Yes, please.'

'Of course.' She took it away.

Paul went in search of food. The canteen operated twenty-four hours a day, as the station did, but the coffee was tasteless and there was nothing to eat but some stale sandwiches and dried-up cake.

A few minutes after eight o'clock, the supervisor came into the canteen. 'Helicopter called in to say he had had no word yet from Leopardess. We're sending him the emergency message now.'

'Thank you.' It would take Brian – or his Gestapo impersonator – at least an hour to decode the message, compose a reply, encode it and transmit it. Paul stared at his plate, wondering how the British had the nerve to call this a sandwich: two pieces of white bread smeared with margarine and one thin slice of ham.

No mustard.

THIRTY-FOUR

The red-light district of Paris was a neighbourhood of narrow, dirty streets on a low hill behind the rue de la Chapelle, not far from the Gare du Nord. At its heart was 'La Charbo', the rue de la Charbonnière. On the north side of the street, the convent of La Chapelle stood like a marble statue in a junkyard. The convent consisted of a tiny church and a house where eight nuns dedicated their lives to helping the most wretched of Parisians. They made soup for starving old men, talked depressed women out of suicide, dragged drunk sailors from the gutter, and taught the children of prostitutes to read and write. Next door to the convent stood the Hôtel de la Chapelle.

The hotel was not exactly a brothel, for there were no whores in residence; but when the place was not full the proprietress was willing to rent rooms by the hour to heavily made-up women in cheap evening gowns who arrived with fat French businessmen, furtive German soldiers, or naïve young men too drunk to see straight.

Flick walked through the door with a mighty sense of relief. The gendarmes had dropped her off half a mile away. She had seen two copies of her 'Wanted' poster on the way. Christian had given her his handkerchief, a clean cotton square, red with white dots, and she had tied it over her head in an attempt to hide her blonde hair, but she knew that anyone who looked hard at her would recognize her from the poster. There had been nothing she could do but keep her eyes down and her fingers crossed. It had seemed like the longest walk of her life.

The proprietress was a friendly, overweight woman wearing a pink silk bathrobe over a whalebone corset. She had once been voluptuous, Flick guessed. Flick had stayed at the place before, but the proprietress did not appear to remember her. Flick addressed her as 'Madame', but she said: 'Call me Régine.' She took Flick's money and gave her a room key without asking any questions.

Flick was about to go upstairs to her room when she glanced through the window and saw Diana and Maude arriving in a strange kind of taxi, a sofa on wheels attached to a bicycle. Their brush with the gendarmes did not seem to have sobered them, and they were giggling about the vehicle.

'Good God, what a dump,' said Diana, when she walked through the door. 'Perhaps we can eat out.'

Paris restaurants had continued to operate during the occupation, but inevitably many of their customers were German officers, and agents avoided them if they could. 'Don't even think about it,' Flick said crossly. 'We're going to lie low here for a few hours then go to the Gare de l'Est at first light.'

Maude looked accusingly at Diana. 'You promised to take me to the Ritz.'

Flick controlled her temper. 'What world are you living in?' she hissed at Maude.

'All right, keep your hair on.'

'Nobody leaves! Is that understood?'

'Yes, yes.'

'One of us will go out and buy food later. I have to get out of sight now. Diana, you sit here and wait for the others while Maude checks into your room. Let me know when everyone's arrived.'

Climbing the stairs, Flick passed a Negro girl in a tight red dress and noticed that she had a full head of straight black hair. 'Wait,' Flick said to her. 'Will you sell me your wig?'

'You can buy one yourself around the corner, honey.' She looked Flick up and down, taking her for an amateur hooker. 'But, frankly, I'd say you need more than a wig.'

'I'm in a hurry.'

The girl pulled it off to reveal black curls cropped close to her scalp. 'I can't work without it.'

Flick took a thousand-franc note from her jacket pocket. 'Buy yourself another.'

She looked at Flick with new eyes, realizing she had too much money to be a prostitute. With a shrug, she accepted the money and handed over the wig.

'Thank you,' said Flick.

The girl hesitated. No doubt she was wondering how many more of those notes Flick had. 'I do girls, too,' she said. She reached out and brushed Flick's breast lightly with her fingertips.

'No, thanks.'

'Maybe you and your boyfriend . . .'

'No.'

The girl looked at the thousand-franc note. 'Well, I guess this is my night off. Good luck, honey.'

'Thanks,' said Flick. 'I need it.'

She found her room, put her case on the bed, and took off her jacket. There was a small mirror over a washbasin. Flick washed her hands then stood looking at her face for a moment.

She combed her short blonde hair back over her ears and pinned it with hair clips. Then she put on the wig and adjusted it. It was a bit big, but it would stay on. The black hair altered her appearance radically. However, her fair eyebrows now looked peculiar. She took the eyebrow pencil from her make-up kit and darkened them. That was much better. Not only did she look like a brunette, she seemed more formidable than the sweet girl in the swimsuit. She had the same straight nose and severe chin, but that seemed like a family resemblance between two otherwise different-looking sisters.

Next she took her identity papers from her jacket pocket. With great care, she retouched the photograph, using the eyebrow pencil to draw faint lines of dark hair and narrow dark eyebrows. When she was done she looked hard at the picture. She did not think anyone would be able to tell it had been doctored unless they rubbed it hard enough to smear the pencil marks.

She took off the wig, stepped out of her shoes and lay on the bed. She had not slept for two nights, because she had spent Thursday night making love to

Paul and Friday night on the metal floor of a Hudson bomber. Now she closed her eyes and dropped off within seconds.

She was awakened by a knock at the door. To her surprise, it was getting dark: she had slept for several hours. She went to the door and said: 'Who is it?'

'Ruby.'

She let her in. 'Is everything all right?'

'I'm not sure.'

Flick closed the curtains then switched on the light. 'What's happened?'

'Everyone has checked in. But I don't know where Diana and Maude are. They're not in their room.'

'Where have you looked?'

'The proprietress's office, the little church next door, the bar across the street.'

'Oh, Christ,' Flick said in dismay. 'The bloody fools, they've gone out.'

'Where would they have gone?'

'Maude wanted to go to the Ritz.'

Ruby was incredulous. 'They can't be that stupid!'

'Maude can.'

'But I thought Diana had more sense.'

'Diana's in love,' Flick said. 'I suppose she'll do anything Maude asks. And she wants to impress her paramour, take her to swanky places, show that she knows her way around the world of high society.'

'They say love is blind.'

'In this case, love is bloody suicidal. I can't believe it – but I bet that's where they've gone. It will serve them right if they end up dead.'

'What'll we do?'

'Go to the Ritz and get them out of there – if we're not too late.'

Flick put on her wig. Ruby said: 'I wondered why your eyebrows had gone dark. It's effective, you look like someone else.'

'Good. Get your gun.'

In the lobby, Régine handed Flick a note. It was addressed in Diana's handwriting. Flick ripped it open and read:

We're going to a better hotel. We'll meet you at the Gare de l'Est at 5 a.m. Don't worry!

She showed it to Ruby then ripped it to shreds. She was most angry with herself. She had known Diana all her life, it was no surprise that she was foolish and irresponsible. Why did I bring her? she asked herself. Because I had no one else, was the answer.

They left the flophouse. Flick did not want to use the Métro, for she knew there were Gestapo checkpoints at some stations and occasional spot checks on the trains. The Ritz was in the Place Vendôme, a brisk half-hour walk from La Charbo. The sun had gone down, and night was falling fast. They would have to keep an eye on the time: there was an eleven o'clock curfew.

Flick wondered how long it would take the Ritz staff to call the Gestapo about Diana and Maude. They would have known immediately that there was something odd about them. Their papers said they were secretaries from Reims – what were two such women doing at the Ritz? They were dressed respectably enough, by the standards of occupied France, but they certainly did not look like typical Ritz clients – the wives of diplomats from neutral countries, the girlfriends of black-marketeers, or the mistresses of German officers. The hotel manager himself might not do anything, especially if he were anti-Nazi, but the Gestapo had informants in every large hotel and restaurant in the city, and strangers with implausible stories were just what they were paid to report. This kind of detail was drummed into people on SOE's training course – but that course lasted three months, and Diana and Maude had been given only two days.

Flick quickened her step.

THIRTY-FIVE

Dieter was exhausted. To get a thousand posters printed and distributed in half a day had taken all his powers of persuasion and intimidation. He had been patient and persistent when he could, and had flown into a mad rage when necessary. In addition, he had not slept the previous night. His nerves were jangled, he had a headache, and his temper was short.

But a feeling of peace descended on him as soon as he entered the grand apartment building at the Porte de la Muette, overlooking the Bois de Boulogne. The job he had been doing for Rommel required him to travel all over northern France, so he needed to be based in Paris; but getting this place had taken a lot of bribery and bullying. It had been worth it. He loved the dark mahogany panelling, the heavy curtains, the high ceilings, the eighteenth-century silver on the sideboard. He walked around the cool, dim apartment, renewing his acquaintance with his favourite possessions: a small Rodin sculpture of a hand, a Degas pastel of a dancer putting on a ballet slipper, a first edition of *The Count of Monte Cristo*. He sat at the Steinway baby grand piano and played a languid version of 'Ain't Misbehavin': 'No one to talk with, all by myself . . .'

Before the war, the apartment and much of the furniture had belonged to an engineer from Lyon who had made a fortune manufacturing small electrical goods, vacuum cleaners and radios and doorbells. Dieter had learned this from a neighbour, a rich widow whose husband had been a leading French Fascist in the thirties. The engineer was a vulgarian, she said: he had hired people to choose the right wallpaper and antiques. For him, the only purpose of objects of beauty had been to impress his wife's friends. He had gone to America, where everyone was vulgar, said the widow. She was pleased the apartment now had a tenant who really appreciated it.

Dieter took off his jacket and shirt and washed the Paris grime from his face and neck. Then he put on a clean white shirt, inserted gold links in the French cuffs, and chose a silver-grey tie. While he was tying it, he switched on the radio. The news from Italy was bad. The newscaster said the Germans were fighting a fierce rearguard action. Dieter concluded that Rome must fall in the next few days.

But Italy was not France.

He now had to wait for someone to spot Felicity Clairet. He could not be certain she would pass through Paris, of course; but it was undoubtedly the likeliest place, after Reims, for her to be seen. Anyway, there was nothing more he could do. He wished he had brought Stéphanie with him from Reims. However, he needed her to occupy the house in the rue du Bois. There was a chance that more Allied agents would land and find their way to her door. It was important to draw them gently into the net. He had left instructions that

411

neither Michel nor Dr Bouler was to be tortured in his absence: he might yet have uses for them.

There was a bottle of Dom Perignon champagne in the icebox. He opened it and poured some into a crystal flute. Then, with a feeling that life was good, he sat down at his desk to read his mail.

There was a letter from his wife, Waltraud.

My beloved Dieter,
   I am so sorry we will not be together on your fortieth birthday.

Dieter had forgotten his birthday. He looked at the date on his Cartier desk clock. It was 3 June. He was forty years old today. He poured another glass of champagne to celebrate.

In the envelope from his wife were two other missives. His seven-year-old daugher Margarete, known as Mausi, had drawn a picture of him in uniform standing by the Eiffel Tower. In the picture, he was taller than the tower: so children magnified their fathers. His son, Rudi, ten years old, had written a grown-up letter, carefully rounded letters in dark blue ink:

My dear Papa,
   I am doing well in school although Dr Richter's classroom has been bombed. Fortunately it was night time and the school was empty.

Dieter closed his eyes in pain. He could not bear the thought of bombs falling on the city where his children

412

JACKDAWS

lived. He cursed the murderers of the RAF, even
though he knew German bombs had fallen on British
schoolchildren.

He looked at the phone on his desk, contemplating
trying to call home. It was difficult to get through: the
French phone system was overloaded, and military
traffic had priority, so you could wait hours for a
personal call to be connected. All the same, he decided
to try. He felt a sudden longing to hear the voices of
his children, and reassure himself that they were still
alive.

He reached for the phone. It rang before he touched
it. He picked it up. 'Major Franck here.'

'This is Lieutenant Hesse.'

Dieter's pulse quickened. 'You have found Felicity
Clairet?'

'No. But something almost as good.'

THIRTY-SIX

Flick had been to the Ritz once, when she was a student in Paris before the war. She and a girlfriend had put on hats and makeup, gloves and stockings, and walked through the door as if they did it every day. They had sauntered along the hotel's internal arcade of shops, giggling at the absurd prices of scarves and fountain pens and perfume. Then they had sat in the lobby, pretending they were meeting someone who was late, and criticized the outfits of the women who came there to tea. They themselves had not dared to order so much as a glass of water. In those days, Flick had saved every spare penny for cheap seats at the Comédie Française.

Since the occupation began, she had heard that the owners were attempting to run the hotel as normally as possible, even though many of the rooms had been taken over permanently by top Nazis. She had no gloves or stockings today, but she had powdered her face and set her beret at a jaunty angle, and she just had to hope that some of the hotel's wartime patrons would be forced into similar compromises.

Lines of grey military vehicles and black limousines were lined up outside the hotel in the Place Vendôme.

On the façade of the building, six blood-red Nazi banners flapped boastfully in the breeze. A commissionaire in top hat and red trousers looked doubtfully at Flick and Ruby. 'You can't come in,' he said.

Flick was in a light blue suit, very creased, and Ruby in a navy frock and a man's raincoat. They were not dressed to dine at the Ritz. Flick tried to imitate the hauteur of a French woman dealing with an irritating inferior. Putting her nose in the air, she said: 'What is the matter?'

'This entrance is reserved for the top brass, Madame. Even German colonels can't come in this way. You have to go around to the rue Cambon and use the back door.'

'As you wish,' Flick said with an air of weary courtesy, but in truth she was pleased he had not told them they were underdressed. She and Ruby walked quickly around the block and found the rear entrance.

The lobby was bright with light, and the bars on either side were full of men in evening dress or uniform. The buzz of conversation clicked and whirred with German consonants, not the languid vowels of French. Flick felt as though she were walking into the enemy's stronghold.

She went up to the desk. A concierge in a coat with brass buttons looked down his nose at her. Judging her to be neither a German nor a wealthy French woman, he said coldly: 'What is it?'

'Check whether Mademoiselle Legrand is in her room,' Flick said peremptorily. Diana must be using the false name on her papers, Simone Legrand. 'I have an appointment.'

He backed off. 'May I tell her who is enquiring?'

'Madame Martigny. I am her employee.'

'Very good. In fact Mademoiselle is in the rear dining room with her companion. Perhaps you would speak to the head waiter.'

Flick and Ruby crossed the lobby and entered the restaurant. It was a picture of elegant living: white tablecloths, silver cutlery, candles, and waiters in black gliding around the room with dishes of food. No one would have guessed that half Paris was starving. Flick smelt real coffee.

Pausing on the threshold, she saw Diana and Maude immediately. They were at a small table on the far side of the room. As Flick watched, Diana took a bottle of wine out of a gleaming bucket beside the table and poured for Maude and herself. Flick could have throttled her.

She turned to make for the table, but the head waiter stood in her way. Pointedly looking at her cheap suit, he said: 'Yes, Madame?'

'Good evening,' she said. 'I must speak with that lady over there.'

He did not move. He was a small man with a worried air, but he was not to be bullied. 'Perhaps I can give her a message for you.'

'I'm afraid not, it's too personal.'

'Then I will tell her that you are here. The name?'

Flick glared in Diana's direction, but Diana did not

look up. 'I am Madame Martigny,' Flick said, giving up. 'Tell her I must speak to her immediately.'

'Very well. If Madame would care to wait here.'

Flick ground her teeth with frustration. As the head waiter walked away, she was tempted just to run past him. Then she noticed a young man in the black uniform of an SS major at a nearby table staring at her. She met his eye and looked away, fear rising in her throat. Had he merely taken an idle interest in her altercation with the head waiter? Was he trying to remember where he had seen her before, having seen the poster but not yet made the connection? Or did he simply find her attractive? In any event, Flick realized, it would be dangerous for her to make a fuss.

Every second she stood here was dangerous. She resisted the temptation to turn and run.

The head waiter spoke to Diana, then turned and beckoned Flick.

Flick said to Ruby: 'You'd better wait here – one is less conspicuous than two.' Then she walked quickly across the room to Diana's table.

Neither Diana nor Maude had the grace to look guilty, Flick observed angrily. Maude appeared pleased with herself, Diana haughty. Flick put her hands on the edge of the table and leaned forward to speak in a low voice. 'This is terribly dangerous. Get up, now, and leave with me. We'll pay the bill on the way out.'

She had been as forceful as she knew how, but they were living in a fantasy world. 'Be reasonable, Flick,' Diana said.

Flick was outraged. How could Diana be such an arrogant idiot? 'You stupid cow,' she said. 'Don't you realize you'll get killed?'

She saw immediately that it had been a mistake to use abuse. Diana looked superior. 'It's my life. I'm entitled to take that risk—'

'You're endangering us too, and the whole mission. Now get up off that chair!'

'Look here—' There was a commotion behind Flick. Diana stopped and looked past her.

Flick turned around and gasped.

Standing in the entrance was the well-dressed German officer she had last seen in the square at Sainte-Cécile. She took him in at a glance: a tall figure in an elegant dark suit with a white handkerchief in the breast pocket.

She quickly turned her back, heart pounding, and prayed that he had not noticed her. With her dark wig, there was a good chance he would not have recognized her at first glance.

His name came back to her: Dieter Franck. She had found his photograph in Percy Thwaite's files. He was a former police detective. She recalled the note on the back of his photo: 'A star of Rommel's intelligence staff, this officer is said to be a skilled interrogator and a ruthless torturer.'

For the second time in a week, she was close enough to shoot him.

Flick did not believe in coincidence. There was a reason he was here at the same time as she.

She soon found out what it was. She looked again

and saw him striding across the restaurant towards her, with four Gestapo types trailing him. The head waiter came after them, a look of panic on his face.

Keeping her face averted, Flick walked away.

Franck went straight to Diana's table.

The whole place suddenly became quiet: customers fell silent in mid-sentence, waiters stopped serving vegetables, the sommelier froze with a decanter of claret in his hand.

Flick reached the doorway, where Ruby stood waiting. Ruby whispered: 'He's going to arrest them.' Her hand moved towards her gun.

Flick again caught the eye of the SS major. 'Leave it in your pocket,' she murmured. 'There's nothing we can do. We might take on him and four Gestapo men, but we're surrounded by German officers. Even if we killed all those five we'd be mown down by the others.'

Franck was questioning Diana and Maude. Flick could not make out the words. Diana's voice took on the tone of supercilious indifference she used when she was in the wrong. Maude became tearful.

Franck must have asked for their papers, because the two women simultaneously reached for their handbags, on the floor beside their chairs. Franck shifted his position so that he was to one side of Diana and slightly behind her, looking over her shoulder, and suddenly Flick knew what was going to happen next.

Maude took out her identity papers, but Diana pulled a gun. A shot rang out, and one of the uniformed Gestapo men doubled over and fell. The restaurant erupted. Women screamed, men dived for cover. There was a second shot, and another Gestapo man cried out. Some diners ran for the exit.

Diana's gun hand moved towards a third Gestapo man. Flick had a flash of memory: Diana in the woods at Somersholme, sitting on the ground smoking a cigarette with dead rabbits all around her. She remembered what she had said to Diana: 'You're a killer.' She had been right.

But Diana did not fire the third shot.

Dieter Franck kept a cool head. He seized Diana's right forearm with both his hands and banged her wrist on the edge of the table. She screamed with pain and the gun fell from her grasp. He yanked her out of her chair, threw her face down on the carpet, and fell on her with both knees in the small of her back. He pulled her hands behind her back and handcuffed her, ignoring the screams of pain she gave as he jerked her injured wrist. He stood up.

Flick said to Ruby: 'Let's get out of here.'

There was a crush at the doorway, panicky men and women all trying to pass through at the same time. Before Flick could move, the young SS major who had been staring at her earlier sprang to his feet and grabbed her arm. 'Wait a moment,' he said in French.

Flick fought down panic. 'Take your hands off me!'

He tightened his grip. 'You seem to know those women over there,' he said.

'No, I don't!' She tried to move away.

He pulled her back with a jerk. 'You'd better stay here and answer some questions.'

There was another shot. Several women screamed,

but no one knew where the shot had come from. The SS officer's face twisted in a grimace of agony. As he slumped to the floor, Flick saw Ruby, behind him, slipping her pistol back into her raincoat pocket.

They both forced their way through the crowd at the door, shoving ruthlessly, and burst out into the lobby. They were able to run without drawing attention to themselves, because everyone else was running.

Cars were parked in a line along the kerb in the rue Cambon, some of them attended by chauffeurs. Most of the chauffeurs were hurrying towards the hotel to see what was happening. Flick picked a black Mercedes 230 sedan with a spare wheel perched on the running-board. She looked into the front: the key was in the dash. 'Get in!' she yelled at Ruby. She got behind the wheel and pulled the self-starter. A big engine rumbled into life. She engaged first gear, heaved the steering wheel around, and accelerated away from the Ritz. The car was heavy and sluggish, but stable: at speed, it cornered like a train.

When she was several blocks away she reviewed her position. She had lost a third of her team, including her best marksman. She considered whether to abandon the operation, and immediately decided to carry on. It would be awkward: she would have to explain why only four cleaners had come to the chateau instead of the usual six, but she could make up some excuse. It meant they might be questioned more closely, but she would take that risk.

She dumped the car in the rue de la Chapelle. She and Ruby were out of immediate danger. They walked quickly to the flophouse. Ruby rounded up Greta and Jelly and brought them to Flick's room. She told them what had happened.

'Diana and Maude will be questioned straight away,' she said. 'Dieter Franck is a capable and ruthless interrogator, so we have to assume they will tell everything they know – including the address of this hotel. That means the Gestapo could be here at any moment. We have to leave now.'

Jelly was crying. 'Poor Maude,' she said. 'She was a silly cow but she didn't deserve to be tortured.'

Greta was more practical. 'Where will we go?'

'We'll hide in the convent next door to the flophouse. They'll take anyone in. I've hidden escaped prisoners-of-war there before now. They'll let us stay until daybreak.'

'Then what?'

'We'll go to the station as planned. Diana is going to tell Dieter Franck our real names, our codenames, and our false identities. He will put out an alert for anyone travelling under our aliases. Fortunately, I have a spare set of papers for all of us, using the same photographs but different identities. The Gestapo don't have photographs of you three, and I've changed my appearance, so the checkpoint guards will have no way of recognizing us. However, to be safe, we won't go to the station at first light – we'll wait until about ten o'clock when it should be busy.'

Ruby said: 'Diana will also tell them what our mission is.'

'She'll tell them we're going to blow up the railway

tunnel at Marles. Fortunately, that's not our real mission. It's a cover story I gave out.'

Jelly said admiringly: 'Flick, you think of everything.'

'Yes,' she said grimly. 'That's why I'm still alive.'

THIRTY-SEVEN

Paul sat in the dismal canteen at Grendon Underwood, brooding anxiously about Flick, for more than an hour. He was beginning to believe that Brian Standish had been compromised. The incident in the cathedral, the fact that Chatelle had been in total darkness, and the unnatural correctness of the third radio message all pointed in the same direction.

In the original plan, Flick would have been met at Chatelle by a reception committee consisting of Michel and the remnants of the Bollinger circuit. Michel would have taken them to a hideaway for a few hours, then arranged transport to Sainte-Cécile. After they entered the chateau and blew up the telephone exchange he would have driven them back to Chatelle to meet their pick-up plane. All that had changed, now, but Flick would still need both transport and a hiding-place when she got to Reims, and she would be relying on the Bollinger circuit to help. However, if Brian had been compromised, would there be any of the circuit left? Was the safe house safe? Was Michel in Gestapo hands too?

At last Lucy Briggs came into the canteen and said: 'Jean asked me to tell you that Helicopter's reply is being decrypted now. Would you like to come with me?'

He followed her to the tiny room – formerly a boot cupboard, he guessed – that served as Jean Bevins's office. Jean had a sheet of paper in her hand. She looked annoyed. 'I can't understand this,' she said.

Paul read it quickly.

CALLSIGN HLCP (HELICOPTER)
SECURITY TAG PRESENT
3 JUN 1944
MESSAGE READS:
TWO STENS WITH SIX MAGAZINES FOR EACH
STOP ONE LEE ENFELD RIFLE WITH TEN CLIPS
STOP SIX COLT AUTOMATICS WITH
APPROXIMATELY ONE HUNDRED ROUNDS STOP
NO GRENADES OVER

Paul stared at the decrypt in dismay, as if hoping the words might change to something less horrifying, but of course they remained the same.

'I expected him to be furious,' Jean said 'He doesn't complain at all, just answers your questions, as nice as pie.'

'Exactly,' said Paul. 'That's because it's not him.' This message had not come from a harassed agent in the field who had been presented with a sudden unreasonable request by his bureaucratic superiors. The reply had been drafted by a Gestapo officer desperate to maintain the smooth appearance of calm normality. The only spelling mistake was 'Enfeld' instead of 'Enfield', and even that suggested a German, for '*feld*' was German for 'field'.

There was no longer any doubt. Flick was in terrible danger.

Paul massaged his temples with his right hand. There was now only one thing to do. The operation was falling apart, and he had to save it – and Flick.

He looked up at Jean, and caught her looking at him with an expression of compassion. 'May I use your phone?' he said.

'Of course.'

He dialled Baker Street. Percy was at his desk. 'This is Paul. I'm convinced Brian has been captured. His radio is being operated by the Gestapo.' In the background, Jean Bevins gasped.

'Oh, hell,' Percy said. 'And without the radio, we have no way to warn Flick.'

'Yes, we do,' said Paul.

'How?'

'Get me a plane. I'm going to Reims – tonight.'

THE EIGHTH DAY:
SUNDAY, 4 JUNE 1944

THIRTY-EIGHT

The Avenue Foch seemed to have been built for the richest people in the world. A wide road running from the Arc de Triomphe to the Bois de Boulogne, it had ornamental gardens on both sides flanked by inner roads giving access to the palatial houses. Number eighty-four was an elegant residence with a broad staircase leading to five storeys of charming rooms. The Gestapo had turned it into a house of torture.

Dieter sat in a perfectly proportioned drawing room, stared at the intricately decorated ceiling for a moment, then closed his eyes, preparing himself for the interrogation. He had to sharpen his wits and at the same time numb his feelings.

Some men enjoyed torturing prisoners. Sergeant Becker in Reims was one. They smiled when their victims screamed, they got erections as they inflicted wounds, and they experienced orgasms during their victims' death throes. But they were not good interrogators, for they focused on pain, rather than information. The best torturers were men such as Dieter, who loathed the process from the bottom of their hearts.

Now he imagined himself closing doors in his soul,

429

shutting his emotions away in cupboards. He thought of the two women as pieces of machinery that would disgorge information as soon as he figured out how to switch them on. He felt a familiar coldness settle over him like a blanket of snow, and he knew he was ready.

'Bring the older one,' he said.

Lieutenant Hesse went to fetch her.

He watched her carefully as she came in and sat in the chair. She had short hair and broad shoulders, and wore a man-tailored suit. Her right hand hung limply, and she was supporting the swollen forearm with her left hand: Dieter had broken her wrist. She was obviously in pain, her face pale and gleaming with sweat, but her lips were set in a line of grim determination.

He spoke to her in French. 'Everything that happens in this room is under your control,' he said. 'The decisions you make, the things you say, will either cause you unbearable pain or bring you relief. It is entirely up to you.'

She said nothing. She was scared, but she did not panic. She was going to be difficult to break, he could tell already.

He said: 'To begin with, tell me where the London headquarters of the Special Operations Executive is located.'

'Eighty-one Regent Street,' she said.

He nodded. 'Let me explain something. I realize that SOE teaches its agents not to remain silent under questioning, but to give false answers which will be difficult to check. Because I know this, I will ask you many questions to which I already know the answers. This way I will know whether you are lying to me. Where is the London headquarters?'

'Carlton House Terrace.'

He walked across to her and slapped her face as hard as he could. She cried out in pain. Her cheek turned an angry red. It was often useful to begin with a slap in the face. The pain was minimal, but the blow was a humiliating demonstration of the helplessness of the prisoner, and it quickly sapped their initial bravery.

But she looked defiantly at him. 'Is that how German officers treat ladies?'

She had a haughty manner, and she spoke French with the accent of the upper classes. She was some kind of aristocrat, he guessed. 'Ladies?' he said scornfully. 'You have just shot and killed two policemen who were going about their lawful business. Specht's young wife is now a widow, and Rolfe's parents have lost their only child. You're not a soldier in uniform, you have no excuse. In answer to your question – no, this is not how we treat ladies, it's how we treat murderers.'

She looked away. He had scored a hit with that remark. He was beginning to undermine her moral foundation.

'Tell me something else,' he said. 'How well do you know Flick Clairet?'

Her eyes widened in an involuntary expression of surprise. That told him he had guessed correctly. These two were part of Major Clairet's team. He had shaken her again.

But she recovered her composure and said: 'I don't know anyone of that name.'

He reached down and knocked her left hand away. She cried out in pain as her broken wrist lost its support and sagged. He took her right hand and jerked it. She screamed.

'Why were you having dinner at the Ritz, for God's sake?' he said. He released her hand.

She stopped screaming. He repeated the question. She caught her breath and said: 'I like the food there.'

She was even tougher than he had thought. 'Take her away,' he said. 'Bring the other one.'

The younger girl was quite pretty. She had put up no resistance when arrested, so she still looked presentable, her dress unruffled and her makeup intact. She appeared much more frightened than her colleague. He asked her the question he had asked the older one: 'Why were you having dinner at the Ritz?'

'I've always wanted to go there,' she replied.

He could hardly believe his ears. 'Weren't you afraid it might be dangerous?'

'I thought Diana would look after me.'

So the other one's name was Diana. 'What's your name?'

'Maude.'

This was suspiciously easy. 'And what are you doing in France, Maude?'

'We were supposed to blow something up.'

'What?'

'I don't remember. Would it have something to do with railways?'

432

Dieter began to wonder whether he was being led up the garden path. 'How long have you known Felicity Clairet?' he tried.

'Do you mean Flick? Only a few days. She's awfully bossy.' A thought crossed her mind. 'She was right, though – we shouldn't have gone to the Ritz.' She began to cry. 'I never meant to do anything wrong. I just wanted to have a good time and see places, that's all I've ever wanted.'

'What's your team's codename?'

'The Blackbirds,' she said in English.

He frowned. The radio message to Helicopter had referred to them as Jackdaws. 'Are you sure?'

'Yes. It's because of some poem, "The Blackbird of Reims", I think. No, "The Jackdaw of Reims", that's it.'

If she was not completely stupid, she was doing a very good imitation. 'Where do you think Flick is now?'

Maude thought for a long moment then said: 'I really don't know.'

Dieter sighed in frustration. One prisoner was too tough to talk, the other too stupid to know anything useful. This was going to take longer than he had hoped.

There might be a way of shortening the process. He was curious about the relationship between these two. Why had the dominant, mannish older woman risked her life to take the pretty, empty-headed girl to dinner at the Ritz? Perhaps I've got a dirty mind, he said to himself. But still . . .

'Take her away,' he said in German. 'Put her in with the other one. Make sure the room has a judas.'

433

When they had been locked away, Lieutenant Hesse showed Dieter to a small room in the attic. He looked through a peephole into the room next door. The two women were sitting side by side on the edge of the narrow bed. Maude was crying and Diana was comforting her. Dieter watched carefully. Diana's broken right wrist rested in her lap. With her left hand she stroked Maude's hair. She was talking in a low voice, but Dieter could not hear the words.

How close a relationship was this? Were they comrades in arms, bosom friends . . . or more? Diana leaned forward and kissed Maude's forehead. That did not mean much. Then Diana put a forefinger on Maude's chin, turned the girl's face to her own, and kissed her lips. It was a gesture of comfort, but surely too intimate for a mere friend?

Finally Diana poked out the tip of her tongue and licked Maude's tears. That made up Dieter's mind. It was not foreplay – no one could have sex in such circumstances – but it was the kind of comfort that would be offered only by a lover, not by a mere friend. Diana and Maude were lesbians. And that solved the problem.

'Bring the older one again,' he said, and he returned to the interview room.

When Diana was brought in the second time, he had her tied to the chair. Then he said: 'Prepare the electrical machinery.' He waited impatiently while the electric-shock machine was rolled in on its trolley and plugged to a socket in the wall. Every minute that passed was taking Flick Clairet farther away from him.

When everything was ready he seized Diana by the

hair with his left hand. Holding her head still, he attached two crocodile clips to her lower lip.

He turned the power on. Diana screamed. He left it on for ten seconds, then switched off.

When her sobbing began to ease he said: 'That was less than half power.' It was true. He had rarely used full power. Only when the torture had gone on a long time, and the prisoner kept passing out, was full power used in an effort to penetrate the subject's fading consciousness. And by then it was generally too late, for madness was setting in.

But Diana did not know that.

'Not again,' she begged. 'Please, please, not again.'

'Are you willing to answer my questions?'

She groaned, but she did not say yes.

Dieter said: 'Bring the other one.'

Diana gasped.

Lieutenant Hesse brought Maude in and tied her to a chair.

'What do you want?' Maude cried.

Diana said: 'Don't say anything – it's better.'

Maude was wearing a light summer blouse. She had a neat, trim figure with full breasts. Dieter tore her blouse open, sending the buttons flying.

'Please!' Maude said. 'I'll tell you anything!'

Under her blouse she wore a cotton chemise with a lacy trim. He took hold of the neckline and ripped it off. Maude screamed.

He stood back and looked. Maude's breasts were round and firm. A part of his mind noticed how pretty they were. Diana must love them, he thought.

He took the crocodile clips from Diana's mouth and carefully fastened one to each of Maude's small pink nipples. Then he returned to the machine and put his hand on the control.

'All right,' Diana said quietly. 'I'll tell you everything.'

* * *

Dieter arranged for the railway tunnel at Marles to be heavily guarded. If the Jackdaws got that far, they would find it almost impossible to enter the tunnel. He felt confident that Flick would not now achieve her objective. But that was secondary. His burning ambition was to capture her and interrogate her.

It was already two o'clock on Sunday morning. Tuesday would be the night of the full moon. The invasion could be hours away. But in those few hours Dieter could break the back of the French Resistance – if he could get Flick into a torture chamber. He only needed the list of names and addresses that she had in her head. The Gestapo in every city in France could be galvanized into action, thousands of trained staff. They were not the brightest of men but they knew how to arrest people. In a couple of hours they could jail hundreds of Resistance cadres. Instead of the massive uprising that the Allies were no doubt hoping for to aid their invasion, there would be calm and order for the Germans to organize their response and push the invaders back into the sea.

He had sent a Gestapo team to raid the Hôtel de la Chapelle, but that was a matter of form: he was certain

Flick and the other three would have left within minutes of the arrest of their comrades. Where was Flick now? Reims was the natural jumping-off point for an attack on Marles, which was why the Jackdaws had originally planned to land near the city. Dieter thought it likely Flick would still pass through Reims. It was on the road and rail routes to Marles, and there was probably some kind of help she needed from the remnants of the Bollinger circuit. He was betting she was now on her way from Paris to Reims.

He arranged for every Gestapo checkpoint between the two cities to be given details of the false identities being used by Flick and her team. However that, too, was something of a formality: either they had alternative identities, or they would find ways to avoid the checkpoints.

He called Reims, got Weber out of bed, and explained the situation. For once Weber was not obstructive. He agreed to send two Gestapo men to keep an eye on Michel's town house, two more to watch Gilberte's building, and two to the house in the rue du Bois to guard Stéphanie.

Finally, as the headache began, Dieter called Stéphanie. 'The British terrorists are on their way to Reims,' he told her. 'I'm sending two men to guard you.'

She was as calm as ever. 'Thank you.'

'But it's important that you continue to go to the rendezvous.' With luck, Flick would not suspect the extent to which Dieter had penetrated the Bollinger circuit, and she would walk into his arms. 'Remember,

437

we changed the location. It's not the cathedral crypt any more, it's the Café de la Gare. If anyone shows up, just drive them back to the house, the way you did with Helicopter. Then the Gestapo can take over from that point.'

'Okay.'

'Are you sure? I've minimized the risk to you, but it's still dangerous.'

'I'm sure. You sound as if you have a migraine.'

'It's just beginning.'

'Do you have the medicine?'

'Hans has it.'

'I'm sorry I'm not there to give it to you.'

He was, too. 'I wanted to drive back to Reims tonight, but I don't think I can make it.'

'Don't you dare. I'll be fine. Take a shot and go to bed. Come back here tomorrow.'

He knew she was right. It was going to be hard enough getting back to his apartment, less than a kilometre away. He could not travel to Reims until he had recovered from the strain of the interrogation. 'Okay,' he said. 'I'll get a few hours' sleep and leave here in the morning.'

'Happy birthday.'

'You remembered! I forgot it myself.'

'I have something for you.'

'A gift?'

'More like . . . an action.'

He grinned, despite his headache. 'Oh, boy.'

'I'll give it to you tomorrow.'

'I can't wait.'

'I love you.'

The words *I love you, too,* came to his lips, but he hesitated, reluctant from old habit to say them; and then there was a click as Stéphanie hung up.

THIRTY-NINE

In the early hours of Sunday morning, Paul Chancellor parachuted into a potato field near the village of Laroque, west of Reims, without the benefit – or the risk – of a reception committee.

The landing gave him a tremendous jolt of pain in his wounded knee. He gritted his teeth and lay motionless on the ground, waiting for it to ease. The knee would probably hurt him every so often for the rest of his life. When he was an old man he would say a twinge meant rain – if he lived to be an old man.

After five minutes he felt able to struggle to his feet and get out of his parachute harness. He found the road, oriented himself by the stars, and started walking, but he was limping badly, and progress was slow.

His identity, hastily cobbled together by Percy Thwaite, was that of a schoolteacher from Épernay, a few miles west. He was hitch-hiking to Reims to visit his father, who was ill. Percy had got him all the necessary papers, some of them hastily forged last night and rushed to Tempsford by motorcycle. The limp fitted quite well with the cover story: a wounded veteran might well be a schoolteacher, whereas an active young man should have been sent to a labour camp in Germany.

Getting here was the simple part. Now he had to find Flick. His only way of contacting her would be via the Bollinger circuit. He had to hope that part of the circuit was left intact, and Brian was the only member in Gestapo custody. Like every new agent dropping into Reims, he would contact Mademoiselle Lemas. He would just have to be especially cautious.

Soon after first light he heard a vehicle. He stepped off the road into the field alongside and concealed himself behind a row of vines. As the noise came closer he realized the vehicle was a tractor. That was safe enough: the Gestapo never travelled by tractor. He returned to the road and thumbed a lift.

The tractor was driven by a boy of about fifteen and was pulling a cartload of artichokes. The driver nodded at Paul's leg and said: 'War wound?'

'Yes,' Paul said. The likeliest moment for a French soldier to have been hurt was during the battle of France, so he added: 'Sedan, nineteen forty.'

'I was too young,' the boy said regretfully.

'Lucky you.'

'But wait till the Allies come back. Then you'll see some action.' He gave Paul a sideways look. 'I can't say any more. But you wait and see.'

Paul thought hard. Was this lad a member of the Bollinger circuit? He said: 'But do our people have the guns and ammunition they need?' If the boy knew anything at all, he would know that the Allies had dropped tons of weaponry in the past few months.

'We'll use whatever weapons come to hand.'

Was he being discreet about what he knew? No, Paul

thought. The boy looked vague. He was fantasizing. Paul said no more.

The lad dropped him off on the outskirts and he limped into town. The rendezvous had changed, from the cathedral crypt to the Café de la Gare, but the time was the same, three o'clock in the afternoon. He had hours to kill.

He went into the café to get breakfast and reconnoitre. He asked for black coffee. The elderly waiter raised his eyebrows, and Paul realized he had made a slip. Hastily, he tried to cover up. 'No need to say "black", I suppose,' he said. 'You probably don't have any milk anyway.'

The waiter smiled, reassured. 'Unfortunately not.' He went away.

Paul breathed out. It was eight months since he had been undercover in France and he had forgotten the minute-to-minute strain of pretending to be someone else.

He spent the morning dozing through services in the cathedral then went back into the café at one thirty for lunch. The place emptied out around two thirty, and he stayed drinking ersatz coffee. Two men came in at two forty-five and ordered beer. Paul looked hard at them. They wore old business suits and talked about grapes in colloquial French. They were eruditely discussing the flowering of the vines, a critical period which had just ended. He did not think they could possibly be agents of the Gestapo.

At exactly three o'clock a tall, attractive woman came in, dressed with unobtrusive elegance in a summer frock of plain green cotton and a straw hat. She wore odd shoes: one black, one brown. This must be Bourgeoise.

Paul was a little surprised. He had expected an older woman. However, that was probably an unwarranted assumption: Flick had never actually described her.

All the same, he was not yet ready to trust her. He got up and left the café.

He walked along the pavement to the railway station and stood in the entrance, watching the café. He was not conspicuous: as usual, there were several people hanging around the station waiting to meet friends.

He monitored the café's clientele. A woman walked by with a child who was demanding pastry and, as they reached the café, the mother gave in and took the child inside. The two grape experts left. A gendarme went in and came out immediately with a packet of cigarettes in his hand.

Paul began to believe this was not a Gestapo trap. There was no one in sight who looked remotely dangerous. Changing the location of the rendezvous had shaken them off.

Only one thing puzzled him. When Brian Standish had been caught at the cathedral, he had been rescued by Bourgeoise's friend Charenton. Where was he today? If he had been keeping an eye on her in the cathedral, why not here too? But the circumstance was not dangerous in itself. And there could be a hundred simple explanations.

The mother and child left the café. Then, at three thirty, Bourgeoise came out. She walked along the pavement away from the station. Paul followed on the other side of the street. She went up to a small black car of Italian design, the one the French called a Simca-Cinq. Paul crossed the street. She got into the car and started the engine.

It was time for Paul to decide. He could not be sure this was safe, but he had gone as far as he could with caution, short of not making the rendezvous at all. At some point, risks had to be taken. Otherwise he might as well have stayed at home.

He went up on the car on the passenger side and opened the door.

She looked coolly at him. 'Monsieur?'

'Pray for me,' he said.

'I pray for peace.'

Paul got in the car. Giving himself a codename, he said: 'I am Danton.'

She pulled away. 'Why didn't you speak to me in the café?' she said. 'I saw you as soon as I walked in. You made me wait there half an hour. It's dangerous.'

'I wanted to be sure this wasn't a trap.'

She glanced over at him. 'You heard what happened to Helicopter.'

'Yes. Where's your friend who rescued him, Charenton?'

She headed south, driving fast. 'He's working today.'

'On Sunday? What does he do?'

'Fireman. He's on duty.'

That explained that. Paul moved quickly to the real purpose of his visit. 'Where's Helicopter?'

She shook her head. 'No idea. My house is a cut-out.

444

I meet people, I pass them on to Monet. I'm not supposed to know anything.'

'Is Monet all right?'

'Yes. He phoned me on Thursday afternoon, checking up on Charenton.'

'Not since?'

'No. But that's not unusual.'

'When did you last see him?'

'In person? I've never seen him.'

'Have you heard from Leopardess?'

'No.'

Paul brooded as the car threaded through the suburbs. Bourgeoise really had no information for him. He would have to move to the next link in the chain.

She pulled into a courtyard alongside a tall house. 'Come inside and get cleaned up,' she said.

He got out of the car. Everything seemed to be in order: Bourgeoise had been at the right rendezvous and had given all the correct signals, and there had been no one following her. On the other hand she had given him no useful information, and he still had no notion how deeply the Bollinger circuit had been penetrated, nor how much danger Flick was in. As Bourgeoise led him to the front door and opened it with her key, he touched the wooden toothbrush in his shirt pocket: it was French-made, so he had been permitted to bring it with him. Now an impulse seized him. As Bourgeoise stepped into the house, he slipped the toothbrush from his pocket and dropped it on the ground just in front of the door.

He followed her inside. 'Big place,' he said. It had

dark old-fashioned wallpaper and heavy furniture, quite out of character with its owner. 'Have you been here long?'

'I inherited it three or four years ago. I'd like to redecorate, but you can't get the materials.' She opened a door and stood aside for him to go first. 'Come into the kitchen.'

He stepped inside and saw two men in uniform. Both held automatic pistols. And both guns were pointed at Paul.

FORTY

Dieter's car suffered a puncture on the RN3 road between Paris and Meaux. A bent nail was stuck in the tyre. The delay irritated him, and he paced the roadside restlessly, but Lieutenant Hesse jacked up the car and changed the wheel with calm efficiency, and they were on their way again within a few minutes.

Dieter had slept late, under the influence of the morphine injection Hans had given him in the early hours, and now he watched with impatience as the ugly industrial landscape east of Paris changed gradually to farming country. He wanted be in Reims. He had set a trap for Flick Clairet and he needed to be there when she fell into it.

The big Hispano-Suiza flew along an arrow-straight road lined with poplars – a road probably built by the Romans. At the start of the war, Dieter had thought the Third Reich would be like the Roman Empire, a pan-European hegemony that would bring unprecedented peace and prosperity to all its subjects. Now he was not so sure.

He worried about his mistress. Stéphanie was in danger, and he was responsible. Everyone's life was at risk now, he told himself. Modern warfare put the entire population on the front line. The best way to protect Stéphanie – and himself, and his family in Germany – was to defeat the invasion. But there were moments when he cursed himself for involving his lover so closely in his mission. He was playing a risky game and using her in an exposed position.

Resistance fighters did not take prisoners. Being in constant peril themselves, they had no scruples about killing French people who collaborated with the enemy.

The thought that Stéphanie might be killed made his chest tighten and his breathing difficult. He could hardly contemplate life without her. The prospect seemed dismal, and he realized he must be in love with her. He had always told himself that she was just a beautiful courtesan, and he was using her the way men always used such women. Now he saw that he had been fooling himself. And he wished all the more that he was already in Reims at her side.

It was Sunday afternoon, so there was little traffic on the road, and they made good progress.

The second puncture occurred when they were less than an hour from Reims. Dieter wanted to scream with frustration. It was another bent nail. Were wartime tyres poor quality? he wondered. Or did French people deliberately drop their old nails on the road, knowing that nine vehicles out of ten were driven by the occupying forces?

The car did not have a second spare wheel, so the tyre had to be mended before they could drive on. They left the car and walked. After a mile or so they came to a farmhouse. A large family was sitting around the remains of a substantial Sunday lunch: on the table were cheese and strawberries and several empty wine bottles. Country folk were the only French people who were well fed. Dieter bullied the farmer into hitching up his horse and cart and driving them to the next town.

In the town square was a single petrol pump on the pavement outside a wheelwright's shop with a closed sign in the window. They banged on the door and woke a surly *garagiste* from his Sunday-afternoon nap. The mechanic fired up an ancient truck and drove off with Hans beside him.

Dieter sat in the living room of the mechanic's house, stared at by three small children in ragged clothes. The mechanic's wife, a tired woman with dirty hair, bustled about in the kitchen but did not offer him so much as a glass of cold water.

Dieter thought of Stéphanie again. There was a phone in the hallway. He looked into the kitchen. 'May I make a call?' he asked politely. 'I will pay you, of course.'

She gave him a hostile glare. 'Where to?'

'Reims.'

She nodded and made a note of the time by the clock on the mantelpiece.

Dieter got the operator and gave the number of the house in the rue du Bois. It was answered immediately by a low, gruff voice reciting the number in a provincial accent. Suddenly alert, Dieter said in French: 'This is Pierre Charenton.'

The voice at the other end changed into Stéphanie's, and she said: 'My darling.'

449

He realized she had answered the phone with her imitation of Mademoiselle Lemas, as a precaution. His heart gladdened with relief. 'Is everything all right?' he asked her.

'I've captured another enemy agent for you,' she said coolly.

His mouth went dry. 'My God ... well done! How did it happen?'

'I picked him up in the Café de la Gare and brought him here.'

Dieter closed his eyes. If something had gone wrong – if she had done anything to make the agent suspect her – she could be dead by now. 'And then?'

'Your men tied him up.'

She had said *him*. That meant the terrorist was not Flick. Dieter was disappointed. All the same, his strategy was working. This man was the second Allied agent to walk into the trap. 'What's he like?'

'A young guy with a limp and half his ear shot off.'

'What have you done with him?'

'He's here in the kitchen, on the floor. I was about to call Sainte-Cécile and have him picked up.'

'Don't do that. Lock him in the cellar. I want to talk to him before Weber does.'

'Where are you?'

'Some village. We have a damn puncture.'

'Hurry back.'

'I should be with you in an hour or two.'

'Okay.'

'How are you?'

'Fine.'

Dieter wanted a serious answer. 'But really, how do you feel?'

'How do I *feel*?' She paused. 'That's a question you don't usually ask.'

Dieter hesitated. 'I don't usually involve you in capturing terrorists.'

Her voice softened. 'I feel fine. Don't worry about me.'

He found himself saying something he had not planned. 'What will we do after the war?'

There was a surprised silence at the other end of the line.

Dieter said: 'Of course, the war could go on for ten years, but on the other hand it might be over in two weeks, and then what would we do?'

She recovered her composure somewhat, but there was an uncharacteristic tremor in her voice as she said: 'What would you like to do?'

'I don't know,' he said, but that left him dissatisfied, and after a moment he blurted out: 'I don't want to lose you.'

'Oh.'

He waited for her to say something else.

'What are you thinking?' he said.

She said nothing. There was an odd sound at the other end, and he realized she was crying. He felt choked up himself. He caught the eye of the mechanic's wife, still timing his phone call. He swallowed hard and turned away, not wanting a stranger to see that he was upset. 'I'll be with you soon,' he said. 'We'll talk some more.'

'I love you,' she said.

He glanced at the mechanic's wife. She was staring at him. To hell with her, he thought. 'I love you, too,' he said. Then he hung up the phone.

FORTY-ONE

It took the Jackdaws most of the day to get from Paris to Reims.

They passed through all the checkpoints without incident. Their new fake identities worked as well as the old, and no one noticed that Flick's photograph had been retouched with eyebrow pencil.

But their train was delayed repeatedly, stopping for an hour at a time in the middle of nowhere. Flick sat in the hot carriage fuming with impatience as the precious minutes leaked away uselessly. She could see the reason for the hold-ups: half the track had been destroyed by the bombers of the US and the RAF. When the train chugged into life and moved forward, they looked out of the windows and saw emergency repair crews cutting through twisted rails, picking up smashed sleepers, and laying new track. Her only consolation was that the delays would be even more maddening for Rommel as he attempted to deploy his troops to repel the invasion.

There was a feeling in her chest like a cold, inert lump, and every few minutes her thoughts returned to Diana and Maude. They had certainly been interrogated by now, probably tortured, possibly killed.

Flick had known Diana all her life. She was going to have to tell Diana's brother, William, what had happened. Flick's own mother would be almost as upset as William. Ma had helped raise Diana.

They began to see vineyards, then champagne warehouses alongside the track, and at last they arrived in Reims a few minutes after four on Sunday afternoon. As Flick had feared, it was too late to carry out their mission the same evening. That meant another nerve-racking twenty-four hours in occupied territory. It also gave Flick a more specific problem: where would the Jackdaws spend the night?

This was not Paris. There was no red-light district with disreputable flophouses whose proprietors asked few questions, and Flick did not know of a convent where the nuns would hide anyone who begged for sanctuary. There were no dark alleys in which down-and-outs slept behind rubbish bins ignored by the police.

Flick knew of three possible hideouts: Michel's town house, Gilberte's apartment, and Mademoiselle Lemas's house in the rue du Bois. Unfortunately, any of them might be under surveillance, depending on how deeply the Gestapo had penetrated the Bollinger circuit. If Dieter Franck was in charge of the investigation, she had to fear the worst.

There was nothing for it but to go and look. 'We must split up into pairs again,' she told the others. 'Four women together is too conspicuous. Ruby and I will go first. Greta and Jelly, follow a hundred metres behind us.'

They walked to Michel's place, not far from the station. It was Flick's marital home, but she always thought of it as his house. There was plenty of room for four women. But the Gestapo almost certainly knew of the place: it would be astonishing if none of the men taken captive last Sunday had revealed the address under torture.

The house was in a busy street with several shops. Walking along the pavement, Flick surreptitiously looked into each parked car while Ruby checked the houses and shops. Michel's property was a high, narrow building in an elegant eighteenth-century row. It had a small front yard with a magnolia tree. The place was still and quiet, with no movement at the windows. The doorstep was dusty.

On their first pass along the street, they saw nothing suspicious: no workmen digging up the road, no watchful loiterers at the pavement tables outside the bar, Chez Régis, no one leaning on a telegraph pole reading a newspaper.

They returned on the opposite side. Outside the baker's shop was a black Citroën Traction Avant with two men in suits sitting in the front, smoking cigarettes and looking bored.

Flick tensed. She was wearing her dark wig, so she felt sure they would not recognize her as the girl on the Wanted poster, but all the same her pulse beat faster and she hurried past them. All along the pavement she listened for a shout behind her, but it did not come, and at last she turned the corner and breathed easier.

She slowed her pace. Her fears had been justified.

Michel's house was no use to her. It did not have a rear entrance, being part of a row with no back alley. The Jackdaws could not enter without being seen by the Gestapo.

She considered the other two possibilities. Michel was presumably still living at Gilberte's apartment, unless he had been captured. The building had a useful back entrance. But it was a tiny place, and four overnight guests at a one-room apartment would not only be uncomfortable but also might be noticed by other people in the building.

The obvious place for them to spend the night was the house in the rue du Bois. Flick had been there twice. It was a big house with lots of bedrooms. Mademoiselle Lemas was completely trustworthy and was more than willing to feed unexpected guests. She had been sheltering British agents, downed airmen and escaping prisoners-of-war for years. And she might know what had happened to Brian Standish.

It was a mile or two from the centre of town. The four women set out to walk there, still in pairs a hundred metres apart.

They arrived half an hour later. The rue du Bois was a quiet suburban street: a surveillance team would have trouble concealing themselves here. There was only one parked car within sight, an impeccably upright Peugot 201 that was much too slow for the Gestapo. It was empty.

Flick and Ruby took a preliminary walk past Mademoiselle Lemas's house. It looked the same as always. Her Simca-Cinq stood in the courtyard, which was unusual only in that she normally parked it in the garage. Flick slowed her pace and surreptitiously looked in at the window. She saw no one. Mademoiselle Lemas used that room only rarely: it was an old-fashioned front parlour, the piano immaculately dusted, the cushions always plumped, the door kept firmly closed except for formal visits. Her secret guests always sat in the kitchen at the back of the house, where there was no chance they would be seen by passers-by.

As Flick passed the door, her eye was caught by something on the ground. It was a wooden toothbrush. Without pausing in her stride, she stooped and picked it up.

Greta said: 'Do you need to clean your teeth?'

'This looks like Paul's.' She almost thought it *was* Paul's, although there must be hundreds like it in France, maybe thousands.

'Do you think he might be here?'

'Maybe.'

'Why would he have come?'

'I don't know. To warn us of danger, perhaps.'

They walked on around the block. Before approaching the house again, she let Greta and Jelly catch up. 'This time we'll go together,' she said. 'Greta and Jelly, knock on the front door.'

Jelly said: 'Thank gordon, my feet are killing me.'

'Ruby and I will go around to the back, just as a precaution. Don't say anything about us, just wait for us to appear.'

They walked along the street again, all together this time. Flick and Ruby went into the courtyard and past

457

the Simca-Cinq and crept around to the back. The kitchen ran almost the whole width of the house at the rear, with two windows and a door between. Flick waited until she heard the metallic ring of the doorbell, then she risked a peep through a window.

Her heart stopped.

There were three people in the kitchen: two men in uniform, and a tall woman with luxuriant red hair who was definitely not the middle-aged Mademoiselle Lemas.

In a frozen fraction of a second, Flick noted that all three were looking away from the windows, reflexively turning in the direction of the front door.

Then she ducked down again.

She thought fast. The men were obviously Gestapo officers. The woman must be a French traitor, posing as Mademoiselle Lemas. She had looked vaguely familiar, even from the back: there was something about the stylish drape of her green summer dress that struck a chord in Flick's memory.

It was dismayingly clear to Flick that the safe house had been betrayed. The place was now a trap for Allied agents. Poor Brian Standish must have fallen straight into it. Flick wondered whether he was still alive.

A feeling of cold determination came over her. She drew her pistol. Ruby did the same.

'Three people,' she told Ruby in a low voice. 'Two men and a woman.' She took a deep breath. It was time to be ruthless. 'We're going to kill the men,' she said. 'Okay?'

Ruby nodded.

Flick thanked heaven for Ruby's cool head. 'I'd prefer to keep the woman alive for questioning, but we'll shoot her if she seems likely to escape.'

'Got it.'

'The men are at the left-hand end of the kitchen. The woman will probably go to the door. You take this window, I'll take the far one. Aim at the man nearest to you. Shoot when I shoot.'

She crept across the width of the house and crouched under the other window. Her breath was coming fast and her heart was beating like a steam hammer, but she was thinking as clearly as if she were playing chess. She had no experience of firing through glass. She decided to shoot three times in rapid succession: once to shatter the window, a second time to kill her man, and a third time to be sure of him. She thumbed the safety catch on her pistol and held it pointing to the sky. Then she straightened up and looked in through the window.

The two men were standing facing the door to the hall. Both had pistols drawn. Flick levelled her gun at the one nearest her.

The woman had gone, but as Flick looked she returned, holding the kitchen door open. Greta and Jelly walked in ahead of her, all unsuspecting; then they saw the Gestapo men. Greta gave a small scream of fear. Something was said – Flick could not hear what – then Greta and Jelly raised their hands in the air.

The fake Mademoiselle Lemas walked into the kitchen behind them. Seeing her full-face, Flick felt a shock of recognition. She had seen her before. An instant later she remembered where. The woman had been in the square at Sainte-Cécile last Sunday with Dieter Franck. Flick had thought she was the officer's mistress. Obviously she was something more than that.

A moment later the woman saw Flick's face at the window. Her mouth dropped open, her eyes widened, and she lifted her hand to point at what she had seen. The two men began to turn.

Flick pulled the trigger. The bang of the gun seemed simultaneous with the crash of breaking glass. Holding the gun level and steady, she fired twice more.

A second later, Ruby fired.

Both men fell to the ground.

Flick threw open the back door and stepped inside.

The young woman had already turned away. She was making a dash for the front door. Flick raised her gun, but too late: in a split second the woman was in the hall and out of Flick's line of sight. Then Jelly, moving surprisingly fast, threw herself through the door. There was a crash of falling bodies and breaking furniture.

Flick crossed the kitchen and looked. Jelly had brought the woman down on the tiled floor of the hall. She had also broken the delicate curved legs of a kidney-shaped table, smashed a Chinese vase that had stood on the table, and scattered a spray of dried grasses that had been in the vase. The French woman struggled to get up. Flick aimed her pistol but did not fire. Jelly, showing remarkably quick reactions, grabbed the woman by the hair and banged her head on the tiles until she stopped wriggling.

The woman was wearing odd shoes, one black and one brown.

Flick turned back and looked at the two Gestapo men on the kitchen floor. Both lay still. She picked up their guns and pocketed them. Loose firearms left lying around might be used by the enemy.

For a moment, the four Jackdaws were safe.

Flick was operating on adrenaline. The time would come, she knew, when she would think about the man she had killed. The end of a life was a dreadful moment. Its solemnity might be postponed, but would return. Hours or days from now, Flick would wonder if the young man in uniform had left behind a wife who was now alone, and children fatherless. But for the present she was able to put that aside and think only of her mission.

She said: 'Jelly, keep the woman covered. Greta, find some string and tie her to a chair. Ruby, go upstairs and make sure there's no one else in the house. I'll check the basement.'

She ran down the stairs to the cellar. There on the dirt floor she saw the figure of a man, tied up and gagged. The gag covered much of his face, but she could see that half his ear had been shot off.

She pulled the gag from his mouth, bent down and gave him a long, passionate kiss. 'Welcome to France.'

He grinned. 'Best welcome I ever had.'

'I've got your toothbrush.'

'It was a last-second thing, because I wasn't perfectly sure of the redhead.'

'It made me just that little bit more suspicious.'

'Thank God.'

She took the sharp little knife from its sheath under her lapel and began to cut the cords that bound him. 'How did you get here?'

'Parachuted in last night.'

'What the hell for?'

'Brian's radio is definitely being operated by the Gestapo. I wanted to warn you.'

She threw her arms around him in a burst of affection. 'I'm so glad you're here!'

He hugged and kissed her. 'In that case I'm glad I came.'

They went upstairs. 'Look who I found in the cellar,' Flick said.

They were all waiting for instructions. She thought for a moment. Five minutes had passed since the shooting. The neighbours must have heard gunfire, but few French citizens were quick to call the police nowadays: they were afraid they would end up answering questions at the Gestapo office. However, she would not take needless risks. They had to be out of here as soon as possible.

She turned her attention to the fake Mademoiselle Lemas, now tied to a kitchen chair. She knew what had to be done, and her heart sank at the prospect. 'What is your name?' she asked her.

'Stéphanie Vinson.'

'You're the mistress of Dieter Franck.'

She was as pale as a sheet, but looked defiant, and Flick thought how beautiful she was. 'He saved my life.'

So that was how Franck had won her loyalty, Flick thought. It made no difference: a traitor was a traitor, whatever the motive. 'You brought Helicopter to this house to be captured.'

She said nothing.

'Is Helicopter alive or dead?'

'I don't know.'

Flick pointed to Paul. 'You brought him here too. You would have helped the Gestapo capture us all.' The anger sounded in her voice as she thought of the danger to Paul.

Stéphanie lowered her gaze.

Flick walked behind the chair and drew her gun. 'You're French, yet you collaborated with the Gestapo. You might have killed us all.'

The others, seeing what was coming, stood aside, out of the line of fire.

Stéphanie could not see the gun, but she sensed what was happening. She whispered: 'What are you going to do with me?'

Flick said: 'If we leave you here now, you will tell Dieter Franck how many we are, and describe us to him, and help him to capture us, so that we can be tortured and killed . . . won't you?'

She did not answer.

Flick pointed the gun at the back of Stéphanie's head. 'Do you have any excuse for helping the enemy?'

'I did what I had to. Doesn't everyone?'

'Exactly,' Flick said, and she pulled the trigger twice.

The gun boomed in the confined space. Blood and something else spurted from the woman's face and splashed on the skirt of her elegant green dress, and she slumped forward soundlessly.

Jelly flinched and Greta turned away. Even Paul went white. Only Ruby remained expressionless.

They were all silent for a moment. Then Flick said: 'Let's get out of here.'

FORTY-TWO

It was six o'clock in the evening when Dieter parked outside the house in the rue du Bois. His sky-blue car was covered with dust and dead insects after the long journey. As he got out, the evening sun slipped behind a cloud, and the suburban street was thrown into shadow. He shivered.

He took off his motoring goggles – he had been driving with the top down – and ran his fingers through his hair to flatten it. 'Wait for me here, please, Hans,' he said. He wanted to be alone with Stéphanie.

Opening the gate and entering the front garden, he noticed that Mademoiselle Lemas's Simca-Cinq was gone. The garage door was open and the garage was empty. Was Stéphanie using the car? But where would she have gone? She should be waiting here for him, guarded by two Gestapo men.

He strode up the garden path and pulled the bell rope. The ring of the bell died away, leaving the house strangely silent. He looked through the window into the front parlour, but that room was always empty. He rang again. There was no response. He bent down to look through the letterbox, but he could not see much: part of the staircase, a painting of a Swiss mountain scene, and the door to the kitchen, half open. There was no movement.

He glanced at the house next door, and saw a face hastily withdraw from a window, and a curtain fall back into place.

He walked around the side of the house and through the courtyard to the rear garden. Two windows were broken and the back door stood open. Fear grew in his heart. What had happened here?

'Stéphanie?' he called. There was no answer.

He stepped into the kitchen.

At first he did not understand what he was looking at. A bundle was tied to a kitchen chair with ordinary household string. It looked like a woman's body with a disgusting mess on top. After a moment, his police experience told him that the disgusting thing was a human head that had been shot. Then he saw that the dead woman was wearing odd shoes, one black and one brown, and he understood she was Stéphanie. He let out a howl of anguish, covered his eyes with his hands, and sank slowly to his knees, sobbing.

After a minute he dragged his hands from his eyes and forced himself to look again. The detective in him noted the blood on the skirt of her dress, and concluded that she had been shot from behind. Perhaps that was merciful; she might not have suffered the terror of knowing she was about to die. There had been two shots, he thought. It was the large exit wounds that had made her lovely face look so dreadful, destroying her eyes and nose, leaving her sensual lips bloodstained but intact. Had it not been for the shoes, he would not have known her. His eyes filled with tears until she became a blur.

The sense of loss was like a wound. He had never known a shock like this sudden knowledge that she was gone. She would not throw him that proud glance again; she would no longer turn heads walking through restaurants; he would never again see her pull silk stockings over her perfect calves. Her style and her wit, her fears and her desires were all cancelled, wiped out, ended. He felt as if *he* had been shot, and had lost part of himself. He whispered her name: at least he had that.

Then he heard a voice behind him.

He cried out, startled.

It came again: a wordless grunt, but human. He leaped to his feet, turning around and wiping the moisture from his eyes. For the first time he noticed two men on the floor. Both wore uniform. They were Stéphanie's Gestapo bodyguards. They had failed to protect her, but at least they had given their lives trying.

Or one of them had.

One lay still, but the other was trying to speak. He was a young chap, nineteen or twenty, with black hair and a small moustache. His uniform cap lay on the linoleum floor beside his head.

Dieter stepped across the room and knelt beside him. He noted exit wounds in the chest: the man had been shot from behind. He was lying in a pool of blood. His head jerked and his lips were moving. Dieter put his ear to the man's mouth.

'Water,' the man whispered.

He was bleeding to death. They always asked for

water near the end, Dieter knew – he had seen it in the desert. He found a cup, filled it at the tap, and held it to the man's lips. He drank it all, the water dribbling down his chin on to his blood-soaked tunic.

Dieter knew he should phone for a doctor, but he had to find out what had happened here. If he delayed, the man might expire without telling what he knew. Dieter hesitated only a moment over the decision. The man was dispensable. Dieter would question him first, then call the doctor. 'Who was it?' he said, and he bent his head again to hear the dying man's whispers.

'Four women,' the man said hoarsely.

'The Jackdaws,' Dieter said bitterly.

'Two at the front . . . two at the back.'

Dieter nodded. He could visualize the course of events. Stéphanie had gone to the front door to answer the knock. The Gestapo men had stood ready, looking towards the hall. The terrorists had sneaked up to the kitchen windows and shot them from behind. And then . . . ?

'Who killed Stéphanie?'

'Water . . .'

Dieter controlled his sense of urgency with an effort of will. He went to the sink, refilled the cup, and put it to the man's mouth again. Once again he drank it all, and sighed with relief, a sigh that turned into a dreadful groan.

'Who killed Stéphanie?' Dieter repeated.

'The small one,' said the Gestapo man.

'Flick,' said Dieter, and his heart filled with a raging desire for revenge.

The man whispered: 'I'm sorry, Major . . .'

'How did it happen?'

'Quick . . . it was very quick.'

'Tell me.'

'They tied her up . . . said she was a traitor . . . gun to the back of the head . . . then they went away.'

'Traitor?' Dieter said.

The man nodded.

Dieter choked back a sob. 'She never shot anyone in the back of the head,' he said in a grief-stricken whisper.

The Gestapo man did not hear him. His lips were still and his breathing had stopped.

Dieter reached out with his right hand and closed the man's eyelids gently with his fingertips. 'Rest in peace,' he said.

Then, keeping his back to the body of the woman he loved, he went to the phone.

FORTY-THREE

It was a struggle to fit five people into the Simca-Cinq. Ruby and Jelly sat on the rudimentary back seat. Paul drove. Greta took the front passenger seat, and Flick sat on Greta's lap.

Ordinarily they would have giggled about it, but they were in sombre mood. They had killed three people, and they had come close to being captured by the Gestapo. Now they were watchful, hyper-alert, ready to react fast to anything that happened. They had nothing on their minds but survival.

Flick guided Paul to the street parallel with Gilberte's. Flick remembered coming here with her wounded husband exactly seven days ago. She directed Paul to park near the end of the alley. 'Wait here,' Flick said. 'I'll check the place.'

Jelly said: 'Be quick, for God's sake.'

'Quick as I can.' Flick got out and ran down the alley, past the back of the factory to the door in the wall. She crossed the garden quickly and slipped through the back entrance into the building. The hallway was empty and the place was quiet. She went softly up the stairs to the attic floor.

She stopped outside Gilberte's apartment. What she

saw filled her with dismay. The door stood open. It had been broken in and was leaning drunkenly from one hinge. She listened, but heard nothing, and something told her the break-in had happened days ago. Cautiously, she stepped inside.

There had been a perfunctory search. In the little living room, the cushions on the seats were disarranged, and in the kitchen corner the cupboard doors stood open. Flick looked into the bedroom and saw a similar scene. The drawers had been pulled out of the chest, the wardrobe was open, and someone had stood on the bed with dirty boots.

She went to the window and looked down into the street. Parked opposite the building was a black Citroën Traction Avant with two men sitting in the front.

This was all bad news, Flick thought despairingly. Someone had talked, and Dieter Franck had made the most of it. He had painstakingly followed a trail that had led him first to Mademoiselle Lemas, then to Brian Standish, and finally to Gilberte. And Michel? Was he in custody? It seemed all too probable.

She thought about Dieter Franck. She had felt a shiver of fear the first time she had looked at the short MI6 biography of him on the back of his file photo. She had not been scared enough, she now knew. He was clever and persistent. He had almost caught her at La Chatelle, he had scattered posters of her face all over Paris, he had captured and interrogated her comrades one after another.

She had set eyes on him just twice, both times for a few moments only. She brought his face to mind. There was intelligence and energy in his look, she thought, plus a determination that could easily become ruthlessness. She was quite sure that he was still on her trail. She resolved to be ever more vigilant.

She looked at the sky. She had about three hours until dark.

She hurried down the stairs and out through the garden back to the Simca-Cinq parked in the next street. 'No good,' she said, as she squeezed into the car. 'The place has been searched and the Gestapo are watching the front.'

'Hell,' Paul said. 'Where do we go now?'

'I know of one more place to try,' said Flick. 'Drive into town.'

She wondered how long they could continue to use the Simca-Cinq, as the tiny 500cc engine struggled to power the overloaded car. Assuming the bodies at the house in the rue du Bois had been discovered within an hour, how long would it be before police and Gestapo men in Reims were alerted to look out for Mademoiselle Lemas's car? Dieter had no way of contacting men who were already out on the streets, but at the next change of shift they would all be briefed. And Flick did not know when the night crews came on duty. She concluded that she had almost no time left. 'Drive to the station,' she said. 'We'll dump the car there.'

'Good idea,' Paul said. 'Maybe they'll think we've left town.'

Flick scanned the streets for military Mercedes cars or black Gestapo Citroëns. She held her breath as they passed a pair of gendarmes patrolling. But they reached the centre of the city without incident. Paul parked near the railway station, and they all got out and hurried away from the incriminating vehicle.

'I'll have to do this alone,' Flick said. 'The rest of you had better go to the cathedral and wait for me there.'

'All my sins have been forgiven several times over, I've spent so much time in church today,' Paul said.

'You can pray for a place to spend the night,' Flick told him, and she hurried away.

She returned to the street where Michel lived. A hundred metres from his house was the bar Chez Régis. Flick went in. The proprietor, Alexandre Régis, sat behind the counter smoking. He gave her a nod of recognition but said nothing.

She went through the door marked 'Toilettes'. She walked along a short passage then opened what looked like a cupboard door. It led to a steep staircase going up. At the top of the stairs was a heavy door with a peephole. Flick banged on it and stood where her face could be seen through the judas. A moment later the door was opened by Mémé Régis, the mother of the proprietor.

Flick entered a large room whose windows were blacked out. It was crudely decorated with matting on the floor, brown-painted walls and several naked bulbs hanging from the ceiling. At one end of the room was a roulette wheel. Around a large circular table a group of men were playing cards. There was a bar in one corner. This was an illegal gambling club.

Michel liked to play poker for high stakes, and he enjoyed louche company, so he occasionally came here for an evening. Flick never played, but she sometimes sat and watched the game for an hour. Michel said she brought him luck. It was a good place to hide from the Gestapo, and Flick had been hoping she might find him here; but as she looked from face to face around the room she was disappointed.

'Thank you, Mémé,' she said to Alexandre's mother. 'It's good to see you. How are you?'

'Fine, have you seen my husband?'

'Ah, the charming Michel. Not tonight, I regret.' The people here did not know Michel was in the Resistance.

Flick went to the bar and sat on a stool, smiling at the barmaid, a middle-aged woman with bright red lipstick. She was Yvette Régis, the wife of Alexandre. 'Have you any Scotch?'

'Of course,' said Yvette. 'For those who can afford it.' She produced a bottle of Dewar's White Label and poured a measure.

Flick said: 'I'm looking for Michel.'

'I haven't seen him for a week or so,' Yvette said.

'Damn.' Flick sipped her drink. 'I'll wait a while, in case he shows up.'

FORTY-FOUR

Dieter was desperate. Flick had proved too clever. She had evaded his trap. She was somewhere in the city of Reims, but he had no way of finding her.

He could no longer have members of the Reims Resistance followed, in the hope that she would contact one of them, for they were all now in custody. Dieter had Michel's house and Gilberte's flat under surveillance, but he felt sure that Flick was too wily to let herself be seen by the average Gestapo flatfoot. There were posters of her all over town, but she must have changed her appearance by now, dyed her hair or something, for no one had reported seeing her. She had outwitted him at every stop.

He needed a stroke of genius.

And he had come up with one – he thought.

He sat on the saddle of a bicycle at the roadside. He was in the centre of town, just outside the theatre. He wore a beret, goggles, and a rough cotton sweater, and his trousers were tucked into his socks. He was unrecognizable. No one would suspect him. The Gestapo never went by bicycle.

He stared west along the street, narrowing his eyes

to look into the setting sun. He was waiting for a black Citroën. He checked his watch: any minute now.

On the other side of the road, Hans was at the wheel of a wheezy old Peugeot which had almost come to the end of its useful life. The engine was running: Dieter did not want to take the risk that it might not start when it was needed. Hans was also disguised, in sunglasses and a cap, and wore a shabby suit and down-at-heel shoes, like a French citizen. He had never done anything like this before, but he had accepted his orders with unflappable stoicism.

Dieter, too, had never done this before. He had no idea whether it would work. All kinds of things could go wrong and anything could happen.

What Dieter had planned was desperate, but what did he have to lose? Tuesday was the night of the full moon. He felt sure the Allies were about to invade. Flick was the grand prize. She was worth a great deal of risk.

But winning the war was no longer what most occupied his mind. His future had been wrecked; he hardly cared who ruled Europe. He thought constantly of Flick Clairet. She had ruined his life: she had murdered Stéphanie. He wanted to find Flick, and capture her, and take her to the basement of the chateau. There he would taste the satisfaction of revenge. He fantasized constantly about how he would torture her: the iron rods that would smash her small bones, the electric-shock machine turned up to maximum, the injections that would render her helpless with great wrenching spasms of nausea, the ice bath that would give her shivering convulsions and freeze the blood in her fingers. Destroying the Resistance, and repelling the invaders, had become merely part of his punishment of Flick.

But first he had to find her.

In the distance he saw a black Citroën.

He stared at it. Was this the one? It was a two-door model, the kind always used when transporting a prisoner. He tried to see inside. He thought there were four people altogether. This had to be the car he was waiting for. It drew nearer, and he recognized the handsome face of Michel in the back, guarded by a uniformed Gestapo man. He tensed.

He was glad now that he had given orders that Michel was not to be tortured while Dieter was away. This scheme would not have been possible otherwise.

As the Citroën came level with Dieter, Hans suddenly pulled away from the kerb in the old Peugeot. The car swung out into the road, leaped forward, and smashed straight into the front of the Citroën.

There was a clatter of crumpling metal and a medley of breaking glass. The two Gestapo men leaped out of the front of the Citroën and began yelling at Hans in bad French – seeming not to notice that their colleague in the back appeared to have banged his head and was slumped, apparently unconscious, beside his prisoner.

This was the critical moment, Dieter thought, his nerves strung like wire. Would Michel take the bait? He stared at the tableau in the middle of the street.

It took Michel a long moment to realize his

opportunity. Dieter almost thought he would fail to seize it. Then he seemed to come to. He reached over the front seats, fumbled at the door catch with bound hands, succeeded in getting the door open, pushed down the seat, and scrambled out.

He glanced at the two Gestapo men still arguing with Hans. They had their backs to him. He turned and walked quickly away. His expression said he could hardly believe his good luck.

Dieter's heart leaped with triumph. His plan was working.

He followed Michel.

Hans followed Dieter on foot.

Dieter rode the bicycle for a few yards, then he found himself catching up with Michel, so he got off and pushed it along the pavement. Michel turned the first corner, limping slightly from his bullet wound but walking fast, holding his bound hands low in front of him to make them less conspicuous. Dieter followed discreetly, sometimes walking, sometimes riding, dropping back out of Michel's sight whenever he could, taking cover behind high-sided vehicles if he got the chance. Michel occasionally glanced back, but made no systematic attempt to shake off a tail. He had no notion that he was being tricked.

After a few minutes, Hans overtook Dieter, by arrangement, and Dieter dropped back to follow Hans. Then they switched again.

Where would Michel go? It was essential to Dieter's plan that Michel should lead him to other Resistance members, so that he could once again pick up Flick's trail.

To Dieter's surprise, Michel headed for his house near the cathedral. Surely he must suspect that his home was under surveillance? Nevertheless he turned into the street. However, he did not go to his own place, but entered a bar across the street called Chez Régis.

Dieter leaned his bicycle against the wall of the next building, a vacant store with a faded *charcuterie* sign. He waited a few minutes, just in case Michel should come out again immediately. When it was clear Michel was staying a while, Dieter went in.

He intended simply to make sure Michel was still there – relying on his goggles and beret to conceal his identity from Michel. He would buy a packet of cigarettes as an excuse and go back outside. But Michel was nowhere in sight. Puzzled, Dieter hesitated.

The barman said: 'Yes, sir?'

'Beer,' said Dieter. 'Draught.' He hoped that if he kept his conversation to a minimum the barman would not notice his slight German accent, and accept him as a cyclist who had stopped to quench his thirst.

'Coming up.'

'Where's the toilet?'

The barman pointed to a door in the corner. Dieter went through it. Michel was not in the men's room. Dieter risked a glance into the ladies': it was empty. He opened what looked like a cupboard door and saw that it led to a staircase. He went up the stairs. At the top was a heavy door with a peephole. He knocked on the door, but there was no answer. He listened for a moment. He could hear nothing, but the door was thick. He felt sure there was someone the other side, looking at him through the peephole, realizing he was not a regular customer. He tried to act as if he had taken a wrong turn on the way to the toilet. He scratched his head, shrugged, and went back down the stairs.

There was no sign of a back entrance to the place. Michel was here, Dieter felt sure, in the locked room upstairs. But what should Dieter do about it?

He took his glass to a table, so that the barman would not try to engage him in small talk. The beer was watery and tasteless. Even in Germany, the quality of beer had declined during the war. He forced himself to finish it, then went out.

Hans was on the other side of the street, looking in the window of a bookshop. Dieter went across. 'He's in some kind of private room upstairs,' he told Hans. 'He may be meeting with other Resistance cadres. On the other hand, it may be a brothel, or something; and I don't want to bust in on him before he's led us to anyone worthwhile.'

Hans nodded, understanding the dilemma.

Dieter made a decision. It was too soon to re-arrest Michel. 'When he comes out, I'll follow him. As soon as we're out of sight, you can raid the place.'

'On my own?'

Dieter pointed to two Gestapo men in a Citroën keeping watch on Michel's house. 'Get them to help you.'

'Okay.'

'Try to make it look like a vice thing – arrest the whores, if there are any. Don't mention the Resistance.'

'Okay.'

'Until then, we wait.'

FORTY-FIVE

Until the moment when Michel walked in, Flick was feeling pessimistic.

She sat at the bar in the little makeshift casino, making desultory conversation with Yvette, indifferently watching the intent faces of the men as they concentrated on their cards, their dice, and the spinning roulette wheel. No one took much notice of her: they were serious gamblers, not to be distracted by a pretty face.

If she did not find Michel, she was in trouble. The other Jackdaws were in the cathedral, but they could not stay there all night. They could sleep in the open – they would survive the weather, in June – but they could so easily be caught.

They also needed transport. If they could not get a car or van from the Bollinger circuit, they would have to steal one. But then they would be forced to carry out the mission using a vehicle for which the police were searching. It added more dangers to an already perilous enterprise.

There was another reason for her gloom: the image of Stéphanie Vinson kept coming back to her. It was the first time Flick had killed a bound, helpless captive, and the first time she had shot a woman.

Any killing disturbed her profoundly. The Gestapo man she had shot a few minutes before Stéphanie had been a combatant with a gun in his hand, but still it seemed dreadful to her that she had brought his life to an end. So it had been with the other men she had killed: two Milice cops in Paris, a Gestapo colonel in Lille, and a French traitor in Rouen. But Stéphanie was worse. Flick had put a gun to the back of her head and executed her. It was exactly how she had taught trainees to do it on the SOE course. Stéphanie had deserved it, of course – Flick had no doubt about that. But she wondered about herself. What kind of person was capable of the cold-blooded killing of a helpless prisoner? Had she become some kind of brutish executioner?

She drained her whisky, but declined a refill for fear of becoming maudlin. Then Michel came through the door.

Overwhelming relief flooded her. Michel knew everyone in town. He would be able to help her. Suddenly the mission seemed possible again.

She felt a wry affection as she took in the lanky figure in a rumpled jacket, the handsome face with the smiling eyes. She would always be fond of him, she imagined. She suffered a painful stab of regret as she thought of the passionate love she had once had for him. That would never come back, she was sure.

As he came closer, she saw that he was not looking so good. His face seemed to have new lines. Her heart filled with compassion for him. Exhaustion and fear showed in his expression, and he might have been fifty rather than thirty-five, she thought anxiously.

But her greatest anxiety came from the thought of telling him that their marriage was over. She was afraid. It struck her as ironic: she had just shot and killed a Gestapo man and a French traitress, and she was undercover in occupied territory, yet her worst fear was of hurting her husband's feelings.

He was visibly delighted to see her. 'Flick!' he cried. 'I knew you would get here!' He crossed the room to her, still limping from his bullet wound.

She said quietly: 'I was afraid the Gestapo had captured you.'

'They did!' He turned, so that his back was to the room and no one could see, and showed her his hands, bound at the wrists with stout rope.

She drew the little knife from the its sheath under her lapel and discreetly cut through his bonds. The gamblers saw nothing. She put the knife away.

Mémé Régis spotted him just as he was stuffing the ropes into his trousers pockets. She embraced and kissed him on both cheeks. Flick watched him flirt with the older woman, talking to her in his come-to-bed voice, giving her the benefit of his sexy grin. Then Mémé resumed her work, serving drinks to the gamblers, and Michel told Flick how he had escaped. She had been afraid he would want to kiss her passionately, and she had not known how she would deal with that but, in the event, he was too full of his own adventures to get romantic with her.

'I was so lucky!' he finished. He sat on a bar stool, rubbing his wrists, and asked for a beer.

Flick nodded. 'Too lucky, perhaps,' she said.

'What do you mean?'

'It could be some kind of trick.'

He was indignant, no doubt resenting the implication that he was gullible. 'I don't think so.'

'Could you have been followed here?'

'No,' he said firmly. 'I checked, of course.'

She was uneasy, but she let it go. 'So Brian Standish is dead, and three others are in custody – Mademoiselle Lemas, Gilberte, and Dr Bouler.'

'The rest are dead. The Germans released the bodies of those killed in the skirmish. And the survivors, Gaston, Geneviève and Bertrand, were shot by a firing squad in the square at Sainte-Cécile.'

'Dear God.'

They were silent for a moment. Flick was weighed down by the thought of the lives lost, and the suffering endured, for the sake of this mission.

Michel's beer came. He drank half in a single draught and wiped his lips. 'I presume you've come back for another attempt on the chateau.'

She nodded. 'But the cover story is that we're going to blow up the railway tunnel at Marles.'

'It's a good idea, we should do it anyway.'

'Not now. Two of my team were taken in Paris, and they must have talked. They will have told the cover story – they had no idea of the real mission – and the Germans are sure to have doubled the guard on the railway tunnel. We'll leave that to the RAF and concentrate on Sainte-Cécile.'

'What can I do?'

'We need somewhere to stay the night.'

He thought for a moment. 'Joseph Laperrière's cellar.'

Laperrière was a champagne maker. Michel's aunt Antoinette had once been his secretary. 'Is he one of us?'

'A sympathizer.' He gave a sour grin. 'Everyone is a sympathizer now. They all think the invasion is coming any day.' He looked enquiringly at her. 'I imagine they're right about that . . .'

'Yes,' she said. She did not elaborate. 'How big is the cellar? There are five of us.'

'It's big, he could hide fifty people down there.'

'Fine. The other thing I need is a vehicle for tomorrow.'

'To drive to Sainte-Cécile?'

'And afterwards, to meet our pick-up plane, if we're still alive.'

'You realize that you can't use the usual drop zone at Chatelle, don't you? The Gestapo know about it – it's where I was picked up.'

'Yes. The plane is coming to the other one at Laroque. I gave instructions.'

'The potato field. Good.'

'And the vehicle?'

'Philippe Moulier has a van. He delivers meat to all the German bases. Monday is his day off.'

'I remember him, he's pro-Nazi.'

'He was. And he's been making money out of them for four years. So now he's terrified that the invasion is going to succeed, and after the Germans have gone he'll be strung up as a collaborator. He's desperate to do something to help us, to prove he's not a traitor. He'll lend us his van.'

'Bring it to the cellar tomorrow at ten o'clock in the morning.'

He touched her cheek. 'Can't we spend the night together?' He smiled his old smile, and looked as roguishly handsome as ever.

She felt a familiar stirring inside, but it was not as strong as it had been in the old days. Once, that smile would have made her wet. Now, it was like the memory of a desire.

She wanted to tell him the truth, for she hated to be anything less than honest. But it might jeopardize the mission. She needed his co-operation. Or was that just an excuse? Perhaps she just did not have the nerve.

'No,' she said. 'We can't spend the night together.'

He looked crestfallen. 'Is it because of Gilberte?'

She nodded, but she could not lie, and she found herself saying: 'Well, partly.'

'What's the other part?'

'I don't really want to have this discussion in the middle of an important mission.'

He looked vulnerable, almost scared. 'Have you got someone else?'

She could not bring herself to hurt him. 'No,' she lied.

He looked hard at her. 'Good,' he said at last. 'I'm glad.'

Flick hated herself.

Michel finished his beer and got off his stool. 'Laperrière's place is in the chemin de la Carrière. It will take you thirty minutes to walk there.'

'I know the street.'

'I'd better go and see Moulier about the van.' He put his arms around Flick and kissed her lips.

She felt dreadful. She could hardly refuse the kiss, having denied that she had someone else; but kissing Michel seemed so disloyal to Paul. She closed her eyes and waited passively until he broke the clinch.

He could not fail to notice her lack of enthusiasm. He looked thoughtfully at her for a moment. 'I'll see you at ten,' he said, and he left.

She decided to give him five minutes to get clear before she followed him out. She asked Yvette for another Scotch.

While she was sipping it, a red light began to flash over the door.

No one spoke, but everyone in the room moved at once. The croupier stopped the roulette wheel and turned it upside-down so that it looked like a normal table top. The card players swept up their stakes and put on their jackets. Yvette picked up the glasses from the bar and dumped them in the sink. Mémé Régis turned out the lights, leaving the room illuminated only by the flashing red bulb over the door.

Flick picked up her bag from the floor and put her hand on her gun. 'What's happening?' she asked Yvette.

'Police raid,' she said.

Flick cursed. What hellish luck it would be to get arrested for illegal gambling.

'Alexandre downstairs has given us the warning,' Yvette explained. 'Get going, quickly!' She pointed across the room.

Flick looked in the direction Yvette indicated and saw Mémé Régis stepping into what looked like a cupboard. As she watched, Mémé shoved aside a couple of old coats hanging from a rail to reveal, at the back of the cupboard, a door which she hurriedly opened. The gamblers began to leave by the hidden door. Maybe, Flick thought, she could get away.

The flashing red light went out, and a banging began on the main door. Flick crossed the room in the dark and joined the men pushing through the cupboard. She followed the crowd into a bare room. The floor was about a foot lower than she expected, and she guessed this was the apartment over the shop next door. They all ran down the stairs and, sure enough, she found herself in the disused *charcuterie*, with a stained marble counter and dusty glass cases. The blind in the front window was drawn down, so that no one could see in from the street.

They all went out through the back door. There was a dirty yard surrounded by a high wall. A door in the wall led to an alley, and the alley led to the next street. When they reached the street the men went in different directions.

Flick walked quickly away and soon found herself alone. Breathing hard, she reoriented herself and headed for the cathedral, where the other Jackdaws were waiting. 'My God,' she whispered to herself, 'that was close.'

As she got her breath back, so she began to see the raid on the gambling club in a different light. It had happened just minutes after Michel had left. Flick did not believe in coincidence.

The more she thought about it, the more convinced she became that whoever was banging on the door had been looking for her. She knew that a small group of men had been playing for high stakes in that room since before the war. The local police certainly knew about the place. Why would they suddenly decide to close it down? If not the police, it must have been the Gestapo. And they were not really interested in gamblers. They went after Communists, Jews, homosexuals – and spies.

The story of Michel's escape had aroused her suspicions from the start, but she had been partly reassured by his insistence that he had not been followed. Now she thought otherwise. His escape must have been faked, like the 'rescue' of Brian Standish. She saw the sly brain of Dieter Franck behind this. Someone had followed Michel to the café, guessed at the existence of the secret upstairs room, and hoped to find her there.

In that case, Michel was still under surveillance. If he continued to be careless, he would be trailed to Philippe Moulier's house tonight, and in the morning, driving the van, he would be followed to the champagne cellar where the Jackdaws were hiding.

And what the hell, Flick thought, am I going to do about that?

THE NINTH DAY:
MONDAY, 5 JUNE 1944

FORTY-SIX

Dieter's migraine began shortly after midnight, as he stood in his room at the Hôtel Frankfort, looking at the bed he would never again share with Stéphanie. He felt that if he could weep, the pain would fade; but no tears came, and he injected himself with morphine and collapsed on the counterpane.

The phone woke him before daylight. It was Walter Goedel, Rommel's aide. Groggily, Dieter said: 'Has the invasion begun?'

'Not today,' Goedel replied. 'The weather is bad in the English Channel.'

Dieter sat upright and shook his head to clear it. 'What, then?'

'The Resistance were clearly *expecting* something. Overnight there has been an eruption of sabotage throughout northern France.' Goedel's voice, already cool, descended to an Arctic chill. 'It was supposed to be your job to prevent that. What are you doing in bed?'

Caught off guard, Dieter struggled to regain his usual poise. 'I'm right on the tail of the most important of all Resistance leaders,' he said, trying hard not to sound as if he were making excuses for failure. 'I almost caught her last night. I'll arrest her today. Don't worry – by tomorrow morning we'll be rounding up terrorists by the hundred. I promise you.' He immediately regretted the pleading tone of the last three words.

Goedel was unmoved. 'After tomorrow, it will probably be too late.'

'I know—' Dieter stopped. The line was dead. Goedel had hung up.

Dieter cradled the phone and looked at his wristwatch. It was four o'clock. He got up.

His migraine had gone, but he felt queasy, either from the morphine or the unpleasant phone call. He drank a glass of water and swallowed three aspirins, then began to shave. As he lathered his face, he nervously ran over the events of the previous evening, asking himself if he had done everything possible.

Leaving Lieutenant Hesse outside Chez Régis, he had followed Michel Clairet to the premises of Philippe Moulier, a supplier of fresh meat to restaurants and military kitchens. It was a storefront property with living quarters above and a yard at the side. Dieter had watched the place for an hour, but no one had come out.

Deciding that Michel intended to spend the night there, Dieter had found a bar and phoned Hans Hesse. Hans had got on a motorcycle and joined him outside the Moulier place at ten. The lieutenant told Dieter the story of the inexplicably empty room above Chez Régis. 'There's some early-warning system,' Dieter speculated. 'The barman downstairs is ready to sound the alarm if anyone comes looking.'

'You think the Resistance were using the place?'

'Probably. I'd guess the Communist Party used to hold meetings there, and the Resistance took over the system.'

'But how did they get away last night?'

'A trapdoor under the carpet, something like that – the Communists would have been prepared for trouble. Did you arrest the barman?'

'I arrested everyone in the place. They're at the chateau now.'

Dieter had left Hans watching the Moulier property and had driven to Sainte-Cécile. There he questioned the terrified proprietor, Alexandre Régis, and learned within minutes that his speculation had been off target. The place was neither a Resistance hideout nor a Communist meeting-place, but an illegal gambling club. Nevertheless, Alexandre confirmed that Michel Clairet had gone there last night. And, he said, Michel had met his wife there.

It was another maddeningly near miss for Dieter. He had captured one Resistance member after another, but Flick always eluded him.

Now he finished shaving, wiped his face, and phoned the chateau to order a car with a driver and two Gestapo men to pick him up. He got dressed and went to the hotel kitchen to beg half a dozen warm croissants which he wrapped in a linen napkin. Then he went out into the cool of the early morning. The towers of the cathedral were silvered by the breaking dawn. One of the fast Citroëns favoured by the Gestapo was waiting.

He gave the driver the address of the Moulier place.

495

He found Hans lurking in a warehouse doorway fifty metres along the street. No one had come or gone all night, Hans said, so Michel must still be inside. Dieter told his driver to wait around the next corner, then stood with Hans, sharing the croissants and watching the sun come up over the roofs of the city.

They had a long wait. Dieter fought to control his impatience as the minutes and hours ticked away uselessly. The loss of Stéphanie weighed on his heart, but he had recovered from the immediate shock, and he had regained his interest in the war. He thought of the Allied forces massing somewhere in the south or east of England, shiploads of men and tanks eager to turn the quiet seaside towns of northern France into battlefields. He thought of the French saboteurs – armed to the teeth, thanks to parachute drops of guns, ammunition and explosives – ready to attack the German defenders from behind, to stab them in the back and fatally cramp Rommel's ability to manoeuvre. He felt foolish and impotent, standing in a doorway in Reims, waiting for an amateur terrorist to finish his breakfast. Today, perhaps, he would be led into the very heart of the Resistance – but all he had was hope.

It was after nine o'clock when the front door opened.

'At last,' Dieter breathed. He moved back, making himself inconspicuous. Hans put out his cigarette.

Michel came out of the building accompanied by a boy of about seventeen who, Dieter guessed, might be a son of Moulier. The lad keyed a padlock and opened the gates of the yard. In the yard was a clean black van with white lettering on the side that read: *Moulier & Fils – Viandes*. Michel got in.

Dieter was electrified. Michel was borrowing a meat-delivery van. It had to be for the Jackdaws. 'Let's go!' he said.

Hans hurried to his motorcycle, which was parked at the kerb, and stood with his back to the road, pretending to fiddle with the engine. Dieter ran to the corner, signalled the Gestapo driver to start the car, then watched Michel.

Michel drove out of the yard and headed away.

Hans started his motorcycle and followed. Dieter jumped into the car and ordered the driver to follow Hans.

They headed east. Dieter, in the front passenger seat of the Gestapo's black Citroën, looked ahead anxiously. Moulier's van was easy to follow, having a high roof with a vent on top like a chimney. That little vent will lead me to Flick, Dieter thought optimistically.

The van slowed in the chemin de la Carrière and pulled into the yard of a champagne house called Laperrière. Hans drove past and turned the next corner, and Dieter's driver followed. They pulled up and Dieter leaped out.

'I think the Jackdaws hid out there overnight,' Dieter said.

'Shall we raid the place?' Hans said eagerly.

Dieter pondered. This was the dilemma he had faced yesterday, outside the café. Flick might be in there. But if he moved too quickly, he might prematurely end Michel's usefulness as a stalking-horse.

'Not yet,' he said. Michel was the only hope he had left. It was too soon to risk losing that weapon. 'We'll wait.'

Dieter and Hans walked to the end of the street and watched the Laperrière place from the corner. There was a tall, elegant house, a courtyard full of empty barrels, and a low industrial building with a flat roof. Dieter guessed the cellars ran beneath the flat-roofed building. Moulier's van was parked in the yard.

Dieter's pulse was racing. Any moment now, Michel would reappear with Flick and the other Jackdaws, he guessed. They would get into the van, ready to drive to their target – and Dieter and the Gestapo would move in and arrest them.

As they watched, Michel came out of the low building. He wore a frown and he stood indecisively in the yard, looking around him in a perplexed fashion. Hans said: 'What's the matter with him?'

Dieter's heart sank. 'Something he didn't expect.' Surely Flick had not evaded him again?

After a minute, Michel climbed the short flight of steps to the door of the house and knocked. A maid in a little white cap let him in.

He came out again a few minutes later. He still looked puzzled, but he was no longer indecisive. He walked to the van, got in, and turned it around.

Dieter cursed. It seemed the Jackdaws were not here. Michel appeared just as surprised as Dieter was, but that was small consolation.

Dieter had to find out what had happened here. He

said to Hans: 'We'll do the same as last night, only this time *you* follow Michel and I'll raid the place.'

Hans started his motorcycle.

Dieter watched Michel drive away in Moulier's van, followed at a discreet distance by Hans Hesse on his motorcycle. When they were out of sight, he summoned the three Gestapo men with a wave, and walked quickly to the Laperrière house.

He pointed at two of the men. 'Check the house. Make sure no one leaves.' Nodding at the third man, he said: 'You and I will search the winery.' He led the way into the low building.

On the ground floor there was a large grape press and three enormous vats. The press was pristine: the harvest was three or four months away. There was no one present but an old man sweeping the floor. Dieter found the stairs and ran down. In the cool underground chamber there was more activity: racked bottles were being turned by a handful of blue-coated workers. They stopped and stared at the intruders.

Dieter and the Gestapo man searched room after room of bottles of champagne, thousands of them, some stacked against the walls, others racked slantwise with the necks down in special A-shaped frames. But there were no women anywhere.

In an alcove at the far end of the last tunnel, Dieter found crumbs of bread, cigarette ends, and a hair clip. His worst fears were dismally confirmed. The Jackdaws had spent the night here. But they had escaped.

He cast about for a focus for his anger. The workers

would probably know nothing about the Jackdaws, but the owner must have given permission for them to hide here. He would suffer for it. Dieter returned to the ground floor, crossed the yard, and went to the house. A Gestapo man opened the door. 'They're all in the front room,' he said.

Dieter entered a large, gracious room with elegant but shabby furnishings: heavy curtains that had not been cleaned for years, a worn carpet, a long dining table and a matching set of twelve chairs. The terrified household staff were standing at the near end of the room: the maid who opened the door, an elderly man who looked like a butler in his threadbare black suit, and a plump woman wearing an apron who must have been the cook. A Gestapo man held a pistol pointed at them. At the far end of the table sat a thin woman of about fifty, with red hair threaded with silver, dressed in a summer frock of pale yellow silk. She had an air of calm superiority.

Dieter turned to the Gestapo men and said in a low voice: 'Where's the husband?'

'He left the house at eight. They don't know where he went. He's expected home for lunch.'

Dieter gave the woman a hard look. 'Madame Laperrière?'

She nodded gravely, but did not deign to speak.

Dieter decided to puncture her dignity. Some German officers behaved with deference to upper-class French people, but Dieter thought they were fools. He would not pander to her by walking the length of the room to speak to her. 'Bring her to me,' he said.

One of the men spoke to her. Slowly, she got up from her chair and approached Dieter. 'What do you want?' she said.

'A group of terrorists from England escaped from me yesterday after killing two German officers and a French woman civilian.'

'I'm sorry to hear that,' said Madame Laperrière.

'They tied the woman up and shot her in the back of the head at point-blank range,' he went on. 'Her brains spilled out on to her dress.'

She closed her eyes and turned her head aside.

Dieter went on: 'Last night your husband sheltered those terrorists in your cellar. Can you think of any reason why he should not be hanged?'

Behind him, the maid began to cry.

Madame Laperrière was shaken. Her face turned pale and she sat down suddenly. 'No, please,' she whispered.

Dieter said: 'You can help your husband by telling me what you know.'

'I don't know anything,' she said in a low voice. 'They came after dinner, and they left before dawn. I never saw them.'

'How did they leave? Did your husband provide them with a car?'

She shook her head. 'We have no petrol.'

'Then how do you deliver the champagne you make?'

'Our customers have to come to us.'

Dieter did not believe her. He felt sure Flick needed transportation. That was why Michel had borrowed a van from Philippe Moulier and brought it here. Yet, when Michel had got here, Flick and the Jackdaws had gone. They *must* have found alternative means of transport, and decided to go on ahead. No doubt Flick had left a message explaining the situation and telling Michel to catch up with her.

Dieter said: 'Are you asking me to believe they left here on foot?'

'No,' she replied. 'I'm telling you that I don't know. When I woke up, they had gone.'

Dieter still thought she was lying, but to get the truth out of her would take time and patience, and he was running out of both. 'Arrest them all,' he said, and his angry frustration injected a petulant note into his voice.

The phone rang in the hall. Dieter stepped out of the dining room and picked it up.

A voice with a German accent said: 'Let me speak to Major Franck.'

'This is he.'

'Lieutenant Hesse here, Major.'

'Hans, what happened?'

'I'm at the station. Michel parked the van and bought a ticket to Marles. The train is about to leave.'

It was as Dieter had thought. The Jackdaws had gone ahead and left instructions for Michel to join them. They were still planning to blow up the railway tunnel. He felt frustrated that Flick was continuing to stay one step ahead of him. However, she had not been able to escape him completely. He was still on her tail. He would catch her soon. 'Get on the train, quickly,' he said to Hans. 'Stay with him. I'll meet you at Marles.'

'Very good,' said Hans, and he hung up.

Dieter returned to the dining room. 'Call the chateau and have them send transportation,' he said to the Gestapo men. 'Turn all the prisoners over to Sergeant Becker for interrogation. Tell him to start with Madame.' He pointed to the driver. 'You can drive me to Marles.'

FORTY-SEVEN

In the Café de la Gare near the railway station, Flick
and Paul had a breakfast of ersatz coffee, black bread,
and sausage with little or no meat in it. Ruby, Jelly and
Greta sat at a separate table, not acknowledging them.
Flick kept an eye on the street outside.

She knew that Michel was in terrible danger. She
had contemplated going to warn him. She could have
gone to the Moulier place – but that would have played
into the hands of the Gestapo, who must be following
Michel in the hope that he would lead them to her.
Even to phone the Moulier place would have risked
betraying her hideout to a Gestapo eavesdropper at the
telephone exchange. In fact, she had decided, the best
thing she could do to help Michel was *not* to contact
him directly. If her theory was right, Dieter Franck
would let Michel remain at large until Flick was caught.

So she had left a message for Michel with Madame
Laperrière. It read:

> Michel –
>   I am sure you are under surveillance. The place we were
> at last night was raided after you left. You have probably
> been followed this morning.

*We will leave before you get here and make ourselves
inconspicuous in the town centre. Park the van near the
railway station and leave the key under the driver's seat. Get
a train to Marles. Shake off your shadow and come back.*

   Be careful – please!
   Flick

Now burn this.

It seemed good in theory, but she waited all morning
in a fever of tension to see whether it would work.

Then, at eleven o'clock, she saw a high van draw up
and park near the station entrance. Flick held her
breath. On the side, in white lettering, she read: *Moulier
& Fils – Viandes.*

Michel got out, and she breathed again.

He walked into the station. He was carrying out her
plan.

She looked to see who might be following him,
but it was impossible. People arrived at the station
constantly, on foot, on bicycles, and in cars, and any of
them might have been shadowing Michel.

She remained in the café, pretending to drink the
bitter, unsatisfying coffee substitute, keeping an eye on
the van, trying to discover whether it was under
surveillance. She studied the people and vehicles
coming and going outside the station, but she did not
spot anyone who might have been watching the van.
After fifteen minutes she nodded to Paul. They got up,
picked up their cases, and walked out.

Flick opened the van door and got into the driving

seat. Paul got in at the other side. Flick's heart was in her mouth. If this was a Gestapo trap, now would be the moment when they arrested her. She fumbled beneath her seat and found a key. She started the van.

She looked around. No one seemed to have noticed her.

Ruby, Jelly and Greta came out of the café. Flick jerked her head to indicate that they should get in the back.

She looked over her shoulder. The van was fitted out with shelves and cupboards, and trays for ice to keep the temperature down. Everything looked as if it had been well scrubbed, but there remained a faint, unpleasant odour of raw meat.

The rear doors opened. The other three women threw their suitcases into the van and clambered in after them. Ruby pulled the doors shut.

Flick put the gearstick into first and drove away.

'We did it!' Jelly said. 'Thank gordon.'

Flick smiled thinly. The hard part was still ahead.

She drove out of town on the road to Sainte-Cécile. She watched for police cars and Gestapo Citroëns, but she felt fairly safe for the moment. The van's lettering announced its legitimacy. And it was not unusual for a woman to be driving such a vehicle, when so many French men were in labour camps in Germany – or had fled to the hills and joined the *maquis* to avoid being sent to the camps.

Soon after midday they reached Sainte-Cécile. Flick noted the sudden miraculous quiet that always fell on

French streets at the stroke of noon, as the people turned their attention to the first serious meal of the day. She drove to Antoinette's building. A pair of tall wooden doors, half open, led to the inner courtyard. Paul leaped out of the van and opened the doors, Flick drove in, and Paul closed the doors behind her. Now the van, with its distinctive legend, could not be seen from the street.

'Come when I whistle,' Flick said, and she jumped out.

She went to Antoinette's door while the others waited in the van. Last time she had knocked on this door, eight days and a lifetime ago, Michel's aunt Antoinette had hesitated to answer, jumpy on account of the gunfire from the square; but today she came right away. She opened the door, a slim middle-aged woman in a stylish but faded yellow cotton dress. She looked blankly at Flick for a moment: Flick still had on the dark wig. Then recognition dawned. 'You!' she said. A look of panic came over her face. 'What do you want?'

Flick whistled to the others, then pushed Antoinette back inside. 'Don't worry,' she said. 'We're going to tie you up so the Germans will think we forced you.'

'What is this?' Antoinette said shakily

'I'll explain in a moment. Are you alone?'

'Yes.'

'Good.'

The others came in and Ruby closed the apartment door. They went into Antoinette's kitchen. A meal was laid out on the table: black bread, a salad of shredded carrots, a heel of cheese, a wine bottle without a label. Antoinette said again: 'What is this?'

'Sit down,' Flick said. 'Finish your lunch.'

She sat down, but she said: 'I can't eat.'

'It's very simple,' Flick said. 'You and your ladies are not going to clean the chateau tonight ... we are.'

She looked baffled. 'How will that happen?'

'We're going to send notes to each of the women on duty tonight, telling them to come here and see you before they go to work. When they arrive, we will tie them up. Then we will go to the chateau instead of them.'

'You can't, you don't have passes.'

'Yes, we do.'

'How ... ?' Antoinette gasped. 'You stole my pass! Last Sunday. I thought I had lost it. I got into the most terrible trouble with the Germans!'

'I'm sorry you got into trouble.'

'But this will be worse – you're going to blow the place up!' Antoinette began to moan and rock. 'They'll blame me, you know what they're like, we'll all be tortured.'

Flick gritted her teeth. She knew that Antoinette could be right. The Gestapo might easily kill the real cleaners just in case they had had something to do with the deception. 'We're going to do everything we can to make you look innocent,' she said. 'You will be our victims, the same as the Germans.' All the same, there remained a risk, Flick knew.

'They won't believe us,' Antoinette moaned. 'We might be killed.'

Flick hardened her heart. 'Yes,' she said. 'That's why it's called a war.'

FORTY-EIGHT

Marles was a small town to the east of Reims, where the railway line began its long climb into the mountains on its way to Frankfurt, Stuttgart and Nuremberg. The tunnel just beyond the town carried a constant stream of supplies from the home country to the German forces occupying France. The destruction of the tunnel would starve Rommel of ammunition.

The town itself looked Bavarian, with half-timbered houses painted in bright colours. The town hall stood on the leafy square opposite the railway station. The local Gestapo chief had taken over the mayor's grand office, and now stood poring over a map with Dieter Franck and a Captain Bern who was in charge of the military guard on the tunnel.

'I have twenty men at each end of the tunnel and another group constantly patrolling the mountain,' said Bern. 'The Resistance would need a large force to overcome them.'

Dieter frowned. According to the confession of the lesbian he had interrogated, Diana Colefield, Flick had started with a team of six women, including herself, and must now be down to four. However, she might have joined up with another group, or made contact with

510

more French Resistance cadres in and around Marles. 'They have plenty of people,' he said. 'The French think the invasion is coming.'

'But a large force is hard to conceal. So far we have seen nothing suspicious.'

Bern was short and slight, and wore spectacles with thick lenses, which was presumably why he was stationed in this backwater rather than with a fighting unit; but he struck Dieter as an intelligent and efficient young officer. Dieter was inclined to take what he said at face value.

Dieter said: 'How vulnerable is the tunnel to explosives?'

'It goes through solid rock. Of course it can be destroyed, but they will need a truckload of dynamite.'

'They have plenty of dynamite.'

'But they need to get it here – again, without our seeing it.'

'Indeed.' Dieter turned to the Gestapo chief. 'Have you received any reports of strange vehicles, or a group of people arriving in the town?'

'None at all. There is only one hotel in town, and at present it has no guests. My men visited the bars and restaurants at lunchtime, as they do every day, and saw nothing unusual.'

Captain Bern said hesitantly: 'Is it conceivable, Major, that the report you received, of an attack on the tunnel, was some kind of deception? A diversion, as it were, to draw your attention away from the real target?'

That infuriating possibility had already begun to dawn on Dieter. He knew from bitter experience that

Flick Clairet was a master of deception. Had she fooled him again? The thought was too humiliating to contemplate. 'I interrogated the informant myself, and I'm sure she was being honest,' Dieter replied, trying hard to keep the rage out of his voice. 'But you could still be right. It's possible *she* had been misinformed, deliberately, as a precaution.'

Bern cocked his head and said: 'A train is coming.'

Dieter frowned. He could hear nothing.

'My hearing is very good,' the man said with a smile. 'No doubt to compensate for my eyesight.'

Dieter had established that the only train to have left Reims for Marles today had been the eleven o'clock, so Michel and Lieutenant Hesse should be on the next one in.

The Gestapo chief went to the window. 'This is a westbound train,' he said. 'Your man is eastbound, I think you said.'

Dieter nodded.

Bern said: 'In fact there are two trains approaching, one from either direction.'

The Gestapo chief looked the other way. 'You're right, so there are.'

The three men went out into the square. Dieter's driver, leaning on the bonnet of the Citroën, stood upright and put out his cigarette. Beside him was a Gestapo motorcyclist, ready to resume surveillance of Michel.

They walked to the station entrance. 'Is there another way out?' Dieter asked the Gestapo man.

'No.'

They stood waiting. Captain Bern said: 'Have you heard the news?'

'No, what?' Dieter replied.

'Rome has fallen.'

'My God.'

'The US army reached the Piazza Venezia yesterday at seven o'clock in the evening.'

As the senior officer, Dieter felt it was his duty to maintain morale. 'That's bad news, but not unexpected,' he said. 'However, Italy is not France. If they try to invade us, they'll get a nasty surprise.' He hoped he was right.

The westbound train came in first. While its passengers were still unloading their bags and stepping on to the platform, the eastbound train chugged in. There was a little knot of people waiting at the station entrance. Dieter studied them surreptitiously, wondering if the local Resistance was meeting Michel off the train. He saw nothing suspicious.

A Gestapo checkpoint stood next to the ticket barrier. The Gestapo chief joined his underling at the table. Captain Bern leaned on a pillar to one side, making himself less conspicuous. Dieter returned to his car and sat in the back, watching the station.

What would he do if Captain Bern were right, and the tunnel was a diversion? The prospect was dismal. He would have to consider alternatives. What other military targets were within reach of Reims? The chateau at Sainte-Cécile was an obvious one, but the Resistance had failed to destroy that only a week ago – surely they would not try again so soon? There was a military camp to the north of the town, some railway marshalling yards between Reims and Paris . . .

That was not the way to go. Guesswork might lead anywhere. He needed information.

He could interrogate Michel right now, as soon as he got off the train, pull out his fingernails one by one until he talked – but would Michel know the truth? He might tell some cover story, believing it to be genuine, as Diana had. Dieter would do better just to follow him until he met up with Flick. She knew the real target. She was the only one worth interrogating now.

Dieter waited impatiently while papers were carefully checked and passengers trickled through. A whistle blew, and the westbound train pulled out. More passengers came out: ten, twenty, thirty. The eastbound train left.

Then Hans Hesse emerged from the station.

Dieter said: 'What the hell . . . ?'

Hans looked around the square, saw the Citroën, and ran towards it.

Dieter jumped out of the car.

Hans said: 'What happened? Where is he?'

'What do you mean?' Dieter shouted angrily. 'You're following him!'

'I did! He got off the train. I lost sight of him in the queue for the checkpoint. After a while I got worried and jumped the queue, but he had already gone.'

'Could he have got back on the train?'

'No – I followed him all the way off the platform.'

'Could he have got on the other train?'

Hans's mouth dropped open. 'I lost sight of him

about the time we were passing the end of the Reims platform . . .'

'That's it,' said Dieter. 'Hell! He's on his way back to Reims. He's a decoy. This whole trip was a diversion.' He was furious that he had fallen for it.

'What do we do?'

'We'll catch up with the train and you can follow him again. I still think he will lead us to Flick Clairet. Get in the car, let's go!'

FORTY-NINE

Flick could hardly believe she had got this far. Four of the original six Jackdaws had evaded capture, despite a brilliant adversary and some mixed luck, and now they were in Antoinette's kitchen, a few steps away from the square at Sainte-Cécile, right under the noses of the Gestapo. In ten minutes time they would walk up to the gates of the chateau.

Antoinette and four of the other five cleaners were firmly tied to kitchen chairs. Paul had gagged all but Antoinette. Each cleaner had arrived carrying a little shopping basket or canvas bag containing food and drink – bread, cold potatoes, fruit, and a flask of wine or ersatz coffee – which they would normally have during their nine-thirty break, not being allowed to use the German canteen. Now the Jackdaws were hastily emptying the bags and reloading them with the things they needed to carry into the chateau: electric torches, guns, ammunition, and yellow plastic explosive in 250-gram sticks. The Jackdaws' own suitcases, which had held the stuff until now, would have looked odd in the hands of cleaners going to work.

Flick realized quickly that the cleaners' own bags were not big enough. She herself had a Sten submachine-gun with a silencer, each of its three parts about a foot long. Jelly had sixteen detonators in a shockproof can, an incendiary thermite bomb, and a chemical block that produced oxygen, for setting fires in enclosed spaces such as bunkers. After loading their ordnance into the bags, they had to conceal it with the cleaners' packets of food. There was not enough room.

'Damn,' Flick said edgily. 'Antoinette, do you have any big bags?'

'What do you mean?'

'Bags, big bags, like shopping bags, you must have some.'

'There's one in the pantry that I use for buying vegetables.'

Flick found the bag, a cheap rectangular basket made of woven reeds. 'It's perfect,' she said. 'Have you any more like it?'

'No, why would I have two?'

Flick needed four.

There was a knock. Flick went to the door. A woman in a flowered overall and a hair-net stood there: the last of the cleaners. 'Good evening,' Flick said.

The woman hesitated, surprised to see a stranger. 'Is Antoinette here? I received a note . . .'

Flick smiled reassuringly. 'In the kitchen. Please come in.'

The woman walked through the apartment, evidently familiar with the place, and entered the kitchen, where she stopped dead and gave a little scream. Antoinette said: 'Don't worry, Françoise – they're tying us up so that the Germans will know we didn't help them.'

Flick relieved the woman of her bag. It was made of knotted string – fine for carrying a loaf and a bottle, but no good to Flick.

This infuriatingly petty detail had Flick stymied just minutes before the climax of the mission. She could not go on until she solved the problem. She forced herself to think calmly, then said to Antoinette: 'Where did you get your basket?'

'At the little shop across the street. You can see it from the window.'

The windows were open, as it was a warm evening, but the shutters were closed for shade. Flick pushed a shutter open a couple of inches and looked out on to the rue du Chateau. On the other side of the street was a store selling candles, firewood, brooms, and clothes pegs. She turned to Ruby. 'Go and buy three more bags, quickly.'

Ruby went to the door.

'If you can, get different shapes and colours.' Flick was afraid the bags might attract attention if they were all the same.

'Right.'

Paul tied the last of the cleaners to a chair and gagged her. He was apologetic and charming, and she did not resist.

Flick gave cleaners' passes to Jelly and Greta. She had held them back until the last minute because they would have given away the mission, if found on the person of a captured Jackdaw. With Ruby's pass in her hand, she went to the window.

Ruby was coming out of the store carrying three

shopping baskets of different kinds. Flick was relieved. She checked her watch: it was two minutes to seven.

Then disaster struck.

As Ruby was about to cross the road, she was accosted by a man in military-style clothes. He wore a blue denim shirt with buttoned pockets, a dark blue tie, a beret, and dark trousers tucked into high boots. Flick recognized the uniform of the Milice, the security militia that did the dirty work of the regime. 'Oh, no!' she said.

Like the Gestapo, the Milice was made up of men too stupid and thuggish to get into the normal police. Their officers were upper-class versions of the same type, snobbish patriots who talked of the glory of France and sent their underlings to arrest Jewish children hiding in cellars.

Paul came and looked over Flick's shoulder. 'Hell, it's a frigging Militian,' he said.

Flick's mind raced. Was this a chance encounter, or part of an organized security sweep directed at the Jackdaws? The Milice were infamous busybodies, revelling in their power to harass their fellow citizens. They would stop people they did not like the look of, examine their papers minutely, and seek a pretext to arrest them. Was the questioning of Ruby such an incident? Flick hoped so. If the police were stopping everyone on the streets of Sainte-Cécile, the Jackdaws might never reach the gates of the chateau.

The cop started to question Ruby aggressively. Flick could not hear clearly, but she picked up the words 'mongrel' and 'black', and she wondered if the man was accusing the dark-skinned Ruby of being a gypsy. Ruby took out her papers. The man examined them, then continued to question her without handing them back.

Paul drew his pistol.

'Put it away,' Flick commanded.

'You're not going to let him arrest her?'

'Yes, I am,' Flick said coldly. 'If we have a shootout now, we're finished – the mission is blown, whatever happens. Ruby's life is not as important as disabling the telephone exchange. Put away the damn gun.'

Paul tucked it under the waistband of his trousers.

The conversation between Ruby and the Militian became heated. Flick watched with trepidation as Ruby shifted the three baskets to her left hand and put her right hand into her raincoat pocket. The man grabbed Ruby's left shoulder in a decisive way, obviously arresting her.

Ruby moved fast. She dropped the baskets. Her right hand came out of her pocket holding a knife. She took a step forward and swung the knife up from hip level with great force, sticking the blade through his uniform shirt just below the ribs, angled up towards the heart.

Flick said: 'Oh, *shit.*'

The man gave a scream that quickly died off into a horrible gurgle. Ruby tugged the knife out and stuck it in again, this time from the side. He threw back his head and opened his mouth in a soundless cry of pain.

Flick was thinking ahead. If she could get the body out of sight quickly, they might get away with this. Had anyone seen the stabbing? Flick's view from the window was restricted by the shutters. She pushed them wide and leaned out. To her left, the rue du Chateau was deserted except for a parked truck and a dog asleep on a doorstep. Looking the other way she saw, coming along the pavement, three young people in police-style uniforms, two men and a woman. They had to be Gestapo personnel from the chateau.

The Militian fell to the pavement, blood coming from his mouth.

Before Flick could shout a warning, the two Gestapo men sprang forward and grabbed Ruby by the arms.

Flick quickly pulled her head back in and drew the shutters together. Ruby was lost.

She continued to watch through a narrow gap between the shutters. One of the Gestapo men banged Ruby's right hand against the shop wall until she dropped the knife. The girl bent over the bleeding Militian. She lifted his head and spoke to him, then said something to the two men. There was a short exchange of barked words. The girl ran into the shop and came out with a storekeeper in a white apron. He bent over the Militian, then stood up again, his face showing distaste – whether for the man's ugly wounds or for the hated uniform, Flick could not tell. The girl ran off, back in the direction of the chateau, presumably to get help; and the two men frogmarched Ruby in the same direction.

Flick said: 'Paul – go and get the baskets Ruby dropped.'

Paul did not hesitate. 'Yes, ma'am.' He went out.

Flick watched him emerge on to the street and cross

the road. What would the storekeeper say? The man looked at Paul and said something. Paul did not reply, but bent down, swiftly picked up the three baskets, and came back.

The storekeeper stared at Paul, and Flick could read his thoughts on his face: at first shocked by Paul's apparent callousness, then puzzled and searching for possible reasons, then beginning to understand.

'Let's move quickly,' Flick said as Paul came into the kitchen. 'Load the bags and out, now! I want us to pass through that checkpoint while the guards are still excited about Ruby.' She quickly stuffed one of the baskets with a powerful torch, her disassembled Sten gun, six 32-round magazines, and her share of the plastic explosive. Her pistol and knife were in her pockets. She covered the weapons in the basket with a cloth and put in a slice of vegetable terrine wrapped in baking paper.

Jelly said: 'What if the guards at the gate search the baskets?'

'Then we're dead,' Flick said. 'We'll just try to take as many of the enemy with us as we can. Don't let the Nazis capture you alive.'

'Oh, my gordon,' said Jelly, but she checked the magazine in her automatic pistol professionally and pushed it home with a decisive click.

The church bell in the town square struck seven.

They were ready.

Flick said to Paul: 'Someone is sure to notice there are only three cleaners instead of the usual six. Antoinette is the supervisor, so they may decide to ask

522

her what's gone wrong. If anyone shows up here, you'll just have to shoot him.'

'Okay.'

Flick kissed Paul on the mouth, briefly but hard, then went out, with Jelly and Greta following.

On the other side of the street, the storekeeper was staring down at the Militian dying on the pavement. He glanced up at the three women, then looked away again. Flick guessed he was already rehearsing his answers to questions: 'I saw nothing. No one else was there.'

The three remaining Jackdaws turned towards the square. Flick set a brisk pace, wanting to get to the chateau as quickly as possible. She could see the gates directly ahead of her, on the far side of the square. Ruby and her two captors were just passing through. Well, Flick thought, at least Ruby is inside.

The Jackdaws reached the end of the street and started across the square. The window of the Café des Sports, smashed in last week's shootout, was boarded over. Two guards from the chateau came across the square at a run, carrying their rifles, their boots clattering on the cobblestones, no doubt heading for the wounded Militian. They took no notice of the little group of cleaning women, who scuttled out of the way.

Flick reached the gate. This was the first really dangerous moment.

One guard was left. He kept looking past Flick at his comrades running across the square. He glanced at Flick's pass and waved her in. She stepped through the gate, then turned to wait for the others.

Greta came next, and the guard did the same. He was more interested in what was going on in the rue du Chateau.

Flick thought they were home and dry, but when he had checked Jelly's pass he glanced into her basket. 'Something smells good,' he said.

Flick held her breath.

'It's some sausage for my supper,' Jelly said. 'You can smell the garlic.'

He waved her on and looked across the square again.

The three Jackdaws walked up the short drive, mounted the steps, and at last entered the chateau.

FIFTY

Dieter spent the afternoon shadowing Michel's train, stopping at every sleepy country halt in case Michel got off. He felt sure he was wasting his time, and that Michel was a decoy; but he had no alternative. Michel was his only lead. He was desperate.

Michel rode the train all the way back to Reims.

A doomy sense of impending failure and disgrace overwhelmed Dieter as he sat in a car beside a bombed building near the Reims station waiting for Michel to emerge. Where had he gone wrong? It seemed to him that he had done everything he could – but nothing had worked.

What if following Michel led nowhere? At some point Dieter would have to cut his losses and interrogate the man. But how much time did he have? Tonight was the night of the full moon, but the English Channel was stormy again. The Allies might postpone the invasion – or they might decide to take their chances with the weather. In a few hours it might be too late.

Michel had come to the station this morning in a van borrowed from Philippe Moulier, the meat supplier, and Dieter looked around for it, but could not see it. He guessed the van had been left here for

Flick Clairet to pick up. By now she might be anywhere within a radius of a hundred miles. He cursed himself for not setting someone to watch the van.

He diverted himself by considering how to interrogate Michel. The man's weak point was probably Gilberte. Right now she was in a cell at the chateau, wondering what was going to happen to her. She would stay there until Dieter was quite sure he had finished with her, then she would be executed or sent to a camp in Germany. How could she be used to make Michel talk – and fast?

The thought of the camps in Germany gave Dieter an idea. Leaning forward, he said to his driver: 'When the Gestapo send prisoners to Germany, they go by train, don't they?'

'Yes, sir.'

'Is it true that you put them in the kind of railway cars normally used for transporting livestock?'

'Cattle trucks, yes, sir, it's good enough for those scum, Communists and Jews and the like.'

'Where do they board?'

'Right here in Reims. The train from Paris stops here.'

'And how often do those trains run?'

'There's one most days. It leaves Paris late in the afternoon and stops here around eight in the evening, if it's on time.'

Before he could progress his idea further, Dieter saw Michel emerge from the station. Ten yards behind him in the crowd was Hans Hesse. They approached Dieter on the other side of the street.

Dieter's driver started the engine.

Dieter turned in his seat to watch Michel and Hans.

They passed Dieter. Then, to Dieter's surprise, Michel turned into the alley alongside the Café de la Gare.

Hans quickened his pace and turned the same corner less than a minute later.

Dieter frowned. Was Michel trying to shake off his tail?

Hans re-emerged from the alley and looked up and down the street with a worried frown. There were not many people on the pavements, just a few travellers walking to and from the station and the last of the city-centre workers heading for home. Hans mouthed a curse and turned back into the alley.

Dieter groaned aloud. Hans had lost Michel.

This was the worst foul-up Dieter had been involved in since the battle of Alam Halfa, when wrong intelligence had led Rommel to defeat. That had been the turning-point of the North African war. Dieter prayed this was not to be the turning-point in Europe.

As he stared despondently at the mouth of the alley, Michel emerged from the front entrance of the café.

Dieter's spirits leaped. Michel had shaken off Hans, but did not realize he had a second shadow. All was not yet lost.

Michel crossed the road, breaking into a run, and headed back the way he had come – towards Dieter in the car.

Dieter thought fast. If he tried to follow Michel, maintaining the surveillance, then he, too, would have to run, and that would make it obvious that he was tailing the man. It was no good: the surveillance was over. It was time to seize Michel.

Michel pounded along the pavement, shoving other pedestrians aside. He ran awkwardly, because of his bullet wound, but he moved fast and rapidly approached Dieter's car.

Dieter made a decision.

He opened the car door.

As Michel drew level, Dieter got out, narrowing the available pavement by holding the door wide. Michel swerved to dodge around the obstacle. Dieter stuck out his leg. Michel tripped over his outstretched foot and went flying. A big man, he fell heavily on to the paved sidewalk.

Dieter drew his pistol and thumbed the safety catch.

Michel lay prone for a second, stunned. Then, groggily, he tried to get to his knees.

Dieter touched the barrel of the gun to Michel's temple. 'Don't get up,' he said in French.

The driver got a pair of handcuffs from the trunk, secured Michel's wrists, and bundled him into the back of the car.

Hans reappeared, looking dismayed. 'What happened?'

'He went in through the back door of the Café de la Gare and came out of the front,' Dieter explained.

Hans was relieved. 'What now?'

'Come with me to the station.' Dieter turned to the driver. 'Do you have a gun?'

'Yes, sir.'

'Keep a close watch on this man. If he tries to escape, shoot him in the legs.'

'Yes, sir.'

Dieter and Hans walked briskly into the station. Dieter buttonholed a uniformed railwayman and said: 'I want to see the stationmaster right away.'

The man looked surly, but he said: 'I'll take you to his office.'

The stationmaster was dressed in a black jacket and waistcoat with striped trousers, an elegant old-fashioned uniform, worn thin at the elbows and knees. He kept his bowler hat on even in his office. He was frightened by this visit from a high-powered German. 'What can I do for you?' he said with a nervous smile.

'Are you expecting a train from Paris with prisoners tonight?'

'Yes, at eight o'clock, as usual.'

'When it comes, hold it here until you hear from me. I have a special prisoner I want to board.'

'Very good. If I could have written authorization . . .'

'Of course. I will arrange it. Do you do anything with the prisoners while the train is here?'

'Sometimes we hose out the cars. Cattle trucks are used, you see, so there are no lavatory facilities, and frankly it becomes extremely unpleasant, without wishing to criticize—'

'Do not clean the trucks tonight, you understand?'

'Of course.'

'Do you do anything else?'

The man hesitated. 'Not really.'

He was guilty about something, Dieter could tell.

'Come on, man, out with it, I'm not going to punish you.'

'Sometimes the railwaymen take pity on the prisoners, and give them water. It's not allowed, strictly speaking, but—'

'No water will be given tonight.'

'Understood.'

Dieter turned to Hans. 'I want you to take Michel Clairet to the police station and lock him in a cell, then return here to the station and make sure my orders are carried out.'

'Of course, Major.'

Dieter picked up the phone on the stationmaster's desk. 'Get me the chateau of Sainte-Cécile.' When he got through he asked for Weber. 'There's a woman in the cells called Gilberte.'

'I know,' said Weber. 'Pretty girl.'

Dieter wondered why Weber sounded so pleased with himself. 'Would you please send her in a car to the railway station in Reims. Lieutenant Hesse is here, he will take charge of her.'

'Very well,' said Weber. 'Hold the line a moment, will you?' He moved the phone away from his mouth and spoke to someone in the room, giving orders for Gilberte to be moved. Dieter waited impatiently. Weber came back on the line. 'I've arranged that.'

'Thank you—'

'Don't hang up. I have some news for you.'

This would be why he was sounding pleased. 'Go on,' Dieter said.

'I have captured an Allied agent myself.'

'What?' Dieter said. This was a lucky break. 'When?'

'A few minutes ago.'

'Where, for God's sake?'

'Right here in Sainte-Cécile.'

'How did that happen?'

'She attacked a Militian, and three of my bright young people happened to witness it. They had the presence of mind to capture the culprit, who was armed with a Colt automatic.'

'Did you say "she"? The agent is a woman?'

'Yes.'

That settled it. The Jackdaws were in Sainte-Cécile. The chateau was their target.

Dieter said: 'Weber, listen to me. I think she is part of a team of saboteurs intending to attack the chateau.'

'They tried that before,' Weber said. 'We gave them a hiding.'

Dieter controlled his impatience with an effort. 'Indeed you did, so they may be more sly this time. May I suggest a security alert? Double the guards, search the chateau, and question all non-German personnel in the building.'

'I have given orders to that effect.'

Dieter was not sure he believed that Weber had already thought of a security alert, but it did not matter, so long as he did so now.

Dieter briefly considered rescinding his instructions about Gilberte and Michel, but decided not to. He might well need to interrogate Michel before the night was over.

'I will return to Sainte-Cécile immediately,' he told Weber.

'As you wish,' Weber said casually, implying he could manage perfectly well without Dieter's assistance.

'I need to interrogate the new prisoner.'

'I have already begun. Sergeant Becker is softening her up.'

'For God's sake! I want her sane and able to speak.'

'Of course.'

'Please, Weber, this is too important for mistakes. I beg you to keep Becker under control until I get there.'

'Very well, Franck. I will make sure he doesn't overdo it.'

'Thank you. I'll be there as fast as I can.' Dieter hung up.

FIFTY-ONE

Flick paused at the entrance to the great hall of the chateau. Her pulse was racing and there was a cold sensation of fear in her chest. She was in the lions' den. If she were captured nothing could save her.

She surveyed the room rapidly. Telephone switchboards had been installed in precise parade-ground rows, incongruously modern against the faded grandeur of the pink and green walls and the podgy cherubs painted on the ceiling. Bundled cables twisted across the chequerboard marble floor like uncoiled ropes on the deck of a ship.

There was a hubbub of chatter from forty operators. Those nearest glanced at the new arrivals. Flick saw one girl speak to her neighbour and point to them. The operators were all from Reims and the surrounding district, many from Sainte-Cécile itself, so they would know the regular cleaners, and would realize the Jackdaws were strangers. But Flick was gambling that they would say nothing to the Germans.

She oriented herself quickly, bringing to mind the plan Antoinette had drawn. The bombed west wing, to her left, was disused. She turned right, and led Greta and Jelly through a pair of tall panelled doors into the east wing.

One room led to another, all palatial reception rooms full of switchboards and equipment racks that buzzed and clicked as numbers were dialled. Flick did not know whether the cleaners normally greeted the operators or passed them in silence: the French were great people for saying good morning, but this place was run by the German military. She contented herself with smiling vaguely and avoiding eye contact.

In the third room, a supervisor in German uniform sat at a desk. Flick ignored her, but the woman called out: 'Where is Antoinette?'

Flick answered without pausing in her stride. 'She's coming.' She heard the tremor of fear in her own voice, and hoped the supervisor had not noticed.

The woman glanced up at the clock, which said five past seven. 'You're late.'

'Very sorry, Madame, we'll get started right away.' Flick hurried into the next room. For a moment she listened, heart in her mouth, for an angry shout calling her back, but none came, and she breathed easier and walked on, with Greta and Jelly close behind.

At the end of the east wing was a stairwell, leading up to the offices or down to the basement. The Jackdaws were headed for the basement, eventually, but first they had preparations to make.

They turned left and moved into the service wing. Following Antoinette's directions, they found a small room where cleaning materials were stored: mops, buckets, brooms, and garbage bins, plus the brown cotton overall coats the cleaners had to wear on duty. Flick closed the door.

'So far, so good,' said Jelly.

Greta said: 'I'm so scared!' She was pale and trembling. 'I don't think I can go on.'

Flick gave her a reassuring smile. 'You'll be fine,' she said. 'Let's get on with it. Put your ordnance into these cleaning buckets.'

Jelly began to transfer her explosives into a bucket, and after a moment's hesitation Greta followed suit. Flick assembled her submachine-gun without its rifle butt, reducing the length by a foot, to make it easier to conceal. She fitted the noise suppressor and flicked the switch for single-shot firing. When using the silencer, the chamber had to be reloaded manually after each shot.

She pushed the weapon under her leather belt. Then she put on an overall coat. It covered the gun. She left the buttons undone for quick access. The other two also put on overalls, concealing the guns and ammunition stuffed into their pockets.

They were almost ready for the basement. However, it was a high-security area, with a guard at the door, and French personnel were not allowed down there – the Germans cleaned it themselves. Before entering, the Jackdaws were going to create a little confusion.

They were about to leave the room when the door opened and a German officer looked in. 'Passes!' he barked.

Flick tensed. She had been expecting some kind of security alert. The Gestapo must have guessed that Ruby was an Allied agent – no one else would be carrying an automatic pistol and a lethal knife – and it made sense for them to take extra precautions at the chateau. However, she had hoped that the Gestapo would move too slowly to interfere with her mission. That wish had not been granted. Probably they were double-checking all French personnel in the building.

'Quickly!' the man said impatiently. He was a Gestapo lieutenant, Flick saw from the badge on his uniform shirt. She took out her pass. He looked at it carefully, comparing the picture with her face, and handed it back. He did the same with Jelly and Greta. 'I must search you,' he said. He looked into Jelly's bucket.

Behind his back, Flick drew the Sten gun from under her overall.

The officer frowned in puzzlement and took from Jelly's bucket the shockproof canister.

Flick disengaged the cocking lever of her gun from the safety slot.

The officer unscrewed the lid of the canister. Amazement dawned on his face as he saw the detonators.

Flick shot him in the back.

The gun was not really silent – the noise suppressor was not perfectly effective – and the shot made a soft bang like a book being dropped on the floor.

The Gestapo lieutenant jerked and fell.

Flick ejected the cartridge and pulled back the bolt, then shot him again in the head to make sure of him.

She reloaded the chamber again and put the gun back under her overall.

Jelly dragged the body to the wall and shoved it behind the door, where it would not be seen by anyone glancing casually into the room.

'Let's get out of here,' said Flick.

Jelly went out. Greta stood frozen and pale, staring at the dead officer.

Flick said: 'Greta. We have a job to do. Let's go.'

At last Greta nodded, picked up her mop and bucket, and walked through the door, moving like a robot.

They went from the cleaning store into the canteen. It was empty but for two girls in uniform drinking coffee and smoking. Speaking French in a low voice, Flick said: 'You know what you have to do.'

Jelly began to sweep the floor.

Greta hesitated.

Flick said: 'Don't let me down.'

Greta nodded. She took a deep breath, straightened her back, and said: 'I'm ready.'

Flick entered the kitchen, and Greta followed.

The fuse boxes for the building were in a cupboard off the kitchen, beside the large electric oven, according to Antoinette, who cleaned the place. There was a young German man at the kitchen range. Flick gave him a sexy smile and said: 'What have you got to offer a hungry girl?'

He grinned at her.

Behind his back, Greta took out a stout pair of pliers

with rubberized handles, then opened the cupboard door.

* * *

The sky was partly cloudy, and the sun disappeared as Dieter Franck drove into the picturesque square of Sainte-Cécile. The clouds were the same shade of dark grey as the slate roof of the church.

He noticed four guards at the chateau gate, instead of the usual two. Although he was in a Gestapo car, the sergeant carefully examined his pass and his driver's before opening the wrought-iron gates and waving the car in. Dieter was pleased: Weber had taken seriously the need for extra security.

A cool breeze blew as he walked from the car to the steps of the grand entrance. Passing into the hall and seeing the rows of women at their switchboards, he thought about the female secret agent Weber had arrested. The Jackdaws were an all-woman team. It occurred to him that they might try to enter the chateau disguised as telephonists. Was it possible? As he passed through the east wing he spoke to the German woman supervisor. 'Have any of these women joined in the last few days?'

'No, Major,' she said. 'One new girl was taken on three weeks ago, and she was the last.'

That put paid to his theory. He nodded and walked on. At the end of the east wing he took the staircase down. The door to the basement stood open, as usual, but there were two soldiers instead of the usual one standing inside. Weber had doubled the guard. The corporal saluted and the sergeant asked for his pass.

Dieter noticed that the corporal stood behind the sergeant while the sergeant checked the pass. He said: 'The way you are now, it's too easy for someone to overpower you both. Corporal, you should stand to the side, and two metres away, so that you have a clear shot if the sergeant is attacked.'

'Yes, sir.'

Dieter entered the basement corridor. He could hear the rumble of the diesel-fuelled generator that supplied electricity to the phone system. He passed the doors of the equipment rooms and entered the interview room. He hoped to find the new prisoner here, but the room was empty.

Puzzled, he stepped inside and closed the door. Then his question was answered. From the inner chamber came a long scream of utter agony.

Dieter threw open the door.

Becker stood at the electric shock machine. Weber sat on a chair nearby. A young woman lay on the operating table with her wrists and ankles strapped and her head clamped in the head restraint. She wore a blue dress, and wires from the electric shock machine ran between her feet and up her dress.

Weber said: 'Hello, Franck. Join us, please. Becker here has come up with an innovation. Show him, Sergeant.'

Becker reached beneath the woman's dress and drew out an ebonite cylinder about fifteen centimetres long and two or three in diameter. The cylinder was ringed by two metal bands a couple of centimetres apart. Two wires from the electric shock machine were attached to the bands.

Dieter was accustomed to torture, but this hellish caricature of the sexual act filled him with loathing, and he shuddered with disgust.

'She hasn't said anything yet, but we've only just started,' Weber said. 'Give her another shock, Sergeant.'

Becker pushed up the woman's dress and inserted the cylinder in her vagina. He picked up a roll of electrician's tape, tore off a strip, and secured the cylinder so that it would not fall out.

Weber said: 'Turn the voltage up this time.'

Becker returned to the machine.

Then the lights went out.

* * *

There was a blue flash and a bang from behind the oven. The lights went out, and the kitchen was filled with the smell of scorched insulation. The motor of the refrigerator ran down with a groan as the power was cut off. The young cook said in German: 'What's going on?'

Flick ran out of the door and through the canteen with Jelly and Greta hard on her heels. They followed a short corridor past the cleaning cupboard. At the top of the stairs Flick paused. She drew her submachine-gun and held it concealed under the flap of her coat.

'The basement will be in total darkness?' she said.

'I cut all the cables, including the wires to the emergency lighting system,' Greta assured her.

'Let's go.'

They ran down the stairs. The daylight coming from the ground-floor windows faded rapidly as they descended, and the entrance to the basement was half-dark.

There were two soldiers standing just inside the door. One of them, a young corporal with a rifle, smiled and said: 'Don't worry, ladies, it's only a power cut.'

Flick shot him in the chest, then swung her weapon and shot the sergeant.

The three Jackdaws stepped through the doorway. Flick held her gun in her right hand and the torch in her left. She could hear a low rumble of machinery and several voices shouting questions in German from distant rooms.

She turned on an electric torch for a second. She was in a broad corridor with a low ceiling. Farther along, doors were opening. She switched off the torch. A moment later she saw the flicker of a match at the far end. About thirty seconds had passed since Greta cut off the power. It would not be long before the Germans recovered from the shock and found torches. She had only a minute, maybe less, to get out of sight.

She tried the nearest door. It was open. She flashed her torch inside. This was a photo lab, with prints hanging to dry and a man in a white coat fumbling his way across the room.

She slammed the door, crossed the corridor in two strides, and tried a door on the opposite side. It was locked. She guessed, from the position of the room at the front of the chateau under a corner of the car park, that the room beyond contained the fuel tanks.

She moved along the corridor and opened the next door. The rumble of machinery became louder. She flashed her torch once more, just for a split-second, long enough to see an electricity generator – the independent power supply to the phone system, she assumed – then she hissed: 'Drag the bodies in here!'

Jelly and Greta pulled the dead guards across the floor. Flick returned to the basement entrance and slammed the steel door shut. Now the corridor was in total darkness. As an afterthought, she shot the three heavy bolts on the inside. That might give her precious extra seconds.

She returned to the generator room, closed the door, and turned on her torch.

Jelly and Greta had pushed the bodies behind the door and stood panting with the effort. 'All done,' Greta murmured.

There was a mass of pipes and cables in the room, but they were all colour-coded with German efficiency, and Flick knew which was which: fresh-air pipes were yellow, fuel lines were brown, water pipes were green, and power lines were striped red-and-black. She directed her torch at the brown fuel line to the generator. 'Later, if we have time, I want you to blow a hole in that.'

'Easy,' said Jelly.

'Now, put your hand on my shoulder and follow me. Greta, you follow Jelly the same way. Okay?'

'Okay.'

Flick turned off her torch and opened the door. Now they had to explore the basement blind. She put her hand to the wall as a guide and began to walk, heading farther inside. A confused babble of raised voices revealed that several men were blundering about the corridor.

An authoritative voice said in German: 'Who closed the main door?'

She heard Greta reply, but in a man's voice: 'It seems to be stuck.'

The German cursed. A moment later there was the scrape of a bolt.

Flick reached another door. She opened it and flashed her torch again. It contained two huge wooden coffers the size and shape of mortuary slabs. Greta whispered: 'Battery room. Go to the next door.'

The German man's voice said: 'Was that a flashlight? Bring it over here!'

'Just coming,' said Greta in her Gerhard voice, but the three Jackdaws walked in the opposite direction.

Flick came to the next room, led the other two inside and closed the door before shining her torch. It was a long, narrow chamber with racks of equipment along both walls. At the near end of the room was a cabinet that probably held large sheets of drawings. At the far end, the beam of her torch revealed a small table. Three men sat at it holding playing cards. They appeared to have remained sitting during the minute or so since the lights went out. Now they moved.

As they rose to their feet, Flick levelled her gun. Jelly

was just as quick. Flick shot one. Jelly's pistol cracked and the man beside him fell. The third man dived for cover, but Flick's torch followed him. Both Flick and Jelly fired again, and he fell still.

Flick refused to let herself think about the dead men as people. There was no time for feelings. She shone her torch around. What she saw gladdened her heart. This was almost certainly the room she was looking for.

Standing a metre from one long wall was a pair of floor-to-ceiling racks bristling with thousands of terminals in tidy rows. From the outside world the telephone cables came through the wall in neat bundles to the backs of the terminals on the nearer rack. At the farther end, similar cables led from the backs of the terminals up through the ceiling to the switchboards above. At the front of the frame, a nightmare tangle of loose jumper wires connected the terminals of the near rack to those of the far one. Flick looked at Greta. 'Well?'

Greta was examining the equipment by the light of her own torch, a fascinated expression on her face. 'This is the MDF – the main distribution frame,' she said, 'but it's a bit different from ours in Britain.'

Flick stared at Greta in surprise. Minutes ago she had said she was too frightened to go on. Now she was unmoved by the killing of three men.

Along the far wall more racks of equipment glowed with the light of vacuum tubes. 'And on the other side?' Flick asked.

Greta swung her torch. 'Those are the amplifiers and carrier circuit equipment for the long-distance lines.'

'Good,' Flick said briskly. 'Show Jelly where to place the charges.'

The three of them went to work. Greta unwrapped the wax-paper packets of yellow plastic explosive while Flick cut the fuse cord into lengths. It burned at one centimetre per second. 'I'll make all the fuses three metres long,' Flick said. 'That will give us exactly five minutes to get out.' Jelly assembled the fire train: fuse, detonator and firing cap.

Flick held a torch while Greta moulded the charges to the frames at the vulnerable places and Jelly stuck the firing cap into the soft explosive.

They worked fast. In five minutes all the equipment was covered with charges like a rash. The fuse cords led to a common source where they were loosely twisted together, so that one light would serve to ignite them all.

Jelly took out a thermite bomb, a black can about the size and shape of a tin of soup, containing finely powdered aluminium and iron oxide. It would burn with intense heat and fierce flames. She took off the lid to reveal two fuses, then placed it on the ground behind the MDF.

Greta said: 'Somewhere in here are thousands of cards showing how the circuits are connected. We should burn them. Then it will take the repair crew two weeks, rather than two days, to reconnect the cables.'

Flick opened the cupboard and found four custom-made card holders containing large diagrams, neatly sorted by labelled file dividers. 'Is this what we're looking for?'

Greta studied a card by the light of her torch. 'Yes.'

Jelly said: 'Scatter them around the thermite bomb. They'll go up in seconds.'

Flick threw the cards on the floor in loose piles.

Jelly placed an oxygen-generating pack on the floor at the blind end of the room. 'This will make the fire hotter,' she said. 'Ordinarily, we could only burn the wooden frames and the insulation around the cables; but with this, the copper cables should melt.'

Everything was ready.

Flick shone her torch around the room. The outer walls were ancient brick, but the inner walls between the rooms were light wooden partitions. The explosion would destroy the partition walls and the fire would spread rapidly to the rest of the basement.

Five minutes had passed since the lights went out.

Jelly took out a cigarette lighter.

Flick said: 'You two, make your way outside the building. Jelly, on your way, go into the generating room and blow a hole in the fuel line, where I showed you.'

'Got it.'

'We meet up at Antoinette's.'

Greta said anxiously: 'Where are *you* going?'

'To find Ruby.'

Jelly warned: 'You have five minutes.'

Flick nodded.

Jelly lit the fuse.

* * *

When Dieter passed from the darkness of the basement into the half-light of the stairwell, he noticed that the guards had gone from the entrance. No doubt they were fetching help, but the ill discipline infuriated him. They should have remained at their post.

Perhaps they had been forcibly removed. Had they been taken away at gunpoint? Was an attack on the chateau already under way?

He ran up the stairs. On the ground floor, there were no signs of battle. The operators were still working: the phone system was on a separate circuit from the rest of the building's electricity, and there was still enough light coming through the windows for them to see their switchboards. He ran through the canteen, heading for the rear of the building where the maintenance workshops were located, but on the way he looked into the kitchen and found three soldiers in overalls staring at a fuse box. 'There's a power cut in the basement,' he said.

'I know,' said one of the men. He had a sergeant's stripes on his shirt. 'All these wires have been cut.'

Dieter raised his voice. 'Then get your tools out and reconnect them, you damn fool!' he said. 'Don't stand here scratching your stupid head!'

The sergeant was startled. 'Yes, sir,' he said.

A worried-looking young cook said: 'I think it's the electric oven, sir.'

'What happened?' Dieter barked.

'Well, Major, they were cleaning behind the oven, and there was a bang—'

'Who? Who was cleaning?'

'I don't know, sir.'

'A soldier, someone you recognized?'

'No, sir . . . just a cleaner.'

Dieter did not know what to think. Clearly the chateau was under attack. But where were the enemy? He left the kitchen, went to the stairwell, and ran up towards the offices on the upper floor.

As he turned at the bend in the stairs, something caught his eye, and he looked back. A tall woman in a cleaner's overall was coming up the stairs from the basement, carrying a mop and a bucket.

He froze, staring at her, his mind racing. She should not have been there. Only Germans were allowed into the basement. Of course, anything could have happened in the confusion of a power cut. But the cook had blamed a cleaner for the power cut. He recalled his brief conversation with the supervisor of the switchboard girls. None of them was new to the job – but he had not asked about the French women cleaners.

He came back down the stairs and met her at ground level. 'Why were you in the basement?' he asked her in French.

'I went there to clean, but the lights are out.'

Dieter frowned. She spoke French with an accent that he could not quite place. He said: 'You're not supposed to go there.'

'Yes, the soldier told me that, they clean it themselves, I didn't know.'

Her accent was not English, Dieter thought. But what was it? 'How long have you worked here?'

'Only a week, and I've always done upstairs until today.'

Her story was plausible, but Dieter was not satisfied. 'Come with me.' He took her arm in a firm grip. She did not resist as he led her through to the kitchen.

Dieter spoke to the cook. 'Do you recognize this woman?'

'Yes, sir. She's the one who was cleaning behind the oven.'

Dieter looked at her. 'Is that true?'

'Yes, sir, I'm very sorry if I damaged something.'

Dieter recognized her accent. 'You're German,' he said.

'No, sir.'

'You filthy traitor.' He looked at the cook. 'Grab her and follow me. She's going to tell me everything.'

* * *

Flick opened the door marked 'Interview Room', stepped inside, closed the door behind her, and swept the room with her torch.

She saw a cheap pine table with ashtrays, several chairs, and a steel desk. The room was empty of people.

She was puzzled. She had located the prison cells on this corridor and had shone her torch through the judas in each door. The cells were empty: the prisoners the Gestapo had taken during the last eight days, including Gilberte, must have been moved somewhere else . . . or killed. But Ruby had to be here somewhere.

Then she saw, on her left, a door leading, presumably, to an inner chamber.

She switched off her torch, opened the door, stepped through, closed the door and switched on her torch.

She saw Ruby right away. She was lying on a table like a hospital operating table. Specially designed straps secured her wrists and ankles and made it impossible for her to move her head. A wire from an electrical machine led between her feet and up her skirt. Flick guessed immediately what had been done to Ruby, and gasped with horror.

She stepped to the table. 'Ruby, can you hear me?'

Ruby groaned. Flick's heart leaped: she was still alive. 'I'll free you,' she said. She put her Sten gun down on the table.

Ruby was trying to speak, but her words came out as a moan. Swiftly, Flick undid the straps that bound Ruby to the table. 'Flick,' Ruby said at last.

'What?'

'Behind you.'

Flick jumped to one side. Something heavy brushed her ear and thumped her left shoulder hard. She cried out in pain, dropped her torch, and fell. Hitting the floor she rolled sideways, moving as far as possible from her original position, so that her assailant could not hit her again.

She had been so shocked by the sight of Ruby that she had not shone her torch all around the room.

Someone else had been lurking in the shadows, waiting for his chance, and had slowly crept up behind her.

Her left arm was momentarily numbed. Using her right hand, she scrabbled on the floor for her torch. Before she found it, there was a loud click, and the lights came on.

She blinked and saw two people. One was a squat, stocky man with a round head and close-cropped hair. Behind him stood Ruby. In the dark she had picked up what looked like a steel bar, and she held it above her head in readiness. As soon as the lights came on, Ruby saw the man, turned, and brought the steel bar down on his head with maximum force. It was a crippling blow, and the man slumped to the floor and lay still.

Flick got up. The feeling was rapidly returning to her arm. She picked up the Sten gun.

Ruby was kneeling over the prone body of the man. 'Meet Sergeant Becker,' she said.

'Are you all right?' Flick said.

'I'm in bloody agony, but I'm going to get my own back on this fucking bastard.' Grasping the front of Becker's uniform tunic, Ruby heaved him upright then, with an effort, pushed him on to the operating table.

He groaned.

'He's coming round!' Flick said. 'I'll finish him off.'

'Give me ten seconds.' Ruby straightened the man's limbs and strapped him in by his wrists and ankles, then she tightened the head restraint so that he could not move. Finally, she took the cylindrical terminal from the electric-shock machine and stuffed it into his mouth. He choked and gagged but could not move his head. She picked up a roll of electrician's tape, tore off a strip with her teeth, and secured the cylinder so that it would not come out of his mouth. Then she went to the machine and fumbled with the switch.

There was a low hum. The man on the table let out a strangled scream. His strapped-down body shook with convulsions. Ruby looked at him for a moment, then she said: 'Let's go.'

They went out, leaving Sergeant Becker writhing on the table, squealing like a pig in the slaughterhouse.

Flick checked her watch. Two minutes had passed since Jelly lit the fuses.

They passed through the interview room and stepped out into the corridor. The confusion had died down. There were just three soldiers near the entrance, talking calmly. Flick walked rapidly towards them with Ruby close behind.

Flick's instinct was to walk straight past the soldiers, relying on a confident air to get her through; but then she glimpsed, through the door, the tall figure of Dieter Franck approaching, followed by two or three other people she could not clearly see. She stopped abruptly. Ruby bumped into her back. Flick turned to the nearest door. It was marked 'Wireless Room'. She opened it. The room was empty. They stepped inside.

She left the door an inch open. She heard Major Franck bark in German: 'Captain, where are the two men who should be guarding this entrance?'

'I don't know, Major, I was just asking.'

Flick took the silencer off her Sten gun and flicked

the switch for rapid fire. She had used only four bullets so far, leaving twenty-eight in the magazine.

'Sergeant, you and this corporal stand guard. Captain, you go up to Major Weber's office and tell him Major Franck strongly recommends he conduct a search of the basement immediately. Off you go, at the double!'

A moment later, Franck's footsteps passed the wireless room. Flick waited, listening. A door slammed. She peeped out. Franck had disappeared.

'Let's go,' she said to Ruby. They left the Wireless Room and walked to the main door.

The corporal said in French: 'What are you doing here?'

Flick had an answer ready. 'My friend Valérie is new to the job, and she came to the wrong place in the confusion of the blackout.'

The corporal looked dubious. 'It's still light upstairs, how could she get lost?'

Ruby said: 'I'm very sorry, sir, I thought I was supposed to clean here, and no one stopped me.'

The sergeant said in German: 'We're supposed to keep them out, not keep them in, corporal.' He laughed and waved them on.

* * *

Dieter tied the prisoner to a chair then dismissed the cook who had escorted her from the kitchen. He looked at the woman for a moment, wondering how much time he had. One agent had been arrested in the street outside the chateau. Another, if she was an agent, had been caught coming up the stairs from the basement. Had the others come and gone? Were they waiting somewhere to be let in? Or were they here in the building right now? It was maddening not to know what was happening. But he had ordered the basement searched. The only other thing he could do was interrogate the prisoner.

Dieter began with the traditional slap in the face, sudden and demoralizing. The woman gasped with shock and pain.

'Where are your friends?' he asked her.

The woman's cheek reddened. He studied her expression. What he saw mystified him.

She looked happy.

'You're in the basement of the chateau,' he told her. 'Through that door is the torture chamber. On the other side, beyond that partition wall, is the telephone switchgear. We are at the end of a tunnel, the bottom of the sack, as the French say. If your friends plan to blow up the building, you and I will surely die here in this room.'

Her expression did not change.

Perhaps the chateau was not about to blow up, Dieter thought. But then what was the mission? 'You're German,' he said. 'Why are you helping your country's enemies?'

At last she spoke. 'I'll tell you,' she said. She spoke German with a Hamburg accent. 'Many years ago, I had a lover. His name was Manfred.' She looked away, remembering. 'Your Nazis arrested him and sent him to a camp. I think he died there – I never heard.' She paused, swallowing. Dieter waited. After a moment she went on. 'When they took him away from me, I swore I would have my revenge – and this is it.' She smiled happily. 'Your foul regime is almost finished. And I've helped to destroy it.'

There was something wrong here. She spoke as if the deed was already done. Furthermore, the power cut had come and gone. Had the blackout already served its purpose? This woman showed no fear. But could it be that she did not mind dying?

'Why was your lover arrested?'

'They called him a pervert.'

'What kind?'

'He was homosexual.'

'But he was your lover?'

'Yes.'

Dieter frowned. Then he looked harder at the woman. She was tall and broad-shouldered, and underneath the makeup she had a masculine nose and chin . . .

'Are you a man?' he said in astonishment.

She just smiled.

A dreadful suspicion dawned on Dieter. 'Why are you telling me this?' he said. 'Are you trying to keep me occupied while your friends get away? Are you sacrificing your life to ensure the success of the mission—'

His train of thought was broken by a faint noise. It sounded like a strangled scream. Now that he noticed it, he realized he had heard it two or three times before and ignored it. The sound seemed to come from the next room.

Dieter sprang up and went into the torture chamber.

He expected to see the other woman agent on the table, and was shocked to find someone else there. It was a man, he saw immediately, but at first he did not know who, because the face was distorted – the jaw dislocated, the teeth broken, the cheeks stained with blood and vomit. Then he recognized the squat figure of Sergeant Becker. The wires from the electric shock machine led to Becker's mouth. Dieter realized that the terminal from the machine was in Becker's mouth, secured there by electrician's tape. Becker was still alive, twitching and emitting a dreadful squealing sound. Dieter was horrified.

He swiftly turned off the machine. Becker stopped twitching. Dieter grasped the electric wire and jerked hard. The terminal came out of Becker's mouth. He threw it to the floor.

He bent over the table. 'Becker!' he said. 'Can you hear me? What happened here?'

There was no reply.

* * *

Upstairs, all was normal. Flick and Ruby walked quickly through the ranks of telephone operators, all busy at their switchboards, murmuring into their headsets in low voices as they plugged jacks into sockets, connecting decision-makers in Berlin, Paris and Normandy. Flick checked her watch. In exactly two minutes all those connections would be destroyed, and the military machine would fall apart, leaving a scatter of isolated components, unable to work together. Now, Flick thought, if only we can get out . . .

They passed out of the building without incident. In seconds they would be in the town square. They had almost made it. But, in the courtyard, they met Jelly – coming back.

'Where's Greta?' she said.

'She left with you!' Flick replied.

'I stopped to set a charge on the diesel fuel line in the generator room, like you said. Greta went on ahead of me. But she never reached Antoinette's place. I've just met Paul, he hasn't seen her. I came back to look for her.' Jelly had a paper packet in her hand. 'I told the guard at the gate that I just went out to fetch my supper.'

Flick was dismayed. 'Greta must be inside – hell!'

'I'm going back for her,' Jelly said determinedly. 'She saved me from the Gestapo, back in Chartres, so I owe her.'

Flick looked at her watch. 'We have less than two minutes. Let's go!'

They ran back inside. The switchboard girls stared at them as they raced through the rooms. Flick was already having second thoughts. In attempting to save one of her team, was she about to sacrifice two more – and herself?

When they reached the stairwell, Flick paused. The two soldiers who had let them out of the basement with a joke would not let them in again so easily. 'As before,' she said quietly to the others. 'Approach the guards innocently and shoot at the last moment.'

A voice from above said: 'What's going on here?'

Flick froze.

She looked back over her shoulder. On the staircase coming down from the top floor stood four men. One, in major's uniform, was pointing a pistol at her. She recognized Major Weber.

This was the search party Dieter Franck had asked for. It had appeared at precisely the wrong moment.

Flick cursed herself for a bad decision. Now four would be lost instead of one.

Weber said: 'You women have a conspiratorial air.'

'What do you want with us?' Flick said. 'We're the cleaners.'

'Perhaps you are,' he said. 'But there is a team of female enemy agents in the district.'

Flick pretended to be relieved. 'Oh, good,' she said. 'If you're looking for enemy agents, we're safe. I was afraid you might be dissatisfied with the cleaning.' She forced a laugh. Ruby joined in. Both sounded false.

Weber said: 'Raise your hands in the air.'

As she lifted her wrist past her face, Flick checked her watch.

Thirty seconds left.

'Down the stairs,' said Weber.

Reluctantly, Flick went down. Ruby and Jelly went with her, and the four men followed. She went as slowly as she could, counting seconds.

She stopped at the foot of the stairs. Twenty seconds.

'You again?' said one of the guards.

Flick said: 'Speak to your major.'

'Keep moving,' said Weber.

'I thought we weren't supposed to go into the basement.'

'Just keep going!'

Five seconds.

They passed through the basement door.

There was a tremendous bang.

At the far end of the corridor, the partition walls of the equipment chamber exploded outwards. There was a series of crashing sounds. Flames billowed over the debris. Flick was knocked down.

She got up on one knee, pulled the submachine-gun from under her overall, and spun around. Jelly and Ruby were either side of her. The basement guards, Weber, and the other three men had also fallen. Flick pulled the trigger.

Of the six Germans, only Weber had kept his presence of mind. As Flick sprayed bullets, Weber fired his pistol. Beside Flick Jelly, struggling to her feet, cried out and fell. Then Flick hit Weber in the chest and he went down.

Flick emptied her gun into the six bodies on the floor. She ejected the magazine, took a fresh one from her pocket, and reloaded.

Ruby bent over Jelly, feeling for a pulse. After a moment she looked up. 'Dead,' she said.

Flick looked towards the far end of the corridor,

where Greta was. Flames were billowing out from the equipment chamber, but the wall of the interview room seemed intact.

She ran towards the inferno.

* * *

Dieter found himself lying on the floor without knowing how he had got there. He heard the roaring of flames and smelt smoke. He struggled to his feet and looked into the interview room.

He realized immediately that the brick walls of the torture chamber had saved his life. The partition between the interview room and the equipment chamber had disappeared. The few pieces of furniture in the interview room had been thrown up against the wall. The prisoner had suffered the same fate, and lay on the ground, still tied to the chair, neck at the horrid angle that indicated it was broken and she – or he – was dead. The equipment chamber was aflame and the fire was spreading rapidly.

Dieter realized he had only seconds to get away.

The door to the interview room opened and Flick Clairet stood there holding a submachine-gun.

She wore a dark wig that had fallen askew to reveal her own blonde hair beneath. Flushed, breathing hard, a wild look in her eyes, she was beautiful.

If he had had a gun in his hand at that moment, he would have mown her down in blind rage. She would be an incomparable prize if captured alive, but he was so enraged and humiliated by her success and his own failure that he could not have controlled himself.

But she had the gun.

At first she did not see Dieter, but stared at the dead body of her comrade. Dieter's hand moved inside his jacket. Then she lifted her gaze and met his eyes. He saw recognition dawn on her face. She knew who he was. She knew whom she had been fighting for the past nine days. There was a light of triumph in her eyes. But he also saw the thirst for revenge in the twist of her mouth, and she raised the Sten gun and fired.

Dieter ducked back into the torture chamber as her bullets chipped fragments of brick off the wall. He drew his Walther P38 automatic pistol, thumbed the safety lever to the fire position, and pointed it at the doorway, waiting for Flick to come through.

She did not appear.

He waited a few seconds then risked a look.

Flick had gone.

He dashed across the burning interview room, threw open the door, and stepped into the corridor. Flick and another woman were running toward the far end. As he raised his gun, they jumped over a group of uniformed bodies on the floor. He aimed at Flick, then a hot pain burned his arm. He cried out and dropped his gun. He saw that his sleeve was on fire. He tore off his jacket.

When he looked up again, the women had gone.

Dieter picked up his pistol and went after them.

As he ran, he smelt fuel. There was a leak – or perhaps the saboteurs had holed a pipe. Any second now, the basement would explode like a giant bomb.

But he might still catch Flick.

He ran out and started up the stairs.

* * *

In the torture chamber, Sergeant Becker's uniform started to smoulder.

The heat and the smoke brought him back to consciousness, and he cried for help, but no one heard.

He struggled against the leather straps that bound him, as so many of his victims had struggled in the past; but, like them, he was helpless.

A few moments later, his clothes burst into flame, and he began to scream.

* * *

Flick saw Dieter coming up the stairs after her with his gun in his hand. She was afraid that if she stopped and turned to take aim at him, he would be able to shoot first. She decided to run rather than stand and fight.

Someone had activated the fire alarm, and a klaxon blared throughout the chateau as she and Ruby raced through the switchboard rooms. All the operators left their stations and crowded to the doors, so that Flick found herself in a crush. The crowd would be making it difficult for Dieter to get a shot at her or Ruby, but the other women were slowing them down. Flick punched and kicked ruthlessly to get people out of her way.

They reached the front entrance and ran down the steps. In the square, Flick could see Moulier's meat van, backed up to the chateau gates with its engine running and its rear doors open. Paul stood beside it, staring anxiously through the iron railings. Flick thought he was the best thing she had ever seen.

However, as the women poured out of the building, two guards were directing them into the vineyard on the west side of the courtyard, away from the parked cars. Flick and Ruby ignored their waved instructions and ran for the gates. When the soldiers saw Flick's submachine-gun, they reached for their weapons.

A rifle appeared in Paul's hands. He aimed through the railings. Two shots rang out, and both guards fell.

Paul threw open the gates.

As Flick dashed through the gateway, shots whistled over her head and hit the van: Dieter was firing.

Paul jumped into the front of the van.

Flick and Ruby threw themselves into the back.

As the van pulled away, Flick saw Dieter turn towards the car park where his sky-blue car stood waiting.

At that moment, down in the basement, the fire reached the fuel tanks.

There was a deep underground boom like an earthquake. The car park erupted, gravel and earth and slabs of concrete flying into the air. Half the cars parked around the old fountain were overturned. Huge stones and chunks of brickwork rained down on the rest.

Dieter was thrown back across the steps. The petrol pump soared into the air, and a gout of flame spurted from the ground where it had stood. Several cars caught fire, and their petrol tanks began to explode, one by one. Then the van left the square, and Flick could see no more.

Paul drove at top speed out of the village. Flick and Ruby bounced on the metal floor of the van. It dawned slowly on Flick that they had accomplished their mission. She could hardly believe it. She thought of Greta and Jelly, both dead, and of Diana and Maude, dead or dying in some concentration camp, and she could not feel happy. But she felt a savage satisfaction as she saw again in her mind the blazing equipment chamber and the exploding car park.

She looked at Ruby.

Ruby grinned at her. 'We did it,' she said.

Flick nodded.

Ruby put her arms around Flick and hugged her hard.

'Yes,' Flick said. 'We did it.'

* * *

Dieter picked himself up off the ground. He felt bruised all over, but he could walk. The chateau was ablaze, and the car park was a shambles. The women were screaming and panicking.

He stared at the carnage all around. The Jackdaws had succeeded in their mission. But it was not over yet. They were still in France. And if he could capture and interrogate Flick Clairet, he could yet turn defeat into victory. Sometime tonight, she must be planning to meet a small plane, in a field not far from Reims. He had to find out where and when.

And he knew who would tell him.

Her husband.

THE LAST DAY:
TUESDAY, 6 JUNE 1944

FIFTY-TWO

Dieter sat on the platform at the Reims railway station. French railwaymen and German troops watched with him, standing patiently under the harsh lights. The prison train was late, hours late, but it was coming, he had been assured of that. He had to wait for it. He had no other cards to play.

His heart was full of rage. He had been humiliated and defeated by a girl. Had she been a German girl, he would have been proud of her. He would have called her brilliant and brave. He might even have fallen in love with her. But she belonged to the enemy, and she had outwitted him at every turn. She had killed Stéphanie, she had destroyed the chateau, and she had escaped. But he would catch her yet. And when he did, she would suffer tortures worse than her most terrifying imaginings – then she would talk.

Everyone talked.

The train rolled in a few minutes after midnight.

He noticed the stink even before it came to a halt. It was like the smell of a farmyard, but disgustingly human.

There was an assortment of rail cars, none of them designed for passengers: goods wagons, cattle trucks, even a mail car with its narrow windows broken. Each was crammed with people.

The livestock wagons had high slatted wooden sides to permit observation of the animals. The prisoners nearest put their arms through the slats, hands open with palms upward, begging. They asked to be let out, they pleaded for something to eat, but most of all they begged for water. The guards looked on impassively: Dieter had given instructions that the prisoners were to have no relief at Reims tonight.

He had two Waffen SS corporals with him, guards from the chateau, both good marksmen. He had extracted them from the shambles at Sainte-Cécile, trading on his authority as a major. He turned to them now and said: 'Bring Michel Clairet.'

Michel was locked in the windowless room where the stationmaster kept the cash. The corporals went away and reappeared with Michel between them. His hands were tied behind his back and his ankles were hobbled so that he could not run. He had not been told what had happened at Sainte-Cécile. All he knew was that he had been captured for the second time in a week. There was little left of his buccaneering persona. He was trying to maintain an air of bravado, to keep his spirits up, but the attempt was a failure. His limp was worse, his clothes were dirty, and his face grim. He looked defeated.

Dieter took Michel's arm and walked him closer to the train. At first, Michel did not understand what he was looking at, and his face showed only mystification and fear. Then, when he made out the begging hands and understood the piteous voices, he staggered, as if he had been struck, and Dieter had to hold him upright.

Dieter said: 'I need some information.'

Michel shook his head. 'Put me on the train,' he said. 'I'd rather be with them than with you.'

Dieter was shocked by the insult and surprised by Michel's courage. He said: 'Tell me where the Jackdaws' plane will land – and when.'

Michel stared at him. 'You haven't caught them,' he said, and hope came back into his face. 'They've blown up the chateau, haven't they? They succeeded.' He threw back his head and gave a whoop of joy. 'Well done, Flick!'

Dieter made Michel walk the length of the train, slowly, showing him the numbers of prisoners and the scale of their suffering. 'The plane,' he said again.

Michel said: 'The field outside La Chatelle, at three a.m.'

Dieter was almost certain that was false. Flick had been scheduled to arrive at La Chatelle, seventy-two hours ago, but had aborted the landing, presumably because she suspected a Gestapo trap. Dieter knew there was a back-up landing place, because Gaston had told him so; but Gaston had known only its codename, Champ d'Or, not its location. Michel, however, would know the exact place. 'You're lying,' Dieter said.

'Then put me on the train,' Michel replied.

Dieter shook his head. 'That's not the choice – nothing so easy.'

He saw puzzlement and the shadow of fear in Michel's eyes.

Dieter walked him back and stopped at the women's car. Their feminine voices begged in French and German, some invoking the pity of God, others asking the men to think of their mothers and sisters, a few offering sexual favours. Michel bowed his head, refusing to look.

Dieter beckoned to two figures standing in the shadows.

Michel looked up, and a terrible dread came over his face.

Hans Hesse walked out of the shadows, escorting a young woman. She might have been beautiful, but her face was ghastly white, her hair lay in greasy strands, and she had sores on her lips. She seemed weak, walking with difficulty.

It was Gilberte.

Michel gasped.

Dieter repeated his question. 'Where will the plane land, and when?'

Michel said nothing.

Dieter said: 'Put her on the train.'

Michel moaned.

A guard opened the gate of a cattle truck. While two others kept the women in with bayonets, the guard pushed Gilberte into the truck. 'No,' she cried. 'No, please!'

The guard was about to close the gate, but Dieter said: 'Wait.' He looked at Michel. Tears were pouring down the man's face.

Gilberte said: 'Please, Michel, I beg you.'

Michel nodded. 'All right,' he said.

'Don't lie again,' Dieter warned.

'Let her out.'

'The time and place.'

'The potato field east of Laroque, at two a.m.'

Dieter looked at his watch. It was twelve fifteen. 'Show me,' he said.

* * *

Five kilometres from Laroque, the village of L'Épine was asleep. Bright moonlight silvered the big church. Behind the church, Moulier's meat van was parked inconspicuously next to a barn. In the deep moon-shadow thrown by a buttress, the surviving Jackdaws sat waiting.

'What are you looking forward to?' said Ruby.

Paul said: 'A steak.'

Flick said: 'A soft bed with clean sheets. How about you?'

'Seeing Jim.'

Flick recalled that Ruby had had a fling with the firearms instructor. 'I thought . . .' She stopped.

'You thought it was just a casual shag?' Ruby said.

Flick nodded, embarrassed.

'So did Jim,' Ruby said. 'But I've got other plans.'

Paul laughed softly. 'I'll bet you get what you want.'

'What about you two?' Ruby asked.

Paul said: 'I'm single.' He looked at Flick.

She shook her head. 'I intended to ask Michel for a

divorce ... but how could I, in the middle of an operation?'

'So we'll wait until after the war to get married,' Paul said. 'I'm patient.'

Typical man, Flick thought. He slips marriage into the conversation like a minor detail, on a level with buying a dog licence. So much for romance.

But in truth she was pleased. It was the second time he had mentioned marriage. Who needs romance? she thought.

She looked at her watch. It was one thirty. 'Time to go,' she said.

* * *

Dieter had commandeered a Mercedes limousine that had been outside the chateau grounds and so had survived the explosion. The car was now parked at the edge of the vineyard next to the potato field at Laroque, camouflaged with leafy vines torn from the ground. Michel and Gilberte were in the back seat, bound hand and foot, guarded by Hans.

Dieter also had with him the two corporals, each armed with a rifle. Dieter and the riflemen looked into the potato field. They could see clearly in the moonlight.

Dieter said: 'The terrorists will be here in the next few minutes. We have the advantage of surprise. They have no idea that we're here. But remember, I must have them alive — especially the leader, the small woman. You have to shoot to wound, not kill.'

One of the marksmen said: 'We can't guarantee that.

This field must be three hundred metres wide. Let's say the enemy is a hundred and fifty metres away. At that distance, no one could be sure of hitting the legs of a running man.'

'They won't be running,' Dieter said. 'They're meeting a plane. They have to form a line, pointing electric torches at the aircraft to guide the pilot down. That means they'll be standing still for several minutes.'

'In the middle of the field?'

'Yes.'

The man nodded. 'Then we can do it.' He looked up. 'Unless the moon goes behind a cloud.'

'In that event, we'll turn on the headlights of the car at the crucial moment.' The Mercedes had huge dinner-plate lamps.

The other marksman said: 'Listen.'

They fell silent. A motor vehicle was approaching. They all knelt. Despite the moonlight, they would not be visible against the dark mass of the vines, provided they kept their heads down.

A van came along the road from the village with its lights off. It pulled up by the gate to the potato field. A female figure jumped out and swung the gate wide. The van pulled in and its engine was silenced. Two more people got out, another woman and a man.

'Quiet, now,' Dieter whispered.

Suddenly the hush was shattered by the blare of a car horn, incredibly loud.

Dieter jumped and cursed. It came from immediately behind him. 'Jesus!' he exploded. It was the Mercedes. He leaped to his feet and ran to the open window of the driver's door. He saw immediately what had happened.

Michel had sprung forward, leaning across the front seat, and before Hans could stop him he had pressed on the horn with his bound hands. Hans, in the front passenger seat, was now trying to aim his gun, but Gilberte had joined in, and she was lying half over Hans, hampering his movements so that he kept having to push her away.

Dieter reached in and shoved Michel, but Michel resisted, and Dieter's position, with his arms extended through the car window, was too awkward for him to exert much force. The horn continued to sound a deafening warning that the Resistance agents could not fail to hear.

Dieter fumbled for his gun.

Michel found the light switch, and the car's headlamps came on. Dieter looked up. The riflemen were hideously exposed in the glare of the lights. They both got up off their knees, but before they could throw themselves out of the beam there was a rattle of machine-gun fire from the field. One rifleman cried out, dropped his gun, clutched his belly and fell across the bonnet of the Mercedes; then the other was shot in the head. A sharp pain stung Dieter's left arm, and he let out a yell of shock.

Then there was a shot from within the car, and Michel cried out. Hans had at last flung Gilberte off himself and got his pistol out. He fired again, and Michel slumped, but Michel's hand was still on the horn, and his body now lay over his hand, pressing it down, so the horn continued to blare. Hans fired a third time, uselessly, for his bullet thudded into the body of a dead man. Gilberte screamed and threw herself at Hans again, grabbing at his gun arm with her manacled hands. Dieter had his gun out but could not shoot at Gilberte for fear of hitting Hans.

There was a fourth shot. It was Hans's gun again, but now it was somehow pointing upwards, and he shot himself, the bullet hitting him under the chin. He gave a horrid gurgle, blood came out of his mouth, and he slumped back against the door, his eyes staring lifelessly.

Dieter took careful aim and shot Gilberte in the head.

He reached through the window with his right arm and shoved the corpse of Michel away from the steering wheel.

The horn was silenced.

He found the light switch and killed the headlamps.

He looked across the field.

The van was still there, but the Jackdaws had disappeared.

He listened. Nothing moved.

He was alone.

* * *

Flick crawled through the vineyard on her hands and knees, heading for Dieter Franck's car. The moonlight, so necessary for clandestine flights across occupied territory, was now her enemy. She wished for a cloud to shade the moon, but for the moment the sky was clear.

She kept close to the row of vines, but she threw a conspicuous moon shadow.

She had firmly instructed Paul and Ruby to stay behind, hiding at the edge of the field near the van. Three people made three times the noise, and she did not want a companion to betray her presence.

As she crawled, she listened for the incoming plane. She had to locate any remaining enemy and kill them before the plane arrived. The Jackdaws could not stand in the middle of the field with torches while there were armed troops aiming at them from the vineyard. And if they did not hold torches, the plane would return to England without touching down. The thought was unbearable.

She was deeper into the vineyard than Dieter Franck's car, which was parked at the edge. She was five rows of vines back. She would approach the enemy from behind. She kept the submachine-gun in her right hand, ready to fire, as she crawled.

She drew level with the car. Franck had camouflaged it with vegetation, but when she peeped over the rows of vines she saw moonlight glint off the rear window.

The shoots of the vines were espaliered crosswise, but she was able to crawl beneath the lowest strand. She pushed her head through and looked up and down the next alley. It was clear. She crawled across the open space and repeated the exercise. She grew ultra-cautious as she approached the car, but she saw no one.

When she was two rows away, she was able to see the wheels of the car and the ground around it. She thought she could make out two motionless bodies in uniform. How many were there in total? It was a long Mercedes limousine, and could easily carry six.

She crept closer. Nothing moved. Were they all dead? Or had one or two survived, and concealed themselves nearby, waiting to pounce?

Eventually she crawled right up to the car.

The doors were wide open, and the interior seemed full of bodies. She looked in the front and recognized Michel. She choked back a sob. He was a bad husband, but he had been her choice, and now he was lifeless, with three red-ringed bullet holes in his blue chambray shirt. She guessed he had been the one to sound the horn. If so, he had died saving her life. There was no time to think of such things now: she would ponder them later, if she lived long enough.

Next to Michel lay a man she did not recognize who had been shot in the throat. He wore the uniform of a lieutenant. There were more bodies in the back. She looked through the open rear door. One was that of a woman. She leaned into the car for a better view. She gasped: the woman was Gilberte, and she seemed to be staring at Flick. A ghastly moment later, Flick realized that the eyes saw nothing, and Gilberte was dead, shot in the head.

She leaned over Gilberte to look at the fourth corpse. It rose up from the floor in a swift motion. Before she had time to scream, it grabbed her by the hair and thrust the barrel of a gun into the soft flesh of her throat.

It was Dieter Franck.

'Drop the gun,' he said in French.

579

She was holding the submachine-gun in her right hand but it was pointing up and, before she could aim it, he would be able to shoot her. She had no choice: she dropped it. The safety catch was disengaged, and she half hoped the impact of its fall would fire the gun, but it landed harmlessly on the earth.

'Back away.'

As she stepped back he followed her, getting out of the car, keeping the gun at her throat. He drew himself upright. 'You're so small,' he said, looking her up and down. 'And you've done so much damage.'

She saw blood on the sleeve of his suit, and guessed she had winged him with her Sten gun.

'Not just to me,' he said. 'That telephone exchange is every bit as important as you obviously believe.'

She found her voice. 'Good.'

'Don't look pleased. Now you're going to damage the Resistance.'

She wished she had not been so fierce in ordering Paul and Ruby to wait in hiding. There was now no chance they would come to her rescue.

Dieter shifted the gun from her throat to her shoulder. 'I don't want to kill you, but I'd be happy to give you a crippling wound. I need you able to talk, of course. You're going to give me all the names and addresses in your head.'

She thought of the suicide pill concealed in the hollow cap of her fountain pen. Would she have a chance to take it?

'It's a pity you've destroyed the interrogation facility

at Sainte-Cécile,' he went on. 'I'll have to drive you to Paris. I've got all the same equipment there.'

She thought with horror of the hospital operating table and the electric-shock machine.

'I wonder what will break you?' he said. 'Sheer pain breaks everyone, eventually, of course, but I feel that you might bear pain for an inconveniently long time.' He raised his left arm. The wound seemed to give him a twinge, and he winced, but he bore it. He touched her face. 'The loss of your looks, perhaps. Imagine this pretty face disfigured: the nose broken, the lips slashed, one eye put out, the ears cut off.'

Flick felt sick, but she maintained a stony expression.

'No?' His hand moved down, stroking her neck, then he touched her breast. 'Sexual humiliation, then. To be naked in front of many people, fondled by a group of drunk men, forced to perform acts of grossness with animals . . .'

'And which of us would be most humiliated by that?' she said defiantly. 'Me, the helpless victim . . . or you, the real perpetrator of obscenity?'

He took his hand away. 'Then again, we have tortures which destroy for ever a woman's ability to bear children.'

Flick thought of Paul, and flinched involuntarily.

'Ah,' he said, with satisfaction. 'I believe I have found the key to unlock you.'

She realized she had been foolish to speak to him. Now she had given him information which he could use to break her will.

'We'll drive straight to Paris,' he said. 'We'll be there by dawn. By midday you will be begging me to stop the torture and listen to you pour out all the secrets you know. Tomorrow night we will arrest every member of the Resistance in northern France.'

Flick was cold with dread. Franck was not bragging. He could do it.

'I think you can travel in the boot of the car,' he said. 'It's not airtight, you won't suffocate. But I'll put the corpses of your husband and his lover in with you. A few hours bumping around with dead people will put you in the right frame of mind, I think.'

Flick shuddered with loathing. She could not help it.

Keeping the pistol pressed to her shoulder, he reached into his pocket with his other hand. He moved his arm cautiously: the bullet wound hurt but did not incapacitate him. He drew out a pair of handcuffs. 'Give me your hands,' he said.

She remained motionless.

'I can either handcuff you, or render your arms useless by shooting you in both shoulders.'

Helpless, she raised her hands.

He closed one cuff over her left wrist. She moved her right towards him. Then she made her last desperate move.

She struck sideways with her handcuffed left hand, knocking his gun away from her shoulder. At the same time she used her right hand to draw the small knife from its hidden sheath behind the lapel of her jacket.

He flinched back, but not fast enough.

She lunged forward and thrust the knife directly into

his left eye. He turned his head, but the knife was already in, and Flick moved farther forward, pressing her body up against his, ramming the knife home. Blood and fluid spurted from the wound. Franck screamed in agony and fired his gun, but the shots went into the air.

He staggered back, but she followed him, still pushing the knife with the heel of her hand. The weapon had no hilt, and she continued to shove until its entire three inches had sunk into his head. He fell backwards and hit the ground.

She fell on him, knees on his chest, and she felt ribs crack. He dropped his gun and clawed at his eye with both hands, trying to get at the knife, but it was sunk too deep. Flick grabbed the gun. It was a Walther P38. She stood upright, held it two-handed, and aimed it at Franck.

Then he fell still.

She heard pounding footsteps. Paul rushed up. 'Flick! Are you all right?'

She nodded.

She was still pointing the Walther at Dieter Franck. 'I don't think that will be necessary,' Paul said softly. After a moment, he moved her hands, then gently took the gun from her and engaged the safety catch.

Ruby appeared. 'Listen!' she cried. 'Listen!'

Flick heard the drone of a Hudson.

'Let's get moving,' Paul said.

They ran out into the field to signal the plane that would take them home.

* * *

They crossed the English Channel in strong winds and intermittent rain. During a quiet spell, the navigator came back into the passenger compartment and said: 'You might want to take a look outside.'

Flick, Ruby and Paul were dozing. The floor was hard, but they were exhausted. Flick was wrapped in Paul's arms, and she did not want to move.

The navigator pressed them. 'You'd better be quick, before it clouds over again. You'll never see anything like this again if you live to be a hundred.'

Curiosity overcame Flick's tiredness. She got up and staggered to the small rectangular window. Ruby did the same. Obligingly, the pilot dipped a wing.

The English Channel was choppy, and a stiff wind blew, but the moon was full and she could see clearly. At first she could hardly believe her eyes. Immediately below the plane was a grey-painted warship bristling with guns. Alongside it was a small ocean liner, its paintwork gleaming white in the moonlight. Behind them, a rusty old steamer pitched into the swell. Beyond them and behind were cargo boats, troop transports, battered old tankers, and great shallow-draught landing ships. There were ships as far as Flick could see, hundreds of them.

The pilot dipped the other wing and she looked out of the other side. It was the same.

'Paul, look at this!' she cried.

He came and stood beside her. 'Jeepers!' he said. 'I've never seen so many ships in all my life!'

'It's the invasion!' she said.

'Take a look out of the front,' said the navigator.

Flick went forward and looked over the pilot's

shoulder. The ships were spread out over the sea like a carpet, stretching for miles and miles, as far as she could see. She heard Paul's incredulous voice say: 'I didn't know there were this many ships in the damn world!'

'How many do you think it is?' Ruby said.

The navigator said: 'I heard five thousand.'

'Amazing,' Flick said.

The navigator said: 'I'd give a lot to be part of that, wouldn't you?'

Flick looked at Paul and Ruby, and they all smiled. 'Oh, we are,' she said. 'We're part of it, all right.'

ONE YEAR LATER: WEDNESDAY, 6 JUNE 1945

FIFTY-THREE

The London street called Whitehall was lined on both sides with grandiose buildings that embodied the magnificence of the British empire as it had once been, a hundred years earlier. Inside those fine buildings, many of the high rooms with their long windows had been subdivided by cheap partitions to form offices for lesser officials and meeting rooms for unimportant groups. As a subcommittee of a subcommittee, the Medals (Clandestine Actions) Working Party met in a windowless room fifteen feet square with a vast, cold fireplace that occupied half of one wall.

Simon Fortescue from MI6 was in the chair, wearing a striped suit, striped shirt and striped tie. The Special Operations Executive was represented by John Graves from the Ministry of Economic Warfare, which had theoretically supervised SOE throughout the war. Like the other civil servants on the committee, Graves wore the Whitehall uniform of black jacket and grey striped trousers. The Bishop of Marlborough was there in a purple clerical shirt, no doubt to give the moral dimension to the business of honouring men for killing other men. Colonel Algernon 'Nobby' Clarke, an intelligence officer, was the only member of the committee who had seen action in the war.

Tea was served by the committee's secretary, and a plate of biscuits was passed around while the men deliberated.

It was mid-morning when they came to the case of the Jackdaws of Reims.

John Graves said: 'There were six women on this team, and only two came back. But they destroyed the telephone exchange at Sainte-Cécile, which was also the local Gestapo headquarters.'

'Women?' said the bishop. 'Did you say six women?'

'Yes.'

'My goodness me.' His tone was disapproving. 'Why women?'

'The telephone exchange was heavily guarded, but they got in by posing as cleaners.'

'I see.'

Nobby Clarke, who had spent most of the morning chain-smoking in silence, now said: 'After the liberation of Paris, I interrogated a Major Goedel, who had been aide to Rommel. He told me they had been virtually paralysed by the breakdown in communications on D-Day. It was a significant factor in the success of the invasion, he thought. I had no idea a handful of girls were responsible. I should think we're talking about the Military Cross, aren't we?'

'Perhaps,' said Fortescue, and his manner became prissy. 'However, there were discipline problems with this group. An official complaint was entered against the leader, Major Clairet, after she insulted a Guards officer.'

'Insulted?' said the bishop. 'How?'

'There was a row in a bar, and I'm afraid she told him to fuck off, saving your presence, Bishop.'

'My goodness me. She doesn't sound like the kind of person who should be held up as a hero to the next generation.'

'Exactly. A lesser decoration than the Military Cross, then – the MBE, perhaps.'

Nobby Clarke spoke again. 'I disagree,' he said mildly. 'After all, if this woman had been a milksop she probably wouldn't have been able to blow up a telephone exchange under the noses of the Gestapo.'

Fortescue was irritated. It was unusual for him to encounter opposition. He hated people who were not intimidated by him. He looked around the table. 'The consensus of the meeting seems to be against you.'

Clarke frowned. 'I presume I can put in a minority recommendation,' he said with stubborn patience.

'Indeed,' said Fortescue. 'Though I doubt if there's much point.'

Clarke drew on his cigarette thoughtfully. 'Why not?'

'The Minister will have some knowledge of one or two of the individuals on our list. In those cases he will follow his own inclinations, regardless of our recommendations. In all other cases he will do as we suggest, having himself no interest. If the committee is not unanimous he will accept the recommendation of the majority.'

'I see,' said Clarke. 'All the same, I should like the record to show that I dissented from the committee, and recommended the Military Cross for Major Clairet.'

Fortescue looked at the secretary, the only woman in the room. 'Make sure of that, please, Miss Gregory.'

'Very good,' she said quietly.

Clarke stubbed out his cigarette and lit another.

And that was the end of that.

* * *

Frau Waltraud Franck came home happy. She had managed to buy a neck of mutton. It was the first meat she had seen for a month. She had walked from her suburban home into the bombed city centre of Cologne and had stood in line outside the butcher's shop all morning. She had also forced herself to smile when the butcher, Herr Beckmann, fondled her behind; for if she had objected, he would have been 'sold out' to her ever afterwards. But she could put up with Beckmann's wandering hands. She would get three days of meals out of a neck of mutton.

'I'm back!' she sang out as she entered the house. The children were at school, but Dieter was at home. She put the precious meat in the pantry. She would save it for tonight, when the children would be here to share it. For lunch she and Dieter would have cabbage soup and black bread.

She went into the living room. 'Hello, darling!' she said brightly.

Her husband sat at the window, motionless. A

piratical black patch covered one eye. He had on one of his beautiful old suits, but it hung loosely on his skinny frame, and he wore no tie. She tried to dress him nicely, every morning, but she had never mastered the tying of a man's tie. His face wore a vacant expression, and a dribble of saliva hung from his open mouth. He did not reply to her greeting.

She was used to this. 'Guess what?' she said. 'I got a neck of mutton!'

He stared at her with his good eye. 'Who are you?' he said.

She bent and kissed him. 'We'll have a meaty stew for supper tonight. Aren't we lucky!'

* * *

That afternoon, Flick and Paul got married in a little church in Chelsea.

It was a simple ceremony. The war in Europe was over, and Hitler was dead, but the Japanese were fiercely defending Okinawa, and wartime austerity continued to cramp the style of Londoners. Flick and Paul both wore their uniforms: wedding-dress material was very hard to find, and Flick, as a widow, did not want to wear white.

Percy Thwaite gave Flick away. Ruby was matron of honour. She could not be bridesmaid because she was already married – to Jim, the firearms instructor from the Finishing School, who was sitting in the second row of pews.

Paul's father, General Chancellor, was best man. He

was still stationed in London, and Flick had got to know him quite well. He had the reputation of an ogre in the US military, but to Flick he was a sweetheart.

Also in the church was Mademoiselle Jeanne Lemas. She had been taken to Ravensbrueck concentration camp, with young Marie; and Marie had died there, but somehow Jeanne Lemas had survived, and Percy Thwaite had pulled a hundred strings to get her to London for the wedding. She sat in the third row, wearing a cloche hat.

Dr Claude Bouler had also survived, but Diana and Maude had both died in Ravensbrueck. Before she died, Diana had become a leader in the camp, according to Mademoiselle Lemas. Trading on the German weakness of showing deference to aristocracy, she had fearlessly confronted the camp commandant to complain about conditions and demand better treatment for all. She had not achieved much, but her nerve and optimism had raised the spirits of the starving inmates, and several survivors credited her with giving them the will to live.

The wedding service was short. When it was over, and Flick and Paul were husband and wife, they simply turned around and stood at the front of the church to receive congratulations.

Paul's mother was there, too. Somehow the general had managed to get his wife on a transatlantic flying boat. She had arrived late last night, and now Flick met her for the first time. She looked Flick up and down, obviously wondering whether this girl was good enough to be the wife of her wonderful son. Flick felt mildly put out. But she told herself this was natural in a proud mother, and kissed Mrs Chancellor's cheek with warmth.

They were going to live in Boston. Paul would take up the reins of his educational-records business. Flick planned to finish her doctorate, then teach American youngsters about French culture. The five-day voyage across the Atlantic would be their honeymoon.

Flick's mother was there in a hat she had bought in 1938. She cried, even though it was the second time she had seen her daughter married.

The last person in the small congregation to kiss Flick was her brother, Mark.

There was one more thing Flick needed to make her happiness perfect. With her arm still around Mark, she turned to her mother, who had not spoken to him for five years. 'Look, Ma,' she said. 'Here's Mark.'

Mark looked terrified.

Ma hesitated for a long moment. Then she opened her arms and said: 'Hello, Mark.'

'Oh, Ma,' he said, and he hugged her.

After that, they all walked out into the sunshine.

From the Official History:

> Women did not normally organize sabotage; but
> Pearl Witherington, a trained British courier, took
> over and ran an active *maquis* of some two
> thousand men in Berry with gallantry and
> distinction after the Gestapo arrested her
> organizer. She was strongly recommended for an
> MC [Military Cross], for which women were held
> ineligible; and received instead a civil MBE, which
> she returned, observing she had done nothing
> civil.

M.R.D. Foot, *S.O.E. in France* (HMSO, London, 1966)

ACKNOWLEDGEMENTS

For information and guidance about the Special Operations Executive, I'm grateful to M.R.D. Foot; on the Third Reich, Richard Overy; on the history of telephone systems, Bernard Green; on weapons, Candice DeLong and David Raymond. For help with research in general I am grateful as always to Dan Starer of Research for Writers in New York City; and to Rachel Flagg. I received much invaluable help from my editors: Phyllis Grann and Neil Nyren in New York, Imogen Taylor in London, Jean Rosenthal in Paris and Helmut Pesch in Cologne; and my agents Al Zuckerman and Amy Berkower. Several family members read the drafts and made helpful criticisms, especially John Evans, Barbara Follett, Emanuele Follett, Jann Turner and Kim Turner.

HORNET
FLIGHT

Some of what follows really happened.

PROLOGUE

A man with a wooden leg walked along a hospital corridor.

He was a short, vigorous type with an athletic build, thirty years old, dressed in a plain charcoal grey suit and black toecapped shoes. He walked briskly, but you could tell he was lame by the slight irregularity in his step: tap-*tap*, tap-*tap*. His face was fixed in a grim expression, as if he were suppressing some profound emotion.

He reached the end of the corridor and stopped at the nurse's desk. 'Flight Lieutenant Hoare?' he said.

The nurse looked up from a register. She was a pretty girl with black hair, and she spoke with the soft accent of County Cork. 'You'll be a relation, I'm thinking,' she said with a friendly smile.

Her charm had no effect. 'Brother,' said the visitor. 'Which bed?'

'Last on the left.'

He turned on his heel and strode along the aisle to the end of the ward. In a chair beside the bed, a figure in a brown dressing-gown sat with his back to the room, looking out of the window, smoking.

The visitor hesitated. 'Bart?'

The man in the chair stood up and turned around. There was a bandage on his head and his left arm was in a sling, but he was smiling. He was younger and taller than the visitor. 'Hello, Digby.'

Digby put his arms around his brother and hugged him hard. 'I thought you were dead,' he said.

Then he began to cry.

* * *

'I was flying a Whitley,' Bart said. The Armstrong Whitworth Whitley was a cumbersome long-tailed bomber that flew in an odd nose-down attitude. In the spring of 1941, Bomber Command had a hundred of them, out of a total strength of about seven hundred aircraft. 'A Messerschmitt fired on us and we took several hits,' Bart continued. 'But he must have been running out of fuel, because he peeled off without finishing us. I thought it was my lucky day. Then we started to lose altitude. The Messerschmitt must have damaged both engines. We chucked out everything that wasn't bolted down, to reduce our weight, but it was no good, and I realized we'd have to ditch in the North Sea.'

Digby sat on the edge of the hospital bed, dry-eyed now, watching his brother's face, seeing the thousand-yard-stare as Bart remembered.

'I told the crew to jettison the rear hatch then get into ditching position, braced against the bulkhead.' The Whitley had a crew of five, Digby recalled. 'When we reached zero altitude I heaved back on the stick and opened the throttles, but the aircraft refused to

4

level out, and we hit the water with a terrific smash. I was knocked out.'

They were step-brothers, eight years apart. Digby's mother had died when he was thirteen, and his father had married a widow with a boy of her own. From the start, Digby had looked after his little brother, protecting him from bullies and helping him with his school work. They had both been mad about aeroplanes, and dreamed of being pilots. Digby lost his right leg in a motorcycle accident, studied engineering, and went into aircraft design; but Bart lived the dream.

'When I came to, I could smell smoke. The aircraft was floating and the starboard wing was on fire. The night was dark as the grave, but I could see by the light of the flames. I crawled along the fuselage and found the dinghy pack. I bunged it through the hatch and jumped. Jesus, that water was cold.'

His voice was low and calm, but he took hard pulls on his cigarette, drawing the smoke deep into his lungs and blowing it out between tight-pursed lips in a long jet. 'I was wearing a life jacket and I came to the surface like a cork. There was quite a swell, and I was going up and down like a tart's knickers. Luckily, the dinghy pack was right in front of my nose. I pulled the string and it inflated itself but I couldn't get in. I didn't have the strength to heave myself out of the water. I couldn't understand it – didn't realize I had a dislocated shoulder and a broken wrist and three cracked ribs and all that. So I just stayed there, holding on, freezing to death.'

There had been a time, Digby recalled, when he thought Bart had been the lucky one.

'Eventually Jones and Croft appeared. They'd held on to the tail until it went down. Neither could swim, but their Mae Wests saved them, and they managed to scramble into the dinghy and pull me in.' He lit a fresh cigarette. 'I never saw Pickering. I don't know what happened to him, but I assume he's at the bottom of the sea.'

He fell silent. There was one crew member unaccounted for, Digby realized. After a pause, he said: 'What about the fifth man?'

'John Rowley, the bomb-aimer, was alive. We heard him call out. I was in a bit of a daze, but Jones and Croft tried to row towards the voice.' He shook his head in a gesture of hopelessness. 'You can't imagine how difficult it was. The swell must have been three or four feet, the flames were dying down so we couldn't see much, and the wind was howling like a bloody banshee. Jones yelled, and he's got a strong voice. Rowley would shout back, then the dinghy would go up one side of a wave and down the other and spin around at the same time, and when he called out again his voice seemed to come from a completely different direction. I don't know how long it went on. Rowley kept shouting, but his voice became weaker as the cold got to him.' Bart's face stiffened. 'He started to sound a bit pathetic, calling to God and his mother and that sort of rot. Eventually he went quiet.'

Digby found he was holding his breath, as if the

mere sound of breathing would be an intrusion on such a dreadful memory.

'We were found soon after dawn, by a destroyer on U-boat patrol. They dropped a cutter and hauled us in.' Bart looked out of the window, blind to the green Hertfordshire landscape, seeing a different scene, far away. 'Bloody lucky, really,' he said.

* * *

They sat in silence for a while, then Bart said: 'Was the raid a success? No one will tell me how many came home.'

'Disastrous,' Digby said.

'What about my squadron?'

'Sergeant Jenkins and his crew got back safely.' Digby drew a slip of paper from his pocket. 'So did Pilot Officer Arasaratnam. Where's he from?'

'Ceylon.'

'And Sergeant Riley's aircraft took a hit but made it back.'

'Luck of the Irish,' said Bart. 'What about the rest?'

Digby just shook his head.

'But there were six aircraft from my squadron on that raid!' Bart protested.

'I know. As well as you, two more were shot down. No apparent survivors.'

'So Creighton-Smith is dead. And Billy Shaw. And . . . oh, God.' He turned away.

'I'm sorry.'

Bart's mood changed from despair to anger. 'It's

7

not enough to be sorry,' he said. 'We're being sent out there to die!'

'I know.'

'For Christ's sake, Digby, you're part of the bloody government.'

'I work for the prime minister, yes.' Churchill liked to bring people from private industry into the government and Digby, a successful aircraft designer before the war, was one of his troubleshooters.

'Then this is your fault as much as anyone's. You shouldn't be wasting your time visiting the sick. Get the hell out of here and do something about it.'

'I am doing something,' Digby said calmly. 'I've been given the task of finding out why this is happening. We lost fifty per cent of the aircraft on that raid.'

'Bloody treachery at the top, I suspect. Or some fool air marshal boasting in his club about tomorrow's raid, and a Nazi barman taking notes behind the beer pumps.'

'That's one possibility.'

Bart sighed. 'I'm sorry, Diggers,' he said, using a childhood nickname. 'It's not your fault, I'm just blowing my top.'

'Seriously, have you any idea why so many are being shot down? You've flown more than a dozen missions. What's your hunch?'

Bart looked thoughtful. 'I wasn't just sounding off about spies. When we get to Germany, they're ready for us. *They know we're coming.*'

'What makes you say that?'

'Their fighters are in the air, waiting for us. You know how difficult it is for defensive forces to time that right. The fighter squadron has to be scrambled at just the right moment, they must navigate from their airfield to the area where they think we might be, then they have to climb above our ceiling, and when they've done all that they have to find us in the moonlight. The whole process takes so much time that we should be able to drop our ordnance and get clear before they catch us. But it isn't happening that way.'

Digby nodded. Bart's experience matched that of other pilots he had questioned. He was about to say so when Bart looked up and smiled over Digby's shoulder. Digby turned to see a Negro in the uniform of a squadron leader. Like Bart, he was young for his rank, and Digby guessed he had received the automatic promotions that came with combat experience – flight lieutenant after twelve sorties, squadron leader after fifteen.

Bart said: 'Hello, Charles.'

'You had us all worried, Bartlett. How are you?' The newcomer's accent was Caribbean overlaid with an Oxbridge drawl.

'I may live, they say.'

With a fingertip, Charles touched the back of Bart's hand where it emerged from his sling. It was a curiously affectionate gesture, Digby thought. 'I'm jolly glad to hear it,' Charles said.

'Charles, meet my brother Digby. Digby, this is Charles Ford. We were together at Trinity until we left to join the air force.'

'It was the only way to avoid taking our exams,' Charles said, shaking Digby's hand.

Bart said: 'How are the Africans treating you?'

Charles smiled and explained to Digby: 'There's a squadron of Rhodesians at our airfield. First class flyers, but they find it difficult to deal with an officer of my colour. We call them the Africans, which seems to irritate them slightly. I can't think why.'

Digby said: 'Obviously you're not letting it get you down.'

'I believe that with patience and improved education we may eventually be able to civilize such people, primitive though they seem now.' Charles looked away, and Digby caught a glimpse of the anger beneath his good humour.

'I was just asking Bart why he thinks we're losing so many bombers,' Digby said. 'What's your opinion?'

'I wasn't on this raid,' Charles said. 'By all accounts, I was lucky to miss it. But other recent operations have been pretty bad. I get the feeling the Luftwaffe can follow us through cloud. Might they have some kind of equipment on board that enables them to locate us even when we're not visible?'

Digby shook his head. 'Every crashed enemy aircraft is minutely examined, and we've never seen anything like what you're talking about. We're working hard to invent that kind of device, and I'm sure the enemy are too, but we're a long way from success, and we're pretty sure they're well behind us. I don't think that's it.'

'Well, that's what it feels like.'

'I still think there are spies,' Bart said.

'Interesting.' Digby stood up. 'I have to get back to Whitehall. Thanks for your opinions. It helps to talk to the men at the sharp end.' He shook hands with Charles and squeezed Bart's uninjured shoulder. 'Sit still and get well.'

'They say I'll be flying again in a few weeks.'

'I can't say I'm glad.'

As Digby turned to go, Charles said: 'May I ask you a question?'

'Of course.'

'On a raid like this one, the cost to us of replacing lost aircraft must be more than the cost to the enemy of repairing the damage done by our bombs.'

'Undoubtedly.'

'Then . . .' Charles spread his arms in a sign of incomprehension. 'Why do we do it? What's the point of bombing?'

'Yes,' Bart said. 'I'd like to know that.'

'What else can we do?' Digby said. 'The Nazis control Europe: Austria, Czechoslovakia, Holland, Belgium, France, Denmark, Norway. Italy is an ally, Spain is sympathetic, Sweden is neutral, and they have a pact with the Soviet Union. We have no military forces on the Continent. We have no other way of fighting back.'

Charles nodded. 'So we're all you've got.'

'Exactly,' Digby said. 'If the bombing stops, the war is over – and Hitler has won.'

* * *

The prime minister was watching *The Maltese Falcon*. A private cinema had recently been built in the old kitchens of Admiralty House. It had fifty or sixty plush seats and a red velvet curtain, but it was usually used to show film of bombing raids and to screen propaganda pieces before they were shown to the public.

Late at night, after all the memoranda had been dictated, the cables sent, the reports annotated, and the minutes initialled, when he was too worried and angry and tense to sleep, Churchill would sit in one of the large VIP seats in the front row with a glass of brandy and lose himself in the latest enchantment from Hollywood.

As Digby walked in, Humphrey Bogart was explaining to Mary Astor that when a man's partner is killed he's supposed to do something about it. The air was thick with cigar smoke. Churchill pointed to a seat. Digby sat down and watched the last few minutes of the movie. As the credits appeared over the statuette of a black falcon, Digby told his boss that the Luftwaffe seemed to have advance notice when Bomber Command was coming.

When he had finished, Churchill stared at the screen for a few moments, as if he were waiting to find out who had played Bryan. There were times when he was charming, with an engaging smile and a twinkle in his blue eyes, but tonight he seemed sunk in gloom. At last he said: 'What does the RAF think?'

'They blame poor formation flying. In theory, if

the bombers fly in close formation, their armament should cover the entire sky, so any enemy fighter that appears should be shot down immediately.'

'And what do you say to that?'

'Rubbish. Formation flying has never worked. Some new factor has entered the equation.'

'I agree. But what?'

'My brother blames spies.'

'All the spies we've caught have been amateurish – but that's why they were caught, of course. It may be that the competent ones have slipped through the net.'

'Perhaps the Germans have made a technical breakthrough.'

'The Secret Intelligence Service tell me the enemy are far behind us in the development of radar.'

'Do you trust their judgement?'

'No.' The ceiling lights came on. Churchill was in evening dress. He always looked dapper, but his face was lined with weariness. He took from his waistcoat pocket a folded sheet of flimsy paper. 'Here's a clue,' he said, and he handed it to Digby.

Digby studied the sheet. It appeared to be a decrypt of a Luftwaffe radio signal, in German and English. It said that the Luftwaffe's new strategy of dark night-fighting – *Dunkel Nachtjagd* – had scored a great triumph, thanks to the excellent information from Freya. Digby read the message in English then again in German. 'Freya' was not a word in either language. 'What does this mean?' he said.

13

'That's what I want you to find out.' Churchill stood up and shrugged into his jacket. 'Walk back with me,' he said. As he left, he called out: 'Thank you!'

A voice from the projectionist's booth replied: 'My pleasure, sir.'

As they passed through the building, two men fell in behind them: Inspector Thompson from Scotland Yard, and Churchill's private bodyguard. They emerged on the parade ground, passed a team operating a barrage balloon, and went through a gate in the barbed-wire fence to the street. London was blacked out, but a crescent moon gave enough light for them to find their way.

They walked side by side a few yards along Horse Guards Parade to Number One Storey's Gate. A bomb had damaged the rear of Number Ten Downing Street, the traditional residence of the prime minister, so Churchill was living at the nearby annexe over the Cabinet War Rooms. The entrance was protected by a bombproof wall. The barrel of a machine gun poked through a hole in the wall.

Digby said: 'Goodnight, sir.'

'It can't go on,' said Churchill. 'At this rate, Bomber Command will be finished by Christmas. I need to know who or what Freya is.'

'I'll find out.'

'Do so with the utmost despatch.'

'Yes, sir.'

'Goodnight,' said the prime minister, and he went inside.

PART ONE

ONE

On the last day of May 1941, a strange vehicle was seen on the streets of Morlunde, a city on the west coast of Denmark.

It was a Danish-made Nimbus motorcycle with a sidecar. That in itself was an unusual sight, because there was no petrol for anyone except doctors and the police and, of course, the German troops occupying the country. But this Nimbus had been modified. The four-cylinder petrol engine had been replaced by a steam engine taken from a scrapped river launch. The seat had been removed from the sidecar to make room for a boiler, firebox and chimney stack. The substitute engine was low in power, and the bike had a top speed of about twenty-two miles per hour. Instead of the customary roar of a motorcycle exhaust, there was only the gentle hiss of steam. The eery quiet and the slow pace gave the vehicle a stately air.

In the saddle was Harald Olufsen, a tall youth of eighteen, with clear skin and fair hair brushed back from a high forehead. He looked like a Viking in a school blazer. He had saved for a year to buy the Nimbus, which had cost him six hundred crowns –

then, the day after he got it, the Germans had imposed the petrol restrictions.

Harald had been furious. What right did they have? But he had been brought up to act rather than complain.

It had taken him another year to modify the bike, working in school holidays, fitting it in with revision for his university entrance exams. Today, home from his boarding school for the Whitsun break, he had spent the morning memorizing physics equations and the afternoon attaching a sprocket from a rusted lawn mower to the back wheel. Now, with the motorcycle working perfectly, he was heading for a bar where he hoped to hear some jazz and perhaps even meet some girls.

He loved jazz. After physics, it was the most interesting thing that had ever happened to him. The American musicians were the best, of course, but even their Danish imitators were worth listening to. You could sometimes hear good jazz in Morlunde, perhaps because it was an international port, visited by sailors from all over the world.

But when Harald drove up outside the Club Hot, in the heart of the dockside district, its door was closed and its windows shuttered.

He was mystified. It was eight o'clock on a Saturday evening, and this was one of the most popular spots in town. It should be swinging.

As he sat staring at the silent building, a passer-by stopped and looked at his vehicle. 'What's that contraption?'

'A Nimbus with a steam engine. Do you know anything about this club?'

'I own it. What does the bike use for fuel?'

'Anything that burns. I use peat.' He pointed to the pile in the back of the sidecar.

'*Peat?*' The man laughed.

'Why are the doors shut?'

'The Nazis closed me down.'

Harald was dismayed. 'Why?'

'Employing Negro musicians.'

Harald had never seen a coloured musician in the flesh, but he knew from records that they were the best. 'The Nazis are ignorant swine,' he said angrily. His evening had been ruined.

The club owner looked up and down the street to make sure no one had heard. The occupying power ruled Denmark with a light hand, but all the same few people openly insulted the Nazis. However, there was no one else in sight. He returned his gaze to the motorcycle. 'Does it work?'

'Of course it does.'

'Who converted it for you?'

'I did it myself.'

The man's amusement was turning to admiration. 'That's pretty clever.'

'Thank you.' Harald opened the tap that admitted steam into the engine. 'I'm sorry about your club.'

'I'm hoping they'll let me open again in a few weeks. But I'll have to promise to employ white musicians.'

'Jazz without Negroes?' Harald shook his head

19

in disgust. 'It's like banning French cooks from restaurants.' He took his foot off the brake and the bike moved slowly away.

He thought of heading for the town centre, to see if there was anyone he knew in the cafés and bars around the square, but he felt so disappointed about the jazz club that he decided it would be depressing to hang around. He steered for the harbour.

His father was pastor of the church on Sande, a small island a couple of miles offshore. The little ferry that shuttled to and from the island was in dock, and he drove straight on to it. It was crowded with people, most of whom he knew. There was a merry gang of fishermen who had been to a football match and had a few drinks afterwards; two well-off women in hats and gloves with a pony and trap and a stack of shopping; and a family of five who had been visiting relations in town. A well-dressed couple he did not recognize were probably going to dine at the island's hotel, which had a high-class restaurant. His motorcycle attracted everyone's interest, and he had to explain the steam engine again.

At the last minute a German-built Ford sedan drove on. Harald knew the car: it belonged to Axel Flemming, owner of the hotel. The Flemmings were hostile to Harald's family. Axel Flemming felt he was the natural leader of the island community, a role which Pastor Olufsen believed to be his own, and the friction between the rival patriarchs affected all other family members. Harald wondered how Flemming had managed to get petrol for his car. He supposed anything was possible to the rich.

The sea was choppy and there were dark clouds in the western sky. A storm was coming in, but the fishermen said they would be home before it arrived, just. Harald took out a newspaper he had picked up in the town. Entitled *Reality*, it was an illegal publication, printed in defiance of the occupying power and given away free. The Danish police had not attempted to suppress it and the Germans seemed to regard it as beneath contempt. In Copenhagen, people read it openly on trains and streetcars. Here people were more discreet, and Harald folded it to hide the masthead while he read a report about the shortage of butter. Denmark produced millions of pounds of butter every year, but almost all of it was now sent to Germany, and Danes had trouble getting any. It was the kind of story that never appeared in the censored legitimate press.

The familiar flat shape of the island came closer. It was twelve miles long and a mile wide, with a village at each end. The fishermen's cottages, and the church with its parsonage, constituted the older village at the south end. Also at the south end, a school of navigation, long disused, had been taken over by the Germans and turned into a military base. The hotel and the larger homes were at the north end. In between, the island was mostly sand dunes and scrub with a few trees and no hills, but all along the seaward side was a magnificent ten-mile beach.

Harald felt a few drops of rain as the ferry approached its dock at the north end of the island. The hotel's horse-drawn taxi was waiting for the well-dressed couple. The fishermen were met by the wife of one of them driving a horse and cart. Harald decided to cross the island and drive home along the beach, which had hard-packed sand – in fact it had been used for speed trials of racing cars.

He was half way from the dock to the hotel when he ran out of steam.

He was using the bike's petrol tank as a water reserve, and he realized now that it was not big enough. He would have to get a five-gallon oil drum and put it in the sidecar. Meanwhile, he needed water to get him home.

There was only one house within sight, and unfortunately it was Axel Flemming's. Despite their rivalry, the Olufsens and the Flemmings were on speaking terms: all members of the Flemming family came to church every Sunday and sat together at the front. Indeed, Axel was a deacon. All the same, Harald did not relish the thought of asking the antagonistic Flemmings for help. He considered walking a quarter of a mile to the next nearest house, then decided that would be foolish. With a sigh, he set off up the long drive.

Rather than knock at the front door, he went around the side of the house to the stables. He was pleased to see a manservant putting the Ford in the garage. 'Hello, Gunnar,' said Harald. 'Can I have some water?'

The man was friendly. 'Help yourself,' he said. 'There's a tap in the yard.'

Harald found a bucket beside the tap and filled it. He went back to the road and poured the water into the tank. It looked as if he might manage to avoid meeting any of the family. But when he returned the bucket to the yard, Peter Flemming was there.

A tall, haughty man of thirty in a well-cut suit of oatmeal tweed, Peter was Axel's son. Before the quarrel between the families, he had been best friends with Harald's brother Arne, and in their teens they had been known as ladykillers, Arne seducing girls with his wicked charm and Peter by his cool sophistication. Peter now lived in Copenhagen but had come home for the holiday weekend, Harald assumed.

Peter was reading *Reality*. He looked up from the paper to see Harald. 'What are you doing here?' he said.

'Hello, Peter, I came to get some water.'

'I suppose this rag is yours?'

Harald touched his pocket and realized with consternation that the newspaper must have fallen out when he reached down for the bucket.

Peter saw the movement and understood its meaning. 'Obviously it is,' he said. 'Are you aware that you could go to jail just for having it in your possession?'

The talk of jail was not an empty threat: Peter was a police detective. Harald said, 'Everyone reads it in the city.' He made himself sound defiant, but in fact he was a little scared: Peter was mean enough to arrest him.

'This is not Copenhagen,' Peter intoned solemnly.

Harald knew that Peter would love the chance to disgrace an Olufsen. Yet he was hesitating. Harald thought he knew why. 'You'll look a fool if you arrest a schoolboy on Sande for doing something half the population does openly. Especially when everyone finds out you've got a grudge against my father.'

Peter was visibly torn between the desire to humiliate Harald and the fear of being laughed at. 'No one is entitled to break the law,' he said.

'Whose law – ours, or the Germans'?'

'The law is the law.'

Harald felt more confident. Peter would not be arguing so defensively if he intended to make an arrest. 'You only say that because your father makes so much money giving Nazis a good time at his hotel.'

That hit home. The hotel was popular with German officers, who had more to spend than the Danes. Peter flushed with anger. 'While your father gives inflammatory sermons,' he retorted. It was true: the pastor had preached against the Nazis, his theme being 'Jesus was a Jew'. Peter continued: 'Does he realize how much trouble will be caused if he stirs people up?'

'I'm sure he does. The founder of the Christian religion was something of a troublemaker himself.'

'Don't talk to me about religion. I have to keep order down here on earth.'

'To hell with order, we've been invaded!' Harald's

frustration over his blighted evening out boiled over. 'What right have the Nazis got to tell us what to do? We should kick the whole evil pack of them out of our country!'

'You mustn't hate the Germans, they're our friends,' Peter said with an air of pious self-righteousness that maddened Harald.

'I don't hate Germans, you damn fool, I've got German cousins.' The pastor's sister had married a successful young Hamburg dentist who came to Sande on holiday, back in the twenties. Their daughter Monika was the first girl Harald had kissed. 'They've suffered more from the Nazis than we have,' Harald added. Uncle Joachim was Jewish and, although he was a baptized Christian and an elder of his church, the Nazis had ruled that he could only treat Jews, thereby ruining his practice. A year ago he had been arrested on suspicion of hoarding gold and sent to a special kind of prison, called a *Konzentrazionslager*, in the small Bavarian town of Dachau.

'People bring trouble on themselves,' Peter said with a worldly-wise air. 'Your father should never have allowed his sister to marry a Jew.' He threw the newspaper to the ground and walked away.

At first Harald was too taken aback to reply. He bent and picked up the newspaper. Then he said to Peter's retreating back: 'You're starting to sound like a Nazi yourself.'

Ignoring him, Peter went in by a kitchen entrance and slammed the door.

Harald felt he had lost the argument, which was

infuriating, because he knew that what Peter had said was outrageous.

It started to rain heavily as he headed back toward the road. When he returned to his bike, he found that the fire under the boiler had gone out.

He tried to relight it. He crumpled up his copy of *Reality* for kindling, and he had a box of good quality wood matches in his pocket, but he had not brought with him the bellows he had used to start the fire earlier in the day. After twenty frustrating minutes bent over the firebox in the rain, he gave up. He would have to walk home.

He turned up the collar of his blazer.

He pushed the bike half a mile to the hotel and left it in the small car park, then set off along the beach. At this time of year, three weeks from the summer solstice, the Scandinavian evenings lasted until eleven o'clock; but tonight clouds darkened the sky and the pouring rain further restricted visibility. Harald followed the edge of dunes, finding his way by the feel of the ground underfoot and the sound of the sea in his right ear. Before long, his clothes were so soaked that he could have swum home without getting any wetter.

He was a strong young man, and as fit as a greyhound, but two hours later he was tired, cold and miserable when he came up against the fence around the new German base and realized he would have to walk two miles around it in order to reach his home a few hundred yards away.

If the tide had been out, he would have continued

along the beach for, although that stretch of sand was officially off limits, the guards would not have been able to see him in this weather. However, the tide was in, and the fence reached into the water. It crossed his mind to swim the last stretch, but he dismissed the idea immediately. Like everyone in this fishing community, Harald had a wary respect for the sea, and it would be dangerous to swim at night in this weather when he was already exhausted.

But he could climb the fence.

The rain had eased, and a quarter moon showed fitfully through racing clouds, intermittently shedding an uncertain light over the drenched landscape. Harald could see the chicken-wire fence six feet high with two strands of barbed wire at the top, formidable enough but no great obstacle to a determined person in good physical shape. Fifty yards inland, it passed through a copse of scrubby trees and bushes that hid it from view. That would be the place to get over.

He knew what lay beyond the fence. Last summer he had worked as a labourer on the building site. At that time, he had not known it was destined to be a military base. The builders, a Copenhagen firm, had told everyone it was to be a new coastguard station. They might have had trouble recruiting staff if they had told the truth – Harald for one would not knowingly have worked for the Nazis. Then, when the buildings were up and the fence had been completed, all the Danes had been sent away, and Germans had been brought in to instal the equipment. But Harald knew the layout. The disused navigation school had been refurbished, and two new buildings put up either side of it. All the buildings were set back from the beach, so he could cross the base without going near them. In addition, much of the ground at this end of the site was covered with low bushes that would help conceal him. He would just have to keep an eye out for patrolling guards.

He found his way to the copse, climbed the fence, eased himself gingerly over the barbed wire at the top, and jumped down the other side, landing softly on the wet dunes. He looked around, peering through the gloom, seeing only the vague shapes of trees. The buildings were out of sight, but he could hear distant music and an occasional shout of laughter. It was Saturday night: perhaps the soldiers were having a few beers while their officers dined at Axel Flemming's hotel.

He headed across the base, moving as fast as he dared in the shifting moonlight, staying close to bushes when he could, orienting himself by the waves on his right and the faint music to the left. He passed a tall structure and recognized it, in the dimness, as a searchlight tower. The whole area could be lit up in an emergency, but otherwise the base was blacked out.

A sudden burst of sound to his left startled him, and he crouched down, his heart beating faster. He looked over toward the buildings. A door stood open, spilling light. As he watched, a soldier came out and ran across the compound; then another door opened in a different building, and the soldier ran in.

Harald's heartbeat eased.

He passed through a stand of conifers and went down into a dip. As he came to the bottom of the declivity, he saw a structure of some kind looming up in the murk. He could not make it out clearly, but he did not recall anything being built in this location. Coming closer, he saw a curved concrete wall about as high as his head. Above the wall something moved, and he heard a low hum, like an electric motor.

This must have been erected by the Germans after the local workers had been laid off. He wondered why he had never seen the structure from outside the fence, then realized that the trees and the dip in the ground would hide it from most viewpoints, except perhaps the beach – which was out of bounds where it passed the base.

When he looked up and tried to make out the details, rain drove into his face, stinging his eyes. But he was too curious to pass by. The moon shone bright for a moment. Squinting, he looked again. Above the circular wall he made out a grid of metal or wire like an oversize mattress, twelve feet on a side. The whole contraption was rotating like a merry-go-round, completing a revolution every few seconds.

Harald was fascinated. It was a machine of a kind he had never seen before, and the engineer in him was spellbound. What did it do? Why did it revolve? The sound told him little – that was just the motor that turned the thing. He felt sure it was not a gun, at least not the conventional kind, for there was no barrel. His best guess was that it was something to do with radio.

29

Nearby, someone coughed.

Harald reacted instinctively. He jumped, got his arms over the edge of the wall, and hauled himself up. He lay for a second on the narrow top, feeling dangerously conspicuous, then eased himself down on the inside. He worried that his feet might encounter moving machinery, but he felt almost sure there would be a walkway around the mechanism to allow engineers to service it, and after a tense moment he touched a concrete floor. The hum was louder, and he could smell engine oil. On his tongue was the peculiar taste of static electricity.

Who had coughed? He presumed a sentry was passing by. The man's footsteps must have been lost in the wind and rain. Fortunately, the same noises had muffled the sound Harald made scrambling over the wall. But had the sentry seen him?

He flattened himself against the curved inside of the wall, breathing hard, waiting for the beam of a powerful flashlight to betray him. He wondered what would happen if he were caught. The Germans were amiable, out here in the countryside: most of them did not strut around like conquerors, but seemed almost embarrassed at being in charge. They would probably hand him over to the Danish police. He was not sure what line the cops would take. If Peter Flemming were part of the local force, he would make sure Harald suffered as much as possible; but he was based in Copenhagen, fortunately. What Harald dreaded, more than any official punishment, was his father's anger. He could already hear the pastor's sarcastic interrogation: 'You climbed the fence? And entered the secret military compound? At night? And used it as a short cut home? Because it was *raining*?'

But no light shone on Harald. He waited, and stared at the dark bulk of the apparatus in front of him. He thought he could see heavy cables coming from the lower edge of the grid and disappearing into the gloom on the far side of the pit. This had to be a means of sending radio signals, or receiving them, he thought.

When a few slow minutes had passed, he felt sure the guard had moved on. He clambered to the top of the wall and tried to see through the rain. On either side of the structure he could make out two smaller dark shapes, but they were static, and he decided they must be part of the machinery. No sentry was visible. He slid down the outside of the wall and set off once again across the dunes.

In a dark moment, when the moon was behind a thick cloud, he walked smack into a wooden wall. Shocked and momentarily scared, he let out a muffled curse. A second later he realized he had run into an old boathouse that had been used by the navigation school. It was derelict, and the Germans had not repaired it, apparently having no use for it. He stood still for a moment, listening, but all he could hear was his heart pounding. He walked on.

He reached the far fence without further incident. He scrambled over and headed for his home.

He came first to the church. Light glowed from the long row of small, square windows in its seaward wall.

Surprised that anyone should be in the building at this hour on a Saturday night, he looked inside.

The church was long and low-roofed. On special occasions it could hold the island's resident population of four hundred, but only just. Rows of seats faced a wooden lectern. There was no altar. The walls were bare except for some framed texts.

Danes were undogmatic about religion, and most of the nation subscribed to Evangelical Lutheranism. However, the fishing folk of Sande had been converted, a hundred years ago, to a harsher creed. For the last thirty years Harald's father had kept their faith alight, setting an example of uncompromising puritanism in his own life, stiffening the resolve of his congregation in weekly brimstone sermons, and confronting backsliders personally with the irresistible holiness of his blue-eyed gaze. Despite the example of this blazing conviction, his son was not a believer. Harald went to services whenever he was at home, not wanting to hurt his father's feelings, but in his heart he dissented. He had not yet made up his mind about religion in general, but he knew he did not believe in a god of petty rules and vengeful punishments.

As he looked through the window he heard music. His brother Arne was at the piano, playing a jazz tune with a delicate touch. Harald smiled with pleasure. Arne had come home for the holiday. He was amusing and sophisticated, and he would enliven the long weekend at the parsonage.

Harald walked to the entrance and stepped inside. Without looking around, Arne changed the music seamlessly to a hymn tune. Harald grinned. Arne had heard the door open and thought their father might be coming in. The pastor disapproved of jazz and certainly would not permit it to be played in his church. 'It's only me,' Harald said.

Arne turned around. He was wearing his brown army uniform. Ten years older than Harald, he was a flying instructor with the army aviation troops, based at the flying school near Copenhagen. The Germans had halted all Danish military activity, and the aircraft were grounded most of the time, but the instructors were allowed to give lessons in gliders.

'Seeing you out of the corner of my eye, I thought you were the old man.' Arne looked Harald up and down fondly. 'You look more and more like him.'

'Does that mean I'll go bald?'

'Probably.'

'And you?'

'I don't think so. I take after Mother.'

It was true. Arne had their mother's thick dark hair and hazel eyes. Harald was fair, like their father, and had also inherited the penetrating blue-eyed stare with which the pastor intimidated his flock. Both Harald and their father were formidably tall, making Arne seem short at an inch under six feet.

'I've got something to play you,' Harald said. Arne got off the stool and Harald sat at the piano. 'I learned this from a record someone brought to school. You know Mads Kirke?'

'Cousin of my colleague Poul.'

'Right. He discovered this American pianist called

33

Clarence Pine Top Smith.' Harald hesitated. 'What's the old man doing at this moment?'

'Writing tomorrow's sermon.'

'Good.' The piano could not be heard from the parsonage, fifty yards away, and it was unlikely that the pastor would interrupt his preparation to take an idle stroll across to the church, especially in this weather. Harald began to play *Pine Top's Boogie-Woogie*, and the room filled with the sexy harmonies of the American south. He was an enthusiastic pianist, though his mother said he had a heavy hand. He could not sit still to play, so he stood up, kicking the stool back, knocking it over, and played standing, bending his long frame over the keyboard. He made more mistakes this way, but they did not seem to matter as long as he kept up the compulsive rhythm. He banged out the last chord and said in English: 'That's what I'm talkin' about!' just as Pine Top did on the record.

Arne laughed. 'Not bad!'

'You should hear the original.'

'Come and stand in the porch. I want to smoke.'

Harald stood up. 'The old man won't like that.'

'I'm twenty-eight,' Arne said. 'I'm too old to be told what to do by my father.'

'I agree – but does he?'

'Are you afraid of him?'

'Of course. So is Mother, and just about every other person on this island – even you.'

Arne grinned. 'All right, maybe just a little bit.'

They stood outside the church door, sheltered from the rain by a little porch. On the far side of a patch of sandy ground they could see the dark shape of the parsonage. Light shone through the diamond-shaped window set into the kitchen door. Arne took out his cigarettes.

'Have you heard from Hermia?' Harald asked him. Arne was engaged to an English girl whom he had not seen for more than a year, since the Germans had occupied Denmark.

Arne shook his head. 'I tried to write to her. I found an address for the British Consulate in Gothenburg.' Danes were allowed to send letters to Sweden, which was neutral. 'I addressed it to her at that house, not mentioning the consulate on the envelope. I thought I'd been quite clever, but the censors aren't so easily fooled. My commanding officer brought the letter back to me and said that if I ever tried anything like that again I'd be court-martialled.'

Harald liked Hermia. Some of Arne's girlfriends had been, well, dumb blondes, but Hermia had brains and guts. She was a little scary on first acquaintance, with her dramatic dark looks and her direct manner of speech; but she had endeared herself to Harald by treating him like a man, not just someone's kid brother. And she was sensationally voluptuous in a swimsuit. 'Do you still want to marry her?'

'God, yes – if she's alive. She might have been killed by a bomb in London.'

'It must be hard, not knowing.'

Arne nodded, then said: 'How about you? Any action?'

Harald shrugged. 'Girls my age aren't interested in schoolboys.' He said it lightly, but he was hiding real resentment. He had suffered a couple of wounding rejections.

'I suppose they want to date a guy who can spend some money on them.'

'Exactly. And younger girls . . . I met a girl at Easter, Birgit Claussen.'

'Claussen? The boatbuilding family in Morlunde?'

'Yes. She's pretty, but she's only sixteen, and she was so boring to talk to.'

'It's just as well. The family are Catholics. The old man wouldn't approve.'

'I know.' Harald frowned. 'He's strange, though. At Easter he preached about tolerance.'

'He's about as tolerant as Vlad the Impaler.' Arne threw away the stub of his cigarette. 'Let's go and talk to the old tyrant.'

'Before we go in . . .'

'What?'

'How are things in the army?'

'Grim. We can't defend our country, and most of the time I'm not allowed to fly.'

'How long can this go on?'

'Who knows? Maybe for ever. The Nazis have won everything. There's no opposition left but the British, and they're hanging on by a thread.'

Harald lowered his voice, although there was no

one to listen. 'Surely someone in Copenhagen must be starting a Resistance movement?'

Arne shrugged. 'If they were, and I knew about it, I couldn't tell you, could I?' Then, before Harald could say more, Arne dashed through the rain toward the light shining from the kitchen.

TWO

Hermia Mount looked with dismay at her lunch – two charred sausages, a dollop of runny mashed potato, and a mound of overcooked cabbage – and she thought with longing of a bar on the Copenhagen waterfront that served three kinds of herring with salad, pickles, warm bread and lager beer.

She had been brought up in Denmark. Her father had been a British diplomat who spent most of his career in Scandinavian countries. Hermia had worked in the British Embassy in Copenhagen, first as a secretary, later as assistant to a naval attaché who was in fact with MI6, the secret intelligence service. When her father died, and her mother returned to London, Hermia stayed on, partly because of her job, but mainly because she was engaged to a Danish pilot, Arne Olufsen.

Then, on 9 April 1940, Hitler invaded Denmark. Four anxious days later, Hermia and a group of British officials had left in a special diplomatic train that brought them through Germany to the Dutch frontier, from where they travelled through neutral Holland and on to London.

Now, at the age of thirty, Hermia was an

intelligence analyst in charge of MI6's Denmark desk. Along with most of the service, she had been evacuated from its London headquarters at 54 Broadway, near Buckingham Palace, to Bletchley Park, a large country house on the edge of a village fifty miles north of the capital.

A Nissen hut hastily erected in the grounds served as a canteen. Hermia was glad to be escaping the Blitz, but she wished that by some miracle they could also have evacuated one of London's charming little Italian or French restaurants, so that she would have something to eat. She forked a little mash into her mouth and forced herself to swallow.

To take her mind off the taste of the food, she put that day's *Daily Express* beside her plate. The British had just lost the Mediterranean island of Crete. The *Express* tried to put a brave face on it, claiming the battle had cost Hitler 18,000 men, but the depressing truth was that this was another in a long line of triumphs for the Nazis.

Glancing up, she saw a short man of about her own age coming towards her, carrying a cup of tea, walking briskly but with a noticeable limp. 'May I join you?' he said cheerfully, and sat opposite her without waiting for an answer. 'I'm Digby Hoare. I know who you are.'

She raised an eyebrow and said: 'Make yourself at home.'

The note of irony in her voice made no apparent impact. He just said: 'Thanks.'

She had seen him around once or twice. He had an energetic air, despite his limp. He was no matinée idol, with his unruly dark hair, but he had nice blue eyes, and his features were pleasantly craggy in a Humphrey Bogart way. She asked him: 'What department are you with?'

'I work in London, actually.'

That was not an answer to her question, she noted. She pushed her plate aside.

He said: 'You don't like the food?'

'Do you?'

'I'll tell you something. I've debriefed pilots who have been shot down over France and made their way home. We think we're experiencing austerity, but we don't know the meaning of the word. The Frogs are starving to death. After hearing those stories, everything tastes good to me.'

'Austerity is no excuse for vile cooking,' Hermia said crisply.

He grinned. 'They told me you were a bit waspish.'

'What else did they tell you?'

'That you're bilingual in English and Danish – which is why you're head of the Denmark desk, I presume.'

'No. The war is the reason for that. Before, no woman ever rose above the level of secretary-assistant in MI6. We didn't have analytical minds, you see. We were more suited to home-making and child-rearing. But since war broke out, women's brains have undergone a remarkable change, and we have become capable of work that previously could only be accomplished by the masculine mentality.'

He took her sarcasm with easy good humour. 'I've noticed that, too,' he said. 'Wonders never cease.'

'Why have you been checking up on me?'

'Two reasons. First, because you're the most beautiful woman I've ever seen.' This time he was not grinning.

He had succeeded in surprising her. Men did not often say she was beautiful. Handsome, perhaps; striking, sometimes; imposing, often. Her face was a long oval, perfectly regular, but with severe dark hair, hooded eyes, and a nose too big to be pretty. She could not think of a witty rejoinder. 'What's the other reason?'

He glanced sideways. Two older women were sharing their table, and although they were chatting to one another, they were probably also half-listening to Digby and Hermia. 'I'll tell you in a minute,' he said. 'Would you like to go out on the tiles?'

He had surprised her again. 'What?'

'Will you go out with me?'

'Certainly not.'

For a moment he seemed nonplussed. Then his grin returned, and he said: 'Don't sugar the pill, give it to me straight.'

She could not help smiling.

'We could go to the pictures,' he persisted. 'Or to the Shoulder of Mutton pub in Old Bletchley. Or both.'

She shook her head. 'No, thank you,' she said firmly.

41

'Oh.' He seemed crestfallen.

Did he think she was turning him down because of his disability? She hastened to put that right. 'I'm engaged,' she said. She showed him the ring on her left hand.

'I didn't notice.'

'Men never do.'

'Who's the lucky fellow?'

'A pilot in the Danish army.'

'Over there, I presume.'

'As far as I know. I haven't heard from him for a year.'

The two ladies left the table, and Digby's manner changed. His face turned serious and his voice became quiet but urgent. 'Take a look at this, please.' He drew from his pocket a sheet of flimsy paper and handed it to her.

She had seen such flimsy sheets before, here at Bletchley Park. As she expected, it was a decrypt of an enemy radio signal.

'I imagine I've no need to tell you how desperately secret this is,' Digby said.

'No need.'

'I believe you speak German as well as Danish.'

She nodded. 'In Denmark, all school children learn German, and English and Latin as well.' She studied the signal for a moment. 'Information from Freya?'

'That's what's puzzling us. It's not a word in German. I thought it might mean something in one of the Scandinavian languages.'

42

'It does, in a way,' she said. 'Freya is a Norse goddess – in fact she's the Viking Venus, the goddess of love.'

'Ah!' Digby looked thoughtful. 'Well, that's something, but it doesn't get us far.'

'What's this all about?'

'We're losing too many bombers.'

Hermia frowned. 'I read about the last big raid in the newspapers – they said it was a great success.'

Digby just looked at her.

'Oh, I see,' she said. 'You don't tell the newspapers the truth.'

He remained silent.

'In fact, my entire picture of the bombing campaign is mere propaganda,' she went on. 'The truth is that it's a complete disaster.' To her dismay, he still did not contradict her. 'For heaven's sake, how many aircraft did we lose?'

'Fifty per cent.'

'Dear God.' Hermia looked away. Some of those pilots had fiancées, she thought. 'But if this goes on . . .'

'Exactly.'

She looked again at the decrypt. 'Is Freya a spy?'

'It's my job to find out.'

'What can I do?'

'Tell me more about the goddess.'

Hermia dug back into her memory. She had learned the Norse myths at school, but that was a long time ago. 'Freya has a gold necklace that is very precious. It was given to her by four dwarves. It's guarded by the watchman of the gods . . . Heimdal, I think his name is.'

'A watchman. That makes sense.'

'Freya could be a spy with access to advance information about air raids.'

'She could also be a machine for detecting approaching aircraft before they come within sight.'

'I've heard that we have such machines, but I've no idea how they work.'

'Three possible ways: infra-red, lidar, and radar. Infra-red detectors would pick up the rays emitted by a hot aircraft engine, or possibly its exhaust. Lidar is a system of optical pulses sent out by the detection apparatus and reflected back off the aircraft. Radar is the same thing with radio pulses.'

'I've just remembered something else. Heimdal can see for a hundred miles by day or night.'

'That makes it sound more like a machine.'

'That's what I was thinking.'

Digby finished his tea and stood up. 'If you have any more thoughts, will you let me know?'

'Of course. Where do I find you?'

'Number Ten, Downing Street.'

'Oh!' She was impressed.

'Goodbye.'

'Goodbye,' she said, and watched him walk away.

She sat there for a few moments. It had been an interesting conversation in more ways than one. Digby Hoare was very high-powered: the prime minister himself must be worried about the loss of bombers.

Was the use of the codename Freya mere coincidence, or was there a Scandinavian connection?

She had enjoyed Digby's asking her out. Although she was not interested in dating another man, it was nice to be asked.

After a while, the sight of her uneaten lunch began to get her down. She took her tray to the slops table and scraped her plate into the pigbin. Then she went to the ladies' room.

While she was in a cubicle, she heard a group of young women come in, chattering animatedly. She was about to emerge when one of them said: 'That Digby Hoare doesn't waste time – talk about a fast worker.'

- Hermia froze with her hand on the door knob.

'I saw him move in on Miss Mount,' said an older voice. 'He must be a tit man.'

The others giggled. In the cubicle, Hermia frowned at this reference to her generous figure.

'I think she gave him the brush-off, though,' said the first girl.

'Wouldn't you? I couldn't fancy a man with a wooden leg.'

A third girl spoke with a Scots accent. 'I wonder if he takes it off when he shags you,' she said, and they all laughed.

Hermia had heard enough. She opened the door, stepped out, and said: 'If I find out, I'll let you know.'

The three girls were shocked into silence, and Hermia left before they had time to recover.

She stepped out of the wooden building. The wide

45

green lawn, with its cedar trees and swan pond, had been disfigured by huts thrown up in haste to accommodate the hundreds of staff from London. She crossed the park to the house, an ornate Victorian mansion built of red brick.

She passed through the grand porch and made her way to her office in the old servants' quarters, a tiny L-shaped space that had probably been the boot room. It had one small window too high to see out of, so she worked with the light on all day. There was a phone on her desk and a typewriter on a side table. Her predecessor had had a secretary, but women were expected to do their own typing. On her desk, she found a package from Copenhagen.

After Hitler's invasion of Poland, she had laid the foundations of a small spy network in Denmark. Its leader was her fiancé's friend, Poul Kirke. He had put together a group of young men who believed that their small country was going to be overrun by its larger neighbour, and the only way to fight for freedom was to cooperate with the British. Poul had declared that the group, who called themselves the Nightwatchmen, would not be saboteurs or assassins, but would pass military information to British Intelligence. This achievement by Hermia – unique for a woman – had won her promotion to head of the Denmark desk.

The package contained some of the fruits of her foresight. There was a batch of reports, already decrypted for her by the code room, on German military dispositions in Denmark: army bases on the central island of Fyn; naval traffic in the Kattegat, the sea that separated Denmark from Sweden; and the names of senior German officers in Copenhagen.

Also in the package was a copy of an underground newspaper called *Reality*. The underground press was, so far, the only sign of resistance to the Nazis in Denmark. She glanced through it, reading an indignant article which claimed there was a shortage of butter because all of it was sent to Germany.

The package had been smuggled out of Denmark to a go-between in Sweden, who passed it to the MI6 man at the British legation in Stockholm. With the package was a note from the go-between saying he had also passed a copy of *Reality* to the Reuters wire service in Stockholm. Hermia frowned at that. On the surface, it seemed a good idea to publicize news of conditions under the occupation, but she did not like agents mixing espionage with other work. Resistance action could attract the attention of the authorities to a spy who might otherwise work unnoticed for years.

Thinking about the Nightwatchmen reminded her painfully of her fiancé. Arne was not one of the group. His character was all wrong. She loved him for his careless *joie de vivre*. He made her relax, especially in bed. But a happy-go-lucky man with no head for mundane detail was not the type for secret work. In her more honest moments, she admitted to herself that she was not sure he had the courage. He was a daredevil on the ski slopes – they had met on a Norwegian mountain, where Arne had been the only skier more proficient than Hermia – but she was not sure how he would face the more subtle terrors of undercover operations.

She had considered trying to send him a message via the Nightwatchmen. Poul Kirke worked at the flying school, and if Arne was still there they must see one another every day. It would have been shamefully unprofessional to use the spy network for a personal communication, but that was not what stopped her. She would have been found out for sure, because her messages had to be encrypted by the code room, but even that might not have deterred her. It was the danger to Arne that held her back. Secret messages could fall into enemy hands. The ciphers used by MI6 were unsophisticated poem codes left over from peacetime, and could be broken easily. If Arne's name appeared in a message from British intelligence to Danish spies, he would probably lose his life. Hermia's inquiry about him could turn into his death warrant. So she sat in her boot room with acid anxiety burning inside her.

She composed a message to the Swedish go-between, telling him to keep out of the propaganda war and stick to his job as courier. Then she typed a report to her boss containing all the military information in the package, with carbon copies to other departments.

At four o'clock she left. She had more work to do, and she would return for a couple of hours this evening, but now she had to meet her mother for tea.

Margaret Mount lived in a small house in Pimlico. After Hermia's father had died of cancer in his late forties, her mother had set up home with an unmarried school friend, Elizabeth. They called one another Mags and Bets, their adolescent nicknames. Today the two had come by train to Bletchley to inspect Hermia's lodgings.

She walked quickly through the village to the street where she rented a room. She found Mags and Bets in the parlour talking to her landlady, Mrs Bevan. Hermia's mother was wearing her ambulance driver's uniform, with trousers and a cap. Bets was a pretty woman of fifty in a flowered dress with short sleeves. Hermia hugged her mother and gave Bets a kiss on the cheek. She and Bets had never become friends, and Hermia sometimes suspected Bets was jealous of her closeness to her mother.

Hermia took them upstairs. Bets looked askance at the drab little room with its single bed, but Hermia's mother said heartily: 'Well, this isn't bad, for wartime.'

'I don't spend much time here,' Hermia lied. In fact she spent long, lonely evenings reading and listening to the radio.

She lit the gas ring to make tea and sliced up a small cake she had bought for the occasion.

Mother said: 'I don't suppose you've heard from Arne?'

'No. I wrote to him via the British legation in Stockholm, and they forwarded the letter, but I never heard back, so I don't know whether he got it.'

'Oh, dear.'

Bets said: 'I wish I'd met him. What's he like?'

Falling in love with Arne had been like skiing

49

downhill, Hermia thought: a little push to get started, a sudden increase in speed, and then, before she was quite ready, the exhilarating feeling of hurtling down the piste at a breakneck pace, unable to stop. But how to explain that? 'He looks like a movie star, he's a wonderful athlete, and he has the charm of an Irishman, but that's not it,' Hermia said. 'It's just so easy to be with him. Whatever happens, he just laughs. I get angry sometimes – though never at him – and he smiles at me and says: "There's no one like you, Hermia, I swear." Dear God, I do miss him.' She fought back tears.

Her mother said briskly: 'Plenty of men have fallen in love with you, but there aren't many who can put up with you.' Mags's conversational style was as unadorned as Hermia's own. 'You should have nailed his foot to the floor while you had the chance.'

Hermia changed the subject and asked them about the Blitz. Bets spent air raids under the kitchen table, but Mags drove her ambulance through the bombs. Hermia's mother had always been a formidable woman, somewhat too direct and tactless for a diplomat's wife, but war had brought out her strength and courage, just as a secret service suddenly short of men had allowed Hermia to flourish. 'The Luftwaffe can't keep this up indefinitely,' said Mags. 'They don't have an unending supply of aircraft and pilots. If our bombers keep pounding German industry, it must have an effect eventually.'

Bets said: 'Meanwhile, innocent German women and children are suffering just as we do.'

'I know, but that's what war is about,' said Mags.

Hermia recalled her conversation with Digby Hoare. People like Mags and Bets imagined that the British bombing campaign was undermining the Nazis. It was a good thing they had no inkling that half the bombers were being shot down. If people knew the truth they might give up.

Mags began to tell a long story about rescuing a dog from a burning building, and Hermia listened with half an ear, thinking about Digby. If Freya was a machine, and the Germans were using it to defend their borders, it might well be in Denmark. Was there anything she could do to investigate? Digby had said the machine might emit some kind of beam, either optical pulses or radio waves. Such emissions ought to be detectable. Perhaps her Nightwatchmen could do something.

She began to feel excited about the idea. She could send a message to the Nightwatchmen. But first, she needed more information. She would start work on it tonight, she decided, as soon as she had seen Mags and Bets back on to their train.

She began to feel impatient for them to go. 'More cake, Mother?' she said.

THREE

Jansborg Skole was three hundred years old, and proud of it.

Originally the school had consisted of a church and one house where the boys ate, slept and had lessons. Now it was a complex of old and new red-brick buildings. The library, at one time the finest in Denmark, was a separate building as large as the church. There were science laboratories, modern dormitories, an infirmary, and a gym in a converted barn.

Harald Olufsen was walking from the refectory to the gym. It was twelve noon, and the boys had just finished lunch – a make-it-yourself open sandwich with cold pork and pickles, the same meal that had been served every Wednesday throughout the seven years he had attended the school.

He thought it was stupid to be proud that the institution was old. When teachers spoke reverently of the school's history, he was reminded of old fishermen's wives on Sande who liked to say: 'I'm over seventy, now,' with a coy smile, as if it were some kind of achievement.

As he passed the headmaster's house, the head's

wife came out and smiled at him. 'Good morning, Mia,' he said politely. The head was always called Heis, the Ancient Greek word for the number one, so his wife was Mia, the feminine form of the same Greek word. The school had stopped teaching Greek five years ago, but traditions died hard.

'Any news, Harald?' she asked.

Harald had a home-made radio that could pick up the BBC. 'The Iraqi rebels have been defeated,' he said. 'The British have entered Baghdad.'

'A British victory,' she said. 'That makes a change.'

Mia was a plain woman with a homely face and lifeless brown hair, always dressed in shapeless clothes, but she was one of only two women at the school, and the boys constantly speculated about what she looked like naked. Harald wondered if he would ever stop being obsessed with sex. Theoretically, he believed that after sleeping with your wife every night for years you must get used to it, and even become bored, but he just could not imagine it.

The next lesson should have been two hours of maths, but today there was a visitor. He was Svend Agger, an old boy of the school who now represented his home town in the Rigsdag, the nation's parliament. The entire school was to hear him speak in the gym, the only room big enough to hold all one hundred and twenty boys. Harald would have preferred to do maths.

He could not remember the precise moment when school work had become interesting. As a small boy, he had regarded every lesson as an infuriating distraction from important business such as damming streams and building tree houses. Around the age of fourteen, almost without noticing it, he had begun to find physics and chemistry more exciting than playing in the woods. He had been thrilled to discover that the inventor of quantum physics was a Danish scientist, Niels Bohr. Bohr's interpretation of the periodic table of the elements, explaining chemical reactions by the atomic structure of the elements involved, seemed to Harald a divine revelation, a fundamental and deeply satisfying account of what the universe was made of. He worshipped Bohr the way other boys adored Kaj Hansen – 'Little Kaj' – the soccer hero who played inside forward for the team known as B93 København. Harald had applied to study physics at the University of Copenhagen, where Bohr was director of the Institute of Theoretical Physics.

Education cost money. Fortunately Harald's grandfather, seeing his own son enter a profession that would keep him poor all his life, had provided for his grandsons. His legacy had paid for Arne and Harald to go to Jansborg Skole. It would also finance Harald's time at university.

He entered the gym. The younger boys had put out benches in neat rows. Harald sat at the back, next to Josef Duchwitz. Josef was very small, and his surname sounded like the English word 'duck', so he had been nicknamed Anaticula, the Latin word for a duckling. Over the years it had got shortened to Tik. The two boys had very different backgrounds – Tik was from a wealthy Jewish family – yet they had been close friends all through school.

A few moments later, Mads Kirke sat next to Harald. Mads was in the same year. He came from a distinguished military family: his grandfather a general, his late father a defence minister in the thirties. His cousin Poul was a pilot with Arne at the flying school.

The three friends were science students. They were usually together, and they looked comically different – Harald tall and blond, Tik small and dark, Mads a freckled redhead – so that when a witty English master had referred to them as the Three Stooges, the nickname had stuck.

Heis, the head teacher, came in with the visitor, and the boys stood up politely. Heis was tall and thin with glasses perched on the bridge of a beaky nose. He had spent ten years in the army, but it was easy to see why he had switched to schoolteaching. A mild-mannered man, he seemed apologetic about being in authority. He was liked rather than feared. The boys obeyed him because they did not want to hurt his feelings.

When they had sat down again, Heis introduced the parliamentary deputy, a small man so unimpressive that anyone would have thought he was the schoolteacher and Heis the distinguished guest. Agger began to talk about the German occupation.

Harald remembered the day it had begun, fourteen months before. He had been woken up in the middle of the night by aircraft roaring overhead. The Three Stooges had gone up on the roof of the dormitory to watch but, after a dozen or so aircraft had passed over, nothing else happened, so they went back to bed.

He had learned no more until morning. He had been brushing his teeth in the communal bathroom when a teacher had rushed in and said: 'The Germans have landed!' After breakfast, at eight o'clock when the boys assembled in the gym for the morning song and announcements, the head had told them the news. 'Go to your rooms and destroy anything that might indicate opposition to the Nazis or sympathy with Britain,' he had said. Harald had taken down his favourite poster, a picture of a Tiger Moth biplane with RAF roundels on its wings.

Later that day – a Tuesday – the older boys had been detailed to fill sandbags and carry them to the church to cover the priceless ancient carvings and sarcophagi. Behind the altar was the tomb of the school's founder, his stone likeness lying in state, dressed in medieval armour with an eye-catchingly large codpiece. Harald had caused great amusement by mounting a sandbag end-up on the protrusion. Heis had not appreciated the joke, and Harald's punishment had been to spend the afternoon moving paintings to the crypt for safety.

All the precautions had been unnecessary. The school was in a village outside Copenhagen, and it was a year before they saw any Germans. There had never been any bombing or even gunfire.

Denmark had surrendered within twenty-four hours. 'Subsequent events have shown the wisdom of that decision,' said the speaker with irritating smugness, and there was a susurration of dissent as the boys shifted uncomfortably in their seats and muttered comments.

'Our king continues on his throne,' Agger went on. Next to Harald, Mads grunted disgustedly. Harald shared Mads's annoyance. King Christian X rode out on horseback most days, showing himself to the people on the streets of Copenhagen, but it seemed an empty gesture.

'The German presence has been on the whole benign,' the speaker went on. 'Denmark has proved that a partial loss of independence, due to the exigencies of war, need not necessarily lead to undue hardship and strife. The lesson, for boys such as yourselves, is that there may be more honour in submission and obedience than in ill-considered rebellion.' He sat down.

Heis clapped politely, and the boys followed suit, though without enthusiasm. If the head had been a shrewder judge of an audience's mood, he would have ended the session then; but instead he smiled and said: 'Well, boys, any questions for our guest?'

Mads was on his feet in an instant. 'Sir, Norway was invaded on the same day as Denmark, but the Norwegians fought for two months. Doesn't that make us cowards?' His tone was scrupulously polite, but the question was challenging, and there was a rumble of agreement from the boys.

'A naive view,' Agger said. His dismissive tone angered Harald.

Heis intervened. 'Norway is a land of mountains and fjords, difficult to conquer,' he said, bringing his military expertise to bear. 'Denmark is a flat country with a good road system – impossible to defend against a large motorized army.'

Agger added: 'To put up a fight would have caused unnecessary bloodshed, and the end result would have been no different.'

Mads said rudely: 'Except that we would have been able to walk around with our heads held high, instead of hanging them in shame.' It sounded to Harald like something he might have heard at home from his military relations.

Agger coloured. 'The better part of valour is discretion, as Shakespeare wrote.'

Mads said: 'In fact, sir, that was said by Falstaff, the most famous coward in world literature.' The boys laughed and clapped.

'Now, now, Kirke,' said Heis mildly. 'I know you feel strongly about this, but there's no need for discourtesy.' He looked around the room and pointed to one of the younger boys. 'Yes, Borr.'

'Sir, don't you think Herr Hitler's philosophy of national pride and racial purity could be beneficial if adopted here in Denmark?' Woldemar Borr was the son of a prominent Danish Nazi.

'Elements of it, perhaps,' Agger said. 'But Germany and Denmark are different countries.' That was plain prevarication, Harald thought angrily. Couldn't the man find the guts to say that racial persecution was wrong?

Heis said plaintively: 'Would any boy like to ask Mr Agger about his everyday work as a member of the Rigsdag, perhaps?'

Tik stood up. Agger's self-satisfied tone had irritated him, too. 'Don't you feel like a puppet?' he said. 'After all, it's the Germans who really rule us. You're just pretending.'

'Our nation continues to be governed by our Danish parliament,' Agger replied.

Tik muttered: 'Yes, so you get to keep your job.' The boys nearby heard him and laughed.

'The political parties remain – even the Communists,' Agger went on. 'We have our own police, and our armed forces.'

'But the minute the Rigsdag does something the Germans disapprove of, it will be closed down, and the police and the military will be disarmed,' Tik argued. 'So you're acting in a farce.'

Heis began to look annoyed. 'Remember your manners, please, Duchwitz,' he said peevishly.

'That's all right, Heis,' said Agger. 'I like a lively discussion. If Duchwitz thinks our parliament is useless, he should compare our circumstances with those prevailing in France. Because of our policy of cooperation with the Germans, life is a great deal better, for ordinary Danish people, than it might be.'

Harald had heard enough. He stood up and spoke

without waiting for permission from Heis. 'And what if the Nazis come for Duchwitz?' he said. 'Will you advise friendly cooperation then?'

'And why should they come for Duchwitz?'

'The same reason they came for my uncle in Hamburg – because he's a Jew.'

Some of the boys looked around with interest. They probably had not realized Tik was Jewish. The Duchwitz family was not religious, and Tik went along to services in the ancient redbrick church just like everyone else.

Agger showed irritation for the first time. 'The occupying forces have demonstrated complete tolerance towards Danish Jews.'

'So far,' Harald argued. 'But what if they change their minds? Suppose they decide that Tik is just as Jewish as my Uncle Joachim? What is your advice to us then? Shall we stand aside while they march in and seize him? Or should we now be organizing a Resistance movement in preparation for that day?'

'Your best plan is to make sure you are never faced with such a decision, by supporting the policy of cooperation with the occupying power.'

The smooth evasiveness of the answer maddened Harald. 'But what if that doesn't work?' he persisted. 'Why won't you answer the question? What do we do when the Nazis come for our friends?'

Heis put in: 'You're asking what's called a hypothetical question, Olufsen,' he said. 'Men in public life prefer not to meet trouble half way.'

'The question is how far his policy of cooperation

will go,' Harald said hotly. 'And there won't be time for debate when they bang on your door in the middle of the night, Heis.'

For a moment, Heis looked ready to reprimand Harald for rudeness, but in the end he answered mildly. 'You've made an interesting point, and Mr Agger has answered it quite thoroughly,' he said. 'Now, I think we've had a good discussion, and it's time to go back to our lessons. But first, let's thank our guest for taking the time out of his busy life to come and visit us.' He raised his hands to lead a round of applause.

Harald stopped him. 'Make him answer the question!' he shouted. 'Should we have a Resistance movement, or will we let the Nazis do anything they like? For God's sake, what lessons could be more important than this?'

The room went quiet. Arguing with the staff was permitted, within reason, but Harald had crossed the line into defiance.

'I think you'd better leave us,' Heis said. 'Off you go, and I'll see you afterwards.'

This made Harald furious. Boiling with frustration, he stood up. The room remained silent as all the boys watched him walk to the door. He knew he should leave quietly, but he could not bring himself to do it. He turned at the door and pointed an accusing finger at Heis. 'You won't be able to tell the Gestapo to leave the damn room!' he said.

Then he went out and slammed the door.

FOUR

Peter Flemming's alarm clock went off at half past five in the morning. He silenced it, turned on the light, and sat upright in bed. Inge was lying on her back, eyes open, staring at the ceiling, as expressionless as a corpse. He looked at her for a moment, then got up.

He went into the little kitchen of their Copenhagen apartment and turned on the radio. A Danish reporter was reading a sentimental statement by the Germans about the death of Admiral Luetjens, who had gone down with the Bismarck ten days ago. Peter put a small pot of oatmeal on the cooker, then laid a tray. He buttered a slice of rye bread and made ersatz coffee.

He felt optimistic, and after a moment he recalled why. Yesterday there had been a break in the case he was working on.

He was a detective-inspector in the security unit, a section of the Copenhagen criminal investigation department whose job was to keep tabs on union organizers, Communists, foreigners and other potential troublemakers. His boss, the head of the department, was superintendent Frederik Juel, clever but lazy. Educated at the famous Jansborg Skole, Juel was fond of the Latin proverb *Quieta non movere*, Let sleeping dogs lie. He was descended from a hero of Danish naval history, but the aggression had long been bred out of his line.

In the past fourteen months their work had expanded, as opponents of German rule had been added to the department's watch list.

So far the only outward sign of resistance had been the appearance of underground newspapers such as *Reality*, the one the Olufsen boy had dropped. Juel believed the illegal newspapers were harmless, if not actually beneficial as a safety valve, and refused to pursue the publishers. This attitude infuriated Peter. Leaving criminals at large, to continue their offences, seemed madness to him.

The Germans did not really like Juel's *laissez-faire* attitude, but so far they had not pushed the matter to a confrontation. Juel's liaison with the occupying power was General Walter Braun, a career soldier who had lost a lung in the battle of France. Braun's aim was to keep Denmark tranquil at all costs. He would not overrule Juel unless forced to.

Recently Peter had learned that copies of *Reality* were being smuggled to Sweden. Until now, he had been obliged to abide by his boss's hands-off rule, but he hoped Juel's complacency would be shaken by the news that the papers were finding their way out of the country. Last night, a Swedish detective who was a personal friend of Peter's had called to say he thought the paper was being carried on a Lufthansa flight from Berlin to Stockholm that stopped at

Copenhagen. That was the breakthrough that accounted for Peter's feeling of excitement when he woke up. He could be on the brink of a triumph.

When the oatmeal was ready, he added milk and sugar then took the tray into the bedroom.

He helped Inge sit upright. He tasted the oatmeal to make sure it was not too hot, then began to feed her with a spoon.

A year ago, just before petrol restrictions came in, Peter and Inge had been driving to the beach when a young man in a new sports car had crashed into them. Peter had broken both his legs and recovered rapidly. Inge had smashed her skull, and she would never be the same.

The other driver, Finn Jonk, the son of a well-known university professor, had been thrown clear and landed in a bush, unharmed.

He had no driving licence – it had been taken from him by the courts after a previous accident – and he had been drunk. But the Jonk family had hired a top lawyer who had succeeded in delaying the trial for a year, so Finn still had not been punished for destroying Inge's mind. The personal tragedy, for Inge and Peter, was also an example of the disgraceful way crimes could go unpunished in modern society. Whatever you might say against the Nazis, they were gratifyingly tough on criminals.

When Inge had eaten her breakfast, Peter took her to the toilet, then bathed her. She had always been scrupulously neat and clean. It was one of the things he had loved about her. She was especially clean about sex, always washing carefully afterwards – something he appreciated. Not all girls were like that. One woman he had slept with, a nightclub singer he had met during a raid and had a brief affair with, had objected to his washing himself after sex, saying it was unromantic.

Inge showed no reaction as he bathed her. He had learned to be equally unmoved, even when he touched the most intimate parts of her body. He dried her soft skin with a big towel, then dressed her. The most difficult part was putting her stockings on. First he rolled the stocking, leaving only the toe sticking out. Then he carefully eased it over her foot and unrolled it up her calf and over her knee, finally fastening the top to the clips of the garter belt. When he started doing this he had laddered them every time, but he was a persistent man, and could be very patient when he had his mind set on achieving something; and now he was expert.

He helped her into a cheerful yellow cotton dress, then added a gold wristwatch and bracelet. She could not tell the time, but he sometimes thought she came near to smiling when she saw jewellery glinting on her wrists.

When he had brushed her hair, they both looked at her reflection in the mirror. She was a pretty, pale blonde, and before the accident she had had a flirtatious smile and a coy way of fluttering her eyelashes. Now her face was blank.

On their Whitsun visit to Sande, Peter's father had tried to persuade him to put Inge into a private nursing home. Peter could not afford the fees, but Axel was willing to pay. He said he wanted Peter to be free, though the truth was he was desperate for a grandson to bear his name. However, Peter felt it was his duty to take care of his wife. For him, duty was the most important of a man's obligations. If he shirked it, he would lose his self-respect.

He took Inge to the living room and sat her by the window. He left the radio playing music at low volume, then returned to the bathroom.

The face in his shaving mirror was regular and well-proportioned. Inge had used to say he looked like a film star. Since the accident he had noticed a few grey hairs in his red morning stubble, and there were lines of weariness around the orange-brown eyes. But there was a proud look in the set of his head, and an immovable rectitude in the straight line of his lips.

When he had shaved he tied his tie and strapped on his shoulder holster with the standard issue Walther 7.65mm pistol, the smaller seven-round 'PPK' version designed as a concealed weapon for detectives. Then he stood in the kitchen and ate three slices of dry bread, saving the scarce butter for Inge.

The nurse was supposed to come at eight o'clock.

Between eight and five past Peter's mood changed. He began to pace up and down the little hallway of the apartment. He lit a cigarette then crushed it out impatiently. He looked at his wristwatch every few seconds.

Between five and ten past he became angry. Did he not have enough to cope with? He combined caring for his helpless wife with a taxing and highly responsible job as a police detective. The nurse had no *right* to let him down.

When she rang the doorbell at eight fifteen, he threw open the door and shouted: 'How dare you be late?'

She was a plump girl of nineteen, wearing a carefully pressed uniform, her hair neatly arranged under her nurse's cap, her round face lightly made up. She was shocked by his anger. 'I'm sorry,' she said.

He stood aside to let her in. He felt a strong temptation to strike her, and she obviously sensed this, for she hurried past him nervously.

He followed her into the living room. 'You had time to do your hair and make-up,' he said angrily.

'I said I'm sorry.'

'Don't you realize that I have a very demanding job? You've got nothing on your mind more important than walking with boys in the Tivoli Garden – yet you can't even get to work on time!'

She looked nervously at his gun in the shoulder holster, as if she was afraid he was going to shoot her. 'The bus was late,' she said in a shaky voice.

'Get an earlier bus, you lazy cow!'

'Oh!' She looked about to cry.

Peter turned away, fighting an urge to slap her fat face. If she walked out, he would be in worse trouble. He put on his jacket and went to the door. 'Don't you ever be late again!' he shouted. Then he left the apartment.

Outside the building he jumped on to a tram

heading for the city centre. He lit a cigarette and smoked in rapid puffs, trying to calm himself. He was still angry when he got off outside the Politigaarden, the daringly modern police headquarters, but the sight of the building soothed him: its squat shape gave a reassuring impression of strength, its blindingly white stone spoke of purity, and its rows of identical windows symbolized order and the predictability of justice. He passed through the dark vestibule. Hidden in the centre of the building was a large open courtyard, circular, with a ring of double pillars marking a sheltered walkway like the cloisters of a monastery. Peter crossed the courtyard and entered his section.

He was greeted by detective constable Tilde Jespersen, one of a handful of women in the Copenhagen force. The young widow of a policeman, she was as tough and smart as any cop in the department. Peter often used her for surveillance work, a role in which a woman was less likely to arouse suspicion. She was rather attractive, with blue eyes and fair curly hair and the kind of small, curvy figure that women would call too fat but men thought just right. 'Bus delayed?' she said sympathetically.

'No. Inge's nurse turned up a quarter of an hour late. Empty-headed flibbertigibbet.'

'Oh, dear.'

'Anything happening?'

'I'm afraid so. General Braun is with Juel. They want to see you as soon as you get here.'

That was bad luck: a visit from Braun on the day

Peter was late. 'Damn nurse,' he muttered, and headed for Juel's office.

Juel's upright carriage and piercing blue eyes would have suited his naval namesake. He spoke German as a courtesy to Braun. All educated Danes could get by in German, and English as well. 'Where have you been, Flemming?' he said to Peter. 'We are waiting.'

'I apologize,' Peter replied in the same language. He did not give the reason for his lateness: excuses were undignified.

General Braun was in his forties. He had probably been handsome once, but the explosion that destroyed his lung had also taken away part of his jaw, and the right side of his face was deformed. Perhaps because of his damaged appearance, he always wore an immaculate field service uniform, complete with high boots and holstered pistol.

He was courteous and reasonable in conversation. His voice was a soft near-whisper. 'Take a look at this, if you would, Inspector Flemming,' he said. He had spread several newspapers on Peter's desk, all folded open to show a particular report. It was the same story in each newspaper, Peter saw: an account of the butter shortage in Denmark, blaming the Germans for taking it all. The newspapers were the *Toronto Globe*, the *Washington Post* and the *Los Angeles Times*. Also on the table was the Danish underground newspaper *Reality*, badly printed and amateur-looking beside the legitimate publications, but containing the original story the others had copied. It was a small triumph of propaganda.

Juel said: 'We know most of the people who produce these home-made newspapers.' He spoke in a tone of languid assurance that irritated Peter. You might imagine, from his manner, that it was he, not his famous ancestor, who had defeated the Swedish navy at the battle of Koge Bay. 'We could pick them all up, of course. But I'd rather leave them alone and keep an eye on them. Then, if they do something serious like blowing up a bridge, we'll know who to arrest.'

Peter thought that was stupid. They should be arrested now, to *stop* them blowing up bridges. But he had had this argument with Juel before, so he clamped his teeth together and said nothing.

Braun said: 'That might have been acceptable when their activities were confined to Denmark. But this story has gone all over the world! Berlin is furious. And the last thing we need is a clampdown. We'll have the damned Gestapo stamping all over town in their jackboots, stirring up trouble and throwing people in jail, and God knows where it will end.'

Peter was gratified. The news was having the effect he wanted. 'I'm already working on this,' he said. 'All these American newspapers got the story from the Reuters wire service, which picked it up in Stockholm. I believe the *Reality* newspaper is being smuggled out to Sweden.'

'Good work!' said Braun.

Peter stole a glance at Juel, who looked angry. So he should. Peter was a better detective than his boss, and incidents such as this proved it. Two years ago, when the post of head of the security unit had fallen vacant, Peter had applied for the job, but Juel had got it. Peter was a few years younger than Juel, but had more successful cases to his credit. However, Juel belonged to a smug metropolitan élite who had all gone to the same schools, and Peter was sure they conspired to keep the best jobs for themselves and hold back talented outsiders.

Now Juel said: 'But how could the newspaper be smuggled out? All packages are inspected by the censors.'

Peter hesitated. He had wanted to get confirmation before revealing what he suspected. His information from Sweden could be wrong. However, Braun was right here in front of him, pawing the earth and champing at the bit, and this was not the moment to equivocate. 'I've had a tip. Last night I spoke to a detective friend in Stockholm who has been discreetly asking questions at the wire service office. He thinks the newspaper comes on the Lufthansa flight from Berlin to Stockholm that stops here.'

Braun nodded excitedly. 'So if we search every passenger boarding the flight here in Copenhagen, we should find the latest edition.'

'Yes.'

'Does the flight go today?'

Peter's heart sank. This was not the way he worked. He preferred to verify information before rushing into a raid. But he was grateful for Braun's aggressive attitude – a pleasing contrast with Juel's laziness and caution. Anyway, he could not hold back the avalanche of Braun's eagerness. 'Yes, in a few hours,' he said, hiding his misgivings.

'Then let's get moving!'

Haste could ruin everything. Peter could not let Braun take charge of the operation. 'May I make a suggestion, General?'

'Of course.'

'We must act discreetly, to avoid forewarning our culprit. Let's assemble a team of detectives and German officers, but keep them here at headquarters until the last minute. Allow the passengers to assemble for the flight before we move in. I'll go alone to Kastrup aerodrome to make arrangements quietly. When the passengers have checked their baggage, the aircraft has landed and refuelled, and they're about to board, it will be too late for anyone to slip away unnoticed – and then we can pounce.'

Braun smiled knowingly. 'You're afraid that a lot of Germans marching around would give the game away.'

'Not at all, sir,' Peter said with a straight face. When the occupiers made fun of themselves it was not wise to join in. 'It will be important for you and your men to accompany us, in case there is any need to question German citizens.'

Braun's face stiffened, his self-deprecating sally rebuffed. 'Quite so,' he said. He went to the door. 'Call me at my office when your team is ready to depart.' He left.

Peter was relieved. At least he had regained control.

His only worry was that Braun's enthusiasm might have forced him to move too soon.

'Well done, for tracing the smuggling route,' Juel said condescendingly. 'Good detective work. But it would have been tactful to tell me before you told Braun.'

'I'm sorry, sir,' Peter said. In fact it would not have been possible: Juel had already left for the day when the Swedish detective had called last night. But Peter did not make the excuse.

'All right,' Juel said. 'Put together a squad and send them to me for briefing. Then go to the aerodrome and phone me when the passengers are ready to board.'

Peter left Juel's room and returned to Tilde's desk in the main office. She was wearing a jacket, blouse and skirt in different shades of light blue, like a girl in a French painting. 'How did it go?' she asked.

'I was late, but I made up for it.'

'Good.'

'There's a raid on at the aerodrome this morning,' he told her. He knew which detectives he wanted with him. 'I'll take Bent Conrad, Peder Dresler and Knut Ellegard.' Detective sergeant Conrad was enthusiastically pro-German. Detective constables Dresler and Ellegard had no strong political or patriotic feelings, but were conscientious policemen who took orders and did a thorough job. 'And I'd like you to come along, too, if you would, in case there are female suspects to be searched.'

'Of course.'

'Juel will brief you all. I'm going ahead to Kastrup.' Peter went to the door, then turned back. 'How's little Stig?' Tilde had a son six years old, looked after by his grandmother during the working day.

She smiled. 'He's fine. His reading is coming along fast.'

'He'll be chief of police one day.'

Her face darkened. 'I don't want him to be a cop.'

Peter nodded. Tilde's husband had been killed in a shootout with a gang of smugglers. 'I understand.'

She added defensively: 'Would you want your son to do this job?'

He shrugged. 'I don't have any children, and I'm not likely to.'

She gave him an enigmatic look. 'You don't know what the future holds.'

'True.' He turned away. He did not want to start that discussion on a busy day. 'I'll call in.'

'OK.'

Peter took one of the police department's unmarked black Buicks, recently equipped with two-way radio. He drove out of the city and across a bridge to the island of Amager, where Kastrup Aerodrome was located. It was a sunny day, and from the road he could see people on the beach.

He looked like a businessman or lawyer in his conservative chalk-stripe suit and discreetly patterned tie. He did not have a briefcase, but for verisimilitude he had brought with him a file folder, filled with papers taken from a waste basket.

He felt anxious as he approached the aerodrome. If he could have had another day or two, he might have been able to establish whether every flight carried illegal packages, or only some. There was a maddening possibility that today he might find nothing, but his raid would alert the subversive group, and they might change to a different route. Then he would have to start again.

The aerodrome was a scatter of low buildings on one side of a single runway. It was heavily guarded by German troops, but civilian flights continued to be operated by the Danish airline, DDL, and the Swedish ABA, as well as Lufthansa.

Peter parked outside the office of the airport controller. He told the secretary he was from the government's Aviation Safety Department, and was admitted instantly. The controller, Christian Varde, was a small man with a salesman's ready smile. Peter showed his police card. 'There will be a special security check on the Lufthansa flight to Stockholm today,' he said. 'It has been authorized by General Braun, who will be arriving shortly. We must get everything ready.'

A frightened look came over the face of the manager. He reached for the phone on his desk, but Peter covered the instrument with his own hand. 'No,' he said. 'Please do not forewarn anyone. Do you have a list of passengers expected to board the flight here?'

'My secretary does.'

'Ask her to bring it in.'

Varde called his secretary and she brought a sheet of paper. He gave it to Peter.

Peter said: 'Is the flight coming in on time from Berlin?'

'Yes.' Varde checked his watch. 'It should land in forty-five minutes.'

That was enough time, just.

It would simplify Peter's task if he had to search only those passengers joining the flight in Denmark. 'I want you to call the pilot and say that no one will be permitted to deplane at Kastrup today. That includes passengers and crew.'

'Very good.'

He looked at the list the secretary had brought. There were four names: two Danish men, a Danish woman and a German man. 'Where are the passengers now?'

'They should be checking in.'

'Take their baggage, but do not load it on to the aircraft until it has been searched by my men.'

'Very well.'

'The passengers, too, will be searched before they board. Is anything else loaded here, in addition to passengers and their luggage?'

'Coffee and sandwiches for the flight, and a bag of mail. And the fuel, of course.'

'The food and drink must be examined, and the mailbag. One of my men will observe the refuelling.'

'Fine.'

'Go now and send the message to the pilot. When

all the passengers have checked in, come and find me in the departure lounge. But please – try to give the impression that nothing special is happening.'

Varde went out.

Peter made his way to the departure area, racking his brains to make sure he had thought of everything. He sat in the lounge and discreetly studied the other passengers, wondering which of them would end up in jail today instead of on a plane. This morning there were scheduled flights to Berlin, Hamburg, the Norwegian capital of Oslo, the southern Swedish city of Malmo, and the Danish holiday island of Bornholm, so he could not be sure which of the passengers were destined for Stockholm.

There were only two women in the room: a young mother with two children, and a beautifully dressed older woman with white hair. The older woman could be the smuggler, Peter thought: her appearance might be intended to allay suspicion.

Three of the passengers wore German uniforms. Peter checked his list: his man was a Colonel von Schwarzkopf. Only one of the soldiers was a colonel. But it was wildly unlikely that a German officer would smuggle Danish underground newspapers.

All the others were men just like Peter, wearing suits and ties, holding their hats in their laps.

Trying to appear bored but patient, as if waiting for a flight, he watched everyone carefully, alert for signs that someone had sensed the imminent security check. Some passengers looked nervous, but that could just be fear of flying. Peter was most concerned to make sure no one tried to throw away a package, or conceal papers somewhere in the lounge.

Varde reappeared. Beaming as if delighted to see Peter again, he said: 'All four passengers have checked in.'

'Good.' It was time to begin. 'Tell them that Lufthansa would like to offer them some special hospitality, then take them to your office. I'll follow.'

Varde nodded and went to the Lufthansa desk. While he was asking the Stockholm passengers to come forward, Peter went to a pay phone, called Tilde, and told her all was ready for the raid. Varde led the group of four passengers away, and Peter tagged on to the little procession.

When they were assembled in Varde's office, Peter revealed his identity. He showed his police badge to the German colonel. 'I'm acting under orders from General Braun,' he said to forestall protests. 'He is on his way here and will explain everything.'

The colonel looked annoyed, but sat down without comment, and the other three passengers – the white-haired lady and two Danish businessmen – did the same. Peter leaned against the wall, watching them, alert for guilty behaviour. Each had a bag of some kind: the old lady a large handbag, the officer a slim document case, the businessmen briefcases. Any of them could be carrying copies of an illegal newspaper.

Varde said brightly: 'May I offer you tea or coffee while you're waiting?'

Peter checked his watch. The flight from Berlin was

78

due now. He looked out of Varde's window and saw it coming in to land. The aircraft was a Junkers Ju-52 trimotor – an ugly machine, he thought: its surface was corrugated, like a shed roof, and the third engine, protruding from the nose, looked like the snout of a pig. But it approached at a remarkably low speed for such a heavy aircraft, and the effect was quite majestic. It touched down and taxied to the terminal. The door opened, and the crew threw down the chocks that secured the wheels when the aircraft was parked.

Braun and Juel arrived, with the four detectives Peter had chosen, while the waiting passengers were drinking the airport's ersatz coffee.

Peter watched keenly while his detectives emptied out the men's briefcases and the white-haired lady's handbag. It was quite possible the spy would have the illegal newspaper in hand baggage, he thought. Then the traitor could claim he had brought it to read on the plane. Not that it would do him any good.

But the contents of the bags were innocent.

Tilde took the lady into another room to be searched, while the three male suspects removed their outer clothing. Braun patted down the colonel, and Sergeant Conrad did the Danes. Nothing was found.

Peter was disappointed, but he told himself it was much more likely that the contraband would be in checked baggage.

The passengers were allowed to return to the lounge, but not to board the aircraft. Their luggage was lined up on the apron outside the terminal building: two new-looking crocodile cases that undoubtedly belonged to the old lady, a duffle bag that was probably the colonel's, a tan leather suitcase and a cheap cardboard one.

Peter felt confident he would find a copy of *Reality* in one of them.

Bent Conrad got the keys from the passengers. 'I bet it's the old woman,' he murmured to Peter. 'She looks like a Jew to me.'

'Just unlock the luggage,' Peter said.

Conrad opened all the bags and Peter began to search them, with Juel and Braun looking over his shoulders, and a crowd of people watching through the window of the departure lounge. He imagined the moment when he would triumphantly produce the newspaper and flourish it in front of everyone.

The crocodile cases were stuffed with expensive old-fashioned clothing, which he dumped on the ground. The duffle bag contained shaving tackle, a change of underwear, and a perfectly pressed uniform shirt. The businessman's tan leather case held papers as well as clothing, and Peter looked through them all carefully, but there were no newspapers nor anything suspicious.

He had left the cheap cardboard suitcase until last, figuring the less affluent businessman was the likeliest of the four passengers to be a spy.

The case was half empty. It held a white shirt and a black tie, supporting the man's story that he was going to a funeral. There was also a well-worn black Bible. But no newspaper.

Peter began to wonder despairingly if his fears had been well founded, and this was the wrong day for the raid. He felt angry that he had let himself be pushed into acting prematurely. He controlled his fury. He was not finished yet.

He took a penknife from his pocket. He pushed its point into the lining of the old lady's expensive luggage and tore a ragged gash in the white silk. He heard Juel grunt with surprise at the sudden violence of the gesture. Peter ran his hand beneath the ripped lining. To his dismay, nothing was hidden there.

He did the same to the businessman's leather case, with the same result. The second businessman's cardboard suitcase had no lining, and Peter could see nothing in its structure that might serve as a hiding place.

Feeling his face redden with frustration and embarrassment, he cut the stitching on the leather base of the colonel's canvas duffle and felt inside for concealed papers. There was nothing.

He looked up to see Braun, Juel, and the detectives staring at him. Their faces showed fascination and a hint of fear. His behaviour was beginning to look a little crazy, he realized.

To hell with that.

Juel said languidly: 'Perhaps your information was wrong, Flemming.'

And wouldn't that please you, Peter thought resentfully. But he was not finished yet.

He saw Varde watching from the departure lounge,

and beckoned him. The man's smile looked strained as he contemplated the wreckage of his customers' luggage. 'Where is the mailbag?' Peter said.

'In the baggage office.'

'Well, what are you waiting for? Bring it here, idiot!'

Varde went off. Peter pointed at the luggage with a disgusted gesture and said to his detectives: 'Get rid of this stuff.'

Dresler and Ellegard repacked the suitcases roughly. A baggage handler came to take them to the Junkers. 'Wait,' Peter said as the man began to pick up the cases. 'Search him, sergeant.' Conrad searched the man and found nothing.

Varde brought the mailbag and Peter emptied the letters on the ground. They all bore the stamp of the censor. There were two envelopes large enough to hold a newspaper, one white and one brown. He ripped open the white one. It held six copies of a legal document, some kind of contract. The brown envelope contained the catalogue of a Copenhagen glassware factory. Peter cursed aloud.

A trolley bearing a tray of sandwiches and several coffee pots was wheeled out for Peter's inspection. This was Peter's last hope. He opened each pot and poured the coffee out on the ground. Juel muttered something about this being unnecessary, but Peter was too desperate to care. He pulled away the linen napkins covering the tray and poked about among the sandwiches. To his horror, there was nothing. In a rage, he picked up the tray and dumped the sandwiches on the ground, hoping to find a newspaper underneath, but there was only another linen napkin.

He realized he was going to be completely humiliated, and that made him madder.

'Begin refuelling,' he said. 'I'll watch.'

A tanker was driven out to the Junkers. The detectives put out their cigarettes and looked on as aviation fuel was pumped into the wings of the aircraft. Peter knew this was useless, but he persevered stubbornly, wearing a wooden expression, because he could not think what else to do. Passengers watched curiously through the rectangular windows of the Junkers, no doubt wondering why a German general and six civilians needed to observe the refuelling.

The tanks were filled and the caps closed.

Peter could not think of any way to delay the take-off. He had been wrong, and now he looked a fool.

'Let the passengers board,' he said with suppressed fury.

He returned to the departure lounge, his humiliation complete. He wanted to strangle someone. He had made a complete mess of things in front of General Braun as well as Superintendent Juel. The appointments board would feel justified in having picked Juel instead of Peter for the top job. Juel might even use this fiasco as an excuse for having Peter shunted sideways to some low-profile department such as Traffic.

He stopped in the lounge to watch the take-off. Juel, Braun and the detectives waited with him. Varde was standing nearby, trying hard to look as if nothing out of the ordinary had happened. They watched while the four angry passengers boarded. The chocks were removed from the wheels by the ground crew and thrown on board, then the door was closed.

As the aircraft moved off its stand, Peter was struck by inspiration. 'Stop the plane,' he said to Varde.

Juel said: 'For God's sake . . .'

Varde looked as if he might cry. He turned to General Braun. 'Sir, my passengers . . .'

'Stop the plane!' Peter repeated.

Varde continued to look pleadingly at Braun. After a moment, Braun nodded. 'Do as he says.'

Varde picked up a phone.

Juel said: 'My God, Flemming, this had better be good.'

The aircraft rolled on to the runway, turned a full circle, and came back to its stand. The door opened, and the chocks were thrown down to the ground crew.

Peter led the rest of the detectives out on to the apron. The propellers slowed and stopped. Two men in overalls were wedging the chocks in front of the main wheels. Peter addressed one of them. 'Hand me that chock.'

The man looked scared, but did as he was told.

Peter took the chock from him. It was a simple triangular block of wood about a foot high – dirty, heavy, and solid.

'And the other one,' Peter said.

Ducking under the fuselage, the mechanic picked up the other and handed it over.

It looked the same, but felt lighter. Turning it over

in his hands, Peter found that one face was a sliding lid. He opened it. Inside was a package carefully wrapped in oilcloth.

Peter gave a sigh of profound satisfaction.

The mechanic turned and ran.

'Stop him!' Peter cried, but it was unnecessary. The man veered away from the men and tried to run past Tilde, no doubt imagining he could easily push her aside. She turned like a dancer, letting him pass, then stuck out a foot and tripped him. He went flying.

Dresler jumped on him, hauled him to his feet, and twisted his arm behind his back.

Peter nodded to Ellegard. 'Arrest the other mechanic. He must have known what was going on.'

Peter turned his attention to the package. He unwrapped the oilcloth. Inside were two copies of *Reality*. He handed them to Juel.

Juel looked at the papers, then up at Peter.

Peter stared at him expectantly, saying nothing, waiting.

Juel said reluctantly: 'Well done, Flemming.'

Peter smiled. 'Just doing my job, sir.'

Juel turned away.

Peter said to his detectives: 'Handcuff both mechanics and take them to headquarters for questioning.'

There was something else in the package. Peter pulled out a sheaf of papers clipped together. They were covered with typed characters in five-letter groups that made no sense. He stared at them in puzzlement for a moment. Then enlightenment dawned, and he realized this was a triumph greater than he had dreamed.

The papers he was holding bore a message in code.

Peter handed the papers to Braun. 'I think we have uncovered a spy ring, General.'

Braun looked at the papers and paled. 'My God, you're right.'

'Perhaps the German military has a department that specializes in breaking enemy ciphers?'

'It certainly does.'

'Good,' said Peter.

FIVE

An old-fashioned carriage drawn by two horses picked up Harald Olufsen and Tik Duchwitz at the railway station in Tik's home village of Kirstenslot. Tik explained that the carriage had been rotting in a barn for years, then had been resurrected when the Germans imposed petrol restrictions. The coachwork gleamed with fresh paint, but the team was a pair of ordinary carthorses borrowed from a farm. The coachman looked as if he might have been more comfortable behind a plough.

Harald was not sure why Tik had invited him for the weekend. The Three Stooges had never visited each other's homes, even though they had been close friends at school for seven years. Perhaps the invitation was a consequence of Harald's anti-Nazi outburst in class. Maybe Tik's parents were curious to meet the pastor's son who was so concerned about the persecution of Jews.

They drove from the station through a small village with a church and a tavern. At the far edge of the village they turned off the road and passed between a pair of massive stone lions. At the far end of a half-mile drive Harald saw a fairy-tale castle with battlements and turrets.

There were hundreds of castles in Denmark. Harald sometimes took comfort from that fact. Although it was a small country, it had not always surrendered abjectly to its belligerent neighbours. There might be something of the Viking spirit left.

Some castles were historic monuments, maintained as museums and visited by tourists. Many were little more than country manor houses occupied by prosperous farming families. In between were a number of spectacular homes owned by the wealthiest people in the land. Kirstenslot – the house had the same name as the village – was one of those.

Harald was intimidated. He had known the Duchwitz family were wealthy – Tik's father and uncle were bankers – but he was not prepared for this. He wondered anxiously if he would know the right ways to behave. Nothing about life at the parsonage had prepared him for a place such as this.

It was late on Saturday afternoon when the carriage dropped them at the cathedral-like front entrance. Harald walked in, carrying his small suitcase. The marbled hall was crammed with antique furniture, decorated vases, small statues and large oil paintings. Harald's family was inclined to take literally the Second Commandment, which forbade the making of a likeness of anything in heaven or on earth, so there were no pictures in the parsonage (though Harald knew that he and Arne had been secretly photographed as babies, for he had found the pictures hidden in his mother's stocking drawer). The wealth of art in the Duchwitz home made him mildly uncomfortable.

Tik led him up a grand staircase into a bedroom. 'This is my room,' he said. There were no old masters or Chinese vases here, just the kind of stuff an eighteen-year-old collected: a football, a picture of Marlene Dietrich looking sultry, a clarinet, and a framed advertisement for a Lancia Aprilla sports car designed by Pininfarina.

Harald picked up a framed photo. It showed Tik about four years before with a girl about the same age. 'Who's the girlfriend?'

'My twin sister, Karen.'

'Oh.' Harald knew, vaguely, that Tik had a twin. She was taller than Tik in the picture. It was a black-and-white photo, but she seemed to have lighter colouring. 'Obviously not an identical twin, she's too good-looking.'

'Identical twins have to be the same sex, idiot.'

'Where does she go to school?'

'The Danish Royal Ballet.'

'I didn't know they ran a school.'

'If you want to be in the corps you have to go to the school. Some girls start at the age of five. They do all the usual lessons, and dancing as well.'

'Does she like it?'

Tik shrugged. 'It's hard work, she says.' He opened a door and went along a short corridor to a bathroom and a second, smaller bedroom. Harald followed him. 'You'll be in here, if it's all right,' Tik said. 'We'll share the bathroom.'

'Great,' said Harald, dropping his case on the bed.

'You could have a grander room, but you'd be miles away.'

'This is better.'

'Come and say hello to my mother.'

Harald followed Tik along the main first-floor corridor. Tik tapped on a door, opened it a little, and said: 'Are you receiving gentlemen callers, Mother?'

A voice replied: 'Come in, Josef.'

Harald followed Tik into Mrs Duchwitz's boudoir, a pretty room with framed photographs on every level surface. Tik's mother looked like him. She was very short, though dumpy where Tik was slim, and she had the same dark eyes. She was about forty, but her black hair was already touched with grey.

Tik presented Harald, who shook her hand with a little bow. Mrs Duchwitz made them sit down and asked them about school. She was amiable and easy to talk to, and Harald began to feel less apprehensive about the weekend.

After a while she said: 'Go along and get ready for dinner, now.' The boys returned to Tik's room. Harald said anxiously: 'You don't wear anything special for dinner, do you?'

'Your blazer and tie are fine.'

It was all Harald had. The school blazer, trousers, overcoat, and cap, plus sports kit, were a major expense for the Olufsen family, and they had to be replaced constantly as he grew a couple of inches every year. He had no other clothes, apart from sweaters for the winter and shorts for the summer. 'What are you going to wear?' he asked Tik.

'A black jacket and grey flannels.'

Harald was glad he had brought a clean white shirt.

'Would you like to bathe first?' Tik said.

'Sure.' The idea that you had to have a bath before dinner seemed odd to Harald, but he told himself he was learning the ways of the rich.

He washed his hair in the bath, and Tik shaved at the same time. 'You don't shave twice a day at school,' Harald said.

'Mother's so fussy. And my beard is dark. She says I look like a coal miner if I don't shave in the evening.'

Harald put on his clean shirt and school trousers, then went into the bedroom to comb his damp hair in the mirror over the dressing table. While he was doing so, a girl walked in without knocking. 'Hello,' she said. 'You must be Harald.'

It was the girl in the photograph, but the monochrome picture had not done her justice. She had white skin and green eyes, and her curly hair was a vivid shade of coppery red. A tall figure in a long dark-green dress, she glided across the room like a ghost. With the easy strength of an athlete, she picked up a heavy chair by its back and turned it around to sit on it. She crossed her long legs and said: 'Well? Are you Harald?'

He managed to speak. 'Yes, I am.' He felt conscious of his bare feet. 'You're Tik's sister.'

'Tik?'

'That's what we call Josef at school.'

'Well, I'm Karen, and I don't have a nickname. I heard about your eruption at school. I think you're absolutely right. I hate the Nazis – who do they think they are?'

Tik emerged from the bathroom wrapped in a towel. 'Have you no regard for a gentleman's privacy?' he said.

'No, I don't,' she retorted. 'I want a cocktail, and they won't serve them until there's at least one male in the room. I believe servants make up these rules themselves, you know.'

'Well, just look the other way for a minute,' Tik said, and to Harald's surprise he dropped the towel.

Karen was unperturbed by her brother's nakedness and did not bother to look away. 'How are you, anyway, you black-eyed dwarf?' she said amiably as he pulled on clean white undershorts.

'I'm fine, though I'll be finer when the exams are over.'

'What will you do if you fail?'

'I suppose I'll work at the bank. Father will probably make me start at the bottom, filling the inkwells of the junior clerks.'

Harald said to Karen: 'He won't fail the exams.'

She replied: 'I suppose you're clever, like Josef.'

Tik said: 'Much cleverer, actually.'

Harald could not honestly deny it. Feeling bashful, he asked: 'What's it like at ballet school?'

'A cross between serving in the army and being in jail.'

Harald stared at Karen in fascination. He did not know whether to regard her as one of the boys or one of the gods. She bantered with her brother like a kid. Nevertheless she was extraordinarily graceful. Just sitting in the chair, waving an arm or pointing or resting her chin on her hand, she seemed to be dancing. All her movements were harmonious. Yet her poise did not restrain her, and Harald watched the changing expressions of her face like one mesmerized. She had a full-lipped mouth and a wide smile that was slightly lopsided. In fact her whole face was a little irregular – her nose was not quite straight and her chin was uneven – but the overall effect was beautiful. In fact, he thought, she was the most beautiful girl he had ever met.

'You'd better put some shoes on,' Tik said to Harald.

Harald retreated to his room and finished dressing. When he returned, Tik was looking spiffy in a black jacket, white shirt and plain dark tie. Harald felt very much the schoolboy in his blazer.

Karen led the way downstairs. They entered a long, untidy room with several large sofas, a grand piano, and an elderly dog on a rug in front of the fireplace. The relaxed air contrasted with the stuffy formality of the hall, although here, too, the walls were crowded with oil paintings.

A young woman in a black dress and a white apron

asked Harald what he would like to drink. 'Whatever Josef is having,' he replied. There was no alcohol at the parsonage. At school, in the final year, the boys were allowed to drink one glass of beer each at the Friday night get-together. Harald had never drunk a cocktail and was not quite sure what one was.

To give himself something to do, he bent down and patted the dog. It was a long, lean red setter with a sprinkling of grey in its gingery fur. It opened an eye and wagged its tail once in polite acknowledgement of Harald's attentions.

Karen said: 'That's Thor.'

'The god of thunder,' Harald said with a smile. 'Silly, I agree, but Josef named him.'

Tik protested: 'You wanted to call him Buttercup!'

'I was only eight years old at the time.'

'So was I. Besides, Thor isn't so silly. He sounds like thunder when he farts.'

At that moment Tik's father came in, and he looked so like the dog that Harald almost laughed. A tall, thin man, he was elegantly dressed in a velvet jacket and a black bow tie, and his curly red hair was turning grey. Harald stood up and shook hands.

Mr Duchwitz addressed him with the same languid courtesy the dog had shown. 'I'm so glad to meet you,' he said in a lazy drawl. 'Josef is always talking about you.'

Tik said: 'So now you know the whole family.'

Mr Duchwitz said to Harald: 'How are things at school, after your outburst?'

'I wasn't punished, oddly enough,' Harald

answered. 'In the past, I've had to cut the grass with nail scissors just for saying "Rubbish" when some teacher made a stupid statement. I was much ruder than that to Mr Agger. But Heis, that's the head, just gave me a quiet lecture about how much more effectively I would have made my point if I had kept my temper.'

'Setting an example himself by not being angry with you,' Mr Duchwitz said with a smile, and Harald realized that was exactly what Heis had been doing.

Karen said: 'I think Heis is wrong. Sometimes you have to make a stink to get people to listen.'

That struck Harald as true, and he wished he had thought to say it to Heis. Karen was shrewd as well as beautiful. But he had a question for Mr Duchwitz and had been looking forward to the chance of asking it. 'Sir, aren't you worried about what the Nazis might do to you? We know how badly Jews are treated in Germany and Poland.'

'I do worry. But Denmark is not Germany, and the Germans seem to regard us as Danes first and Jews second.'

'So far, anyway,' Tik put in.

'True. But then there's the question of what options are open to us. I suppose I could make a business trip to Sweden, then apply for a visa to the United States. Getting the whole family out would be more difficult. And think what we would be leaving behind: a business that was started by my great-grandfather, this house where my children were born, a collection of paintings it has taken me a lifetime to put together . . . When you look at it that way, it seems simplest to sit tight and hope for the best.'

'Anyway, it's not as if we're shopkeepers, for heaven's sake,' Karen said airily. 'I hate the Nazis, but what are they going to do to the family that owns the largest bank in the country?'

Harald thought that was stupid. 'The Nazis can do anything they like, you should know that by now,' he said scornfully.

'Oh, should I?' Karen said coldly, and he realized he had offended her. He was about to explain how Uncle Joachim had been persecuted but, at that moment, Mrs Duchwitz joined them, and they started talking about the Royal Danish Ballet's current production, which was *Les Sylphides*.

'I love the music,' Harald said. He had heard it on the radio and could play snatches of it on the piano.

'Have you seen the ballet?' Mrs Duchwitz asked him.

'No.' He felt the urge to give the impression that he had seen many ballets, but had happened to miss this one. Then he realized just how risky it would be to fake it in front of this highly knowledgeable family. 'To be honest, I've never been to the theatre,' he confessed.

'How dreadful,' Karen said with a supercilious air.

Mrs Duchwitz shot her a look of disapproval. 'Then Karen must take you,' she said.

'Mother, I'm terribly busy,' Karen protested. 'I'm understudying a principal role!'

Harald felt hurt by her rejection, but guessed he

was being punished for speaking dismissively to her about the Nazis.

He drained his glass. He had enjoyed the bittersweet taste of the cocktail, and it had given him a relaxed sense of wellbeing, but perhaps it had also made him careless of what he said. He regretted affronting Karen. Now that she had suddenly cooled, he realized how much he had come to like her.

The maid who had been serving drinks announced that dinner was ready, and opened a pair of doors that led to the dining room. They walked through and sat at one end of a long table. The maid offered wine, but Harald declined.

They had vegetable soup, cod in white sauce, and lamb chops with gravy. There was plenty of food, despite rationing, and Mrs Duchwitz explained that much of what they ate came from the estate.

Throughout the meal, Karen said nothing directly to Harald, but addressed her conversation to the company in general. Even when he asked her a question, she looked at the others as she answered. Harald was dismayed. She was the most enchanting girl he had ever met, and he had got on the wrong side of her within a couple of hours.

Afterwards, they returned to the drawing room and had real coffee. Harald wondered where Mrs Duchwitz had bought it. Coffee was like gold dust, and she certainly had not grown it in a Danish garden.

Karen went out on to the terrace for a cigarette, and Tik explained that their old-fashioned parents did not like to see girls smoking. Harald was awestruck at the sophistication of a girl who drank cocktails *and* smoked.

When Karen came back in, Mr Duchwitz sat at the piano and began turning over the pages on the music stand. Mrs Duchwitz stood behind him. 'Beethoven?' he said, and she nodded. He played a few notes, and she began to sing a song in German. Harald was impressed, and at the end he applauded.

Tik said: 'Sing another one, Mother.'

'All right,' she said. 'But then you have to play something.'

The parents performed another song, then Tik fetched his clarinet and played a simple Mozart lullaby. Mr Duchwitz returned to the piano and played a Chopin waltz, from *Les Sylphides*, and Karen kicked off her shoes and showed them one of the dances she was understudying.

Then they all looked expectantly at Harald.

He realized he was supposed to perform. He could not sing, except for roaring out Danish folk songs, so he would have to play. 'I'm not very good at classical music,' he said.

'Rubbish,' Tik said. 'You play the piano in your father's church, you told me.'

Harald sat at the keyboard. He really could not inflict inspirational Lutheran hymns on a cultured Jewish family. He hesitated, then began to play *Pine Top's Boogie-Woogie*. It started with a melodic trill played by the right hand. Then the left hand began the insistently rhythmic bass pattern, and the right played the blues discords that were so seductive. After a few moments, he lost his self-consciousness and began to feel the music. He played louder and more emphatically, calling out in English at the high points: 'Everybody, boogie-woogie!' just like Pine Top. The tune came to its climax and he said: 'That's what I'm talkin' about!'

When he finished, there was silence in the room. Mr Duchwitz wore the pained expression of a man who has accidentally swallowed something rotten. Even Tik looked embarrassed. Mrs Duchwitz said: 'Well, I must say, I don't think anything quite like that has ever been heard in this room.'

Harald realized he had made a mistake. The highbrow Duchwitz family disapproved of jazz as much as his own parents. They were cultured, but that did not make them open-minded. 'Oh, dear,' he said. 'I see that was not the right sort of thing.'

'Indeed not,' said Mr Duchwitz.

From behind the sofa, Karen caught Harald's eye. He expected to see a supercilious smile on her face but, to his surprise and delight, she gave him a broad wink.

That made it worthwhile.

* * *

On Sunday morning, he woke up thinking about Karen.

He hoped she might come into the boys' room to chat, as she had yesterday, but they did not see her.

She did not appear at breakfast. Trying hard to sound casual, Harald asked Tik where she was. Uninterested, Tik said she was probably doing her exercises.

After breakfast, Harald and Tik did two hours of exam revision. They both expected to pass easily, but they were not taking any chances, as the results would decide whether they could go to university. At eleven o'clock they went for a walk around the estate.

Near the end of the long drive, partly hidden from view by a stand of trees, was a ruined monastery. 'It was taken over by the king after the Reformation, and used as a home for a hundred years,' Tik said. 'Then Kirstenslot was built, and the old place fell into disuse.'

They explored the cloisters where the monks had walked. The cells were now storerooms for garden equipment. 'Some of this stuff hasn't been looked at for decades,' Tik said, poking a rusty iron wheel with the toe of his shoe. He opened a door into a large, well-lit room. There was no glass in the narrow windows, but the place was clean and dry. 'This used to be the dormitory,' Tik said. 'It's still used in summer, by seasonal workers on the farm.'

They entered the disused church, now a junk room. There was a musty smell. A thin black-and-white cat stared at them as if to ask what right they had to walk in like that, then it escaped through a glassless window.

Harald lifted a canvas sheet to reveal a gleaming Rolls-Royce sedan mounted on blocks. 'Your father's?' Harald said.

'Yes – put away until petrol goes on sale again.'

There was a scarred wooden work bench with a vice, and a collection of tools that had presumably been used to maintain the car when it was running. In the corner was a wash basin with a single tap. Up against the wall were stacks of wooden boxes that had once held soap and oranges. Harald looked inside one and found a jumble of toy cars made of painted tin. He picked one up. A driver was depicted on the windows, in profile on the side window, full face on the windscreen. He remembered when such toys had been infinitely desirable to him. He put the car back carefully.

In the far corner was a single-engined aeroplane with no wings.

Harald looked at it with interest. 'What's this?'

'A Hornet Moth, made by de Havilland, the English company. Father bought it five years ago, but he never learned to fly it.'

'Have you been up in it?'

'Oh, yes, we had great rides when it was new.'

Harald touched the great propeller, at least six feet long. The mathematically precise curves made it a work of art in his eyes. The aircraft leaned slightly to one side, and he saw that the undercarriage was damaged and one tyre was flat.

He felt the fuselage and was surprised to find it was made of some kind of fabric, stretched taut over a frame, with small rips and wrinkles in places. It was painted light blue with a black coachline edged in white, but the paintwork that might once have been cheerful was now dull, dusty and streaked with oil. It did have wings, he now saw – biplane wings, painted silver – but they were hinged, and had been swung around to point backwards.

He looked through the side window into the cabin. It was much like the front of a car. There were two seats side by side and a varnished wooden instrument panel with an assortment of dials. The upholstery of one seat had burst, and the stuffing was coming out. It looked as if mice had nested there.

He found the door handle and clambered inside, ignoring the soft scuttling sounds he heard. He sat on the one intact seat. The controls appeared simple. In the middle was a Y-shaped joystick that could be operated from either seat. He put his hand on the stick and his feet on the pedals. He thought flying would be even more thrilling than driving a motorcycle. He imagined himself soaring over the castle like a giant bird, with the roar of the engine in his ears.

'Did you ever fly it yourself?' he asked Tik.

'No. Karen took lessons, though.'

'Did she?'

'She wasn't old enough to qualify, but she was very good.'

Harald experimented with the controls. He saw a pair of 'On–Off' switches and flicked them both, but nothing happened. The stick and the pedals seemed loose, as if they were not connected to anything. Seeing what he was doing, Tik said: 'Some of the cables were taken out last year – they were needed to repair one of the farm machines. Let's go.'

Harald could have spent another hour fiddling with the aircraft, but Tik was impatient, so he climbed out.

They left from the back of the monastery and followed a cart track through a wood. Attached to Kirstenslot was a large farm. 'It's been rented to the Nielsen family since before I was born,' Tik said. 'They raise pigs for bacon, they keep a dairy herd that wins prizes, and they have several hundred acres under cereal crops.'

They tramped around a broad wheat field, crossed a pasture full of black-and-white cows, and smelled the pigs from a distance. On the dirt road leading to the farmhouse, they came across a tractor and trailer. A young man in overalls was peering at the engine. Tik shook hands with the man and said: 'Hello, Frederik, what's wrong?'

'Engine died on me in the middle of the road. I was taking Mr Nielsen and the family to church in the trailer.' Harald looked again at the trailer and saw that it contained two benches. 'Now the grown-ups are walking to church and the kiddies have been took home.'

'My friend Harald here is a wizard with all kinds of engines.'

'I wouldn't mind if he'd take a look.'

The tractor was an up-to-date model, with a diesel engine, and rubber tyres rather than steel wheels. Harald bent down to study the innards. 'What happens when you turn her over?'

'I'll show you.' Frederik pulled a handle. The starter motor whined, but the engine would not catch.

'She needs a new fuel pump, I think.' Frederik shook his head despairingly. 'We can't get spare parts for none of our machines.'

Harald frowned sceptically. He could smell fuel, which suggested to him that the pump was working, but the diesel was not reaching the cylinders. 'Would you try the starter once more?'

Frederik pulled the handle. Harald thought he saw the fuel filter outlet pipe move. Looking more closely, he saw that diesel was leaking from the release valve. He reached in and wiggled the nut. The entire valve assembly came away from the filter. 'There's the problem,' he said. 'The screw thread inside this nut has worn down, for some reason, and it's letting the fuel escape. Have you got a piece of wire?'

Frederik reached into the pockets of his tweed trousers. 'I've got a stout bit of string here.'

'That will do temporarily.' Harald put the valve back in position and tied it to the filter with the string so that it could not wobble. 'Try the starter now.'

Frederik pulled the handle, and the engine started. 'Well, I'm damned,' he said. 'You've mended it.'

'When you get a chance, replace the string with wire. Then you won't need a spare part.'

'I don't suppose you're going to be here for a week or two?' Frederik said. 'This farm has got broken machinery all over the place.'

'No, sorry – I have to go back to school.'

'Well, good luck.' Frederik climbed on his tractor. 'I can get to the church in time to bring the Nielsens back home, anyhow, thanks to you.' He drove off.

Harald and Tik strolled back towards the castle. 'That was impressive,' Tik said.

Harald shrugged. For as long as he could remember, he had been able to fix machines.

'Old Nielsen is keen on all the latest inventions,' Tik added. 'Machines for sowing, reaping, even milking.'

'Can he get fuel for them?'

'Yes. You can if it's for food production. But no one can find spare parts for anything.'

Harald checked his watch: he was looking forward to seeing Karen at lunch. He would ask her about her flying lessons.

In the village they stopped at the tavern. Tik bought two glasses of beer and they sat outside to enjoy the sunshine. Across the street, people were coming out of the small red-brick church. Frederik drove by on the tractor and waved. Seated in the trailer behind him were five people. The big man with white hair and a ruddy outdoor face must be Farmer Nielsen, Harald thought.

A man in black police uniform came out with a mousy woman and two small children. He gave Tik a hostile glare as he approached.

One of the children, a girl of about seven, said in a loud voice: 'Why don't they go to church, Daddy?'

'Because they're Jews,' the man said. 'They don't believe in Our Lord.'

Harald looked at Tik.

'The village policeman, Per Hansen,' Tik said

105

quietly. 'And local representative of the Danish National Socialist Workers Party.'

Harald nodded. The Danish Nazis were a weak party. In the last general election, two years ago, they had won only three seats in the Rigsdag. But the occupation had raised their hopes and, sure enough, the Germans had pressed the Danish government to give a ministerial post to the Nazi leader, Fritz Clausen. However, King Christian had dug in his heels and blocked the move, and the Germans had backed off. Party members such as Hansen were disappointed, but appeared to be waiting for a change of mood. They seemed confident that their time would come. Harald was afraid they might be right.

Tik drained his glass. 'Time for lunch.'

They returned to the castle. In the front courtyard Harald was surprised to see Poul Kirke, the cousin of their classmate Mads and friend of Harald's brother Arne. Poul was wearing shorts, and a bicycle was propped against the grand brick portico. Harald had met him several times, and now he stopped to talk while Tik went inside.

'Are you working here?' Poul asked him.

'No, visiting. School isn't over yet.'

'The farm hires students for the harvest, I know. What are you planning to do this summer?'

'I'm not sure. Last year I worked as a labourer at a building site on Sande.' He grimaced. 'Turned out to be a German base, although they didn't say so until later.'

Poul seemed interested 'Oh? What sort of base?'

'Some kind of radio station, I think. They fired all the Danes before they installed the equipment. I'll probably work on the fishing boats this summer, and do the preliminary reading for my university course. I'm hoping to study physics under Niels Bohr.'

'Good for you. Mads always says you're a genius.'

Harald was about to ask what Poul was doing here at Kirstenslot, when the answer became obvious. Karen came around the side of the house pushing a bicycle.

She looked ravishing in khaki shorts that showed off her long legs.

'Good morning, Harald,' she said. She went up to Poul and kissed him. Harald noted enviously that it was a kiss on the lips, though a brief one. 'Hi,' she said.

Harald was dismayed. He had been counting on an hour with Karen at the lunch table. But she was off on a bicycle ride with Poul, who was obviously her boy-friend, even though he was ten years older. Harald now saw, for the first time, that Poul was very good looking, with regular features and a movie-star smile that showed perfect teeth.

Poul held Karen's hands and looked her up and down. 'You are completely delectable,' he said. 'I wish I had a photo of you like this.'

She smiled graciously. 'Thank you.'

'Ready to go?'

'All set.'

They climbed on their bikes.

Harald felt sick. He watched them set off side by side down the half-mile drive in the sunshine. 'Have a nice ride!' he called.

Karen waved without turning around.

SIX

Hermia Mount was about to get the sack.

This had never happened to her before. She was bright and conscientious, and her employers had always regarded her as a treasure, despite her sharp tongue. But her current boss, Herbert Woodie, was going to tell her she was fired, as soon as he worked up the courage.

Two Danes working for MI6 had been arrested at Kastrup aerodrome. They were now in custody and undoubtedly being interrogated. It was a bad blow to the Nightwatchmen network. Woodie was a peacetime MI6 man, a long-serving bureaucrat. He needed someone to blame, and Hermia was a suitable candidate.

Hermia understood this. She had worked for the British civil service for a decade, and she knew its ways. If Woodie were forced to accept that the blame lay with his department, he would pin it on the most junior person available. Woodie had never been comfortable working with a woman anyway, and he would be happy to see her replaced by a man.

At first Hermia was inclined to offer herself up as the sacrificial victim. She had never met the two aircraft mechanics – they had been recruited by Poul Kirke – but the network was her creation and she was responsible for the fate of the arrested men. She was as upset as if they had already died, and she did not want to go on.

After all, she thought, how much had she actually done to help the war effort? She was just accumulating information. None of it had ever been used. Men were risking their lives to send her photographs of Copenhagen harbour with nothing much happening. It seemed foolish.

But in fact she knew the importance of this laborious routine work. At some future date, a reconnaissance plane would photograph the harbour full of ships, and military planners would need to know whether this represented normal traffic or the sudden build-up of an invasion force – and at that point Hermia's photographs would become crucial.

Furthermore, the visit of Digby Hoare had given an immediate urgency to her work. The Germans' aircraft detection system could be the weapon that would win the war. The more she thought about it, the more likely it seemed that the key to the problem could lie in Denmark. The Danish west coast seemed the ideal location for a warning station designed to detect bombers approaching Germany.

And there was no one else in MI6 who had her ground-level knowledge of Denmark. She knew Poul Kirke personally and he trusted her. It could be disastrous if a stranger took over. She had to keep her job. And that meant outwitting her boss.

'This is bad news,' Woodie said sententiously as she stood in front of his desk.

His office was a bedroom in the old house of Bletchley Park. Flowered wallpaper and silk-shaded wall lights suggested it had been occupied by a lady before the war. Now it had filing cabinets instead of wardrobes full of dresses, and a steel map table where once there might have been a dressing table with spindly legs and a triple mirror. And instead of a glamorous woman in a priceless silk negligee, the room was occupied by a small, self-important man in a grey suit and glasses.

Hermia faked the appearance of calm. 'There's always danger when an operative is interrogated, of course,' she said. 'However—' She thought of the two brave men being interrogated and tortured, and her breath caught in her throat for a moment. Then she recovered. 'However, in this case I feel the risk is slight.'

Woodie grunted sceptically. 'We may need to set up an inquiry.'

Her heart sank. An inquiry meant an investigator from outside the department. He would have to come up with a scapegoat, and she was the obvious choice. She began the defence she had prepared. 'The two men arrested don't have any secrets to betray,' she said. 'They were ground crew at the aerodrome. One of the Nightwatchmen would give them papers to be smuggled out, and they would stow the contraband in a hollow wheel chock.' Even so, she knew, they might reveal apparently innocent details about how they were recruited and run, details which a clever spycatcher could use to track down other agents.

'Who passed them the papers?'

'Matthies Hertz, a lieutenant in the army. He's gone into hiding. And the mechanics don't know anyone else in the network.'

'So our tight security has limited the damage to the organization.'

Hermia guessed that Woodie was rehearsing a line he might speak to his superiors, and she forced herself to flatter him. 'Exactly, sir, that's a good way of putting it.'

'But how did the Danish police get to your people in the first place?'

Hermia had anticipated this question, and her answer was carefully prepared. 'I think the problem is at the Swedish end.'

'Ah.' Woodie brightened. Sweden, being a neutral country, was not under his control. He would welcome the chance of shifting the blame to another department. 'Take a seat, Miss Mount.'

'Thank you.' Hermia felt encouraged: Woodie was reacting as she had hoped. She crossed her legs and went on: 'I think the Swedish go-between has been passing copies of the illegal newspapers to Reuters in Stockholm, and this may have alerted the Germans. You have always had a strict rule that our agents stick to information gathering, and avoid ancillary activities such as propaganda work.' This was more flattery: she had never heard Woodie say any such thing, though it was a general rule in espionage.

However, he nodded sagely. 'Indeed.'

'I reminded the Swedes of your ruling as soon as I found out what was happening, but I fear the damage had been done.'

Woodie looked thoughtful. He would be happy if he could claim that his advice had been ignored. He did not really like people to do as he suggested, because when things went well they just took the credit themselves. He preferred it if they ignored his counsel and things went wrong. Then he could say: 'I told you so.'

Hermia said: 'Shall I do you a memo, mentioning your rule and quoting my signal to the Swedish legation?'

'Good idea.' Woodie liked this even better. He would not be allocating blame himself, merely quoting an underling who would incidentally be giving him credit for sounding the alarm.

'Then we'll need a new way of getting information out of Denmark. We can't use radio for this kind of material, it takes too long to broadcast.'

Woodie had no idea how to organize an alternative smuggling route. 'Ah, that's a problem,' he said with a touch of panic.

'Fortunately we have set up a fallback option, using the boat train that crosses from Elsinore in Denmark to Helsingborg in Sweden.'

Woodie was relieved. 'Splendid,' he said.

'Perhaps I should say in my memo that you've authorized me to action that.'

'Fine.'

She hesitated. 'And . . . the inquiry?'

'You know, I'm not sure that will be necessary. Your memo should serve to answer any questions.'

She concealed her relief. She was not going to be fired after all.

She knew she should quit while she was ahead. But there was another problem she was desperate to raise with him. This seemed like an ideal opportunity. 'There is one thing we could do that would improve our security enormously, sir.'

'Indeed?' Woodie's expression said that if there were such a procedure he would already have thought of it.

'We could use more sophisticated codes.'

'What's wrong with our poem and book codes? Agents of MI6 have been using them for years.'

'I fear the Germans may have figured out how to break them.'

Woodie smiled knowingly. 'I don't think so, my dear.'

Hermia decided to take the risk of contradicting him. 'May I show you what I mean?' Without waiting for his answer, she went on: 'Take a look at this coded message.' She quickly scribbled on her pad:

gsff cffs jo uif dbouffo

She said: 'The commonest letter is *f*.'

'Obviously.'

'In the English language, the letter used most commonly is *e*, so the first thing a codebreaker would do is assume that *f* stands for *e*, which gives you this.'

114

gsEE cEEs jo uiE dbouEEo

'It could still mean anything,' Woodie said.

'Not quite. How many four-letter words are there ending in double *e*?'

'I'm sure I've no idea.'

'Only a few common ones: *flee, free, glee, thee,* and *tree.* Now look at the second group.'

'Miss Mount, I don't really have time—'

'Just another few seconds, sir. There are many four-letter words with a double *e* in the middle. What could the first letter be? Not *a*, certainly, but it could be *b*. So think of words beginning *bee* that might logically come next. *Flee been* makes no sense, *free bees* sounds odd, although *tree bees* might be right—'

Woodie interrupted. 'Free beer!' he said triumphantly.

'Let's try that. The next group is two letters, and there aren't many two-letter words: *an, at, in, if, it, on, of, or,* and *up* are the commonest. The fourth group is a three-letter word ending in *e*, of which there are many, but the commonest is *the.*'

Woodie was getting interested despite himself. 'Free beer at the something.'

'Or in the something. And that something is a seven-letter word with a double *e* in it, so it ends *eed, eef, eek, eel, eem, een, eep*—'

'Free beer in the canteen!' said Woodie triumphantly.

'Yes,' Hermia said. She sat in silence, looking at Woodie, letting the implications of what had just

115

happened sink in. After a few moments she said: 'That's how easy our codes are to break, sir.' She looked at her watch. 'It took you three minutes.'

He grunted. 'A good party trick, Miss Mount, but the old hands at MI6 know more about this sort of thing than you, take it from me.'

It was no good, she thought despairingly. He would not be moved on this today. She would have to try again later. She forced herself to give in gracefully. 'Very good, sir.'

'Concentrate on your own responsibilities. What are the rest of your Nightwatchmen up to?'

'I'm about to ask them to keep their eyes open for any indications that the Germans have developed long-distance aircraft detection.'

'Good Lord, don't do that!'

'Why not?'

'If the enemy finds out we're asking that question, he'll guess we've got it!'

'But, sir – what if he does have it?'

'He doesn't. You can rest assured.'

'The gentleman who came here from Downing Street last week seemed to think otherwise.'

'In strict confidence, Miss Mount, an MI6 committee looked into the whole radar question quite recently, and concluded that it would be another eighteen months before the enemy developed such a system.'

So, Hermia thought, it was called radar. She smiled. 'That's so reassuring,' she lied. 'I expect you were on the committee yourself, sir?'

Woodie nodded. 'In fact I chaired it.'

'Thank you for setting my mind at rest. I'll get on with that memo.'

'Jolly good.'

Hermia went out. Her face ached with smiling and she was exhausted by the effort of constantly deferring to Woodie. She had saved her job, and she permitted herself a moment of satisfaction as she walked back to her own office. But she had failed with the codes. She had found out the name of the long-distance aircraft detection system – radar – but it was clear Woodie would not let her investigate whether the Germans had such a system in Denmark.

She longed to do something of immediate value to the war effort. All this routine work made her impatient and frustrated. It would be so satisfying to see some real results. And it might even justify what had happened to those two poor aircraft mechanics at Kastrup.

She could investigate enemy radar without Woodie's permission, of course. He might find out, but she was willing to take that risk. However, she did not know what to tell her Nightwatchmen. What should they be looking for, and where? She needed more information before she could brief Poul Kirke. And Woodie was not going to give it to her.

But he was not her only hope.

She sat down at her desk, picked up the phone, and said: 'Please connect me with Number Ten, Downing Street.'

* * *

She met Digby Hoare in Trafalgar Square. She stood at the foot of Nelson's Column and watched him cross the road from Whitehall. She smiled at the energetic, lopsided stride that already seemed to her characteristic of him. They shook hands, then walked towards Soho.

It was a warm summer evening, and the West End of London was busy, its pavements thronged with people heading for theatres, cinemas, bars and restaurants. The happy scene was marred only by bomb damage, the occasional blackened ruin in a row of buildings standing out like a rotten tooth in a smile.

She had thought they were going for a drink in a pub, but Digby led her to a small French restaurant. The tables either side of them were empty, so they could talk without being overheard.

Digby was wearing the same dark grey suit, but this evening he had on a light blue shirt that set off his blue eyes. Hermia was pleased she had decided to wear her favourite piece of jewellery, a panther brooch with emerald eyes.

She was keen to get down to business. She had refused to go on a date with Digby and she did not want him to get the idea that she might have changed her mind. As soon as they had ordered, she said: 'I want to use my agents in Denmark to find out whether the Germans have radar.'

He looked at her through narrowed eyes. 'The question is more complicated than that. It's now beyond doubt that they have radar, as we do. But theirs is more effective than ours – devastatingly so.'

'Oh.' She was taken aback. 'Woodie told me . . . never mind.'

'We're desperate to find out why their system is so good. Either they have invented something better than we've got, or they've devised a way of using it more effectively – or both.'

'All right.' She rapidly readjusted her ideas in the light of this new information. 'Just the same, it seems likely that some of this machinery is in Denmark.'

'It would be a logical place – and the codename "Freya" suggests Scandinavia.'

'So what are my people looking for?'

'That's difficult.' He frowned. 'We don't know what their machinery looks like – that's the point, isn't it?'

'I presume it gives out radio waves.'

'Yes, of course.'

'And presumably the signals travel a good distance – otherwise the warning wouldn't be early enough.'

'Yes. It would be useless unless the signals travelled at least, say, fifty miles. Probably more.'

'Could we listen for them?'

He raised his eyebrows in surprise. 'Yes, with a radio receiver. Clever notion – I don't know why no one else thought of it.'

'Can the signals be distinguished from other transmissions, such as normal broadcasts, the news and so on?'

He nodded. 'You'd be listening for a series of pulses, probably very rapid, say a thousand per second. You'd hear it as a continuous musical note. So you'd know it wasn't the BBC. And it would be quite different from the dots and dashes of military traffic.'

'You're an engineer. Could you put together a radio receiver suitable for picking up such signals?'

He looked thoughtful. 'It's got to be portable, presumably.'

'It should pack into a suitcase.'

'And work off a battery, so it can be used anywhere.'

'Yes.'

'It might be possible. There's a team of boffins in Welwyn who do this stuff all day.' Welwyn was a small town between Bletchley and London. 'Exploding turnips, radio transmitters concealed in bricks, that sort of thing. They could probably cobble something together.'

Their food came. Hermia had ordered a tomato salad. It came with a sprinkling of chopped onion and a sprig of mint, and she wondered why British cooks could not produce food that was simple and delicious like this, instead of tinned sardines and boiled cabbage.

'What made you set up the Nightwatchmen?' Digby asked her.

She was not sure what he meant. 'It seemed like a good idea.'

'Still, not an idea that would occur to the average young woman, if I may say so.'

She thought back, remembering the struggle she had had with another bureaucratic boss, and asked herself why she had persisted. 'I wanted to strike a blow against the Nazis. There's something about them that I find absolutely loathsome.'

'Fascism blames problems on a false cause – people of other races.'

'I know, but it's not that. It's the uniforms, the strutting and posturing, and the way they howl out those hateful speeches. It just makes me sick.'

'When did you experience all this? There aren't many Nazis in Denmark.'

'I spent a year in Berlin in the thirties. I watched them marching and saluting and spitting on people and smashing the windows of Jewish shopkeepers. I remember thinking: these people have to be stopped before they spoil the whole world. I still think so. I'm more sure of that than anything.'

He smiled. 'Me, too.'

Hermia had a seafood fricassee, and once again she was struck by what a French cook could do with common ingredients, despite rationing. The dish contained sliced eel, some of the winkles beloved of Londoners, and flaked cod, but it was all fresh and well seasoned, and she tucked in with relish.

Every now and again she caught Digby's eye, and he always had the same look, a mixture of adoration and lust. It alarmed her. If he fell in love with her, it could only lead to trouble and heartbreak. But it was pleasing, as well as embarrassing, to have a man so obviously desire her. At one point she felt herself flush, and put her hand to her throat to hide her blushes.

She deliberately turned her thoughts to Arne. The first time she talked to him, in the bar of a ski hotel in Norway, she knew she had found what was missing in her life. 'Now I understand why I've never had a satisfactory relationship with a man,' she had written to her mother. 'It's because I hadn't met Arne.' When he proposed to her, she had said: 'If I'd known there were men like you, I'd have married one years ago.'

She said yes to everything he suggested. She was normally so intent on having her own way that she had never been able to share an apartment with a girlfriend, but with Arne she lost her will power. Every time he asked her to go out with him she accepted; when he kissed her, she kissed him back; when he stroked her breasts under her ski sweater she just sighed with pleasure; and when he knocked on the door of her hotel room at midnight she said: 'I'm so glad you're here.'

Thinking of Arne helped her to feel cooler towards Digby, and as they finished their meal she turned the conversation to the war. An Allied army including British, Commonwealth and Free French forces had invaded Syria. It was a skirmish on the far fringes, and they both found it hard to see the outcome as important. The conflict in Europe was all that really counted. And here it was a war of bombers.

When they left the restaurant it was dark, but there was a full moon. They walked south, heading for her mother's house in Pimlico, where Hermia was going to spend the night. As they were crossing St James's

Park the moon went behind a cloud, and Digby turned to her and kissed her.

She could not help admiring the swift sureness of his moves. His lips were on hers before she could turn away. With a strong hand he pulled her body to his, and her breasts pressed against his chest. She knew she should be indignant, but to her consternation she found herself responding. She suddenly remembered what it was like to feel a man's hard body and hot skin, and in a rush of desire she opened her mouth to him.

They kissed hungrily for a minute, then his hand went to her breast, and that broke the spell. She was too old and respectable to be groped in a park. She broke the clinch.

The thought of taking him home crossed her mind. She imagined the pained disapproval of Mags and Bets, and the picture made her laugh.

'What is it?' he said.

She saw that he looked hurt. He probably imagined her laughter had to do with his disability. I must remember how vulnerable he might be to mockery, she thought. She hastened to explain. 'My mother is a widow who lives with a middle-aged spinster. I just thought how they would react if I told them I wanted to bring a man home for the night.'

The hurt look went away. 'I like your thinking,' he said, and he tried to kiss her again.

She was tempted, but thought of Arne, and put a resisting hand on Digby's chest. 'No more,' she said firmly. 'Walk me home.'

They left the park. The momentary euphoria left her, and she began to feel troubled. How could she enjoy kissing Digby when she loved Arne? As they passed Big Ben and Westminster Abbey, an air-raid warning put all such thoughts out of her mind.

Digby said: 'Do you want to find a shelter?'

Many Londoners no longer took cover during air raids. Fed up with sleepless nights, some had decided it was worth risking the bombs. Others had become fatalistic, saying that a bomb either had your number on it or not, and there was nothing you could do either way. Hermia was not quite so blasé, but on the other hand she had no intention of spending the night in an air-raid shelter with the amorous Digby. She nervously twisted the engagement ring on her left hand. 'We're only a few minutes away,' she replied. 'Do you mind if we keep going?'

'I may be forced to spend the night at your mother's house after all.'

'At least I'll be chaperoned.'

They hurried through Westminster into Pimlico. Searchlights probed the scattered clouds, then they heard the sinister low drone of heavy aircraft, like a large beast growling hungrily, deep in its throat. An anti-aircraft gun boomed somewhere, and flak burst in the sky like fireworks. Hermia wondered whether her mother was out driving her ambulance tonight.

To Hermia's horror, bombs started to fall nearby, although it was normally the industrial East End that was hardest hit. There was a deafening crump that seemed to come from the next street. A minute later, a fire engine roared by. Hermia walked on as fast as she could.

Digby said: 'You're so cool – aren't you scared?'

'Of course I'm scared,' she said impatiently. 'I'm just not panicking.'

They turned a corner and saw a blazing building. The fire engine was outside and the men were unrolling hoses.

'How much farther?' Digby asked.

'Next street,' Hermia said, panting.

When they rounded the next corner, they saw another fire engine at the far end of the street, near Mags's house. 'Oh, God,' Hermia said, and she broke into a run. Her heart pounded with fear as she dashed along the pavement. There was an ambulance, she saw, and at least one house in her mother's section had been hit. 'No, please,' she said aloud.

Coming closer, she was perplexed that she could not identify her mother's house, though she saw clearly that the house next door was on fire. She stopped and stared, trying to understand what she was looking at. Then, at last, she realized that her mother's house was gone. Nothing was left of it but a gap in the terrace and a pile of debris. She groaned in despair.

Digby said: 'Is that the house?'

Hermia nodded, unable to speak.

Digby called to a fireman in an authoritative voice. 'You!' he said. 'Any sign of the occupants of this building?'

'Yes, sir,' said the fireman. 'One person was blown clear by the blast.' He pointed to the small front yard of the undamaged house on the far side. There was a body on a stretcher lying on the ground. The face was covered.

Hermia felt Digby take her arm. Together they entered the yard.

Hermia knelt down and Digby uncovered the face.

'It's Bets,' Hermia said, with a sickeningly guilty feeling of relief.

Digby was looking around. 'Who's that, sitting on the wall?'

Hermia looked up, and her heart lurched as she recognized the figure of her mother, dressed in her ambulance uniform and tin hat, slumped on the low wall as if all the life had gone out of her. 'Mother?' she said.

Her mother looked up, and Hermia saw that tears were streaming down her face.

Hermia went to her and put her arms around her.

'Bets is dead,' her mother said.

'I'm sorry, Mother.'

'She loved me so much,' her mother sobbed.

'I know.'

'Do you? Do you know? She waited all her life for me. Did you realize that? All her life.'

Hermia hugged her mother hard. 'I'm so sorry,' she said.

* * *

There had been about two hundred Danish ships at sea on the morning of 9 April 1940, when Hitler invaded Denmark. All that day, Danish-language broadcasts by the BBC appealed to sailors to head for Allied ports rather than return home to a conquered country. In total, about five thousand men accepted the offer of refuge. Most sought harbour on the east coast of England, hoisted the Union Jack, and continued to sail throughout the war under the British flag. Consequently, by the middle of the following year small communities of Danes had settled in several English ports.

Hermia decided to go to the fishing town of Stokeby. She had visited the place twice previously to talk to the Danes there. On this occasion she told her boss, Herbert Woodie, that her mission was to check her somewhat out-of-date plans of the main Danish ports and make any alterations necessary.

He believed her.

She had a different story for Digby Hoare.

Digby came to Bletchley, two days after the bomb destroyed her mother's house, with a radio receiver and direction finder neatly packed into a used-looking tan leather suitcase. As he showed her how to use the equipment, she thought guiltily of the kiss in the park, and how much she had enjoyed it, and wondered uneasily how she would be able to look Arne in the eye.

Her original plan had been to attempt to smuggle the radio receiver to the Nightwatchmen, but she had since thought of something simpler. The signals from the radar apparatus could probably be picked up at sea just as easily as on land. She told Digby she was going to pass the suitcase to the captain of a fishing boat and teach him how to use it. Digby approved.

That plan might well have worked, but in truth she did not want to hand such an important job over to someone else. So she intended to go herself.

In the North Sea, between England and Denmark, there was a large sandbank known as Dogger Bank, where the sea was as shallow as fifty feet in places, and the fishing was good. Both British and Danish ships trawled there. Strictly speaking, Denmark-based vessels were banned from venturing so far from their coast, but Germany needed herrings, so the ban was irregularly enforced and constantly defied. For some time, Hermia had had it in the back of her mind that messages – or even people – might travel between the two countries on fishing boats, transferring from Danish to British or vice versa in the middle. Now, however, she had a better idea. The far end of the Dogger Bank was only a hundred miles from the Danish coast. If all her guesswork turned out to be right, the signals from the Freya machine should be detectable from the fishing ground.

She took a train on Friday afternoon. She was dressed for the sea in trousers, boots, and a loose sweater, with her hair pushed under a man's checked cap. As the train rolled through the flat fen country of eastern England, she worried whether her plan would work. Would she find a ship willing to take her? Would she pick up the signals she was expecting? Or was the whole thing a waste of time?

After a while her mind turned to her mother. Mags had been under control again yesterday at Bets's funeral, appearing calmly sorrowful rather than stricken by grief, and today she had gone to Cornwall to stay with her sister, Hermia's Aunt Bella. But on the night of the bomb her soul had been laid bare.

The two women had been devoted friends, but it was clearly more than that. Hermia did not really want to think what else could be involved, but she could not help being intrigued. Setting aside the embarrassing thought of what physical relation there might have been between Mags and Bets, Hermia was shocked that her mother had nourished a passionate lifelong attachment that had remained carefully disguised, all those years, from Hermia herself and presumably from Mags's husband, Hermia's father.

She arrived in Stokeby at eight o'clock on a mild summer evening and went from the railway station straight to the Shipwright's Arms pub on the dockside. It took her only a few minutes of asking around to learn that Sten Munch, a Danish captain she had met on her last visit here, was due to sail in the morning in his vessel *Morganmand*, which meant 'early riser'. She found Sten at his house on the hillside, clipping the hedge in his front garden like a born Englishman. He invited her in.

He was a widower and lived with his son, Lars, who had been on the boat with him on 9 April 1940. Lars had since married a local girl, Carol. When Hermia went inside, Carol was nursing a tiny baby a few days old. Lars made tea. They all spoke English for Carol's sake.

Hermia explained that she needed to get as close as possible to the Danish coast in an attempt to listen to a German wireless transmission – she did not say what kind. Sten did not question her story. 'Of course!' he said expansively. 'Anything to help defeat the Nazis! But my boat is not really suitable.'

'Why not?'

'It's very small – only thirty-five feet – and we'll be away for about three days.'

Hermia had been expecting this. She had told Woodie she needed to get her mother settled in new accommodation and would be back some time next week. 'That's all right,' she told Sten. 'I've got time.'

'My boat has only three berths. We sleep in shifts. It's not designed for ladies. You should go in a larger vessel.'

'Is there one leaving in the morning?'

Sten looked at Lars, who said: 'No. Three set off yesterday, won't return until next week. Peter Gorning should be back tomorrow. He'll go out again about Wednesday.'

She shook her head. 'Too late.'

Carol looked up from her baby. 'They sleep in their clothes, you know. That's why they stink when they get home. It's worse than the smell of the fish.'

Hermia immediately liked her for her down-to-earth directness. 'I'll be fine,' she said. 'I can sleep in my clothes, in a bed still warm from the previous occupant. It won't kill me.'

Sten said: 'You know I want to help. But the sea is not for women. You were made for the gracious things in life.'

Carol snorted scornfully. 'Like giving birth?'

Hermia smiled, grateful to have Carol as an ally. 'Exactly. We can put up with discomfort.'

Carol nodded vigorously. 'Think of what Charlie's going through in the desert.' She explained to Hermia: 'My brother Charlie's in the army somewhere in North Africa.'

Sten looked cornered. He did not want to take Hermia, but he was reluctant to say so, wanting to appear patriotic and brave. 'We leave at three o'clock in the morning.'

'I'll be there.'

Carol said: 'You might as well stay here, now. We've got a spare room.' She looked at her father-in-law. 'If that's all right with you, Pa.'

He had run out of excuses. 'Of course!' he said.

'Thank you,' said Hermia. 'You're very kind.'

They went to bed early. Hermia did not undress, but sat up in her room with the light on. She was afraid that, if she overslept, Sten would leave without her. The Munch family were not great readers, and the only book she could find was the Bible in Danish, but it kept her awake. At two o'clock she went to the bathroom and washed quickly, then tiptoed downstairs and put the kettle on. Sten appeared at half past two. When he saw Hermia in the kitchen he looked surprised and disappointed. She poured tea into a big cup and he took it gratefully enough.

Hermia, Sten and Lars walked down the hill to the quay a few minutes before three o'clock. Two more Danish men were waiting at the dockside. The *Morganmand* was very small. Thirty-five feet was about the length of a London bus. The vessel was made of wood, and had one mast and a diesel engine. On deck was a small wheelhouse and a series of hatches over the hold. From the wheelhouse, a companionway led down to the living quarters. At the stern end were the massive spars and the winding gear for the nets.

Dawn was breaking as the little vessel threaded its way through the defensive minefield at the mouth of the harbour. The weather was fine, but they encountered a swell of five or six feet as soon as they left the shelter of the land. Fortunately, Hermia was never seasick.

Throughout the day, she tried to make herself useful around the boat. She knew no seamanship, so she kept the galley clean. The men were used to preparing food for themselves, but she washed their dishes and the frying pan in which they cooked almost everything they ate. She made sure she talked to the two crewmen, speaking Danish, getting on terms of respectful friendliness with each of them. When she had nothing else to do, she sat on the deck and enjoyed the sunshine.

Towards midday they reached the Outer Silver Pit, on the south-east corner of the Dogger Bank, and began to trawl. The boat reduced speed and headed north-east. At first they could not find the fish, and the nets came up almost empty. Then, towards the end of the afternoon, the fish started running.

At nightfall, Hermia went below and lay on a bunk. She thought she would not sleep, but she had been up for thirty-six hours, and tiredness got the better of tension. She dropped off within minutes.

During the night she was awakened, briefly, by the volcanic rumble of a flight of bombers overhead. She wondered vaguely whether it was the RAF heading for Germany or the Luftwaffe going the other way, then drifted off to sleep again.

The next thing she knew, Lars was shaking her. 'We're approaching our nearest point to Denmark,' he said. 'We're about a hundred and twenty miles off Morlunde.'

Hermia took her suitcase receiver up on deck. It was already full daylight. The men were hauling in a net full of flapping fish, mainly herrings and mackerel, and tipping them into the hold. Hermia found it a gruesome sight, and looked away.

She connected the battery to the radio and was relieved to see the dials flicker. She fixed the aerial to the mast with a length of wire thoughtfully provided by Digby. She let the set warm up, then put on the headphones.

As the boat motored north-east, Hermia roamed up and down the wireless frequencies. As well as the BBC's broadcasts in English, she picked up French, Dutch, German and Danish radio programmes, plus a host of Morse transmissions which she presumed were military signals from both sides. At the first pass up and down, she heard nothing that might have been radar.

She repeated the exercise more slowly, making sure she missed nothing. She had plenty of time. But once again she did not hear what she was listening for.

She kept trying.

After two hours she noticed that the men had stopped fishing and were watching her. She caught the eye of Lars, who said: 'Any luck?'

She pulled off the headphones. 'I'm not picking up the signal I was expecting,' she said in Danish.

Sten replied in the same language. 'The fish were running all night. We've done well – our hold is full. We're ready to go home.'

'Would you motor north for a while? I must try to find this signal – it's really important.'

Sten looked doubtful, but his son said: 'We can afford it, we've had a good night.'

Sten was reluctant. 'What if a German spotter plane flies overhead?'

Hermia said: 'You could throw out nets and pretend to be fishing.'

'There are no fishing grounds where you want to go.'

'German pilots don't know that.'

One of the crew put in: 'If it's to help free Denmark . . .'

The other hand nodded vigorously.

Once again, Hermia was saved by Sten's reluctance

to appear cowardly in front of others. 'All right,' he said. 'We'll head north.'

'Keep a hundred miles off the coast,' Hermia said as she put the headphones back on.

She continued to scan the frequencies. As time went by, she became less hopeful. The likeliest place for a radar station was at the southern end of Denmark's coast, near the border with Germany. She had thought she would pick up the broadcast early. But her hopes fell by the hour as the boat headed north.

She was not willing to leave the set alone for more than a minute or two, so the fishermen brought her tea at intervals, and a bowl of canned stew at supper time. While listening, she gazed east. She could not see Denmark, but she knew Arne was there somewhere, and she enjoyed feeling closer to him.

Towards nightfall, Sten knelt on the deck beside her to talk, and she took off the headphones. 'We're off the northern point of the Jutland peninsula,' he said. 'We have to turn back.'

In desperation she said: 'Could we go closer? Maybe a hundred miles offshore is too far away to pick up the signal.'

'We need to head for home.'

'Could we follow the coast southward, retracing our course, but fifty miles closer to land?'

'Too dangerous.'

'It's almost dark. There are no spotter planes at night.'

'I don't like it.'

'Please. It's very important.' She shot an appealing look at Lars, who was standing nearby, listening. He was bolder than his father, perhaps because he saw his future in Britain, with his English wife.

As she was hoping, Lars joined in. 'How about seventy-five miles offshore?'

'That would be great.'

Lars looked at his father. 'We have to go south anyway. It won't add more than a few hours to our voyage.'

Sten said angrily: 'We'll be putting our crew in danger!'

Lars replied mildly: 'Think of Carol's brother in Africa. He's put himself in danger. This is our chance to do something to help.'

'All right, you take the wheel,' Sten said sulkily. 'I'm going to sleep.' He stepped into the wheelhouse and flung himself down the companionway.

Hermia smiled at Lars. 'Thanks.'

'We should thank you.'

Lars turned the boat around and Hermia continued to scan the airwaves. Night fell. They sailed without lights, but the sky was clear and there was a three-quarter moon, which made Hermia feel that the boat must be conspicuous. However, they saw no aircraft and no other shipping. Periodically, Lars checked their position with a sextant.

Her mind drifted back to the air raid she and Digby had been in a few days ago. It was the first time she had been caught out of doors during a raid. She had managed to remain calm, but it had been a terrifying scene: the drone of the aircraft, the searchlights and the flak, the crump of falling bombs and the hellish light of burning houses. Yet here she was doing her best to help the RAF inflict the same horrors on German families. It seemed mad – but the only alternative was to let the Nazis take over the world.

It was a short midsummer night, and dawn broke early. The sea was unusually calm. A morning mist rose from the surface, reducing visibility and making Hermia feel safer. As the boat continued south, she became more anxious. She must pick up the signal soon – unless she and Digby were wrong, and Herbert Woodie right.

Sten came on deck with a mug of tea in one hand and a bacon sandwich in the other. 'Well?' he said. 'Have you got what you wanted?'

'It's most likely to come from the south of Denmark,' she said.

'Or nowhere at all.'

She nodded despondently. 'I'm beginning to think you're right.' Then she heard something. 'Wait!' She had been scanning upwards through the frequencies, and thought she had heard a musical note. She reversed the knob and went down, searching for the spot. She got a lot of static, then the note again – a pure machine-like tone about an octave above middle C. 'I think this could be it!' she said joyfully. The wavelength was 2.4 metres. She made a note in the little book Digby had tucked into the suitcase.

Now she had to determine the direction.

Incorporated into the receiver was a dial graduated from one to three hundred and sixty with a needle pointing to the source of the signal. Digby had emphasized that the dial had to be aligned precisely with the centre line of the boat. Then the direction of the signal could be calculated from the heading of the boat and the needle on the dial. 'Lars!' she called. 'What's our heading?'

'East south-east,' he said.

'No, exactly.'

'Well . . .' Although the weather was fine and the sea was calm, nevertheless the boat was moving all the time, and the compass was never still.

'As best you can,' she said.

'One hundred and twenty degrees.'

The needle on her dial pointed to 340. Adding 120 to that brought the direction around to 100. Hermia made a note. 'And what is our position?'

'Wait a minute. When I shot the stars, we were crossing the fifty-sixth parallel.' He looked at the log, checked his wristwatch, and called out their latitude and longitude. Hermia wrote down the numbers, knowing they were only an estimate.

Sten said: 'Are you satisfied now? Can we go home?'

'I need another reading so that I can triangulate the source of the broadcast.'

He grunted in disgust and walked away.

Lars winked at her.

She kept the receiver tuned to the note as they motored south. The needle on the direction finder moved imperceptibly. After half an hour she again asked Lars for the boat's heading.

'Still one-twenty.'

The needle on her dial now pointed to 335. The direction of the signal was therefore 095. She asked him to estimate their position again, and wrote the numbers down.

'Home?' he said.

'Yes. And thank you.'

He turned the wheel.

Hermia was triumphant, but she could not wait to find out where the signal was coming from. She went into the wheelhouse and found a large-scale chart. With Lars's help she marked the two positions she had noted and drew lines for the bearing of the signal from each position, correcting for True North. The lines intersected off the coast, near the island of Sande.

'My God,' Hermia said. 'That's where my fiancé comes from.'

'Sande? I know it – I went to watch the racing car speed trials there a few years back.'

She was jubilant. Her guess had been right and her method had worked. The signal she had been expecting was coming from the most logical place.

Now she needed to send Poul Kirke, or one of his team, to Sande to look around. As soon as she returned to Bletchley she would send a coded message.

A few minutes later, she took another heading. The

signal was weak now, but the third line on the map made a triangle with the other two, and the island of Sande lay mainly within that triangle. All the calculations were approximate, but the conclusion seemed clear. The radio signal was coming from the island.

She could hardly wait to tell Digby.

SEVEN

Harald thought the Tiger Moth was the most beautiful machine he had ever seen. It looked like a butterfly poised for flight, its upper and lower wings spread wide, its toy-car wheels resting lightly on the grass, its long tail tapering behind. The weather was fine with gentle breezes, and the little aircraft trembled in the wind, as if eager to take off. It had a single engine in the nose, driving the big cream-painted propeller. Behind the engine were two open cockpits, one in front of the other.

It was cousin to the dilapidated Hornet Moth he had seen in the ruined monastery at Kirstenslot, and the two aircraft were mechanically similar, except that the Hornet Moth had an enclosed cabin with seats side by side. However, the Hornet Moth had looked sorry for itself, leaning to one side on its broken undercarriage, its fabric torn and oil-stained, its upholstery bursting. By contrast, the Tiger Moth had a sprightly look, with new paint bright on its fuselage and the sun glinting off its windscreen. Its tail rested on the ground and its nose pointed up, as if it were sniffing the air.

'You'll notice that the wings are flat underneath

but curved above,' said Harald's brother, Arne Olufsen. 'When the aircraft is moving, the air travelling over the top of the wing is forced to move faster than the air passing underneath.' He gave the engaging grin that made people forgive him anything. 'For reasons I have never understood, this lifts the aircraft off the ground.'

'It creates a pressure difference,' Harald said.

'Indeed,' Arne replied drily.

The senior class at Jansborg Skole were spending the day at the Army Aviation School at Vodal. They were being shown around by Arne and his friend Poul Kirke. It was a recruiting exercise by the army, who were having trouble persuading bright young men to join a military force that had nothing to do. Heis, with his army background, liked Jansborg to send one or two pupils into the military each year. For the boys, the visit was a welcome break from exam revision.

'The hinged surfaces on the lower wings are called ailerons,' Arne told them. 'They are connected by cables to the control column, which is sometimes called the joystick, for reasons you are too young to understand.' He grinned again. 'When the stick is moved to the left, the left aileron moves up and the right one down. This causes the aircraft to tilt and turn left. We call it banking.'

Harald was fascinated, but he wanted to get in and fly.

'You'll observe that the rear half of the tailplane is also hinged,' Arne said. 'This is called the elevator, and it points the aircraft up or down. Pull back on the

stick and the elevator tilts up, depressing the tail, so
that the aircraft climbs.'

Harald noticed that the upright part of the tail also
had a flap. 'What's that for?' he asked, pointing at it.

'This is the rudder, controlled by a pair of pedals
in the footwell of the cockpit. It works in the same way
as the rudder of a boat.'

Mads put in: 'Why do you need a rudder? You use
the ailerons to change direction.'

'Good point!' Arne said. 'Shows that you're
listening. But can't you figure it out? Why would we
need a rudder as well as ailerons to steer the aircraft?'

Harald guessed. 'You can't use the ailerons when
you're on the runway.'

'Because . . .?'

'The wings would hit the ground.'

'Correct. We use the rudder while taxiing, when we
can't tilt the wings because they would hit the ground.
We also use the rudder in the air, to control unwanted
sideways movement of the aircraft, which is called
yaw.'

The fifteen boys had toured the air base, sat
through a lecture – on opportunities, pay and training
in the army – and had lunch with a group of young
pupil pilots. Now they were eager for the individual
flying lesson which had been promised to each of
them as the climax of the day. Five Tiger Moths were
lined up on the grass. Danish military aircraft had
been officially grounded since the beginning of the
occupation, but there were exceptions. The flying
school was allowed to give lessons in gliders, and

special permission had been granted for today's exercise in Tiger Moths. Just in case anyone had the idea of flying a Tiger Moth all the way to Sweden, two Messerschmitt Me-109 fighter aircraft stood on the runway, ready to give chase and shoot down anyone who tried to escape.

Poul Kirke took over the commentary from Arne. 'I want you to look into the cockpit, one at a time,' he said. 'Stand on the black walkway on the lower wing. Don't step anywhere else or your foot will go through the fabric and you won't be able to fly.'

Tik Duchwitz went first. Poul said: 'On the left side you see a silver-coloured throttle lever, which controls the speed of the engine, and lower down a green trim lever which applies a spring loading to the elevator control. If the trim is correctly set when cruising, the aircraft should fly level when you take your hand off the stick.'

Harald went last. He could not help being interested, despite his resentment of the smoothly arrogant way Poul had swept Karen Duchwitz off on her bicycle.

As he stepped down, Poul said: 'So, what do you think, Harald?'

Harald shrugged. 'It seems straightforward.'

'Then you can go first,' Poul said with a grin.

The others laughed, but Harald was pleased.

'Let's all get kitted up,' Poul said.

They returned to the hangar and put on flying suits – step-in overalls that buttoned in front. Helmets and goggles were also given out. To Harald's annoyance, Poul made a point of helping him.

'Last time we met was at Kirstenslot,' Poul said as he adjusted Harald's goggles.

Harald nodded curtly, not wishing to be reminded. Still, he could not help wondering exactly what Poul's relationship with Karen was. Were they just dating, or something more? Did she kiss him passionately and let him touch her body? Did they talk of getting married? Had they had sexual intercourse? He did not want to think about these things, but he could not help it.

When they were ready, the first five students returned to the field, each with a pilot. Harald would have liked to go up with his brother, but once again Poul chose Harald. It was almost as if he wanted to get to know Harald better.

An airman in oily overalls was refuelling the aircraft, standing with one foot in a toehold in the fuselage. The tank was in the centre of the upper wing where it passed above the front seat – a worrying position, Harald felt. Would he be able to forget the gallons of inflammable fluid over his head?

'First, the pre-flight inspection,' Poul said. He leaned into the cockpit. 'We check that the magneto switches are off and the throttle is closed.' He looked at the wheels. 'Chocks in place.' He kicked the tyres and wiggled the ailerons. 'You mentioned that you had worked on the new German base at Sande,' he said casually.

145

'Yes.'

'What sort of work?'

'Just general labouring – digging holes, mixing concrete, carrying bricks.'

Poul moved to the back of the aircraft and checked the movement of the elevators. 'Did you find out what the place is for?'

'Not then, no. As soon as the basic construction work was done, the Danish workers were dismissed, and the Germans took over. But I'm pretty sure it's a radio station of some kind.'

'I think you mentioned that last time. But how do you know?'

'I've seen the equipment.'

Poul looked at him sharply, and Harald realized this was no casual inquiry. 'Is it visible from outside?'

'No. The place is fenced and guarded, and the radio equipment is screened by trees, except on the side facing the sea, and that part of the beach is off limits.'

'So how come you saw it?'

'I was in a hurry to get home, so I took a short cut across the base.'

Poul crouched down behind the rudder and checked the tail skid shoe. 'So,' he said, 'what did you see?'

'A large aerial, the biggest I've ever come across, maybe twelve feet square, on a rotating base.'

The airman who had been refuelling the aircraft interrupted the conversation. 'Ready when you are, sir.'

Poul said to Harald: 'Ready to fly?'

'Front or back?'

'The trainee always sits in the back.'

Harald climbed in. He had to stand on the bucket seat then ease himself down. The cockpit was narrow, and he wondered how fat pilots managed, then he realized there were no fat pilots.

Because of the nose-up angle at which the aircraft sat on the grass, he could see nothing in front of him but the clear blue sky. He had to lean out to one side to see the ground ahead.

He put his feet on the rudder pedals and his right hand on the control stick. Experimentally, he moved the stick from side to side and saw the ailerons move up and down at his command. With his left hand he touched the throttle and trim lever.

On the fuselage just outside his cockpit were two small knobs which he assumed were the twin magneto switches.

Poul leaned in to adjust Harald's safety harness. 'These aircraft were designed for training, so they have dual controls,' he said. 'While I'm flying, rest your hands and feet lightly on the controls and feel how I'm moving them. I'll tell you when to take over.'

'How will we talk?'

Poul pointed to a Y-shaped rubber pipe like a doctor's stethoscope. 'This works like the speaking tube on a ship.' He showed Harald how to fix the ends to earpieces in his flying helmet. The foot of the Y was plugged into an aluminium pipe which undoubtedly led to the front cockpit. Another tube with a mouthpiece was used for speaking.

Poul climbed into the front seat. A moment later Harald heard his voice through the speaking tube. 'Can you hear me?'

'Loud and clear.'

The airman stood by at the left front of the aircraft, and a shouted dialogue ensued, with the airman asking questions and Poul answering.

'Ready to start, sir?'

'Ready to start.'

'Fuel on, switches off, throttle closed?'

'Fuel is on, switches are off, throttle is closed.'

Harald expected the airman to turn the propeller at that point, but instead he moved to the right side of the aircraft, opened the cowling panel in the fuselage, and fiddled with the engine – priming it, Harald assumed. Then he closed the panel and returned to the nose of the aircraft.

'Sucking in, sir,' he said, then he reached up and pulled the propeller blade down. He repeated the action three times, and Harald guessed this procedure drew fuel into the cylinders.

The airman reached over the lower wing and flicked the two little switches just outside Harald's cockpit. 'Throttle set?'

Harald felt the throttle lever move forward half an inch under his hand, then heard Poul say: 'Throttle set.'

'Contact.'

Poul reached out and flicked the switches forward of his cockpit.

Once again the airman swung the propeller, this time stepping back smartly immediately afterwards. The engine fired and the propeller turned. There was a roar, and the little aircraft trembled. Harald had a sudden vivid sense of how light and frail it was, and remembered with a sense of shock that it was made, not of metal, but of wood and linen. The vibration was not like that of a car or even a motorcycle, which felt solid and firmly grounded by comparison. This was more like climbing a young tree and feeling the wind shake its slender branches.

Harald heard Poul's voice over the speaking tube. 'We have to let the engine warm up. It takes a few minutes.'

Harald thought about Poul's questions on the subject of the base at Sande. This was not idle curiosity, he felt sure. Poul had a purpose. He wanted to know the strategic importance of the base. Why? Was Poul part of some secret Resistance movement? What else could it be?

The engine note rose, and Poul reached out and turned magneto switches off and on again in turn – performing yet another safety check, Harald assumed. Then the note declined to idling pitch, and at last Poul signalled to the airman to remove the wheel chocks. Harald felt a lurch, and the aircraft moved forward.

The pedals at his feet moved as Poul used the

rudder to steer the aircraft across the grass. They taxied to the runway, which was marked by little flags, and turned into the wind, then they stopped, and Poul said: 'A few more checks before we take off.'

For the first time, it occurred to Harald that what he was about to do was dangerous. His brother had been flying for years without an accident, but other pilots had crashed, and some had died. He told himself that people died in cars, on motorcycles, and aboard boats – but somehow this felt different. He made himself stop thinking about the dangers. He was not about to panic and disgrace himself in front of the class.

Suddenly the throttle lever beneath his hand moved smoothly forward, the engine roared louder, and the Tiger Moth eagerly moved along the runway. After only a few seconds, the control stick eased away from Harald's knees, and he felt himself tip forward slightly as the tail lifted behind him. The little aircraft gathered speed, rattling and shaking over the grass. Harald's blood seemed to thrill with excitement. Then the stick eased back under his hand, the aircraft seemed to jump from the ground, and they were airborne.

It was exhilarating. They climbed steadily. To one side, Harald could see a small village. In crowded Denmark, there were not many places from which you could not see a village. Poul banked right. Feeling himself tipped sideways, Harald fought the panicky notion that he was going to fall out of the cockpit.

To calm himself, he looked at the instruments. The

rev counter showed two thousand rpm, and their speed was sixty miles per hour. They were at an altitude of one thousand feet already. The needle on the turn-and-slip indicator pointed straight up.

The aircraft straightened out and levelled off. The throttle lever moved back, the engine note dipped, and the revs slipped back to nineteen hundred. Poul said: 'Are you holding the stick?'

'Yes.'

'Check the line of the horizon. It probably goes through my head.'

'In one ear and out the other.'

'When I release the controls, I want you to simply keep the wings level and the horizon in the same place relative to my ears.'

Feeling nervous, Harald said: 'OK.'

'You have control.'

Harald felt the aircraft come alive in his hands, as every slight movement he made affected its flight. The line of the horizon fell to Poul's shoulders, showing that the nose had lifted, and he realized that a barely conscious fear of diving to the ground was making him pull back on the stick. He pushed it forward infinitesimally, and had the satisfaction of seeing the horizon line slowly rise to Poul's ears.

The aircraft lurched sideways and banked. Harald felt he had lost control and they were about to fall out of the sky. 'What was that?' he cried.

'Just a gust of wind. Correct for it, but not too much.'

Fighting back panic, Harald moved the stick against

the direction of bank. The aircraft lurched in the other direction, but at least he felt he was controlling it, and he corrected again with another small movement. Then he saw that he was climbing again, and brought the nose down. He found he had to concentrate fiercely on responding to the aircraft's slightest motion just to keep a steady course. He felt that a mistake could send him crashing to the ground.

When Poul spoke, Harald resented the interruption. 'That's very good,' Poul said. 'You're getting the hang of it.'

Harald felt he just needed to practise for another year or two.

'Now press lightly on the rudder pedals with both feet,' Poul said.

Harald had not thought about his feet for a while. 'All right,' he said brusquely.

'Look at the turn-and-slip indicator.'

Harald wanted to say *For God's sake, how can I do that and fly the aircraft at the same time?* He forced himself to take his eyes off the horizon for a second and look at the instrument panel. The needle was still in the twelve noon position. He looked back at the horizon and found that he had lifted the nose again. He corrected.

'When I take my feet off the rudder, you'll find the nose will yaw left and right with the turbulence. In case you're not sure, check the indicator. When the aircraft yaws left, the needle will move to the right, telling you to press down with your right foot to correct.'

'All right.'

Harald felt no sideways movement but a few moments later, when he managed to steal a glance at the dial, he saw he was yawing left. He pressed down on the rudder pedal with his right foot. The needle did not move. He pressed harder. Slowly, the pointer edged back to the central position. He looked up and saw that he was diving slightly. He pulled the stick back. He checked the turn-and-slip indicator again. The needle was steady.

It would have seemed simple and easy if he had not been fifteen hundred feet up in the air.

Poul said: 'Now let's try a turn.'

'Oh, shit,' said Harald.

'First, look left to see if there's anything in the way.'

Harald glanced to the left. In the far distance he could see another Tiger Moth, presumably with one of his classmates aboard, doing the same as he. That was reassuring. 'Nothing nearby,' he said.

'Ease the stick to the left.'

Harald did so. The aircraft banked left and he again experienced the sickening feeling that he was going to fall out. But the aircraft began to swing around to the left, and Harald felt a surge of excitement as he realized he was actually steering the Tiger Moth.

'In a turn, the nose tends to dip,' Poul said. Harald saw that indeed the aircraft was heading downwards, and he pulled back on the stick.

'Watch that turn-and-slip indicator,' Poul said. 'You're doing the equivalent of a skid.'

Harald checked the dial and saw that the needle had

moved to the right. He pressed the rudder pedal with his right foot. Once again, it responded only slowly.

The aircraft had turned through ninety degrees, and Harald was eager to straighten up and feel safe again, but Poul seemed to read his mind – or perhaps all pupils felt the same way at this point – and said: 'Keep turning, you're doing fine.'

The angle of bank seemed dangerously steep to Harald but he held the turn, keeping the nose up, checking the slip indicator every few seconds. Out of the corner of his eye he noticed a bus driving along the road below, just as if nothing in the least dramatic was happening in the sky, and there was no danger of a Jansborg schoolboy dropping out of the heavens to his death on its roof.

He had turned through three-quarters of a circle before Poul at last said: 'Straighten up.'

With relief, Harald eased the stick right, and the aircraft straightened.

'Watch that slip indicator.'

The needle had moved left. Harald pressed the rudder pedal with his left foot.

'Can you see the airfield?'

At first Harald could not. The countryside beneath him was a meaningless pattern of fields dotted with buildings. He had no idea what the air base would look like from above.

Poul helped him out. 'A row of long white buildings beside a bright green field. Look to the left of the propeller.'

'I see it.'

'Head that way, keeping the airfield on the left of our nose.'

Until now, Harald had not thought about the course they were following. It had been all he could manage to keep the aircraft steady. Now he had to do all the things he had previously learned and at the same time head for home. There was always one thing too many to think about.

'You're climbing,' Poul said. 'Throttle back an inch and bring us down to a thousand feet as we approach the buildings.'

Harald checked the altimeter and saw that the aircraft was indeed at two thousand feet. It had been fifteen hundred last time he looked. He throttled back and eased the stick forward.

'Dip the nose a bit more,' said Poul.

Harald felt the aircraft was in danger of diving vertically to the ground, but he forced himself to push the stick farther forward.

'Good,' said Poul.

By the time they were at a thousand feet, the base was below them.

'Turn left around the far side of that lake and bring us in line with the runway,' Poul ordered.

Harald levelled out and checked the slip indicator.

As he drew parallel with the end of the lake, he moved the stick left. This time, the feeling that he was going to fall out was not so bad.

'Watch that slip indicator.'

He had forgotten. Correcting with his foot, he brought the aircraft around.

KEN FOLLETT

'Throttle back an inch.'

Harald brought the lever back, and the engine note dipped sharply.

'Too much.'

Harald eased it forward again.

'Dip the nose.'

Harald pushed the control stick forward.

'That's it. But try to keep heading for the runway.'

Harald saw that he had wandered off course and was headed for the hangars. He put the aircraft into a shallow turn, correcting with the rudder, then lined it up with the runway again. But now he could see that he was too high.

'I'll take over from here,' Poul said.

Harald had thought Poul might talk him through a landing, but clearly he had not gained sufficient control for that. He felt disappointed.

Poul closed the throttle. The engine note fell abruptly, giving Harald the worrying feeling that there was nothing to keep the aircraft from falling straight down, but in fact it glided gradually to the runway. A few seconds before touchdown, Poul eased the stick back. The aircraft seemed to float along a few inches above the earth. Harald felt the footwell pedals moving constantly, and realized Poul was steering with the rudder now they were too close to the ground to dip a wing. At last there was a bump as the wheels and the tailskid touched earth.

Poul turned off the runway and taxied towards their parking space. Harald was thrilled. It had been even more exciting than he had imagined. He was also

156

exhausted from concentrating so hard. It had only been a short time, he thought, then he glanced at his watch, and saw to his astonishment that they had been airborne for forty-five minutes. It had felt like five.

Poul shut down the engine and climbed out. Harald pushed back his goggles, took off his helmet, fumbled with his safety harness, and struggled out of his seat. He stepped on to the reinforced strip on the wing and jumped to the ground.

'You did very well,' said Poul. 'Showed quite a talent for it, in fact – just like your brother.'

'I'm sorry I couldn't bring it in to the runway.'

'I doubt if any of the other boys will even be allowed to try. Let's go and get changed.'

When Harald had got out of his flying suit, Poul said: 'Come to my office for a minute.' Harald went with him to a door marked 'Chief Flying Instructor' and entered a small room with a filing cabinet, a desk and a couple of chairs.

'Would you mind making a drawing of that radio equipment you were describing to me earlier?' Poul's tone was casual, but his body was stiff with tension.

Harald had wondered whether that subject would come up again. 'Sure.'

'It's quite important. I won't go into the reasons why.'

'That's all right.'

'Sit at the desk. There's a box of pencils and some paper in the drawer. Take your time. Do it over until you're satisfied.'

'OK.'

'How long do you think you might need?'

'Maybe a quarter of an hour. It was dark so I can't draw details. But I have a clear outline in my head.'

'I'll leave you alone so you don't feel pressured. I'll come back in fifteen minutes.'

Poul left and Harald began to draw. He cast his mind back to that Saturday night in the pouring rain. There had been a circular concrete wall, he recalled, about six feet high. The aerial had been a grid of wires looking like bedsprings. Its rotating base was inside the circular wall, and cables had run from the back of the aerial into a duct.

First he drew the wall with the aerial above. He vaguely recalled that there had been one or two similar structures nearby, so he sketched them in lightly. Then he drew the machinery as if the wall were not there, showing its base and the cables. He was no artist but he could render machinery accurately, probably because he liked it.

When he had finished, he turned the sheet of paper over and made a plan of the island of Sande, showing the position of the base and the restricted area of beach.

Poul came back after fifteen minutes. He studied the drawings intently, then said: 'This is excellent – thank you.'

'You're welcome.'

He pointed to the ancillary structures Harald had sketched. 'What are these?'

'I really don't know. I didn't look closely. But I thought I should put them in.'

'Quite right. One more question. This grid of wires, which is presumably an aerial. Is it flat, or dished?'

Harald racked his brains, but could not remember. 'I'm not sure,' he said. 'Sorry.'

'That's all right.' Poul opened the filing cabinet. All the files were labelled with names, presumably of past and present pupils at the school. He selected one marked 'Andersen, H.C.' It was not an unusual name, but Hans Christian Andersen was Denmark's most famous writer, and Harald guessed the file might be a hiding place. Sure enough, Poul put the drawings in the folder and returned the file to its place.

'Let's go back to the others,' he said. He went to the door. Stopping with his hand on the doorknob, he said: 'Making drawings of German military installations is a crime, technically. It would be best not to mention this to anyone – not even Arne.'

Harald felt a pang of dismay. His brother was not involved in this. Even Arne's best friend did not think he had the nerve.

Harald nodded. 'I'll agree to that – on one condition.'

Poul was surprised. 'Condition? What?'

'That you tell me something honestly.'

He shrugged. 'All right, I'll try.'

'There is a Resistance movement, isn't there?'

'Yes,' Poul said, looking serious. After a moment's pause, he added: 'And now you're in it.'

EIGHT

Tilde Jespersen wore a light, flowery perfume that wafted across the pavement table and teased Peter Flemming's nostrils, never quite strong enough for him to identify it, like an elusive memory. He imagined how the fragrance would rise from her warm skin as he slipped off her blouse, her skirt, and her underwear.

'What are you thinking about?' she said.

He was tempted to tell her. She would pretend shock, but secretly be pleased. He could tell when a woman was ready for that kind of talk, and he knew how to do it: lightly, with a self-deprecating smile, but an underlying tone of sincerity.

Then he thought of his wife, and held back. He took his marital vows seriously. Other people might think he had a good excuse for breaking them, but he set himself higher standards.

So he said: 'I was thinking about you tripping up the runaway mechanic at the aerodrome. You showed great presence of mind.'

'I didn't even think about it, just stuck out my foot.'

'You have good instincts. I was never in favour of

160

women police and, to tell you the truth, I still have my doubts – but no one could deny you're a first class cop.'

She shrugged. 'I have doubts myself. Maybe women ought to stay home and look after babies. But after Oskar died . . .' Oskar had been her husband, a Copenhagen detective and friend of Peter's. 'I had to work, and law enforcement is the only life I know anything about. My father was a customs officer, my older brother is a military police officer, and my younger brother a uniformed policeman in Aarhus.'

'I'll tell you the great thing about you, Tilde – you never try to get men to do your work by playing the helpless female.'

He intended his remark as a compliment, but she did not look as pleased as he had hoped. 'I never ask for help at all,' she said crisply.

'Probably a good policy.'

She gave him a look he could not read. Puzzling over the sudden chill in the atmosphere, he wondered whether she might be afraid to ask for assistance in case she was immediately classed as a helpless female. He could see how she might resent that. After all, men asked one another for help all the time.

She said: 'But why are you a cop? Your father has a successful business – don't you want to take it over, one day?'

He shook his head ruefully. 'I used to work at the hotel in the school holidays. I hated the guests, with their demands and complaints: this beef is

161

overcooked, my mattress is lumpy, I've been waiting twenty minutes for a cup of coffee. I couldn't stand it.'

The waiter came. Peter resisted the temptation to have herrings and onions on his smorrebrod, thinking, vaguely, that he might get close enough to Tilde for her to smell his breath, so he ordered soft cheese and cucumbers instead. They handed their ration cards to the waiter.

Tilde said: 'Any progress in the spy case?'

'Not really. The two men we arrested at the aerodrome told us nothing. They were sent to Hamburg for what the Gestapo calls "deep interrogation", and they gave the name of their contact – Matthies Hertz, an army officer. But he has disappeared.'

'A dead end, then.'

'Yes.' The phrase made him think of another dead end he had run into. 'Do you know any Jews?'

She looked surprised. 'One or two, I should think. None in the police force. Why?'

'I'm making a list.'

'A list of Jews?'

'Yes.'

'Where, in Copenhagen?'

'In Denmark.'

'Why?'

'The usual reason. It's my job to keep tabs on troublemakers.'

'And Jews are troublemakers?'

'The Germans think so.'

162

'You can see why *they* might have problems with Jews – but do we?'

He was taken aback. He had expected her to see this from his point of view. 'It's as well to be prepared. We have lists of union organizers, communists, foreign nationals, and members of the Danish Nazi Party.'

'And you think that's the same thing?'

'It's all information. Now, it's easy to identify new Jewish immigrants, who've come here in the last fifty years. They dress funny, they speak with a peculiar accent, and most of them live in the same few Copenhagen streets. But there are also Jews whose families have been Danish for centuries. *They* look and talk the same as everyone else. Most of them eat roast pork and go to work on Saturday mornings. If we ever need to find them, we could have trouble. So I'm making a list.'

'How? You can't just go round asking people if they know any Jews.'

'It's a problem. I have two junior detectives going through the phone book, and one or two other lists, making notes of Jewish-sounding names.'

'That's not very reliable. There are lots of people called Isaksen who aren't Jewish.'

'And lots of Jews with names like Jan Christiansen. What I'd really like to do is raid the synagogue. They probably have a membership list.'

To his surprise, she was looking disapproving, but she said: 'Why don't you?'

'Juel won't allow it.'

'I think he's right.'

'Really? Why?'

'Peter, can't you see? What use might your list be put to in the future?'

'Isn't it obvious?' Peter said irritably. 'If Jewish groups start to organize resistance to the Germans, we'll know where to look for suspects.'

'And what if the Nazis just decide to round up all the Jews and send them to those concentration camps they have in Germany? They'll use your list!'

'But why would they send the Jews to camps?'

'Because Nazis hate Jews. But we're not Nazis, we're police officers. We arrest people because they've committed crimes, not because we hate them.'

'I know that,' Peter said angrily. He was astonished to be attacked from this angle. Tilde should know that his motive was to uphold the law, not subvert it. 'There's always a risk that information will be misused.'

'So wouldn't it be better not to make the damn list?'

How could she be so stupid? It maddened him to be opposed by someone he thought of as a comrade in the war against lawbreakers. 'No!' he shouted. He lowered his voice with an effort. 'If we thought that way, we wouldn't have a security department at all!'

Tilde shook her head. 'Look, Peter, the Nazis have done a lot of good things, we both know that. They're on the side of the police, basically. They've clamped down on subversion, they maintain law and order, they've reduced unemployment, and so on. But on the subject of Jews, they're insane.'

'Maybe, but they're making the rules now.'

'Just look at the Danish Jews – they're law-abiding, hard-working, they send their children to school ... It's ludicrous to make a list of their names and addresses as if they were all part of some Communist conspiracy.'

He sat back and said accusingly: 'So, you'd refuse to work on this with me?'

It was her turn to be offended. 'How can you say that? I'm a professional police officer, and you're my boss. I'll do what you say. You ought to know that.'

'Do you mean it?'

'Look, if you wanted to make a complete list of witches in Denmark, I'd tell you I didn't think witches were criminals or subversives – but I'd help you make the list.'

Their food arrived. There was an awkward silence as they began to eat. After a few minutes, Tilde said: 'How are things at home?'

Peter had a sudden memory of himself and Inge, a few days before the accident, walking to church on Sunday morning, two healthy, happy young people in their best clothes. With all the scum and riff-raff in the world, why did it have to be his wife whose mind was destroyed by that drunken boy in his sports car? 'Inge is the same,' he said.

'No improvement?'

'When the brain is damaged that badly, it doesn't mend. There will never be any improvement.'

'It must be hard for you.'

'I'm fortunate to have a generous father. I couldn't afford a nurse on police wages – Inge would have to go into an asylum.'

Once again Tilde gave him a look that was hard to read. It was almost as if she felt the asylum might not be a bad solution. 'What about the driver of the sports car?'

'Finn Jonk. His trial started yesterday. It should be over in a day or two.'

'At last! What do you think will happen?'

'He's pleading guilty. I assume he'll be jailed for five or ten years.'

'It doesn't seem enough.'

'For destroying someone's mind? What would be enough?'

After lunch, when they were walking back to the Politigaarden, Tilde put her arm through Peter's. It was an affectionate gesture, and he felt she was telling him that she liked him despite their disagreement. As they approached the ultramodern police headquarters building, he said: 'I'm sorry you disapprove of my Jewish list.'

She stopped and turned to him. 'You're not a bad man, Peter.' To his surprise, she seemed to be on the edge of tears. 'Your sense of duty is your great strength. But doing your duty isn't the only law.'

'I don't really understand what you mean.'

'I know.' She turned away and went into the building alone.

Making his way to his office, he tried to see the

issue from her point of view. If the Nazis imprisoned law-abiding Jews, that would be a crime, and his list would help the criminals. But you could say that about a gun, or even a car: the fact that something might be used by criminals did not mean it was wrong to have it.

As he was crossing the open central courtyard, he was hailed by his boss, Frederik Juel. 'Come with me,' Juel said briskly. 'We've been summoned by General Braun.' He marched ahead, his military bearing giving an impression of decisiveness and efficiency that Peter knew to be quite false.

It was a short walk from the Politigaarden to the town square, where the Germans had taken over a building called the Dagmarhus. It was surrounded by barbed wire and had cannons and anti-aircraft guns on the flat roof. They were shown to Walter Braun's office, a corner room overlooking the square, comfortably furnished with an antique desk and a leather couch. There was a rather small picture of the Fuehrer on the wall and a framed photograph on the desk of two small boys in school uniform. Braun wore his pistol even here, Peter noted, as if to say that although he had a cosy office, nevertheless he meant business.

Braun was looking pleased with himself. 'Our people have decoded the message you found in the hollow aeroplane chock,' he said in his habitual near-whisper.

Peter was elated.

'Very impressive,' Juel murmured.

'Apparently it was not difficult,' Braun went on. 'The British use simple codes, often based on a poem or famous passage of prose. Once our cryptanalysts get a few words, a professor of English can usually fill in the rest. I have never before known the study of English literature to serve any useful purpose.' He laughed at his own wit.

Peter said impatiently: 'What was in the message?'

Braun opened a file on his desk. 'It comes from a group calling themselves the Nightwatchmen.' Although they were speaking German, he used the Danish word *natvaegterne*. 'Does that mean anything to you?'

Peter was taken by surprise. 'I'll check the files, of course, but I'm pretty sure we haven't come across this name before.' He frowned, considering. 'Real-life nightwatchmen are usually police or soldiers, aren't they?'

Juel bridled. 'I hardly think that Danish police officers—'

'I didn't say they were Danish,' Peter interrupted. 'The spies could be German traitors.' He shrugged. 'Or they may just aspire to military status.' He looked at Braun. 'What's the content of the message, General?'

'Details of our military dispositions in Denmark. Take a look.' He passed a sheaf of papers across the desk. 'Locations of anti-aircraft batteries in and around Copenhagen. German naval vessels in the harbour during the last month. Regiments stationed in Aarhus, Odense and Morlunde.'

'Is the information accurate?'

Braun hesitated. 'Not precisely. Close to the truth, but not exact.'

Peter nodded. 'Then the spies probably are not Germans with inside information, for such people would be able to get correct details from the files. More likely, they are Danes who are careful observers making educated estimates.'

Braun nodded. 'A shrewd deduction. But can you find these people?'

'I certainly hope so.'

Braun's focus of attention had switched entirely to Peter, as if Juel were not there, or just an underling in attendance rather than the senior officer. 'Do you think the same people are putting out the illegal newspapers?'

Peter was pleased that Braun recognized his expertise, but frustrated that Juel was nevertheless the boss. He hoped that Braun himself had noted this irony. He shook his head. 'We know the underground editors and we keep an eye on their activities. If they had been making meticulous observations of German military dispositions, we would have noticed. No – I believe this is a new organization we haven't encountered.'

'Then how will you catch them?'

'There is one group of potential subversives whom we have never properly investigated – the Jews.'

Peter heard a sharp intake of breath from Juel.

Braun said: 'You had better take a look at them.'

'It's not always easy to know who the Jews are, in this country.'

'Then go to the synagogue!'

'Good idea,' Peter said. 'They may have a membership list. That would be a start.'

Juel gave Peter a thunderous look, but said nothing.

Braun said: 'My superiors in Berlin are impressed with the loyalty and efficiency of the Danish police in intercepting this message to British intelligence. Nevertheless, they were keen to send in a team of Gestapo investigators. I have dissuaded them, by promising that you will vigorously investigate the spy ring and bring the traitors to justice.' It was a long speech for a man with one lung, and it left him breathless. He paused, looking from Peter to Juel and back again. When he had caught his breath, he finished: 'For your own sakes, and for the good of everyone in Denmark, you'd better succeed.'

Juel and Peter stood up, and Juel said tightly: 'We will do everything possible.'

They left. As soon as they were outside the building, Juel rounded on Peter with a blazing blue-eyed stare. 'You know perfectly well this has nothing to do with the synagogue, damn you.'

'I know nothing of the kind.'

'You're just toadying to the Nazis, you disgusting creep.'

'Why shouldn't we help them? They represent the law, now.'

'You think they'll help your career.'

'And why not?' Peter said, stung to retaliate. 'The

170

Copenhagen élite are prejudiced against men from the provinces – but the Germans may be more fair-minded.'

Juel was incredulous. 'Is *that* what you believe?'

'At least they're not blind to the abilities of boys who did not go to Jansborg Skole.'

'So you think you were passed over because of your background? Idiot – you didn't get the job because you're too extreme! You've got no sense of proportion. You'd wipe crime out by arresting everyone who looked suspicious!' He made a disgusted sound. 'If I have anything to do with it, you'll never get another promotion. Now get out of my sight.' He walked away.

Peter burned with resentment. Who did Juel think he was? Having a famous ancestor did not make him better than anyone else. He was a cop, just like Peter, and he had no right to talk as if he were a higher life form.

But Peter had got his way. He had defeated Juel. He had permission to raid the synagogue.

Juel would hate him for ever for that. But did it matter? Braun, not Juel, was the power now. Better to be Braun's favourite and Juel's enemy than the other way around.

Back at headquarters, Peter swiftly assembled his team, choosing the same detectives he had used at Kastrup: Conrad, Dresler, and Ellegard. He said to Tilde Jespersen: 'I'd like to take you along, if you don't object.'

'Why would I object?' she said testily.

'After our conversation over lunch . . .'

'Please! I'm a professional. I told you that.'

'Good enough,' he said.

They drove to a street called Krystalgade. The yellow-brick synagogue stood side-on to the street, as if hunching a shoulder against a hostile world. Peter stationed Ellegard at the gate to make sure no one could sneak out.

An elderly man in a yarmulke appeared from the Jewish old people's home next door. 'May I help you?' he said politely.

'We're police officers,' Peter said. 'Who are you?'

The man's face took on a look of such abject fear that Peter almost felt sorry for him. 'Gorm Rasmussen, I'm the day manager of the home,' he said in a shaky voice.

'You have keys to the synagogue?'

'Yes.'

'Let us in.'

The man took a bunch of keys from his pocket and opened a door.

Most of the building was taken up by the main hall, a richly decorated room with gilded Egyptian columns supporting galleries over the side aisles. 'These Jews have plenty of money,' Conrad muttered.

Peter said to Rasmussen: 'Show me your membership list.'

'Membership? What do you mean?'

'You must have the names and addresses of your congregation.'

'No – all Jews are welcome.'

Peter's instinct told him the man was telling the truth, but he would search the place anyway. 'Are there any offices here?'

'No. Just small robing rooms for the rabbi and other officials, and a cloakroom for the congregation to hang their coats.'

Peter nodded to Dresler and Conrad. 'Check them out.' He walked up the centre of the room to the pulpit end and climbed a short flight of steps to a raised dais. Behind a curtain he found a concealed niche. 'What have we here?'

'The Torah scrolls,' said Rasmussen.

There were six large, heavy-looking scrolls lovingly wrapped in velvet cloth, providing perfect hiding-places for secret documents. 'Unwrap them all,' he said. 'Spread them out on the floor so I can see there's nothing else inside.'

'Yes, right away.'

While Rasmussen was doing his bidding, Peter walked a short distance away with Tilde, and talked to her while keeping a suspicious eye on the manager. 'Are you OK?'

'I told you.'

'If we find something, will you admit I was right?'

She smiled. 'If we don't, will you admit you were wrong?'

He nodded, pleased that she was not angry with him.

Rasmussen spread out the scrolls, covered with Hebrew script. Peter saw nothing suspicious. He supposed it was possible they had no register of

173

members. More likely, they used to have one but destroyed it as a precaution the day the Germans invaded. He felt frustrated. He had gone to a lot of trouble for this raid, and had made himself even more unpopular with his boss. It would be maddening if it came to nothing.

Dresler and Conrad returned from opposite ends of the building. Dresler was empty-handed, but Conrad was carrying a copy of the newspaper *Reality*.

Peter took the newspaper and showed it to Rasmussen. 'This is illegal.'

'I'm sorry,' the man said. He looked as if he might cry. 'They push them through the letter box.'

The people who printed the newspaper were not being sought by the police, so those who merely read it were in no danger at all – but Rasmussen did not know that, and Peter pushed his moral advantage. 'You must write to your people sometimes,' he said.

'Well, of course, to leading members of the Jewish community. But we don't have a list. We know who they are.' He tried a weak smile. 'So do you, I imagine.'

It was true. Peter knew the names of a dozen or more prominent Jews: a couple of bankers, a judge, several professors at the university, some political figures, a painter. They were not who he was after: they were too well known to be spies. Such people could not stand at the dockside counting ships without being noticed. 'Don't you send letters to the ordinary people, asking them to donate to charities, telling them of events you're organizing, celebrations, picnics, concerts?'

'No,' said the man. 'We just put up a notice at the community centre.'

'Ah,' said Peter with a satisfied smile. 'The community centre. And where is that?'

'Near Christiansborg, in Ny Kongensgade.'

It was about a mile away. 'Dresler,' said Peter. 'Keep this guy here for fifteen minutes and make sure he doesn't warn anyone.'

They drove to the street called Ny Kongensgade. The Jewish community centre was a large eighteenth-century building with an internal courtyard and an elegant staircase, though it needed redecorating. The cafeteria was closed, and there was no one playing ping-pong in the basement. A well-dressed young man with a disdainful air was in charge of the office. He said they had no list of names and addresses, but the detectives searched the place anyway.

The young man's name was Ingemar Gammel, and something about him made Peter thoughtful. What was it? Unlike Rasmussen, Gammel was not frightened; but whereas Peter had felt Rasmussen was scared but innocent, Gammel gave him the opposite impression.

Gammel sat at a desk, wearing a waistcoat with a watch chain, and looked on coolly while his office was ransacked. His clothes seemed expensive. Why was a wealthy young man acting as secretary here? This kind of work was normally done by underpaid girls, or middle-class housewives whose children had flown the nest.

'I think this is what we're looking for, boss,' said Conrad, passing Peter a black ringbinder. 'A list of rat holes.'

Peter looked inside and saw page after page of names and addresses, several hundred of them. 'Bang,' he said. 'Well done.' But instinct told him there was more to find here. 'Keep looking, everyone, in case something else turns up.'

He flicked through the pages, looking for anything odd, or familiar, or ... something. He had that dissatisfied feeling. But nothing caught his eye.

Gammel's jacket hung from a hook behind the door. Peter read the tailor's label. The suit had been made by Anderson & Sheppard of Savile Row, London, in 1938. Peter was jealous. He bought his clothes from the best shops in Copenhagen, but he could never afford an English suit. There was a silk handkerchief in the outside breast pocket. He found a well-stuffed money clip in the left side pocket. In the right pocket was a train ticket to Aarhus, return, with a neat hole made by a ticket inspector's punch. 'Why did you go to Aarhus?'

'To visit friends.'

The decoded message had included the name of the German regiment stationed at Aarhus, Peter recalled. However, Aarhus was Denmark's largest town after Copenhagen, and hundreds of people travelled between the two cities every day.

In the inside pocket of the jacket was a slim diary. Peter opened it.

Gammel said with contempt: 'Do you enjoy your work?'

Peter looked up with a smile. He did enjoy infuriating pompous rich men who thought they were superior to ordinary people. But what he said was: 'Like a plumber, I see a lot of shit.' He pointedly returned his gaze to Gammel's diary.

Gammel's handwriting was stylish, like his suit, with big capitals and full loops. The entries in the diary all looked normal: lunch dates, theatre, Mother's birthday, phone Jorgen about Wilder. 'Who is Jorgen?' Peter asked.

'My cousin, Jorgen Lumpe. We exchange books.'

'And Wilder?'

'Thornton Wilder.'

'And he is . . .?'

'The American writer. *The Bridge of San Luis Rey.* You must have read it.'

There was a sneer in that, an implication that policemen were not sufficiently cultured to read foreign novels, but Peter ignored it and turned to the back of the diary. As he expected, he found a list of names and addresses, some with phone numbers. He glanced up at Gammel, and thought he saw the hint of a flush on his clean-shaven cheeks. That was promising. He scrutinized the address list with care.

He picked a name at random. 'Hilde Bjergager – who is she?'

'A lady friend,' Gammel answered coolly.

Peter tried another. 'Bertil Bruun?'

Gammel remained unflustered. 'We play tennis.'

'Fred Eskildsen.'

'My bank manager.'

The other detectives had stopped searching and fallen silent, sensing the tension.

'Poul Kirke?'

'Old friend.'

'Preben Klausen.'

'Picture dealer.'

For the first time, Gammel showed a hint of emotion, but it was relief, rather than guilt. Why? Did he think he had got away with something? What was the significance of the picture dealer Klausen? Or was the previous name the important one? Had Gammel shown relief because Peter had *moved on* to Klausen?

'Poul Kirke is an old friend?'

'We were at university together.' Gammel's voice was even, but there was just the suggestion of fear in his eyes.

Peter glanced at Tilde, and she gave a slight nod. She, too, had seen something in Gammel's reaction.

Peter looked again at the diary. There was no address for Kirke, but beside the phone number was a capital 'N', written uncharacteristically small. 'What does this mean – the letter N?' Peter said.

'Naestved. It's his number at Naestved.'

'What's his other number?'

'He doesn't have another.'

'So why do you need the annotation?'

'To tell you the truth, I don't remember,' Gammel said, showing irritation.

It might have been true. On the other hand, 'N' might stand for 'Nightwatchman'.

Peter said: 'What does he do for a living?'

'Pilot.'

'With whom?'

'The army.'

'Ah.' Peter had speculated that the Nightwatchmen might be army people, because of their name and because they were accurate observers of military details. 'At which base?'

'Vodal.'

'I thought you said he was at Naestved.'

'It's nearby.'

'It's twenty miles away.'

'Well, that's how I remember it.'

Peter nodded thoughtfully, then said to Conrad: 'Arrest this lying prick.'

* * *

The search of Ingemar Gammel's apartment was disappointing. Peter found nothing of interest: no code book, no subversive literature, no weapons. He concluded that Gammel must be a minor figure in the spy ring, one whose role was simply to make observations and report them to a central contact. That key man would compile the messages and send them to England. But who was the pivotal figure? Peter hoped it might be Poul Kirke.

Before driving the fifty miles to the flying school at Vodal where Poul Kirke was stationed, Peter spent an hour at home with his wife, Inge. As he fed her apple-

and-honey sandwiches in tiny squares, he found himself daydreaming about domestic life with Tilde Jespersen. He imagined himself watching Tilde getting ready to go out in the evening – washing her hair and drying it vigorously with a towel, sitting at the dressing-table in her underwear polishing her nails, looking in the mirror as she tied a silk scarf around her neck. He realized he was yearning to be with a woman who could do things for herself.

He had to stop thinking this way. He was a married man. The fact that a man's wife was sick did not provide an excuse for adultery. Tilde was a colleague and a friend, and she should never be any more to him than that.

Feeling restless and discontented, he turned on the radio and listened to the news while he waited for the evening nurse to arrive. The British had launched a new attack in North Africa, crossing the Egyptian border into Libya with a tank division in an attempt to relieve the besieged city of Tobruk. It sounded like a major operation, though the censored Danish radio station naturally predicted that German antitank guns would decimate the British forces.

The phone rang, and Peter crossed the room to pick it up.

'Allan Forslund here, Traffic Division.' Forslund was the officer dealing with Finn Jonk, the drunk driver who had crashed into Peter's car. 'The trial has just ended.'

'What happened?'

'Jonk got six months.'

180

'Six *months?*'

'I'm sorry—'

Peter's vision blurred. He felt he was going to fall over, and he put a hand on the wall to steady himself. 'For destroying my wife's mind and ruining my life? Six months?'

'The judge said he had already suffered torment and he would have to live with the guilt for the rest of his life.'

'That's shit!'

'I know.'

'I thought the prosecution was going to ask for a severe sentence.'

'We did. But Jonk's lawyer was very persuasive. Said the boy has stopped drinking, rides around on a bicycle, is studying to be an architect—'

'Anyone can say that.'

'I know.'

'I don't accept this! I refuse to accept it!'

'Nothing we can do—'

'Like hell there isn't.'

'Peter, don't take any hasty action.'

Peter tried to calm himself. 'Of course I won't.'

'Are you alone?'

'I'm going back to work in a few minutes.'

'So long as you have someone to talk to.'

'Yes. Thanks for calling, Allan.'

'I'm very sorry we didn't do better.'

'Not your fault. A slick lawyer and a stupid judge. We've seen that before.' Peter hung up. He had forced himself to sound calm, but he was boiling. If

181

Jonk had been at large he might have sought him out and killed him – but the kid was safe in jail, if only for a few months. He thought of finding the lawyer, arresting him on a pretext, and beating the shit out of him; but he knew he would not do it. The lawyer had not broken any laws.

He looked at Inge. She was sitting where he had left her, watching him blank-faced, waiting for him to continue feeding her. He noticed that some of the chewed apple had dribbled from her mouth on to the bodice of her dress. She was not normally a messy eater, despite her condition. Before the accident she had been extraordinarily fastidious about her appearance. Seeing her with food on her chin and stains on her clothing suddenly made him want to weep.

He was saved by the doorbell. He pulled himself together rapidly and answered it. The nurse had arrived at the same time as Bent Conrad, who had come to pick him up for the journey to Vodal. He shrugged on his jacket and left the nurse to clean Inge up.

They went in two cars, standard black police Buicks. Peter thought the army might put obstacles in his way, so he had asked General Braun to detail a German officer to impose authority if necessary, and a Major Schwarz from Braun's staff was in the lead car.

The journey took an hour and a half. Schwarz smoked a large cigar, filling the car with fumes. Peter tried not to think about the outrageously light sentence on Finn Jonk. He might need his wits about him at the air base, and he did not want his judgement to be skewed by rage. He tried to smother his blazing fury, but it smouldered on under a blanket of false calm, stinging his eyes with its smoke, like Schwarz's cigar.

Vodal was a grass airfield with a scatter of low buildings along one side. Security was light – it was only a training school, so nothing remotely secret went on here – and a single guard at the gate casually waved them through without asking their business. Half a dozen Tiger Moths were parked in a line, like birds on a fence. There were also some gliders and two Messerschmitt Me109s.

As Peter got out of the car, he saw Arne Olufsen, his boyhood rival from Sande, sauntering across the car park in his smart brown army uniform. The sour taste of resentment came into Peter's mouth.

Peter and Arne had been friends, all through childhood, until the quarrel between their families twelve years before. It had started when Axel Flemming, Peter's father, had been accused of tax fraud. Axel felt the prosecution was outrageous: he had only done what everyone else did, and understated his profits by inflating his costs. He had been convicted, and had to pay a hefty fine on top of all the back tax.

He had persuaded his friends and neighbours to see the case as an argument about an accounting technicality, rather than an accusation of dishonesty. Then Pastor Olufsen had intervened.

There was a church rule that any member who

committed a crime should be 'read out', or expelled from the congregation. The offender could rejoin the following Sunday, if he wished, but for one week he was an outsider. The procedure was not invoked for trivial crimes such as speeding, and Axel had argued that his transgression fell into that category. Pastor Olufsen thought otherwise.

This humiliation had been much worse for Axel than the fine with which the court had punished him. His name had been read to the congregation, he had been obliged to leave his place and sit at the back of the church throughout the service, and to complete his mortification the pastor had preached a sermon on the text: 'Render unto Caesar that which is Caesar's.'

Peter winced every time he remembered it. Axel was proud of his position as a successful businessman and community leader, and there could be no greater punishment for him than to lose the respect of his neighbours. It had been torture to Peter to see his father publicly reprimanded by a pompous, self-righteous prig like Olufsen. He believed his father had deserved the fine, but not the humiliation in church. He had sworn then that if any member of the Olufsen family ever transgressed, there would be no mercy.

He hardly dared to hope that Arne was involved in the spy ring. That would be a sweet revenge.

Arne caught his eye. 'Peter!' He looked surprised, but not afraid.

'Is this where you work?' Peter said.

'When there's any work to do.' Arne was as

debonair and relaxed as ever. If he had anything to feel guilty about, he was concealing it well.

'Of course, you're a pilot.'

'This is a training school, but we don't have many pupils. More to the point, what are you doing here?' Arne glanced at the major in German uniform standing behind Peter. 'Is there a dangerous outbreak of littering? Or has someone been cycling after dark without lights?'

Peter did not find Arne's raillery very funny. 'Routine investigation,' he replied shortly. 'Where will I find your commanding officer?'

Arne pointed to one of the low buildings. 'Base headquarters. You need Squadron Leader Renthe.'

Peter left him and went into the building. Renthe was a lanky man with a bristly moustache and a sour expression. Peter introduced himself and said: 'I'm here to interview one of your men, a Flight Lieutenant Poul Kirke.'

The squadron leader looked pointedly at Major Schwarz and said: 'What's the problem?'

The reply 'None of your damn business' sprang to Peter's lips, but he was resolved to be calm, so he told a polite lie. 'He's been dealing in stolen property.'

'When military personnel are *suspected* of crimes, we prefer to investigate the matter ourselves.'

'Of course you do. However . . .' He moved a hand in the direction of Schwarz. 'Our German friends want the police to deal with it, so your *preferences* are irrelevant. Is Kirke on the base at this moment?'

'He happens to be flying.'

Peter raised his eyebrows. 'I thought your planes were grounded.'

'As a rule, yes, but there are exceptions. We're expecting a visit from a Luftwaffe group tomorrow, and they want to be taken up in our training aircraft, so we have permission to do test flights today to make sure the aircraft are in readiness. Kirke should land in a few minutes.'

'I'll search his quarters meanwhile. Where does he bed down?'

Renthe hesitated, then answered reluctantly. 'Dormitory A, at the far end of the runway.'

'Does he have an office, or a locker, or anywhere else he might keep things?'

'He has a small office three doors along this corridor.'

'I'll start there. Tilde, come with me. Conrad, go out to the airfield to meet Kirke when he comes back – I don't want him to slip away. Dresler and Ellegard, search Dormitory A. Squadron Leader, thank you for your help . . .' Peter saw the commander's eyes stray to the phone on the desk, and added: 'Don't make any phone calls for the next few minutes. If you were to warn anyone that we're on our way, that would constitute obstruction of justice. I'd have to throw you in jail, and that wouldn't do the army's reputation much good, would it?'

Renthe made no reply.

Peter, Tilde and Schwarz went along the corridor to a door marked 'Chief Flying Instructor'. A desk and a filing cabinet were squeezed into a small room with no windows. Peter and Tilde began to search and Schwarz lit another cigar. The filing cabinet contained pupil records. Peter and Tilde patiently looked at every sheet of paper. The little room was airless, and Tilde's elusive perfume was lost in Schwarz's cigar smoke.

After fifteen minutes, Tilde made a surprised noise and said: 'This is odd.'

Peter looked up from the exam results of a student called Keld Hansen who had failed his navigation test.

Tilde handed him a sheet of paper. Peter studied it, frowning. It bore a careful sketch of a piece of apparatus that Peter did not recognize: a large square aerial on a stand, surrounded by a wall. A second drawing of the same apparatus without the wall showed more details of the stand, which looked as if it might revolve.

Tilde looked over his shoulder. 'What do you think it can be?'

He was intensely aware of how close she was. 'I've never seen anything like it, but I'd bet the farm it's secret. Anything else in the file?'

'No.' She showed him a folder marked 'Andersen, H.C.'

Peter grunted. 'Hans Christian Andersen – that's suspicious in itself.' He turned the sheet over. On its reverse was a sketch map of an island whose long, thin shape was as familiar to Peter as the map of Denmark itself. 'This is Sande, where my father lives!' he said.

Looking more closely, he saw that the map showed the new German base and the area of the beach that was off limits.

'Bang,' he said softly.

Tilde's blue eyes were shining with excitement. 'We've caught a spy, haven't we?'

'Not yet,' Peter said. 'But we're about to.'

They went outside, followed by the silent Schwarz. The sun had set, but they could see clearly in the soft twilight of the long Scandinavian summer evening.

They walked on to the airfield and stood beside Conrad, near where the planes were parked. The aircraft were being put away for the night. One was being wheeled into the hangar, two airmen pushing its wings and a third lifting its tail off the ground.

Conrad pointed to an incoming aircraft downwind of the airfield and said: 'I think this must be our man.'

It was another Tiger Moth. As it descended in a textbook circuit and turned into the wind for landing, Peter reflected that there was no doubt Poul Kirke was a spy. The evidence found in the filing cabinet would be enough to hang him. But before that happened, Peter had a lot of questions to ask him. Was he simply a reporter, like Ingemar Gammel? Had Kirke travelled to Sande himself to check out the air base and sketch the mystery apparatus? Or did he play the more important role of coordinator, assembling information and transmitting it to England in coded messages? If Kirke was the central contact, who had gone to Sande and made the sketch? Could it have been Arne

Olufsen? That was possible, but Arne had shown no sign of guilt an hour ago when Peter had arrived unexpectedly at the base. Still, it might be worthwhile to put Arne under surveillance.

As the aircraft touched down and bumped along the grass, one of the police Buicks came from the upwind end of the runway in a tearing hurry. It skidded to a stop, and Dresler jumped out, carrying something bright yellow.

Peter threw him a nervous look. He did not want a kerfuffle that might forewarn Poul Kirke. Glancing around, he realized that he had relaxed his guard for a moment, and failed to notice that the group at the edge of the runway appeared somewhat out of place: himself in a dark suit, Schwarz in German uniform smoking a cigar, a woman, and now a man jumping out of a car in an obvious hurry. They looked like a reception committee, and the setup might ring alarm bells in Kirke's mind.

Dresler came up to him excitedly waving the yellow object, a book with a brightly coloured dust jacket. 'This is his code book!' he said.

That meant Kirke *was* the key man. Peter looked at the little aircraft, which had turned off the runway before drawing level with the waiting group, and was now taxiing past them to the parking area. 'Put the book under your coat, you damn fool,' he said to Dresler. 'If he sees you waving that about, he'll know we're on to him!'

He looked again at the Tiger Moth. He could see

Kirke in the open cockpit, but could not read the man's expression behind the goggles, scarf and helmet.

However, there was no room to misinterpret what happened next.

The engine suddenly roared louder as the throttle was opened wide. The aircraft swung around, turning into the wind but also heading straight for the little group around Peter. 'Damn, he's going to run for it!' Peter cried.

The plane picked up speed and came directly at them.

Peter drew his pistol.

He wanted to take Kirke alive, and interrogate him – but he would rather have him dead than let him get away. Holding the gun with both hands, he pointed it at the oncoming aircraft. It was virtually impossible to shoot down a plane with a handgun, but perhaps he might hit the pilot with a lucky shot.

The Tiger Moth's tail came up off the ground, levelling the fuselage and bringing Kirke's head and shoulders into view. Peter took careful aim at the flying helmet and pulled the trigger. The aircraft lifted off the ground, and Peter raised his aim, emptying the seven-shot magazine of the Walther PPK. He saw with bitter disappointment that he had shot too high, for a series of small holes like ink blots appeared in the fuel tank over the pilot's head, and petrol was spurting into the cockpit in small jets. The aircraft did not falter.

The others threw themselves flat.

A suicidal rage seized Peter as the spinning propeller approached him at sixty miles per hour. At the controls with Poul Kirke were all the criminals who had ever escaped justice, including Finn Jonk, the driver who had injured Inge. Peter was going to stop Kirke getting away if it killed him.

Out of the corner of his eye, he saw Major Schwarz's cigar smouldering on the grass, and he was seized by inspiration.

As the biplane swept lethally towards him he stooped, picked up the burning cigar, and threw it at the pilot.

Then he flung himself sideways.

He felt the rush of wind as the lower wing passed within inches of his head.

He hit the ground, rolled over and looked up.

The Tiger Moth was climbing. The bullets and the lighted cigar seemed to have had no effect. Peter had failed.

Would Kirke get away? The Luftwaffe would scramble the two Messerschmitts to chase him, but that would take a few minutes, by which time the Tiger Moth would be out of sight. Kirke's fuel tank was damaged, but the holes might not be at the lowest point of the tank, in which case he might retain sufficient petrol to get him across the water to Sweden, which was only twenty miles away. And darkness was falling.

Kirke had a chance, Peter concluded bitterly.

Then there was the whoosh of a sudden fire, and a single big flame rose from the cockpit.

It spread with ghastly speed all over the visible head and shoulders of the pilot, whose clothing must have been soaked with petrol. The flames licked back along the fuselage, rapidly consuming the linen fabric.

For a few seconds the aircraft continued to climb, although the head of the pilot had turned to a charred stump. Then Kirke's body slumped, apparently pushing the control stick forward, and the Tiger Moth turned nose-down and dived the short distance to earth, plunging like an arrow into the ground. The fuselage crumpled like a concertina.

There was a horrified silence. The flames continued to lick around the wings and the tail, stripping the fabric, eating into the wooden wing spars, and revealing the square steel tubes of the fuselage like the skeleton of a burned martyr.

Tilde said: 'My God, how dreadful – the poor man.' She was shaking.

Peter put his arms around her. 'Yes,' he said. 'And the worst of it is, now he can't answer questions.'

PART TWO

NINE

The sign outside the building read 'Danish Institute of Folk Song and Country Dancing', but that was just to fool the authorities. Down the steps, through the double curtain that served as a light trap, and inside the windowless basement, there was a jazz club.

The room was small and dim. The damp concrete floor was littered with cigarette ends, and sticky with spilled beer. There were a few rickety tables and some wooden chairs, but most of the audience was standing. There were sailors and dockers shoulder to shoulder with well dressed young people and a sprinkling of German soldiers.

On the tiny stage, a young woman sat at the piano, crooning ballads into a microphone. Perhaps it was jazz, but it was not the music Harald was passionate about. He was waiting for Memphis Johnny Madison, who was coloured, even though he had lived most of his life in Copenhagen and had probably never seen Memphis.

It was two o'clock in the morning. Earlier this evening, after lights out at school, the Three Stooges – Harald, Mads and Tik – had put their clothes back on, sneaked out of the dormitory building, and caught the last train into the city. It was risky – they would be in deep trouble if they were found out – but it would be worth it to see Memphis Johnny.

The aquavit Harald was drinking with draft beer chasers was making him even more euphoric.

In the back of his mind was the thrilling memory of his conversation with Poul Kirke, and the frightening fact that he was now in the Resistance. He hardly dared to think about it, for it was something he could not share even with Mads and Tik. He had passed secret military information to a spy.

After Poul had admitted that there was a secret organization, Harald had said he would do anything else he could to help. Poul had promised to use Harald as one of his observers. His task would be to collect information on the occupying forces and give it to Poul for onward transmission to Britain. He was proud of himself, and eager for his first assignment. He was also frightened, but he tried not to think about what might happen if he were caught.

He still hated Poul for dating Karen Duchwitz. He had the sour taste of jealousy in the pit of his stomach every time he thought about it. But he suppressed the feeling for the sake of the Resistance.

He wished Karen were here now. She would appreciate the music.

Just as he was thinking that female company was lacking, he noticed a new arrival: a woman with curly dark hair, wearing a red dress, sitting on a stool at the bar. He could not see her too clearly – the air was smoky, or perhaps there was something wrong with his vision – but she seemed to be alone. 'Hey, look,' he said to the others.

'Nice, if you like older women,' said Mads.

Harald peered at her, trying to focus better. 'Why, how old is she?'

'She's got to be thirty at least.'

Harald shrugged. 'That's not really *old*. I wonder if she'd like someone to talk to?'

Tik, who was not as drunk as the other two, said: 'She'll talk to you.'

Harald was not sure why Tik was grinning like a fool. Ignoring him, Harald stood up and headed for the bar. As he got closer, he saw that the woman was quite plump, and her round face was heavily made up. 'Hello, schoolboy,' she said, but her smile was friendly.

'I noticed that you were alone.'

'For the moment.'

'I thought you might want someone to talk to.'

'That's not really what I'm here for.'

'Ah – you prefer to listen to the music. I'm a great jazz fan, have been for years. What do you think of the singer? She's not American, of course, but—'

'I hate the music.'

Harald was nonplussed. 'Then why—'

'I'm a working girl.'

She seemed to think that explained everything, but he was mystified. She continued to smile warmly at him, but he had the sense they were talking at cross-purposes. 'A working girl,' he repeated.

'Yes. What did you think I was?'

He was inclined to be nice to her, so he said: 'You look like a princess to me.'

She laughed.

He asked her: 'What's your name?'

'Betsy.'

It was an unlikely name for a working-class Danish girl, and Harald guessed it was assumed.

A man appeared at Harald's elbow. Harald was taken aback by the newcomer's appearance: he was unshaven, he had rotten teeth, and one eye was half closed by a big bruise. He wore a stained tuxedo and a collarless shirt. Despite being short and skinny, he looked intimidating. He said: 'Come on, sonny, make up your mind.'

Betsy said to Harald: 'This is Luther. Leave the boy alone, Lou, he's not doing anything wrong.'

'He's driving other customers away.'

Harald realized he had no idea what was going on, and he decided he must be drunker than he had imagined.

Luther said: 'Well – do you want to fuck her, or not?'

Harald was astonished. 'I don't even know her!'

Betsy burst out laughing.

'It's ten crowns, you can pay me,' Luther said.

Enlightenment dawned. Harald turned to her and said in a voice loud with astonishment: 'Are you a prostitute?'

'All right, don't shout,' she said with annoyance.

Luther grabbed Harald by the shirt front and

pulled him forwards. His grip was strong, and Harald staggered. 'I know you educated types,' Luther spat. 'You think this kind of thing is funny.'

Harald smelled the man's bad breath. 'Don't get upset,' he said. 'I just wanted to talk to her.'

A barman with a rag around his head leaned over the bar and said: 'No trouble, please, Lou. The lad means no harm.'

'Doesn't he? I think he's laughing at me.'

Harald was beginning to wonder anxiously whether Luther had a knife, when the club manager picked up the microphone and announced Memphis Johnny Madison, and there was a burst of applause.

Luther pushed Harald away. 'Get out of my sight, before I slit your fool throat,' he said.

Harald went back to the others. He knew he had been humiliated, but he was too drunk to care. 'I made an error of etiquette,' he said.

Memphis Johnny walked on stage, and Harald instantly forgot Luther.

Johnny sat at the piano and leaned towards the microphone. Speaking perfect Danish with no trace of an accent, he said: 'Thank you. I'd like to open with a composition by the greatest boogie-woogie pianist of them all, Clarence Pine Top Smith.'

There was renewed applause, and Harald shouted in English: 'Play it, Johnny!'

Some kind of disturbance broke out near the door, but Harald took no notice. Johnny played four bars of introduction then stopped abruptly and said into the microphone: 'Heil Hitler, baby.'

A German officer walked on stage.

Harald looked around, bewildered. A group of military police had come into the club. They were arresting the German soldiers, but not the Danish civilians.

The officer snatched the microphone from Johnny and said in Danish: 'Entertainers of inferior race are not permitted. This club is closed.'

'No!' cried Harald in dismay. 'You can't do that, you Nazi peasant!'

Fortunately, his voice was drowned in the general hubbub of protest.

'Let's get out before you make any more errors of etiquette,' said Tik. He took Harald's arm.

Harald resisted. 'Come on!' he yelled. 'Let Johnny play!'

The officer handcuffed Johnny and walked him out.

Harald was heartbroken. It had been his first chance to hear a real boogie pianist, and the Nazis had stopped the show after a few bars. 'They have no right!' he shouted.

'Of course not,' Tik said soothingly, and steered him to the door.

The three young men made their way up the steps to the street. It was midsummer, and the short Scandinavian night was already over. Dawn had broken. The club was on the waterfront, and the broad channel of water gleamed in the half light. Sleeping ships floated motionless at their moorings. A cool, salty breeze blew in from the sea. Harald breathed deeply then felt momentarily dizzy.

'We might as well go to the railway station and wait for the first train home,' Tik said. Their plan was to be in bed, pretending to sleep, before anyone at school got up.

They headed for the town centre. At the main intersections, the Germans had erected concrete guard posts, octagonal in plan and about four feet high, with room in the middle for a soldier to stand, visible from the chest up. They were not manned at night. Harald was still furious about the closure of the club, and he was further enraged by these ugly symbols of Nazi domination. Passing one, he gave it a futile kick.

Mads said: 'They say the sentries at these posts wear lederhosen, because no one can see their legs.' Harald and Tik laughed.

A moment later, they passed a pile of builder's rubble outside a shop that had been newly refitted, and Harald happened to notice a cluster of paint cans on top of the pile – whereupon he was struck by an idea. He leaned across the rubbish and picked up a can.

'What the hell are you doing?' Tik said.

There was a little black paint left in the bottom, still liquid. From among the odd bits of timber on the pile, Harald selected a piece of wooden slat an inch wide that would serve as a brush.

Ignoring bemused questions from Tik and Mads, he walked back to the guard post. He knelt in front of it with the paint and the stick. He heard Tik say something in a warning voice, but ignored him. With great care, he wrote in black paint on the concrete wall:

THIS NAZI

HAS NO

TROUSERS

ON

He stepped back to admire his work. The letters were large and the words could be read at a distance. Later this morning, thousands of Copenhageners on their way to work would see the joke and smile.

'What do you think of that?' he said. He looked around. Tik and Mads were nowhere to be seen, but two uniformed Danish policemen stood immediately behind him.

'Very amusing,' said one of them. 'You're under arrest.'

* * *

He spent the rest of the night in the Politigaarden, in the drunk tank with an old man who had urinated in his trousers and a boy his own age who vomited on the floor. He was too disgusted with them and himself to sleep. As the hours went by, he developed a headache and a raging thirst.

But the hangover and the filth were not his worst worries. He was more concerned about being interrogated about the Resistance. What if he were turned over to the Gestapo and tortured? He did not know how much pain he could stand. Eventually he might betray Poul Kirke. And all for a stupid joke! He could not believe how childish he had been. He was bitterly ashamed.

At eight o'clock in the morning, a uniformed policeman brought a tray with three mugs of ersatz tea and a plate of black bread, thinly smeared with a butter substitute. Harald ignored the bread – he could not eat in a place like a toilet – but he drank the tea greedily.

Shortly afterwards, he was taken from the cell to an interview room. He waited a few minutes, then a sergeant came in carrying a folder and a typed sheet of paper. 'Stand up!' the sergeant barked, and Harald leaped to his feet.

The sergeant sat at the table and read the report. 'A Jansborg schoolboy, eh?' he said.

'Yes, sir.'

'You ought to know better, lad.'

'Yes, sir.'

'Where did you get the liquor?'

'At a jazz club.'

He looked up from the typed sheet. 'The Danish Institute?'

'Yes.'

'You must have been there when the Krauts closed it down.'

'Yes.' Harald was confused by his use of the mildly

derogatory slang word 'Kraut' for 'German'. It jarred with his formal tone.

'Do you often get drunk?'

'No, sir. First time.'

'And then you saw the guard post, and you happened to come across a pot of paint . . .'

'I'm very sorry.'

The cop grinned suddenly. 'Well, don't be too sorry. I thought it was pretty funny, myself. No trousers!' He laughed.

Harald was bewildered. The man had seemed hostile, but now he was enjoying the joke. Harald said: 'What's going to happen to me?'

'Nothing. We're the police, not the joke patrol.' The sergeant tore the report in half and dropped it in the waste-paper basket.

Harald could hardly believe his luck. Was he really going to be let off? 'What . . . what should I do?'

'Go back to Jansborg.'

'Thank you!' Harald wondered if he could sneak back into school unnoticed, even at this late stage. He would have some time, on the train, to think of a story. Perhaps no one need ever find out about this.

The sergeant stood up. 'But take a word of advice. Keep off the booze.'

'I will,' Harald said fervently. If he could get out of this scrape, he would never drink alcohol again.

The sergeant opened the door, and Harald suffered a dreadful shock.

Standing outside was Peter Flemming.

Harald and Peter stared at one another for a long moment.

The sergeant said: 'Can I help you, Inspector?'

Peter ignored him and spoke to Harald. 'Well, well,' he said in the satisfied tone of a man who has been proved right at last. 'I wondered, when I saw the name on the overnight arrest list. Could Harald Olufsen, graffiti writer and drunk, be Harald Olufsen, son of the pastor of Sande? Lo and behold, they are one and the same.'

Harald was dismayed. Just when he had started to hope that this dreadful incident could be kept secret, the truth had been discovered by one who had a grudge against his whole family.

Peter turned to the sergeant and said dismissively: 'All right, I'll deal with it now.'

The sergeant looked resentful. 'There are to be no charges, sir, the superintendent has decided.'

'We'll see about that.'

Harald felt he could weep. He had been on the point of getting away with it. This seemed so unfair.

The sergeant hesitated, seeming disposed to argue, and Peter said firmly: 'That will be all.'

'Very good, sir.' He left.

Peter stared at Harald, saying nothing, until at last Harald said: 'What are you going to do?'

Peter smiled, then said: 'I think I'll take you back to school.'

* * *

They entered the grounds of Jansborg Skole in a police Buick driven by a uniformed officer, with Harald in the back like a prisoner.

The sun was shining on the old red-brick buildings and the lawns, and Harald felt a stab of regret for the simple, safe life he had lived here over the past seven years. Whatever happened now, this reassuringly familiar place was not going to be a home to him much longer.

The sight aroused different feelings in Peter Flemming, who muttered sourly to the driver: 'This is where they breed our future rulers.'

'Yes, sir,' the driver said neutrally.

It was the time of the mid-morning sandwich, and the boys were eating outside, so most of the school was watching as the car drove up to the main office and Harald got out.

Peter showed his police badge to the school secretary, and he and Harald were immediately taken to Heis's study.

Harald did not know what to think. It seemed Peter was not going to hand him over to the Gestapo, his worst fear. He was reluctant to let his hopes rise too soon, but all the signs were that Peter regarded him as a mischievous schoolboy, not a member of the Danish Resistance. For once he was grateful to be treated as a child rather than a man.

But in that case, what *was* Peter up to?

As they walked in, Heis unwound his lanky frame from behind his desk and stared at them, with vague concern, through the glasses perched on his beaky nose. His voice was kindly, but a tremor betrayed his nervousness. 'Olufsen? What's all this?'

Peter did not give Harald the chance to answer the question. Jerking a thumb in his direction, he said to Heis in a grating tone: 'Is this one of yours?'

The gentle Heis flinched as if he had been struck. 'Olufsen is a pupil here, yes.'

'He was arrested last night for defacing a German military installation.'

Harald realized that Peter was enjoying the humiliation of Heis, and was determined to make the most of it.

Heis looked mortified. 'I'm very sorry to hear that.'

'He was also drunk.'

'Oh, dear.'

'The police have to decide what to do about it.'

'I'm not sure I—'

'Frankly, we'd rather not prosecute a schoolboy for a childish prank.'

'Well, I'm glad to hear that . . .'

'On the other hand, he can't go unpunished.'

'Indeed not.'

'Apart from anything else, our German friends will want to know that the perpetrator has been dealt with firmly.'

'Of course, of course.'

Harald felt sorry for Heis, but at the same time wished he were not such a weakling. So far, he had done nothing but agree with the bullying Peter.

Peter went on: 'So the outcome depends on you.'

'Oh? In what way?'

'If we let him go, will you expel him from school?'

Harald immediately saw what Peter was up to. He just wanted to be sure that Harald's transgression would become public knowledge. He was only interested in the embarrassment of the Olufsen family.

The arrest of a Jansborg schoolboy would make headlines. The shame of Heis would be exceeded only by that of Harald's parents. His father would be volcanic and his mother suicidal.

But, Harald realized, Peter's enmity towards the Olufsen family had blunted his policeman's instincts. He was so happy to have caught an Olufsen drunk that he had overlooked a greater crime. He had not even considered whether Harald's dislike of the Nazis went beyond slogan-daubing to espionage. Peter's malice had saved Harald's skin.

Heis showed the first sign of opposition. 'Expulsion seems a bit harsh—'

'Not as harsh as a prosecution and possible jail sentence.'

'No, indeed.'

Harald did not enter the argument himself, because he could see no way out of this that would enable him to keep the incident secret. He consoled himself with the thought that he had escaped the Gestapo. Any other punishment would seem minor.

Heis said: 'It's almost the end of the academic year. He wouldn't miss much schooling if he were expelled now.'

'Then it will not permit him to avoid much work.'

'Something of a technicality, considering that he is only a couple of weeks away from leaving.'

'But it will satisfy the Germans.'

'Will it? That's important, of course.'

'If you can assure me that he will be expelled, I can release him from custody. Otherwise, I'll have to take him back to the Politigaarden.'

Heis threw a guilty look at Harald. 'It does seem as if the school has no real choice in the matter, doesn't it?'

'Yes, sir.'

Heis looked at Peter. 'Very well, then. I will expel him.'

Peter gave a satisfied smile. 'I'm glad we've resolved this so sensibly.' He stood up. 'Try to keep out of trouble in future, young Harald,' he said pompously.

Harald looked away.

Peter shook hands with Heis. 'Well, thank you, Inspector,' Heis said.

'Pleased to help.' Peter went out.

Harald felt all his muscles relax. He had got away with it. There would be hell to pay at home, of course, but the important thing was that his foolishness had not compromised Poul Kirke and the Resistance.

Heis said: 'A dreadful thing has happened, Olufsen.'

'I know I've done wrong—'

'No, not that. I think you know Mads Kirke's cousin.'

'Poul, yes.' Harald tensed again. Now what? Had

Heis somehow found out about Harald's involvement with the Resistance? 'What about Poul?'

'He has been in a plane crash.'

'My God! I was flying with him a few days ago!'

'It happened last night at the flying school.' Heis hesitated.

'What . . .?'

'I'm sorry to have to tell you that Poul Kirke is dead.'

TEN

'Dead?' said Herbert Woodie with a squeak in his voice. 'How can he be dead?'

'They're saying he crashed his Tiger Moth,' Hermia replied. She was angry and distraught.

'The damn fool,' Woodie said callously. 'This could ruin everything.'

Hermia stared at him in disgust. She would have liked to slap his stupid face.

They were in Woodie's office at Bletchley Park with Digby Hoare. Hermia had sent a message to Poul Kirke, instructing him to get an eyewitness description of the radar installation on the island of Sande. 'The reply came from Jens Toksvig, one of Poul's helpers,' she said, making an effort to be calm and factual. 'It was sent via the British legation in Stockholm, as usual, but it wasn't even enciphered – Jens obviously doesn't know the code. He said the crash was being passed off as an accident, but in fact Poul was trying to escape from the police and they shot at the aircraft.'

'The poor man,' said Digby.

'The message came in this morning,' Hermia added. 'I was about to come and tell you, Mr Woodie, when you sent for me.' In fact she had been in tears.

She did not cry often, but her heart was touched by the death of Poul, so young, handsome, and full of energy. She knew, too, that she was responsible for his being killed. It was she who had asked him to spy for Britain, and his courageous assent had led directly to his death. She thought of his parents, and his cousin Mads, and she had wept for them, too. Most of all, she longed to finish the job he had started, so that his killers would not prevail in the end.

'I'm so sorry,' Digby said, and he put his arm around Hermia's shoulders in a sympathetic squeeze. 'Lots of men are dying, but it hurts when it's someone you know.'

She nodded. His words were simple and obvious, but she was grateful for the thought. What a good man he was. She felt a surge of affection for him, then remembered her fiancé and felt guilty. She wished she could see Arne again. Talking to him and touching him would reinforce her love and make her immune to the appeal of Digby.

'But where does that leave us?' Woodie asked.

Hermia collected her thoughts rapidly. 'According to Jens, the Nightwatchmen have decided to lie low, at least for a while, and see how far the police carry their investigation. So, to answer your question, it leaves us without any sources of information in Denmark.'

'Makes us appear damned incompetent,' Woodie said.

'Never mind that,' Digby said crisply. 'The Nazis

have found a war-winning weapon. We thought we were years ahead with radar – now we learn that they have it too, and theirs is better than ours! I don't give a fuck about how you appear. The only question is how we find out more.'

Woodie looked outraged but said nothing. Hermia asked: 'What about other sources of intelligence?'

'We're trying them all, of course. And we've picked up one more clue: the word *himmelbett* has appeared in Luftwaffe decrypts.'

Woodie said: '*Himmelbett?* That means heaven bed. What does it signify?'

'It's their word for a four-poster bed,' Hermia told him.

'Makes no sense,' Woodie said grumpily, as if it were her fault.

She asked Digby: 'Any context?'

'Not really. It seems that their radar operates in a *himmelbett*. We can't figure it out.'

Hermia reached a decision. 'I'll have to go to Denmark myself,' she said.

'Don't be ridiculous,' Woodie said.

'We have no agents in the country, so someone has to be infiltrated,' she said. 'I know the ground better than anyone else in MI6, that's why I'm chief of the Denmark desk. And I speak the language like a native. I've got to go.'

'We don't send women on missions like that,' Woodie said dismissively.

Digby said: 'Yes, we do.' He turned to Hermia.

'You'll leave for Stockholm tonight. I'll come with you.'

* * *

'Why did you say that?' Hermia asked Digby the following day, as they walked through the Golden Room in the Stadhuset, Stockholm's famous City Hall.

Digby paused to study a wall mosaic. 'I knew the prime minister would want me to keep the closest possible watch on such an important mission.'

'I see.'

'And I wanted the chance to have you to myself. This is the next best thing to a slow boat to China.'

'But you know I have to get in touch with my fiancé. He's the only person I can trust to help us.'

'Yes.'

'And I'll probably see him all the sooner in consequence.'

'That suits me fine. I can't compete with a man who is trapped in a country hundreds of miles away, heroically silent and unseen, holding on to your affection by invisible cords of loyalty and guilt. I'd rather have a flesh-and-blood rival with human failings, someone who gets grumpy with you and has dandruff on his collar and scratches his bum.'

'This isn't a contest,' she said with exasperation. 'I love Arne. I'm going to marry him.'

'But you're not married yet.'

Hermia shook her head as if to detach herself from this irrelevant talk. Previously, she had enjoyed Digby's romantic interest in her – albeit guiltily – but now it was a distraction. She was here for a rendezvous. She and Digby were only pretending to be tourists with time to kill.

They left the Golden Room and went down the broad marble staircase and out into the cobbled courtyard. They crossed an arcade of pink granite pillars and found themselves in a garden overlooking the grey water of Lake Malaren. Turning to look up at the three-hundred-foot tower that rose over the red-brick building, Hermia checked that their shadow was with them.

A bored-looking man in a grey suit and well-worn shoes, he made little effort to conceal his presence. As Digby and Hermia had pulled away from the British legation, in a chauffeur-driven Volvo limousine that had been adapted to run on charcoal, they had been followed by two men in a black Mercedes 230. When they stopped outside the Stadhuset, the man in the grey suit had followed them inside.

According to the British air attaché, a group of German agents kept all British citizens in Sweden under constant surveillance. They could be shaken off, but it was unwise. Losing your tail was taken as proof of guilt. Men who evaded surveillance had been arrested and accused of espionage, and the Swedish authorities had been pressured to expel them.

Therefore, Hermia had to escape without the shadow realizing it.

Following a prearranged plan, Hermia and Digby wandered across the garden and turned around the corner of the building to look at the cenotaph of the city's founder, Birger Jarl. The gilded sarcophagus lay in a canopied tomb with stone pillars at each corner. 'Like a *himmelbett*,' Hermia said.

Concealed from view on the far side of the cenotaph was a Swedish woman of the same height and build as Hermia, with similar dark hair.

Hermia looked inquiringly at the woman, who nodded decisively.

Hermia suffered an instant of fear. Until now she had done nothing illegal. Her visit to Sweden had been as innocent as it seemed. From this moment on, she would be on the wrong side of the law, for the first time in her life.

'Quickly,' the woman said in English.

Hermia slipped off her light summer raincoat and red beret, and the other woman put them on. Hermia took from her pocket a dull brown scarf and tied it around her head, covering her distinctive hair and partly concealing her face.

The Swedish woman took Digby's arm, and the two of them moved away from the cenotaph and sauntered back into the garden in full view.

Hermia waited a few moments, pretending to study the elaborate wrought-iron railing around the monument, fearful that the tail would be suspicious and come to check. But nothing happened.

She moved out from behind the cenotaph, half-expecting him to be lying in wait, but there was no one nearby. Pulling the scarf a little farther over her face, she walked around the corner into the garden.

She saw Digby and the decoy heading for the gate

at the far end. The shadow was following them. The plan was working.

Hermia went in the same direction, tailing the tail. As arranged, Digby and the woman went straight to their car, which was waiting in the square. Hermia saw them get into the Volvo and drive away. The tail followed in the Mercedes. They would lead him all the way back to the legation, and he would report that the two visitors from Britain had spent the afternoon as innocent tourists.

And Hermia was free.

She crossed the Stadhusbron bridge and headed for Gustav Adolf Square, the centre of the city, walking fast, eager to get on with her task.

Everything had happened with bewildering rapidity in the last twenty-four hours. Hermia had been given only a few minutes to throw a few clothes into a suitcase, then she and Digby had been driven in a fast car to Dundee, in Scotland, where they checked into a hotel a few minutes after midnight. That morning at dawn they had been taken to Leuchars Aerodrome, on the Fife coast, and an RAF crew wearing civilian British Overseas Airways Corporation uniforms had flown them to Stockholm, a three-hour journey. They had had lunch at the British legation then put into operation the plan they had devised in the car between Bletchley and Dundee.

As Sweden was neutral, it was possible to phone or write from here to people in Denmark. Hermia was going to try to call her fiancé, Arne. At the Danish end, calls were monitored and letters opened by the censors, so she would have to be extraordinarily careful in what she said. She had to mount a deception that would sound innocent to an eavesdropper yet bring Arne into the Resistance.

Back in 1939, when she had set up the Nightwatchmen, she had deliberately excluded Arne. It was not because of his convictions: he was as anti-Nazi as she was, albeit in a less passionate way – he thought they were stupid clowns in silly uniforms who wanted to stop people having fun. No, the problem was his careless nature. He was too open and friendly for clandestine work. Perhaps also she had been unwilling to put him in danger, although Poul had agreed with her about Arne's unsuitability. But now she was desperate. Arne was as happy-go-lucky as ever, but she had no one else.

Besides, everyone felt differently about danger today from at the outbreak of war. Thousands of fine young men had given their lives already. Arne was a military officer: he was supposed to take risks for his country.

All the same, her heart felt cold at the thought of what she was going to ask him to do.

She turned into the Vasagatan, a busy street in which there were several hotels, the central railway station, and the main post office. Here in Sweden, telephone services had always been separate from the mail, and there were special public phone bureaus. Hermia was heading for the one in the railway station.

She could have telephoned from the British legation, but that would almost certainly have aroused suspicion. At the phone bureau, there would be nothing unusual about a woman who spoke hesitant Swedish with a Danish accent coming in to phone home.

She and Digby had talked about whether the phone call would be listened to by the authorities. In every telephone exchange in Denmark there was at least one young German woman in uniform listening in. They could not possibly eavesdrop on every phone call, of course. However, they were more likely to pay attention to international calls, and calls to military bases, so there was a strong chance that Hermia's conversation with Arne would be monitored. She would have to communicate in hints and doubletalk. But that should be possible. She and Arne had been lovers, so she ought to be able to make him understand without being explicit.

The station was built like a French château. The grand entrance lobby had a coffered ceiling and chandeliers. She found the phone bureau and stood in line.

When she got to the counter, she told the clerk that she wanted to make a person-to-person call to Arne Olufsen, and gave the number of the flying school. She waited impatiently, full of apprehension, while the operator tried to get Arne on the line. She did not even know whether he was at Vodal today. He might be flying, or away from the base for the afternoon, or on leave. He might have been transferred to another base or have resigned from the army.

But she would try to track him down, wherever he was. She could speak to his commanding officer and ask where he had gone, she could call his parents on Sande, and she had numbers for some of his friends in Copenhagen. She had all afternoon to spend, and plenty of money for phone calls.

It would be strange to talk to him after more than a year. She was thrilled but anxious. The mission was the important thing, but she could not help fretting about how Arne would feel about her. Perhaps he no longer loved her as he once had. What if he were cold to her? It would break her heart. But he might have met someone else. After all, she had enjoyed a flirtation with Digby. How much more easily might a man find his heart straying?

She remembered skiing with him, racing down a sunlit slope, the two of them leaning to one side then the other in perfect rhythm, perspiring in the icy air, laughing with the sheer joy of being alive. Would those days ever come back?

She was called to a booth.

She picked up the phone and said: 'Hello?'

Arne said: 'Who is it?'

She had forgotten his voice. It was low and warm and sounded as if it might break into laughter at any minute. He spoke educated Danish, with a precise diction he had learned in the military and the hint of a Jutland accent left over from his childhood.

She had planned her first sentence. She intended to use the pet names they had for each other, hoping this would alert Arne to the need to speak discreetly.

But for a moment she could not speak at all.

'Hello?' he said. 'Is anyone there?'

She swallowed and found her voice. 'Hello, Toothbrush, this is your black cat.' She called him 'Toothbrush' because that was what his moustache felt like when he kissed her. Her nickname came from the colour of her hair.

It was his turn to be dumbstruck. There was a silence.

Hermia said: 'How are you?'

'I'm OK,' he said at last. 'My God, is it really you?'

'Yes.'

'Are you all right?'

'Yes.' Suddenly she could not stand any more small talk. Abruptly she said: 'Do you still love me?'

He did not answer immediately. That made her think his feelings had changed. He would not say so directly, she thought; he would equivocate, and say they needed to reassess their relationship after all this time, but she would know—

'I love you,' he said.

'Do you?'

'More than ever. I've missed you terribly.'

She closed her eyes. Feeling dizzy, she leaned against the wall.

'I'm so glad you're still alive,' he said. 'I'm so happy to be talking to you.'

'I love you, too,' she said.

'What's been happening? How are you? Where are you calling from?'

She pulled herself together. 'I'm not far away.'

He noticed her guarded manner and responded in a similar tone. 'OK, I understand.'

She had prepared the next part. 'Do you remember the castle?' There were many castles in Denmark, but one was special to them.

'You mean the ruins? How could I forget?'

'Could you meet me there?'

'How could you get there – Never mind. Do you mean it?'

'Yes.'

'It's a long way.'

'It's really very important.'

'I'd go a lot farther to see you. I'm just figuring out how. I'll ask for leave, but if it's a problem I'll just go AWOL—'

'Don't do that.' She did not want the military police looking for him. 'When's your next day off?'

'Saturday.'

The operator came on the line to tell them they had ten seconds.

Hastily, Hermia said: 'I'll be there on Saturday – I hope. If you don't make it, I'll come back every day for as long as I can.'

'I'll do the same.'

'Be careful. I love you.'

'I love you—'

The line went dead.

Hermia kept the receiver pressed to her ear, as if she could hold on to him a little longer that way. Then the operator asked her if she wanted to make another call, and she declined and hung up.

She paid at the counter then went out, dazed with happiness. She stood in the station concourse, under the high curved roof, with people hurrying past her in all directions. He still loved her. In two days' time she would see him. Someone bumped into her, and she got out of the crowd into a café where she slumped in a chair. Two days.

The ruined castle to which they had both enigmatically referred was Hammershus, a tourist attraction on the Danish holiday island of Bornholm, in the Baltic Sea. They had spent a week on the island in 1939, posing as man and wife, and had made love among the ruins one warm summer evening. Arne would take the ferry from Copenhagen, a trip of seven or eight hours, or fly from Kastrup, which took about an hour. The island was a hundred miles from mainland Denmark, but only twenty miles from the south coast of Sweden. Hermia would have to find a fishing boat to take her across that short stretch of water illegally.

But it was the danger to Arne, not herself, that she kept thinking about. He was going to meet secretly with an agent of the British secret service. She would ask him to become a spy.

If he were caught, the punishment would be death.

ELEVEN

On the second day after his arrest, Harald returned home.

Heis had allowed him to stay at school another two days to take the last of his exams. He would be permitted to graduate, though not to attend the ceremony, which was a week away. But the important thing was that his university place was safe. He would study physics under Niels Bohr – if he lived that long.

During those two days he had learned, from Mads Kirke, that the death of Poul had not been a straightforward crash. The army was refusing to reveal details, saying they were still investigating, but other pilots had told the family that the police had been on the base at the time, and shots had been fired. Harald was sure, though he could not say this to Mads, that Poul had been killed because of his Resistance work.

Nevertheless, he was more afraid of his father than of the police as he made his way home. It was a tediously familiar journey across the width of Denmark from Jansborg, in the east, to Sande, off the west coast. He knew every small-town railway station and fish-smelling ferry dock and all the flat green landscape in between. The journey took the whole day, because of multiple train delays, but he wished it could be longer.

He spent the time anticipating his father's wrath. He composed indignant speeches of self-justification which even he found unconvincing. He tried out a variety of more or less grovelling apologies, unable to find a formula that was sincere but not abject. He wondered whether to tell his parents to be grateful he was alive, when he might have met the same fate as Poul Kirke; but that seemed to make cheap use of a heroic death.

When he reached Sande, he further postponed his arrival by walking home along the beach. The tide was out, and the sea was barely visible a mile away, a narrow strip of dark blue touched with inconstant smears of white surf, sandwiched between the bright blue of the sky and the buff-coloured sand. It was evening, and the sun was low. A few holidaymakers strolled through the dunes, and a group of boys around twelve or thirteen years old were playing football. It would have been a happy scene, but for the new grey concrete bunkers at intervals of a mile along the high-tide mark, bristling with artillery and manned by steel-helmeted soldiers.

He came to the new military base and left the beach to follow the long diversion around it, welcoming the additional delay. He wondered whether Poul had managed to send off his sketch of the radio equipment to the British. If not, the police must have found it. Would they wonder who had drawn it? Fortunately there was nothing to connect it with Harald. All the same, the thought was frightening. The police still did not know he was a criminal, but now they knew about his crime.

At last he came within sight of his home. Like the church, the parsonage was built in the local style, with red-painted bricks and a thatched roof that swept low over the windows, like a hat pulled over the eyes to keep out the rain. The lintel over the front door was painted in slanting stripes of black, white and green, a local tradition.

Harald went to the back and looked through the diamond-shaped pane of glass in the kitchen door. His mother was alone. He studied her for a moment, wondering what she had been like when she was his age. Ever since he could remember, she had looked tired; but she must have been pretty, once.

According to family legend Harald's father, Bruno, had been thought by everyone to be a confirmed bachelor at the age of thirty-seven, wholly dedicated to the work of his little sect. Then he had met Lisbeth, ten years younger, and lost his heart. So madly in love was he that he had worn a coloured tie to church in an attempt to appear romantic, and the deacons had been obliged to reprimand him for inappropriate attire.

Watching his mother as she bent over the sink, scrubbing a pot, Harald tried to imagine the tired grey hair as it had once been, jet black and gleaming, and the hazel eyes twinkling with humour; the lines of the face smoothed away, and the weary body full of energy. She must have been irresistibly sexy, Harald supposed, to have turned his father's remorselessly holy thoughts to the lusts of the flesh. It was hard to imagine.

He went in, put down his suitcase, and kissed his mother.

'Your father's out,' she said.

'Where has he gone?'

'Ove Borking is sick.' Ove was an elderly fisherman and faithful member of the congregation.

Harald was relieved. Any postponement of the confrontation was a reprieve.

His mother looked solemn and tearful. Her expression touched his heart. He said: 'I'm sorry to have caused you distress, Mother.'

'Your father is mortified,' she said. 'Axel Flemming has called an emergency meeting of the Board of Deacons to discuss the matter.'

Harald nodded. He had anticipated that the Flemmings would make the most of this.

'But why did you do it?' his mother asked plaintively.

He had no answer.

She made him a ham sandwich for his supper. 'Is there any news of Uncle Joachim?' he asked.

'Nothing. We get no answers to our letters.'

Harald's own troubles seemed nothing when he thought about his cousin Monika, penniless and persecuted, not even knowing whether her father was dead or alive. While Harald was growing up, the annual visit of the Goldstein cousins had been the highlight of the year. For two weeks the monastic atmosphere of the parsonage was transformed, and the place was full of people and noise. The pastor had for his sister and her family an indulgent fondness that he showed no one else, certainly not his own children, and he would smile benignly as they committed transgressions, such as buying ice-cream on a Sunday, for which he would have punished Harald and Arne. For Harald, the sound of the German language meant laughter and pranks and fun. Now he wondered if the Goldsteins would ever laugh again.

He turned on the radio to hear the war news. It was bad. The British assault in North Africa had been abandoned, a catastrophic failure, half their tanks lost, either crippled in the desert by mechanical failures or destroyed by experienced German antitank gunners. The Axis grip on North Africa was unshaken. Danish radio and the BBC told essentially the same story.

At midnight a flight of bombers crossed overhead. Harald looked out and saw they were heading east. That meant they were British. The bombers were all the British had, now.

When he went back inside, his mother said: 'Your father could be out all night. You'd better go to bed.'

He lay awake for a long time. He asked himself why he was scared. He was too big to be beaten. His father's wrath was formidable, but how bad could a tongue-lashing be? Harald was not easily intimidated. Rather the reverse: he was inclined to resent authority and defy it out of sheer rebelliousness.

The short night came to an end, and a rectangle of

grey dawn light appeared around the curtain at his window like a picture frame. He drifted into sleep. His last thought was that perhaps what he really feared was not some hurt to himself, but his father's suffering.

He was awakened brusquely an hour later.

The door burst open, the light came on, and the pastor stood beside the bed, fully dressed, hands on his hips, chin thrust forward. 'How could you do it?' he shouted.

Harald sat up, blinking at his father, tall, bald, dressed in black, staring at Harald with the blue-eyed glare that terrified his congregation.

'What were you thinking of?' his father raged. 'What possessed you?'

Harald did not want to cower in his bed like a child. He threw off the sheet and stood up. Because the weather was warm, he had slept in his undershorts.

'Cover yourself, boy,' his father said. 'You're practically naked.'

The unreasonableness of this criticism stung Harald into a rejoinder. 'If underwear offends you, don't enter bedrooms without knocking.'

'Knocking? Don't tell me to knock on doors in my own house!'

Harald suffered the familiar feeling that his father had an answer for everything. 'Very well,' he said sulkily.

'What devil took hold of you? How could you bring such disgrace upon yourself, your family, your school and your church?'

Harald pulled on his trousers and turned to face his father.

'Well?' the pastor raged. 'Are you going to answer me?'

'I'm sorry, I thought you were asking rhetorical questions.' Harald was surprised by his own cool sarcasm.

His father was infuriated. 'Don't try to use your education to fence with me – I went to Jansborg too.'

'I'm not fencing. I'm asking whether there's any chance you'll listen to anything I say.'

The pastor raised his hand as if to strike. It would have been a relief, Harald thought as his father hesitated. Whether he took the blow passively, or hit back, violence would have been some kind of resolution.

But his father was not going to make it that easy. He dropped his hand and said: 'Well, I'm listening. What have you got to say for yourself?'

Harald gathered his thoughts. On the train he had rehearsed many versions of this speech, some of them most eloquent, but now he forgot all his oratorical flourishes. 'I'm sorry I daubed the guard post, because it was an empty gesture, a childish act of defiance.'

'At the least!'

For a moment he considered whether to tell his father about his connection with the Resistance, but he quickly decided not to risk further ridicule. Besides, now that Poul was dead, the Resistance might no longer exist.

Instead, he concentrated on the personal. 'I'm sorry to have brought disgrace on the school, because Heis is a kindly man. I'm sorry I got drunk, because it made me feel dreadful the next morning. Most of all, I'm sorry to have caused my mother distress.'

'And your father?'

Harald shook his head. 'You're upset because Axel Flemming knows all about this and he's going to rub your nose in it. Your pride has been hurt, but I'm not sure you're worried about me at all.'

'Pride?' his father roared. 'What has pride to do with anything? I've tried to bring up my sons to be decent, sober, God-fearing men – and you've let me down.'

Harald felt exasperated. 'Look, it's not that much of a disgrace. Most men get drunk—'

'Not my sons!'

'—once in their lives, at least.'

'But you were *arrested.*'

'That was bad luck.'

'It was bad *behaviour*—'

'And I wasn't charged – the police sergeant actually thought that what I did was funny. "We're not the joke patrol," he said. I wouldn't even have been expelled from school if Peter Flemming hadn't threatened Heis.'

'Don't you dare try to minimize this. No member of this family has ever been to jail for any reason. You've dragged us into the gutter.' The pastor's face changed suddenly. For the first time, he showed sadness rather than anger. 'And it would be shocking and tragic even if no one in the world knew of it but me.'

Harald saw that his father was sincere in this, and the realization threw him off balance. It was true that the old man's pride was wounded, but that was not all. He genuinely feared for his son's spiritual welfare. Harald was sorry he had been sarcastic.

But his father gave him no chance to be conciliatory. 'There remains the question of what is to be done with you.'

Harald was not sure what this meant. 'I've only missed a few days of school,' he said. 'I can do the preliminary reading for my university course here at home.'

'No,' his father said. 'You're not getting off so lightly.'

Harald had a dreadful foreboding. 'What do you mean? What are you planning?'

'You're not going to university.'

'What are you talking about? Of course I am.' Suddenly Harald felt very afraid.

'I'm not going to send you to Copenhagen to pollute your soul with strong drink and jazz music. You've proved you aren't mature enough for the city. You'll stay here, where I can supervise your spiritual development.'

'But you can't phone the university and say: "Don't teach this boy." They've given me a place.'

'They haven't given you any money, though.'

Harald was shocked. 'My grandfather bequeathed money for my education.'

'But he left it to me to dispense. And I'm not going to give it to you to spend in nightclubs.'

'It's not your money – you don't have the right!'

'I most certainly do. I'm your father.'

Harald was stunned. He had not dreamed of this. It was the only punishment that could really hurt him. Bewildered, he said: 'But you've always told me that education was so important.'

'Education is not the same as godliness.'

'Even so . . .'

His father saw that he was genuinely shocked, and his attitude softened a little. 'An hour ago, Ove Borking died. He had no education worth speaking of – he could barely write his name. He spent his life working on other men's boats, and never made enough to buy a carpet for his wife to put on the parlour floor. But he raised three God-fearing children, and every week he gave a tenth of his meagre wages to the church. That's what God considers a good life.'

Harald knew and liked Ove, and was sorry he had died. 'He was a simple man.'

'Nothing wrong with simplicity.'

'Yet if all men were like Ove, we'd still be fishing from dugout canoes.'

'Perhaps. But you're going to learn to emulate him before you do anything else.'

'And what does that mean?'

'Get dressed. Put on your school clothes and a clean shirt. You're going to work.' He left the room.

Harald stared at the closed door. What next?

He washed and shaved in a daze. He could hardly believe what was happening.

He might go to university without his father's help, of course. He would have to get a job to support himself, and he would not be able to afford the private tuition that most people considered essential to supplement the free lectures. But could he achieve all he wanted in those circumstances? He did not want merely to pass his exams. He wanted to be a great physicist, the successor to Niels Bohr. How could he do that if he did not have the money to buy books?

He needed time to think. And while he was thinking, he had to go along with whatever his father was planning.

He went downstairs and ate without tasting the porridge his mother had made.

His father saddled the horse, Major, a broad-backed Irish gelding strong enough to carry them both. The pastor mounted, and Harald got up behind.

They rode the length of the island. The journey took Major more than an hour. When they reached the dock, they watered the horse at the quayside trough and waited for the ferry. The pastor still had not told Harald where they were going.

When the boat docked, the ferryman touched his cap to the pastor, who said: 'Ove Borking was called home early this morning.'

'I expected as much,' said the ferryman.

234

'He was a good man.'

'Rest his soul.'

'Amen.'

They crossed to the mainland and rode up the hill to the town square. The stores were not yet open, but the pastor knocked at the door of the haberdashery. It was opened by the owner, Otto Sejr, a deacon of the Sande church. He seemed to be expecting them.

They stepped inside, and Harald looked around. Glass cases displayed balls of coloured wool. The shelves were stacked with lengths of material, wool cloth and printed cotton and a few silks. Below the shelves were drawers, each neatly marked.

Ribbon – white

Ribbon – fancy

Elastic

Buttons – shirt

Buttons – horn

Pins

Knitting needles

There was a dusty smell of mothballs and lavender, like an old lady's wardrobe. The odour brought to Harald's mind a childhood memory, suddenly vivid: standing here as a small boy while his mother bought black satin for his father's clerical shirts.

The shop had a run-down air now, probably because of wartime austerity. The higher shelves were empty, and it seemed to him there was not the astonishing variety of colours of knitting wool he recalled from his childhood.

But what was he doing here today?

His father soon answered the question. 'Brother Sejr has kindly agreed to give you a job,' he said. 'You'll be helping in the shop, serving customers and doing anything else you can to make yourself useful.'

He stared at his father, speechless.

'Mrs Sejr is in poor health, and can't work any longer, and their daughter has recently married and gone to live in Odense, so he needs an assistant,' the pastor went on, as if that were what needed explaining.

Sejr was a small man, bald with a little moustache. Harald had known him all his life. He was pompous, mean and sly. He wagged a fat finger and said: 'Work hard, pay attention, and be obedient, and you may learn a valuable trade, young Harald.'

Harald was flabbergasted. He had been thinking for two days about how his father would respond to his crime, but nothing he anticipated had come close to this. It was a life sentence.

His father shook hands with Sejr and thanked him, then said to Harald in parting: 'You'll take your lunch with the family here, and come straight home when you finish work. I'll see you tonight.' He waited a moment as if expecting an answer, but when Harald said nothing he went out.

'Right,' said Sejr. 'There's just time to sweep the floor before we open. You'll find a broom in the cupboard. Start at the back, sweep towards the front, and push the dust out through the door.'

Harald began his task. Seeing him brush one-handed, Sejr snapped: 'Put both hands on that broom, boy!'

Harald obeyed.

At nine o'clock, Sejr put the 'Open' sign in the door. 'When I want you to deal with a customer, I'll say: "Forward," and you step forward,' he said. 'You say: "Good morning, how may I serve you?" But watch me with one or two customers first.'

Harald watched Sejr sell six needles on a card to an old woman who counted out her coins as carefully as if they were pieces of gold. Next was a smartly dressed woman of about forty who bought two yards of black braid. Then it was Harald's turn to serve. The third customer was a thin-lipped woman who looked familiar. She asked for a reel of white cotton thread.

Sejr snapped: 'On your left, top drawer.'

Harald found the cotton. The price was marked in pencil on the wooden end of the reel. He took the money and made change.

Then the woman said: 'So, Harald Olufsen, you've been in the fleshpots of Babylon, I hear.'

Harald flushed. He had not prepared himself for this. Did the whole town know what he had done? He was not going to defend himself to gossip-mongers. He made no reply.

Sejr said: 'Young Harald will come under a more steady influence here, Mrs Jensen.'

'I'm sure it will do him good.'

They were thoroughly enjoying his humiliation, Harald realized. He said: 'Will there be anything else, then?'

'Oh, no thank you,' said Mrs Jensen, but she made no move to leave. 'So you won't be going to the university?'

Harald turned away and said: 'Where's the toilet, Mr Sejr?'

'Through the back and upstairs.'

As he left, he heard Sejr say apologetically: 'He's embarrassed, of course.'

'And no wonder,' the woman replied.

Harald climbed the stairs to the apartment over the shop. Mrs Sejr was in the kitchen, dressed in a pink quilted housecoat, washing breakfast cups at the sink. 'I've only got a few herrings for lunch,' she said. 'I hope you don't eat much.'

He lingered in the bathroom, and when he returned to the shop he was relieved to see that Mrs Jensen had gone. Sejr said: 'People are bound to be curious – you must be polite, whatever they say.'

'My life is none of Mrs Jensen's business,' he replied angrily.

'But she's a customer, and the customer is always right.'

The morning wore on with painful slowness. Sejr checked stock, wrote orders, did his books, and dealt with phone calls, but Harald was expected to stand waiting, ready for the next person to come through the door. It left him plenty of time to ponder. Was he really going to spend his life selling reels of cotton to housewives? It was unthinkable.

By midmorning, when Mrs Sejr brought him and

Sejr a cup of tea, he had decided he could not even spend the rest of the summer working here.

By lunch time he knew he was not going to last the day.

As Sejr flipped the 'Closed' sign, Harald said: 'I'm going for a walk.'

Sejr was startled. 'But Mrs Sejr has prepared lunch.'

'She told me she doesn't have enough food.' Harald opened the door.

'You've only got an hour,' Sejr called after him. 'Don't be late!'

Harald walked down the hill and got on the ferry.

He crossed to Sande and walked along the beach towards the parsonage. He felt a strange, tight sensation in his chest when he looked at the dunes, the miles of damp sand, and the endless sea. The view was as familiar as his own face in the mirror, yet now it gave him an aching sense of loss. He almost felt like crying, and after a while he realized why.

He was going to leave this place today.

The rationale came after the realization. He did not have to do the job selected for him – but he could not continue to live in the house after defying his father. He would have to go.

The thought of disobeying his father was no longer frightening, he realized as he strode along the sand. The drama had gone out of it. When had this change taken place? It was when the pastor had said he would withhold the money grandpa had left, Harald decided. That had been a shocking betrayal which could not possibly leave their relationship intact. At that moment, Harald had understood that he could no longer trust his father to have his best interests at heart. He had to look after himself now.

The conclusion was strangely anticlimactic. Of course he had to take responsibility for his own life. It was like realizing that the Bible was not infallible: he found it hard to imagine how he had formerly been so trusting.

When he reached the parsonage, the horse was not in the paddock. Harald guessed his father had returned to the Borking house to make arrangements for Ove's funeral. He went in by the kitchen door. His mother was at the table peeling potatoes. She looked frightened when she saw him. He kissed her, but gave no explanations.

He went to his room and packed his case as if he were going to school. His mother came to the bedroom door and stood watching him, wiping her hands in a towel. He saw her face, lined and sad, and he looked quickly away. After a while, she said: 'Where will you go?'

'I don't know.'

He thought of his brother. He went into his father's study, picked up the telephone, and placed a call to the flying school. After a few minutes, Arne came on the line. Harald told him what had happened.

'The old man overplayed his hand,' Arne commented. 'If he'd put you into a tough job, like cleaning fish at the canning plant, you'd have stuck it out just to prove your manhood.'

'I suppose I might.'

'But you were never going to stay long working in a damn shop. Our father can be a fool, sometimes. Where will you go now?'

Harald had not decided until this moment, but now he had a flash of inspiration. 'Kirstenslot,' he said. 'Tik Duchwitz's place. But don't tell Father. I don't want him coming after me.'

'Old man Duchwitz might tell him.'

That was a good point, Harald reflected. Tik's respectable father would have little sympathy for a boogie-playing, slogan-daubing runaway. But the ruined monastery was used as a dormitory by seasonal workers on the farm. 'I'll sleep in the old monastery,' he said. 'Tik's father won't even know I'm there.'

'How will you eat?'

'I may be able to get a job on the farm. They employ students in summer.'

'Tik is still at school, I presume.'

'But his sister might help me.'

'I know her, she went out with Poul a couple of times. Karen.'

'Only a couple of times?'

'Yes. Why – are you interested in her?'

'She's out of my league.'

'I suppose she is.'

'What happened to Poul . . . exactly?'

'It was Peter Flemming.'

'Peter!' Mads Kirke had not known that detail.

'He came with a car full of cops, looking for Poul.

Poul tried to escape in his Tiger Moth, and Peter shot at him. The aircraft crashed and burned.'

'Good God! Did you see it?'

'No, but one of my airmen did.'

'Mads told me some of this, but he didn't know it all. So Peter Flemming killed Poul. That's terrible.'

'Don't talk about it too much, you might get into trouble. They're trying to pass it off as an accident.'

'All right.' Harald noticed that Arne was not saying *why* the police had come after Poul. And Arne must have noticed that Harald did not ask.

'Let me know how you get on at Kirstenslot. Phone if you need anything.'

'Thanks.'

'Good luck, kid.'

As Harald hung up, his father walked in. 'And what do you think you're doing?'

Harald stood up. 'If you want money for the phone call, ask Sejr for my morning's wages.'

'I don't want money, I want to know why you're not at the shop.'

'It's not my destiny to be a haberdasher.'

'You don't know what your destiny is.'

'Perhaps not.' Harald left the room.

He went outside to the workshop and lit the boiler of his motorcycle. While he waited for it to build up steam, he stacked peat in the sidecar. He did not know how much he would need to get him to Kirstenslot, so he took it all. He returned to the house and picked up his suitcase.

His father waylaid him in the kitchen. 'Where do you think you're going?'

'I'd rather not say.'

'I forbid you to leave.'

'You can't really forbid things any more, Father,' Harald said quietly. 'You're no longer willing to support me. You're doing your best to sabotage my education. I'm afraid you've forfeited the right to tell me what to do.'

The pastor looked stunned. 'You have to tell me where you're going.'

'No.'

'Why not?'

'If you don't know where I am, you can't interfere with my plans.'

The pastor looked mortally wounded. Harald felt regret like a sudden pain. He had no desire for revenge, and it gave him no satisfaction to see his father's distress; but he was afraid that if he showed remorse he would lose his strength of purpose, and allow himself to be bullied into staying. So he turned his face away and walked outside.

He strapped his suitcase to the back of the bike and drove it out of the workshop.

His mother came running across the yard and thrust a bundle into his hands. 'Food,' she said. She was crying.

He stowed the food in the sidecar with the peat.

She threw her arms around him as he sat on the bike. 'Your father loves you, Harald. Do you understand that?'

'Yes, Mother, I think I do.'

She kissed him. 'Let me know that you're all right. Telephone, or send a postcard.'

'OK.'

'Promise.'

'I promise.'

She released him, and he drove away.

TWELVE

Peter Flemming undressed his wife.

She stood passively in front of the mirror, a warm-blooded statue of a pale, beautiful woman. He took off her wristwatch and necklace, then patiently undid the hooks and eyes of her dress, his blunt fingers expert from months of practice. There was a smear on the side, he noticed with a disapproving frown, as if she touched something sticky then wiped her hand on her hip. She was not normally dirty. He pulled the dress over her head, careful not to disarrange her hair.

Inge was as lovely today as she had been the first time he had seen her in her underwear. But then she had been smiling, speaking fond words, her expression showing eagerness and a trace of apprehension. Today her face was blank.

He hung her dress in the wardrobe then took off her brassiere. Her breasts were full and round, the nipples so light in colour they were almost invisible. He swallowed hard and tried not to look at them. He made her sit on the dressing-table stool, then removed her shoes, unfastened her stockings and rolled them down, and took off her garter belt. He stood her up again to pull down her underpants. Desire rose in him as he uncovered the blonde curls between her legs. He felt disgusted with himself.

He knew he could have sexual intercourse with her if he wished. She would lie still and accept it with blank impassivity, as she took everything that happened to her. But he could not bring himself to do it. He had tried, one time, not long after she came home from the hospital, telling himself that perhaps this would rekindle in her the spark of awareness; but he had been revolted by himself, and had stopped after a few seconds. Now the desire came back, and he had to fight it off even though he knew that giving in would bring no relief.

He threw her underwear into the linen basket with an angry gesture. She did not move as he opened a drawer and took out a white cotton nightdress embroidered with small flowers, a gift to Inge from his mother. She was innocent in her nakedness, and to desire her seemed as wrong as to desire a child. He drew the nightdress over her head, put her arms into it, and smoothed it down her back. He looked over her shoulder into the mirror. The flower pattern suited her, and she looked pretty. He thought he saw a faint smile touch her lips, but it was probably his imagination.

He took her to the bathroom then put her to bed. As he undressed himself, he looked at his own body in the mirror. There was a long scar across his belly, souvenir of a Saturday-night street brawl he had broken up as a young policeman. He no longer had the athletic physique of his youth, but he was still fit. He wondered how long it would be before a woman touched his skin with hungry hands.

He put on pyjamas, but he did not feel sleepy. He decided to return to the living room and smoke another cigarette. He looked at Inge. She lay still with her eyes open. He would hear her if she moved. He generally knew when she needed something. She would simply stand up, and wait, as if she could not figure out what to do next; and he would have to guess what she wanted: a drink of water, the toilet, a shawl to keep her warm, or something more complicated. Occasionally she would move about the apartment, apparently at random, but she would soon come to a halt, perhaps at a window, or staring helplessly at a closed door, or just in the middle of the room.

He left the bedroom and crossed the little hallway to the living room, leaving both doors open. He found his cigarettes then, on impulse, took a half-empty bottle of aquavit from a cupboard and poured some into a glass. Sipping his drink and smoking, he thought about the week past.

It had started well and finished badly. He had begun by catching two spies, Ingemar Gammel and Poul Kirke. Better still, they were not like his usual targets, union organizers who intimidated strike-breakers, or Communists who sent coded letters to Moscow saying that Jutland was ripe for revolution.

No, Gammel and Kirke were real spies, and the sketches Tilde Jespersen had found in Kirke's office constituted important military intelligence.

Peter's star seemed in the ascendant. Some of his colleagues had begun to act coolly towards him, disapproving of his enthusiastic cooperation with the German occupiers, but they hardly mattered. General Braun had called him in to say that he thought Peter should be head of the security department. He did not say what would happen to Frederik Juel. But he had made it clear that the job was Peter's if he could wrap this case up.

It was a pity Poul Kirke had died. Alive, he might have revealed who his collaborators were, where his orders came from, and how he sent information to the British. Gammel was still alive, and had been handed over to the Gestapo for 'deep interrogation', but he had revealed nothing further, probably because he did not know any more.

Peter had pursued the investigation with his usual energy and determination. He had questioned Poul's commanding officer, the supercilious Squadron Leader Renthe. He had interviewed Poul's parents, his friends, and even his cousin Mads, and had got nothing from any of them. He had detectives tailing Poul's girlfriend, Karen Duchwitz, but so far she appeared to be no more than a hard-working student at the ballet school. Peter also had Poul's best friend, Arne Olufsen, under surveillance. Arne was the best prospect, for he could easily have drawn the sketches of the military base on Sande. But Arne had spent the week blamelessly going about his duties. Tonight, Friday, he had taken the train into Copenhagen, but there was nothing unusual about that.

After a brilliant start, the case seemed to have dead-ended.

The week's minor triumph had been the humiliation of Arne's brother, Harald. However, Peter felt sure Harald was not involved in espionage. A man who was risking his life as a spy did not daub silly slogans.

Peter was wondering where to go next with the investigation when there was a knock at the door.

He glanced at the clock on the mantelpiece. It was ten-thirty, not outrageously late but still an unusual time for an unexpected visit. The caller certainly could not be surprised to find him in pyjamas. He stepped into the hallway and opened the door. Tilde Jespersen stood there, a sky-blue beret perched on her fair curly hair.

'There's been a development,' she said. 'I thought we should discuss it.'

'Of course. Come in. You'll have to excuse my appearance.'

She glanced at the pattern on his pyjamas with a grin. 'Elephants,' she said as she walked into the living room. 'I wouldn't have guessed.'

He felt embarrassed and wished he had put on a robe, although it was too warm.

Tilde sat down. 'Where's Inge?'

'In bed. Would you like some aquavit?'

'Thank you.'

He got a fresh glass and poured for both of them.

She crossed her legs. Her knees were round and her calves plump, quite different from Inge's slender legs. She said: 'Arne Olufsen bought a ticket for tomorrow's ferry to Bornholm.'

Peter froze with the glass half way to his lips. 'Bornholm,' he said softly. The Danish holiday island was tantalizingly close to the Swedish coast. Could this be the break he was waiting for?

She took out a cigarette and he lit it. Blowing out smoke, she said: 'Of course, he might simply be due for some leave, and have decided to take a vacation . . .'

'Quite so. On the other hand, he may be planning to escape to Sweden.'

'That's what I thought.'

Peter swallowed his drink with a satisfying gulp. 'Who's with him now?'

'Dresler. He relieved me fifteen minutes ago. I came straight here.'

Peter forced himself to be sceptical. It was too easy, in an investigation, to let wishful thinking mislead you. 'Why would Olufsen want to leave the country?'

'He might have been scared by what happened to Poul Kirke.'

'He hasn't been acting scared. Until today he's been doing his job, apparently happily.'

'Maybe he's just noticed the surveillance.'

Peter nodded. 'They always do, sooner or later.'

'Alternatively, he might be going to Bornholm to spy. The British could have ordered him there.'

Peter made a doubtful face. 'What's on Bornholm?'

Tilde shrugged. 'Maybe that's the question they want answered. Or perhaps it's a rendezvous. Remember, if he can get from Bornholm to Sweden, the journey the other way is probably just as easy.'

'Good point.' Tilde was very clear-thinking, he reflected. She kept all possibilities in view. He looked at her intelligent face and clear blue eyes. He watched her mouth as she spoke.

She seemed unaware of his scrutiny. 'The death of Kirke probably broke their normal line of communication. This could be an emergency fall-back plan.'

'I'm not convinced – but there's only one way to find out.'

'Continue to shadow Olufsen?'

'Yes. Tell Dresler to get on the ferry with him.'

'Olufsen has a bicycle with him. Shall I tell Dresler to take one?'

'Yes. Then book yourself and me on tomorrow's flight to Bornholm. We'll get there first.'

Tilde stubbed out her cigarette and stood up. 'Right.'

Peter did not want her to go. The aquavit was warm in his belly, he felt relaxed, and he was enjoying having an attractive woman to talk to. But he could not think of an excuse to detain her.

He followed her into the hallway. She said: 'I'll see you at the airport.'

'Yes.' He put his hand on the doorknob but did not open it. 'Tilde . . .'

She looked at him with a neutral expression. 'Yes?'

'Thanks for this. Good work.'

She touched his cheek. 'Sleep well,' she said, but she did not move away.

He looked at her. The trace of a smile touched the corners of her mouth, but he could not tell whether it was inviting or mocking. He leaned forward, and suddenly he was kissing her.

She kissed him back with fierce passion. He was taken by surprise. She pulled his head to hers, thrust her tongue into his mouth. After a moment of shock he responded. He grabbed her soft breast and squeezed roughly. She made a noise deep in her throat, and thrust her hips against his body.

He saw a movement out of the corner of his eye. He broke the kiss and turned his head.

Inge stood in the bedroom doorway, like a ghost in her pale nightdress. Her face wore its perpetual blank expression, but she was looking straight at them. Peter heard himself make a sound like a sob.

Tilde slipped from his embrace. He turned to speak to her, but no words came. She opened the apartment door and stepped outside. She was gone in a breath.

The door slammed shut.

* * *

The daily flight from Copenhagen to Bornholm was operated by the Danish airline, DDL. It departed at nine a.m. and took an hour. The plane landed at an airstrip a mile or so outside Bornholm's main town, Ronne. Peter and Tilde were met by the local police chief, who gave them the loan of a car as if entrusting them with royal jewels.

They drove into the town. It was a sleepy place, with more horses than cars. The half-timbered houses were painted in striking deep colours: dark mustard, terracotta pink, forest green, and rust red. Two German soldiers stood in the central square, smoking and chatting to passers-by. From the square, a cobbled street led downhill to the harbour. There was a Kriegsmarine torpedo boat in the dock, with a group of small boys clustered on the quayside staring at it. Peter located the ferry port, across from the brick custom house, the largest building in town.

Peter and Tilde drove around to familiarize themselves with the streets, then returned to the port in the afternoon to meet the ferry. Neither mentioned last night's kiss, but Peter was intensely aware of her physical presence: that elusive flowery perfume, her alert blue eyes, the mouth that had kissed him with such urgent passion. At the same time, he kept remembering Inge standing in the bedroom doorway, her expressionless white face a reproach more agonizing than any explicit accusation.

As the ship came into the harbour, Tilde said: 'I hope we're right, and Arne is a spy.'

'You haven't lost your enthusiasm for this work?'

Her reply was sharp. 'Whatever makes you say that?'

'Our discussion about Jews.'

'Oh, that.' She shrugged it off. 'You were right, weren't you? You proved it. We raided the synagogue and it led us to Gammel.'

'Then, I wondered if the death of Kirke might have been too gruesome . . .'

'My husband died,' she said crisply. 'I don't mind seeing criminals die.'

She was even tougher than he had thought. He hid a pleased smile. 'So you'll stay in the police.'

'I don't see any other future. Besides, I might be the first woman to get promotion to sergeant.'

Peter doubted that would ever happen. It would involve men taking orders from a woman, and that seemed beyond the bounds of possibility. But he did not say so. 'Braun virtually promised me promotion if I can round up this spy ring.'

'Promotion to what?'

'Head of the department. Juel's job.' And a man who was head of the security department at thirty could well end up chief of the entire Copenhagen police, he thought. His heart beat faster as he envisioned the crackdown he would impose, with the backing of the Nazis.

Tilde smiled warmly. Putting a hand on his arm, she said: 'Then we'd better make sure we catch them all.'

The ship docked and the passengers began to disembark. As they watched, Tilde said: 'You've known Arne since childhood – is he the type for espionage?'

'I'd have to say no,' Peter replied thoughtfully. 'He's too happy-go-lucky.'

'Oh.' Tilde looked glum.

'In fact, I might have dismissed him as a suspect, but for his English fiancée.'

She brightened. 'That puts him right in the frame.'

'I don't know whether they're still engaged. She went back to England hot-foot when the Germans came. But the possibility is enough.'

A hundred or so passengers got off, some on foot, a handful in cars, many with bicycles. The island was only twenty miles from end to end, and cycling was the easiest way to get around.

'There,' said Tilde, pointing.

Peter saw Arne Olufsen disembarking, wearing his army uniform, pushing his bicycle. 'But where's Dresler?'

'Four people behind.'

'I see him.' Peter put on sunglasses and pulled his hat low, then started the engine. Arne cycled up the cobbled street toward the town centre, and Dresler did the same. Peter and Tilde followed slowly in the car.

Arne headed out of town to the north. Peter began to feel conspicuous. There were few other cars on the roads, and he had to drive slowly to stay with the bikes. Soon he was obliged to fall behind and drop out of sight for fear of being noticed. After a few minutes, he speeded up until he caught sight of Dresler, then slowed again. Two German soldiers on a motorcycle with a sidecar passed them, and Peter wished he had borrowed a motorbike instead of a car.

A few miles out of town, they were the only people on the road. 'This is impossible,' Tilde said in a high, anxious voice. 'He's bound to spot us.'

Peter nodded. She was right, but now a new

thought occurred to him. 'And when he does, his reaction will be highly revealing.'

She gave him an inquiring look, but he did not explain.

He increased speed. Rounding a bend, he saw Dresler crouching in the woods at the side of the road and, a hundred yards ahead, Arne sitting on a wall, smoking a cigarette. Peter had no option but to drive past. He continued another mile then reversed down a farm track.

'Was he checking on us, or just taking a rest?' Tilde said.

Peter shrugged.

A few minutes later Arne cycled past, followed by Dresler. Peter pulled on to the road again.

The daylight was fading. Three miles farther on, they came to a crossroads. Dresler had stopped there and was looking perplexed.

There was no sign of Arne.

Dresler came up to the car window, looking distraught. 'I'm sorry, boss. He put on a burst of speed and got ahead of me. I lost sight of him, and I don't know which way he went at this crossroads.'

Tilde said: 'Hell. He must have planned it. He obviously knows the road.'

'I'm sorry,' Dresler said again.

Tilde said quietly: 'There goes your promotion – and mine.'

'Don't be so gloomy,' Peter said. 'This is good news.'

Tilde was bewildered. 'What do you mean?'

'If an innocent man thinks he's being followed, what does he do? He stops, turns around, and says: "Who the hell do you think you are, following me around?" Only a guilty man deliberately shakes off a surveillance team. Don't you see? This means we were right: Arne Olufsen is a spy.'

'But we've lost him.'

'Oh, don't worry. We'll find him again.'

* * *

They spent the night at a seaside hotel with a bathroom at the end of each corridor. At midnight, Peter put a robe over his pyjamas and knocked on the door of Tilde's room. She called: 'Come in.'

He stepped inside. She was sitting up in the single bed, wearing a light blue silk nightdress, reading an American novel called *Gone with the Wind*. He said: 'You didn't ask who it was at the door.'

'I knew.'

His detective's mind noticed that she wore lipstick, her hair was carefully brushed, and the flowery perfume was in the air, as if she had dressed for a date. He kissed her lips, and she stroked the back of his head. After a moment he looked back to the door, to make sure he had closed it.

'She's not there,' Tilde said.

'Who?'

'Inge.'

He kissed her again, but after a few moments he realized he was not getting excited. He broke the kiss and sat on the edge of the bed.

'It's the same for me,' Tilde said.

'What?'

'I keep thinking about Oskar.'

'He's dead.'

'Inge might as well be.'

He winced.

She said: 'I'm sorry. But it's true. I'm thinking about my husband, and you're thinking about your wife, and neither of them cares.'

'It wasn't like this last night, at my apartment.'

'We didn't give ourselves time to think then.'

This was ridiculous, he thought. In his youth he had been a confident seducer, able to persuade many women to yield to him, and leaving most of them well satisfied. Was he just out of practice?

He shrugged off his robe and slipped into bed beside her. She was warm and welcoming, and her round body under the nightdress was soft to his touch. She turned off the light. He kissed her, but he could not rekindle last night's passion.

They lay side by side in the dark. 'It's all right,' she said. 'You have to leave the past behind. It's difficult for you.'

He kissed her again, briefly, then he got up and returned to his own room.

THIRTEEN

Harald's life was in ruins. All his plans were cancelled and he had no future. Yet, instead of agonizing over his fate, he was looking forward to renewing his acquaintance with Karen Duchwitz. He recalled her white skin and vivid red hair, and the way she walked across the room as if she were dancing, and nothing seemed as important as seeing her again.

Denmark was a small, pretty country, but at twenty miles per hour it seemed like the endless desert. Harald's peat-burning motorcycle took a day and a half to get from his home on Sande across the width of the country to Kirstenslot.

The bike's progress over the monotonous undulating landscape was further slowed by breakdowns. He suffered a puncture before he was thirty miles from home. Next, on the long bridge that linked the Jutland peninsula with the central island of Fyn, his chain broke. The Nimbus motorcycle originally had a shaft drive, but that was difficult to connect to a steam engine, so Harald had taken a chain and sprockets from an old lawn mower. Now he had to push the bike miles to a garage and have a new link inserted. By the time he had crossed Fyn, he had missed the last ferry to the main island of Zealand. He parked the bike, ate the food his mother had given him – three thick slices of ham and a slab of cake – and spent a chill night waiting on the dockside. When he relit the boiler the next morning, the safety valve had developed a leak, but he managed to plug it with chewing gum and sticking plaster.

He arrived at Kirstenslot late on Saturday afternoon. Although he was impatient to see Karen, he did not go immediately to the castle. He drove past the ruined monastery and the entrance to the castle grounds, passed through the village with its church and tavern and railway station, and found the farm he had visited with Tik. He was confident he could get a job here. It was the right time of year, and he was young and strong.

There was a large farmhouse in a neat yard. As he parked the bike, he was watched by two little girls – granddaughters, he imagined, of Farmer Nielsen, the white-haired man he had seen driving away from the church.

He found the farmer at the rear of the house, dressed in muddy corduroys and a collarless shirt, leaning on a fence and smoking a pipe. 'Good evening, Mr Nielsen,' he said.

'Hello, young man,' Nielsen said guardedly. 'What can I do for you?'

'My name is Harald Olufsen. I need a job, and Josef Duchwitz told me you hire summer labourers.'

'Not this year, son.'

Harald was dismayed. He had not even considered the possibility of refusal. 'I'm a hard worker—'

'I don't doubt it, and you look strong enough, but I'm not hiring.'

'Why not?'

Nielsen raised an eyebrow. 'I might say it's none of your business, my lad, but I was a brash young man myself, once, so I'll tell you that times are hard, the Germans buy most of what I produce at a price decided by them, and there's no cash to pay casual labourers.'

'I'll work for food,' Harald said desperately. He could not return to Sande.

Nielsen gave him a penetrating look. 'You sound as if you're in some kind of trouble. But I can't hire you on those terms. I'd have trouble with the union.'

It seemed hopeless. Harald cast about for an alternative. He might find work in Copenhagen, but then where would he live? He could not even go to his brother, who lived on a military base where overnight guests were not permitted.

Nielsen saw his distress and said: 'Sorry, son.' He knocked his pipe out against the top rail of the fence. 'Come on, I'll see you off the premises.'

The farmer probably thought he was desperate enough to steal, Harald thought. The two of them walked around the house to the front yard.

'What the hell's that?' said Nielsen when he saw the bike, with its boiler gently puffing steam.

'It's just an ordinary motorcycle, but I've rigged it to run on peat.'

'How far have you come on it?'

'From Morlunde.'

'Good God! It looks ready to blow up any minute.'

Harald felt offended. 'It's perfectly safe,' he said indignantly. 'I know about engines. In fact, I mended one of your tractors, a few weeks ago.' For a moment, Harald wondered whether Nielsen might hire him out of gratitude, but then he told himself not to be foolish. Gratitude would not pay wages. 'You had a leak in the fuel supply.'

Nielsen frowned. 'What do you mean?'

Harald threw another slab of peat into the firebox. 'I was staying at Kirstenslot for the weekend. Josef and I came across one of your men, Frederik, trying to start a tractor.'

'I remember. So you're that lad?'

'Yes.' He climbed on the bike.

'Wait a minute. Maybe I can hire you.'

Harald looked at him, hardly daring to hope.

'I can't afford labourers, but a mechanic is a different matter. Do you know about all kinds of machinery?'

This was no time for modesty, Harald decided. 'I can usually fix anything with an engine.'

'I've got half a dozen machines lying idle for lack of spares. Do you think you could make them work?'

'Yes.'

Nielsen looked at the motorcycle. 'If you can do this, maybe you can repair my seed drill.'

'I don't see why not.'

'All right,' the farmer said decisively. 'I'll give you a trial.'

'Thank you, Mr Nielsen!'

'Tomorrow's Sunday, so come here on Monday morning at six o'clock. We farmers start early.'

'I'll be here.'

'Don't be late.'

Harald opened the regulator to let steam into the cylinder and drove off before Nielsen could change his mind.

As soon as he was out of earshot, he let out a triumphant yell. He had a job – one much more interesting than serving customers in a haberdashery – and he had done it himself. He felt full of confidence. He was on his own, but he was young and strong and smart. He was going to be all right.

Daylight was fading as he drove back through the village. He almost failed to see a man in police uniform who stepped into the road and waved him down. He braked hard at the last minute, and the boiler sighed a cloud of steam through the safety valve. He recognized the policeman as Per Hansen, the local Nazi.

'What the hell is this?' Hansen said, pointing to the bike.

'It's a Nimbus motorcycle, converted to steam power,' Harald told him.

'It looks dangerous to me.'

Harald had little patience with this kind of officious busybody, but he forced himself to answer politely. 'I assure you, officer, it's perfectly safe. Are you making official inquiries, or just indulging your curiosity?'

'Never mind the cheek, lad. I've seen you before, haven't I?'

Harald told himself not to get on the wrong side of the law. He had already spent one night in jail this week. 'My name is Harald Olufsen.'

'You're a friend of the Jews at the castle.'

Harald lost his temper. 'It's none of your damn business who my friends are.'

'Oho! Is it not?' Hansen looked satisfied, as if he had the result he wanted. 'I've got the measure of you, young man,' he said maliciously. 'I shall keep a close eye on you. Off you go, now.'

Harald pulled away. He cursed his short temper. He had now made an enemy of the local policeman, just because of a throwaway remark about Jews. When would he learn to keep out of trouble?

A quarter of a mile from the gates of Kirstenslot, he turned off the road on to the cart track that led through the wood to the back of the monastery. He could not be seen from the house, and he was betting no one would be working in the garden on a Saturday evening.

He stopped the bike at the west front of the disused church, then walked through the cloisters and entered the church by a side door. At first he could see only ghostly shapes in the dim evening light coming through the high windows. As his eyesight adjusted, he made out the long Rolls-Royce car under its tarpaulin, the boxes of old toys, and the Hornet Moth biplane with its folded wings. He had the feeling that no one had entered the church since last time he was here.

He opened the large main door, drove his bike inside, and closed the door.

He permitted himself a moment of satisfaction as he shut down the steam engine. He had crossed the country on his improvised motorcycle, got himself a job, and found a place to stay. Unless he was unlucky, his father could not find out where he was; but if there should be any important family news, his brother knew how to get in touch with him. Best of all, there was a good chance he would see Karen Duchwitz. He recalled that she liked to smoke a cigarette on the terrace after dinner. He decided to go and look out for her. It was risky – he might be seen by Mr Duchwitz – but he felt lucky today.

In a corner of the church, next to the workbench and tool rack, was a sink with a cold water tap. Harald had not washed for two days. He stripped off his shirt and got cleaned up as best he could without soap. He rinsed out the shirt, hung it on a nail to dry, and put on the spare one from his bag.

An arrow-straight drive half a mile long led from the main gates to the castle, but it was too exposed, and Harald took a roundabout route to approach the place through the wood. He passed the stables, crossed the kitchen garden, and studied the back of the house from the shelter of a cedar tree. He was able to identify the drawing room by its French windows, which were open to the terrace. Next to it was the dining room, he recalled. The blackout curtains were not yet drawn, for the electric lights had not yet been switched on, although he saw the flicker of a candle.

He guessed the family was having dinner. Tik would be at school – Jansborg boys were allowed home once a fortnight, and this was a school weekend – so the dinner party would consist of Karen and her parents, unless there were guests. He decided to risk a closer look.

He crossed the lawn and crept up to the house. He heard the sound of a BBC announcer saying that Vichy French forces had abandoned Damascus to an army of British, Commonwealth and Free French. It made a pleasant change to hear of a British victory, but he found it hard to see how good news from Syria was going to help his cousin Monika in Hamburg. Peeping in through the dining room window, he saw that dinner was over, and a maid was clearing the table.

A moment later, a voice behind him said: 'What do you think you're doing?'

He spun around.

Karen was walking along the terrace towards him. Her pale skin was luminous in the evening light. She wore a long silk dress in a watery shade of blue-green. Her dancer's carriage made it seem as if she were gliding. She looked like a ghost.

'Hush!' he said.

She did not recognize him in the fading light. 'Hush?' she said indignantly. There was nothing ghostly about her challenging tone. 'I find an intruder peering through a window into my house and he tells me to *hush*?' There was a bark from inside.

Harald could not decide whether Karen was genuinely outraged or just amused. 'I don't want your father to know I'm here!' he said in a low, urgent voice.

'You should worry about the police, not my father.'

The old red setter, Thor, came bounding out, ready to savage a burglar, but he recognized Harald and licked his hand.

'I'm Harald Olufsen, I was here two weeks ago.'

'Oh – the boogie-woogie boy! What are you doing skulking on the terrace? Have you come back to rob the place?'

To Harald's dismay, Mr Duchwitz came to the French window and looked out. 'Karen?' he said. 'Is someone there?'

Harald held his breath. If Karen betrayed him now, she could spoil everything.

After a moment, she said: 'It's all right, Daddy – just a friend.'

Mr Duchwitz peered at Harald in the gloom, but did not seem to recognize him, and after a moment he grunted and went back inside.

'Thanks,' Harald breathed.

Karen sat on a low wall and lit a cigarette. 'You're welcome, but you have to tell me what this is all about.' The dress matched her green eyes, which shone out of her face as if lit from within.

He sat on the wall facing her. 'I quarrelled with my father and left home.'

'Why did you come here?'

Karen herself was half the reason, but he decided not to say so. 'I've got a job with Farmer Nielsen, repairing his tractors and machines.'

'You are enterprising. Where are you living?'

'Um . . . in the old monastery.'

'Presumptuous, too.'

'I know.'

'I assume you brought blankets and things.'

'Actually, no.'

'It may be chilly at night.'

'I'll survive.'

'Hmm.' She smoked in silence for a while, watching darkness fall like a mist over the garden. Harald studied her, mesmerized by the twilight on the shapes of her face, the wide mouth and the slightly crooked nose and the mass of wiry hair that somehow combined to be bewitchingly lovely. He watched her full lips as she blew out smoke. Eventually she threw her cigarette into a flower bed, stood up, and said: 'Well, good luck.' Then she went back into the house and closed the French window behind her.

That was abrupt, Harald thought. He felt deflated. He stayed where he was for a minute. He would have been happy to talk to her all night, but she had got bored with him in five minutes. He remembered, now, that she had made him feel alternately welcomed and rejected during his weekend visit. Perhaps it was a game she played. Or maybe it reflected her own vacillating feelings. He liked the thought that she might have feelings about him, even if they were unstable.

He walked back to the monastery. The night air was already cooling. Karen was right, it would be chilly. The church had a tiled floor that looked cold. He wished he had thought to bring a blanket from home.

He looked around for a bed. The starlight that came through the windows faintly illuminated the interior of the church. The east end had a curved wall that had once enclosed the altar. To one side, a broad ledge was incorporated into the wall. A tiled canopy stood over it, and Harald guessed it had once framed some object of veneration – a holy relic, a jewelled chalice, a painting of the Virgin. Now, however, it looked more like a bed than anything else he could see, and he lay down on the ledge.

Through a glassless window he could see the tops of trees and a scatter of stars against a midnight-blue sky. He thought about Karen. He imagined her touching his hair with a fond gesture, brushing his lips with hers, putting her arms around him and hugging him. These images were different from the scenes he had imagined with Birgit Claussen, the Morlunde girl he had dated at Easter. When Birgit starred in his fantasies, she was always taking off her brassiere, or rolling on a bed, or ripping his shirt in her haste to get at him. Karen played a subtler part, more loving than lustful, although there was always the promise of sex deep in her eyes.

He was cold. He got up. Maybe he could sleep in

the aeroplane. Fumbling in the dark, he found the
door handle. But when he opened it he heard
scuttling sounds, and recalled that mice had nested in
the upholstery. He was not afraid of scuttling
creatures, but he could not quite bring himself to bed
down with them.

He considered the Rolls-Royce. He could curl up
on the back seat. It would be roomier than the Hornet
Moth. Taking the canvas cover off, in the dark, might
take a while, but perhaps it would be worth it. He
wondered if the car doors were locked.

He was fumbling with the cover, looking for some
kind of fastening that he could undo, when he heard
light footsteps. He froze. A moment later, the beam of
an electric torch swept past the window. Did the
Duchwitzes have a security patrol at night?

He looked through the door that led to the
cloisters. The torch was approaching. He stood with
his back to the wall, trying not to breathe. Then he
heard a voice. 'Harald?'

His heart leaped with pleasure. 'Karen.'

'Where are you?'

'In the church.'

Her beam found him, then she pointed it upward
to shed a general light. He saw that she was carrying a
bundle. 'I brought you some blankets.'

He smiled. He would be grateful for the warmth,
but he was even more happy that she cared. 'I was just
thinking of sleeping in the car.'

'You're too tall.'

When he unfolded the blankets he found something inside.

'I thought you might be hungry,' she explained.

In the light of her torch he saw half a loaf of bread, a small basket of strawberries, and a length of sausage. There was also a flask. He unscrewed the lid and smelled fresh coffee.

He realized he was ravenous. He fell on the food, trying not to eat like a starved jackal. He heard a mew, and a cat came into the circle of light. It was the skinny black-and-white tom he had seen the first time he entered the church. He dropped a piece of sausage on the ground. The cat sniffed it, turned it over with a paw, then began to eat it daintily. 'What's the cat called?' Harald asked Karen.

'I don't think it has a name. It's a stray.'

At the back of its head it had a tuft of hair like a pyramid. 'I think I'll call him Pinetop,' Harald said. 'After my favourite pianist.'

'Good name.'

He ate everything. 'Boy, that was great. Thank you.'

'I should have brought more. When was the last time you ate?'

'Yesterday.'

'How did you get here?'

'Motorcycle.' He pointed across the church to where he had parked the bike. 'But it's slow, because it runs on peat, so I took two days to get here from Sande.'

'You're a determined character, Harald Olufsen.'

'Am I?' He was not sure whether this was a compliment.

'Yes. In fact, I've never met anyone quite like you.'

On balance, he thought this was good. 'Well, to tell the truth, I feel the same about you.'

'Oh, come on. The world is full of spoiled rich girls who want to be ballet dancers, but how many people have crossed Denmark on a peat-burning motorcycle?'

He laughed, pleased. They were quiet for a minute. 'I was very sorry about Poul,' Harald said eventually. 'It must have been a terrible shock for you.'

'It was completely devastating. I cried all day.'

'Were you very close?'

'We only had three dates, and I wasn't in love with him, but all the same it was dreadful.' Tears came to her eyes, and she sniffed and swallowed.

Harald was shamefully pleased to learn that she had not been in love with Poul. 'It's very sad,' he said, and felt hypocritical.

'I was heartbroken when my grandma died, but somehow this was worse. Gran was old and sick, but Poul was so full of energy and fun, so good-looking and fit.'

'Do you know how it happened?' Harald said tentatively.

'No – the army has been ridiculously secretive about it,' she said, her voice becoming angry. 'They just say he crashed his plane, and the details are classified.'

'Perhaps they're covering something up.'

'Such as what?' she said sharply.

Harald realized he could not tell her what he thought without revealing his own connection to the Resistance. 'Their own incompetence?' he improvised. 'Perhaps the aircraft wasn't properly serviced.'

'They couldn't use the excuse of military secrecy to hide something like that.'

'Of course they could. Who would know?'

'I don't believe our officers would be so dishonourable,' she said stiffly.

Harald realized he had offended her, as he had when he first met her – and in the same way, by being scornful about her credulity. 'I expect you're right,' he said hastily. That was insincere: he felt sure she was wrong. But he did not want to quarrel with her.

Karen stood up. 'I must get back before they lock up.' Her voice was cold.

'Thanks for the food and blankets – you're an angel of mercy.'

'Not my usual role,' she said, softening a little.

'Perhaps I'll see you tomorrow?'

'Maybe. Goodnight.'

'Goodnight.'

Then she was gone.

FOURTEEN

Hermia slept badly. She had a dream in which she was talking to a Danish policeman. The conversation was amiable, though she was anxious not to give herself away; but she realized, after a while, that they were speaking English. The man continued to talk as if nothing had happened, while she trembled and waited for him to arrest her.

She woke up to find herself on a narrow bed in a lodging-house on the island of Bornholm. She was relieved to find that the conversation with the policeman had been a dream – but there was nothing unreal about the danger that faced her now that she had woken up. She was in occupied territory, carrying forged papers, pretending to be a secretary on vacation, and if she were found out, she would be hanged as a spy.

Back in Stockholm, she and Digby had again deceived their German followers with substitutes and, having shaken them off, had taken a train to the south coast. In the tiny fishing village of Kalvsby they had found a boatman willing to take her across the twenty miles or so of sea to Bornholm. She had said goodbye to Digby – who could not possibly pass for Danish –

and climbed aboard. He was going to London for a
day to report to Churchill, but he would fly back
immediately and be waiting for her on the jetty in
Kalvsby when she returned – if she returned.

The fisherman had put her ashore, with her bicycle,
on a lonely beach at dawn yesterday. The man had
promised to return to the same spot four days later at
the same hour. To make sure of him, Hermia had
promised him double the fee for the return journey.

She had cycled to Hammershus, the ruined castle
that was her rendezvous with Arne, and had waited
there for him all day. He had not come.

She told herself not to be surprised. Arne had been
working the previous day, and she guessed he had not
been able to get away early enough to catch the
evening ferry. He had probably taken the Saturday
morning boat and arrived on Bornholm too late
to reach Hammershus before dark. In those
circumstances, he would find somewhere to spend
the night, and come to the rendezvous first thing
in the morning.

That was what she believed in her more cheerful
moments. But at the back of her mind was the
constant thought that he might have been arrested. It
was useless to ask herself what he could have been
arrested for, or to argue that he had not yet
committed a crime, for that only led her to imagine
fanciful scenarios in which he confided in a
treacherous friend, or wrote everything in a diary, or
confessed to a priest.

Late in the day, she had given up on Arne and

cycled to the nearest village. In summer many of the islanders offered bed and breakfast to tourists, and she found a place to stay without difficulty. She fell into bed anxious and hungry, and had bad dreams.

Getting dressed, she recalled the holiday she and Arne had spent on this island, registering at their hotel as Mr and Mrs Olufsen. That was when she had felt most intimate with him. He loved to gamble, and he would make bets with her for sexual favours: 'If the red boat gets into harbour first, you have to go around with no panties all day tomorrow, and if the blue boat wins, you can be on top tonight.' You can have anything you want, my love, she thought, if you just show up today.

She decided to have breakfast that morning before cycling back to Hammershus. She might be waiting all day again, and she did not want to faint from hunger. She dressed in the cheap new clothes she had bought in Stockholm – English clothes might have given her away – and went downstairs.

She felt nervous as she walked into the family dining room. It was more than a year since she had been in the habit of speaking Danish daily. After landing yesterday she had had only a few brief exchanges of words. Now she would have to make small talk.

There was one other guest in the room, a middle-aged man with a friendly smile who said: 'Good morning. I'm Sven Fromer.'

Hermia forced herself to relax. 'Agnes Ricks,' she said, using the name on her false papers. 'It's a beautiful day.' She had nothing to fear, she told herself. She spoke Danish with the accent of the metropolitan bourgeoisie, and Danes never knew she was English until she told them. She helped herself to porridge, poured cold milk over it, and began to eat. The tension she felt made it difficult for her to swallow.

Sven smiled at her and said: 'English style.'

She stared at him, appalled. How had he found her out so fast? 'What do you mean?'

'The way you eat porridge.'

He had his milk in a glass, and took sips from it between mouthfuls of porridge. That was how Danes ate porridge, she knew perfectly well. She cursed her carelessness and tried to bluff it out. 'I prefer it this way,' she said as casually as she could. 'The milk cools the porridge and you can eat it faster.'

'A girl in a hurry. Where are you from?'

'Copenhagen.'

'Me, too.'

Hermia did not want to get into a conversation about exactly where in Copenhagen they both lived. That could too easily lead her into more errors. Her safest plan would be to ask him questions. She had never met a man who did not like to talk about himself. 'Are you on holiday?'

'Unfortunately not. I'm a surveyor, working for the government. However, the job is done, and I don't have to be home until tomorrow, so I'm going to spend today driving around, and catch the overnight ferry this evening.'

'You have a car?'

'I need one for my work.'

The landlady brought bacon and black bread. When she had left the room, Sven said: 'If you're on your own, I'd be happy to take you around.'

'I'm engaged to be married,' Hermia said firmly.

He smiled ruefully. 'Your fiancé is a lucky man. I'd still be glad of your company.'

'Please don't be offended, but I want to be alone.'

'I quite understand. I hope you don't mind my asking.'

She gave him her most charming smile. 'On the contrary, I'm flattered.'

He poured himself another cup of ersatz coffee, and seemed inclined to linger. Hermia began to relax. So far she had aroused no suspicion.

Another guest came in, a man of about Hermia's age, neatly dressed in a suit. He bowed stiffly to them and spoke Danish with a German accent. 'Good morning. I am Helmut Mueller.'

Hermia's heart raced. 'Good morning,' she said. 'Agnes Ricks.'

Mueller turned expectantly to Sven, who stood up, pointedly ignoring the newcomer, and stalked out of the room.

Mueller sat down, looking hurt. 'Thank you for your courtesy,' he said to Hermia.

Hermia tried to behave normally. She pressed her hands together to stop their shaking. 'Where are you from, Herr Mueller?'

'I was born in Luebeck.'

She asked herself what a friendly Dane might say to a German by way of small talk. 'You speak our language well.'

'When I was a boy, my family came often here to Bornholm for holidays.'

He was not suspicious, Hermia saw, and she felt emboldened to ask a less superficial question. 'Tell me, do many people refuse to speak to you?'

'Such rudeness as our fellow guest has just displayed is unusual. In the present circumstances, Germans and Danes have to live together, and most Danes are polite.' He gave her a look of curiosity. 'But you must have observed this – unless you have from another country recently arrived.'

She realized she had made another slip. 'No, no,' she said hastily, covering up. 'I'm from Copenhagen where, as you say, we live together as best we can. I just wondered if things were different here on Bornholm.'

'No, much the same.'

All conversation was dangerous, she realized. She stood up. 'Well, I hope you enjoy your breakfast.'

'Thank you.'

'And have a pleasant day here in our country.'

'I wish you the same.'

She left the room, wondering if she had been too nice. Over-friendliness might arouse suspicion as easily as hostility. But he had shown no sign of mistrust.

As she was leaving on her bicycle, she saw Sven putting his luggage in his car. It was a slope-backed Volvo PV444, a popular Swedish car often seen in

Denmark. She saw that the rear seat had been removed to make room for his equipment, tripods and a theodolite and other gear, some in an assortment of leather cases, some wrapped in blankets for protection. 'I apologize for creating a scene,' he said. 'I didn't wish to be rude to you.'

'That's all right.' She could see that he was still angry. 'You obviously feel strongly.'

'I come from a military family. It's difficult for me to accept that we surrendered so quickly. I believe we should have fought. We should be fighting now!' He made a gesture of frustration, as if throwing something away. 'I shouldn't speak this way. I'm embarrassing you.'

She touched his arm. 'You have nothing to apologize for.'

'Thank you.'

She rode off.

* * *

Churchill was pacing the croquet lawn at Chequers, the official country residence of the British prime minister. He was writing a speech in his head: Digby knew the signs. His weekend guests were the American ambassador, John Winant, and the foreign secretary, Anthony Eden, with their wives; but none of them were to be seen. Digby sensed there was some crisis, but no one had told him what. Churchill's private secretary, Mr Colville, gestured towards the brooding premier. Digby approached Churchill across the smooth grass.

The prime minister lifted his bent head. 'Ah, Hoare,' he said. He stopped walking. 'Hitler has invaded the Soviet Union.'

'Christ!' said Digby Hoare. He wanted to sit down but there were no chairs. 'Christ!' he repeated. Yesterday, Hitler and Stalin had been allies, their friendship cemented by the Nazi–Soviet pact of 1939. Today they were at war. 'When did that happen?'

'This morning,' Churchill said grimly. 'General Dill has just been here to give me the details.' Sir John Dill was chief of the Imperial General Staff, therefore the most senior man in the military. 'Early intelligence estimates put the size of the invading army at three million men.'

'Three *million?*'

'They have attacked along a two-thousand-mile front. There is a northern group heading for Leningrad, a central one making for Moscow, and a southern force on its way to the Ukraine.'

Digby was dazed. 'Oh, my God. Is this the end, sir?'

Churchill drew on his cigar. 'It may be. Most people believe the Russians can't win. They will be slow to mobilize. With heavy air support from the Luftwaffe, Hitler's tanks could wipe out the Red Army in a few weeks.'

Digby had never seen his boss look so defeated. In the face of bad news Churchill normally became even more pugnacious, always wanting to respond to defeat by going on the attack. But today he looked worn down. 'Is there any hope?' Digby asked.

'Yes. If the Reds can survive until the end of

281

summer, it may be a different story. The Russian winter defeated Napoleon and it might yet undo Hitler. The next three or four months will be decisive.'

'What are you going to do?'

'I shall go on the BBC tonight at nine.'

'And say . . .?'

'That we must give whatever help we can to Russia and the Russian people.'

Digby raised his eyebrows. 'A hard thing for a passionate anti-Communist to propose.'

'My dear Hoare, if Hitler invaded Hell, I would at least make a favourable reference to the Devil in the House of Commons.'

Digby smiled, wondering whether that line was being considered for inclusion in tonight's speech. 'But is there any help we *can* give?'

'Stalin has asked me to step up the bombing campaign against Germany. He hopes it will force Hitler to bring aircraft home to defend the Fatherland. That would weaken the invading army and might give the Russians an even chance.'

'Are you going to do it?'

'I have no choice. I've ordered a bombing raid for the next full moon. It will be the largest air operation of the war so far, which means the largest in the history of mankind. There will be more than five hundred bombers, over half our entire strength.'

Digby wondered if his brother would be on the raid. 'But if they suffer the kind of losses we've been experiencing . . .'

'We will be crippled. That's why I've called you in. Do you have an answer for me?'

'Yesterday I infiltrated an agent into Denmark. Her orders are to get photographs of the radar installation on Sande. That will answer the question.'

'It had better. The bombing raid is scheduled in sixteen days' time. When do you hope to have the photographs in your hands?'

'Within a week.'

'Good,' Churchill said dismissively.

'Thank you, prime minister.' Digby turned away.

'Don't fail me,' said Churchill.

* * *

Hammershus was on the northern tip of Bornholm. The castle stood on a hill that looked across the sea to Sweden, and had once guarded the island against invasion by its neighbour. Hermia wheeled her bicycle along the winding path up the rocky slopes, wondering if today would be as fruitless as yesterday. The sun was shining, and she was warm from the effort of cycling.

The castle had been built of mixed brick and stone. Solitary walls remained, their features forlornly suggestive of family life: large sooty fireplaces exposed to the sky, cold stone cellars for storing apples and ale, broken staircases that led nowhere, narrow windows through which thoughtful children must once have stared at the sea.

Hermia was early, and the place was deserted.

Judging by yesterday's experience, she would have it to herself for another hour or more. What would it be like if Arne did turn up today, she wondered as she pushed her bike through ruined archways and across grass-grown floors.

In Copenhagen before the invasion she and Arne had been a glamorous couple, the centre of a social set of young officers and pretty girls with government connections, always having parties and picnics, going dancing and playing sports, sailing and riding horses and driving to the beach. Now that those days were over, would she seem to Arne like part of his past? On the phone, he had said he still loved her – but he had not seen her for more than a year. Would he find her the same, or changed? Would he still like the smell of her hair and the taste of her mouth? She began to feel nervous.

She had spent all day yesterday looking at the ruins, and they held no more interest for her. She walked to the seaward side, leaned her bike against a low stone wall, and looked down at the beach far below.

A familiar voice said: 'Hello, Hermia.'

She whirled around and saw Arne walking towards her, smiling, his arms spread wide. He had been waiting behind a tower. Her nervousness vanished. She ran into his arms and hugged him hard enough to hurt.

'What's the matter?' he said. 'Why are you weeping?'

She realized she was crying, her chest heaving with

sobs, tears running down her face. 'I'm so happy,' she said.

He kissed her wet cheeks. She held his face in both hands, feeling his bones with her fingertips to prove to herself that he was real, this was not one of the imaginary reunion scenes she had dreamed so often. She nuzzled his neck, breathing in the smell of him, army soap and brilliantine and aeroplane fuel. There were no smells in her dreams.

She was overwhelmed by emotion, but the feeling slowly changed from excitement and happiness to something else. Their tender kisses turned searching and hungry, their gentle caresses became urgently demanding. When her knees felt weak she sank to the grass, pulling him down with her. She licked his neck, sucked his lip, and bit his earlobe. His erection pressed against her thigh. She fumbled with the buttons of his uniform trousers, opening the fly so that she could feel him properly. He pushed up the skirt of her dress and slid his hand beneath the elastic of her underwear. She suffered a moment of coy embarrassment at how wet she was, then it was forgotten in a wave of pleasure. Impatiently, she broke the embrace long enough to take off her panties and throw them aside, then pulled him on top of her. It occurred to her that they were in full view of any early tourists coming to see the ruins, but she did not care. She knew that later, when the madness had left her, she would shudder with horror at the risk she had taken, but she could not hold back. She gasped as he entered her, then clung to him with her arms and legs, pressing his belly to hers, his chest to her breasts, his face into her neck, insatiably hungry for the touch of his body. Then that, too, passed as she focused on a node of intense pleasure that began small and hot, like a distant star, and grew steadily, seeming to possess more and more of her body, until it exploded.

They lay still for a while. She enjoyed the weight of his body on her, the breathless feeling it gave her, his slow detumescence. Then a shadow fell on them. It was only a cloud passing over the sun, but it reminded her that the ruins were open to the public, and someone could come along at any time. 'Are we still alone?' she murmured.

He lifted his head and looked around. 'Yes.'

'We'd better get up before the tourists arrive.'

'OK.'

She grabbed him as he pulled away. 'One more kiss.'

He kissed her softly, then stood up.

She found her underpants and pulled them on quickly, then stood up and brushed grass off her dress. Now that she was decent the sense of urgency left her, and all the muscles of her body felt pleasantly lassitudinous, as they sometimes did when she lay in bed on Sunday morning, dozing and listening to church bells.

She leaned on the wall, looking at the sea, and Arne put his arm around her. It was hard to wrench her mind back to war, deception and secrecy.

'I'm working for British Intelligence,' she said abruptly.

He nodded. 'I was afraid of that.'

'Afraid? Why?'

'It means you're in even more danger than if you had come here just to see me.'

She was pleased that his first thought was of the peril to her. He really did love her. But she brought trouble. 'Now you're at risk, too, just because you're with me.'

'You'd better explain.'

She sat on the wall and gathered her thoughts. She had failed to think of a censored version of the story that included only what he absolutely had to know. No matter how she chopped it up, half the truth made no sense, so she had to tell him everything. She was going to ask him to risk his life, and he needed to know why.

She told him about the Nightwatchmen, the arrests at Kastrup aerodrome, the devastating rate of bomber losses, the radar installation on his home island of Sande, the *himmelbett* clue, and the involvement of Poul Kirke. As she talked, his face changed. The merriment went from his eyes, and his perennial smile was replaced by a look of anxiety. She wondered whether he would accept the mission.

If he were a coward, surely he would not have chosen to fly the flimsy wood-and-linen machines of the Army Aviation Troops? On the other hand, being a pilot was part of his dashing image. And he often put pleasure before work. It was one of the reasons she loved him: she was too serious, and he made her enjoy herself. Which was the real Arne – the hedonist or the airman? Until now he had never been put to the test.

'I've come to ask you to do what Poul would have done, if he had lived: go to Sande, get into the base, and examine the radar installation.'

Arne nodded, looking solemn.

'We need photographs, good ones.' She leaned across to her bicycle, opened the saddlebag, and took out a small 35mm camera, a German-made Leica IIIa. She had considered a miniature Minox Riga, which was easier to conceal, but in the end had preferred the precision of the Leica's lens. 'This is probably the most important job you'll ever be asked to do. When we understand their radar system, we will be able to devise ways to defeat it, and that will save the lives of thousands of airmen.'

'I can see that.'

'But if you're caught, you'll be executed – shot or hanged – for spying.' She held out the camera.

She half wanted him to refuse the mission, for she could hardly bear the thought of the danger he would be in if he accepted. But, if he refused, could she ever respect him?

He did not take the camera. 'Poul was the head of your Nightwatchmen.'

She nodded.

'I suppose most of our friends were in it.'

288

'Better that you don't know—'

'Just about everyone except me.'

She nodded. She feared what was coming.

'You think I'm a coward.'

'It didn't seem like your kind of thing—'

'Because I like parties, and I make jokes, and flirt with girls, you thought I didn't have the guts for secret work.' She said nothing, but he was insistent. 'Answer me.'

She nodded miserably.

'In that case, I'll have to prove you wrong.' He took the camera.

She did not know whether to be happy or sad. 'Thank you,' she said, fighting back tears. 'You'll be careful, won't you?'

'Yes. But there's a problem. I was followed to Bornholm.'

'Oh, hell.' This was something she had not anticipated. 'Are you sure?'

'Yes. I noticed a couple of people hanging around the base, a man and a young woman. She was on the train to Copenhagen with me, then he was on the ferry. When I got here, he followed me on a bicycle, and there was a car behind. I shook them off a few miles outside Ronne.'

'They must suspect you of working with Poul.'

'Ironically, as I wasn't.'

'Who do you think they are?'

'Danish police, acting under orders from the Germans.'

'Now that you've given them the slip, they undoubtedly feel sure you're guilty. They must still be looking for you.'

'They can't search every house in Bornholm.'

'No, but they'll have people watching the ferry port and the aerodrome.'

'I hadn't thought of that. So how am I going to get back to Copenhagen?'

He was not yet thinking like a spy, Hermia noted. 'We'll have to smuggle you on to the ferry somehow.'

'And then where would I go? I can't return to the flying school – it's the first place they'll look.'

'You'll have to stay with Jens Toksvig.'

Arne's face darkened. 'So he's one of the Nightwatchmen.'

'Yes. His address—'

'I know where he lives,' Arne snapped. 'He was my friend before he was a Nightwatchman.'

'He may be jumpy, because of what happened to Poul—'

'He won't turn me away.'

Hermia pretended not to notice Arne's anger. 'Let's assume you get tonight's ferry. How long will it take you to get to Sande?'

'First I'll talk to my brother, Harald. He worked as a labourer on the site when they were building the base, so he can give me the layout. Then you have to allow a full day to get to Jutland, because the trains are always delayed. I could get there late on Tuesday, sneak into the base on Wednesday, and return to

Copenhagen on Thursday. Then how do I get in touch with you?'

'Come back here next Friday. If the police are still watching the ferry, you'll have to find some way of disguising yourself. I'll meet you right here. We'll cross to Sweden with the fisherman who brought me. Then we'll get you false papers at the British legation and fly you to England.'

He nodded grimly.

She said: 'If this works out, we could be together again, and free, in a week's time.'

He smiled. 'It seems too much to hope for.'

He did love her, she decided, even though he was still feeling wounded at having been left out of the Nightwatchmen. And still, in her heart of hearts, she was not sure he had the nerve for this work. But she was undoubtedly going to find out.

While they had been talking, the first few tourists had arrived, and a handful of people were now strolling around the ruins, peering into cellars and touching the ancient stones. 'Let's get out of here,' Hermia said. 'Did you come on a bicycle?'

'It's behind that tower.'

Arne fetched his bike and they left the castle, Arne wearing sunglasses and a cap to make him hard to recognize. The disguise would not pass a careful check of passengers boarding a ferry, but might protect him if he chanced to meet his pursuers on the road.

Hermia considered the problem of escape as they freewheeled down the hillside. Could she devise a better disguise for Arne? She had no wigs or costumes, nor any make-up other than the minimal lipstick and powder she used herself. He had to look like a different person, and for that he needed professional help. He could surely find it in Copenhagen, but not here.

At the foot of the hill she spotted her fellow guest at the boarding house, Sven Fromer, getting out of his Volvo. She did not want him to see Arne, and she hoped to ride past without his noticing her, but she was unlucky. He caught her eye, waved, and stood expectantly beside the path. It would have been conspicuously rude to ignore him, so she felt obliged to stop.

'We meet again,' he said. 'This must be your fiancé.'

She was not in any danger from Sven, she told herself. There was nothing suspicious about what she was doing, and anyway Sven was anti-German. 'This is Oluf Arnesen,' she said, reversing Arne's name. 'Oluf, meet Sven Fromer. He stayed at the same place as me last night.'

The two men shook hands. Arne said conversationally: 'Have you been here long?'

'A week. I leave tonight.'

Hermia was struck by a thought. 'Sven,' she said. 'This morning you told me we should be fighting the Germans.'

'I talk too much. I ought to be more circumspect.'

'If I gave you a chance to help the British, would you take a risk?'

He stared at her. 'You?' he said. 'But how . . . Do you mean to say that you are—'

'Would you be willing?' she pressed him.

'This isn't some kind of trick, is it?'

'You'll have to trust me. Yes or no?'

'Yes,' he said. 'What do you want me to do?'

'Could a man hide in the back of your car?'

'Sure. I could conceal him behind my equipment. He wouldn't be comfortable, but there's room.'

'Would you be willing to smuggle someone on the ferry tonight?'

Sven looked at his car, then at Arne. 'You?'

Arne nodded.

Sven smiled. 'Hell, yes,' he said.

FIFTEEN

Harald's first day working at the Nielsen farm was more successful than he had dared to hope. Old Nielsen had a small workshop with enough equipment for Harald to repair just about anything. He had patched the water pump on a steam plough, welded a hinge on a caterpillar track, and found the short circuit that caused the farmhouse lights to fuse every night. He had eaten a hearty lunch of herrings and potatoes with the farmhands.

In the evening he had spent a couple of hours at the village tavern with Karl, the farmer's youngest son – although he had drunk only two small glasses of beer, remembering what a fool he had made of himself with liquor a week before. Everyone was talking about Hitler's invasion of the Soviet Union. The news was bad. The Luftwaffe claimed to have destroyed 1,800 Soviet aircraft on the ground in lightning raids. In the tavern, everyone thought Moscow would fall before winter, except the local Communist, and even he seemed worried.

Harald left early because Karen had said she might see him after dinner. He felt weary but pleased with himself as he walked back to the old monastery. When he entered the ruined building, he was astonished to find his brother in the church, staring at the derelict aircraft. 'A Hornet Moth,' Arne said. 'The gentleman's aerial carriage.'

'It's a wreck,' Harald said.

'Not really. The undercarriage is a bit bent.'

'How do you think it happened?'

'On landing. The back end of a Hornet tends to swing out of control, because the main wheels are too far forward. But the axle tubes aren't designed to withstand sideways pressure, so when you swerve violently they can buckle.'

Arne looked terrible, Harald saw. Instead of his army uniform, he wore what seemed to be someone else's old clothes, a worn tweed jacket and faded corduroy trousers. He had shaved off his moustache, and a greasy cap covered his curly hair. In his hands he held a small, neat 35mm camera. There was a strained expression on his face instead of his usual insouciant smile. 'What happened to you?' Harald said anxiously.

'I'm in trouble. Have you got anything to eat?'

'Not a thing. We can go to the tavern—'

'I can't show my face. I'm a wanted man.' Arne tried a wry grin, but it finished up as a grimace. 'Every policeman in Denmark has my description, and there are posters of me all over Copenhagen. I was chased by a cop all along the Stroget and only just got away.'

'Are you in the Resistance?'

Arne hesitated, shrugged, then said: 'Yes.'

Harald was thrilled. He sat on the ledge he used as

a bed and Arne sat next to him. Pinetop the cat appeared and rubbed his head against Harald's leg. 'So you were working with them when I asked you, at home, three weeks ago?'

'No, not then. I was left out at first. Apparently they thought I wasn't suitable for secret work. By Christ, they were right. But now they're desperate, so I'm in it. I have to take pictures of some machinery at the military base on Sande.'

Harald nodded. 'I drew a sketch of it for Poul.'

'Even you were in it before me,' Arne said bitterly. 'Well, well.'

'Poul told me not to tell you.'

'Apparently everyone thought I was a coward.'

'I could redraw my sketches . . . although they were only from memory.'

Arne shook his head. 'They need accurate photos. I came to ask you if there's a way to sneak inside.'

Harald found this talk of espionage exciting, but it bothered him that Arne did not seem to have a well thought out plan. 'There's a place where the fence is concealed by trees, yes – but how are you going to get to Sande if the police are looking for you?'

'I've changed my appearance.'

'Not much. What papers are you carrying?'

'Only my own – how would I get any others?'

'So if you're stopped by the police for any reason, it will take them about ten seconds to establish that you're the man they're all looking for.'

'That's about it.'

Harald shook his head. 'It's crazy.'

'It has to be done. This equipment enables the Germans to detect bombers when they're still miles away – in time to scramble their fighters.'

'It must use radio waves,' Harald said excitedly.

'The British have a similar system, but the Germans seem to have refined it, and they're shooting down as many as half the aircraft on a raid. The RAF is desperate to figure out how they're doing it. It's worth risking my life.'

'Not pointlessly. If you're caught, you won't be able to pass the information to the British.'

'I have to try.'

Harald took a deep breath. 'Why don't I go?'

'I knew you were going to say that.'

'No one's looking for me. I know the site. I've already been over the fence – I took a short cut one night. And I know more about radio than you, so I'll have a better idea of what to photograph.' Harald thought the logic of his argument irresistible.

'If you're caught, you'll be shot as a spy.'

'Same applies to you – only you're virtually certain to be caught, whereas I'll probably get away with it.'

'The police may have found your sketches when they came for Poul. If so, the Germans must know that someone's interested in the base on Sande, and they will probably have improved their security as a result. Getting over the fence may not be as easy as it was.'

'I still have a better chance than you.'

'I can't send you into danger. What if you're caught – what will I say to Mother?'

'You'll say that I died fighting for freedom. I've as

much right as you to take the risk. Give me the damn camera.'

Before Arne could reply, Karen came in.

She walked softly and appeared without warning, so Arne had no chance to hide, although reflexively he made a move to get up, then stopped himself.

'Who are you?' Karen said with her customary directness. 'Oh! Hello, Arne. You've shaved off your moustache – I suppose that's because of all the posters I saw in Copenhagen today. Why are you an outlaw?' She sat on the covered bonnet of the Rolls-Royce, crossing her long legs like a fashion model.

Arne hesitated, then said: 'I can't tell you.'

Karen's mind raced ahead, drawing inferences with impressive speed. 'My God, you're in the Resistance! Was Poul in it too? Is that why he died?'

Arne nodded. 'He didn't crash his aircraft. He was trying to escape from the police, and they shot at him.'

'Poor Poul.' She looked away for a moment. 'So you've taken up where he left off. But now the police are on to you. Someone must be sheltering you – probably Jens Toksvig, he was Poul's closest friend after you.'

Arne shrugged and nodded.

'But you can't move around without risking arrest, so . . .' She looked at Harald, and her voice went quiet. 'You're in it now, Harald.'

To Harald's surprise, she looked concerned, as if she were afraid for him. He was pleased that she cared.

He looked at Arne. 'Well? Am I in it?'

Arne sighed and gave him the camera.

* * *

Harald arrived in Morlunde late the following day. He left the steam bike in a car park next to the ferry dock, feeling it would be too conspicuous on Sande. He had nothing with which to cover it, and no way of locking it, but he trusted that a casual thief would be unable to figure out how to make it go.

He was in time for the last ferry of the day. As he waited on the dockside, the evening slowly dimmed, and stars appeared like the lights of distant ships on a dark sea. A drunk islander came staggering along the quay, peered rudely at Harald, muttered: 'Ah, young Olufsen,' then sat on a capstan some distance away and tried to light a pipe.

The boat docked and a handful of people got off. To Harald's surprise, a Danish policeman and a German soldier stood at the head of the gangway. As the drunk boarded, they checked his identity card. Harald's heartbeat seemed to falter. He hesitated, scared, unsure whether to board. Had they simply stepped up security after finding his sketches, as Arne had forecast? Or were they looking for Arne himself? Would they know Harald was the brother of the wanted man? Olufsen was a common name – but they might have been briefed on the family. He had an expensive camera in his satchel. It was a popular German make, but all the same it could arouse suspicion.

He tried to calm his mind and consider his options. There were other ways of getting to Sande. He was not sure he could swim two miles in the open sea, but he might be able to borrow or steal a small boat. However, if he were seen beaching the boat on Sande he would be sure to be questioned. He might do better to act innocent.

He boarded the ferry.

The policeman asked him: 'What is your reason for wanting to travel to Sande?'

Harald suppressed his indignation that anyone should presume to ask such a question. 'I live there,' he said. 'With my parents.'

The policeman looked at his face. 'I don't remember seeing you before, and I've been doing this for four days.'

'I've been away at school.'

'Tuesday is a strange day to come home.'

'It's the end of term.'

The policeman grunted, apparently satisfied. He checked the address on Harald's card and showed it to the soldier, who nodded and let Harald on board.

He went to the far end of the boat and stood looking out to sea, waiting for his heart to stop racing. He was relieved to have passed the checkpoint, but furious that he had to justify himself to a policeman when moving around his own country. It seemed a silly reaction, when he thought about it logically, but he could not help feeling outraged.

At midnight the boat left the dock.

There was no moon. In the starlight, the flat island

of Sande was a dark swell like another wave on the horizon. Harald had not expected to return so soon. In fact, when he left on Friday he had wondered if he would ever see the place again. Now he was back as a spy, with a camera in his bag and a mission to photograph the Nazis' secret weapon. He vaguely recalled thinking what a thrill it would be to become part of the Resistance. In reality, it was no fun at all. On the contrary, he was sick with fear.

He felt worse as he disembarked on the familiar quay and looked across the road to the post office and the grocery store that had not changed since he could remember. His life had been secure and stable for the first eighteen years. Now he felt he would never be safe again.

He made his way to the beach and began to tramp south. The wet sand gleamed silver in the starlight. He heard a girlish giggle from an unseen source in the dunes, and he felt a pang of jealousy. Would he ever make Karen giggle like that?

It was near dawn when he came within sight of the base. He could make out the fence posts. The trees and bushes inside the site showed as dark patches on the dunes. If he could see, so could the guards, he realized. He dropped to his knees and began to crawl forward.

A minute later he was glad of his caution. He spotted two guards patrolling inside the fence, side by side, with a dog.

That was new. They had not patrolled in pairs before, and there had been no dogs.

He dropped flat. The two men did not seem especially alert. They were strolling, not marching. The one holding the dog was talking animatedly while the other smoked. As they came nearer, Harald could hear the voice over the sound of the waves breaking on the beach. He had learned German in school, like all Danish children. The man was telling a boastful story about a woman called Margareta.

Harald was fifty yards from the fence. As the guards approached the nearest point to him, the dog sniffed the air. It could probably smell Harald, but did not know where he was. It barked uncertainly. The guard holding the lead was not as well trained as the dog, and he told the animal to shut up, then carried on explaining how he got Margareta to meet him in the wood shed. Harald lay completely still. The dog barked again, and one of the guards turned on a powerful flashlight. Harald hid his face in the sand. The beam of the torch played along the dunes but passed over him without stopping.

The guard said: 'Then she said all right, but you'll have to pull it out at the last minute.' They walked on, and the dog became quiet again.

Harald lay still until they were out of sight. Then he turned inland and approached the section of the fence that was concealed by vegetation. He feared the soldiers might have cut down the trees, but the copse was still there. He crawled through the bushes, reached the fence, and stood up.

He hesitated. He could back out at this point, and he would have broken no law. He could return to

Kirstenslot and concentrate on his new job, spending his evenings in the tavern and his nights dreaming of Karen. He could take the attitude that war and politics were none of his concern, as many Danes did. But even as he contemplated that line, he was revolted. He imagined himself explaining his decision to Arne and Karen, or Uncle Joachim and cousin Monika, and he felt ashamed just for thinking about it.

The fence was unchanged, six feet of chicken wire topped by two strands of barbed wire. Harald swung his satchel around to his back, to keep it out of the way, then climbed the fence, stepped gingerly over the barbed wire, and jumped down the other side.

Now he was committed. He was inside a military base with a camera. If they caught him, they would kill him.

He walked quickly forward, treading softly, keeping close to bushes and trees, looking around constantly. He passed the searchlight tower, and thought with trepidation how utterly exposed he would be if someone decided to switch on the powerful beams. He listened hard for patrolling footsteps, but heard only the constant hushing urged by the waves. After a few minutes he descended a gentle slope and entered a stand of conifers which provided him with good cover. He wondered for a moment why the soldiers had not thought of chopping down the trees, for better security, then he realized that they served to conceal the secret radio equipment from prying eyes.

A moment later he reached his destination. Now that he knew what he was looking for, he could see quite clearly the circular wall and the big rectangular grid rising from its hollow core, the aerial slowly rotating, like a mechanical eye scanning the dark horizon. He heard again the low hum of the electric motor. On either side of the structure he could make out the two smaller shapes, and now in the starlight he saw that they were miniature versions of the big rotating aerial.

So there were three machines. He wondered why. Might that somehow explain the remarkable superiority of German radar? Looking more closely at the smaller aerials, he thought they were constructed differently. He would need to look again in daylight, but it seemed to him they might tilt as well as rotate. Why would that be? He must make sure to get good photographs of all three pieces of apparatus.

The first time he was here, he had jumped over the circular wall in a fright, after hearing a guard cough nearby. Now that he had time to think, he felt sure there must be an easier way in. The walls were needed to protect the equipment from accidental damage, but engineers surely needed to get inside for maintenance. He walked around the circle, peering at the brickwork in the dim light, and came across a wooden door. It was not locked, and he passed through, quietly closing it behind him.

He felt a little safer. No one could see him from outside. Engineers would not do maintenance at this time of night except in an emergency. If someone did come in, he might just have time to leap over the wall before he was spotted.

He looked up at the great revolving grid. It must pick up radio beams reflected off aircraft, he guessed. The aerial must act like a lens, focusing the signals received. The cable protruding from the base carried the data back to the new buildings Harald had helped to construct last summer. There, presumably, monitors displayed the results, and operators stood ready to alert the Luftwaffe.

In the half dark, with the humming machinery looming over him and the ozone smell of electricity in his nostrils, he felt he was inside the beating heart of the war machine. The struggle between the scientists and engineers on both sides could be as important as the battlefield clash of tanks and machine guns. And he had become part of it.

He heard an aircraft. There was no moon, so it was not likely to be a bomber. It might be a German fighter on a local flight, or a civilian transport that had got lost. He wondered if the big aerial had detected its approach an hour ago. He wondered whether the smaller aerials were pointed at it. He decided to step outside and take a look.

One of the smaller aerials faced the sea, in the direction from which the aircraft was approaching. The other pointed inland. Both were tilted at angles different from previously, he thought. As the aircraft roared closer, he noticed the first aerial tilt more, as if following it. The other continued to move, though in response to what he could not figure.

The aircraft crossed Sande and headed inland, the aerial dish continuing to follow it until after its sound died away to nothing. Harald returned to his hiding place inside the circular wall, musing on what he had seen.

The sky was turning from black to grey. At this time of year, dawn broke before three o'clock. In another hour, the sun would rise.

He took the camera out of his satchel. Arne had shown him how to use it. As daylight strengthened, he moved quietly around inside the wall, figuring out the best angles for photographs that would reveal every detail of the machinery.

He and Arne had agreed he would take the shots at about a quarter to five. The sun would be up, but it would not be shining over the wall into the installation. Sunshine was not necessary – the film in the camera was sensitive enough to record details without it.

As time went by, Harald's thoughts turned anxiously to escape. He had arrived at night, and entered the base cloaked by darkness, but he could not wait until tomorrow night before leaving. It was almost certain that an engineer would routinely inspect the equipment at least once during the course of a day, even if nothing went wrong. So Harald had to get away as soon as he had taken the photos – when it would be full daylight. His departure would be a lot more dangerous than his arrival.

He considered which way to go. To the south of where he was, in the direction of his parents' home, the fence was only a couple of hundred yards away, but the route lay across open dunes without trees or bushes. Going north, retracing his steps, under cover of vegetation much of the way, would take longer but might be safer.

He wondered how he would face a firing squad. Would he be calm and proud, keeping his terror under control, or would he break and turn into a gibbering fool, pleading for mercy and wetting himself?

He forced himself to wait calmly. The light grew stronger and the minute hand crawled around the face of his watch. He heard no new sounds from outside. A soldier's day started early, but he was hoping there would not be much activity before six o'clock – by which time he would be gone.

At last it was time to take the pictures. The sky was cloudless and there was a clear morning light. He could see every rivet and terminal of the complex piece of machinery in front of him. Focusing the lens carefully, he photographed the revolving base of the apparatus, the cables, and the grid of the aerial. He unfolded a yard rule from the monastery tool rack and placed it in some of the pictures to show scale – his own bright idea.

Next he had to go outside the wall.

He hesitated. In here he felt safe. But he had to have pictures of the two smaller aerials.

He cracked the door. All was still. He could tell, by the sound of the surf, that the tide was coming in. The base was bathed in the watery light of a seaside morning. There was no sign of life. It was the hour when men sleep heavily, and even dogs have dreams.

He took careful shots of the two smaller aerials, which were protected only by low walls. Thinking about their function, he realized that one of them had been tracking an aircraft that was within visual range. The whole point of this apparatus was to detect bombers *before* they came in sight, he had thought. Presumably the second small aerial was tracking another aircraft.

Snapping photographs, he turned the puzzle over in his mind. How could three devices work together to increase the kill rate of Luftwaffe fighters? Perhaps the large aerial gave advance warning of a bomber's approach and the smaller one tracked the bomber within German air space. But then what did the second smaller aerial do?

It occurred to him that there would be another aircraft in the sky – the fighter that had been scrambled to attack the bomber. Could the second aerial be used by the Luftwaffe to track *their own aircraft?* It seemed crazy, but as he stepped back to photograph the three aerials together, showing their placement relative to one another, he realized it made perfect sense. If a Luftwaffe controller knew the positions of the bomber and the fighter, he could direct the fighter by radio until it made contact with the bomber.

He began to see how the Luftwaffe might be working. The large aerial gave advance warning of a raid so that the fighters could be scrambled in time. One of the smaller aerials picked up a bomber as it came closer. The other tracked a fighter, enabling the controller to direct the pilot precisely to the bomber's location. After that, it was like shooting fish in a barrel.

That thought made Harald realize how exposed he was: standing upright, in full daylight, in the middle of a military base, photographing top secret equipment. Panic surged through his veins like poison. He tried to calm himself and take the last few photos he had planned, showing the three aerials from different angles, but he was too terrified. He had taken at least twenty shots. It must be enough, he told himself.

He thrust the camera into his satchel and started walking quickly away. Forgetting his resolution to take the longer but safer route north, he headed south, across the open dunes. In that direction the fence was visible, just beyond the old boathouse he had bumped into last time. Today he would pass it on the seaward side, and it would hide him from sight for a few paces.

As he approached it, a dog barked.

He looked around wildly but saw no soldiers and no dog. Then he realized the sound had come from the boathouse. The soldiers must be using the derelict building as a kennel. A second dog joined the barking.

Harald broke into a run.

The dogs excited one another, more joined in, and the noise became hysterically loud. Harald reached the building then turned seaward, trying to keep the boathouse between himself and the main buildings while he sprinted for the fence. Fear gave him speed. Every second he expected a shot to ring out.

He reached the fence, not knowing whether he had

been seen or not. He climbed it like a monkey and vaulted over the barbed wire at the top. He came down hard on the other side, splashing in shallow water. He scrambled to his feet and glanced back through the fence. Beyond the boathouse, partly obscured by trees and bushes, he could see the main buildings, but no soldiers were in view. He turned away and ran. He stayed in the shallow water for a hundred yards, so that the dogs could not follow his scent, then he turned inland. He left shallow footprints in the hard sand, but he knew the fast-moving tide would cover them in a minute or two. He reached the dunes, where he left no visible trace.

A few minutes later he came to the dirt road. He glanced back and saw no one following. Breathing hard, he headed for the parsonage. He ran past the church to the kitchen door.

It was open. His parents were always up early.

He stepped inside. His mother was at the stove, wearing a dressing gown, making tea. When she saw him she gave a cry of shock and dropped the earthenware teapot. It hit the tiled floor and the spout broke off. Harald picked up the two pieces. 'I'm sorry to startle you,' he said.

'Harald!'

He kissed her cheek and hugged her. 'Is my father at home?'

'In the church. There wasn't time to tidy up last night, so he's gone to straighten the chairs.'

'What happened last night?' There was no service on a Monday evening.

'The board of deacons met to discuss your case. They're going to read you out next Sunday.'

'The revenge of the Flemmings.' Harald found it strange that he had once thought that sort of thing important.

By now, guards would have gone to find out what had disturbed the dogs. If they were thorough, they might check nearby houses, and look for a fugitive in sheds and barns. 'Mother,' he said, 'if the soldiers come here, will you tell them I've been in bed all night?'

'Whatever has happened?' she said fearfully.

'I'll explain later.' It would be more natural if he were in bed, he thought. 'Tell them I'm still asleep – will you?'

'All right.'

He left the kitchen and went upstairs to his bedroom. He slung his satchel over the back of the chair. He took the camera out and put it in a drawer. He thought of hiding it, but there was no time, and a hidden camera was proof of guilt. He shed his clothes quickly, put on his pyjamas, and got into bed.

He heard his father's voice in the kitchen. He got out of bed and went to the top of the stairs to listen.

'What's he doing here?' the pastor said.

His mother replied: 'Hiding from the soldiers.'

'For goodness' sake, what has the boy got himself into now?'

'I don't know, but—'

His mother was interrupted by a loud knocking. A young man's voice said in German: 'Good morning.

311

We're looking for someone. Have you seen a stranger at any time in the last few hours?'

'No, nobody at all.' The nervousness in his mother's voice was so evident that the soldier must have noticed it – but perhaps he was used to people being frightened of him.

'How about you, sir?'

His father said firmly: 'No.'

'Is there anyone else here?'

Harald's mother replied: 'My son. He's still asleep.'

'I need to search the house.' The voice was polite, but it was making a statement, not asking permission.

'I'll show you around,' said the pastor.

Harald returned to his bed, heart thudding. He heard booted footsteps on the tiled floors downstairs, and doors opening and closing. Then the boots came up the wooden staircase. They entered his parents' bedroom, then Arne's old room and finally approached Harald's. He heard the handle of his door turn.

He closed his eyes, feigning sleep, and tried to make his breathing slow and even.

The German voice said quietly: 'Your son.'

'Yes.'

There was a pause.

'Has he been here all night?'

Harald held his breath. He had never known his father to tell even a white lie.

Then he heard: 'Yes. All night.'

He was flabbergasted. His father had lied for him. The hard-hearted, stiff-necked, self-righteous old tyrant had broken his own rules. He was human after all. Harald felt tears behind his closed eyelids.

The boots receded along the passage and down the stairs, and Harald heard the soldier take his leave. He got out of bed and went to the top of the stairs.

'You can come down now,' his father said. 'He's gone.'

He went down. His father looked solemn. 'Thank you for that, Father,' Harald said.

'I committed a sin,' his father said. For a moment, Harald thought he was going to be angry. Then the old face softened. 'However, I believe in a forgiving God.'

Harald realized the agony of conflict his father had been through in the last few minutes, but he did not know how to say that he understood. The only thing he could think of was to shake hands. He held out his hand.

His father looked at it, then took it. He drew Harald to him and put his left arm around Harald's shoulders. He closed his eyes, struggling to contain a profound emotion. When he spoke, the resonant boom of the preacher had gone from his voice, and his words came out in a murmur of anguish. 'I thought they would kill you,' he said. 'My dear son, I thought they would kill you.'

SIXTEEN

Arne Olufsen had slipped through Peter Flemming's fingers.

Peter brooded over this as he boiled an egg for Inge's breakfast. After Arne shook off the surveillance on Bornholm, Peter had said blithely that they would soon pick him up again. Peter's confidence had been badly misplaced. He believed Arne was not cunning enough to get off the island unobserved – and he had been wrong. He did not yet know how Arne had managed it, but there was no doubt he had returned to Copenhagen, for a uniformed policeman had spotted him in the city centre. The patrolman had given chase, but Arne had outrun him – and vanished again.

Some kind of espionage was obviously still going on, as Peter's boss, Frederik Juel, had pointed out with icy scorn. 'Olufsen is apparently performing evasive manoeuvres,' he had said.

General Braun had been more blunt. 'The killing of Poul Kirke has clearly failed to disable the spy ring,' he had said. There had been no further talk of promoting Peter to head of department. 'I shall call in the Gestapo.'

It was so unfair, Peter thought angrily. He had uncovered this spy ring, found the secret message in the aeroplane chock, arrested the mechanics, raided the synagogue, arrested Ingemar Gammel, raided the flying school, killed Poul Kirke, and flushed out Arne Olufsen. Yet people such as Juel who had done nothing were able to denigrate his achievements and prevent his getting the recognition that was his due.

But he was not finished yet. 'I can find Arne Olufsen,' he had said to General Braun the night before. Juel had started to object, but Peter had overridden him. 'Give me twenty-four hours. If he's not in custody tomorrow night, call in the Gestapo.'

Braun had agreed.

Arne had not returned to barracks, nor was he with his parents on Sande, so he had to be hiding out at the home of a fellow spy. But they would all be lying low. However, one person who probably knew most of the spies was Karen Duchwitz. She had been Poul's girlfriend, and her brother was at school with Poul's cousin. She was not a spy, Peter felt sure, so she had no reason to lie low. She might lead Peter to Arne.

It was a long shot, but it was all he had.

He mashed the soft-boiled egg up with salt and a little butter, then took the tray into the bedroom. He sat Inge up and gave her a spoonful of egg. He got the feeling she did not much like it. He tasted it, and it was fine, so he gave her another spoonful. After a moment she pushed it out of her mouth, like a baby. The egg ran down her chin and on to the bodice of her nightdress.

Peter stared in despair. She had made a mess of herself several times in the past week or two. This was a new development. 'Inge would never have done that,' he said.

He put the tray down, left her and went to the phone. He dialled the hotel on Sande and asked for his father, who was always at work early. When he got through, he said: 'You were right. It's time to put Inge in a home.'

* * *

Peter studied the Royal Theatre, a domed nineteenth-century building of yellow stone. Its façade was carved with columns, pilasters, capitals, corbels, wreaths, shields, lyres, masks, cherubs, mermaids and angels. On the roof were urns, torchères, and four-legged creatures with wings and human breasts. 'It's a bit overdone,' he said. 'Even for a theatre.'

Tilde Jespersen laughed.

They were sitting on the verandah of the Hotel d'Angleterre. They had a good view across the Kongens Nytorv, the largest square in Copenhagen. Inside the theatre, the students of the ballet school were watching a dress rehearsal of *Les Sylphides*, the current production. Peter and Tilde were waiting for Karen Duchwitz to come out.

Tilde was pretending to read today's newspaper. The front-page headline said: LENINGRAD AFLAME. Even the Nazis were surprised at how well the Russian campaign was going, saying their success 'baffled the imagination'.

Peter was talking to release tension. So far, his plan was a complete failure. Karen had been under surveillance all day and had done nothing but go to school. But fruitless anxiety was debilitating, and led to mistakes, so he tried to relax. He said: 'Do you think architects deliberately make theatres and opera houses intimidating, to discourage ordinary people from going in?'

'Do you consider yourself an ordinary person?'

'Of course.' The entrance was flanked by two green statues of sitting figures, larger than life-size. 'Who are those two?'

'Holberg and Oehlenschläger.'

He recognized the names. They were both great Danish playwrights. 'I don't much like drama – too many speeches. I'd rather see a movie, something to make me laugh, Buster Keaton or Laurel and Hardy. Did you see the one where these guys are whitewashing a room, and someone comes in carrying a plank on his shoulder?' He chuckled at the recollection. 'I nearly fell on the damn floor laughing.'

She gave him one of her enigmatic looks. 'Now you have surprised me. I wouldn't have put you down as a lover of slapstick.'

'What did you imagine I would like?'

'Western movies, where gunplay ensures that justice is triumphant.'

'You're right, I like those too. What about you? Do you enjoy theatre? Copenhageners approve of culture in theory, but most of them have never been inside that building.'

'I like opera – do you?'

'Well . . . the tunes are OK but the stories are silly.'

She smiled. 'I've never thought of it that way, but you're right. How about ballet?'

'I don't really see the point. And the costumes are peculiar. To tell the truth, I find the men's tights a bit embarrassing.'

She laughed again. 'Oh, Peter, you're so funny, but I like you all the same.'

He had not intended to be amusing, but he accepted the compliment cheerfully. He glanced down at the photograph in his hand. He had taken it from Poul Kirke's bedroom. It showed Poul sitting on a bicycle with Karen perched on the crossbar. They were both wearing shorts. Karen had wonderful long legs. They looked such a happy couple, full of energy and fun, that for a moment Peter felt sad that Poul had died. He had to remind himself sternly that Poul had chosen to be a spy and to flout the law.

The purpose of the photo was to help him identify Karen. She was attractive, with a big smile and masses of curly hair. She seemed the antithesis of Tilde, who had small, neat features in a round face. Some of the men said Tilde was frigid, because she repelled their advances – but I know better, Peter thought.

They had not talked about the fiasco in the hotel on Bornholm. Peter was too embarrassed to raise it. He was not going to apologize – that would just be further humiliation. But a plan was forming in his mind, something so dramatic he preferred to think about it only vaguely.

'Here she comes,' said Tilde.

Peter looked across the square and saw a group of young people emerging from the theatre. He picked out Karen immediately. She was wearing a straw boater at a jaunty angle and a mustard-yellow summer dress with a flared skirt that danced enticingly around her knees. The black-and-white photograph had not shown her white skin and flaming red hair, nor had it done justice to the spirited air that was obvious to Peter even at a distance. She looked as if she were making an entrance on the stage of the theatre, rather than merely walking down the steps outside.

She crossed the square and turned into the main drag, the Stroget.

Peter and Tilde stood up.

'Before we go,' Peter said.

'What?'

'Will you come to my apartment this evening?'

'Any special reason?'

'Yes, but I'd rather not explain.'

'All right.'

'Thanks.' He said no more, but hurried after Karen. Tilde followed him at a distance, by prearrangement.

The Stroget was a narrow street crowded with shoppers and buses, frequently blocked by illegally parked cars. Double the fines and ticket every car and the problem would go away, Peter felt sure. He kept Karen's straw hat in sight. He prayed she was not simply heading for home.

At the end of the Stroget was the town hall square. Here the group of students dispersed. Karen walked

on with just one of the girls, chatting animatedly.
Peter drew closer. They passed the Tivoli Garden and
stopped, as if about to part company, but continued
their conversation. They looked pretty and carefree in
the afternoon sunshine. Peter wondered impatiently
how much more two girls could have to say to one
another after having spent all day together.

At last Karen's friend walked towards the main
railway station and Karen went the opposite way.
Peter's hopes rose. Did she have a rendezvous with
one of the circle of spies? He followed her, but to his
dismay she approached Vesterport, a suburban railway
station from which she could catch a train to her
home village of Kirstenslot.

This was no good. He had only a few hours left.
Clearly she was not going to lead him to one of the
circle. He would have to force the situation.

He caught up with her at the entrance to the
station. 'Excuse me,' he said. 'I must speak to you.'

She gave him a level look and kept walking. 'What
is it?' she said with cool politeness.

'Could we talk for just a minute?'

She passed through the entrance and started down
the steps to the platform. 'We're talking.'

He pretended to be nervous. 'I'm taking a terrible
risk just speaking to you.'

That got to her. She stopped on the platform and
glanced around nervously. 'What's this about?'

She had wonderful eyes, he noticed: a striking clear
green. 'It's about Arne Olufsen.' He saw fear in those

320

eyes, and was gratified. His instinct had been right. She knew something.

'What about him?' She managed to keep her voice low and even.

'Aren't you a friend of his?'

'No. I've met him – I used to go out with a friend of his. But I don't really know him. Why are you asking me?'

'Do you know where he is?'

'No.'

She spoke firmly, and he thought with dismay that she looked as if she was telling the truth.

But he was not yet ready to give up. 'Could you get a message to him?'

She hesitated, and Peter's heart leaped with hope. He guessed she was wondering whether to lie or not. 'Possibly,' she said after a moment. 'I can't be sure. What sort of message?'

'I'm with the police.'

She took a frightened step back.

'It's all right, I'm on your side.' He could tell that she did not know whether to believe him. 'I'm nothing to do with the security department, I do road accidents. But our office is next to theirs, and sometimes I hear what's going on.'

'What have you heard?'

'Arne is in great danger. The security department know where he's hiding.'

'My God.'

Peter noted that she did not ask what the security

department was, nor what crime Arne was supposed to have committed, and she showed no surprise about his being in hiding. She must therefore know what Arne was up to, he concluded with a sense of triumph.

On that basis, he could arrest and interrogate her. But he had a better plan. He put a note of dramatic urgency into his voice. 'They're going to arrest him tonight.'

'Oh, no!'

'If you know how to reach Arne please, for God's sake, try to get a warning to him in the next hour.'

'I don't think—'

'I can't risk being seen with you. I have to go. I'm sorry. Do your best.' He turned and walked rapidly away.

At the top of the steps he passed Tilde, who was pretending to read a timetable. She did not look at him, but he knew she had seen him, and she would now follow Karen.

Across the street, a man in a leather apron was unloading crates of beer from a wagon drawn by two big horses. Peter stepped behind the cart. He took off his trilby hat, stuffed it inside his jacket, and replaced it with a peaked cap. He knew from experience that this simple switch effected a remarkable change in his appearance. It would not defy careful scrutiny, but at a casual glance he looked like a different person.

Standing half concealed by the wagon, he watched the station entrance. After a few moments, Karen came out.

Tilde was a few paces behind her.

Peter followed Tilde. They turned a corner and walked along the street that lay between the Tivoli and the main railway station. On the next block, Karen turned into the main post office, a grand classical building of red brick and grey stone. Tilde followed her in.

She was going to make a phone call, Peter thought with exhilaration. He ran to the staff entrance. He showed his police badge to the first person he met, a young woman, and said: 'Bring the duty manager, quick.'

A few moments later, a stooped man in a well-worn black suit appeared. 'How may I help you?'

'A young woman in a yellow dress has just entered the main hall,' Peter told him. 'I don't want her to see me, but I need to know what she does.'

The manager looked thrilled. This was probably the most exciting thing that had ever happened in the post office, Peter thought. 'My goodness,' said the man. 'You'd better come with me.'

He hurried along a corridor and opened a door. Peter could see a counter with a row of stools facing small windows. The manager stepped through the door. 'I think I see her,' he said. 'Curly red hair and a straw hat?'

'That's the one.'

'I'd never have guessed she was a criminal.'

'What is she doing?'

'Looking in the telephone directory. Amazing that someone so pretty—'

'If she makes a call, I need to listen.'

The manager hesitated.

Peter had no right to listen to private phone calls without a warrant – but he was hoping the manager would not know that. 'It's very important,' he said.

'I'm not sure I can—'

'Don't worry, I'll take responsibility.'

'She's putting the phone book down.'

Peter was not going to let Karen phone Arne without listening in. If necessary he would pull his gun and threaten this dozy post office clerk, he decided. 'I must insist.'

'We have rules here.'

'Nevertheless—'

'Ah!' said the manager. 'She's put the book down, but she's not coming to the counter.' His face cleared with relief. 'She's leaving!'

Peter cursed with frustration and ran for the exit.

He cracked the door and peeped out. He saw Karen crossing the road. He waited until Tilde emerged, following Karen. Then he tagged along.

He was disappointed, but not defeated. Karen knew the name of someone who could get in touch with Arne. She had looked that name up in the phone book. Why the hell had she not phoned the person? Perhaps she feared – rightly – that the conversation might be overheard by police or German security staff doing routine surveillance.

Still, if she had not wanted the phone number, she must have been looking for the address. And now, if Peter's luck was in, she was heading for that address.

He let Karen get out of sight but kept Tilde in view.

Walking behind Tilde was always a pleasure. It was good to have an excuse to watch her rounded rear. Did she know he was staring at her? Was she exaggerating the sway of her hips deliberately? He had no idea. Who could tell what was in a woman's mind?

They crossed to the small island of Christiansborg and followed the waterfront, with the harbour on their right and the ancient buildings of the government island on their left. The sun-warmed air of the city was refreshed here by a salty breeze from the Baltic Sea. The broad channel of water was lined by freighters, fishing boats, ferries, and ships of the Danish and German navies. Two young sailors fell in behind Tilde and cheerfully tried to pick her up, but she spoke sharply to them and they peeled off immediately.

Karen walked as far as the palace of Amalienborg, then turned inland. Following Tilde, Peter crossed the wide square formed by the four rococo mansions where the royal family lived. From there they headed into Nyboder, a neighbourhood of small houses originally built as cheap accommodation for sailors.

They entered a street called St Paul's Gade. Peter could see Karen in the distance, looking at a row of yellow houses with red roofs, apparently searching for a number. He had a strong, exciting feeling of being close to his quarry.

Karen paused and looked up and down the street, as if checking whether she was observed. It was far too late for that, of course, but she was an amateur. In any case, she did not appear to register Tilde, and Peter was too far away to be recognized.

She knocked on a door.

As Peter caught up with Tilde, the door opened. He could not see who was there. Karen said something and stepped inside, and the door closed. It was number fifty-three, Peter noted.

Tilde said: 'Do you think Arne is in there?'

'Either him, or someone who knows where he is.'

'What do you want to do?'

'Wait.' He looked up and down the street. On the opposite side was a corner shop. 'Over there.' They crossed the road and stood looking in the window. Peter lit a cigarette.

Tilde said: 'The shop probably has a phone. Should we call headquarters? We might as well go in in force. We don't know how many spies might be in there.'

Peter considered summoning reinforcements. 'Not yet,' he said. 'We're not sure what's happening. Let's see how this develops.'

Tilde nodded. She removed her sky-blue beret and put a nondescript patterned scarf over her head. Peter watched her tuck the curls of her fair hair under the scarf. She would look somewhat different when Karen came out of the house, so that Karen was less likely to notice her.

Tilde took the cigarette from Peter's fingers, put it to her own mouth, drew in smoke, and handed the cigarette back. It was an intimate gesture, and he felt almost as if she had kissed him. He sensed that he was blushing, and looked away, towards number fifty-three.

The door opened and Karen came out.

'Look,' he said, and Tilde followed his gaze.

The door closed behind Karen and she walked away alone.

'Damn,' Peter said.

'What do we do now?' Tilde asked.

Peter thought fast. Suppose Arne was inside the little yellow house. Then Peter needed to summon reinforcements, bust into the house and arrest him and anyone with him. On the other hand, Arne might be somewhere else, and Karen could be on her way there – in which case Peter needed to follow her.

Or she might have failed in her quest and decided to give up and go home.

He made a decision. 'We'll split up,' he told Tilde. 'You follow Karen. I'll call headquarters and raid that house.'

'OK.' Tilde hurried after Karen.

Peter went into the shop. It was a general store, selling vegetables and bread and household necessities such as soap and matches. There were cans of food on the shelves, and the floor was obstructed by bundles of firewood and sacks of potatoes. The place looked dirty but prosperous. He showed his police badge to a grey-haired woman in a stained apron. 'Do you have a phone?'

'I'll have to charge you.'

He fumbled in his pocket for change. 'Where is it?' he said impatiently.

She jerked her head towards a curtain at the back. 'Through there.'

He threw some coins on the counter and passed

327

into a small parlour that smelled of cats. He snatched up the phone, called the Politigaarden, and got Conrad. 'I think I may have found Arne's hideout. Number fifty-three St Paul's Gade. Get Dresler and Ellegaard and come here in a car as fast as you can.'

'Right away,' said Conrad.

Peter hung up and hurried outside. He had been less than a minute. If anyone had left the house during that time, they should still be visible on the street. He looked up and down. He saw an old man in a collarless shirt walking an arthritic dog, the two of them moving with painful slowness. A lively pony was drawing a flatbed cart carrying a sofa with holes in the leather upholstery. A group of boys was playing football in the road, using an old tennis ball worn bald with use. There was no sign of Arne. He crossed the street.

Indulging himself for a moment, he thought how satisfying it would be to arrest the elder son of the Olufsen family. What a revenge that would be for the humiliation of Axel Flemming all those years ago. Coming immediately after the expulsion from school of the younger son, the unmasking of Arne as a spy would surely mean the end of Pastor Olulfsen's hegemony. How could he strut and preach when both his sons had gone wrong? He would have to resign.

Peter's father would be pleased.

The door of number fifty-three opened. Peter reached under his jacket and touched the grip of his gun in its shoulder holster as Arne stepped out of the house.

Peter was filled with elation. Arne had shaved off

his moustache and covered his black hair with a workman's cap, but Peter had known him all his life, and recognized him immediately.

After a moment, triumph was replaced by caution. There was often trouble when a lone officer tried to make an arrest. The possibility of escape looked tempting to the suspect who was up against only one cop. Being a plain-clothes detective, lacking the authority of a uniform, made it worse. If there was a fight, passers-by had no way of knowing that one of the two was an officer, and might even intervene on the wrong side.

Peter and Arne had fought once before, twelve years before, at the time of the quarrel between their families. Peter was bigger, but Arne was fit and strong from all the sports he did. There was no clear result. They had traded several blows then been separated. Today Peter had a gun. But perhaps Arne did too.

Arne slammed the house door and turned on to the street, walking towards Peter.

As they came closer, Arne avoided his eye, walking on the inside of the pavement, near the house walls, in the manner of a fugitive. Peter walked on the kerb side, furtively watching Arne's face.

When they were ten yards apart, Arne stole a glance at Peter's face. Peter met his eye, watching his expression. He saw a frown of puzzlement, then recognition, then shock, fear and panic.

Arne stopped, momentarily frozen.

'You're under arrest,' Peter said.

Arne partly recovered his composure, and for a

moment the familiar careless grin flickered across his face. 'Gingerbread Pete,' he said, using a childhood nickname.

Peter saw that Arne was about to make a run for it. He drew his gun. 'Lie on the ground face down with your hands behind your back.'

Arne looked worried rather than frightened. In a moment of insight, Peter saw that it was not the gun Arne was scared of, but something else.

Arne said in a challenging tone: 'Are you ready to shoot me?'

'If necessary,' Peter said. He levelled the gun threateningly, but in truth he was desperate to take Arne alive. Poul Kirke's death had dead-ended the investigation. He wanted to interrogate Arne, not kill him.

Arne smiled enigmatically, then turned and ran.

Peter held his gun arm straight and sighted along the barrel. He aimed at Arne's legs, but it was impossible to shoot accurately with a pistol, and he knew he might hit any part of Arne's body, or none. But Arne was getting farther away, and Peter's chances of stopping him were diminishing with every split second that passed.

Peter pulled the trigger.

Arne kept running.

Peter fired again repeatedly. After the fourth shot, Arne seemed to stagger. Peter fired again, and Arne fell, hitting the ground with the heavy thud of a dead weight, rolling on to his back.

'Oh, Christ, no, not again,' Peter said.

He ran forward, still pointing the gun at Arne.

The figure on the ground lay still.

Peter knelt beside it.

Arne opened his eyes. His face was white with pain. 'You stupid pig, you should have killed me,' he said.

* * *

Tilde came to Peter's apartment that evening. She was wearing a new pink blouse with flowers embroidered on the cuffs. Pink suited her, Peter thought. It brought out her femininity. The weather was warm, and she seemed to have nothing on under the blouse.

He showed her into the living room. The evening sun shone in, lighting the room with a weird glow, giving a fuzzy edge to the furniture and the pictures on the walls. Inge sat in a chair by the fireplace, gazing into the room with the expressionless look she always wore.

Peter drew Tilde to him and kissed her. She froze for a moment, surprised, then she kissed him back. He stroked her shoulders and her hips.

She pulled back and looked in his face. He could see desire in her eyes, but she was troubled. She glanced at Inge. 'Is this all right?' she said.

He touched her hair. 'Hush.' He kissed her again, hungrily. They became more passionate. Without breaking the kiss, he unbuttoned her blouse, exposing her soft breasts. He stroked the warm skin.

She pulled away again, breathing hard. Her breasts rose and fell as she panted. 'What about her?' she said. 'What about Inge?'

Peter looked at his wife. She was regarding the two of them with a blank stare, showing no emotion at all, as always. 'There's no one there,' he told Tilde. 'No one there at all.'

She looked into his eyes. Her face showed compassion and understanding mingled with curiosity and lust. 'All right,' she said. 'All right.'

He bent his head to her naked breasts.

PART THREE

PART THREE

SEVENTEEN

The quiet village of Jansborg was creepy by twilight. The villagers seemed to go to bed early, so the streets were deserted and the houses dark and still. Harald felt as if he were driving through a place where something dreadful had happened, and he was the only person who did not know about it.

He parked the motorcycle outside the railway station. It did not look as conspicuous as he had feared, for next to it was a gas-powered Opel Olympia cabriolet, with a wooden structure like a shed over its rear roof to house the giant fuel bag.

He left the bike and set off to walk to the school in the gathering darkness.

After his escape from the guards on Sande he had got back into his old bed and slept heavily until midday. His mother woke him, fed him a vast lunch of cold pork and potatoes, pushed money into his pocket, and pleaded with him to tell her where he was living. Weakened by her affection and his father's unexpected mellowing, he had told her he was staying in Kirstenslot. However, he had not mentioned the disused church, for fear she would worry about him sleeping rough, and he had left her with the impression he was a guest at the big house.

Then he had set out to drive across Denmark from west to east again. Now, in the evening of the following day, he was approaching his old school.

He had decided to develop the film before going to Copenhagen to hand it over to Arne, who was hiding out at Jens Toksvig's house in the Nyboder district. He needed to be sure that his photography had been successful, and there were clear images on the roll. Cameras could go wrong, and photographers made mistakes. He did not want Arne to risk his life travelling to England with a film that turned out to be blank. The school had its own darkroom, with all the chemicals necessary for processing. Tik Duchwitz was secretary of the Camera Club, and had a key.

Harald avoided the main gates and cut across the neighbouring farm to enter the school via the stables. It was ten o'clock. The younger boys were already in bed, and the middle school was getting undressed. Only the seniors were still about, and most of them were in their study-bedrooms. It was graduation day tomorrow, and they would be packing for home.

Threading through the familiar cluster of buildings, Harald fought the temptation to skulk furtively along walls and dash across open spaces. If he walked naturally and confidently he would appear, to the casual glance, to be a senior boy heading for his room. He was surprised at how difficult it was to fake an identity that had been genuinely his only ten days before.

He saw no one on his way to the Red House, the building where Tik and Mads had their rooms. There was no way he could conceal himself as he climbed the stairs to the top floor: if he met someone, he would be recognized instantly. But his luck held. The upper corridor was deserted. He hurried past the rooms of the housemaster, Mr Moller. He quietly opened Tik's door and stepped inside.

Tik was sitting on the lid of his suitcase, trying to close it. 'You!' he said. 'Good God!'

Harald sat beside him and helped him snap the catches closed. 'Looking forward to going home?'

'No such luck,' Tik said. 'I'm being exiled to Aarhus. I've got to spend the summer working in a branch of the family bank. It's my punishment for going to that jazz club with you.'

'Oh.' Harald had been looking forward to having Tik's company at Kirstenslot, but now he decided there was no need to mention that he was living there.

'What are you doing here?' Tik asked when they had the suitcase shut and strapped.

'I need your help.'

Tik grinned. 'What now?'

Harald took the small roll of thirty-five-millimetre film from his trousers pocket. 'I want to develop this.'

'Why can't you take it to a shop?'

'Because I would be arrested.'

Tik's grin faded and he became solemn. 'You're involved in a conspiracy against the Nazis.'

'Something like that.'

'You're in danger.'

'Yes.'

There was a tap at the door.

Harald dropped to the floor and slid under the bed.

Tik said: 'Yes?'

Harald heard the door opening, then Moller's voice saying: 'Lights out, please, Duchwitz.'

'Yes, sir.'

'Goodnight.'

'Goodnight, sir.'

The door closed, and Harald rolled out from under the bed.

They listened while Moller progressed along the corridor, saying goodnight to each boy. They heard his footsteps returning to his own rooms, then his door closing. They knew he would not reappear until morning, unless there should be an emergency.

Keeping his voice low, Harald said to Tik: 'Have you still got the key to the darkroom?'

'Yes, but first we'd have to get into the labs.' The science building was locked at night.

'We can break a window at the back.'

'When they see the smashed glass, they'll know someone broke in.'

'What do you care? You're leaving tomorrow!'

'All right.'

They took off their shoes and crept out into the corridor. They went down the stairs silently and put their shoes back on when they reached the door. Then they stepped outside.

It was now after eleven, and night had fallen. At

this hour, no one would normally be moving about the grounds, so they had to take care not to be seen from a window. Fortunately there was no moon. They hurried away from the Red House, their footsteps muffled by grass. As they reached the church Harald glanced back, and saw a light in one of the senior rooms. A figure crossed the window and paused. A split-second later, Harald and Tik had turned the corner of the church.

'I think we might have been seen,' Harald whispered. 'There's a light on in the Red House.'

'Staff bedrooms all look out on to the back,' Tik pointed out. 'If we were seen by someone, it must have been a boy. Nothing to worry about.'

Harald hoped he was right.

They circled the library and approached the science building from the rear. Although new, it had been designed to match the older structures around, so it had red brick walls and composite casement windows each made up of six panes of glass.

Harald took off a shoe and tapped a window with its heel. It seemed quite strong. 'When you're playing football, glass is so fragile,' he murmured. He put his hand inside the shoe and hit the pane hard. It broke with a noise like the last trump. The two boys stood still, aghast at how loud it had been; but silence descended as if nothing had happened. There was no one in the nearby buildings – the church, the library and the gymnasium – and, when Harald's heartbeat quietened, he realized that the smash had gone unheard.

339

He used his shoe to knock out the jagged edges from the frame. They fell inside on to a laboratory bench. He put his arm through and unlatched the window. Still using the shoe to protect his hand from cuts, he reached inside and swept the shards to one side. Then he climbed in.

Tik followed, and they closed the window behind them.

They were in the chemistry lab. Astringent smells of acids and ammonia stung Harald's nostrils. He could see almost nothing, but the room was familiar, and he made his way to the door without crashing into anything. He passed into the corridor and found the door to the darkroom.

Once they were both inside, Tik locked the door and switched on the light. Harald realized that, as no light could get into the darkroom, none could escape either.

Tik rolled up his sleeves and went to work. He ran warm water into a sink and busied himself with chemicals from a row of jars. He took the temperature of the water in the sink and added hot until he was satisfied. Harald understood the principles, but had never tried to do this himself, so he had to trust his friend.

What if something had gone wrong – the shutter had not operated properly, or the film had been fogged, or the image was blurred? The pictures would be useless. Did he have the nerve to try again? He would have to go back to Sande, climb that fence in the dark, sneak into the installation, wait for sunrise, take more pictures, then attempt to escape in daylight, all over again. He was not sure he could summon up the strength of will.

When all was ready, Tik set a timer and turned off the light. Harald sat patiently in the dark while Tik unrolled the exposed film and began the process that would develop the pictures – if there were any pictures. He explained that he was bathing the film first in pyrogallol, which would react with the silver salts to form a visible image. They sat and waited until the clockwork timer rang its bell, then Tik washed the film in acetic acid to stop the reaction. Finally he bathed it in hypo to fix the image.

At last he said: 'That should do it.'

Harald held his breath.

Tik turned on the light. Harald was dazzled for a few moments, and could not see anything. When his vision cleared, he peered at the length of greyish film in Tik's hands. Harald had risked his life for this. Tik held it up to the light. At first Harald could not make out any images, and he thought he would have to do it all again. Then he remembered he was looking at a negative, on which black appeared white and vice versa; and he began to make out the shapes. He saw a reverse image of the large rectangular aerial that had so intrigued him when he first saw it four weeks before.

He had succeeded.

He looked along the row of images and recognized each one: the rotating base, the clustered cables, the grid taken from several angles, the smaller machines with their tilting aerials, and finally the last picture, the general view of all three structures, taken when he was on the edge of panic. 'They came out!' he said triumphantly. 'They're great!'

Tik looked pale. 'What are these pictures of?' he said in a frightened voice.

'Some new machinery the Germans have invented for detecting approaching aircraft.'

'I wish I hadn't asked. Do you realize what the punishment is for what we're doing?'

'I took the pictures.'

'And I developed the film. God in heaven, I could be hanged.'

'I told you it was this kind of thing.'

'I know, but I didn't really think it through.'

'I'm sorry.'

Tik rolled the film and put it in its cylindrical container. 'Here, take it,' he said. 'I'm going back to bed to forget that this ever happened.'

Harald put the canister in his trousers pocket.

Then they heard voices.

Tik groaned.

Harald froze, listening. At first he could not make out the words, but he felt sure the sounds came from within the building, not outside. Then he heard the distinctive voice of Heis say: 'There doesn't seem to be anyone here.'

The next voice belonged to a boy. 'They definitely came this way, sir.'

Harald frowned at Tik. 'Who . . .?'

Tik whispered: 'It sounds like Woldemar Borr.'

'Of course,' Harald groaned. Borr was the school Nazi. It must have been he who saw them from the window. What bad luck – any other boy would have kept his mouth shut.

Then there was a third voice. 'Look, there's a broken pane in this window.' It was Mr Moller. 'This must be how they got in – whoever they are.'

'I'm sure Harald Olufsen was one of them, sir,' said Borr. He sounded pleased with himself.

Harald said to Tik: 'Let's get out of this darkroom. Maybe we can prevent their learning that we've been doing photography.' He flicked off the light, turned the key in the lock, and opened the door.

All the lights were on, and Heis was standing right outside.

'Oh, shit,' said Harald.

Heis was wearing a shirt without a collar: he had obviously been on his way to bed. He looked down his long nose. 'So it is you, Olufsen.'

'Yes, sir.'

Borr and Mr Moller appeared behind Heis.

'You're no longer a pupil at this school, you know,' Heis went on. 'It's my duty to call the police and have you arrested for burglary.'

Harald suffered a moment of panic. If the police found the film in his pocket, he would be finished.

'And Duchwitz is with you – I might have known,' Heis added, seeing Tik behind Harald. 'But what on earth are you doing?'

Harald had to persuade Heis not to call the police – but he could not explain in front of Borr. He said: 'Sir, if I could speak to you alone?'

Heis hesitated.

Harald decided that if Heis refused, and called the police, he would not surrender gracefully. He would make a run for it. But how far would he get? 'Please, sir,' he said. 'Give me a chance to explain.'

'Very well,' Heis said reluctantly. 'Borr, go back to bed. And you, Duchwitz. Mr Moller, perhaps you'd better see them to their rooms.' They all departed.

Heis walked into the chemistry lab, sat on a stool, and took out his pipe. 'All right, Olufsen,' he said. 'What is it this time?'

Harald wondered what to say. He could not think of a plausible lie, but he feared the truth would be more incredible than anything he might invent. In the end he simply took the little cylinder out of his pocket and gave it to Heis.

Heis took out the roll of film and held it up to the light. 'This looks like some kind of new-fangled radio installation,' he said. 'Is it military?'

'Yes, sir.'

'Do you know what it does?'

'It tracks aircraft by radio beams, I think.'

'So that's how they're doing it. The Luftwaffe claim they've been shooting down RAF bombers like flies. This explains it.'

'I believe they track the bomber and the fighter that has been sent to intercept it, so that the controller can direct the fighter precisely.'

344

Heis looked over his glasses. 'My God. Do you realize how important this is?'

'I think so.'

'There's only one way the British can help the Russians, and that's by forcing Hitler to bring aircraft back from the Russian front to defend Germany from air raids.'

Heis was ex-army, and military thinking came naturally to him. Harald said: 'I'm not sure I see what you're getting at.'

'Well, the strategy won't work while the Germans can shoot bombers down easily. But if the British find out how it's done, they can devise countermeasures.' Heis looked around. 'There must be an almanac here somewhere.'

Harald did not see why he needed an almanac, but he knew where it was. 'In the physics office.'

'Go and get it.' Heis put the film down on the laboratory bench and lit his pipe while Harald stepped into the next room, found the almanac on the bookshelf, and brought it back. Heis flipped through the pages. 'The next full moon is on the eighth of July. I'd bet there will be a big bombing raid that night. It's twelve days away. Can you get this film to England by then?'

'It's someone else's job.'

'Good luck to him. Olufsen, do you know how much danger you're in?'

'Yes.'

'The penalty for spying is death.'

'I know.'

'You always had guts, I'll give you that.' He handed back the film. 'Is there anything you need? Food, money, petrol?'

'No, thanks.'

Heis stood up. 'I'll see you off the premises.'

They went out by the main door. The night air cooled the perspiration on Harald's forehead. They walked side by side along the road to the gate. 'I don't know what I'm going to tell Moller,' said Heis.

'If I might make a suggestion?'

'By all means.'

'You could say we were developing dirty pictures.'

'Good idea. They'll all believe that.'

They reached the gate, and Heis shook Harald's hand. 'For God's sake, be careful, boy,' said the head.

'I will.'

'Good luck.'

'Goodbye.'

Harald walked away in the direction of the village.

When he reached the bend in the road, he looked back. Heis was still at the gate, watching him. Harald waved, and Heis waved back. Then Harald walked on.

* * *

He crawled under a bush and slept until sunrise, then retrieved his motorcycle and drove into Copenhagen.

He felt good as he steered through the outskirts of the city in the morning sunshine. He had suffered some close shaves, but in the end he had done what he promised. He was going to enjoy handing over the film. Arne would be impressed. Then Harald's job would be done, and it would be up to Arne to get the pictures to Britain.

After seeing Arne, he would drive back to Kirstenslot. He would have to beg Farmer Nielsen for his job back. He had only worked one day before disappearing for the rest of the week. Nielsen would be annoyed – but he might need Harald's services badly enough to hire him again.

Being at Kirstenslot would mean seeing Karen. He looked forward eagerly to that. She was not interested in him romantically, and she never would be, but she seemed to like him. For his part, he was content to talk to her. The idea of kissing her was too remote even to wish for.

He made his way to Nyboder. Arne had given Harald the address of Jens Toksvig. St Paul's Gade was a narrow street of small terraced houses. There were no front gardens: the doors opened directly on to the pavement. Harald parked the bike outside fifty-three and knocked.

It was answered by a uniformed policeman.

For a moment, Harald was struck dumb. Where was Arne? He must have been arrested—

'What is it, lad?' the policeman said impatiently. He was a middle-aged man with a grey moustache and sergeant's stripes on his sleeve.

Harald was inspired. Displaying a panic that was all too real, he said: 'Where's the doctor, he must come right away, she's having the baby now!'

The policeman smiled. The terrified father-to-be was a perennial figure of comedy. 'There's no doctor here, lad.'

'But there must be!'

'Calm down, son. There were babies before there were doctors. Now, what address have you got?'

'Doctor Thorsen, fifty-three Fischer's Gade, he must be here!'

'Right number, wrong street. This is St Paul's Gade. Fischer's Gade is one block south.'

'Oh, my God, the wrong street!' Harald turned away and jumped on to the bike. 'Thank you!' he shouted. He opened the steam regulator and pulled away.

'All part of the job,' the policeman said.

Harald drove to the end of the street and turned the corner.

Very clever, he thought, but what the hell do I do now?

EIGHTEEN

Hermia spent all Friday morning in the beautiful ruin of Hammershus castle, waiting for Arne to arrive with the vital film.

It was now even more important than it had been five days ago, when she had sent him on the mission. In the interim, the world had changed. The Nazis were set fair to conquer the Soviet Union. They had already taken the key fortress of Brest. Their total air superiority was devastating the Red Army.

Digby had told her, in a few grim sentences, of his conversation with Churchill. Bomber Command would commit every plane it could get off the ground to the biggest air raid of the war, in a desperate attempt to draw Luftwaffe strength away from the Russian front and give the Soviet soldiers a chance to fight back. That raid was now eleven days away.

Digby had also talked to his brother, Bartlett, who was fit again, back on active service, and certain to be piloting one of the bombers.

The raid would be a suicide mission, and Bomber Command would be fatally weakened, unless they could develop tactics for evading German radar in the next few days. And that depended on Arne.

Hermia had persuaded her Swedish fisherman to bring her across the water again – although he had warned her that this would be the last time, as he felt it dangerous to fall into a pattern. At dawn she had splashed through the shallows, carrying her bike, on to the beach below Hammershus. She had climbed the steep hill to the castle, where she stood on the ramparts, like a medieval queen, and watched the sun rise on a world that was increasingly ruled by the strutting, shouting, hate-filled Nazis she so loathed.

During the day she moved, every half hour or so, from one part of the ruins to another, or strolled through the woods, or descended to the beach, just so that it would not be obvious to tourists that she was waiting to meet someone. She suffered a combination of terrible tension and yawn-making boredom that she found strangely wearying.

She diverted herself by recalling their last meeting. The memory was sweet. She was shocked at herself for making love to Arne right there on the grass in broad daylight. But she did not regret it. She would remember that all her life.

She expected him on the overnight ferry. The distance from the harbour at Ronne to the castle of Hammershus was only about fifteen miles. Arne could bike it in an hour or walk it in three. However, he did not show up during the morning.

This made her anxious, but she told herself not to worry. The same thing had happened last time: he had missed the overnight boat and taken the morning sailing. She assumed he would arrive that evening.

Last time she had sat tight and waited for him, and he had not shown up until the following morning. Now she was too impatient for that. When she felt sure he could not have come on the overnight ferry, she decided to cycle to Ronne.

She felt increasingly nervous as she passed from the lonely country roads into the more populous streets of the little town. She told herself this was safer – she was more conspicuous in the countryside and could lose herself in the town – but it felt the opposite. She saw suspicion in everyone's eyes, not just policemen and soldiers but shopkeepers in their doorways, carters leading horses, old men smoking on benches, and dockers drinking tea on the quay. She walked around the town for a while, trying not to meet anyone's eye, then went into a hotel on the harbour and ate a sandwich. When the ferry docked, she stood with a small group of people waiting to meet passengers. As they disembarked she scrutinized every face, expecting Arne to be in some kind of disguise.

It took a few minutes for them all to come ashore. When the flow stopped, and passengers started boarding for the return journey, Hermia realized Arne was not on the boat.

She fretted over what to do next. There were a hundred possible explanations for his non-appearance, ranging from the trivial to the tragic. Had he lost his nerve and abandoned the mission? She felt ashamed of such a suspicion, but she had always doubted whether Arne was hero material. He might be dead, of course. But it was most likely he had been held up by something stupid like a delayed train. Unfortunately, he had no way of letting her know.

But, she realized, she might be able to contact him.

She had told him to hide out at Jens Toksvig's house in the Nyboder district of Copenhagen. Jens had a phone, and Hermia knew the number.

She hesitated. If the police were listening in on Jens's phone, for any reason, they could trace the call, and then they would know . . . what? That something might be going on on Bornholm. That would be bad, but not fatal. The alternative was for her to find overnight accommodation and wait to see whether Arne came in on the next ferry. She did not have the patience for that.

She returned to the hotel and placed the call.

As the operator was putting her through, she wished she had taken more time to plan what to say. Should she ask for Arne? If anyone happened to be listening in, that would give away his whereabouts. No, she would have to speak in riddles, as she had when calling from Stockholm. Jens would probably answer the phone. He would recognize her voice, she thought. If not, she would say: 'It's your friend from Bredgade, remember me?' Bredgade was the street where the British Embassy had been located when she worked there. That should be enough of a hint for him – though it might also be enough to alert a detective.

Before she had time to think it through, the phone was picked up, and a man's voice said: 'Hello?'

It certainly was not Arne. It might have been Jens, but she had not heard his voice for more than a year.

She said: 'Hello.'

'Who is that speaking?' The voice was that of an older man. Jens was twenty-nine.

She said: 'Let me speak to Jens Toksvig, please.'

'Who is calling?'

Who the hell was she speaking to? Jens lived alone. Maybe his father had come to stay. But she was not going to give her real name. 'It's Hilde.'

'Hilde who?'

'He'll know.'

'May I have your second name, please?'

This was ominous. She decided to try to bully him. 'Look, I don't know who the hell you are, but I didn't call to play stupid games, so just put Jens on the damn phone, will you?'

It did not work. 'I must have your surname.'

This was not someone playing games, she decided. 'Who are you?'

There was a long pause, then he replied. 'I am Sergeant Egill of the Copenhagen police.'

'Is Jens in trouble?'

'What is your full name, please?'

Hermia hung up.

She was shocked and frightened. This was as bad as it could be. Arne had taken refuge in Jens's house, and now the house was under police guard. It could only mean that they had found out that Arne was hiding there. They must have arrested Jens and perhaps Arne too. Hermia fought back tears. Would she ever see her lover again?

She walked out of the hotel and looked across the harbour towards Copenhagen, a hundred miles away in the direction of the setting sun. Arne was probably in jail there.

There was no way she was going to meet up with her fisherman and return to Sweden empty-handed. She would be letting down Digby Hoare and Winston Churchill and thousands of British airmen.

The ferry's horn sounded the all-aboard with a noise like a bereaved giant. Hermia jumped on her bicycle and cycled furiously to the dock. She had a complete set of forged papers, including identity card and ration book, so she could pass any checkpoint. She bought a ticket and hurried on board. She had to go to Copenhagen. She had to find out what had happened to Arne. She had to get his film, if he had taken any pictures. When she had done that, she would worry about how to escape from Denmark and get the film to England.

The ferry hooted mournfully again and moved slowly away from the dock.

NINETEEN

Harald drove along the Copenhagen quayside at sundown. The dirty water of the harbour was an oily grey in daytime, but now it glowed with the reflection of the sunset, a red and yellow sky broken up, by the wavelets, into dabs of colour like strokes of a paint brush.

He stopped the motorcycle near a line of Daimler-Benz trucks partly loaded with timber from a Norwegian freighter. Then he saw two German soldiers guarding the cargo. The roll of film in his pocket suddenly felt burning hot against his leg. He put his hand in his pocket and told himself not to be panicky. No one suspected him of any wrongdoing – and the bike would be safe near the soldiers. He parked next to the trucks.

The last time he was here he had been drunk, and now he struggled to remember exactly where the jazz club was. He walked along the row of warehouses and taverns. The grimy buildings were transformed, like the dirty water of the harbour, by the romantic glow of the setting sun. Eventually he spotted the sign that read: 'Danish Institute of Folk Song and Country

Dancing.' He went down the steps to the cellar and pushed the door. It was open.

The time was ten o'clock, early for night clubs, and the place was half empty. No one was playing the beer-stained piano on the little stage. Harald crossed the room to the bar, scanning the faces. To his disappointment, he did not recognize anyone.

The barman wore a rag tied around his head like a gypsy. He nodded warily to Harald, who did not look like the usual type of customer.

'Have you seen Betsy today?' Harald asked.

The barman relaxed, apparently reassured that Harald was just another young man looking for a prostitute. 'She's around,' he said.

Harald sat on a stool. 'I'll wait.'

'Trude's over there,' the barman said helpfully.

Harald glanced in the direction he pointed and saw a blonde woman drinking from a lipstick-stained glass. He shook his head. 'I want Betsy.'

'These things are very personal,' said the barman sagely.

Harald suppressed a smile at the obviousness of this remark. What could be more personal than sexual intercourse? 'That's very true,' he said. Were tavern conversations always stupid?

'A drink while you're waiting for her?'

'Beer, please.'

'Chaser?'

'No, thanks.' The thought of aquavit still made Harald feel nauseated.

He sipped his beer thoughtfully. He had spent the

day brooding over his plight. The presence of police at Arne's hideout almost certainly meant that Arne had been found out. If by some miracle he had evaded arrest, the only place he might be hiding was the ruined monastery at Kirstenslot; so Harald had driven there and checked. He found the place empty.

He had sat on the floor of the church for several hours, alternately grieving at his brother's fate and trying to figure out what he should do next.

If he were to finish the job Arne had started, he had to get the film to London in the next eleven days. Arne must have had a plan for this, but Harald did not know what it was, and could not think of any way to find out. So he had to devise his own.

He considered simply putting the negatives in an envelope and mailing them to the British legation in Stockholm. However, he felt sure all mail for that address was routinely opened by the censors.

He did not have the luck to be acquainted with any of the small group of people who travelled legitimately between Denmark and Sweden. He could simply go to the ferry dock in Copenhagen, or the boat train station at Elsinore, and ask a passenger to take the envelope; but that seemed almost as risky as mailing it.

He had concluded, after a day of racking his brains, that he had to go himself.

He could not do so openly. He would not be given a permit to travel, now that his brother was known to be a spy. He would have to find a clandestine route. Danish ships went to and from Sweden every day.

There had to be a way to get on board one and slip off unnoticed on the other side. He could not get a job on a boat – sailors had special identity papers. But there was always underworld activity around docks: smuggling, theft, prostitution, drugs. So he needed to make contact with criminals and find someone willing to smuggle him to Sweden.

When the afternoon began to cool, and the tiled floor of the monastery became chilly, he had got back on his motorcycle and returned to the jazz club, in the hope of seeing the only criminal he had ever met.

He did not have to wait long for Betsy. He had drunk only half his beer when she arrived. She came down the rear staircase with a man whom, Harald presumed, she had just serviced in a bedroom upstairs. The client had pale, unhealthy skin and a brutally short haircut, and there was a cold sore on his left nostril. He was about seventeen. Harald guessed he was a sailor. He walked quickly across the room and out of the door, looking furtive.

Betsy came to the bar, saw Harald, and did a double-take. 'Hello, schoolboy,' she said amiably.

'Hello, princess.'

She tossed her head coquettishly, shaking her dark curls. 'Changed your mind? Want to have a go?'

The thought of having sex with her only minutes after the sailor was vile, but he answered with a joke. 'Not before we're married.'

She laughed. 'What would your mother say?'

He looked at her plump figure. 'That you need feeding up.'

358

She smiled. 'Flatterer. You're after something, aren't you? You didn't come back for the watery beer.'

'As a matter of fact, I need a word with your Luther.'

'Lou?' She looked disapproving. 'What do you want with him?'

'A little problem he may be able to help me with.'

'What?'

'I probably shouldn't tell you—'

'Don't be stupid. Are you in trouble?'

'Not exactly.'

She looked across at the door and said: 'Oh, shit.'

Following her gaze, Harald saw Luther come in. Tonight he was wearing a silk sports coat, very dirty, over an undershirt. With him was a man of about thirty who was so drunk he could hardly stand. Holding the man's arm, Luther steered him to Betsy. The man stood peering lustfully at her.

Betsy said to Luther: 'How much did you take off him?'

'Ten.'

'Lying turd.'

Luther handed her a five-crown note. 'Here's your half.'

She shrugged, pocketed the money, and took the man upstairs.

Harald said: 'Would you like a drink, Lou?'

'Aquavit.' His manners had not improved. 'What are you after, then?'

'You're a man with many contacts along the waterfront.'

'Don't bother to butter me up, son,' Luther interrupted. 'What do you want? A little boy with a nice bum? Cheap cigarettes? Dope?'

The barman filled a small glass with aquavit. Luther emptied it at a gulp. Harald paid and waited until the barman moved away. Lowering his voice, he said: 'I want to go to Sweden.'

Luther narrowed his eyes. 'Why?'

'Does it matter?'

'It might.'

'I've got a girlfriend in Stockholm. We want to get married.' Harald began to improvise. 'I can get a job in her father's factory. He makes leather goods, wallets and handbags and—'

'So apply to the authorities for a permit to go abroad.'

'I did. They turned me down.'

'Why?'

'They wouldn't say.'

Luther looked thoughtful. After a minute he said: 'Fair enough.'

'Can you get me on a ship?'

'Anything's possible. How much money have you got?'

Harald recalled Betsy's mistrust of Luther a minute ago. 'None,' he said. 'But I can get some. So, can you arrange something for me?'

'I know a man I can ask.'

'Great! Tonight?'

'Give me ten crowns.'

'What for?'

'For going to see this man. You think I'm a free public service, like the library?'

'I told you, I haven't got any money.'

Luther grinned, showing his rotten teeth. 'You paid for that drink with a twenty, and got a ten in your change. Give it to me.'

Harald hated to yield to a bully, but he seemed to have no choice. He handed over the note.

'Wait here,' said Luther, and he went out.

Harald waited, sipping his beer slowly to make it last. He wondered where Arne was now. Probably in a cell in the Politigaarden, being interrogated. Perhaps Peter Flemming would do the questioning – espionage was his department. Would Arne talk? Not at first, Harald felt sure. Arne would not crumble immediately. But would he have the strength to hold out? Harald had always felt there was a part of Arne he did not fully know. What if he were tortured? How long would it be before he betrayed Harald?

There was a commotion from the back staircase, and Betsy's latest client, the drunk, fell down the stairs. Betsy followed him, picked him up, and walked him through the door and up the outside steps.

She returned with another client, this one a respectable middle-aged man in a grey suit that was old but neatly pressed. He looked as if he had worked all his life in a bank and never got promoted. As they crossed the room, Betsy said to Harald: 'Where's Lou?'

'Gone to see a man for me.'

She stopped and came over to the bar, leaving the bank clerk looking embarrassed in the middle of the room. 'Don't get involved with Lou, he's a bastard.'

'I've got no choice.'

'Then take a tip.' She lowered her voice. 'Don't trust him a single inch.' She wagged her finger like a schoolteacher. 'Watch your back, for God's sake.' Then she went upstairs with the man in the worn suit.

At first Harald felt annoyed with her for being so sure he could not take care of himself. Then he told himself not to be stupid. She was right – he was out of his depth. He had never dealt with people like Luther, and he had no idea how to protect himself.

Don't trust him, Betsy had said. Well, he had only given the man ten crowns. He could not see how Luther could cheat him at this stage, though later he might take a larger sum then fail to deliver.

Watch your back. Be prepared for treachery. Harald could not think how Luther could betray him, but were there any precautions he could take? It occurred to him that he was trapped in this bar, with no back door. Maybe he should leave and watch the entrance from a distance. There might be some safety in unpredictable behaviour.

He swallowed the last of his beer and went out with a wave to the barman.

He walked along the quay, in the twilight, to where a big grain ship was tied up with hawsers as thick as his arm. He sat on the domed top of a steel capstan and turned to face the club. He could see the entrance clearly, and he thought he would probably recognize

Luther. Would Luther spot him here? He thought not, for he would be hard to see against the dark bulk of the ship. That was good. It put Harald in control. When Luther returned, if all seemed well, Harald would go back into the bar. If he smelled a rat he would vanish. He settled down to wait.

After ten minutes, a police car appeared.

It came along the quayside very fast, but with no siren. Harald stood up. His instinct was to run, but he realized that would call attention to him, and he forced himself to sit down again and keep very still.

The car pulled up sharply outside the jazz club.

Two men got out. One, the driver, wore a police uniform. The other was in a light-coloured suit. Peering at him in the dim light, Harald recognized the face, and gasped. It was Peter Flemming.

The two cops went into the club.

Harald was about to hurry away when another figure appeared, slouching along the cobblestones with a familiar gait. It was Luther. He stopped a few yards from the police car and leaned against the wall, like an idle bystander waiting to see what would happen.

Presumably he had told the police of Harald's planned flight to Sweden. No doubt he hoped to be paid for the tip-off. How wise Betsy had been – and what a good thing Harald had acted on her advice.

The police came out of the club after a few minutes. Peter Flemming talked to Luther. Harald could hear the voices, for they both spoke angrily, but he was too far away to make out the words. However, it seemed that Peter was reprimanding Luther, who kept throwing his hands in the air in a gesture of helpless frustration.

After a while the two policemen drove away, and Luther went inside.

Harald walked quickly away, shaken by his narrow escape. He found his motorcycle and drove off in the last of the twilight. He would spend the night in the ruined monastery at Kirstenslot.

Then what would he do?

* * *

Harald told Karen the whole story the following evening.

They sat on the floor in the disused church, while evening darkened outside and the draped shapes and boxes around them turned to ghosts in the twilight. She sat with her legs crossed, like a schoolgirl, and hiked the skirt of her silk evening gown above her knees, for comfort. Harald lit her cigarettes, and felt he was becoming intimate with her.

He told her about getting into the base on Sande, then pretending to be asleep while the soldier searched his parents' house. 'You've got such nerve!' she exclaimed. He was pleased by her admiration, and glad she could not see the dampness in his eyes as he explained that his father had told a lie to save him.

He explained Heis's deduction that there would be a major air raid at the next full moon, and his reasons for thinking the film had to get to London before then.

When he related how a police sergeant had answered the door of Jens Toksvig's house, she interrupted him. 'I got a warning,' she said.

'What do you mean?'

'A stranger came up to me at the railway station and told me the police knew where Arne was. This man was a cop himself, in the traffic department, but he happened to have overheard something, and he wanted to let us know because he was sympathetic.'

'Didn't you warn Arne?'

'Yes, I did! I knew he was with Jens, so I looked Jens up in the phone book then went to his house. I saw Arne and told him what had happened.'

It sounded a bit odd to Harald. 'What did Arne say?'

'He told me to leave first, and said he was going to get out immediately after me – but obviously he left it too late.'

'Or your warning was a ruse,' Harald mused.

'What do you mean?' she said sharply.

'Maybe your policeman was lying. Suppose he wasn't sympathetic at all. He might have followed you to Jens's place and arrested Arne the minute you left.'

'That's ridiculous – policemen don't do things like that!'

Harald realized that once again he had run up against Karen's faith in the integrity and good will of those around her. Either she was credulous or he was unduly cynical – he was not sure which. It reminded him of her father's belief that the Nazis would not harm Danish Jews. He wished he thought they were right. 'What did the man look like?'

'Tall, handsome, heavy, red hair, nice suit.'

'A kind of oatmeal tweed?'

'Yes.'

That settled it. 'He's Peter Flemming.' Harald did not feel bitter towards Karen: she had thought she was saving Arne. She was the victim of a clever ruse. 'Peter is more of a spy than a policeman. I know his family, back on Sande.'

'I don't believe you!' she said hotly. 'You've got too much imagination.'

He did not want to argue with her. It pierced his heart to know that his brother was in custody. Arne should never have got involved in deception. There was no slyness in his nature. Harald wondered grievingly if he would ever see his brother again.

But there were more lives at stake. 'Arne won't be able to get this film to England.'

'What are you going to do with it?'

'I don't know. I'd like to take it myself, but I can't figure out how.' He told her about the jazz club and Betsy and Luther. 'And perhaps it's just as well that I can't get to Sweden. I'd probably be jailed for not having the right papers.' It was part of the Swedish government's neutrality agreement with Hitler's Germany that Danes who travelled illegally to Sweden would be arrested. 'I don't mind taking a risk, but I need a better-than-even chance of success.'

'There must be a way – how was Arne going to do it?'

'I don't know, he didn't tell me.'

'That was silly.'

'In retrospect, perhaps, but he probably thought the fewer people who knew, the safer he would be.'

'Someone must know.'

'Well, Poul must have had a means of communication with the British – but it's in the nature of these things that they're kept secret.'

They were silent for a while. Harald felt depressed. Had he risked his life for nothing?

'Have you heard any news?' he asked her. He missed his radio.

'Finland declared war on the Soviet Union. So did Hungary.'

'Vultures scenting death,' Harald said bitterly.

'It's so maddening to be sitting here helpless while the filthy Nazis are conquering the world. I just wish there was something we could do.'

Harald touched the film canister in his trousers pocket. 'This would make a difference, if I could get it to London in the next ten days. A big difference.'

Karen glanced at the Hornet Moth. 'It's a pity that thing won't fly.'

Harald looked at the damaged undercarriage and the torn fabric. 'I might be able to repair it. But I've only had one lesson, I couldn't pilot it.'

Karen looked thoughtful. 'No,' she said slowly. 'But I could.'

TWENTY

Arne Olufsen proved surprisingly resistant to interrogation.

Peter Flemming questioned him on the day of his arrest, and again on the following day, but he pretended to be innocent and revealed no secrets. Peter was disappointed. He had expected the fun-loving Arne to break as easily as a champagne glass.

He had no more luck with Jens Toksvig.

He considered arresting Karen Duchwitz, but he felt sure she was peripheral to the case. Besides, she was more use to him roaming around freely. She had already led him to two spies.

Arne was the prime suspect. He had all the connections: he knew Poul Kirke, he was familiar with the island of Sande, he had an English fiancée, he had gone to Bornholm which was so close to Sweden, and he had shaken off his police tail.

The arrest of Arne and Jens had restored Peter in General Braun's favour. But now Braun wanted to know more: how the spy ring worked, who else was in it, what means they used to communicate with England. Peter had arrested a total of six spies, but none of them had talked. The case would not be wound up until one of them cracked and revealed all. Peter had to break Arne.

He planned the third interrogation carefully.

At four o'clock on Sunday morning he burst into Arne's cell with two uniformed policemen. They woke Arne by shining a torch in his eyes and yelling, then pulled him out of bed and marched him along the corridor to the interrogation room.

Peter sat on the only chair, behind a cheap table, and lit a cigarette. Arne looked pale and frightened in his prison pyjamas. His left leg was bandaged and strapped from mid-thigh to shin, but he could stand upright – Peter's two bullets had damaged muscles but had not broken any bones.

Peter said: 'Your friend Poul Kirke was a spy.'

'I didn't know that,' Arne replied.

'Why did you go to Bornholm?'

'For a little holiday.'

'Why would an innocent man on holiday evade police surveillance?'

'He might dislike being followed around by a lot of nosey flatfoots.' Arne had more spirit than Peter had expected, despite the early hour and the rude awakening. 'But, as it happens, I didn't notice them. If, as you say, I evaded surveillance, I did it unintentionally. Perhaps your people are just bad at their job.'

'Rubbish. You deliberately shook off your tail. I know, I was part of the surveillance team.'

Arne shrugged. 'That doesn't surprise me, Peter.

You were never very bright as a kid. We were at school together, remember? In fact we were best friends.'

'Until they sent you off to Jansborg, where you learned to disrespect the law.'

'No. We were friends until our families quarrelled.'

'Because of your father's malice.'

'I thought it was over your father's tax fiddle.'

This was not going the way Peter planned it. He switched his line. 'Whom did you meet on Bornholm?'

'No one.'

'You walked around for days and never spoke to anyone?'

'I picked up a girl.'

Arne had not mentioned this in previous interrogations. Peter felt sure it was untrue. Maybe he could catch Arne out. 'What was her name?'

'Annika.'

'Surname?'

'I didn't ask.'

'When you came back to Copenhagen, you went into hiding.'

'Hiding? I was staying with a friend.'

'Jens Toksvig – another spy.'

'He didn't tell me that.' He added sarcastically: 'These spies are a bit secretive.'

Peter was dismayed that Arne had not been more weakened by his time in the cells. He was sticking to his story, which was unlikely but not impossible. Peter began to fear that Arne might never talk. He told himself this was just a preliminary skirmish. He pressed on. 'So you had no idea the police were searching for you?'

'No.'

'Not even when a policeman chased you in the Tivoli Garden?'

'That must have been someone else. I've never been chased by a policeman.'

Peter let the sarcasm sound in his voice. 'You didn't happen to see any of the one thousand posters of your face that have been put up around the city?'

'I must have missed them.'

'Then why did you change your appearance?'

'Did I change my appearance?'

'You shaved off your moustache.'

'Someone told me I looked like Hitler.'

'Who?'

'The girl I met on Bornholm, Anne.'

'You said her name was Annika.'

'I called her Anne for short.'

Tilde Jespersen came in with a tray. The smell of hot toast made Peter's mouth water. He trusted it was having the same effect on Arne. Tilde poured tea. She smiled at Arne and said: 'Would you like some?'

He nodded.

Peter said: 'No.'

Tilde shrugged.

This little exchange was an act. Tilde was pretending to be nice in the hope that Arne would warm to her.

Tilde brought in another chair and sat down to

drink her tea. Peter ate some buttered toast, taking his time. Arne had to stand and watch them.

When Peter had finished eating, he resumed the questioning. 'In Poul Kirke's office, I found a sketch of a military installation on the island of Sande.'

'I'm shocked,' Arne said.

'If he had not been killed, he would have sent those sketches to the British.'

'He might have had an innocent explanation for them, had he not been shot down by a trigger-happy fool.'

'Did you make those drawings?'

'Certainly not.'

'Sande is your home. Your father is pastor of a church there.'

'It's your home, too. Your father runs a hotel where off-duty Nazis get drunk on aquavit.'

Peter ignored that. 'When I met you in St Paul's Gade, you ran away. Why?'

'You had a gun. If not for that, I would have punched your ugly head, the way I did behind the post office twelve years ago.'

'I knocked you down behind the post office.'

'But I got up again.' Arne turned to Tilde with a smile. 'Peter's family and mine have been at loggerheads for years. That's the real reason he's arrested me.'

Peter ignored that. 'Four nights ago, there was a security alert at the base. Something disturbed the guard dogs. The sentries saw someone running across the dunes in the direction of your father's church.' As

Peter talked, he watched Arne's face. So far, Arne did not look surprised. 'Was that you running across the dunes?'

'No.'

Arne was telling the truth, Peter felt. He continued: 'Your parents' home was searched.' Peter saw a flicker of fear in Arne's eyes: he had not known about this. 'The guards were looking for a stranger. They found a young man asleep in bed, but the pastor said it was his son. Was that you?'

'No. I haven't been home since Whitsun.'

Once again, Peter thought he was telling the truth.

'Two nights ago, your brother Harald returned to Jansborg Skole.'

'From which he was expelled because of your malice.'

'He was expelled because he disgraced the school!'

'By daubing a joke on a wall?' Once again Arne turned to Tilde. 'The police superintendent had decided to release my brother without charges – but Peter went to his school and insisted they expel him. You see how much he hates my family?'

Peter said: 'He broke into the chemistry lab and used the darkroom to develop a film.'

Arne's eyes widened visibly. Clearly this was news to him. He was rattled, at last.

'Fortunately, he was discovered by another boy. I learned of this from the boy's father, who happens to be a loyal citizen and a believer in law and order.'

'A Nazi?'

'Was it your film, Arne?'

373

'No.'

'The head teacher says the film consisted of photographs of naked women, and claims he confiscated it and burned it. He's lying, isn't he?'

'I have no idea.'

'I believe the photographs were of the military installation on Sande.'

'Do you?'

'They were your pictures, weren't they?'

'No.'

Peter felt he was at last beginning to intimidate Arne, and he pressed his advantage. 'Next morning, a young man called at Jens Toksvig's house. One of our officers answered the door – a middle-aged sergeant, not one of the force's intellectual giants. The boy pretended to have come to the wrong address, looking for a doctor, and our man was gullible enough to believe him. But it was a lie. The young man was your brother, wasn't he?'

'I'm quite sure he was not,' Arne said, but he looked frightened.

'Harald was bringing you the developed film.'

'No.'

'That evening, a woman in Bornholm, who called herself Hilde, telephoned Jens Toksvig's house. Didn't you say you had picked up a girl called Hilde?'

'No, Anne.'

'Who is Hilde?'

'Never heard of her.'

'Perhaps it was a false name. Could she have been your fiancée, Hermia Mount?'

374

'She's in England.'

'There you are mistaken. I have been talking to the Swedish immigration authorities.' It had been hard to force them to cooperate, but in the end Peter had got the information he wanted. 'Hermia Mount flew in to Stockholm ten days ago, and has not yet departed.'

Arne feigned surprise, but the act was unconvincing. 'I know nothing of that,' he said, too mildly. 'I haven't heard from her for more than a year.'

If that had been true, he would have been astonished and shocked to learn that she had certainly been in Sweden and possibly in Denmark. He was definitely lying now. Peter continued: 'The same night – this is the day before yesterday – a young man nicknamed Schoolboy went to a waterfront jazz club, met with a small-time criminal called Luther Gregor, and asked for help to escape to Sweden.'

Arne looked horrified.

Peter said: 'It was Harald, wasn't it?'

Arne said nothing.

Peter sat back. Arne was badly shaken now, but overall he had put up an ingenious defence. He had explanations for everything Peter threw at him. Worse, he was cleverly turning the personal hostility between them to his advantage, claiming that his arrest had been motivated by malice. Frederik Juel might be gullible enough to believe that. Peter was worried.

Tilde poured tea into a mug and gave it to Arne without consulting Peter. Peter said nothing: this was all part of the prearranged scenario. Arne took the mug in a shaky hand and drank thirstily.

Tilde spoke in a kindly voice. 'Arne, you're in over your head. This isn't just about you any more. You've involved your parents, your fiancée and your young brother. Harald is in deep trouble. If this goes on, he'll end up hanged as a spy – and it will be your fault.'

Arne held the mug in both hands, saying nothing, looking bewildered and scared. Peter thought he might be weakening.

'We can make a deal with you,' Tilde went on. 'Tell us everything, and both you and Harald will escape the death penalty. You don't have to take my word for that – General Braun will be here in a few minutes, and he will guarantee that you'll live. But first you have to tell us where Harald is. If you don't, you'll die, and so will your brother.'

Doubt and fear crossed Arne's face. There was a long silence. At last Arne seemed to come to a resolution. He reached out and put the mug on the tray. He looked at Tilde, then turned his gaze to Peter. 'Go to Hell,' he said quietly.

Peter sprang to his feet, furious. 'You're the one who's going to Hell!' he shouted. He kicked his chair over backwards. 'Don't you understand what's happening to you?'

Tilde got to her feet and left quietly.

'If you don't talk to us, you'll be turned over to the Gestapo,' Peter went on angrily. '*They* won't give you tea and ask polite questions. They'll pull out your fingernails, and light matches under the soles of your feet. They'll fasten electrodes to your lips, and throw cold water over you to make the shocks more excruciating. They'll strip you naked and beat you with hammers. They'll smash the bones of your ankles and kneecaps so that you can never walk again, and then they'll carry on beating you, keeping you alive and conscious and screaming. You'll beg and plead with them to let you die, but they won't – not until you talk. And you will talk. Get that into your head. In the end, *everyone talks*.'

White-faced, Arne said quietly: 'I know.'

Peter was taken aback by the poise and resignation behind the fear. What did it mean?

The door opened and General Braun came in. It was now six o'clock, and Peter had been expecting him: his appearance was part of the scenario. Braun was the picture of cold efficiency in his crisp uniform with his holstered pistol. As always, his damaged lungs made his voice a gentle near-whisper. 'Is this the man to be sent to Germany?'

Arne moved fast, despite his injury.

Peter was looking the other way, towards Braun, and he saw only a blur as Arne reached for the tea tray. The heavy earthenware teapot flew through the air and struck the side of Peter's head, splashing tea over his face. When he had dashed the liquid from his eyes he saw Arne charge into Braun. Arne moved clumsily on his wounded leg, but he knocked the general over. Peter sprang to his feet, but he was too slow. In the second for which Braun lay still on the floor, gasping, Arne unbuttoned the general's holster and snatched out the pistol.

He swung the gun toward Peter, holding it two-handed.

Peter froze. The gun was a 9mm Luger. It held eight rounds of ammunition in the grip magazine – but was it loaded? Or did Braun wear it just for show?

Arne remained in a sitting position but pushed himself backward until he was up against the wall.

The door was still open. Tilde stepped inside, saying: 'What—?'

'Stay still!' Arne barked.

Peter asked himself urgently how familiar Arne was with weapons. He was a military officer, but in the air force he might not have had much practice.

As if to answer the unspoken question, Arne switched off the safety catch on the left side of the pistol with a deliberate movement that everyone could see.

Behind Tilde, were the two uniformed policemen who had escorted Arne from his cell. None of the four policemen was carrying a gun. They did not bring weapons into the cell area. It was a strict regulation imposed to prevent prisoners doing exactly what Arne had just done. But Braun did not consider himself subject to the regulations, and no one had had the nerve to ask him to hand in his weapon.

Now Arne had them all at his mercy.

Peter said: 'You can't get away, you know. This is the largest police station in Denmark. You've got the drop on us, but there are dozens of armed police outside. You can't get past them all.'

'I know,' Arne said.

There was that ominous note of resignation again.

Tilde said: 'And would you want to kill so many innocent Danish policemen?'

'No, I wouldn't.'

It all began to make sense. Peter remembered Arne's words when Peter had shot him: *You stupid pig, you should have killed me.* That fitted with the fatalistic attitude Arne had displayed since his arrest. He feared he was going to betray his friends – perhaps even his brother.

Suddenly Peter knew what was going to happen next. Arne had figured out that the only way to be completely safe was to be dead. But Peter wanted Arne to be tortured by the Gestapo and to reveal his secrets. He could not let Arne die.

Despite the gun pointed straight at him, Peter dashed at Arne.

Arne did not shoot him. Instead, he jerked back the gun and pressed its nose into the soft skin under his chin.

Peter flung himself on Arne.

The gun barked once.

Peter struck it from Arne's hand, but he was too late. A gush of blood and brain sprayed from the top of Arne's head, making a fan-shaped stain on the pale wall behind him. Peter fell on Arne, and some of the mess splashed on Peter's face. He rolled away and scrambled to his feet.

Arne's face was strangely unchanged. The damage was all behind, and he still had the ironic smile he had worn as he put the gun to his throat. After a moment, he fell sideways, the smashed back of his skull leaving a red smear on the wall. His body hit the floor with a lifeless thud. He lay still.

Peter wiped his face with his sleeve.

General Braun got to his feet, struggling for breath.

Tilde bent down and picked up the pistol.

They all looked at the body.

'Brave man,' said General Braun.

TWENTY-ONE

When Harald woke up, he knew that something wonderful had happened, but for a moment he could not recall what it was. He lay on the ledge in the apse of the church, with Karen's blanket around him and Pinetop the cat curled up against his chest, and waited for his memory to work. It seemed to him that the wonderful event was interwoven with something worrying, but he was so excited that he did not care about the danger.

It all came back in a rush: Karen had agreed to fly him to England in the Hornet Moth.

He sat upright suddenly, displacing Pinetop, who leaped to the floor with an indignant yowl.

The danger was that they might both be caught, arrested, and killed. What made him happy, despite that, was that he would be spending hours alone with Karen. Not that he thought anything romantic would happen. He realized she was out of his league. But he could not help how he felt about her. Even if he was never going to kiss her, he was thrilled at the thought of how long they would be together. It was not just the journey, though that would be the climax. Before they could take off they would have to spend days working on the aircraft.

But the whole plan depended on whether he could repair the Hornet Moth. Last night, with only a flashlight for illumination, he had not been able to inspect it thoroughly. Now, with the rising sun shining through the high windows over the apse, he could assess the magnitude of the task.

He washed at the cold tap in the corner, pulled on his clothes, and began his examination.

The first thing he noticed was a long piece of stout rope tied to the undercarriage. What was that for? He thought for a minute, then realized it was for moving the aircraft when the engine was off. With the wings folded, it might be difficult to find a point at which to push the machine, but the rope would enable someone to pull it around like a cart.

Just then, Karen arrived.

She was casually dressed in shorts and sandals, showing off her long, strong legs. Her curly hair was freshly washed and stood out around her head in a coppery cloud. Harald thought angels must look like that. What a tragedy it would be if she died in the adventure that was ahead of them.

It was too early to talk of dying, he told himself. He had not even begun to repair the aircraft. And, in the clear light of morning, it looked a more daunting task.

Like Harald, Karen was pessimistic this morning. Yesterday she had been excited by the prospect of adventure. Today she took a more gloomy view. 'I've been thinking about mending this thing,' she said.

'I'm not sure it can be done, especially in ten days – nine, now.'

Harald felt the onset of the stubborn mood that always came over him when someone told him he could not do something. 'We'll see,' he said.

'You've got that look,' she observed.

'What?'

'The look that says you don't want to hear what's being said.'

'I haven't got a look,' he said tetchily.

She laughed. 'Your teeth are clenched, your mouth is turned down at the corners, and you're frowning.'

He was forced to smile, and in truth he was pleased that she noticed his expression.

'That's better,' she said.

He began to study the Hornet Moth with an engineer's eye. When he had first seen it, he had thought its wings were broken, but Arne had explained that they were folded back for easy storage. Harald looked at the hinges by which they were attached to the fuselage. 'I think I could refit the wings,' he said.

'That's easy. Our instructor, Thomas, did it every time he put the aircraft away. It only takes a few minutes.' She touched the nearer wing. 'The fabric is in a bad state, though.'

The wings and the fuselage were made of wood covered with a fabric that had been treated with some kind of paint. On the upper surface, Harald could see the stitches where the fabric was attached to the ribs with thick thread. The paint was cracked and crazed, and the fabric was torn in places. 'It's only superficial damage,' Harald said. 'Does it matter?'

'Yes. The rips in the fabric might interfere with the air flow over the wings.'

'So we need to patch them. I'm more worried about the undercarriage.'

The aircraft had been in some kind of accident, probably an awkward landing such as Arne had described. Harald knelt down to look more closely at the damaged landing gear. The solid steel stub axle appeared to have two prongs that fitted into a V-shaped strut. The V-strut was made of oval steel tube, and both arms of the V had creased and buckled at their weakest point, presumably just beyond the ends of the stub axle. They looked as if they would easily break. A third strut, that looked to Harald like a shock absorber, appeared undamaged. Nevertheless, the undercarriage was clearly too weak for a landing.

'I did that,' Karen said.

'You crashed?'

'I landed in a crosswind and swerved sideways. The wing tip hit the ground.'

It sounded terrifying. 'Were you scared?'

'No, I just felt such a fool, but Tom said it's not uncommon in a Hornet Moth. In fact he confessed he had done it himself once.'

Harald nodded. That fitted with what Arne had said. But there was something in the way she spoke about Thomas the instructor that made him feel jealous. 'Why was it never repaired?'

'We don't have the facilities here.' She waved at the

workbench and the tool rack. 'Tom could do minor repairs, and he was good with the engine, but this isn't a metalwork shop, and we have no welding gear. Then Daddy had a minor heart attack. He's fine, but it meant he would never get a pilot's licence, and he lost interest in learning to fly. So the work never got done.'

That was discouraging, Harald thought. How was he going to do metalwork? He walked to the tail and examined the wing that had hit the ground. 'It doesn't seem to be fractured,' he said. 'I can easily repair the tip.'

'You can't tell,' she said gloomily. 'One of the wooden spars inside might have been overloaded. There's no way to be sure just by looking at the outside. And if a wing is weakened, the plane will crash.'

Harald studied the tailplane. Its rear half was hinged, and moved up and down: this was the elevator, he recalled. The upright rudder moved right and left. Looking more closely, he saw that they were controlled by wire cables that emerged from the fuselage. But the cables had been cut and removed. 'What happened to the wire?' he said.

'I remember it being taken to repair some other machine.'

'That's going to be a problem.'

'Only the last ten feet of each cable is missing – as far forward as the turnbuckle behind the access panel under the fuselage. The rest was too difficult to get at.'

'All the same, that's forty feet, and you can't buy cables – no one can get spare parts for anything. No doubt that's why they were cannibalized in the first place.' Harald was beginning to feel overwhelmed by misgivings, but he deliberately spoke cheerfully. 'Well, let's see what else is wrong.' He moved to the nose. He found two catches on the right side of the fuselage, turned them, and opened the cowling, which was made of a thin metal that felt like tin but was probably aluminium. He studied the engine.

'It's a four-cylinder in-line layout,' Karen said.

'Yes, but it seems to be upside-down.'

'By comparison with a car engine, yes. The crankshaft is at the top. That's to raise the level of the propeller for ground clearance.'

Harald was surprised by her expertise. He had never met a girl who knew what a crankshaft was. 'What was this Tom like?' he said, trying hard to keep the note of suspicion out of his voice.

'He was a great teacher, patient but encouraging.'

'Did you have a love affair with him?'

'Please! I was fourteen!'

'I bet you had a crush on him.'

She was miffed. 'I suppose you think that's the only reason a girl would learn about engines.'

Harald did think that, but he said: 'No, no, I just noticed that you talked about him in a fond way. None of my business. The engine is air-cooled, I see.' There was no radiator, but the cylinders had cooling fins.

'I think all aero-engines are, to save weight.'

He moved to the other side and opened the right

cowling. All the fuel and oil hoses seemed to be firmly attached, and there were no outward signs of damage. He unscrewed the oil cap and checked the dipstick. There was still a little oil in the tank. 'It looks OK,' he said. 'Let's see if it starts.'

'It's easier with two people. You can sit inside while I swing the propeller.'

'Won't the battery be flat after all these years?'

'There's no battery. The electricity comes from two magnetos which are driven by the engine itself. Let's get into the cabin and I'll show you what to do.'

Karen opened the door then let out a squeal and fell back – into Harald's arms. It was the first time he had touched her body, and an electric thrill went through him. She seemed hardly to notice that they were hugging, and he felt guilty for enjoying a fortuitous embrace. He hastily set her upright and detached himself. 'Are you all right?' he said. 'What happened?'

'Mice.'

He opened the door again. Two mice jumped through the gap and ran down his trousers to the floor. Karen made a disgusted noise.

There were holes in the cloth upholstery of one seat, and Harald guessed they had nested in the stuffing. 'That problem is quickly solved,' he said. He made a kissing sound with his lips, and Pinetop appeared, hoping for food. Harald picked the cat up and handed him into the cabin.

Pinetop suddenly became energized. He darted from one side of the little cockpit to the other, and

Harald thought he saw a mouse tail disappear into the hole under the left-hand seat through which a copper pipe ran. Pinetop leaped on to the seat, then on to the luggage shelf behind, without catching a mouse. Then he investigated the holes in the upholstery. There he found a baby mouse, and began to eat it with great delicacy.

On the luggage shelf, Harald noticed two small books. He reached into the cabin and picked them up. They were manuals, one for the Hornet Moth and one for the Gipsy Major engine that powered it. He was delighted. He showed them to Karen.

'But what about the mice?' she said. 'I hate them.'

'Pinetop chased them off. In future, I'll leave the cabin doors open, so he can get in and out. He'll keep them away.' Harald opened the Hornet Moth manual.

'What's he doing now?'

'Pinetop? Oh, he's eating the babies. Look at these diagrams, this is great!'

'Harald!' she yelled. 'That's disgusting! Go and stop him!'

He was taken aback. 'What's the matter?'

'It's revolting!'

'It's natural.'

'I don't care if it is.'

'What's the alternative?' Harald said impatiently. 'We have to get rid of the nest. I could dig the babies out with my hands, and throw them into the bushes, but Pinetop would still eat them, unless the birds got them first.'

'It's so cruel.'

'They're *mice*, for God's sake!'

'How can you not understand? Can't you see that I hate it!'

'I do understand, I just think it's silly—'

'Oh, you're just a stupid engineer who thinks about how things work and never about how people feel.'

Now he was wounded. 'That's not true.'

'It is,' she said, and she stamped off.

Harald was astonished. 'What the hell was that all about?' he said aloud. Did she really believe he was a stupid engineer who never thought about how people felt? It was very unfair.

He stood on a box to look out of one of the high windows. He saw Karen marching off up the drive towards the castle. She seemed to change her mind, and veered off into the woods. Harald thought of following her, then decided not to.

On the first day of their great collaboration, they had had a row. What chance was there that they could fly to England?

He returned to the aircraft. He might as well try to start the engine. If Karen backed out, he would find another pilot, he told himself.

The instructions were in the manual.

Chock the wheels and put handbrake hard on.

He could not find the chocks, but he dragged two boxes of junk across the floor and pushed them hard up against the wheels. He located the handbrake lever in the left-hand door and checked that it was fully engaged. Pinetop was sitting on the seat, licking his paws, wearing a sated look. 'The lady thinks you're

389

disgusting,' Harald told him. The cat looked disdainful and hopped out of the cabin.

Turn on petrol (control in cabin).

He opened the door and leaned into the cabin. It was small enough for him to reach the controls without climbing in. The fuel gauge was partly hidden between the two seat backs. Next to it was a knob in a slot. He moved it from 'Off' to 'On'.

Flood carburetter by actuating the lever on either side of the engine pumps. Flow of petrol through the jet is then caused by operating the tickler of the carburetter.

The left cowling was still open, and he immediately spotted the two fuel pumps, each with a small lever sticking out. The carburetter tickler was harder to identify, but he eventually guessed it was a ring-pull with a spring-back mechanism. He pulled the ring and worked one of the levers up and down. He had no way of telling whether what he was doing was having any effect. For all he knew, the tank might be dry.

He felt dejected now that Karen had gone. Why was he so clumsy with her? He was desperately keen to be friendly and charming and do whatever it took to please her, but he could not figure out what she wanted. Why could girls not be more like engines?

Put throttle in 'shut' position, or nearly so.

He hated manuals that could not make up their minds. Should the throttle be closed, or slightly open? He found the control, a lever in the cabin just forward of the left door. Thinking back to his flight in a Tiger Moth two weeks ago, he recalled that Poul Kirke had set the throttle at about half an inch from the 'Off' end. The Hornet Moth ought to be similar. It had an engraved scale graduated from one to ten, where the Tiger Moth had nothing. Guessing, Harald set the throttle at one.

Put switches in 'on' position.

There was a pair of switches on the dashboard marked simply 'On' and 'Off'. Harald guessed they must operate the twin magnetos. He put them on.

Swing airscrew.

Harald stood at the front and grasped one of the blades of the propeller. He pulled it down. It was very stiff, and he had to put all his strength into moving it. When finally it turned, it gave a sharp click then stopped.

He turned it again. This time it moved more easily. It clicked again.

The third time, he gave it a vigorous heave, hoping the engine would fire.

Nothing happened.

He tried again. The propeller moved easily, and clicked each time, but the engine remained silent and still.

Karen came in. 'Won't it start?' she said.

He looked at her in surprise. He had not expected to see her again today. He was elated, but replied in a matter-of-fact tone. 'Too early to say – I've only just begun.'

She seemed contrite. 'I'm sorry I stormed off.'

This was a new aspect of her. He would have guessed she was too proud to apologize. 'That's all right,' he said.

'It was just the thought of the cat eating the baby mice. I couldn't stand it. I know it's foolish to think about mice when men like Poul are losing their lives.'

That was how Harald saw it, but he did not say so. 'Pinetop's gone now, anyway.'

'I'm not surprised the engine won't start,' she said, reverting to practical problems – just as he did when embarrassed, he thought. 'It hasn't been turned over for at least three years.'

'It might be a fuel problem. Over a couple of winters, water must have condensed in the tank. But oil floats, so the fuel will lie on top. We might be able to drain off the water.' He consulted the manual again.

'We should turn off the switches, for safety,' Karen said. 'I'll do it.'

Harald learned from the manual that there was a panel on the underside of the fuselage that gave access to the fuel drain plug. He took a screwdriver from the tool rack then lay on the floor and wriggled under the aircraft to unscrew the panel. Karen lay beside him and he handed her the screws. She smelled good, a mixture of warm skin and shampoo.

When the panel came off, Karen handed him an adjustable spanner. The drain plug was awkwardly placed, being slightly to one side of the access hole. This was the kind of fault that made Harald long to be in charge, so that he could force lazy designers to do things properly. When his hand was in the gap, he could no longer see the drain plug, so he had to work blind.

He turned the plug slowly but, when it opened, he was startled by the sudden spurt of freezing liquid on to his hand. He withdrew his hand quickly, banging his numbed fingers on the edge of the access hole and, to his intense irritation, he dropped the plug.

With dismay he heard it roll down the fuselage. Fuel poured from the drain. He and Karen quickly wriggled out of the way of the gush. Then there was nothing they could do except watch until the system was empty and the church reeked of petroleum.

Harald cursed Captain de Havilland and the careless British engineers who had designed the aircraft. 'Now we've got no fuel,' he said bitterly.

'We could syphon some out of the Rolls-Royce,' Karen suggested.

'That's not aeroplane fuel.'

'The Hornet Moth runs on car petrol.'

'Does it? I didn't realize that.' Harald perked up again. 'Right. Let's see if we can get that drain plug back.' He guessed the plug had rolled back until it stopped up against a cross-member. He put his arm into the hole, but could not reach far enough. Karen got a wire brush from the work bench and retrieved it with that. Harald replaced the plug in the drain.

Next they had to take fuel from the car. Harald found a funnel and a clean bucket, while Karen used a pair of heavy pliers to cut a length off a garden hose. They pulled the cover off the Rolls-Royce. Karen undid the fuel cap and fed the hose into the tank.

Harald said: 'Shall I do that?'

'No,' she said. 'My turn.'

He guessed she wanted to prove she could do dirty work, especially after the mice incident, so he stood back and watched.

Karen put the end of the hose between her lips and sucked. When the petrol came into her mouth she quickly directed the hose into the bucket, while at the same time grimacing and spitting. Harald watched the grotesque expressions on her face. Miraculously, she was no less beautiful when screwing up her eyes and pursing her lips. She caught his gaze and said: 'What are you staring at?'

He laughed and said: 'You, of course – you're so pretty when you're spitting.' He realized immediately that he had revealed more of his feelings than he wanted to, and he waited for a sharp retort, but she just laughed.

He had only said she was pretty, of course. That was not news to her. But he had said it affectionately, and girls always noticed tones of voice, especially when you did not want them to. If she had been annoyed, she would have shown it with a disapproving look or an impatient toss of her head. But, on the contrary, she had seemed pleased – almost, he thought, as if she were glad he was fond of her.

He felt he had crossed a bridge.

The bucket filled up and the hose ran dry. They had emptied the tank of the car. There was only a gallon or so of petrol in the bucket, Harald guessed, but it was plenty for testing the engine. He had no idea where they would get enough fuel to cross the North Sea.

Harald carried the bucket over to the Hornet Moth. He flipped open the access cover and pulled the petrol cap. It had a hook to fix it to the lip of the filler neck. Karen held the funnel while Harald poured the fuel into the tank.

'I don't know where we're going to get any more,' Karen said. 'We certainly can't buy it.'

'How much do we need?'

'The tank takes thirty-five gallons. But that's another problem. The Hornet Moth's range is six hundred miles – in ideal conditions.'

'And it's about that distance to Britain.'

'So if conditions are less than perfect – for example, if we have head winds, which is not unlikely . . .'

'We'll come down in the sea.'

'Exactly.'

'One problem at a time,' said Harald. 'We haven't started the engine yet.'

Karen knew what to do. 'I'll flood the carburettor,' she said.

Harald turned on the fuel.

Karen worked the priming mechanism until fuel dribbled on the floor, then called: 'Mags on.'

Harald switched on the magnetos and checked that the throttle was still at the just-open position.

Karen grasped the propeller and pulled it down. Again there was a sharp click. 'Hear that?' she said.

'Yes.'

'It's the impulse starter. That's how you know it's working, by the click.' She swung the propeller a second time, then a third. Finally she gave it a mighty heave and stepped smartly back.

The engine gave a shocking bark which echoed around the church, then it died.

Harald cheered.

Karen said: 'What are you so pleased about?'

'It fired! There can't be much wrong.'

'It didn't start, though.'

'It will, it will. Try again.'

She swung the propeller again, but with the same result. The only change was that Karen's cheeks became attractively flushed with the effort.

After a third try, Harald turned the switches off. 'The fuel is flowing freely now,' he said. 'It sounds to me as if the problem is with the ignition. We need some tools.'

'There's a tool kit.' Karen reached into the cabin and lifted a cushion to reveal a large locker under the seat. She took out a canvas bag with leather straps.

Harald opened the bag and took out a spanner with a cylindrical head on a swivelling joint, designed to operate around corners. 'A universal spark plug spanner,' he said. 'Captain de Havilland did something right.'

There were four spark plugs on the right side of the engine. Harald removed one and examined it. There was oil on the points. Karen took a lace-edged handkerchief from the pocket of her shorts and wiped the plug clean. She found a feeler gauge in the tool kit and checked the gap. Then Harald replaced the plug. They repeated the process with the other three.

'There are four more on the other side,' Karen said.

Although the engine had only four cylinders, there were two magnetos, each operating its own set of spark plugs – a safety measure, Harald presumed. The left side plugs were harder to get at, behind two cooling baffles which first had to be removed.

When all the plugs had been checked, Harald removed the Bakelite caps over the contact breakers and checked the points. Finally, he removed the distributor cap from each magneto in turn, and wiped out the inside with Karen's handkerchief, which had now become a filthy rag.

'We've done all the obvious things,' he said. 'If it doesn't start now, we've got serious trouble.'

Karen primed the engine again then turned the propeller slowly three times. Harald opened the cabin door and threw the magneto switches. Karen gave the propeller a final heave and stepped back.

The engine turned over, barked, and hesitated. Harald, standing by the door with his head in the cabin, pushed the throttle forward. The engine roared to life.

Harald whooped with triumph as the propeller turned, but he could hardly hear his own voice over the noise. The sound of the engine bounced off the church walls and made a deafening racket. He saw Pinetop's tail disappear through a window.

Karen came up to him, her hair blowing wildly in the slipstream from the propeller. In his exuberance, Harald hugged her. 'We did it!' he yelled. She hugged

him back, to his intense pleasure, then said
something. He shook his head, to indicate that he
could not hear her. She came delightfully close to him
and spoke into his ear. He felt her lips brush his
cheek. He could hardly think of anything except how
easy it would be to kiss her now. 'We should turn it
off, before someone hears!' she shouted.

Harald remembered that this was not a game, and
that the purpose of repairing the aircraft was to fly a
dangerous secret mission. He put his head inside the
cabin, moved the throttle back to the closed position,
and switched off the magnetos. The engine stopped.

When the noise died away, the inside of the church
should have been silent, but it was not. A strange
sound came from outside. At first, Harald thought his
ears were still registering the din of the engine, but
gradually he realized it was something else. Still he
could not credit what he heard, for it sounded like
the tramp of marching feet.

Karen stared at him, bewilderment and fear
showing on her face.

They both turned and ran to the windows. Harald
leaped on the box he used for looking out over the
high sills. He gave his hand to Karen, who jumped up
beside him. They looked out together.

A troop of about thirty soldiers in German uniform
was marching up the drive.

At first he assumed they were coming for him, but
he quickly saw that they were in no shape for a
manhunt. Most of them appeared to be unarmed.
They had a heavy wagon drawn by four weary horses,

loaded with what looked like camping gear. They marched past the monastery and continued up the drive. 'What the hell is this?' he said.

'They mustn't get in here!' Karen said.

They both looked around the interior of the church. The main entrance, at the western end, consisted of two enormous wooden doors. This was the way the Hornet Moth must have come in, with its wings folded back. Harald had also driven his bike through there. It had a huge old lock on the inside with a giant key, plus a wooden bar that rested in brackets.

There was only one other entrance, the small side door that led in from the cloisters. This was the one Harald normally used. It had a lock, but Harald had never seen a key. There was no bar.

'We could nail the small door shut, then come in and out through the windows like Pinetop,' Karen said.

'We have a hammer and nails . . . we need a piece of wood.'

In a room full of junk it should have been easy to find a stout plank but, to Harald's disappointment, there was nothing suitable. In the end he prised one of the shelves from the wall above the workbench. He placed it diagonally across the door and nailed it firmly to the door frame.

'A couple of men could break it down without much effort,' he said. 'But at least no one can walk in casually and stumble over our secret.'

'They might look through the windows, though,'

Karen said. 'They would only have to find something to stand on.'

'Let's conceal the propeller.' Harald grabbed the canvas cover they had removed from the Rolls-Royce. Together they draped it over the nose of the Hornet Moth. It reached far enough to cover the cabin.

They stood back. Karen said: 'It still looks like an aircraft with its nose covered and its wings folded back.'

'To you, yes. But you already know what it is. Someone looking in through the window is just going to see a junk room.'

'Unless he happens to be an airman.'

'That wasn't the Luftwaffe out there, was it?'

'I don't know,' she said. 'I'd better go and find out.'

TWENTY-TWO

Hermia had lived more years in Denmark than England, but suddenly it was a foreign country. The familiar streets of Copenhagen had a hostile air, and she felt she stood out. She hurried like a fugitive down streets where she had walked as a child, hand-in-hand with her father, innocent and carefree. It was not just the checkpoints, the German uniforms, and the grey-green Mercedes cars. Even the Danish police made her jumpy.

She had friends here, but she did not contact them. She was afraid of bringing more people into danger. Poul had died, Jens had presumably been arrested and she did not know what had happened to Arne. She felt cursed.

She was exhausted and stiff from her overnight ferry trip, and racked with worry about Arne. Excruciatingly aware of the hours ticking by toward the full moon, she forced herself to move with the utmost caution.

The home of Jens Toksvig in St Paul's Gade was one of a row, all single storey, with front doors that gave immediately on to the pavement. Number fifty-three appeared empty. No one went to the door except the postman. On the previous day, when Hermia telephoned from Bornholm, it had been occupied by at least one policeman, but the guard must have been withdrawn.

Hermia also observed the neighbours. On one side was a dilapidated house occupied by a young couple with a child – the kind of people who might be too absorbed in their own life to take an interest in their neighbours. But in the freshly painted and neatly curtained house on the other side was an older woman who looked out of the window frequently.

After watching for three hours, Hermia went to the neat house and knocked.

A plump woman of about sixty years came to the door in an apron. Looking at the little suitcase Hermia was carrying, she said: 'I never buy anything on the doorstep.' She smiled in a superior way, as if her refusal was a mark of social distinction.

Hermia smiled back. 'I've been told that number fifty-three might be available to rent.'

The neighbour's attitude changed. 'Oh?' she said with interest. 'Looking for a place to live, are you?'

'Yes.' The woman was as nosey as Hermia had hoped. Indulging her, Hermia said: 'I'm getting married.'

The woman's glance went automatically to Hermia's left hand, and Hermia showed her the engagement ring. 'Very nice. Well, I must say, it would be a relief to have a respectable family next door, after the goings-on.'

'Goings-on?'

She lowered her voice. 'It was a nest of Communist spies.'

'No, really?'

The woman folded her arms over her corseted bosom. 'They were arrested last Wednesday, the whole pack of them.'

Hermia felt a chill of fear, but she made herself keep up the pretence of idle gossip. 'Goodness! How many?'

'I couldn't say, exactly. There was the tenant, young Mr Toksvig, who I wouldn't have taken for a wrongdoer, though he wasn't always as respectful to his elders as he might have been, then lately an airman seemed to be living there, a nice-looking boy, though he never said much; but there were all sorts in and out of the place, mostly military types.'

'And they were arrested on Wednesday?'

'On that very pavement, where you see Mr Schmidt's spaniel cocking his leg against the lamp post, there was a shooting.'

Hermia gasped, and her hand flew to her mouth. 'Oh, no!'

The old woman nodded, pleased with this reaction to her story, not suspecting that she might be speaking of the man Hermia loved. 'A plain-clothes policeman shot one of the Communists.' She added superfluously: 'With a gun.'

Hermia was so afraid of what she might learn that she could hardly speak. She forced out three words: 'Who was shot?'

'I didn't actually see it myself,' the woman said with

infinite regret. 'I happened to be over at my sister's house in Fischer's Gade, borrowing a knitting pattern for a cardigan. It wasn't Mr Toksvig himself, that I can say for sure, because Mrs Eriksen in the shop saw it, and she said it was a man she didn't know.'

'Was he . . . killed?'

'Oh, no. Mrs Eriksen thought he might have been wounded in the leg. Anyhow, he cried out when the ambulance men lifted him on to the stretcher.'

Hermia felt sure it was Arne who had been shot. She seemed to feel the pain of a bullet wound herself. She was breathless and dizzy. She needed to get away from this awful old busybody who told the tragic story with such relish. 'I must be going,' she said. 'What a dreadful thing to happen.' She turned away.

'Anyway, I should think the place will be to rent, before too long,' the woman said to her back.

Hermia walked away, paying no attention.

She turned corners at random until she came to a café, where she sat down to gather her thoughts. A hot cup of ersatz tea helped her recover from the shock. She had to find out for sure what had happened to Arne and where he was now. But first she needed somewhere to spend the night.

She got a room at a cheap hotel near the waterfront. It was a sleazy place, but her bedroom door had a stout lock. At about midnight, a slurred voice outside asked if she would like a little drink, and she got up to jam the door with a tilted chair.

She spent most of the night awake, wondering if Arne had been the man shot in St Paul's Gade. If so, how badly was he hurt? If not, had he been arrested with the others, or was he still at large? Whom could she ask? She could contact Arne's family, but they probably would not know, and it would scare them to death to be asked whether he had been shot. She knew many of his friends, but the only ones likely to know what had happened were dead, or in custody, or in hiding.

In the early hours of the morning, it occurred to her that there was one person who was almost certain to know if Arne had been arrested: his commanding officer.

At first light, she went to the railway station and caught a train to Vodal.

As the train crawled south, stopping at every sleepy village, she thought of Digby. By now he would be back in Sweden, waiting impatiently on the quay at Kalvsby for her to arrive with Arne and the film. The fisherman would come back alone, and tell Digby that Hermia had not appeared at their rendezvous. Digby would not know whether she had been captured or merely delayed. He would be as distraught about her as she was about Arne.

The flying school had a desolate feel. There were no aircraft on the field and none in the sky. A few machines were being serviced and, in one of the hangars, some trainees were being shown the innards of an engine. She was directed to the headquarters building.

She had to give her real name, for there were people here who knew her. She asked to see the base commander, adding: 'Tell him I'm a friend of Arne Olufsen's.'

She knew she was taking a risk. She had met Squadron Leader Renthe, and remembered him as a tall, thin man with a moustache. She had no idea what his politics were. If he happened to be pro-Nazi, she could be in trouble. He might phone the police and report an Englishwoman asking questions. But he was fond of Arne, as so many people were, so she was hoping that for Arne's sake he would not betray her. Anyway, she was going to take the chance. She had to find out what had happened.

She was admitted immediately, and Renthe recognized her. 'My God – you're Arne's fiancée!' he said. 'I thought you'd gone back to England.' He hurried to close the door behind her – a good sign, she thought, for if he wanted privacy that suggested he was not going to alert the police, at least not immediately.

She decided to offer no explanation of why she was in Denmark. Let him draw his own conclusions. 'I'm trying to find out where Arne is,' she said. 'I fear he may be in trouble.'

'It's worse than that,' said Renthe. 'You'd better sit down.'

Hermia remained standing. 'Why?' she cried. 'Why sit down? What's happened?'

'He was arrested last Wednesday.'

'Is that all?'

'He was shot and wounded while trying to escape from the police.'

'So it was him.'

'I beg your pardon?'

'A neighbour told me one of them had been shot. How is he?'

'Please do sit down, my dear.'

Hermia sat down. 'It's bad, isn't it?'

'Yes.' Renthe hesitated. Then, in a low voice, he said slowly: 'I'm dreadfully sorry to have to tell you that I'm afraid Arne is dead.'

She cried out in anguish. In her heart she had known this might be so, but the possibility of losing him had been too dreadful to think about. Now that it had come, she felt as if she had been struck by a train. 'No,' she said. 'It's not true.'

'He died in police custody.'

'What?' With an effort, she made herself listen.

'He died at police headquarters.'

A terrible possibility entered her mind. 'Did they torture him?'

'I don't think so. It seems that, in order to avoid revealing information under torture, he took his own life.'

'Oh, God!'

'He sacrificed himself to protect his friends, I'd guess.'

Renthe looked blurred, and Hermia realized she was seeing him through tears which were streaming down her face. She fumbled for a handkerchief, and Renthe passed her his own. She wiped her face, but the tears kept coming.

Renthe said: 'I've only just heard. I've got to phone Arne's parents and tell them.'

Hermia knew them well. She found the steely pastor difficult to deal with: it seemed he could relate to people only by dominating them, and subservience did not come easily to Hermia. He loved his sons, but expressed his love by laying down rules. What Hermia remembered most vividly about Arne's mother was that her hands were always chapped from being in water too much, washing clothes and preparing vegetables and scrubbing floors. Thinking of them drew Hermia's thoughts away from her own loss, and she felt a surge of compassion. They would be distraught. 'How dreadful for you to be the bearer of such news,' she said to Renthe.

'Indeed. Their firstborn son.'

That made her think of the other son, Harald. He was fair where Arne was dark, and they were different in other ways: Harald was more serious, somewhat intellectual, with little of Arne's easy charm, but likeable in his own way. Arne had said he was going to talk to Harald about ways to sneak into the base on Sande. How much did Harald know? Had he got involved?

Her mind was turning to practical matters, but she felt hollow. The state of shock she was in would permit her to carry on with her life, but she felt as if she would never be whole again. 'What else did the police tell you?' she asked Renthe.

'Officially, they would say only that he had died while giving information, and that "No other person is thought to have been involved," which is their euphemism for suicide. But a friend at the

Politigaarden told me Arne did it to avoid being turned over to the Gestapo.'

'Did they find anything in his possession?'

'What do you mean?'

'Such as photographs?'

Renthe stiffened. 'My friend didn't say so, and it's dangerous for you and me to even discuss such a possibility. Miss Mount, I was fond of Arne, and for his sake I would like to do anything I can for you, but please remember that as an officer I have sworn loyalty to the King, whose orders to me are to cooperate with the occupying power. Whatever my personal opinions might be, I can't countenance espionage – and, if I thought someone was involved in such activity, it would be my duty to report the facts.'

Hermia nodded. It was a clear warning. 'I appreciate your frankness, Squadron Leader.' She stood up, wiping her face. She remembered that the handkerchief was his, and said: 'I'll launder this, and send it back to you.'

'Don't even think about it.' He came around his desk and put his hands on her shoulders. 'I really am most dreadfully sorry. Please accept my deepest sympathy.'

'Thank you,' she said, and she left.

As soon as she was out of the building, the tears came again. Renthe's handkerchief was a wet rag. She would not have thought she had so much fluid in her. Seeing everything through a watery screen, she made her way somehow to the railway station.

The hollow calm came back as she considered

where to go next. The mission that had killed Poul and Arne was not done. She still had to get photographs of the radar equipment on Sande before the next full moon. But now she had an additional motive: revenge. Completion of the task would be the most painful retribution she could inflict upon the men who had driven Arne to his death. And she found a new asset to help her. She no longer cared for her own safety. She felt ready to take any risk. She would walk down the streets of Copenhagen with her head held high, and woe betide anyone who tried to stop her.

But what, exactly, would she do?

Arne's brother might be the key. Harald would probably know whether Arne had returned to Sande before the police got him, and he might even know whether Arne had had photographs in his possession when he was arrested. Furthermore, she thought she knew where to find Harald.

She took a train back to Copenhagen. It travelled so slowly that by the time she got to the city it was too late for another journey. She went to bed in her flophouse, with the door locked against amorous drunks, and cried herself to sleep. On the following morning she got the first train to the suburban village of Jansborg.

The newspaper she bought at the station had the headline HALF WAY TO MOSCOW. The Nazis had made astonishing leaps. In only a week they had taken Minsk and were in sight of Smolensk, two hundred miles inside Soviet territory.

The full moon was eight days away.

She told the school secretary that she was Arne Olufsen's fiancée, and she was shown in to Heis's office immediately. The man who had been responsible for the education of Arne and Harald made her think of a giraffe in spectacles, looking down a long nose at the world below. 'So you're Arne's wife-to-be,' he said amiably. 'How very nice to meet you.'

He appeared to have no knowledge of the tragedy. Without preamble, Hermia said: 'Haven't you heard the news?'

'News? I'm not sure I have . . .'

'Arne is dead.'

'Oh, my goodness me!' Heis sat down heavily.

'I thought you might have heard.'

'No. When did it happen?'

'Early yesterday, at police headquarters in Copenhagen. He took his own life to avoid interrogation by the Gestapo.'

'How very dreadful.'

'Does this mean that his brother doesn't know yet?'

'I've no idea. Harald is no longer here.'

She was surprised. 'Why not?'

'I'm afraid he was expelled.'

'I thought he was a star pupil!'

'Yes, but he misbehaved.'

Hermia did not have time to discuss schoolboy transgressions. 'Where is he now?'

'Back at his parents' home, I presume.' Heis frowned. 'Why do you ask?'

'I'd like to talk to him.'

Heis looked thoughtful. 'About anything in particular?'

Hermia hesitated. Caution dictated that she say nothing to Heis about her mission, but his last two questions suggested to her that he knew something. She said: 'Arne may have had something of mine in his possession when he was arrested.'

Heis was pretending that his questions were casual, but he was gripping the edge of his desk hard enough to turn his knuckles white. 'May I ask what?'

She hesitated again, then took a chance. 'Some photographs.'

'Ah.'

'That means something to you?'

'Yes.'

Hermia wondered whether Heis would trust her. For all he knew, she could have been a detective posing as Arne's fiancée. 'Arne died for those photos,' she said. 'He was trying to get them to me.'

Heis nodded, and seemed to come to a decision. 'After Harald had been expelled, he returned to the school at night and broke into the photographic darkroom in the chemistry lab.'

Hermia gave a sigh of satisfaction. Harald had developed the film. 'Did you see the pictures?'

'Yes. I have been telling people they were photographs of young ladies in risqué poses, but that's just a story. The pictures were of a military installation.'

Hermia was thrilled. The photos had been taken.

The mission had succeeded to that extent. But where was the film now? Had there been time for Harald to give it to Arne? If so, the police had it now, and Arne's sacrifice had been for nothing. 'When did Harald do this?'

'Last Thursday.'

'Arne was arrested on Wednesday.'

'So Harald still has your photographs.'

'Yes.' Hermia's spirits lifted. Arne's death had not been futile. The crucial film was still in circulation, somewhere. She stood up. 'Thank you for your help.'

'You're going to Sande?'

'Yes. To find Harald.'

'Good luck,' said Heis.

TWENTY-THREE

The German army had a million horses. Most divisions included a veterinary company, dedicated to healing sick and wounded beasts, finding fodder, and catching runaways. One such company had now been billeted on Kirstenslot.

It was the worst possible stroke of luck for Harald. The officers were living in the castle, and about a hundred men were bedded down in the ruined monastery. The old cloisters, adjacent to the church where Harald had his hideout, had been turned into a horse hospital.

The army had been persuaded not to use the church itself. Karen had pleaded with her father to negotiate this, saying she did not want the soldiers to damage the childhood treasures that were stored there. Mr Duchwitz had pointed out to the commanding officer, Captain Kleiss, that the junk in the church left little usable room anyway. After a glance through a window – Harald being absent, warned away by Karen – Kleiss had agreed to its remaining locked up. As a quid pro quo, he had requested three rooms in the castle for offices, and the deal had been struck.

The Germans were polite, friendly – and curious. On top of all the difficulties Harald faced repairing the Hornet Moth, he now had to do everything under the noses of the soldiers.

He was undoing the nuts that held the buckled wishbone axle. His plan was to detach the damaged section, then sneak past the soldiers and go to Farmer Nielsen's workshop. If Nielsen would let him, he would repair it there. Meanwhile, the intact third leg, with the shock absorber, would hold the weight of the aircraft while stationary.

The wheel brake was probably damaged, but Harald was not going to worry about brakes. They were used mainly when taxiing, and Karen had told him she could manage without them.

As he worked, Harald kept glancing up at the windows, expecting at any moment to see the face of Captain Kleiss looking in. Kleiss had a big nose and a thrusting chin, which gave him a belligerent look. But no one came, and after a few minutes Harald had the V-shaped strut in his hand.

He stood on a box to look through a window. The eastern end of the church was partly obscured by a chestnut tree that was now in full leaf. There seemed to be no one in the immediate vicinity. Harald pushed the strut through the window and dropped it on the ground outside, then jumped after it.

Beyond the tree, he could see the wide lawn in front of the castle. The soldiers had pitched four large tents and parked their vehicles there, jeeps and horse boxes and a fuel tanker. A few men were visible, passing from one tent to another, but it was afternoon, and most of the company were away on missions, taking horses to and from the railway station, negotiating with farmers for hay, or treating sick horses in Copenhagen and other towns.

He picked up the strut and walked quickly into the wood.

As he turned the corner of the church, he saw Captain Kleiss.

The captain was a big man with an aggressive air, and he was standing with his arms crossed and his legs apart, talking to a sergeant. They both turned and looked straight at Harald.

Harald suffered the sudden nausea of fear. Was he to be caught so early? He stopped, wanting to turn back, then realized that to run away would be incriminating. He hesitated then walked forward, conscious that his behaviour looked guilty, and that he was carrying part of the undercarriage of an aeroplane. He had been caught red-handed, and all he could do was try to bluff it out. He tried to hold the strut in a casual way, as he might carry a tennis racket or a book.

Kleiss addressed him in German. 'Who are you?'

He swallowed, trying to remain calm. 'Harald Olufsen.'

'And what's that you've got?'

'This?' Harald could hear his own heartbeat. He tried desperately to think of a plausible lie. 'It's, um . . .' He felt himself blush, then was saved by inspiration. 'Part of the mower assembly from a reaping machine.' It occurred to him that an uneducated Danish farm boy would not speak such good German, and he wondered anxiously whether Kleiss was subtle enough to spot the anomaly.

Kleiss said: 'What's wrong with the machine?'

'Er, it ran over a boulder and buckled the frame.'

Kleiss took the strut from him. Harald hoped he did not know what he was looking at. Horses were the man's business, and there was no reason why he should be able to recognize part of the undercarriage of an aircraft. Harald stopped breathing, waiting for Kleiss's verdict. At last the man gave him back the strut. 'All right, on your way.'

Harald walked into the woods.

When he was out of sight, he stopped and leaned against a tree. That had been an awful moment. He thought he might vomit, but managed to suppress the reaction.

He pulled himself together. There might be more such moments. He would have to get used to it.

He walked on. The weather was warm but cloudy, a summer combination dismally familiar in Denmark, where no place was far from the sea. As he approached the farm, he wondered how angry old Nielsen was that he had left without warning after working only one day.

He found Nielsen in the farmyard staring truculently at a tractor with steam pouring from its engine.

Nielsen gave him a hostile glare. 'What do you want, runaway?'

417

That was a bad start. 'I'm sorry I left without explanation,' Harald said. 'I was called home to my parents' place quite suddenly, and I didn't have time to speak to you before I left.'

Nielsen did not ask what the emergency had been. 'I can't afford to pay unreliable workers.'

That made Harald hopeful. If money was what the mean old farmer was concerned about, he could keep it. 'I'm not asking you to pay me.'

Nielsen only grunted at that, but he looked a shade less malign. 'What do you want, then?'

Harald hesitated. This was the difficult bit. He did not want to tell Nielsen too much. 'A favour,' he said.

'What sort?'

Harald showed him the strut. 'I'd like to use your workshop to repair a part from my motorcycle.'

Nielsen looked at him. 'By Christ, you've got a nerve, lad.'

I know that, Harald thought. 'It's really important,' he pleaded. 'Perhaps you could do that instead of paying me for the day I worked.'

'Perhaps I could.' Nielsen hesitated, obviously reluctant to do anything helpful, but his parsimony got the better of him. 'All right, then.'

Harald concealed his elation.

Nielsen added: 'If you fix this damn tractor first.'

Harald cursed under his breath. He did not want to waste time on Nielsen's tractor when he had such a short time to repair the Hornet Moth. But it was only a boiling radiator. 'All right,' he said.

Nielsen stomped off to find something else to grumble about.

The tractor soon ran out of steam, and Harald was able to look at the engine. He immediately saw that a hose had perished where it was clamped to a pipe, allowing water to leak out of the cooling system. There was no chance of getting a replacement hose, of course, but fortunately the existing one had some slack in it, so he was able to cut off the rotten end and reattach the hose. He got a bucket of hot water from the farmhouse kitchen and refilled the radiator – it was damaging to run cold water through an overheated engine. Finally he started the tractor to make sure the clamp held. It did.

At last he went into the workshop.

He needed some thin sheet steel to reinforce the fractured part of the axle strut. He already knew where to get it. There were four metal shelves on the wall. He took everything off the top shelf and rearranged the items on the three lower shelves. Then he lifted the top shelf down. Using Nielsen's metal shears, he trimmed off the flanged edges of the shelf, then cut four strips.

He would use these as splints.

He put one strip in a vice and hammered it into a rough curve to fit over the oval tube of the strut. He did the same with the other three strips. Then he welded them in place over the dents in the strut.

He stood back to look at his work. 'Unsightly, but effective,' he said aloud.

Tramping back through the woods to the castle, he could hear the sounds of the army camp: men calling to one another, engines revving, horses whinnying. It was early evening, and the soldiers would have returned from their day's duties. He wondered whether he would have trouble getting back into the church unnoticed.

He approached the monastery from the back. At the north side of the church, a young private was leaning against the wall, smoking a cigarette. Harald nodded to him, and the soldier said in Danish: 'Good day, I am Leo.'

Harald tried to smile. 'I'm Harald, nice to meet you.'

'Would you like a cigarette?'

'Thank you, another time, I'm in a hurry.'

Harald walked around to the side of the church. He had found a log and rolled it under one of the windows. Now he stood on it and looked into the church. He passed the wishbone strut through the glassless window and dropped it on to the box that stood below the window on the inside. It bounced off the box and fell to the floor. Then he wriggled through.

A voice said: 'Hello!'

His heart stopped, then he saw Karen. She was at the tail, partly concealed by the aircraft, working on the wing with the damaged tip. Harald picked up the axle strut and went to show it to her.

Then a voice said in German: 'I thought this place was empty!'

Harald spun around. The young private, Leo, was looking in through the window. Harald stared at him aghast, cursing his luck. 'It's a storeroom,' he said.

Leo wriggled through the window and dropped to the floor. Harald shot a glance back to the tail of the aircraft. Karen had vanished. Leo looked around, seeming curious rather than suspicious.

The Hornet Moth was covered from propeller to cabin, and the wings were folded back, but the fuselage was visible, and the tail fin could be made out at the far side of the church. How observant was Leo?

Luckily, the soldier seemed more interested in the Rolls-Royce. 'Nice car,' he said. 'Is it yours?'

'Unfortunately not,' said Harald. 'The motorcycle is mine.' He held up the axle strut from the Hornet Moth. 'This is for my sidecar. I'm trying to fix it up.'

'Ah!' Leo showed no sign of scepticism. 'I'd like to help you, but I don't know anything about machinery. Horseflesh is my specialty.'

'Of course.' They were about the same age, and Harald felt sympathy for the lonely young man far from home. But he wished all the same that Leo would go before he saw too much.

A shrill whistle sounded. 'Supper time,' Leo said.

Thank God, Harald thought.

'It was a pleasure talking to you, Harald. I look forward to seeing you again.'

'Me, too.'

Leo stood on the box and pulled himself out through the window.

'Jesus,' Harald said aloud.

Karen emerged from behind the tail of the Hornet Moth, looking shaken. 'That was a nasty moment.'

'He wasn't suspicious, he just wanted to talk.'

'God preserve us from friendly Germans,' she said with a smile.

'Amen.' He loved it when she smiled. It was like the sun coming up. He looked at her face as long as he dared.

Then he turned to the wing she had been working on. She was repairing the rips, he saw. He went closer and stood next to her. She was dressed in old corduroy trousers that looked as if they had been worn for gardening, and a man's shirt with the sleeves rolled. 'I'm gluing patches of linen over the damaged areas,' she explained. 'When the glue is dry, I'll paint over the patches to make them airtight.'

'Where did you get the material, and the glue, and the paint?'

'From the theatre. I fluttered my eyelashes at a set builder.'

'Good for you.' It was obviously easy for her to get men to do anything she wanted. He was jealous of the set builder. 'What do you do at the theatre all day, anyway?' he said.

'I'm understudying the lead in *Les Sylphides*.'

'Will you get to dance it on stage?'

'No. There are two casts, so both the other dancers would have to fall ill.'

'Shame. I'd love to see you.'

'If the impossible happens, I'll get you a ticket.' She

returned her attention to the wing. 'We have to make sure there are no internal fractures.'

'That means we have to examine the wooden spars under the fabric.'

'Yes.'

'Well, now that we've got the material to repair rips, I suppose we could cut an inspection panel in the fabric and just look inside.'

She looked dubious. 'OK . . .'

He did not think a knife would easily cut the treated linen, but he found a sharp chisel on the tool shelf. 'Where should we cut?'

'Near the struts.'

He pressed the chisel into the surface. Once the initial breach had been made, the chisel cut the fabric relatively easily. Harald made an L-shaped incision and folded back a flap, making a sizable opening.

Karen pointed a flashlight into the hole, then put her face down and peered inside. She took her time looking around, then withdrew her head and put her arm in. She grasped something and shook vigorously. 'I think we're in luck,' she said. 'Nothing shifts.'

She stepped back and Harald took her place. He reached inside, grasped a strut, and pushed and pulled it. The entire wing moved, but he felt no weakness.

Karen was pleased. 'We're making progress,' she said. 'If I can finish the work on the fabric tomorrow, and you can bolt the axle strut back on, the airframe will be complete, except for the missing cables. And we've still got eight days to go.'

'Not really,' Harald said. 'We probably need to reach England at least twenty-four hours before the raid, for our information to have any effect. That brings it down to seven. To arrive on the seventh day, we need to leave the previous evening and fly overnight. So we really have six days at the most.'

'Then I'll have to finish the fabric tonight.' She looked at her watch. 'I'd better show up at the house for dinner, but I'll come back as soon as I can.'

She put away the glue and washed her hands at the sink, using soap she had brought from the house for Harald. He watched her. He was always sorry when she left. He thought he would like to be with her all day, every day. He guessed that was the feeling that made people want to get married. Did he want to marry Karen? It seemed like a foolish question. Of course he did. He had no doubt. He sometimes tried to imagine the two of them after ten years, fed up with one another and bored, but it was impossible. Karen would never be boring.

She dried her hands on a scrap of towel. 'What are you so thoughtful about?'

He felt himself blush. 'Wondering what the future holds.'

She gave him a startlingly direct look, and for a moment he felt she could read his mind; then she looked away. 'A long flight across the North Sea,' she said. 'Six hundred miles without landfall. So we'd better be sure this old kite can make it.'

She went to the window and stood on the box.

'Don't look – this is an undignified manoeuvre for a lady.'

'I won't, I swear,' he said with a laugh.

She pulled herself up. Breaking his promise cheerfully, he watched her rear as she wriggled through. Then she dropped out of sight.

He turned his attention back to the Hornet Moth. It should not take long to reattach the braced axle strut. He found the nuts and bolts where he had left them, on the work bench. He knelt by the wheel, fitted the strut in place, and began to attach the bolts that held it to the fuselage and the wheel mounting.

Just as he was finishing, Karen came back in, much sooner than expected.

He smiled, pleased at her early return, then saw that she looked distraught. 'What's happened?' he said.

'Your mother telephoned.'

Harald was angry. 'Damn! I shouldn't have told her where I was going. Who did she speak to?'

'My father. But he told her you definitely weren't here, and she seems to have believed him.'

'Thank God.' He was glad he had decided not to tell Mother he was living in the disused church. 'What did she want, anyway?'

'There's bad news.'

'What?'

'It's about Arne.'

Harald realized, with a guilty start, that in the last few days he had hardly given a thought to his brother, languishing in jail. 'What's happened?'

'Arne is . . . he's dead.'

At first Harald could not take it in. 'Dead?' he said as if he did not understand the meaning of the word. 'How could that be?'

'The police say he took his own life.'

'Suicide?' Harald had the feeling the world was crumbling around him, the walls of the church collapsing and the trees in the park falling over and the castle of Kirstenslot blowing away in a strong wind. 'Why would he do that?'

'To avoid interrogation by the Gestapo, Arne's commanding officer told her.'

'To avoid . . .' Harald saw immediately what that meant. 'He was afraid he wouldn't be able to withstand the torture.'

Karen nodded. 'That was the implication.'

'If he had talked, he would have betrayed me.'

She was silent, neither agreeing with him nor contradicting him.

'He killed himself to protect me.' Harald suddenly needed Karen to confirm his inference. He took her by the shoulders. 'I'm right, am I not?' he shouted. 'That must be it! He did it for me! Say something, for God's sake.'

At last she spoke. 'I think you're right,' she whispered.

In an instant Harald's anger was transformed into grief. It swamped him, and he lost control. Tears flooded his eyes, and his body shook with sobs. 'Oh, God,' he said, and he covered his wet face with his hands. 'Oh, God, this is awful.'

He felt Karen's arms enfold him. Gently, she drew his head down to her shoulder. His tears soaked into her hair and ran down her throat. She stroked his neck and kissed his wet face.

'Poor Arne,' Harald said, his voice choked by sorrow. 'Poor Arne.'

'I'm sorry,' Karen murmured. 'My darling Harald, I'm so sorry.'

TWENTY-FOUR

In the middle of the Politigaarden, Copenhagen's police headquarters, was a spacious circular courtyard open to the sunshine. It was ringed by an arcade with classical double pillars in a perfect repeating pattern. To Peter Flemming, the design stood for the way order and regularity permitted the light of truth to shine in on human wickedness. He often wondered whether the architect had intended that, or had just thought a courtyard might look nice.

He and Tilde Jespersen stood in the arcade, leaning against a pair of pillars, smoking cigarettes. Tilde wore a sleeveless blouse that showed the smooth skin of her arms. She had fine blonde hair on her forearms. 'The Gestapo have finished with Jens Toksvig,' he told her.

'And?'

'Nothing.' He felt exasperated, and he shook his shoulders as if to shrug off the feeling of frustration. 'He has told everything he knows, of course. He is one of the Nightwatchmen, he passed information to Poul Kirke, and he agreed to shelter Arne Olufsen when Arne was on the run. He also said that this whole project had been organized by Arne's fiancée, Hermia Mount, who is with MI6 back in England.'

'Interesting – but it doesn't get us anywhere.'

'Exactly. Unfortunately for us, Jens doesn't know who sneaked into the base on Sande, and he has no knowledge of the film Harald developed.'

Tilde drew in smoke. Peter watched her mouth. She seemed to be kissing the cigarette. She inhaled, then blew smoke out through her nostrils. 'Arne killed himself to protect someone,' she said. 'I assume that person has the film.'

'His brother Harald either has it or has passed it to someone else. Either way, we have to talk to him.'

'Where is he?'

'At the parsonage on Sande, I assume. It's the only home he's got.' He looked at his watch. 'I'm catching a train in an hour.'

'Why not phone?'

'I don't want to give him the chance to run away.'

Tilde looked troubled. 'What will you say to the parents? Don't you think they might blame you for what happened to Arne?'

'They don't know I was there when Arne shot himself. They don't even know I arrested him.'

'I suppose not,' she said dubiously.

'Anyway, I don't give a shit what they think,' Peter said impatiently. 'General Braun hit the roof when I told him that the spies may have photographs of the base on Sande. God knows what the Germans have there but it's deadly secret. And he blames me. If that film leaves Denmark, I don't know what he'll do to me.'

'But you're the one who uncovered the spy ring!'

'And I almost wish I hadn't.' He dropped his cigarette end and stamped on it, grinding it with the sole of his shoe. 'I'd like you to come to Sande with me.'

Her clear blue eyes gave him an appraising look. 'Of course, if you want my help.'

'And I'd like you to meet my parents.'

'Where would I stay?'

'I know a small hotel in Morlunde, quiet and clean, that I think would suit you.' His father owned a hotel, of course, but that was too close to home. If Tilde stayed there, the entire population of Sande would know what she was doing every minute of the day.

Peter and Tilde had not spoken about what had happened in his apartment, even though it was six days ago. He was not sure what to say. He had felt driven to do it, to have sex with Tilde in front of Inge, and Tilde had gone along with it, sharing his passion and seeming to understand his need. Afterwards, she had seemed troubled, and he had driven her home and left her with a goodnight kiss.

They had not repeated it. Once was enough to prove whatever he had to prove. He had gone to Tilde's apartment the following evening, but her son had been awake, asking for drinks of water and complaining of bad dreams, and Peter had left early. Now he saw the trip to Sande as a chance to get her alone.

But she seemed to hesitate. She asked another practical question: 'What about Inge?'

'I'll get the nursing agency to provide twenty-four-hour cover, as I did when we went to Bornholm.'

'I see.'

She looked across the courtyard, considering, and he studied her profile: the small nose, the bow-shaped mouth, the determined chin. He remembered the overwhelming thrill of possessing her. Surely she could not have forgotten that. He said: 'Don't you want to spend a night together?'

She turned to him with a smile. 'Of course I do,' she said. 'I'd better go and pack a case.'

* * *

On the following morning, Peter woke up in the Oesterport Hotel in Morlunde. The Oesterport was a respectable establishment but its owner, Erland Berten, was not married to the woman who called herself Mrs Berten. Erland had a wife in Copenhagen who would not give him a divorce. No one in Morlunde knew this except Peter Flemming, who had discovered it by chance, while investigating the murder of one Jacob Berten, who was no relation. Peter had let Erland know he had found out about the real Mrs Berten, but had otherwise kept the news to himself, knowing that the secret gave him power over Erland. Now he could rely on Erland's discretion. Whatever happened between Peter and Tilde in the Oesterport Hotel, Erland would tell no one.

However, Peter and Tilde had not slept together in the end. Their train had been delayed, and had finally arrived in the middle of the night, long after the last ferry to Sande. Weary and bad-tempered after the frustrating journey, they had checked in to separate single rooms and grabbed a couple of hours' sleep. Now they were going to catch the first ferry of the morning.

He dressed quickly then went and tapped on Tilde's door. She was putting on a straw hat, looking in the mirror over the fireplace as she adjusted it. He kissed her cheek, not wanting to spoil her make-up.

They walked down to the harbour. A local policeman and a German soldier asked them for their identity cards as they boarded the ferry. The checkpoint was new. Peter guessed it was an additional security precaution brought in by the Germans because of the spies' interest in Sande. But it could be useful to Peter, too. He showed his police badge and asked them to write down the names of everyone visiting the island over the next few days. It would be interesting to see who came to Arne's funeral.

On the other side of the channel, the hotel's horse-drawn taxi was waiting for them. Peter told the driver to take them to the parsonage.

The sun was edging up over the horizon, gleaming off the little windows of the low houses. There had been rain overnight, and the coarse grass of the sand dunes glistened with droplets. A light breeze ruffled the surface of the sea. The island seemed to have put on its best clothes for Tilde's visit. 'What a pretty place,' she said. He was glad she liked it. He pointed out the sights as they drove: the hotel, his father's

432

house – the largest on the island – and the military base that was the target of the spy ring.

Approaching the parsonage, Peter noticed that the door to the little church stood open, and he heard a piano. 'That might be Harald,' he said. He heard the excitement in his own voice. Could it be this easy? He coughed, and made his voice deeper and calmer. 'Let's see, shall we?'

They dismounted from the buggy. The driver said: 'What time shall I come back, Mr Flemming?'

'Wait here, please,' Peter said.

'I've got other customers—'

'Just wait!'

The driver muttered something under his breath.

Peter said: 'If you're not here when I come out, you're fired.' The driver looked sulky, but he stayed put.

Peter and Tilde entered the church. At the far end of the room a tall figure was seated at the piano. He had his back to the door, but Peter knew the broad shoulders and domed head. It was Bruno Olufsen, Harald's father.

Peter winced with disappointment. He was hungry for this arrest. He must be careful not to let his need take control.

The pastor was playing a slow hymn tune in a minor key. Peter glanced at Tilde and saw that she looked sorrowful. 'Don't be fooled,' he murmured. 'The old tyrant is as hard as gunmetal.'

The verse ended and Olufsen began another. Peter was not willing to wait. 'Pastor!' he said loudly.

The pastor did not stop playing immediately, but finished the line, and let the music hang in the air for a moment. Finally he turned around. 'Young Peter,' he said in a flat voice.

Peter was momentarily shocked to see that the pastor seemed to have aged. His face was lined with weariness and his blue eyes had lost their icy glitter. After an instant of surprise, Peter said: 'I'm looking for Harald.'

'I didn't imagine this was a condolence call,' the pastor said coldly.

'Is he here?'

'Is this an official inquiry?'

'Why do you ask? Is Harald involved in some wrongdoing?'

'Certainly not.'

'I'm glad to hear it. Is he in the house?'

'No. He's not on the island. I don't know where he went.'

Peter looked at Tilde. This was a letdown – but, on the other hand, it suggested that Harald was guilty. Why else would he disappear? 'Where do you think he might be?'

'Go away.'

Arrogant as ever – but this time the pastor was not going to get away with it, Peter thought with relish. 'Your elder son killed himself because he was caught spying,' he said harshly.

The pastor flinched as if Peter had struck him.

Peter heard Tilde gasp beside him, and realized he had shocked her by his cruelty, but he pressed on.

'Your younger son may be guilty of similar crimes. You're in no position to act high and mighty with the police.'

The pastor's normally proud face looked hurt and vulnerable. 'I've told you that I don't know where Harald is,' he said dully. 'Do you have any other questions?'

'What are you hiding?'

The pastor sighed. 'You're one of my flock, and if you come to me for spiritual help I won't turn you away. But I will not speak to you for any other reason. You're arrogant and cruel, and as near worthless as one of God's creatures can be. Get out of my sight.'

'You can't throw people out of the church – it doesn't belong to you.'

'If you want to pray, you're welcome here. Otherwise, go away.'

Peter hesitated. He did not want to submit to being thrown out, but he knew he had been defeated. After a moment he took Tilde's arm and led her outside. 'I told you he was hard,' he said.

Tilde seemed shaken. 'I think the man is in pain.'

'No doubt. But was he telling the truth?'

'Obviously Harald has gone into hiding – which means almost certainly that he has the film.'

'So we have to find him.' Peter reflected on the conversation. 'I wonder if his father really doesn't know where he is.'

'Have you ever known the pastor to lie?'

'No – but he might make an exception to protect his son.'

Tilde made a dismissive gesture. 'We're not going to get anything out of him, either way.'

'I agree. But we're on the right track, that's the main thing. Let's try the mother. She at least is made of flesh and blood.'

They went to the house. Peter steered Tilde to the back. He tapped on the kitchen door and went in without waiting for an answer, as was usual on the island.

Lisbeth Olufsen was sitting at the kitchen table, doing nothing. Peter had never in his life seen her idle: she was always cooking or cleaning. Even in church she was busy, straightening rows of chairs, putting out hymn books or gathering them up, stoking the peat boiler that warmed the big room in winter. Now she sat looking at her hands. The skin was cracked and raw in places, like a fisherman's.

'Mrs Olufsen?'

She turned her face to him. Her eyes were red and her cheeks were drawn. After a moment, she recognized him. 'Hello, Peter,' she said expressionlessly.

He decided to take a softer approach with her. 'I'm sorry about Arne.'

She nodded vaguely.

'This is my friend Tilde. We work together.'

'Pleased to meet you.'

He sat at the table and nodded to Tilde to do the same. Perhaps a simple, practical question would bring Mrs Olufsen out of her daze. 'When is the funeral?'

She thought for a moment, then answered: 'Tomorrow.'

That was better.

'I've spoken to the pastor,' Peter said. 'We saw him in the church.'

'His heart is broken. He doesn't show it to the world, though.'

'I understand. Harald must be dreadfully upset, too.'

She glanced at him and looked quickly down at her hands again. It was the briefest of looks, but Peter read fear and deceit in it. She muttered: 'We haven't spoken to Harald.'

'Why is that?'

'We don't know where he is.'

Peter could not tell whether she was lying from moment to moment, but he felt sure of her intention to deceive. It angered him that the pastor and his wife, who pretended to be morally superior to others, should deliberately hide the truth from the police. He raised his voice. 'You'd be well advised to cooperate with us!'

Tilde put a restraining hand on his arm and looked an inquiry at him. He nodded for her to go ahead. She said: 'Mrs Olufsen, I'm sorry to have to tell you that Harald may have been involved in the same illegal activities as Arne.'

Mrs Olufsen looked frightened.

Tilde continued: 'The longer he goes on, the worse trouble he'll be in when finally we catch up with him.'

The old woman shook her head from side to side, looking distressed, but she said nothing.

'If you would help us find him, you'd be doing the best thing for him.'

'I don't know where he is,' she repeated, but less firmly.

Peter sensed weakness. He stood up and leaned across the kitchen table, pushing his face into hers. 'I saw Arne die,' he said gratingly.

Mrs Olufsen's eyes widened in horror.

'I saw your son put the gun to his own throat and pull the trigger,' he went on.

Tilde said: 'Peter, no—'

He ignored her. 'I saw his blood and brains spatter the wall behind him.'

Mrs Olufsen cried out with shock and grief.

She was about to crack, Peter saw with satisfaction. He pressed his advantage. 'Your elder son was a spy and a criminal, and he met a violent end. They that live by the sword shall die by the sword, that's what the Bible says. Do you want the same to happen to your other son?'

'No,' she whispered. 'No.'

'Then tell me where he is!'

The kitchen door burst open and the pastor strode in. 'You filth,' he said.

Peter straightened up, startled but defiant. 'I'm entitled to question—'

'Get out of my house.'

Tilde said: 'Let's go, Peter.'

'I still want to know—'

'Now!' the pastor roared. 'Leave now!' He advanced around the table.

Peter backed away. He knew he should not allow himself to be shouted down. He was on legitimate police business and he had a right to ask questions. But the towering presence of the pastor scared him, despite the gun under his jacket, and he found himself reversing steadily to the door.

Tilde opened it and went out.

'I haven't finished with you two,' Peter said feebly as he backed through the doorway.

The pastor slammed the door in his face.

Peter turned away. 'Damned hypocrites,' he said. 'The pair of them.'

The buggy was waiting. 'To my father's house,' Peter said, and they got in.

As they drove away, he tried to put the humiliating scene out of his mind and concentrate on his next steps. 'Harald must be living somewhere,' he said.

'Obviously.' Tilde's tone was curt, and he guessed she was distressed by what she had just witnessed.

'He's not at school and he's not at home, and he has no relations except for some cousins in Hamburg.'

'We could circulate a picture of him.'

'We'll have trouble finding one. The pastor doesn't believe in photos – they're a sign of vanity. You didn't see any pictures in that kitchen, did you?'

'What about a school photo?'

'Not a Jansborg tradition. The only picture of Arne we could find was the one in his army record. I doubt there's a photo of Harald anywhere.'

'So what's our next move?'

'I think he's staying with friends – don't you?'

'Makes sense.'

She would not look at him. He sighed. She was in a bad mood with him. So be it. 'This is what you do,' he said in a tone of command. 'Call the Politigaarden. Send Conrad to Jansborg Skole. Get a list of the home addresses of all the boys in Harald's class. Then have someone call at each house, ask a few questions, snoop around a bit.'

'They must be all over Denmark. It would take a month to visit them all. How much time do we have?'

'Very little. I don't know how long it will take for Harald to figure out a way to get the film to London, but he's a cunning young villain. Use local police where necessary.'

'Very well.'

'If he's not staying with friends, he must be hiding out with another member of the spy ring. We're going to stay for the funeral and see who shows up. We'll check out every mourner. One of them must know where Harald is.'

The buggy slowed as it approached the entrance to Axel Flemming's house. Tilde said: 'Do you mind if I go back to the hotel?'

His parents were expecting them for lunch, but Peter could see that Tilde was not in the mood. 'All right.' He tapped the driver on the shoulder. 'Go to the ferry dock.'

They drove in silence for a while. As they approached the dock, Peter said: 'What will you do at the hotel?'

'In fact I think I should return to Copenhagen.'

That made him angry. As the horse stopped at the quayside, he said: 'What the hell is wrong with you?'

'I didn't like what just happened.'

'We had to do it!'

'I'm not sure.'

'It was our duty to try to make those people tell what they knew.'

'Duty isn't everything.'

She had said that during their argument about Jews, he recalled. 'That's just playing with words. Duty is what you have to do. You can't make exceptions. That's what's wrong with the world.'

The ferry was in dock. Tilde got down from the buggy. 'It's just life, Peter, that's all.'

'It's why we have crime! Wouldn't you rather live in a world where everyone did their duty? Just imagine it! Well-behaved people in smart uniforms getting things done, with no slacking, no lateness, no half-measures. If all crimes were punished and no excuses accepted there would be a lot less for the police to do!'

'Is that really what you want?'

'Yes – and if I ever get to be chief of police, and the Nazis are still running things, that's what it will be like! What's wrong with that?'

She nodded, but did not answer his question. 'Goodbye, Peter,' she said.

As she walked away he shouted after her: 'Well? What's wrong with it?' But she boarded the ferry without turning around.

PART FOUR

TWENTY-FIVE

Harald knew the police were looking for him.

His mother had phoned Kirstenslot again, ostensibly to tell Karen the date and time of Arne's funeral. During the conversation, she had said she had been questioned by the police about Harald's whereabouts. 'But I don't know where he is, so I couldn't tell them,' she had said. It was a warning, and Harald admired his mother for having the courage to send it and the shrewdness to figure out that Karen could probably deliver it.

Despite the warning, he had to go to the flying school.

Karen purloined some of her father's old clothes, so that Harald would not have to wear his distinctive school blazer. He put on a marvellously lightweight sports jacket from America and a linen cap, and wore sunglasses. He looked more like a millionaire playboy than a fugitive spy as he got on the train at Kirstenslot. Nevertheless he was nervous. He felt trapped in the railway carriage. If a policeman accosted him he could not run away.

In Copenhagen he walked the short distance from the Vesterport suburban station to the main line station without seeing a single police uniform. A few minutes later he was on another train to Vodal.

On the way, he thought about his brother. Everyone had thought Arne unsuited to Resistance work: too playful, too careless, perhaps not brave enough. And in the end he had turned out to be the greatest hero of all. The thought brought tears to Harald's eyes behind the sunglasses.

Squadron Leader Renthe, commanding officer of the flying school, reminded him of his old headmaster, Heis. Both men were tall and thin and long-nosed. Because of the resemblance, Harald found it difficult to lie to Renthe. 'I've come to, er, pick up my brother's effects,' he said. 'Personal stuff. If that's all right.'

Renthe did not appear to notice his embarrassment. 'Of course,' he said. 'One of Arne's colleagues, Hendrik Janz, has packed everything up. There's just a suitcase and a duffle bag.'

'Thanks.' Harald did not want Arne's effects, but he had needed an excuse to come here. What he was really after was about fifty feet of steel cable to replace the missing control cables of the Hornet Moth. And this was the only place he could think of where he might get it.

Now that he was here, the task seemed more daunting than it had from a distance. He felt a wave of mild panic. Without the cable, the Hornet Moth could not fly. Then he thought again of the sacrifice his brother had made, and told himself to stay calm. If he kept a cool head, he might find a way.

'I was going to send the bags to your parents,' Renthe added.

'I'll do it.' Harald wondered whether he could confide in Renthe.

'I only hesitated because I thought perhaps they should go to his fiancée.'

'Hermia?' Harald said, surprised. 'In England?'

'Is she in England? She was here three days ago.'

Harald was astonished. 'What was she doing here?'

'I assumed she had taken Danish citizenship and was living here. Otherwise, her presence in Denmark would have been illegal, and I would have been obliged to report her visit to the police. But obviously she would not have come here if that had been the case. She would know, wouldn't she, that as an army officer I'm obliged to report anything illegal to the police.' He looked hard at Harald and added: 'Do you see what I mean?'

'I think I do.' Harald realized he was being given a message. Renthe suspected that he and Hermia were involved in espionage with Arne, and he was warning Harald not to say anything about it to him. He obviously sympathized, but was not willing to break any rules. Harald stood up. 'You've made things very clear – thank you.'

'I'll get someone to show you to Arne's quarters.'

'No need – I can find my way.' He had seen Arne's room two weeks before, when he was here for a flight in a Tiger Moth.

Renthe shook his hand. 'My deepest condolences.'

'Thank you.'

447

Harald left the headquarters building and walked along the single road that connected all the low buildings that made up the base. He moved slowly, taking a good look inside the hangars. There was not much activity. What was there to do at an air base where the aircraft could not fly?

He felt frustrated. The cable he needed must be here, somewhere. All he had to do was find out where, and get hold of it. But it was not that simple.

In one hangar he saw a Tiger Moth completely dismantled. The wings were detached, the fuselage stood on trestles, the engine on a stand. His hopes rose. He walked in through the giant doorway. A mechanic in overalls was sitting on an oil can, drinking tea from a big mug. 'Amazing,' Harald said to him. 'I've never seen one taken to pieces like that.'

'Has to be done,' the man replied. 'Parts wear out, and you can't have them failing in mid-air. On aircraft, everything has to be perfect. Otherwise you fall out of the sky.'

Harald found that a sobering thought. He was planning to cross the North Sea in an aircraft that had not been looked at by a mechanic for years. 'So you replace everything?'

'Everything that moves, yes.'

Harald thought optimistically that this man might be able to give him what he wanted. 'You must get through a lot of spares.'

'That's right.'

'There's what, a hundred feet of control cables in each aircraft?'

'A Tiger Moth requires one hundred and fifty-nine feet of ten-hundredweight cable.'

And that's what I need, Harald thought with mounting excitement. But once again he hesitated to ask, for fear of giving himself away to someone unsympathetic. He looked around. He had vaguely imagined that aeroplane parts would be lying around for anyone to pick up. 'So, where do you keep it all?'

'Stores, of course. This is the army. Everything in its place.'

Harald grunted with exasperation. If only he could have seen a length of cable and picked it up casually ... but it was pointless to wish for easy solutions. 'Where's the store?'

'Next building along.' The mechanic frowned. 'Why all the questions?'

'Idle curiosity.' Harald guessed he had pushed this man far enough. He should move on before arousing serious suspicion. He gave a sketchy wave and turned away. 'Nice talking to you.'

He walked to the next building and stepped inside. A sergeant sat behind a counter, smoking and reading a newspaper. Harald saw a photograph of Russian soldiers surrendering, and the headline: STALIN TAKES CONTROL OF SOVIET DEFENCE MINISTRY.

Harald studied the rows of steel shelves that stretched out on the other side of the counter. He felt like a child in a sweet shop. Here was everything he could want, from washers to entire engines. He could build a whole aircraft out of these parts.

And one entire section was given over to miles of

cable of different kinds, all neatly wound on wooden cylinders like cotton reels.

Harald was delighted. He had learned exactly where the cable was. Now he had to figure out how to get his hands on it.

After a moment, the sergeant looked up from the newspaper. 'Yes?'

Could the man be bribed? Yet again, Harald hesitated. He had a pocketful of money, given to him for this purpose by Karen. But he did not know how to phrase an offer. Even a corrupt warehouseman might be offended by a crass proposal. He wished he had thought more about his approach. But he had to do it. 'Can I ask you something?' he said. 'All these spare parts – is there any way that someone, a civilian I mean, could buy, or—'

'No,' the sergeant said abruptly.

'Even if the price was, you know, not a major consideration—'

'Absolutely not.'

Harald did not know what else to say. 'If I've given offence . . .'

'Forget it.'

At least the man had not called the police. Harald turned away.

The door was solid wood with three locks, he noted as he left. It would not be easy to break in to this warehouse. Perhaps he was not the first civilian to realize that scarce components might be found in military stores.

Feeling defeated, he made his way to the officers'

quarters and found Arne's room. As Renthe had promised, there were two bags neatly lined up at the foot of the bed. The room was otherwise bare.

It struck Harald as pathetic that his brother's life could be packed into two bags, and that his room should then bear no trace of his existence. The thought brought tears to his eyes again. But the important thing was what a man left behind in the minds of others, he told himself. Arne would always live in Harald's memory – teaching him to whistle, making their mother laugh like a schoolgirl, combing his glossy hair in a mirror. He thought of the last time he had seen his brother, sitting on the tiled floor of the disused church in Kirstenslot, weary and scared but determined to fulfil his mission. And, once again, he saw that the way to honour Arne's memory was to finish the job he had started.

A corporal looked in at the door and said: 'Are you related to Arne Olufsen?'

'His brother. My name is Harald.'

'Benedikt Vessell, call me Ben.' He was a man in his thirties with a friendly grin that showed tobacco-stained teeth. 'I was hoping to run into someone from the family.' He fished in his pocket and pulled out money. 'I owe Arne forty crowns.'

'What for?'

The corporal looked sly. 'Well, don't say a word, I run a little book on the horse races, and Arne picked a winner.'

Harald took the money, not knowing what else to do. 'Thank you.'

'Is that all right, then?'

Harald did not really understand the question. 'Of course.'

'Good.' Ben looked furtive.

It crossed Harald's mind that the sum owed might have been more than forty crowns. But he was not going to argue. 'I'll give it to my mother,' he said.

'Deepest sympathy, son. He was a good sort, your brother.'

The corporal obviously was not a rule keeper. He seemed the type who would murmur 'Don't say a word' quite frequently. His age suggested he was a career soldier, but his rank was lowly. Perhaps he put his energies into illegal activities. He probably sold pornographic books and stolen cigarettes. Maybe he could solve Harald's problem. 'Ben,' Harald said. 'Can I ask you something?'

'Anything at all.' Ben took a tobacco pouch from his pocket and began to hand-roll a cigarette.

'If a man wanted, for private purposes, to get hold of fifty feet of control cable for a Tiger Moth, do you know of any way it could be done?'

Ben looked at him through narrowed eyes. 'No,' he said.

'Say, the person had a couple of hundred crowns to pay for it.'

Ben lit his cigarette. 'This is to do with what Arne was arrested for, isn't it?'

'Yes.'

Ben shook his head. 'No, lad, it can't be done. Sorry.'

'Never mind,' Harald said lightly, though he was bitterly disappointed. 'Where can I find Hendrik Janz?'

'Two doors along. If he's not in his room, try the canteen.'

Harald found Hendrik seated at a small desk, studying a book on meteorology. Pilots had to understand the weather, to know when it was safe to fly and if there was a storm coming. 'I'm Harald Olufsen.'

Hendrik shook his hand. 'Damn shame about Arne.'

'Thank you for packing up his stuff.'

'Glad to be able to do something.'

Did Hendrik approve of what Arne had done? Harald needed some indication before sticking his neck out. He said: 'Arne did what he thought was right for his country.'

Hendrik immediately looked wary. 'I know nothing of that,' he said. 'To me he was a reliable colleague and a good friend.'

Harald was dismayed. Hendrik obviously was not going to help him steal the cable. What was he going to do?

'Thanks again,' he said. 'Goodbye.'

He returned to Arne's room and picked up the bags. He was at a loss to know what else to do. He could not leave without the cable he needed – but how could he take it? He had tried everything.

Maybe there was another place he could get cable. But he could not think where. And he was running out of time. The full moon was six days away. That meant he had only four days left to work on the aircraft.

He left the building and headed for the gate, carrying the bags. He was going to return to Kirstenslot – but for what purpose? Without the cable, the Hornet Moth would not fly. He wondered how he was going to tell Karen he had failed.

As he passed the stores building, he heard his name called. 'Harald!'

A truck was parked to one side of the warehouse, and Ben stood half-concealed by the vehicle, beckoning. Harald hurried over.

'Here,' said Ben, and he held out a thick coil of steel cable. 'Fifty feet, and a bit extra.'

Harald was thrilled. 'Thank you!'

'Take it, for God's sake, it's heavy.'

Harald took the cable and turned away.

'No, no!' Ben said. 'You can't walk through the gate with that in your hand, for Christ's sake! Put it in one of the bags.'

Harald opened Arne's suitcase. It was full.

Ben said: 'Give me that uniform, quick.'

Harald took out Arne's uniform and replaced it with the coil.

Ben picked up the uniform. 'I'll get rid of this, don't worry. Now clear off!'

Harald shut the case and reached into his pocket. 'I promised you two hundred crowns—'

'Keep the money,' Ben said. 'And good luck to you, son.'

'Thanks!'

'Now get lost! I never want to see you again.'

'Right,' said Harald, and he walked rapidly away.

* * *

Next morning, Harald stood outside the castle in the grey gleam of dawn. It was half past three. In his hand he held a four-gallon oil can, empty and clean. The tank of the Hornet Moth would take thirty-five gallons of petrol, just under nine canfuls. There was no legitimate way to get fuel, so Harald was going to steal it from the Germans.

He had everything else he needed. The Hornet Moth required only a few more hours of work and it would be ready to take off. But its fuel tank was empty.

The kitchen door opened quietly and Karen stepped out. She was accompanied by Thor, the old red setter that made Harald smile because it looked so much like Mr Duchwitz. Karen paused on the doorstep, staring around warily, like a cat when there are strangers in the house. She wore a chunky green sweater that concealed her figure, and the old brown corduroys that Harald thought of as her gardening trousers. But she looked wonderful. She called me darling, he said to himself, hugging the memory. She called me darling.

She smiled brilliantly, dazzling him. 'Good morning!'

Her voice seemed dangerously loud. He put a finger on his lips for quiet. It would be safer to remain completely silent. There was nothing to discuss: they had made their plan last night, sitting on the floor in the disused church, eating chocolate cake from the Kirstenslot pantry.

Harald led the way into the woods. Under cover, they walked half the length of the park. When they drew level with the soldiers' tents, they peeked cautiously from the bushes. As expected, they saw a single man on guard duty, standing outside the mess tent, yawning. At this hour, everyone else was asleep. Harald was relieved to have his expectations fulfilled.

The veterinary company's fuel supply came from a small petrol tanker that was parked a hundred yards from the tents – no doubt as a safety precaution. The separation would be helpful to Harald, though he wished it were greater. The tanker had a hand pump, he had already observed, and there was no locking mechanism.

The truck was parked alongside the drive that led to the castle door, so that vehicles could approach it on a hard surface. The hose was on the drive side, for convenience. In consequence, the bulk of the truck shielded anyone using it from view by the encampment.

Everything was as expected, but Harald hesitated. It seemed madness to steal petrol from under the noses of the soldiers. But it was dangerous to think too much. Fear could paralyse. Action was the antidote. Without further reflection he broke cover, leaving Karen and the dog behind, and walked quickly across the damp grass to the tanker.

He took the nozzle from its hook and fed it into his

can, then reached for the pump lever. As he pulled it down, there was a gurgling sound from inside the tank, and the noise of petrol sloshing into the can. It seemed very loud, but perhaps not loud enough to be heard by the sentry a hundred yards away.

He glanced anxiously back at Karen. As agreed, she was watching from the screen of vegetation, ready to alert Harald if anyone approached.

The can filled quickly. He screwed on the cap and picked it up. It was heavy. He returned the nozzle tidily to its hook then hurried back to the trees. Once out of sight, he paused, grinning triumphantly at Karen. He had stolen four gallons of petrol and got away with it. The plan was working!

Leaving her there, he cut through the woods to the monastery. He had already opened the big church door so that he could slip in and out. It would have been too awkward and time-consuming to pass the heavy can through the high window. He stepped inside. With relief, he put down the can. He popped open the access panel and undid the petrol cap of the Hornet Moth. He fumbled awkwardly because his fingers were numb from carrying the heavy can, but he got the cap open. He emptied the can into the aircraft's tank, replaced both caps to minimize the smell of fuel, and went out.

While he was filling the can for the second time, the sentry decided to make a patrol.

Harald could not see the man, but knew something was wrong when Karen whistled. He looked up to see her emerging from the wood with Thor at her heel.

He let go of the hand pump and dropped to his knees to look under the tanker and across the lawn. He saw the soldier's boots approaching.

They had foreseen this problem and prepared for it. Still on his knees, Harald watched Karen stroll across the grass. She met up with the sentry while he was still fifty yards away from the tanker. The dog amiably sniffed the man's crotch. Karen took out cigarettes. Would the sentry be friendly, and smoke with a pretty girl? Or would he be a stickler for routine, and ask her to walk her dog somewhere else while he continued his patrol? Harald held his breath. The sentry took a cigarette, and they lit up.

The soldier was a small man with a bad complexion. Harald could not hear their words, but he knew what Karen was saying: she could not sleep, she felt lonely, she wanted someone to talk to. 'Don't you think he might be suspicious?' Karen had said while discussing this plan last night. Harald had assured her that the victim would enjoy being flirted with far too much to question her motives. Harald had not been as certain as he pretended, but to his relief the sentry was fulfilling his prediction.

He saw Karen point to a tree stump a little way off and then lead the soldier to it. She sat down, placing herself so that the sentry had to have his back to the tanker if he wanted to sit next to her. Now, Harald knew, she would be saying that the local boys were so dull, she liked to talk to men who had travelled a little and seen the world, they seemed more mature. She patted the surface beside her to encourage him. Sure enough, he sat down.

Harald resumed pumping.

He filled the can and hurried into the woods. Eight gallons!

When he returned, Karen and the sentry were in the same positions. While he refilled the can, he calculated how long he needed. Filling the can took about a minute, the walk to the church about two, pouring the petrol into the Hornet Moth another minute, the return journey another two. Six minutes for the round trip, then, making fifty-four minutes for nine canfuls. Assuming he would tire towards the end, call it an hour.

Could the sentry be kept chatting that long? The man had nothing else to do. The soldiers rose at five thirty, still more than an hour away, and began their duties at six. Assuming the British did not invade Denmark in the next hour, the sentry had no reason to stop talking to a pretty girl. But he was a soldier, under military discipline, and he might feel it his duty to patrol.

All Harald could do was hope for the best, and hurry.

He took the third canful to the church. Twelve gallons already, he thought optimistically; more than two hundred miles – a third of the way to England.

He continued his shuttle. According to the manual he had found in the cockpit, the DH87B Hornet Moth should fly 632 miles on a full tank. That figure

459

assumed no wind. The distance to the English coast, as best he could reckon it from the atlas, was about 600 miles. The margin of safety was nowhere near enough. A head wind would reduce their mileage and bring them down in the sea. He would take a full can of petrol in the cabin, he decided. That would add seventy miles to the Hornet Moth's range, assuming he could figure out a way to top up the tank in flight.

He pumped with his right hand and toted with his left, and both arms were aching by the time he emptied the fourth canful into the aircraft. Returning for the fifth, he saw that the sentry was standing up, as if preparing to move off, but Karen still had him talking. She laughed at something the man said, and slapped his shoulder playfully. It was a coquettish gesture that was most uncharacteristic of her, but all the same Harald felt a pang of jealousy. She never slapped his shoulder playfully.

But she had called him darling.

He carried the fifth and sixth canfuls, and felt he was two thirds of the way to the English coast.

Whenever he felt scared, he thought of his brother. It was difficult, he found, to accept that Arne was dead. He kept thinking about whether his brother would approve of what he was doing, what he would say when Harald told him about some aspect of his plans, how he would be amused or sceptical or impressed. In that way, Arne was still part of Harald's life.

Harald did not believe in the obstinately irrational fundamentalism of his father. Talk of heaven and hell seemed mere superstition to him. But now he saw that in a way dead people lived on in the minds of those who had loved them, and that was a kind of afterlife. Any time his resolution weakened, he recalled that Arne had given everything for this mission, and felt an impulse of loyalty that gave him strength – even though the brother to whom he owed that loyalty was no more.

Returning to the church with the seventh canful, he was seen.

As he approached the church door, a soldier in underwear emerged from the cloisters. Harald froze, the can of petrol in his hand as incriminating as a hot gun. The soldier, half asleep, walked to a bush and began to urinate and yawn at the same time. Harald saw that it was Leo, the young private who had been so intrusively friendly three days ago.

Leo caught his eye, was startled to find himself observed, and looked guilty. 'Sorry,' he mumbled.

Harald guessed it was against the rules to pee in the bushes. They had dug a latrine behind the monastery, but it was a long walk, and Leo was being lazy. Harald tried to smile reassuringly. 'Don't worry,' he said in German. But he could hear the tremor of fear in his own voice.

Leo did not seem to notice it. Readjusting his clothing, he frowned. 'What's in the can?'

'Water, for my motorcycle.'

'Oh.' Leo yawned. Then he jerked a thumb at the bush. 'We're not supposed to . . .'

'Forget it.'

Leo nodded, and stumbled away.

Harald stepped into the church. He paused a moment, closing his eyes, getting over the tension. Then he poured the fuel into the Hornet Moth.

As he approached the petrol tanker for the eighth time, he saw that his plan was beginning to fall apart. Karen was walking away from the tree stump, back towards the woods. She gave the sentry a friendly wave, so they must have parted on good terms, but Harald guessed the man had some duty he was obliged to perform. However, he was walking away from the tanker, towards the mess tent, so Harald felt able to carry on, and he refilled the can.

As he carried it into the woods, Karen caught up with him and murmured: 'He has to light the kitchen stove.'

Harald nodded and hurried on. He poured the eighth canful into the aircraft's tank and returned for the ninth. The sentry was nowhere to be seen, and Karen gave him the thumbs-up sign to indicate that he could go ahead. He filled the can for the ninth time and returned to the church. As he had calculated, this brought the level to the brim, with some left over. But he needed an extra canful to carry in the cabin. He returned for the last time.

Karen stopped him at the edge of the wood and pointed. The sentry was standing beside the petrol tanker. Harald saw with dismay that, in his hurry, he had forgotten to return the nozzle to its hook, and the petrol hose dangled untidily. The soldier looked up and down the park with a puzzled frown, then returned the nozzle to its proper place. He remained standing there for a while. He took out cigarettes, put one in his mouth, and opened a box of matches; then moved away from the tanker before striking his match.

Karen whispered to Harald: 'Haven't you got enough petrol yet?'

'I need one more can.'

The sentry was strolling away with his back to the lorry, smoking, and Harald decided to take a chance. He walked fast across the grass. To his dismay, he found that the tanker did not quite conceal him from the soldier's angle of view. Nevertheless he put the nozzle in the can and started to pump, knowing he would be seen if the man chanced to turn around. He filled the can, replaced the nozzle, screwed the cap on the can and walked away.

He was almost at the woods when he heard a shout.

He pretended to be deaf and walked on without turning around or increasing his pace.

The sentry shouted again, and Harald heard running boots.

He passed into the trees. Karen appeared. 'Get out of sight!' she whispered. 'I'll head him off.'

Harald darted into a patch of shrubbery. Lying flat, he wriggled under a rambling bush, dragging the can with him. Thor tried to follow him, thinking this was a game. Harald smacked him sharply on the nose, and the dog retreated, his feelings hurt.

Harald heard the sentry say: 'Where's that man?'

'You mean Christian?' Karen said.

'Who is he?'

'One of the gardeners. You're terribly handsome when you're cross, Ludie.'

'Never mind that, what was he doing?'

'Treating diseased trees with the stuff in that can, something that kills those ugly mushroom growths you see on tree trunks.'

That was inventive of her, Harald thought, even if she's forgotten the German word for fungicide.

'This early?' Ludie said sceptically.

'He told me the treatment works best when it's cool.'

'I saw him walking away from the petrol tanker.'

'Petrol? What would Christian do with petrol? He doesn't have a car. I expect he was taking a short cut across the lawn.'

'Hm.' Ludie was still uneasy. 'I haven't noticed any diseased trees.'

'Well, look at this.' Harald heard them take a few paces. 'See that growing out of the bark like a great big wart? It would kill the tree unless Christian treated it.'

'I suppose it would. Well, please tell your servants to keep clear of the encampment.'

'I will, and I apologize. I'm sure Christian meant no harm.'

'Very well.'

'Goodbye, Ludie. Perhaps I'll see you tomorrow morning.'

'I'll be here.'

'Bye.'

Harald waited a few minutes, then he heard Karen say: 'All clear.'

He crawled out from the bush. 'You were brilliant!'

'I'm becoming such a good liar, it's worrying.'

They walked towards the monastery – and suffered another shock.

As they were about to leave the shelter of the woods, Harald saw Per Hansen, the village policeman and local Nazi, standing outside the church.

He cursed. What the hell was Hansen doing here? And at this time of the morning?

Hansen was standing still, legs apart and arms folded, looking across the park at the military encampment. Harald put a restraining hand on Karen's arm, but he was too late to stop Thor, who instantly sensed the hostility Karen felt. The dog erupted from the woods at a run, made for Hansen, stopped at a safe distance, and barked. Hansen looked scared and angry, and his hand went to the holstered gun at his belt.

Karen whispered: 'I'll deal with him.' Without waiting for Harald to reply she went forward and whistled to the dog. 'Come here, Thor!'

Harald put down his can of petrol, dropped to a crouch, and watched through the leaves.

Hansen said to Karen: 'You should keep that dog under control.'

'Why? He lives here.'

'It's aggressive.'

'He barks at intruders. It's his job.'

'If it attacks a member of the police force, it might be shot.'

'Don't be ridiculous,' Karen said, and Harald could not help observing that she displayed all the arrogance of her wealth and social position. 'What are you doing, snooping around my garden at the crack of dawn?'

'I'm on official business, young lady, so you mind your manners.'

'Official business?' she said sceptically. Harald guessed she was pretending to be incredulous in order to get more information out of him. 'What business?'

'I'm looking for someone called Harald Olufsen.'

Harald murmured: 'Oh, shit.' He had not been expecting this.

Karen was shocked, but she managed to cover up. 'Never heard of him,' she said.

'He's a school friend of your brother's, and he's wanted by the police.'

'Well, I can't be expected to know all my brother's schoolmates.'

'He's been to the castle.'

'Oh? What does he look like?'

'Male, eighteen years old, six feet one inch, fair hair and blue eyes, probably wearing a blue school blazer with a stripe on the sleeve.' Hansen sounded as if he were reciting something he had memorized from a police report.

'He sounds terribly attractive, apart from the blazer, but I don't recall him.' Karen was maintaining her air of careless disdain, but Harald could see the tension and worry on her face.

'He's been here twice at least,' Hansen said. 'I've seen him myself.'

'I must have missed him. What's his crime, failing to return a library book?'

'I don't – that is, I can't say. I mean, it's a routine inquiry.'

Hansen obviously did not know what the crime was, Harald thought. He must be asking on behalf of some other policeman – Peter Flemming, presumably.

Karen was saying: 'Well, my brother has gone to Aarhus, and there's no one staying here now – apart from a hundred soldiers, of course.'

'Last time I saw Olufsen, he had a very dangerous-looking motorcycle.'

'Oh, *that* boy,' Karen said, pretending to remember. 'He was expelled from school. Daddy won't let him come here any more.'

'No? Well, I think I'll have a word with your father anyway.'

'He's still asleep.'

'I'll wait.'

'As you please. Come on, Thor!' Karen walked away, and Hansen continued up the drive.

Harald waited. Karen approached the church, turned to check that Hansen was not watching her, then slipped through the door. Hansen walked up the drive towards the castle. Harald hoped he would not stop to talk to Ludie, and discover that the sentry had seen a tall blond man behaving suspiciously near the petrol tanker. Fortunately, Hansen walked past the encampment and eventually disappeared behind the castle, presumably heading for the kitchen door.

Harald hurried to the church and slipped inside. He put the last can of petrol down on the tiled floor.

Karen closed the big door, turned the key in the lock, and dropped the bar into place. Then she turned to Harald. 'You must be exhausted.'

He was. Both arms hurt, and his legs ached from hurrying through the woods with a heavy weight. As soon as he relaxed, he felt slightly nauseated from the petrol fumes. But he was ecstatically happy. 'You were wonderful!' he said. 'Flirting with Ludie as if he were the most eligible bachelor in Denmark.'

'He's two inches shorter than me!'

'And you completely fooled Hansen.'

'Not difficult, that.'

Harald picked up the can again and put it in the cabin of the Hornet Moth, stowing it on the luggage shelf behind the seats. He closed the door and turned around to see Karen standing right behind him, grinning broadly. 'We did it,' she said.

'My God, we did.'

She put her arms around him and looked at him expectantly. It was almost as if she wanted him to kiss her. He thought of asking, then decided to be more decisive. He closed his eyes and leaned forward. Her lips were soft and warm. He could have stayed that way, motionless, enjoying the touch of her lips, for a long time, but she had other ideas. She broke contact, then kissed him again. She kissed his upper lip, then the lower, then his chin, then his lips again. Her mouth was busily playful, exploring. He had never kissed like this before. He opened his eyes and was startled to see that she was looking at him with bright merriment in her eyes.

'What are you thinking?' she said.

'Do you really like me?'

'Of course I do, stupid.'

'I like you, too.'

'Good.'

He hesitated, then said: 'As a matter of fact, I love you.'

'I know,' she said, and she kissed him again.

TWENTY-SIX

Walking through the centre of Morlunde in the bright light of a summer morning, Hermia Mount was in more danger than she had been in Copenhagen. People in this small town knew her.

Two years before, after she and Arne had become engaged, he had brought her to his parents' home on Sande. She had been to church, watched a football match, visited Arne's favourite bar, and gone shopping with Arne's mother. It broke her heart to remember that happy time.

But the consequence was that plenty of local people would remember the Olufsen boy's English fiancée, and there was a serious danger she would be recognized. If that happened, people would start talking, and before long the police would hear.

This morning she wore a hat and sunglasses, but still she felt perilously conspicuous. All the same, she had to take the risk.

She had spent the previous evening in the town centre, hoping to run into Harald. Knowing how much he loved jazz, she had gone first to the Club Hot, but it was closed. She had not found him in any

470

of the bars and cafés where young people gathered. It had been a wasted evening.

This morning she was going to his home.

She had thought of telephoning, but it was hazardous. If she gave her real name she risked being overheard and betrayed. If she gave a false name, or called anonymously, she might spook Harald and cause him to flee. She had to visit in person.

This would be even more risky. Morlunde was a town, but on the small island of Sande every resident knew all the others. She could only hope that islanders might take her for a holidaymaker, and not look too closely. She had no better option. The full moon was five days away.

She made her way to the harbour, carrying her small suitcase, and boarded the ferry. At the top of the gangway stood a German soldier and a Danish policeman. She showed her papers in the name of Agnes Ricks. The documents had already passed three inspections, but nevertheless she suffered a shiver of fear as she offered the forgeries to the two uniformed men.

The policeman studied her identity card. 'You're a long way from home, Miss Ricks.'

She had prepared her cover story. 'I'm here for the funeral of a relative.' It was a good pretext for a long journey. She was not sure when Arne's interment was scheduled, but there was nothing suspicious about a family member arriving a day or two early, especially given the hazards of wartime travel.

'That would be the Olufsen funeral.'

'Yes.' Hot tears came to her eyes. 'I'm a second cousin, but my mother was very close to Lisbeth Olufsen.'

The policeman sensed her grief, despite the sunglasses, and he said gently: 'My condolences.' He handed the papers back. 'You're in plenty of time.'

'Am I?' That suggested it was today. 'I wasn't sure, I couldn't get through on the telephone to check.'

'I believe the service is at three o'clock this afternoon.'

'Thank you.'

Hermia went forward and leaned on the rail. As the ferry chugged out of the harbour, she looked across the water to the flat, featureless island and recalled her first visit. She had been shocked to see the cold, unadorned rooms where Arne had grown up, and to meet his stern parents. It was a mystery how that solemn family had produced someone as much fun as Arne.

She was a somewhat severe person herself, or so her colleagues seemed to think. In that way she had played a role in Arne's life similar to that of his mother. She had made him punctual, and discouraged him from getting drunk, while he had taught her to relax and have fun. She had once said to him: 'There's a time and place for spontaneity,' and he had laughed about it all day.

She had returned to Sande once more, for the Christmas festival. It had seemed more like Lent. For the Olufsens, Christmas was a religious event, not a bacchanal. Yet she had found the holiday enjoyable in

472

its quiet way, doing crossword puzzles with Arne, getting to know Harald, eating Mrs Olufsen's plain food, and walking along the cold beach in a fur coat, hand in hand with her lover.

She had never imagined returning here for his funeral.

She longed to go to the service, but she knew it was impossible. Too many people would see her and recognize her. There might even be a police detective present, studying the faces. After all, if Hermia could figure out that Arne's mission was being carried on by someone else, the police could make the same deduction.

In fact, she now realized, the funeral was going to delay her by some hours. She would have to wait until after the service before going to the house. Beforehand there would be neighbours in the kitchen preparing food, parishioners in the church arranging flowers, and an undertaker fussing about timings and pallbearers. It would be almost as bad as the service itself. But afterwards, as soon as the mourners had had their tea and smorrebrod, they would all depart, leaving the immediate family to grieve alone.

It meant she would have to kill time now, but caution was everything. If she could get the film from Harald this evening she could catch the first train to Copenhagen in the morning, sail to Bornholm tomorrow night, cross to Sweden the following day, and be in London twelve hours later, with two days to go before the full moon. It was worth wasting a few hours.

She disembarked on to the quay at Sande and walked to the hotel. She could not go into the building, for fear she might encounter someone who remembered her, so she walked on to the beach. It was not really sunbathing weather – there was patchy cloud, and a cool breeze off the water – but the old-fashioned striped bathing huts had been wheeled out, and a few people were splashing in the waves or picnicking on the sand. Hermia was able to find a sheltered dip in the dunes and disappear into the holiday scene.

She waited there while the tide came in and a horse from the hotel pulled the wheeled bathing huts back up the beach. She had spent so much of the last two weeks sitting and waiting.

She had met Arne's parents a third time, on their once-a-decade trip to Copenhagen. Arne had taken them all to the Tivoli Garden and had been his most debonair, amusing self, charming waitresses, making his mother laugh, even getting his dour father to reminisce about schooldays at Jansborg. A few weeks later the Nazis had come and Hermia had left the country, ignominiously she felt, in a closed train with a crowd of diplomats from countries hostile to Germany.

And now she was back, seeking out a deadly secret, risking her life and the lives of others.

She left her position at half past four. The parsonage was ten miles from the hotel, a brisk walk of two and a half hours, so she would arrive at seven. She felt sure all the guests would have left by then, and she would find Harald and his parents sitting quietly in the kitchen.

The beach was not deserted. Several times on her long walk she encountered people. She gave them a wide berth, letting them assume she was an unfriendly holidaymaker, and no one recognized her.

At last she saw the outlines of the low church and the parsonage. The thought that this had been Arne's home struck her with sadness. There was no one in sight. As she came nearer, she saw the fresh grave in the little cemetery.

With a full heart, she crossed the churchyard and stood by the grave of her fiancé. She took off her sunglasses. There were lots of flowers, she observed: people were always touched by the death of a young man. Grief took hold of her, and she began to shake with sobs. Tears streamed down her face. She fell to her knees and took a handful of the piled-up earth, thinking of his body lying below. I doubted you, she said in her mind, but you were the bravest of us all.

At last the storm abated and she was able to stand up. She wiped her face dry with her sleeve. She had work to do.

When she turned away, she saw the tall figure and domed head of Arne's father, standing a few yards off, watching her. He must have approached silently, and waited for her to rise. 'Well, Hermia,' he said. 'God bless you.'

'Thank you, pastor.' She wanted to hug him, but he was not a hugging man, so she shook his hand.

'You arrived too late for the funeral.'

'That was intentional. I can't afford to be seen.'

'You'd better come into the house.'

Hermia followed him across the rough grass. Mrs Olufsen was in the kitchen, but for once she was not at the sink. Hermia guessed that neighbours had cleared up after the wake and washed the dishes. Mrs Olufsen was sitting at the kitchen table in a black dress and hat. When she saw Hermia she burst into tears.

Hermia hugged her, but her compassion was distracted. The person she wanted was not in the room. As soon as she decently could, she said: 'I was hoping to see Harald.'

'He's not here,' said Mrs Olufsen.

Hermia had a dreadful feeling that this long and dangerous journey would turn out to have been for nothing. 'Didn't he come to the funeral?'

She shook her head tearfully.

Curbing her exasperation as best she could, Hermia said: 'So where is he?'

The pastor said: 'You'd better sit down.'

She forced herself to be patient. The pastor was used to being obeyed. She would not get anywhere by defying his will.

Mrs Olufsen said: 'Will you have a cup of tea? It's not the real thing, of course.'

'Yes, please.'

'And a sandwich? There's such a lot left over.'

'No, thank you.' Hermia had had nothing all day, but she was too tense to eat. 'Where is Harald?' she said impatiently.

'We don't know,' said the pastor.

'How come?'

The pastor looked ashamed, a rare expression on his face. 'Harald and I had harsh words. I was as stubborn as he. Since then, the Lord has reminded me how precious is the time a man spends with his sons.' A tear rolled down his lined face. 'Harald left in anger, refusing to say where he was going. Five days later he returned, just for a few hours, and there was something of a reconciliation. On that occasion, he told his mother he was going to stay at the home of a school mate, but when we telephoned, they said he was not there.'

'Do you think he is still angry with you?'

'No,' said the pastor. 'Well, perhaps he is, but that's not why he has disappeared.'

'What do you mean?'

'My neighbour, Axel Flemming, has a son in the Copenhagen police.'

'I remember,' Hermia said. 'Peter Flemming.'

Mrs Olufsen put in: 'He had the nerve to come to the funeral.' Her tone was uncharacteristically bitter.

The pastor went on: 'Peter claims that Arne was a spy for the British, and Harald is continuing his work.'

'Ah.'

'You don't seem surprised.'

'I won't lie to you,' Hermia said. 'Peter is right. I asked Arne to take photographs of the military base here on the island. Harald has the film.'

Mrs Olufsen cried: 'How could you? Arne is dead because of that! We lost our son and you lost your fiancé! How could you?'

477

'I'm sorry,' Hermia whispered.

The pastor said: 'There's a war, Lisbeth. Many young men have died fighting the Nazis. It's not Hermia's fault.'

'I have to get the film from Harald,' Hermia said. 'I have to find him. Won't you help me?'

Mrs Olufsen said: 'I don't want to lose my other son! I couldn't bear it!'

The pastor took her hand. 'Arne was working against the Nazis. If Hermia and Harald can finish the job he started, his death will have some meaning. We have to help.'

Mrs Olufsen nodded. 'I know,' she said. 'I know. I'm just so scared.'

Hermia said: 'Where did Harald say he was going?'

Mrs Olufsen answered. 'Kirstenslot. It's a castle outside Copenhagen, the home of the Duchwitz family. The son, Josef, is at school with Harald.'

'But they say he's not there?'

She nodded. 'But he's not far away. I spoke to Josef's twin sister, Karen. She's in love with Harald.'

The pastor said incredulously: 'How do you know that?'

'By the sound of her voice when she spoke about him.'

'You didn't mention it to me.'

'You would have said I couldn't possibly tell.'

The pastor smiled ruefully. 'Yes, I would.'

Hermia said: 'So you think Harald is in the vicinity of Kirstenslot, and Karen knows where he is?'

'Yes.'

'Then I'll have to go there.'

The pastor took a watch out of his waistcoat pocket. 'You've missed the last train. You'd better stay the night. I'll take you to the ferry first thing in the morning.'

Hermia's voice dropped to a whisper. 'How can you be so kind? Arne died because of me.'

'The Lord giveth, and the Lord taketh away,' said the pastor. 'Blessed be the name of the Lord.'

TWENTY-SEVEN

The Hornet Moth was ready to fly.

Harald had installed the new cables from Vodal. His final task had been the punctured tyre. He had used the car jack from the Rolls-Royce to lift the aircraft, then he had taken the wheel to the nearest garage and paid a mechanic to repair the tyre. He had devised a method of refuelling in flight, knocking out a cabin window and passing a hose through it and into the petrol filler pipe. Finally he had unfolded the wings, fixing them in flying position with the simple steel pins provided. Now the aircraft filled the width of the church.

He looked outside. It was a calm day, with a light wind, and patchy low cloud that would serve to hide the Hornet Moth from the Luftwaffe. They would go tonight.

His stomach clenched with anxiety when he thought of it. Simply circling the Vodal training school in a Tiger Moth had seemed like a hair-raising adventure. Now he was planning to fly hundreds of miles over the open sea.

An aircraft such as this should hug the coast, so that it could glide to land in case of trouble. Flying to

England from here, it was theoretically possible to follow the coastlines of Denmark, Germany, Holland, Belgium and France. But Harald and Karen would be many miles out to sea, well away from German-occupied land. If anything went wrong, they would have nowhere to go.

Harald was still worrying when Karen slipped through the window, carrying a basket like Little Red Riding Hood. His heart leaped with pleasure at the sight of her. All day, as he worked on the aircraft, he had thought about the way they had kissed early this morning, after stealing the petrol. He kept touching his lips with his fingertips to bring back the memory.

Now she looked at the Hornet Moth and said: 'Wow.'

He was pleased to have impressed her. 'Pretty, isn't it?'

'But you can't get it through the door like that.'

'I know. I'll have to fold the wings again, then unfold them outside.'

'So why have you rigged them now?'

'For practice. I'll be able to do it faster the second time.'

'How fast?'

'I'm not sure.'

'What about the soldiers? If they see us . . .'

'They'll be asleep.'

She looked solemn. 'We're ready, aren't we?'

'We're ready.'

'When shall we go?'

'Tonight, of course.'

'Oh, my God.'

'Waiting just increases the chance that we'll be found out before we get away.'

'I know, but . . .'

'What?'

'I suppose I just didn't think it would come so quickly.' She took a package out of her basket and handed it to him absent-mindedly. 'I brought you some cold beef.' She fed him every night.

'Thanks.' He studied her carefully. 'You're not having second thoughts, are you?'

She shook her head decisively. 'No. I'm just remembering that it's three years since I sat in a pilot's seat.'

He went over to the work bench and selected a small hatchet and a ball of stout cord. He stowed them in the locker under the dashboard of the aircraft.

Karen said: 'What are they for?'

'If we come down in the sea, I figure the aircraft will sink, because of the weight of the engine. But the wings on their own would float. So if we could chop the wings off, we could lash them together for a makeshift raft.'

'In the North Sea? I think we'd die of cold before long.'

'It's better than drowning.'

She shivered. 'If you say so.'

'We ought to take some biscuits and a couple of bottles of water.'

'I'll get some from the kitchen. Speaking of water

482

... we're going to be in the air for more than six hours.'

'So?'

'How do we pee?'

'Open the door and hope for the best.'

'That's all right for you.'

He grinned. 'Sorry.'

She looked around and picked up a handful of old newspapers. 'Put these inside.'

'What for?'

'In case I have to pee.'

He frowned. 'I don't see how . . .'

'Pray that you never have to find out.'

He put the newspapers on the seat.

'Do we have any maps?' she asked.

'No. I assumed we would just fly west until we see land, and that will be England.'

She shook her head. 'It's quite difficult to know where you are in the air. I used to get lost just flying around here. Suppose we get blown off course? We could come down in France by mistake.'

'My God, I didn't think of that.'

'The only way to check your position is to compare the terrain features below you with a map. I'll see what we've got in the house.'

'OK.'

'I'd better go and get all the stuff we need.' She slipped out through the window again, carrying the empty basket.

Harald was too tense to eat the beef she had

brought him. He began to refold the wings. The process was quick, by design: the intention was that the gentleman owner would do this every night, and garage the aircraft alongside the family car.

To prevent the upper wing fouling the cabin roof when the wings were folded, the inner section of the trailing edge was hinged to swing up out of the way. So Harald's first step was to unlock the hinged sections and push them up.

On the underside of each upper wing was stowed a brace, called a jury strut, which Harald detached then fixed between the inner ends of the upper and lower wings, to prevent their collapsing together.

The wings were held in the flying position by L-shaped sliding pins in the front spars of all four wings. On the upper wings, the pin was locked in place by the jury strut, which Harald had now removed, so all he had to do was turn the pin through ninety degrees and pull it forward about four inches.

The pins on the lower wings were locked in place by leather straps. Harald undid the strap on the left wing, then turned the pin and pulled it.

As soon as it came free, the wing started to move.

Harald realized he should have expected this. In its parked position, with its tail on the ground, the aircraft was tilted, with its nose in the air; and now the heavy double wing was swinging backwards by force of gravity. He grabbed at it, terrified that it would crash against the fuselage and cause damage. He tried to seize the leading edge of the lower wing, but it was too thick for him to get a grasp. 'Hell!' he cried. He stepped forward, chasing the wing, and grabbed at the steel rigging wires between upper and lower wings. He got a purchase, and slowed the swing, then the wire bit into the skin of his hand. He cried out and automatically let go. The wing swivelled back and came to rest with a painful thud against the fuselage.

Cursing his carelessness, Harald went to the tail, took hold of the lower wing tip in both hands, and swung it out so that he could check for damage. To his intense relief there seemed to be none. The trailing edges of the upper and lower wings were intact, and the fuselage was unmarked. Nothing was broken but the skin of Harald's right hand.

Licking the blood from his hand, he went to the right side. This time he braced the lower wing with a tea-chest full of old magazines, so that it could not move. He pulled the pins, then walked around the wing, shoved the chest out of the way, and held the wing, allowing it to swing slowly back into the folded position.

Karen came back.

'Did you get everything?' Harald said anxiously.

She dropped her basket on the floor. 'We can't go tonight.'

'What?' He felt cheated. He had got scared for nothing. 'Why not?' he said angrily.

'I'm dancing tomorrow.'

'*Dancing?*' He was outraged. 'How can you put that before our mission?'

'It's really special. I told you I've been understudying the lead role. Half the company has gone down with some kind of gastric illness. There are two casts, but the leads in both are sick, so I've been called in. It's a great piece of luck!'

'Damn bad luck, it seems to me.'

'I'll be on the main stage at the Royal Theatre, and guess what? The King will be there!'

He ran his fingers through his hair distractedly. 'I can't believe you're saying this.'

'I reserved a ticket for you. You can pick it up at the box office.'

'I'm not going.'

'Don't be so grumpy! We can fly tomorrow night, after I dance. The ballet isn't on again for another week after that, and one of the other two is sure to be better by then.'

'I don't care about the damn ballet – what about the war? Heis reckoned the RAF must be planning a massive air raid. They need our photographs before then! Think of the lives at stake!'

She sighed, and her voice softened. 'I knew you would feel this way, and I thought about forgoing the opportunity, but I just can't. Anyway, if we fly tomorrow, we'll be in England three days before the full moon.'

'But we'll be in deadly danger here for an extra twenty-four hours!'

'Look, no one knows about this plane – why would they find out tomorrow?'

'It's possible.'

'Oh, don't be so childish, anything's *possible*.'

'Childish? The police are looking for me, you know

that. I'm a fugitive and I want to get out of this country as soon as I can.'

Now she was getting angry. 'You really ought to understand how I feel about this performance.'

'Well, I don't.'

'Look, I might die in this damn plane.'

'So might I.'

'While I'm drowning in the North Sea, or freezing to death on your makeshift raft, I'd like to be able to think that before I died I achieved my life's ambition, and danced wonderfully on the stage of the Royal Danish Theatre in front of the King. Can't you understand that?'

'No, I can't!'

'Then you can go to Hell,' she said, and she went out through the window.

Harald stared after her. He was thunderstruck. A minute passed before he moved. Then he looked inside the basket she had brought. There were two bottles of mineral water, a packet of crackers, a flashlight, a spare battery and two spare bulbs. There were no maps, but she had put in an old school atlas. He picked up the book and opened it. On the end-paper was written, in a girlish hand: 'Karen Duchwitz, Class 3.'

'Oh, Hell,' he said.

TWENTY-EIGHT

Peter Flemming stood on the quay at Morlunde, watching the last ferry of the day come in from Sande, waiting for a mystery woman.

He had been disappointed, though not really surprised, that Harald had not shown up yesterday for his brother's funeral. Peter had carefully scrutinized all the mourners. Most were islanders whom Peter had known since childhood. It was the others who interested him. After the service, taking tea in the parsonage, he had spoken to all the strangers. There were a couple of old school pals, some army buddies, friends from Copenhagen, and the headmaster of Jansborg Skole. He had ticked their names on the list given him by the policeman on the ferry. And he noticed one name not ticked: Miss Agnes Ricks.

Returning to the ferry dock, he had asked the policeman if Agnes Ricks had gone back to the mainland. 'Not yet,' the man had said. 'I'd remember her. She's a bit of all right.' He grinned and cupped his hands over his chest to signify large breasts.

Peter had gone to his father's hotel and learned that no Agnes Ricks had checked in.

He was intrigued. Who was Miss Ricks and what was

she doing? Instinct told him she had some connection with Arne Olufsen. Perhaps it was wishful thinking. But she was the only lead he had.

He was too conspicuous loitering at the quay on Sande, so he crossed to the mainland and made himself unobtrusive at the large commercial harbour there. However, Miss Ricks did not appear. Now, as the ferry docked for the last time until morning, Peter retired to the Oesterport Hotel.

There was a phone in a little booth in the hotel lobby, and he used it to call Tilde Jespersen at home in Copenhagen.

'Was Harald at the funeral?' she said immediately.

'No.'

'Damn.'

'I checked out the mourners. No clues there. But there's one more lead I'm following up, a Miss Agnes Ricks. What about you?'

'I've spent the day on the phone to local police stations all over the country. I've got men checking on each of Harald's classmates. I should hear from all of them tomorrow.'

'You walked off the job,' he said with an abrupt change of subject.

'It wasn't a normal job, though, was it?' She was obviously prepared for this.

'Why not?'

'You took me because you wanted to sleep with me.'

Peter ground his teeth. He had compromised his own professionalism by having sex with her, and now he could not admonish her. Angrily, he said: 'Is that your excuse?'

'It's not an excuse.'

'You said you disliked the way I interrogated the Olufsens. That's not a reason for a police officer to run away.'

'I didn't run away from the job. I just didn't want to sleep with a man who could do that.'

'I was just doing my duty!'

Her voice changed. 'Not quite.'

'What do you mean?'

'It would be all right if you had been tough just for the sake of getting the job done. I could respect that. But you liked what you were doing. You tortured the pastor and bullied his wife, and you enjoyed it. Their grief gave you satisfaction. I can't get into bed with a man like that.'

Peter hung up.

He spent much of the night awake, thinking about Tilde. Lying in bed, angry with her, he imagined himself slapping her. He would have liked to go to her apartment, and pull her out of bed in her nightgown, and punish her. In his fantasy she pleaded for mercy, but he ignored her cries. Her gown became torn in the struggle, and he became aroused and raped her. She screamed and fought him off, but he held her down. Afterwards, she begged forgiveness with tears in her eyes, but he left her without a word.

Eventually he fell asleep.

In the morning he went to the dock to meet the first ferry from Sande. He looked hopefully at the salt-caked boat as it steamed into the dock. Agnes Ricks was his only hope. If she turned out to be innocent, he was not sure what to do next.

A handful of passengers disembarked. Peter's plan had been to ask the policeman if one of them was Miss Ricks, but there was no need. He immediately noticed, among the men in work clothes headed for the early shift at the cannery, a tall woman wearing sunglasses and a headscarf. As she came closer, he realized he knew her. He saw black hair escaping from under the scarf, but it was the large, curved nose that gave her away. She walked with a confident, mannish stride, he observed, and he remembered noticing that gait when he first met her, two years before.

She was Hermia Mount.

She looked thinner and older than the woman who had been introduced as Arne Olufsen's fiancée back in 1939, but Peter had no doubt.

'You treacherous bitch, I've got you,' he said with profound satisfaction.

Anxious that she might recognize him, he put on heavy-rimmed glasses and pulled his hat forward to cover the distinctive red of his hair. Then he followed her to the station, where she bought a ticket to Copenhagen.

After a long wait they boarded an old, slow, coal-burning train that meandered across Denmark from west to east, stopping at half-timbered stations in seaweed-smelling resorts and sleepy market towns. Peter sat in a first-class carriage, fidgeting with impatience. Hermia was in the next carriage, in a third-class seat. She could not get away from him while they were on the train, but on the other hand he could make no progress until she got off.

It was mid-afternoon when the train pulled into Nyborg, on the central island of Fyn. From here they had to transfer to a ferry across the Great Belt to Zealand, the largest island, where they would board another train to Copenhagen.

Peter had heard talk of an ambitious plan to replace the ferry with a huge bridge twelve miles long. Traditionalists liked the numerous Danish ferries, saying their slow progress was part of the country's relaxed attitude to life, but Peter would have liked to scrap them all. He had a lot to do; he preferred bridges.

While waiting for the ferry, he found a phone and called Tilde at the Politigaarden.

She was coolly professional. 'I haven't found Harald, but I've got a clue.'

'Good!'

'Twice in the last month he's visited Kirstenslot, the home of the Duchwitz family.'

'Jews?'

'Yes. The local policeman recalls meeting him. He says Harald had a steam-driven motorcycle. But he swears Harald is not there now.'

'Make double sure. Go there yourself.'

'I was planning to.'

He wanted to talk to her about what she had said yesterday. Did she really mean that she could not sleep with him again? But he could not think of a way to raise the subject, so he kept talking about the case. 'I found Miss Ricks. She's Hermia Mount, Arne Olufsen's fiancée.'

'The English girl?'

'Yes.'

'Good news!'

'It is.' Peter was glad Tilde had not lost her enthusiasm for the case. 'She's on her way to Copenhagen now, and I'm following her.'

'Isn't there a chance she'll recognize you?'

'Yes.'

'In case she tries to give you the slip, why don't I meet the train?'

'I'd rather you go to Kirstenslot.'

'Maybe I can do both. Where are you?'

'Nyborg.'

'You're at least two hours away.'

'More. This train is torpid.'

'I can drive out to Kirstenslot, snoop around for an hour, and still meet you at the station.'

'Good,' he said. 'Do it.'

TWENTY-NINE

When Harald cooled down, he saw that Karen's decision to postpone their flight for a day was not completely mad. He put himself in her place by imagining that he had been offered the chance to perform an important experiment with the physicist Neils Bohr. He might have delayed the escape to England for the sake of such an opportunity. Perhaps he and Bohr together would change mankind's understanding of how the universe worked. If he were going to die, he would like to know he had done something like that.

Nevertheless he spent a tense day. He checked everything on the Hornet Moth twice. He studied the instrument panel, familiarizing himself with the gauges so that he could help Karen. The panel was not illuminated, for the aircraft was not designed to be used at night, so they would have to shine the torch on the dials to read the instruments. He practised folding and unfolding the wings, improving his time. He tried out his in-flight refuelling system, pouring a little petrol through the hose that led from the cabin, through the smashed-out window, into the tank. He watched the weather, which was fine, with patchy cloud and a light breeze. A three-quarter moon rose late in the afternoon. He put on clean clothes.

He was lying on his ledge bed, stroking Pinetop the cat, when someone rattled the big church door.

Harald sat upright, putting Pinetop on the floor, and listened.

He heard the voice of Per Hansen. 'I told you it was locked.'

A woman replied: 'All the more reason to look inside.'

The voice was authoritative, Harald noted fearfully. He pictured a woman in her thirties, attractive but businesslike. Obviously she was with the police. Presumably she had sent Hansen to look for Harald at the castle yesterday. Clearly she had not been satisfied with Hansen's inquiries and had come herself today.

Harald cursed. She would probably be more thorough than Hansen. It would not take her long to find a way into the church. There was nowhere for him to hide except the trunk of the Rolls-Royce, and any serious searcher was sure to open that.

Harald was afraid he might already be too late to exit by his usual window, which was just around the corner from the main door. But there were windows all around the curved chancel, and he quickly made his escape through one of those.

When he hit the ground, he looked around warily. This end of the church was only partly concealed by trees, and he might have been seen by a soldier; but he was in luck, and no one was nearby.

He hesitated. He wanted to get away, but he needed

to know what happened next. He flattened himself against the wall of the church and listened. He heard Hansen's voice say: 'Mrs Jespersen? If we stand on that log we could get through the window.'

'No doubt that's why the log is there,' the woman replied crisply. She was obviously a lot smarter than Hansen. Harald had a dreadful feeling she was going to learn everything.

He heard the scrape of feet on the wall, a grunt from Hansen as, presumably, he squeezed himself through the window, then a thud as he hit the tiled floor of the church. A lighter thud followed a few seconds afterwards.

Harald crept around the side of the church, stood on the log, and peeped through the window.

Mrs Jespersen was a pretty woman of about thirty, not fat but well rounded, smartly dressed in practical clothes, a blouse and skirt with flat shoes and a sky-blue beret over her blonde curls. As she was not in uniform, she must be a detective, Harald deduced. She carried a shoulder bag which presumably had a gun in it.

Hansen was red-faced from the exertion of getting through the window, and he looked harassed. Harald guessed the village policeman was finding it a strain dealing with the quick-thinking detective.

She looked first at the bike. 'Well, here's the motorcycle you told me about. I see the steam engine. Ingenious.'

'He must have left it here,' Hansen said in a

defensive tone. Obviously he had told the detective that Harald had gone away.

But she was not convinced. 'Perhaps.' She moved to the car. 'Very nice.'

'It belongs to the Jew.'

She ran a finger along the curve of a mudguard and looked at the dust. 'He hasn't been out in it for a while.'

'Of course not – its wheels are off.' Hansen thought he had caught her out, and looked pleased.

'That doesn't mean much – wheels can be put on quickly. But it's difficult to fake a layer of dust.'

She crossed the room and picked up Harald's discarded shirt. He groaned inwardly. Why had he not put it away somewhere? She sniffed it.

Pinetop appeared from somewhere and rubbed his head against Mrs Jespersen's leg. She stooped to stroke him. 'What are you after?' she said to the cat. 'Has someone been feeding you?'

Nothing could be hidden from this woman, Harald saw with dismay. She was too thorough. She moved to the ledge where Harald slept. She picked up his neatly folded blanket, then put it down again. 'Someone's living here,' she said.

'Perhaps it's a vagrant.'

'And perhaps it's Harald fucking Olufsen.'

Hansen looked shocked.

She turned to the Hornet Moth. 'What have we here?' Harald watched in despair as she pulled off the cover. 'I do believe it's an aeroplane.'

497

That's the end, Harald thought. It's all over now.

Hansen said: 'Duchwitz used to have a plane, I remember now. He hasn't flown it for years, though.'

'It's not in bad condition.'

'It's got no wings!'

'The wings are folded back – that's how they got it through the door.' Reaching inside the cabin, she moved the control stick, looking at the tailplane at the same time, seeing the elevator move. 'The controls seem to work.' She peered at the fuel gauge. 'The tank is full.' Looking around the little cabin, she added: 'And there's a four-gallon can behind the seat. And the locker contains two bottles of water and a packet of biscuits. Plus an axe, a ball of good strong cord, a flashlight, and an atlas – with no dust on any of them.'

She withdrew her head from the cabin and looked at Hansen. 'Harald is planning to fly.'

'Well, I'm damned,' said Hansen.

The wild thought of killing them both occurred to Harald. He was not sure he could kill another human being in any circumstances, but he immediately realized he could not overpower two armed police officers with his bare hands, and he dismissed the thought.

Mrs Jespersen became very brisk. 'I have to go into Copenhagen. Inspector Flemming, who's in charge of this case, is coming in by train. Given the way the railways are nowadays, he could arrive any time in the next twelve hours. When he does, we'll come back.

We'll arrest Harald, if he's here, and set a trap for him if he's not.'

'What do you want me to do?'

'Stay here. Find a vantage point in the woods, and watch the church. If Harald appears, don't speak to him, just phone the Politigaarden.'

'Aren't you going to send someone to help me?'

'No. We mustn't do anything to scare Harald off. If he sees you, he won't panic – you're just the village policeman. But a couple of strange cops might spook him. I don't want him to run away and hide somewhere. Now that we've tracked him down, we mustn't lose him again. Is that clear?'

'Yes.'

'On the other hand, if he tries to fly that plane, stop him.'

'Arrest him?'

'Shoot him, if you have to – but don't for God's sake let him take off.'

Harald found her matter-of-fact tone absolutely terrifying. If she had been over-dramatic, he might not have felt so scared. But she was an attractive woman speaking calmly about practicalities – and she had just told Hansen to shoot him if necessary. Until this moment, Harald had not confronted the possibility that the police might simply kill him. Mrs Jespersen's quiet mercilessness shook him.

'You can open this door, to save me scrambling through the window again,' she said. 'Lock it up when I've gone, so that Harald won't suspect anything.'

Hansen turned the key and removed the bar, and they went out.

Harald jumped to the ground and retreated around the end of the church. Moving away from the building, he stood behind a tree and watched from a distance as Mrs Jespersen walked to her car, a black Buick. She looked at her reflection in the car's window and adjusted her sky-blue beret in a very feminine gesture. Then she reverted to cop mode, shook hands briskly with Hansen, got into the car and drove away fast.

Hansen came back, and disappeared from Harald's view, screened by the church.

Harald leaned against the trunk of the tree for a moment, thinking. Karen had promised to come to the church as soon as she got home from the ballet. If she did that she might find the police waiting for her. And how would she explain what she was doing? Her guilt would be obvious.

Harald had to head her off somehow. Thinking about the best way to intercept her and warn her, he decided the simplest thing would be to go to the theatre. That way he could be sure he would not miss her.

He felt a moment of anger towards her. If they had taken off last night they might be in England now. He had warned her that she was putting them both in danger, and now he had been proved right. But recriminations were fruitless. It was done, and he had to deal with the consequences.

Unexpectedly, Hansen came walking around the

corner of the church. He saw Harald and stopped dead.

They were both astonished. Harald had thought Hansen had gone back into the church to lock up. Hansen, for his part, could not have imagined that his quarry was so close. They stared at each other for a paralysed moment.

Then Hansen reached for his gun.

Mrs Jespersen's words flashed through Harald's mind: 'Shoot him, if you have to.' Hansen, a village constable, had probably never shot at anyone in his life. But he might jump at the chance.

Harald reacted instinctively. Without thought for the consequences, he rushed at Hansen. As Hansen drew his pistol from the holster, Harald cannoned into him. Hansen was thrown back, and hit the church wall with a thud, but he did not lose his grip on the gun.

He raised the gun to point it. Harald knew he had only a fraction of a second to save himself. He drew back his fist and hit Hansen on the point of the chin. The blow had the force of desperation behind it. Hansen's head jerked back and hit the brickwork with a sound like the crack of a rifle. His eyes rolled up, his body slumped, and he fell to the ground.

Harald was dreadfully afraid the man was dead. He knelt beside the unconscious body. He saw immediately that Hansen was breathing. Thank God, he thought. It was horrifying to think he might have killed a man – even a vicious fool such as Hansen.

The fight had lasted only a few seconds, but had it

been observed? He looked across the park to the soldiers' encampment. A few men were walking around, but no one was looking Harald's way.

He stuffed Hansen's gun into his pocket then lifted the limp body. Slinging it over his shoulder in a fireman's lift, he hurried around the church to the main door, which was still open. His luck held, and no one saw him.

He put Hansen down, then quickly closed and locked the church door. He got the cord out of the cabin of the Hornet Moth and tied Hansen's feet together. He rolled the man over and tied his hands behind his back. Then he picked up his discarded shirt, stuffed half of it in Hansen's mouth so the man could not cry out, and tied string around Hansen's head so that the gag would not fall out.

Finally he put Hansen in the boot of the Rolls-Royce and closed the lid.

He looked at his watch. He still had time to get to the city and warn Karen.

He lit the boiler on his motorcycle. He might well be seen driving out of the church, but there was no longer any time for caution.

However, he could get into trouble with a policeman's gun making a bulge in his pocket. Not knowing what to do with the pistol, he opened the right door of the Hornet Moth and put it on the floor, where no one would see it unless they got in the aircraft and trod on it.

When the motorcycle engine had a head of steam he opened the doors, drove the bike out, locked up from inside and exited by the window. He was lucky, and saw no one.

He drove into the city, keeping a nervous eye out for policemen, and parked at the side of the Royal Theatre. A red carpet led up to the entrance, and he recalled that the King was attending this performance. A notice informed him that *Les Sylphides* was the last of three ballets on the programme. A crowd of well-dressed people stood on the steps with drinks, and Harald gathered that he had arrived during the interval.

He went to the stage door, where he encountered an obstacle. The entrance was guarded by a uniformed commissionaire. 'I need to speak to Karen Duchwitz,' Harald said.

'Out of the question,' the commissionaire told him. 'She's about to go on stage.'

'It's really important.'

'You'll have to wait until afterwards.'

Harald could see that the man was immovable. 'How long is the ballet?'

'About half an hour, depending how fast the orchestra play.'

Harald remembered that Karen had left a ticket for him at the box office. He decided he would watch her dance.

He went into the marble foyer, got his ticket, and entered the auditorium. He had never been in a theatre before, and he gazed in wonder at the lavish gilded decoration, the rising tiers of the circle, and the rows of red plush seats. He found his place in the fourth row and sat down. There were two German officers in uniform immediately in front of him. He checked his watch. Why did the ballet not start? Every minute brought Peter Flemming nearer.

He picked up a programme that had been left on the seat beside him and flicked through it, looking for Karen's name. She was not on the cast list, but a slip of paper which fell out of the booklet said that the prima ballerina was indisposed and her place would be taken by Karen Duchwitz. It also revealed that the lone male dancer in the ballet would also be played by an understudy, Jan Anders, presumably because the principal man had also fallen victim to the gastric illness that had spread through the cast. This must be a worrying moment for the company, Harald thought, the leading roles being taken by students when the King was in the audience.

A few moments later he was startled to see Mr and Mrs Duchwitz take their seats two rows in front of him. He should have known they would not miss their daughter's big moment. At first he worried that they would see him. Then he realized it no longer mattered. Now that the police had found his hiding-place, he did not need to keep it secret from anyone else.

He remembered guiltily that he was wearing Mr Duchwitz's American sports jacket. It was fifteen years old, according to the tailor's label in the inside pocket, but Karen had not actually asked her father's permission to take it. Would Pa Duchwitz recognize it? Harald told himself he was foolish even to think about it. Being accused of stealing a jacket was the least thing he had to worry about.

He touched the roll of film in his pocket and wondered if there was any chance he and Karen could still escape in the Hornet Moth. A lot depended on Peter Flemming's train. If it came in early, Flemming and Mrs Jespersen would be back at Kirstenslot before Harald and Karen. Perhaps they could avoid getting caught, but it was hard to see how they could get access to the aircraft with the police watching over it. On the other hand, with Hansen out of the way there was no guard on the aircraft at the moment. If Flemming's train did not get in until the early hours of the morning, perhaps there was a chance they could yet take off.

Mrs Jespersen did not know that Harald had seen her. She thought she had plenty of time. That was the only thing in Harald's favour.

When would the damn show start?

After everyone was seated in the auditorium, the King came into the royal box. The audience stood up. It was the first time Harald had seen King Christian X in person, but the face was familiar from photographs, the downturned moustache giving it a permanently grim expression that was appropriate to the monarch of an occupied country. He was in evening dress and stood very upright. In pictures the King always wore some kind of hat, and now Harald saw for the first time that he was losing his hair.

When the King sat, the audience followed suit, and the lights went down. At last, Harald thought.

The curtain rose on twenty or more women motionless in a circle and one man standing at the twelve o'clock position. The dancers, all dressed in white, posed in a pale blueish light like moonlight, and the bare stage disappeared into dark shadows at its edges. It was a dramatic opening, and Harald was fascinated despite his worries.

The music played a slow, descending phrase, and the dancers moved. The circle widened, leaving four people motionless upstage, the man and three women. One of the women lay on the ground as if asleep. A slow waltz began.

Where was Karen? All the girls were in identical dresses, with tight bodices that left their shoulders bare, and full skirts that billowed as they danced. It was a sexy outfit, but the atmospheric lighting made them all look the same, and Harald could not tell which was Karen.

Then the sleeping one moved, and he recognized Karen's red hair. She glided to the centre of the stage. Harald was taut with anxiety, fearing she would do something wrong and spoil her great day; but she seemed assured and controlled. She began to dance on the tips of her toes. It looked painful, and made Harald wince, but she seemed to float. The company formed patterns around her, lines and circles. The audience was silent and still, captivated by her, and Harald's heart filled with pride. He was glad she had decided to do this, no matter what the consequences.

The music changed key and the male dancer

moved. As he leaped across the stage, Harald thought he seemed uncertain and remembered that he, too, was an understudy, Anders. Karen had danced with confidence, making every move seem effortless, but there was tension in the boy's movements that gave his dancing a sense of risk.

The dance closed with the slow phrase that had opened it, and Harald realized there was no story, the dances would be as abstract as the music. He checked his watch. Only five minutes had passed.

The ensemble dispersed and reformed in new configurations that framed a series of solo dances. All the music seemed to be in three-four time, and very melodic. Harald, who loved the discords of jazz, found it almost too sweet.

The ballet fascinated him, but nevertheless his mind wandered to the Hornet Moth, and Hansen tied up in the boot of the Rolls, and Mrs Jespersen. Could Peter Flemming have found the only punctual train in Denmark? If so, had he and Mrs Jespersen gone to Kirstenslot yet? Had they found Hansen? Were they already lying in wait? How could Harald check? Perhaps he would approach the monastery through the woods, in the hope of spotting any ambush.

Karen began a solo dance, and he found himself more tense about her than about the police. He need not have worried: she was relaxed and self-possessed, swirling and tiptoeing and leaping as happily as if she were making it up as she went along. He was astonished at how she could perform some vigorous step, running or jumping across the stage, then come to an abrupt stop in a perfectly graceful pose, as if she had no inertia. She seemed to flout the laws of physics.

Harald became even more nervous when Karen began a dance with Jan Anders. It was called a *pas de deux*, he thought, although he was not sure how he knew that. Anders kept lifting her dramatically high in the air. Her skirt would billow up, showing her fabulous legs. Anders would hold her up, sometimes with one hand, while he struck a pose or moved around the stage. Harald feared for her safety, but again and again she came down with ease and grace. Nevertheless Harald was relieved when the *pas de deux* ended and the ensemble began. He checked his watch again. This must be the last dance, thank God.

Anders performed several spectacular leaps during the last dance, and reprised some of his lifts with Karen. Then, as the music built to a climax, disaster struck.

Anders lifted Karen again, then held her in the air with his hand in the small of her back. She stretched out parallel to the ground. Her legs curved forward with pointed toes, and her arms reached backwards over her head, making an arch. They held the pose for a moment. Then Anders slipped.

His left foot shot out from under him. He staggered and fell flat on his back. Karen tumbled to the stage beside him, landing on her right arm and leg.

The audience gasped with horror. The other dancers rushed to the two fallen figures. The music played on for a few bars then died away. A man in black trousers and a black sweater came on from the wings.

Anders got to his feet, holding his elbow, and Harald saw that he was crying. Karen tried to get up but fell back. The figure in black made a gesture, and the curtain came down. The audience burst into excited chatter.

Harald realized he was standing up.

He saw Mr and Mrs Duchwitz, two rows in front of him, get to their feet and push urgently along the row, excusing themselves to the people they were passing. They were obviously intending to go backstage. Harald decided to do the same.

It was painfully slow getting out of the row of seats. In his anxiety, he had to restrain himself from simply walking along everyone's knees. But he reached the aisle at the same time as the Duchwitzes. 'I'm coming with you,' he said.

'Who are you?' said her father.

Her mother answered the question. 'It's Josef's friend Harald, you've met him before, Karen is sweet on him, let him come.'

Mr Duchwitz grunted assent. Harald had no idea how Mrs Duchwitz knew that Karen was 'sweet' on him, but he was relieved to be accepted as part of the family.

As they reached the exit, the audience fell silent. The Duchwitzes and Harald turned at the door. The curtain had come up. The stage was empty but for the man in black.

'Your majesty, ladies and gentlemen,' he began. 'By

good fortune, the company doctor was in the audience tonight.' Harald guessed that everyone associated with the ballet company would want to be present for a royal performance. 'The doctor is already backstage, and is examining our two principals. He has told me that neither appears to be gravely injured.'

There was a scatter of applause.

Harald was relieved. Now that he knew she was going to be all right, he thought for the first time about how the accident might affect their escape. Even if they could get at the Hornet Moth, would Karen be able to fly it?

The man in black resumed. 'As you know from your programme, both lead roles were played by understudies tonight, as were many of the other parts. Nevertheless, I hope you agree with me that they all danced wonderfully well, and gave a superb performance almost to the very end. Thank you.'

The curtain came down, and the audience applauded. It came up again to reveal the cast, minus Karen and Anders, and they took a bow.

The Duchwitzes went out, and Harald followed.

They hurried to the stage door. An usher took them to Karen's dressing room.

She was sitting with her right arm in a sling. She looked stunningly beautiful in the creamy-white gown, with her shoulders bare and the rise of her breasts showing above the bodice. Harald felt breathless, and did not know whether the cause was anxiety or desire.

The doctor was kneeling in front of her, wrapping a bandage around her right ankle.

Mrs Duchwitz rushed to Karen, saying: 'My poor baby!' She put her arms around Karen and hugged her. It was what Harald would have liked to do.

'Oh, I'm all right,' Karen said, though she looked pale.

Mr Duchwitz spoke to the doctor. 'How is she?'

'She's fine,' the man said. 'She's sprained her wrist and ankle. They'll be painful for a few days, and she must take it easy for at least two weeks, but she'll get over it.'

Harald was relieved that her injuries were not serious, but his immediate thought was: Can she fly?

The doctor fastened the bandage with a safety pin and stood up. He patted her bare shoulder. 'I'd better go and see Jan Anders. He didn't fall as hard as you, but I'm a bit worried about his elbow.'

'Thank you, doctor.'

His hand lingered on her shoulder, to Harald's annoyance. 'You'll dance as wonderfully as ever, don't you worry.' He left.

Karen said: 'Poor Jan, he can't stop crying.'

Harald thought Anders should be shot. 'It was his fault – he dropped you!' he said indignantly.

'I know, that's why he's so upset.'

Mr Duchwitz looked at Harald with irritation. 'What are you doing here?'

Once again it was his wife who answered. 'Harald has been living at Kirstenslot.'

Karen was shocked. 'Mother, how did you know?'

'Do you think nobody noticed how the leftovers disappeared from the kitchen every night? We mothers aren't stupid, you know.'

Mr Duchwitz said: 'But where does he sleep?'

'In the disused church, I expect,' his wife replied. 'That would be why Karen was so keen to keep it locked.'

Harald was horrified that his secret had been so easily unveiled. Mr Duchwitz was looking angry but, before he could explode, the King walked in.

Everyone fell silent.

Karen tried to stand up, but he stopped her. 'My dear girl, please stay just where you are. How do you feel?'

'It hurts, your majesty.'

'I'm sure it does. But no permanent damage, I gather?'

'That's what the doctor said.'

'You danced divinely, you know.'

'Thank you, sir.'

The King looked inquiringly at Harald. 'Good evening, young man.'

'I'm Harald Olufsen, your majesty, a school friend of Karen's brother.'

'Which school?'

'Jansborg Skole.'

'Do they still call the headmaster Heis?'

'Yes – and his wife Mia.'

'Well, be sure to take good care of Karen.' He turned to the parents. 'Hello, Duchwitz, it's good to see you again. Your daughter is marvellously talented.'

'Thank you, your majesty. You remember my wife, Hanna.'

'Of course.' The King shook her hand. 'This is very worrying for a mother, Mrs Duchwitz, but I'm sure Karen will be all right.'

'Yes, your majesty. The young heal fast.'

'Indeed they do! Now, then, let's have a look at the poor fellow who dropped her.' The King moved to the door.

For the first time, Harald noticed the King's companion, a young man who was assistant, or bodyguard, or perhaps both. 'This way, sir,' said the young man, and he held the door.

The King went out.

'Well!' said Mrs Duchwitz in a thrilled voice. 'How very charming!'

Mr Duchwitz said: 'I suppose we'd better get Karen home.'

Harald wondered when he would get a chance to speak to her alone.

Karen said: 'Mother will have to help me out of this dress.'

Mr Duchwitz moved to the door, and Harald followed him, not knowing what else to do.

Karen said: 'Before I change, do you mind if I have a word alone with Harald?'

Her father looked irritated, but her mother said: 'All right – just be quick.' They left the room, and Mrs Duchwitz closed the door.

'Are you really all right?' Harald asked Karen.

'I will be when you've kissed me.'

He knelt beside the chair and kissed her lips. Then, unable to resist the temptation, he kissed her bare shoulders and her throat. His lips travelled downwards, and he kissed the swell of her breasts.

'Oh, my goodness, stop, it's too nice,' she said.

Reluctantly, Harald drew back. He saw that the colour had returned to her face, and she was breathless. He was amazed to think his kisses had done that.

'We have to talk,' she said.

'I know. Are you fit to fly the Hornet Moth?'

'No.'

He had feared as much. 'Are you sure?'

'It hurts too much. I can't even open a damn door. And I can hardly walk, so I couldn't possibly operate the rudder with my feet.'

Harald buried his face in his hands. 'Then it's all over.'

'The doctor said it would only hurt for a few days. We could go as soon as I feel better.'

'There's something I haven't told you yet. Hansen came snooping around again tonight.'

'I wouldn't worry about him.'

'This time he was with a woman detective, Mrs Jespersen, who is a lot cleverer. I listened to their conversation. She went into the church and figured out everything. She guessed that I'm living there and that I'm planning to escape in the aircraft.'

'Oh, no! What did she do?'

'Went to fetch her boss, who happens to be Peter Flemming. She left Hansen on guard and told him to shoot me if I try to take off.'

'To *shoot* you? What are you going to do?'

'I knocked Hansen out and tied him up,' Harald said, not without a touch of pride.

'Oh, my God! Where is he now?'

'In the boot of your father's car.'

She found that funny. 'You fiend!'

'I thought we had just one chance. Peter is on a train and she didn't know when he would get in. If you and I could have got back to Kirstenslot tonight before Peter and Mrs Jespersen, we could still have taken off. But now that you can't fly . . .'

'We could still do it.'

'How?'

'You can be the pilot.'

'I can't – I've only had one lesson!'

'I'll talk you through everything. Poul said you had a natural talent for it. And I could operate the control stick with my left hand some of the time.'

'Do you really mean it?'

'Yes!'

'All right.' Harald nodded solemnly. 'That's what we'll do. Just pray for Peter's train to be late.'

THIRTY

Hermia had spotted Peter Flemming on the ferry.

She saw him leaning on the rail, looking at the sea, and recalled a man with a ginger moustache and a smart tweed suit on the platform at Morlunde. No doubt several people from Morlunde were travelling all the way to Copenhagen, as she was, but the man looked vaguely familiar. The hat and glasses put her off for a while, but eventually her memory dredged him up: Peter Flemming.

She had met him with Arne, in the happy days. The two men had been boyhood friends, she seemed to recall, then had fought when their families quarrelled.

Now Peter was a cop.

As soon as she remembered that, she realized he must be following her. She felt a chill of fear like a cold wind.

She was running out of time. The full moon was three nights away, and she still had not found Harald Olufsen. If she got the film from him tonight, she was not sure how she could get it home in time. But she was not going to give up – for the sake of Arne's memory, for the sake of Digby, and for all the airmen risking their lives to stop the Nazis.

But why had Peter not arrested her already? She was a British spy. What was he up to? Perhaps, like her, Peter was looking for Harald.

When the ferry docked, Peter followed her on to the Copenhagen train. As soon as the train got going, she walked along the corridor, and spotted him in a first-class compartment.

She returned to her seat, worried. This was a very bad development. She must not lead Peter to Harald. She had to throw him off.

She had plenty of time to think about how. The train was delayed repeatedly, and got into Copenhagen at ten o'clock in the evening. By the time it pulled into the station, she had made a plan. She would go into the Tivoli Garden and lose Peter in the crowd.

As she left the train, she glanced back along the platform and saw Peter stepping down from the first-class carriage.

She walked at a normal pace up the stairs from the platform, through the ticket barrier and out of the station. It was dusk. The Tivoli Garden was a few steps from the station. She went to the main entrance and bought a ticket. 'Closing at midnight,' the vendor warned her.

She had come here with Arne in the summer of 1939. It had been a festival night, and fifty thousand people had crammed into the park to watch the fireworks. Now the place was a sad version of its former self, like a black-and-white photograph of a bowl of fruit. The paths still wound charmingly between flower beds, but the fairy lights in the trees had been switched off, and the paths were illuminated by special low-intensity lamps to conform with blackout regulations. The air raid shelter outside the Pantomime Theatre added a dismal touch. Even the bands seemed muted. Most dismaying for Hermia, the crowds were not as dense, making it easier for someone to follow her.

She stopped, pretending to watch a juggler, and glanced back. She saw Peter close behind her, buying a glass of beer from a stall. How was she going to shake him off?

She moved into a crowd around an open-air stage on which an operetta was being sung. She pushed her way through to the front then out at the far side but, when she walked on, Peter was still behind her. If this went on much longer, he would realize she was trying to lose him. Then he might cut his losses and arrest her.

She began to feel frightened. She circled the lake and came to an open-air dance floor where a large orchestra was playing a foxtrot. There were at least a hundred couples dancing energetically, and many more watching. Hermia at last felt something of the atmosphere of the old Tivoli. Seeing a good-looking young man standing alone at the side, she was inspired. She went up to him and turned on her biggest smile. 'Would you like to dance with me?' she said.

'Of course!' He took her in his arms and they were off. Hermia was not a good dancer, but she could get by with a competent partner. Arne had been superb, stylish and masterful. This man was confident and decisive.

'What's your name?' he said.

She almost told him, then stopped herself at the last minute. 'Agnes.'

'I am Johan.'

'I'm very happy to meet you, Johan, and you foxtrot wonderfully.' She looked back to the path and saw Peter watching the dancers.

Inconveniently, the tune came to an abrupt end. The dancers applauded the orchestra. Some couples left the floor and others came on. Hermia said: 'Another dance?'

'It would be my pleasure.'

She decided to level with him. 'Listen, there's a horrid man following me and I'm trying to get away from him. Will you steer us all the way over to the far side?'

'How exciting!' He looked across the floor to the spectators. 'Which one is it? That fat man with the red face?'

'No. The one in the light brown suit.'

'I see him. He's quite handsome.'

The band struck up a polka. 'Oh, dear,' said Hermia. The polka was difficult, but she had to try.

Johan was expert enough to make it easier for her. He could also converse at the same time. 'The man who is bothering you – is he a complete stranger, or someone you know?'

'I have met him before. Take me to the far end, by the orchestra – that's right.'

'Is he your boyfriend?'

'No. I'm going to leave you in a minute, Johan. If he runs after me, will you trip him up, or something?'

'If you wish.'

'Thank you.'

'I think he is your husband.'

'Absolutely not.' They were close to the orchestra. Johan steered her to the edge of the dance floor. 'Perhaps you are a spy, and he is a policeman hoping to catch you stealing military secrets from the Nazis.'

'Something like that,' she said gaily, and she slipped from his arms.

She walked quickly off the floor and around the bandstand into the trees. She ran across the grass until she came to another path, then she made for a side exit. She looked back: Peter was not behind her.

She left the park and hurried to the suburban railway station across the street from the main line terminus. She bought a ticket for Kirstenslot. She felt exhilarated. She had shaken Peter off.

There was no one on the platform with her but an attractive woman in a sky-blue beret.

THIRTY-ONE

Harald approached the church cautiously.

There had been a shower, and the grass was wet, but the rain had stopped. A light breeze blew the clouds along, and a three-quarter moon shone brightly through the gaps. The shadow of the bell tower came and went with the moonlight.

He saw no strange cars parked nearby, but that did not much reassure him. The police would have concealed their vehicles if they were serious about setting a trap.

There were no lights anywhere in the ruined monastery. It was midnight, and the soldiers were in bed, all but two: the sentry in the park outside the mess tent, and a veterinary nurse on duty in the horse hospital.

Harald listened outside the church. He heard a horse snort in the cloisters. With utmost caution, he stood on the log and peeped over the windowsill.

He could see the vague outlines of the car and the aircraft in the dim reflected moonlight. There could be someone hiding in there, lying in wait.

He heard a muffled grunt and a thud. The noise was repeated after a minute, and he guessed it was

Hansen, struggling with his bonds. Harald's heart leaped with hope. If Hansen was still tied up, that meant Mrs Jespersen had not yet returned with Peter. There was still a chance Harald and Karen could take off in the Hornet Moth.

He slipped through the window and padded across the floor to the aircraft. He got the flashlight out of the cabin and shone it around the church. There was no one here.

He opened the boot of the car. Hansen was still tied and gagged. Harald checked the knots. They were holding firm. He closed the boot again.

He heard a loud whisper: 'Harald! Is that you?'

He shone the torch on the windows and saw Karen looking through.

She had been brought home in an ambulance. Her parents had ridden with her. Before they parted, at the theatre, she had promised to slip out of the house as soon as she could, and join him in the church if the coast was clear.

He turned off the torch, then opened the big church door for her. She limped in, wearing a fur coat over her shoulders and carrying a blanket. He put his arms around her gently, careful of her right arm in its sling, and hugged her. For a brief moment he thrilled to the warmth of her body and the scent of her hair.

Then he returned to practicalities. 'How do you feel?'

'I hurt like hell, but I'll live.'

He looked at her coat. 'Are you cold?'

'Not yet, but I will be at five thousand feet over the North Sea. The blanket is for you.'

He took the blanket from her and held her good hand. 'Are you ready to do this?'

'Yes.'

He kissed her softly. 'I love you.'

'I love you, too.'

'Do you? You've never said that before.'

'I know – I'm telling you now in case I don't survive this trip,' she said in her usual matter-of-fact tone. 'You're the best man I've ever met, by a factor of ten. You're brainy, but you never put people down. You're gentle and kind, but you've got courage enough for an army.' She touched his hair. 'You're even nice-looking, in a funny way. What more could I want?'

'Some girls like a man to be well dressed.'

'Good point. We can fix that, though.'

'I'd like to tell you why I love you, but the police could get here any minute.'

'That's all right, I know why, it's because I'm wonderful.'

Harald opened the cabin door and tossed the blanket in. 'You'd better get on board now,' he said. 'The less we have to do once we're outside in plain view, the more chance we have of getting away.'

'OK.'

He saw that it was going to be difficult for her to get into the cabin. He dragged a box over, and she stood on it, but then she could not put her injured foot inside. Getting in was awkward anyway – the cabin was more cramped than the front seat of a small car –

and it seemed impossible with two injured limbs. Harald realized he would have to lift her in.

He picked her up with his left arm under her shoulders and his right under her knees, then he stood on the box and eased her into the passenger seat on the right-hand side of the cabin. That way, she could operate the Y-shaped central control stick with her good left hand, and Harald, beside her in the pilot's seat, would be able to use his right.

'What's this on the floor?' she said, reaching down.

'Hansen's gun. I didn't know what else to do with it.' He closed the door. 'Are you OK?'

She slid the window open. 'I'm fine. The best place to take off will be along the drive. The wind is just right, but blowing towards the castle, so you're going to have to push the aircraft all the way to the door of the castle, then turn it around to take off into the wind.'

'OK.'

He opened the church doors wide. Next he had to get the aircraft out. Fortunately it had been parked intelligently, pointing directly at the door. There was a length of rope firmly tied to the undercarriage which, Harald had surmised when he first saw it, was used to pull the aircraft. He got a firm grasp on the rope and heaved.

The Hornet Moth was heavier than he had thought. As well as its engine, it was carrying thirty-nine gallons of petrol plus Karen. That was a lot to pull.

To overcome its inertia, Harald managed to rock the aircraft on its wheels, get a rhythm going, then heave it into motion. Once it was moving, the strain was less, but it was still heavy. With considerable effort he pulled it out of the church into the park and got it as far as the drive.

The moon came from behind a cloud. The park was lit up almost like day. The aircraft was in full view of anyone who looked in the right direction. Harald had to work fast.

He undid the catch holding the left wing against the fuselage and swung the wing into position. Next, he flipped down the foldaway flap at the inner end of the upper wing. That held the wing in place while he moved around the wing to the front edge. There he turned the lower wing pin and eased it into its slot. It seemed to catch against an obstruction. He had encountered this problem when practising. He wiggled the wing gently, and that enabled him to slide the pin home. He locked it with the leather strap. He repeated the exercise with the upper wing pin, locking it by stowing the jury strut.

It had taken him three or four minutes. He looked across the park to the soldiers' encampment. The sentry had seen him and was walking over.

He went through the same procedure with the right wing. By the time he had finished, the sentry was standing behind him, watching. It was friendly Leo. 'What are you doing?' he said curiously.

Harald had a story ready. 'We're going to take a photograph. Mr Duchwitz wants to sell the aircraft because he can't get fuel for it.'

'Photography? At night?'

'It's a moonlight shot, with the castle in the background.'

'Does my captain know?'

'Oh, yes, Mr Duchwitz spoke to him, and Captain Kleiss said there would be no problem.'

'Oh, good,' Leo said, then he frowned again. 'It's strange that the captain didn't tell me about it, though.'

'He probably didn't think it was important.' Harald realized he was probably on a loser. If the German military were careless, they would not have conquered Europe.

Leo shook his head. 'A sentry must be briefed on any unusual events scheduled to take place during his watch,' he said as if repeating from a rule book.

'I'm sure Mr Duchwitz wouldn't have told us to do this without speaking to Captain Kleiss.' Harald leaned on the tailplane, pushing.

Seeing him struggle to move the tail, Leo helped him. Together they swung the back around in a quarter-circle so that the aircraft was facing along the drive.

Leo said: 'I'd better check with the captain.'

'If you're sure he won't mind being woken up.'

Leo looked doubtful and worried. 'Perhaps he's not asleep yet.'

Harald knew that the officers slept in the castle. He thought of a way to delay Leo and speed up his own task. 'Well, if you've got to go all the way to the castle, you could help me move this crate.'

'OK.'

'I'll take the left wing, you take the right.'

Leo shouldered his rifle and leaned on the metal strut between the upper and lower wings. With the two of them pushing, the Hornet Moth moved more easily.

* * *

Hermia caught the last train of the evening from the Vesterport station. It pulled into Kirstenslot after midnight.

She was not sure what to do when she reached the castle. She did not want to call attention to herself by banging on the door and waking the household. She might have to wait until morning before asking for Harald. That would mean spending the night in the open. But that would not kill her. On the other hand, if there were lights on in the castle she might find someone with whom she could have a discreet word, a servant perhaps. And she was nervous about losing precious time.

One other person got off the train with her. It was the woman in the sky-blue beret.

She suffered a moment of fear. Had she made a mistake? Could this woman be following her, having taken over from Peter Flemming?

She would just have to check.

Outside the darkened station she stopped and opened her suitcase, pretending to search for something. If the woman were tailing her she, too, would have to find a pretext for waiting.

527

The woman came out of the station and walked past her without hesitating.

Hermia continued to fumble in her case while watching from the corner of her eye.

The woman walked briskly to a black Buick parked nearby. Someone was sitting at the wheel, smoking. Hermia could not see the face, just the glow of the cigarette. The woman got in. The car started up and pulled away.

Hermia breathed easier. The woman had spent the evening in the city, and her husband had come to the station to drive her home. False alarm, Hermia thought with relief.

She started walking.

* * *

Harald and Leo pushed the Hornet Moth along the drive, past the petrol tanker from which Harald had stolen fuel, all the way to the courtyard in front of the castle, then turned it into the wind. Leo ran inside to wake Captain Kleiss.

Harald had only a minute or two.

He took the torch from his pocket, switched it on, and held it in his mouth. He turned the catches on the left side of the fuselage nose and opened the cowling. 'Fuel on?' he called.

'Fuel on,' Karen called back.

Harald tugged on the pull-ring of the tickler and worked the lever of one of the two fuel pumps to flood the carburettor. He closed the cowling and secured the catches. Taking the torch from his mouth, he called: 'Throttle set and mags on?'

'Throttle set, mags on.'

He stood in front of the aircraft and swung the propeller. Imitating what he had seen Karen do, he turned it a second time, then a third. Finally he gave it a vigorous heave and stepped smartly back.

Nothing happened.

He cursed. There was no time to deal with snags.

He repeated the procedure. Something was wrong, he thought even as he tried it. Before, when he turned the propeller, something had happened that was not happening now. He tried desperately to remember what it was.

Once again the engine failed to start.

In a flash of recollection he realized what was missing. There was no click when he turned the propeller. He recalled Karen telling him that the click was the impulse starter. Without that, there would be no spark.

He ran to her open window. 'There's no click!' he said.

'Magneto jam,' she said calmly. 'It often happens. Open the right cowling. You'll see the impulse starter between the magneto and the engine. Give it a sharp tap with a stone or something. That usually does the trick.'

He opened the right cowling and shone his torch on the engine. The impulse starter was a flat metal cylinder. He scanned the ground at his feet. There were no stones. 'Give me something from the tool kit,' he said to Karen.

She found the kit and handed him a spanner. He tapped the impulse starter.

A voice behind him called: 'Stop that right now.'

He turned to see Captain Kleiss, dressed in uniform trousers and a pyjama jacket, striding across the courtyard towards him, with Leo close behind. Kleiss was not armed, but Leo had a rifle.

Harald stuffed the spanner into his pocket, closed the cowling, and moved to the nose.

'Stand away from that aircraft!' Kleiss shouted. 'This is an order!'

Suddenly Karen's voice rang out. 'Stop right where you are or I'll shoot you dead!'

Harald saw her arm sticking out of the window, pointing Hansen's pistol straight at Kleiss.

Kleiss stopped, and so did Leo.

Whether Karen knew how to fire the thing, Harald had no idea – but nor did Kleiss.

'Drop the rifle on the ground, Leo,' said Karen.

Leo dropped his weapon.

Harald reached for the propeller and swung it.

It turned with a loud, deeply satisfying click.

* * *

Peter Flemming drove to the castle ahead of Hermia, with Tilde Jespersen in the passenger seat beside him. 'We'll park out of sight, and watch what she does when she gets here,' he said.

'OK.'

'About what happened on Sande—'

'Please don't speak of it.'

He suppressed his anger. 'What, never?'

'Never.'

He wanted to strangle her.

The car's headlights showed a small village with a church and a tavern. Just beyond the village they approached a grand entrance.

'I'm sorry, Peter,' Tilde said. 'I made a mistake, but it's over. Let's just be friends and colleagues.'

He felt he did not care about anything any more. 'To Hell with that,' he said, and turned into the castle grounds.

On the right of the drive was a ruined monastery. 'That's odd,' Tilde said. 'The church doors are wide open.'

Peter hoped there would be some action to take his mind off Tilde's rejection. He stopped the Buick and turned off the engine. 'Let's have a look.' He took a flashlight out of the glove box.

They got out of the car and went into the church. Peter heard a muffled grunt followed by a thud. It seemed to come from the Rolls-Royce car that was standing on blocks in the middle of the room. He opened the boot and shone his torch on a policeman, bound and gagged.

'Is this your man Hansen?' he said.

Tilde said: 'The aeroplane isn't here! It's gone!'

At that moment, they heard an aircraft engine start.

* * *

The Hornet Moth roared into life and seemed to lean forward as if eager to go.

Harald walked quickly to where Kleiss and Leo stood. He picked up the rifle and held it menacingly, putting on an air of confidence that he did not feel. He backed away from them slowly and walked around the spinning propeller to the left side door. He reached for the handle, flung open the door, and threw the rifle on to the luggage shelf behind the seats.

As he climbed in, a sudden movement made him glance past Karen out of the far window. He saw Captain Kleiss throw himself forward, towards the aircraft, and dive to the ground. There was a bang, deafening even over the noise of the engine, as Karen fired Hansen's pistol. But Harald could see that the window frame prevented her bringing her wrist low enough, and her shot missed the captain.

Kleiss rolled under the fuselage, came up the other side, and jumped on the wing.

Harald tried to slam the door, but Kleiss was in the way. The captain grabbed Harald by the lapels and tried to pull him out of his seat. Harald struggled, trying to dislodge Kleiss's grip. Karen was holding the pistol in her left hand and could not turn around, in the cramped cabin, to get a shot at Kleiss. Leo came running up but, because of the door and the wing, he was unable to get close enough to join in the fight.

Harald pulled the spanner from his pocket and lashed out with all his might. The sharp end of the tool hit Kleiss under the eye, drawing blood, but he held on.

Karen reached past Harald and thrust the throttle lever all the way forward. The engine roared louder and the aircraft moved forward. Kleiss lost his balance. He flung one arm out, but held on to Harald with the other.

The Hornet Moth moved faster, bumping over the grass. Harald hit Kleiss again, and this time he cried out, let go, and fell to the ground.

Harald slammed the door.

He reached for the control column in the centre, but Karen said: 'Leave the stick to me – I can do it left handed.'

The aircraft was pointing down the drive but, as soon as it began to pick up speed, it veered off to the right. 'Use the rudder pedals!' Karen shouted. 'Keep it in a straight line!'

Harald pushed the left pedal to bring the aircraft back on to the drive. Nothing happened, so he pressed it with all his might. After a moment, the aircraft swung all the way over to the left. It crossed the drive and plunged into the long grass on the other side.

She yelled: 'There's a lag, you have to anticipate.'

He understood what she meant. It was like steering a boat, only worse. He pushed with his right foot to bring the aircraft back then, as soon as it began to turn, he corrected with his left foot. This time it did not swing so wildly. As it came back to the drive he managed to line it up.

'Now keep it like that,' Karen shouted.

The aircraft accelerated.

At the far end of the drive, a car's headlights came on.

* * *

Peter Flemming thrust the gearstick into first and floored the pedal. Just as Tilde was opening the passenger door to get in, the car jerked away. She let go of the door with a cry and fell back. Peter hoped she had broken her neck.

He steered along the drive, letting the passenger door flap. When his engine started to scream he changed up into second. The Buick gathered speed.

In his headlights he saw a small biplane rolling down the drive, coming straight at him. Harald Olufsen was in that plane, he felt sure. He was going to stop Harald, even if it killed them both.

He changed up into third.

* * *

Harald felt the Hornet Moth tilt as Karen pushed the stick forward, bringing the tail up. He shouted: 'Do you see that car?'

'Yes – is he trying to ram us?'

'Yes.' Harald was staring along the drive, concentrating on keeping the aircraft on a straight course with the rudder pedals. 'Can we take off in time to fly over him?'

'I'm not sure—'

'You have to make up your mind!'

'Get ready to turn if I say!'

'I'm ready!'

The car was dangerously close. Harald could see they were not going to lift over it. Karen yelled: 'Turn!'

He pressed the left pedal. The aircraft, responding less sluggishly at higher speed, swung sharply off the drive – too sharply: he feared his undercarriage repair job might not stand the strain. He corrected quickly.

Out of the corner of his eye he saw the car turn the same way, still aiming to ram the Hornet Moth. It was a Buick, he saw, just like the one in which Peter Flemming had driven him to Jansborg Skole. It turned sharply, trying to maintain a collision course with the aircraft.

But the aircraft had a rudder, whereas the car was steered by its wheels, and this made a difference on the wet grass. As soon as the Buick hit the grass it went into a skid. As it slid sideways, the moonlight momentarily caught the face of the man behind the wheel, fighting for control, and Harald recognized Peter Flemming.

The aircraft wobbled and straightened out. Harald saw that he was about to crash into the petrol tanker. He stamped on the left pedal, and the right wingtip of the Hornet Moth missed the truck by inches.

Peter Flemming was not so lucky.

Glancing back, Harald saw the Buick, completely out of control, slide with terrible inevitability towards the tanker. It smashed into the truck at top speed. There was a booming explosion, and a second later the entire park was lit up with a yellow glow. Harald tried to see if the tail of the Hornet Moth might have caught fire, but it was impossible to look directly behind, so he just hoped for the best.

The Buick was a furnace.

'Steer the aircraft!' Karen yelled at him. 'We're about to take off!'

He returned his attention to the rudder. He saw that he was heading for the mess tent. He pressed the right pedal to miss it.

When they were on a straight course again the aircraft accelerated.

* * *

Hermia had begun to run when she heard the aero engine start up. As she came into the grounds of Kirstenslot she saw a dark car, very like the one at the station, tearing along the drive. As she watched, it went into a skid and crashed into a truck parked alongside the drive. There was a terrific explosion, and both car and truck burst into flame.

She heard a woman cry: 'Peter!'

In the fire's light she saw the woman in the blue beret. Everything fell into place. The woman *had* been following her. The man waiting in the Buick had been Peter Flemming. They had not needed to follow her, because they knew where she was going. They had come to the castle ahead of her. Then what?

She saw a small biplane rolling across the grass, looking as if it was about to take off. Then she saw the woman in the blue beret kneel down, pull a gun from her shoulder bag, and aim at the aircraft.

What was happening here? If the woman in the beret was a colleague of Peter Flemming's, the pilot must be on the side of the angels, Hermia deduced. It could even be Harald, escaping with the film in his pocket.

She had to stop the woman shooting the aircraft down.

* * *

The park was lit up by the flames from the petrol tanker, and in the brightness Harald saw Mrs Jespersen aim a gun at the Hornet Moth.

There was nothing he could do. He was heading straight for her and, if he turned to one side or the other, he would merely present her with a better target. He gritted his teeth. The bullets might pass through the wings or the fuselage without causing serious damage. On the other hand they might disable the engine, damage the controls, hole the petrol tank, or kill him or Karen.

Then he saw a second woman runnning across the grass, carrying a suitcase. 'Hermia!' he shouted in astonishment as he recognized her. She hit Mrs Jespersen over the head with her case. The detective fell sideways and dropped her gun. Hermia hit her again, then grabbed the gun.

Then the aircraft passed over them and Harald realized it had left the ground.

Looking up, he saw that it was about to crash into the bell tower of the church.

537

THIRTY-TWO

Karen thrust the Y-shaped control column sharply to the left, banging it against Harald's knee. The Hornet Moth banked as it climbed, but Harald could see that the turn was not sharp enough, and the aircraft was going to hit the bell tower.

'Left rudder!' Karen screamed.

He remembered that he, too, could steer. He jammed his left foot down hard on the pedal and immediately felt the aircraft bank more steeply. Still he felt sure the right wing would smash into the brickwork. The aircraft came around with excruciating slowness. He braced himself for the crash. The wingtip missed the tower by inches.

'Jesus Christ,' he said.

The gusty wind made the aircraft buck like a pony. Harald felt they could fall out of the sky at any second. But Karen continued the climbing turn. Harald gritted his teeth. The aircraft came around a hundred and eighty degrees. At last, when it was heading back over the castle, she straightened out. As they gained altitude, the aircraft steadied, and Harald recalled Poul Kirke saying there was more turbulence near the ground.

He looked down. Flames still flickered in the petrol tanker, and by their light he could see the soldiers emerging from the monastery in their nightwear. Captain Kleiss was waving his arms and shouting orders. Mrs Jespersen lay still, apparently out cold. Hermia Mount was nowhere to be seen. At the door of the castle, a few servants stood looking up at the aircraft.

Karen pointed to a dial on the instrument panel. 'Keep an eye on this,' she said. 'It's the turn-and-slip indicator. Use the rudder to hold the needle straight upright, at the twelve o'clock position.'

Bright moonlight came through the transparent roof of the cabin, but it was not enough to read the instruments. Harald shone the torch on the dial.

They continued to climb, and the castle shrank behind them. Karen kept looking to left and right as well as ahead, although there was nothing much to see but the moonlit Danish landscape.

'Fasten your lap strap,' she said. He saw that hers was done up. 'It will save you banging your head on the cabin roof if the ride gets bumpy.'

Harald fastened his belt. He began to believe that they had escaped. He allowed himself to feel triumphant. 'I thought I was going to die,' he said.

'So did I – several times!'

'Your parents will go out of their minds with worry.'

'I left them a note.'

'That's more than I did.' He had not thought of it.

'Let's just stay alive, that will make them happy.'

He touched her cheek. 'How do you feel?'

539

'A bit feverish.'

'You've got a temperature. You should sip water.'

'No, thanks. We've got a six-hour flight ahead of us, and no bathroom. I don't want to have to pee on a newspaper in front of you. It could be the end of a beautiful friendship.'

'I'll close my eyes.'

'And fly the aircraft with your eyes shut? Forget it. I'll be all right.'

She was being jocular, but he was anxious about her. He felt shattered by what they had been through, and she had done all the same things with a sprained ankle and a sprained wrist. He hoped she would not pass out.

'Look at the compass,' she said. 'What's our course?'

He had examined the compass while the aircraft was in the church, and knew how to read it. 'Two hundred and thirty.'

Karen banked right. 'I figure our heading for England is two-fifty. Tell me when we're on course.'

He shone the torch on the compass until it showed the right course, then said: 'That's it.'

'Time?'

'Twelve-forty.'

'We should write all this down, but we didn't bring pencils.'

'I don't think I'll forget any of it.'

'I'd like to get above this patchy cloud,' she said. 'What's our altitude?'

Harald shone the torch on the altimeter. 'Four thousand seven hundred feet.'

'So this cloud is at about five thousand.'

A few moments later the aircraft was engulfed by what looked like smoke, and Harald realized they had entered the cloud.

'Keep the light on the airspeed indicator,' Karen said. 'Let me know if our speed changes.'

'Why?'

'When you're flying blind, it's difficult to keep the aircraft in the correct attitude. I could put the nose up or down without realizing it. But if that happens we'll know because our speed will increase or decrease.'

He found it unnerving to be blind. This must be how accidents happen, he thought. An aircraft could easily hit the side of a mountain in cloud. Fortunately there were no mountains in Denmark. But if another aircraft happened to be flying through the same cloud, neither pilot would know until it was too late.

After a couple of minutes, he found that enough moonlight was penetrating the cloud for him to see it swirling against the windows. Then, to his relief, they emerged, and he could see the Hornet Moth's moon shadow on the cloud below.

Karen eased the stick forward to level out. 'See the rev counter?'

Harald shone the torch. 'It says two thousand, two hundred.'

'Bring the throttle smoothly back until it drops to nineteen hundred.'

Harald did as she said.

'We use power to change our altitude,' she explained. 'Throttle forward, we go up; throttle back, we go down.'

'So how do we control our speed?'

'By the attitude of the aircraft. Nose down to go faster, nose up to go slower.'

'Got it.'

'But never lift the nose too sharply, or you will stall. That means you lose lift, and the aircraft falls out of the sky.'

Harald found that a terrifying thought. 'What do you do then?'

'Put the nose down and increase the revs. It's easy – except that your instinct tells you to pull the nose up, and that makes it worse.'

'I'll remember that.'

Karen said: 'Take the stick for a while. See if you can fly straight and level. All right, you have control.'

He grasped the control stick in his right hand.

She said: 'You're supposed to say: "I have control." That's so that the pilot and copilot never get into a situation where each thinks the other is flying the aircraft.'

'I have control,' he said, but he did not feel it. The Hornet Moth had a life of its own, turning and dipping with air turbulence, and he found himself using all his powers of concentration to keep the wings level and the nose in the same position.

Karen said: 'Do you find that you're constantly pulling back on the stick?'

'Yes.'

'That's because we've used some fuel and changed the aircraft's centre of gravity. Do you see that lever by the top forward corner of your door?'

He glanced up briefly. 'Yes.'

'That's the elevator trim lever. I set it all the way forward for take-off, when the tank was full and the tail was heavy. Now the aircraft needs to be retrimmed.'

'How do we do that?'

'Simple. Ease your grip on the stick. You feel it wanting to go forward of its own accord?'

'Yes.'

'Move the trim lever back. You'll find less need for constant back pressure on the stick.'

She was right.

'Adjust the trim lever until you no longer need to pull on the stick.'

Harald drew the lever back gradually. Before he knew it, the control column was pressing back on his hand. 'Too much,' he said. He pushed the trim lever forward a fraction. 'That's about right.'

'You can also trim the rudder, by moving the knob in that toothed rack at the bottom of the instrument panel. When the aircraft is correctly trimmed, it should fly straight and level with no pressure on the controls.'

Harald took his hand off the column experimentally. The Hornet Moth continued to fly level.

He returned his hand to the stick.

543

The cloud below them was not continuous, and at intervals they were able to see through gaps to the moonlit earth below. Soon they left Zealand behind and flew over the sea. Karen said: 'Check the altimeter.'

He found it difficult to look down at the instrument panel, feeling instinctively that he needed to concentrate on flying the aircraft. When he tore his gaze away from the exterior, he saw that they had reached seven thousand feet. 'How did that happen?' he said.

'You're holding the nose too high. It's natural. Unconsciously, you're afraid of hitting the ground, so you keep trying to climb. Dip the nose.'

He pushed the stick forward. As the nose came down, he saw another aircraft. It had large crosses on its wings. Harald felt sick with fear.

Karen saw it at the same time. 'Hell,' she said. 'The Luftwaffe.' She sounded as scared as Harald felt.

'I see it,' Harald said. It was to their left and down, a quarter of a mile or so away, and climbing towards them.

She took the stick and put the nose sharply down. 'I have control.'

'You have control.'

The Hornet Moth went into a dive.

Harald recognized the other aircraft as a Messerschmitt Bf110, a twin-engined night fighter with a distinctive double-finned tailplane and long, greenhouse-like cockpit canopy. He remembered

Arne talking about the Bf110's armament with a mixture of fear and envy: it had cannons and machine guns in the nose, and Harald could see the rear machine guns poking up from the back end of the canopy. This was the aircraft used to shoot down Allied bombers after the radio station on Sande had detected them.

The Hornet Moth was completely defenceless.

Harald said: 'What are we going to do?'

'Try to get back into that cloud layer before he gets within range. Damn, I shouldn't have let you climb so high.'

The Hornet Moth was diving steeply. Harald glanced at the airspeed indicator and saw that they had reached one hundred and thirty knots. It felt like the downhill stretch of a roller-coaster. He realized he was grasping the edge of his seat. 'Is this safe?' he said.

'Safer than being shot.'

The other aircraft came rapidly closer. It was much faster than the Moth. There was a flash and a rattle of gunfire. Harald had been expecting the Messerschmitt to fire on them, but he could not restrain a yell of shock and fear.

Karen turned right, trying to spoil the gunner's aim. The Messerschmitt flashed past below. The gunfire stopped, and the Hornet Moth's engine droned on. They had not been hit.

Harald recalled Arne saying that it was difficult for a fast aircraft to shoot at a slow one. Perhaps that had saved them.

As they turned, he looked out of the window and saw the fighter receding into the distance. 'I think he's out of range,' he said.

'Not for long,' Karen replied.

Sure enough, the Messerschmitt was turning. The seconds dragged by as the Hornet Moth dived toward the protection of the cloud and the fast-moving fighter swept through a wide turn. Harald saw that their airspeed had reached one hundred and sixty. The cloud was tantalizingly close – but not close enough.

He saw the flashes and heard the bangs as the fighter opened up. This time the aircraft were closer and the fighter had a better angle of attack. To his horror he saw a jagged rip appear in the fabric of the lower left wing. Karen shoved the stick over and the Hornet Moth banked.

Then, suddenly, they were plunged into cloud.

The gunfire stopped.

'Thank God,' Harald said. Although it was cold, he was sweating.

Karen pulled back on the stick and brought them out of the dive. Harald shone the torch on the altimeter and watched the needle slow its anticlockwise movement and steady at just above five thousand feet. The airspeed returned gradually to the normal cruising speed of eighty knots.

She banked the aircraft again, changing direction, so that the fighter would not be able to overtake them simply by following their previous course.

'Bring the revs down to about sixteen hundred,' she said. 'We'll get just below this cloud.'

'Why not stay in it?'

'It's difficult to fly in cloud for long. You get disoriented. You don't know up from down. The instruments tell you what's happening but you don't believe them. It's how a lot of crashes happen.'

Harald found the lever in the dark and drew it back.

'Was it just luck that the fighter turned up?' Karen said. 'Maybe they can see us with their radio beams.'

Harald frowned, thinking. He was glad to have a puzzle to take his mind off the danger they were in. 'I doubt it,' he said. 'Metal interferes with radio waves, but I don't think wood or linen does. A big aluminium bomber would reflect the beams back to their aerials, but only our engine would do that, and it's probably too small to show up on their detectors.'

'I hope you're right,' she said. 'If not, we're dead.'

They came out below the cloud. Harald increased the revs to nineteen hundred, and Karen pulled the stick back.

'Keep looking around,' Karen said. 'If we see him again, we have to go up fast.'

Harald did as she said, but there was not much to see. A mile ahead, the moon was shining through a gap in the clouds, and Harald could make out the irregular geometry of fields and woodland. They must be over the large central island of Fyn, he thought. Nearer, a bright light moved perceptibly across the dark landscape, and he guessed it was a railway train or a police car.

Karen banked right. 'Look up to your left,' she said.

Harald could see nothing. She banked the other way, and looked up out of her window. 'We have to watch every angle,' she explained. He noticed that she was getting hoarse with the constant shouting over the noise of the engine.

The Messerschmitt appeared ahead.

It dropped out of the cloud a quarter of a mile in front of them, dimly revealed by moonlight reflected off the ground, heading away. 'Full power!' Karen shouted, but Harald had already done it. She jerked back on the stick to lift the nose.

'Maybe he won't even see us,' Harald said optimistically, but his hopes were immediately dashed as the fighter went into a steep turn.

The Hornet Moth took several seconds to respond to the controls. At last they began to rise towards the cloud. The fighter came around in a wide circle and pitched up to follow their climb. As soon as he was lined up, he fired.

Then the Hornet Moth was in the cloud.

Karen changed direction immediately. Harald cheered. 'Dodged him again!' he said. But his underlying fear gave a brittle tone to the triumph in his voice.

They climbed through the cloud. When the glow of moonlight began to illuminate the swirling mist around them, Harald realized they were near the top of the cloud layer. 'Throttle back,' Karen said. 'We'll have to stay in the cloud as long as we can.' The aircraft levelled. 'Watch that airspeed indicator,' she said. 'Make sure I'm not climbing or diving.'

'OK.' He checked the altimeter, too. They were at five thousand eight hundred feet.

Just then the Messerschmitt appeared only yards away.

It was slightly lower and to the right, heading across their path. For a split-second, Harald saw the terrified face of the German pilot, his mouth opening in a shout of horror. They were all an inch from death. The fighter's wing passed under the Hornet Moth, missing the undercarriage by a hair.

Harald trod on the left rudder pedal and Karen jerked back on the control stick, but the fighter was already gone from view.

Karen said: 'My God, that was close.'

Harald stared into the swirling cloud, expecting the Messerschmitt to appear. A minute went by, then another. Karen said: 'I think he was as scared as us.'

'What do you think he'll do?'

'Fly above and below the cloud for a while, hoping we'll pop out. With luck, our courses will diverge, and we'll lose him.'

Harald checked the compass. 'We're going north,' he said.

'I went off-heading in all that dodging about,' she said. She banked left, and Harald helped with the rudder. When the compass read two-fifty he said: 'Enough,' and she straightened up.

They came out of the cloud. They both scanned the sky in all directions, but there were no other aircraft.

'I feel so tired,' Karen said.

'It's not surprising. Let me take control. Rest for a while.'

Harald concentrated on flying straight and level. The endless minor adjustments started to become instinctive.

'Keep an eye on the dials,' Karen warned him. 'Watch the air speed indicator, the altimeter, the compass, the oil pressure and the fuel gauge. When you're flying, you're supposed to check all the time.'

'OK.' He forced himself to look at the dashboard every minute or two and he found, contrary to what his instincts told him, that the aircraft did not fall to earth as soon as he did so.

'We must be over Jutland now,' Karen said. 'I wonder how far north we strayed?'

'How can we tell?'

'We'll have to fly low as we cross the coast. We should be able to identify some terrain features and establish our position on the map.'

The moon was low on the horizon. Harald checked his watch and was astonished to see that they had been flying for almost two hours. It seemed like a few minutes.

'Let's take a look,' said Karen after a while. 'Pull the revs back to fourteen hundred and dip the nose.' She found the atlas and studied it by the light of the torch. 'We'll have to go lower,' she said. 'I can't see the land well enough.'

Harald brought the aircraft down to three thousand feet, then two. The ground was visible in the moonlight, but there were no distinguishing elements, just fields. Then Karen said: 'Look – is that a town ahead?'

Harald peered down. It was hard to tell. There were no lights because of the blackout – which had been imposed precisely in order to make towns hard to see from the air. But the ground ahead certainly seemed to have a different texture in the moonlight.

Suddenly, small burning lights began to appear in the air. 'What the hell is that?' Karen yelled.

Was someone aiming fireworks at the Hornet Moth? Fireworks had been banned since the invasion.

Karen said: 'I've never seen tracer bullets, but—'

'Shit, is that what they are?' Without waiting for instructions, Harald pushed the throttle forward all the way and lifted the nose to gain altitude.

As he did so, searchlights came on.

There was a bang and something exploded nearby. 'What was that?' Karen cried.

'I think it must have been a shell.'

'Someone's firing at us?'

Harald suddenly realized where they were. 'This must be Morlunde! We're right over the port defences!'

'Turn!'

He banked.

'Don't climb too steeply,' she said. 'You'll stall.'

Another shell burst above them. Searchlight beams scythed the darkness all around. Harald felt as if he were lifting the aircraft by will power.

They came around one hundred and eighty degrees. Harald straightened out and continued to climb. Another shell exploded, but it was behind them. He began to feel they might yet survive.

The firing stopped. He turned again, flying on their original heading, still climbing.

A minute later they passed over the coast.

'We're leaving the land behind,' he said.

She made no reply, and he turned to see that her eyes were closed.

He glanced back at the coastline disappearing behind him in the moonlight. 'I wonder if we'll ever see Denmark again,' he said.

THIRTY-THREE

The moon set, but for a while the sky was clear of cloud, and Harald could see stars. He was grateful for them, as they were the only way he could tell up from down. The engine gave a reassuringly constant roar. He flew at five thousand feet and eighty knots. There was less turbulence than he remembered from his first flight, and he wondered whether that was because he was over the sea, or because it was night – or both. He kept checking his heading by the compass, but he did not know how much the Hornet Moth might be blown off course by wind.

He took his hand off the control stick and touched Karen's face. Her cheek was burning. He trimmed the aircraft to fly straight and level, then took a bottle of water from the locker under the dashboard. He poured some on his hand then dabbed her forehead to cool her. She was breathing normally, though her breath was hot on his hand. She seemed to be in a feverish sleep.

When he returned his attention to the outside world, he saw that dawn was breaking. He checked his watch: it was just after three o'clock in the morning. He must be half way to England.

By the faint light, he saw cloud ahead. There seemed to be no top or bottom to it, so he flew into it. There was also rain, and the water stayed on the windscreen. Unlike a car, the Hornet Moth had no windscreen wipers.

He remembered what Karen had said about disorientation, and resolved not to make any sudden moves. However, staring constantly into swirling nothingness was strangely hypnotic. He wished he could talk to Karen, but he felt she needed sleep after what she had been through. He lost track of the passage of time. He started to imagine shapes in the cloud. He saw a horse's head, the bonnet of a Lincoln Continental, and the moustached face of Neptune. Ahead of him, at eleven o'clock and a few feet below, he saw a fishing boat, with sailors on deck gazing up at him in wonderment.

That was no illusion, he realized, snapping back to full consciousness. The mist had cleared and he was seeing a real boat. He looked at the altimeter. Both hands pointed up. He was at sea level. He had lost altitude without noticing.

Instinctively, he pulled the stick back, lifting the nose, but as he did so he heard Karen's voice in his head saying: 'But never lift the nose too sharply, or you will stall. That means you lose lift, and the aircraft falls out of the sky.' He realized what he had done, and remembered how to correct it, but he was not sure he had time. The aircraft was already losing altitude. He put the nose down and pushed the throttle all the way forward. He was level with the fishing boat as he passed it. He risked pulling the nose up a fraction. He waited for the wheels to hit the waves. The aircraft flew on. He pulled the nose up a little more. He risked a glance at the altimeter. He was climbing. He let out a long breath.

'Pay attention, you fool,' he said aloud. 'Stay awake.'

He continued climbing. The cloud dissipated, and he emerged into a clear morning. He checked his watch. It was four o'clock. The sun was about to rise. Looking up through the transparent roof of the cabin, he could see the North Star to his right. That meant his compass was accurate, and he was still heading west.

Frightened of getting too close to the sea, he climbed for half an hour. The temperature dropped, and cold air came in through the window he had smashed out for his improvised fuel line. He wrapped the blanket around himself for warmth. At ten thousand feet, he was about to level off when the engine coughed.

At first he could not figure out what the noise was. The engine sound had been steady for so many hours that he had ceased to hear it.

Then it came again, and he realized the engine had misfired.

He felt as if his heart had stopped. He was about two hundred miles from land in any direction. If the engine failed now, he would come down in the sea.

It coughed again.

'Karen!' he shouted. 'Wake up!'

She slept on. He took his hand off the stick and shook her shoulder. 'Karen!'

Her eyes opened. She appeared better for her sleep, calmer and less flushed, but a look of fear came over her face as soon as she heard the engine. 'What's happening?'

'I don't know!'

'Where are we?'

'Miles from anywhere.'

The engine continued to cough and splutter.

'We may have to land in the sea,' Karen said. 'What's our altitude?'

'Ten thousand feet.'

'Is the throttle fully open?'

'Yes, I was climbing.'

'That's the problem. Bring it back half way.'

He pulled the throttle back.

Karen said: 'When the throttle is on full, the engine draws air from outside, rather than from within the engine compartment, so it's colder – at this altitude, cold enough to form ice in the carburettor.'

'What can we do?'

'Descend.' She took the stick and pushed it forward. 'As we go down, the air temperature should rise, and the ice will melt – eventually.'

'If it doesn't . . .'

'Look for a ship. If we can splash down near one, we may be rescued.'

Harald scanned the sea from horizon to horizon, but he could see no shipping.

With the engine misfiring they had little thrust and

lost altitude rapidly. Harald took the axe from the locker, ready to carry out his plan of hacking off a wing to use as a float. He put the bottles of water in his jacket pockets. He did not know if they would survive in the sea long enough to die of thirst.

He watched the altimeter. They came down to a thousand feet, then five hundred. The sea looked black and cold. There was still no shipping in sight.

A weird calm settled over Harald. 'I think we're going to die,' he said. 'I'm sorry I got you into this.'

'We're not finished yet,' she said. 'See if you can give me a few more revs, so that we don't splash down too hard.'

Harald pushed the throttle forward. The engine note rose. It missed, fired, and missed again.

Harald said: 'I don't think—'

Then the engine seemed to catch.

It roared steadily for several seconds, and Harald held his breath; then it misfired again. Finally it burst into a steady roar. The aircraft began to climb.

Harald realized they were both cheering.

The revs rose to nineteen hundred without missing a beat. 'The ice melted!' Karen said.

Harald kissed her. It was quite difficult. Although they were shoulder to shoulder and thigh to thigh in the cramped cabin, it was awkward to turn in the seat, especially with a lap strap on. But he managed it.

'That was nice,' she said.

'If we survive this, I'm going to kiss you every day for the rest of my life,' he said happily.

'Really?' she said. 'The rest of your life could be a long time.'

'I hope so.'

She looked pleased. Then she said: 'We should check the fuel.'

Harald twisted in his seat to look at the gauge between the seat backs. It was difficult to read, having two scales, one for use in the air and the other for on the ground when the aircraft was tilted.

But they both read near to Empty.

'Hell, the tank is almost dry,' Harald said.

'There's no land in sight.' She looked at her watch. 'We've been in the air five and a half hours, so we're probably still half an hour from land.'

'That's all right, I can top up the tank.' He unbuckled his lap strap and turned awkwardly to kneel on his seat. The petrol can stood on the luggage shelf behind the seats. Beside it was a funnel and one end of a length of garden hose. Before take-off, Harald had broken the window and passed the hose through the hole, lashing the other end to the petrol inlet in the side of the fuselage.

But now he could see the outside end of the hose flapping in the slipstream. He cursed.

Karen said: 'What's the matter?'

'The hose has worked loose in flight. I didn't tie it tight enough.'

'What are we going to do? We have to refuel!'

Harald looked at the petrol can, the funnel, the hose, and the window. 'I've got to put the hose into the filler neck. And it can't be done from in here.'

'You can't go outside!'

'What will it do to the aircraft if I open the door?'

'My God, it's like a giant airbrake. It will slow us down and turn us left.'

'Can you cope with that?'

'I can maintain air speed by putting the nose down. I suppose I could press down on the right rudder pedal with my left foot.'

'Let's try it.'

Karen put the aircraft into a gentle dive, then put her left foot on the right rudder pedal. 'OK.'

Harald opened the door. The aircraft immediately veered sharply to the left. Karen pushed down on the right rudder pedal, but they continued to turn. She eased the stick over to the right and banked, but the aircraft still went left. 'It's no good, I can't hold it!' she cried.

Harald closed the door. 'If I smash these windows out, that will almost halve the area of wind resistance,' he said. He took the spanner from his pocket. The windows were made of some kind of celluloid that was tougher than glass, but he knew it was not unbreakable, for he had knocked out a rear window two days ago. He drew back his right arm as far as he could and hit the window hard, and the celluloid shattered. He tapped the remaining material out of the frame.

'Ready to try again?'

'Just a minute – we need more air speed.' She leaned across and pushed the throttle open, then eased the trim lever forward an inch. 'OK.'

Harald opened the door.

Once again the aircraft veered left, but this time less sharply, and Karen seemed to be able to correct with the rudder.

Kneeling on the seat, Harald put his head out of the door. He could see the end of the hose flapping around the petrol access cover. Holding the door open with his right shoulder, he stretched out his right arm and grasped the hose. Now he had to feed it into the tank. He could see the open access panel but not the filler neck. He got the end of the hose positioned roughly over the panel, but the length of rubber in his hand constantly flopped around with the movement of the aircraft, and he could not get the end into the pipe. It was like trying to thread a needle in a hurricane. He tried for several minutes, but it became more hopeless as his hand got colder.

Karen tapped his shoulder.

He drew his hand back into the cabin and closed the door.

'We're losing altitude,' she said. 'We need to climb.' She pulled the stick back.

Harald blew on his hand to warm it. 'I can't do it this way,' he told her. 'I can't get the hose into the pipe. I need to be able to hold the other end of the tube.'

'How?'

He thought for a minute. 'Maybe I can put one foot out of the door.'

'Oh, God.'

'Let me know when we've gained enough altitude.'

After a couple of minutes she said: 'OK, but be ready to close the door as soon as I tap your shoulder.'

Facing backwards with his left knee on the seat, Harald put his right foot out through the door and on to the reinforced strip on the wing. Holding his lap strap with his left hand for security, he leaned out and grasped the hose. He ran his hand along its length until he was holding the tip. Then he leaned out farther to put the end into the pipe.

The Hornet Moth hit an air pocket. The aircraft bucked in the air. Harald lost his balance and thought he was going to fall off the wing. He jerked hard on the hose and his lap strap at the same time, trying to stay upright. The other end of the hose, inside the cabin, broke free of the string holding it. As it came loose, Harald involuntarily let go of it. The slipstream whisked it away.

Shaking with fear, he eased back into the cabin and closed the door.

'What happened?' she said. 'I couldn't see!'

For a moment he was unable to reply. When he had recovered, he said: 'I dropped the hose.'

'Oh, no.'

He checked the fuel gauge. 'We're running on empty.'

'I don't know what we can do!'

'I'll have to stand on the wing and pour the petrol in directly from the can. It will take two hands – I can't hold a four-gallon can with one hand, it's too heavy.'

'But you won't be able to hold on.'

561

'You'll have to hold my belt with your left hand.' Karen was strong, but he was not sure she could take his weight if he slipped. However, there was no alternative.

'Then I won't be able to move the control stick.'

'We'll just have to hope you don't need to.'

'All right, but let's gain more altitude.'

He looked around. There was no land in sight.

Karen said: 'Warm your hands. Put them under my coat.'

He turned, still kneeling on the seat, and pressed his hands to her waist. Under the fur coat she was wearing a light summer sweater.

'Put them under my sweater. Go on, feel my skin, I don't mind.'

She was hot to his touch.

He kept his hands there as they climbed. Then the engine missed. 'We're out of fuel,' Karen said.

The engine caught again, but he knew she was right. 'Let's do it,' he said.

She trimmed the aircraft. Harald unscrewed the cap of the four-gallon can, and the tiny cabin filled with the unpleasant smell of petrol, despite the wind blowing in at the broken windows.

The engine missed again and began to falter.

Harald lifted the can. Karen took hold of his belt. 'I've got you tight,' she said. 'Don't worry.'

He opened the door and put his right foot out. He moved the can to the seat. He put his left foot out, so that he was standing on the wing and leaning inside the cabin. He was absolutely terrified.

He lifted the can and stood upright on the wing. He made the mistake of looking beyond the trailing edge of the wing to the sea below. His stomach lurched with nausea. He almost dropped the can. He closed his eyes, swallowed, and got himself under control.

He opened his eyes, resolving not to look down. He leaned over the petrol inlet. His belt tightened over his stomach as Karen took the strain. He tilted the can.

The constant movement of the aircraft made it impossible to pour straight, but after a few moments he got the knack of compensating. He leaned forwards and back, relying on Karen to keep him safe.

The engine continued to misfire for a few seconds, then returned to normal.

He wanted desperately to get back inside, but they needed fuel to reach land. The petrol seemed to flow as slowly as honey. Some blew away in the air flow, and more spilled around the access plate and was wasted, but most of it seemed to go into the pipe.

At last the can was empty. He dropped it into the air and gratefully grabbed the door frame with his left hand. He eased himself back into the cabin and closed the door.

'Look,' said Karen, pointing ahead.

In the far distance, right on the horizon, was a dark shape. It was land.

'Hallelujah,' he said softly.

'Just pray that it's England,' Karen said. 'I don't know how far we might have been blown off course.'

It seemed to take a long time, but eventually the dark shape turned green and became a landscape. Then it resolved into a beach, a town with a harbour, an expanse of fields, and a range of hills.

'Let's take a closer look,' Karen said.

They descended to two thousand feet to examine the town.

'I can't tell whether it's France or England,' Harald said. 'I've never been to either place.'

'I've been to Paris and London, but neither of them looks like this.'

Harald checked the fuel gauge. 'We're going to have to land soon anyway.'

'But we need to know whether we're in enemy territory.'

Harald glanced up through the roof and saw two aircraft. 'We're about to find out,' he said. 'Look up.'

They both stared at the two small aircraft that were rapidly approaching from the south. As they came closer, Harald stared at their wings, waiting for the markings to become distinct. Would they turn out to be German crosses? Had all this been for nothing?

The aircraft came closer, and Harald saw that they were Spitfires with RAF roundels. This was England.

He let out a whoop of triumph. 'We made it!'

The aircraft came closer and flew either side of the Hornet Moth. Harald could see the pilots, staring at them. Karen said: 'I hope they don't think we're enemy spies and shoot us down.'

It was dreadfully possible. Harald tried to think of some way of telling the RAF they were friendly. 'Flag of truce,' he said. He pulled off his shirt and pushed it out of the broken window. The white cotton fluttered in the wind.

It seemed to do the trick. One of the Spitfires moved in front of the Hornet Moth and waggled its wings. Karen said: 'That means "Follow me," I think. But I haven't got enough fuel.' She looked at the landscape below. 'Sea breeze from the east, to judge by the smoke from that farmhouse. I'll come down in that field.' She put the nose down and turned.

Harald looked anxiously at the Spitfires. After a moment they turned and began to circle, but maintained their altitude, as if watching to see what would happen next. Perhaps they had decided that a Hornet Moth could not be much of a threat to the British Empire.

Karen came down to a thousand feet and flew downwind past the field she had chosen. There were no obstructions visible. She turned into the wind for landing. Harald operated the rudder, helping keep the aircraft in a straight line.

When they were twenty feet above the grass, Karen said: 'Throttle all the way back, please.' Harald pulled the lever back. She lifted the nose of the aircraft gently with the stick. When it seemed to Harald that they were almost touching the ground, they continued to fly for fifty yards or more. Then there was a bump as the wheels made contact with the earth.

The aircraft slowed down in a few seconds. As it came to a halt, Harald looked through the broken window and saw, just a few yards away, a young man on a bicycle, watching from a pathway alongside the field, staring at them open-mouthed.

'I wonder where we are?' Karen said.

Harald called out to the bicyclist. 'Hello there!' he said in English. 'What is this place?'

The young man looked at him as if he had come from outer space. 'Well,' he said at last, 'it's not the bloody airport.'

EPILOGUE

Twenty-four hours after Harald and Karen landed in England, the photographs Harald had taken at the radar station on Sande had been printed, enlarged, and pinned up on one wall of a big room in a grand building in Westminster. Some had been marked with arrows and notes. In the room were three men in RAF uniforms, examining the pictures and talking in low, urgent voices.

Digby Hoare ushered Harald and Karen into the room and closed the door, and the officers turned around. One of them, a tall man with a grey moustache, said: 'Hello, Digby.'

'Good morning, Andrew,' Digby said: 'This is Air Vice Marshal Sir Andrew Hogg. Sir Andrew, may I present Miss Duchwitz and Mr Olufsen.'

Hogg shook Karen's left hand, as her right was still in a sling. 'You're an exceptionally brave young woman,' he said. He spoke English with a clipped accent that made him sound as if he had something in his mouth, and Harald had to listen hard to understand him. 'An experienced pilot would hesitate to cross the North Sea in a Hornet Moth,' Hogg added.

'To tell the truth, I had no idea how dangerous it was when I set off,' she replied.

Hogg turned to Harald. 'Digby and I are old friends. He's given me a full report on your debriefing, and frankly I can't tell you how important this information is. But I want you to go over again your theory about how these three pieces of apparatus work together.'

Harald concentrated, retrieving from his memory the English words he needed. He pointed to the general shot he had taken of the three structures. 'The large aerial rotates steadily, as if constantly scanning the skies. But the smaller ones tilt up and down and side to side, and it seemed to me they must be tracking aircraft.'

Hogg interrupted him to say to the other two officers: 'I sent a radio expert on a reconnaissance flight over the island this morning at dawn. He picked up waves of two point four metres wavelength, presumably emanating from the big Freya, and also fifty centimetre waves, presumably from the smaller machines, which must be Wurtzburgs.' He turned back to Harald. 'Carry on, please.'

'So I guessed that the large machine gives long-range warning of the approach of bombers. Of the smaller machines, one tracks a single bomber, and the other tracks the fighter sent up to attack it. That way, a controller could direct a fighter to the bomber with great accuracy.'

Hogg turned to his colleagues again. 'I believe he's right. What do you think?'

One of them said: 'I'd still like to know the meaning of *himmelbett*.'

Harald said: '*Himmelbett?* That's the German word for one of those beds . . .'

'A four-poster bed, we call it in English,' Hogg told him. 'We've heard that the radar equipment operates in a *himmelbett*, but we don't know what that means.'

'Oh!' said Harald. 'I've been wondering how they would organize things. This explains it.'

The room went quiet. 'Does it?' said Hogg.

'Well, if you were in charge of German air defence, it would make sense to divide your borders up into blocks of air space, say five miles wide and twenty miles deep, and assign a set of three machines to each block . . . or *himmelbett*.'

'You might be right,' Hogg said thoughtfully. 'That would give them an almost impenetrable defence.'

'If the bombers fly side by side, yes,' said Harald. 'But if you made your RAF pilots fly in line, and sent them all through one single *himmelbett*, the Luftwaffe would be able to track only one bomber, and the others would have a much better chance of getting through.'

Hogg stared at him for a long moment. Then he looked at Digby, and at his two colleagues, then back at Harald.

'Like a stream of bombers,' Harald said, not sure they understood.

The silence stretched out. Harald wondered if there was something wrong with his English. 'Do you see what I mean?' he said.

'Oh, yes,' said Hogg at last. 'I see exactly what you mean.'

* * *

On the following morning Digby drove Harald and Karen out of London to the north-east. After three hours they arrived at a country house that had been commandeered by the air force as officers' quarters. They were each given a small room with a cot, then Digby introduced them to his brother, Bartlett.

In the afternoon they all went with Bart to the nearby RAF station where his squadron was based. Digby had arranged for them to attend the briefing, telling the local commander it was part of a secret intelligence exercise; and no further questions were asked. They listened as the commanding officer explained the new formation the pilots would use for that night's raid – the bomber stream.

Their target was Hamburg.

The same scene was repeated, with different targets, on airfields up and down eastern England. Digby told Harald that more than six hundred bombers would take part in tonight's desperate attempt to draw some of the Luftwaffe's strength back from the Russian front.

The moon rose a few minutes after six o'clock in the evening, and the twin engines of the Wellingtons began to roar at eight. On the big blackboard in the operations room, take-off times were noted beside the code letter for each aircraft. Barty was piloting G for George.

As night fell, and the wireless operators reported in from the bombers, their positions were marked on a big map table. The markers moved ever closer to Hamburg. Digby smoked one anxious cigarette after another.

The lead aircraft, C for Charlie, reported that it was under attack from a fighter, then its transmissions stopped. A for Able approached the city, reported heavy flak, and dropped incendiaries to light the target for the bombers following.

When they began to drop their bombs, Harald thought of his Goldstein cousins in Hamburg, and hoped they would be safe. As part of his school work last year he had had to read a novel in English, and he had chosen *War in the Air* by H. G. Wells, which had given him a nightmare vision of a city under attack from the air. He knew this was the only way to defeat the Nazis, but all the same he dreaded what might happen to Monika.

An officer came over to Digby and said in a quiet voice that they had lost radio contact with Bart's aircraft. 'It may just be a wireless problem,' he said.

One by one, the bombers called in to report that they were heading back – all but C for Charlie and G for George.

The same officer came over to say: 'The rear gunner of F for Freddie saw one of ours go down. He doesn't know which, but I'm afraid it sounds like G for George.'

Digby buried his face in his hands.

The counters representing the aircraft moved back

across the map of Europe on the table. Only 'C' and 'G' remained over Hamburg.

Digby made a phone call to London, then said to Harald: 'The bomber stream worked. They're estimating a lower level of losses than we've had for a year.'

Karen said: 'I hope Bart's all right.'

In the early hours, the bombers began to come back in. Digby went outside, and Karen and Harald joined him, watching the big aircraft land on the runway and disgorge their crews, tired but jubilant.

When the moon went down, they were all back but Charlie and George.

Bart Hoare never did come home.

* * *

Harald felt low as he undressed and put on the pyjamas Digby had loaned him. He should have been jubilant. He had survived an incredibly dangerous flight, given crucial intelligence to the British, and seen the information save the lives of hundreds of airmen. But the loss of Bart's aircraft, and the grief on Digby's face, reminded Harald of Arne, who had given his life for this, and Poul Kirke, and the other Danes who had been arrested and would almost certainly be executed for their parts in the triumph; and all he could feel was sadness.

He looked out of the window. Dawn was breaking. He drew the flimsy yellow curtains across the little window and got into bed. He lay there, unable to sleep, feeling bad.

After a while Karen came in. She, too, was wearing borrowed pyjamas, with the sleeves and the trousers rolled to shorten them. Her face was solemn. Without speaking, she climbed into bed next to him. He held her warm body in his arms. She pressed her face into his shoulder and began to cry. He did not ask why. He felt sure she had been having the same thoughts as he. She cried herself to sleep in his arms.

After a while he drifted into a doze. When he opened his eyes again, the sun was shining through the thin curtains. He gazed in wonderment at the girl in his arms. He had often daydreamed about sleeping with her, but he had never foreseen it quite like this.

He could feel her knees, and one hip that dug into his thigh, and something soft against his chest that he thought might be a breast. He watched her face as she slept, studying her lips, her chin, her reddish eyelashes, her eyebrows. He felt as if his heart would burst with love.

Eventually she opened her eyes. She smiled at him and said: 'Hello, my darling.' Then she kissed him.

After a while, they made love.

* * *

Three days later, Hermia Mount appeared.

Harald and Karen walked into a pub near the Palace of Westminster, expecting to meet Digby, and there she was, sitting at a table with a gin-and-tonic in front of her.

'But how did you get home?' Harald asked her.

575

'Last time we saw you, you were hitting Detective Constable Jespersen over the head with your suitcase.'

'There was so much confusion at Kirstenslot that I was able to slip away before anyone noticed me,' Hermia said. 'I walked into Copenhagen under cover of darkness and reached the city at sunrise. Then I came out the way I had gone in: Copenhagen to Bornholm by ferry, then a fishing boat across to Sweden, and a plane from Stockholm.'

Karen said: 'I'm sure it wasn't as easy as you make it sound.'

Hermia shrugged. 'It was nothing compared with your ordeal. What a journey!'

'I'm very proud of you all,' said Digby, though Harald thought, by the fond look on his face, that he was especially proud of Hermia.

Digby looked at his watch. 'And now we have an appointment with Winston Churchill.'

An air raid warning sounded as they were crossing Whitehall, so they met the prime minister in the underground complex known as the Cabinet War Rooms. Churchill sat at a small desk in a cramped office. On the wall behind him was a large-scale map of Europe. A single bed covered with a green quilt stood against one wall. He was dressed in a chalk stripe suit and had taken off the jacket, but he looked immaculate.

'So you're the lass who flew the North Sea in a Tiger Moth,' he said to Karen, shaking her left hand.

'A Hornet Moth,' she corrected him. The Tiger

Moth was an open aircraft. 'I think we might have frozen to death in a Tiger Moth.'

'Ah, yes, of course.' He turned to Harald. 'And you're the lad who invented the bomber stream.'

'One of those ideas that came out of a discussion,' he said with some embarrassment.

'That's not the way I heard the story, but your modesty does you credit.' Churchill turned to Hermia. 'And you organized the whole thing. Madam, you're worth two men.'

'Thank you, sir,' she said, although Harald could tell by her wry smile that she did not think that was much of a compliment.

'With your help, we have forced Hitler to withdraw hundreds of fighter aircraft from the Russian Front and bring them back for the defence of the Fatherland. And, partly thanks to that success, it may interest you to know that I have today signed a co-belligerency pact with the Union of Soviet Socialist Republics. Britain no longer stands alone. We have as an ally one of the world's greatest powers. Russia may be bowed, but she is by no means beaten.'

'My God,' said Hermia.

Digby murmured: 'It will be in tomorrow's papers.'

'And what are you two young people thinking of doing next?' Churchill asked.

'I'd like to join the RAF,' Harald said immediately. 'Learn to fly properly. Then help to free my country.'

Churchill turned to Karen. 'And you?'

'Something similar. I'm sure they won't let me be a

pilot, even though I can fly much better than Harald. But I'd like to join the women's air force, if there is one.'

'Well,' said the prime minister, 'we have an alternative to suggest to you.'

Harald was surprised.

Churchill nodded to Hermia, who said: 'We want you both to go back to Denmark.'

It was the one thing Harald had not been expecting. 'Go back?'

Hermia went on: 'First, we'd send you on a training course – quite long, six months. You'd learn radio operation, the use of codes, handling firearms and explosives, and so on.'

Karen said: 'For what purpose?'

'You'd parachute into Denmark equipped with radio sets, weapons, and false papers. Your task would be to start a new Resistance movement, to replace the Nightwatchmen.'

Harald's heart beat faster. It was a remarkably important job. 'I had my heart set on flying,' he said. But the new idea was even more exciting – though dangerous.

Churchill intervened. 'I've got thousands of young men who want to fly,' he said brusquely. 'But so far we haven't found anyone who could do what we're asking of you two. You're unique. You're Danish, you know the country, you speak the language as natives, which you are. And you have proved yourselves quite extraordinarily courageous and resourceful. Let me put it this way: if you don't do it, it won't be done.'

It was hard to resist the force of Churchill's will – and Harald did not really want to. He was being offered the chance to do what he had longed for, and he was thrilled at the prospect. He looked at Karen. 'What do you think?'

'We'd be together,' she said, as if that was the most important thing for her.

'Then you'll go?' said Hermia.

'Yes,' said Harald.

'Yes,' said Karen.

'Good,' said the prime minister. 'Then that's settled.'

Afterword

The Danish resistance eventually became one of the most successful underground movements in Europe. It provided a continuous flow of military intelligence to the Allies, undertook thousands of acts of sabotage against the occupying forces, and provided secret routes by which almost all Denmark's Jews escaped from the Nazis.

Acknowledgments

As always, I was helped in my research by Dan Starer of Research for Writers, New York City (*dstarer@researchforwriters.com*). He put me in touch with most of the people named below.

Mark Miller of de Havilland Support Ltd was my consultant on Hornet Moth planes, what goes wrong with them, and how to repair them. Rachel Lloyd of the Northamptonshire Flying School did her best to teach me to fly a Tiger Moth. Peter Gould and Walt Kessler also helped in this area, as did my flying friends Ken Burrows and David Gilmour.

My guide to all things Danish was Erik Langkjaer. For details of life in wartime Denmark I'm also grateful to Claus Jessen, Bent Jorgensen, Kurt Hartogsen, Dorph Petersen, and Soren Storgaard.

For help with life at a Danish boarding school I thank Klaus Eusebius Jakobsen of Helufsholme Skole og Gods, Erik Jorgensen of the Birkerod Gymnasium, and Helle Thune of Bagsvaerd Kostkole og Gymnasium, all of whom welcomed me to their schools and patiently answered my questions.

I'm grateful for information from Hanne Harboe of the Tivoli Garden, Louise Lind of the Stockholm

Postmuseum, Anita Kempe, Jan Garnert and K.V. Tahvanainen of the Stockholm Telemuseum, Hans Schroder of the Flyvevabnets Bibliotek, Anders Lunde of the Dansk Boldspil-Union, and Henrik Lundbak of the Museum of Danish Resistance in Copenhagen.

Jack Cunningham told me about the Admiralty Cinema, and Neil Cook of HOK International gave me photographs of it. Candice DeLong and Mike Condon helped with weapons. Josephine Russell told me what it was like to be a student ballerina. Titch Allen and Pete Gagan helped with antique motorcycles.

I'm grateful to my editors and agents: Amy Berkower, Leslie Gelbman, Phyllis Grann, Neil Nyren, Imogen Tate, and Al Zuckerman.

Finally, I thank members of my family for reading outlines and drafts: Barbara Follett, Emanuele Follett, Marie-Claire Follett, Richard Overy, Kim Turner, and Jann Turner.

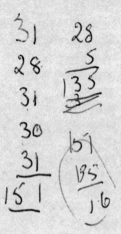

31   28

28   5

31   135

30

31

151

51

135

16